TOME OF HORRORS

Authors: Kevin Baase, Erica Balsley, John "Pexx" Barnhouse, Christopher Bishop, Casey Christofferson, Jim Collura, Andrea Costantini, Jayson 'Rocky' Gardner, Zach Glazar, Skeeter Green, Meghan Greene, Scott Greene, Lance Hawvermale, Travis Hawvermale, Ian S. Johnston, Bill Kenower, Patrick Lawinger, Rhiannon Louve, Ian McGarty, Edwin Nagy, James Patterson, Nathan Paul, Patrick N. Pilgrim, Clark Peterson, Anthony Pryor, Greg Ragland, Robert Schwalb, G. Scott Swift, Greg A. Vaughan, and Bill Webb
Project Manager: Zach Glazar

Developers: Edwin Nagy, Patrick Pilgrim, and Bill Webb
Editors: Edwin Nagy and G. Scott Swift
Layout and Graphic Design: Charles A. Wright
Fifth Edition Ruleset Conversion: Richard Anthony Meyer, Keith Hershey, Jr., Edwin Nagy, Patrick N. Pilgrim, Michael G. Potter, and Jason Whitesitt
Cover Illustration: Rasmus Jensen
Creature Illustration: Dan Houser, Chris McFann, Terry Pavlet; Steven Punter, Artem Shukayev, Joshua Stewart and Michael Syrigos

A Very Special Thanks to Scott Greene and Alex Kammer for their ongoing support of Frog God Games!

FROG GOD GAMES IS

CEO
Bill Webb

COO (Wizard of Whim)
Zach Glazar

Creative Director: Swords & Wizardry
Matthew J. Finch

Art Director (and still kickin')
Charles A. Wright

FROG GOD GAMES

5TH EDITION RULES, 1ST EDITION FEEL

ISBN 978-1-62283-828-8

Product Identity: The following items are hereby identified as Necromancer Games Inc.'s Product Identity, as defined in the Open Game License version 1.0a, Section 1(e), and are not Open Game Content: product and product line names, logos and identifying marks including trade dress; artifacts; creatures; characters; stories, storylines, plots, thematic elements, dialogue, incidents, language, artwork, symbols, designs, depictions, likenesses, formats, poses, concepts, themes and graphic, photographic and other visual or audio representations; names and descriptions of characters, spells, enchantments, personalities, teams, personas, likenesses and special abilities; places, locations, environments, creatures, equipment, magical or supernatural abilities or effects, logos, symbols, or graphic designs; and any other trademark or registered trademark clearly identified as Product Identity. Previously released Open Game Content is excluded from the above list.

Note: This work contains creatures previously published by Frog God Games for the Fifth Edition rules. Since then, thanks to the original design team behind the Fifth Edition rules, clarifications have been widely available. The material published previous to the Tome of Horrors has been updated and could differ from originally published content.

Foreword

Back in the days of 3.0 yesteryear, a little but scrappy company called Necromancer Games made a sweet deal with Wizards of the Coast to convert and publish all of the old monsters from the more obscure AD&D sources—the *Fiend Folio* and *Monster Manual II*. This initial book was called the *Tome of Horrors*.

After that, Necromancer published two more books in the series—each one capturing both old monsters from the halcyon days of 1.0 as well as a myriad of new beasts from modules and other sources. These books were very popular, in fact *Tome of Horrors II* sold out its first print in hours.

Time traveling to 2010, when I re-invented Necromancer as Frog God Games. One of the first major products we completed was *Tome of Horrors Complete*, a 900+ compilation of the first three Necromancer books, updated for Pathfinder and Swords and Wizardry. These books were once again popular (the Pathfinder book blowing through its initial print run in 3 hours!) and very few copies still exist for sale (and the Swords and Wizardry version is long sold out). This was followed by *Tome of Horrors 4* (all new monsters created by Scott Greene) in 2014.

After all, no one ever has enough monsters.

Well, now here we are in 5th Edition. Frog God Games has published a couple of hundred books over the last few years, and of course it makes sense to ensure that this generation of the game has many of these old favorites.

What? A straight reprint you say? Why would I want the same material again?

Well, gentle reader, we didn't think you would, and in any event, putting a giant Tome of Horrors that contained all of the originals, plus *Tome of Horrors 4* , plus the several hundred new monsters we have created in the past 7 years would have pushed us into the 1600 page range. Frog God staff, and in particular me, love a huge book mas much (ok, well probably more than) as the next gamer . . . but sadly the printer told me no way, the projected price point ($300 or so) would have been far too high (though a bargain IMO) and Chuck would likely have threatened me with an ice pick had we decided to go that route.

Besides, what does "complete" mean anyway, especially since we are still creating new material all the time (and we love us some monsters!).

So in light of my mania with giant tomes, and applying a thick layer of Zach wisdom (not his dump stat), we decided to do these in a series once a year or so, turning the old black and white versions of these books into full color, beautifully illustrated volumes of 300-400 monsters each.

What you have in your hands represents the first in a series of Tome 5E's. It consists of many old favorites from the 1980's, more of our original creations from the last 18 years, and even more new monsters that you have never seen before from our own home games and future products. The idea here is to provide the maximum value to you as a GM (yes Matt, I used a "G", not a "D") while making a manageable book both in terms of bulk and price.

That means lots of usable material and lots of value to you the gamer.

Welcome to Tome of Horrors 5th Edition. These guys are hungry, and their favorite meal is still adventurers.

BW

041318

Table of Contents

Abyssal Harvester

This gigantic beast stands at least 40 feet tall. It is a squat, bloated mass of grayish, leathery flesh, somewhat oval in shape with six long, serpentine tentacles protruding from its form. A massive gaping maw dominates its top surface extending around its entire top half. Hundreds of smaller tentacles adorn the lower part of its body, apparently aiding in locomotion.

Abyssal harvesters are horrid monsters found primarily on the Abyssal planes and rarely anywhere else (for an extended amount of time at least). They were created by foul and demonic magic to aid in harvesting bodies and living creatures from other planes for use by the various demon lords and princes (uses include slaves, food, concubines, and so on).

An Abyssal harvester spends most of its time scouring the planes for potential prey. It does so by injecting a single tentacle into the plane and using it to survey its surroundings. If nothing of interest is located, the harvester withdraws its tentacle and moves on. Much of its time is spent scouring the planes as directed by a demon prince, lord, or other powerful demon (though Abyssal harvesters loathe answering to non-princes and rarely do so unless said demon poses a direct threat to the harvester's existence). When not under the direct orders of a prince or demon, any creature a harvester harvests becomes a meal for itself.

A typical Abyssal harvester is 40 feet tall, 20 feet wide at its base, and weighs around 40 tons. Its flesh is gray and usually carries a stench of ozone. Abyssal harvesters are deadly opponents in battle and have no reservations about engaging an enemy in combat. The creature is smart enough to know when it is beaten and will withdraw if combat is going against it.

Most of the time, however, an Abyssal harvester simply injects its tentacles into a plane, grapples its foes, and when they are sufficiently weakened, draws them through a temporary gate onto its plane where it devours them.

Abyssal Harvester

Gargantuan aberration, chaotic evil
Armor Class 17 (natural armor)
Hit Points 370 (20d20 + 160)
Speed 20 ft.

STR	DEX	CON	INT	WIS	CHA
27 (+8)	10 (+0)	26 (+8)	10 (+0)	16 (+3)	13 (+1)

Skills Perception +9
Damage Resistances acid, cold, fire
Damage Immunities poison
Condition Immunities poisoned, prone
Senses darkvision 120 ft., passive Perception 19
Languages Abyssal
Challenge 20 (25,000 XP)

Far Reaching (3/day). An Abyssal harvester can remain on its Abyssal plane and inject up to four of its tentacles across the dimensions and into the Ethereal Plane, Astral Plane, material planes, or Nine Hells.

All of its tentacles must be injected into the same plane, and all appear within the same 20-foot square. While using this ability, it uses sensory organs on its tentacles to see, hear, smell, and feel its surroundings. It can attack normally while using this ability, but it cannot move from its current location. It can withdraw its tentacles as an action and reinject them into the same plane (or a different plane) on its next turn.

The dismissal effect of a *dispel evil or good* spell causes an Abyssal harvester to withdraw a single tentacle if it fails its Charisma saving throw. It cannot reinject that same tentacle into the same plane for one day.

A *banishment* spell forces an Abyssal harvester to withdraw all of its tentacles if it fails its Wisdom saving throw. It cannot reinject any tentacles that were banished into the same plane for one day.

Harvest. A target that has been grappled for 4 consecutive rounds must succeed on a DC 18 Wisdom saving throw or be drawn through an invisible planar gate (created around the Abyssal harvester's tentacles) into the same plane where the Abyssal harvester currently resides. An opponent drawn into the same plane with the harvester is still grappled upon arrival. This ability can only be used when the Abyssal harvester is on its Abyssal Plane and injects its tentacles into the Ethereal Plane, Astral Plane, a material plane, or the Nine Hells.

Innate Spellcasting. The Abyssal harvester's spellcasting ability is Wisdom (spell save DC 17).

It can innately cast the following spells, requiring no material components:

At will: *plane shift* (functions in Astral Plane, the Abyss, the Nine Hells, or the Material Plane only)

Keen Hearing and Smell. The Abyssal harvester has advantage on Wisdom (Perception) checks that rely on hearing or smell.

Magic Weapons. The Abyssal harvester's attacks are magical.

Tentacles. An Abyssal harvester has 4 tentacles, each of which is 20 feet long, has an AC of 20, 30 hit points, resistance to acid, cold, and fire damage, immunity to poison and psychic damage, and the same senses as the Abyssal harvester. A severed tentacle deals no damage to the Abyssal harvester. A tentacle cannot be broken by mere feats of strengths. A tentacle regrows in 1 week.

Actions

Multiattack. The Abyssal harvester makes four tentacle attacks.

Tentacles. The Abyssal harvester makes an attack with its tentacles using one of the following options:

Debilitating Slam. *Melee Weapon Attack:* +14 to hit, reach 20 ft., one target. *Hit:* 29 (6d6 + 8)

bludgeoning damage and the target's maximum hit points are reduced by an equal amount. The target dies if this reduces its maximum hit points to 0. Otherwise, the reduction lasts until the target finishes a long rest.

Grapple. *Melee Weapon Attack:* +14 to hit, reach 20 ft., one target. *Hit:* 29 (6d6 + 8) bludgeoning damage and the target is grappled (escape DC 22). A grappled creature is restrained. An Abyssal harvester can grapple one creature of Huge size or smaller for each tentacle it has remaining.

Constrict. Each creature the Abyssal harvester has grappled takes 22 (4d6 + 8) bludgeoning damage at the start of the harvester's turn.

Abyssal Larva

This creature looks like a puffy and bloated human-sized whitish-yellow maggot with purplish veins pulsating under its fleshy form. A vaguely humanoid head sits atop its body, and its facial features are twisted and distraught as if the creature was in a constant state of pain. A pair of large, downward-curving horns juts from its head, just above its sunken eyes. Its mouth is lined with filthy and sharpened fangs.

Abyssal larvae are believed to be the final form of an evil soul deemed too weak to become a demon or even the servant of a demon. Another theory suggests that the larvae are the imprisoned forms of slain demon princes and lords. Whatever their true origin, Abyssal larvae are plentiful throughout the Abyssal planes and are some of the most disgusting and loathsome creatures encountered there.

These creatures feed on anything they can consume, be it rotting carcasses, freshly slain creatures, and even waste. Consumables are first liquefied through a process requiring the Abyssal larva to regurgitate stomach acids onto its meal. As the food breaks down, the larva slurps it up and consumes it.

While loathed by the more civilized, some demons such as dretches and babaus savor the juicy flesh of these creatures and often engage in hunting expeditions across the Abyss, killing and devouring as many as they can find.

Acting as if almost mindless, Abyssal larvae attack any living creature they encounter. They have no real tactics other than swarming a foe and biting relentlessly. These creatures fight until destroyed.

Abyssal Larva

Medium fiend, chaotic evil
Armor Class 12 (natural armor)
Hit Points 39 (6d8 + 12)
Speed 20 ft.

STR	DEX	CON	INT	WIS	CHA
10 (+0)	13 (+1)	14 (+2)	3 (–4)	10 (+0)	7 (–2)

Skills Perception +2, Stealth +2
Damage Resistances acid, cold, fire
Damage Immunities psychic
Condition Immunities charmed, frightened
Senses darkvision 60 ft., passive Perception 12
Languages Abyssal
Challenge 1/2 (100 XP)

Tortured Mind. The mind of an Abyssal larva cannot be read. If a creature attempts to read an Abyssal larva's mind, it takes 7 (2d6) psychic damage and must succeed on a DC 12 Wisdom saving throw. On a failed saving throw, the creature is poisoned for 1 minute. While poisoned, the creature cannot take reactions and uses their action to Dash in a random direction, even if that leads them into dangerous areas.

Actions

Bite. *Melee Weapon Attack:* +3 to hit, reach 5 ft., one target. *Hit:* 6 (2d4 + 1) piercing damage plus 5 (2d4) acid damage.

Maggot Spray. *Ranged Spell Attack:* +3 to hit, range 10 ft., one target. *Hit:* 1 poison damage and the target must succeed a DC 12 Dexterity saving throw or be poisoned for 1 minute. A poisoned creature can make a DC 12 Constitution saving throw at the end of each of its turns, ending the poisoned effect on a success.

Aerial Assault Gnome

An incessant clicking and whirring grows louder with each passing second. Something glints of metal in the sun on the horizon. The aerial assault gnome buzzes overhead, laying waste to the feeble creatures on the land below with a savage and explosive strafing run.

Aerial Assault Gnome

Small humanoid (gnome), chaotic neutral
Armor Class 18 (armored flight suit)
Hit Points 44 (8d6 + 16)
Speed 20 ft., fly 60 ft.

STR	DEX	CON	INT	WIS	CHA
8 (−1)	16 (+3)	14 (+2)	16 (+3)	10 (+0)	10 (+0)

Skills History +6, Perception +6, Investigation +6, Acrobatics +8
Senses darkvision 60 ft., tremorsense 120 ft., passive Perception 12
Languages Common, Gnome
Challenge 8 (3,900 XP)

Agile Flight. The gnome may use his mechawings to hover in place and may make hairpin turns, granting him an AC bonus of +2 while flying.

Gnome Cunning. The aerial assault gnome has advantage on all spells and magical effects that require an Intelligence, Wisdom, or Charisma saving throw.

Armored Flight Suit. The aerial assault gnome wears a futuristic suit of lightweight, yet extremely strong, mechanized armor that provides comfort and protection.

Actions

Multiattack. The aerial assault gnome can make two attacks: one with his cog thrower and one with Last Resort.

Cog Thrower. *Ranged Weapon Attack:* +8 to hit, range 80/320 ft., one target. *Hit:* 10 (3d6) slashing damage. A stream of razor-sharp cogs is propelled from the gnome's hollow metallic club.

Last Resort. *Melee Weapon Attack:* +4 to hit, range 5 ft., one target. *Hit:* 3 (1d6) bludgeoning damage. The gnome whips his enemy with the still hot metal barrels of his cog thrower.

Strafing Run (3/day). *Ranged Weapon Attack:* +8 to hit, range 120/400 ft., one target. *Hit:* a point the gnome can see. A blast of fire emanates from the target point. Any creatures in a 20-foot radius of the target must succeed on a DC 16 Dexterity saving throw, taking 28 (8d6) fire damage on a failed save, or half as much damage on a successful one.

Reactions

Point Defense. Any creature moving within 20 feet of the aerial assault gnome is blasted by his point defense cannons for 7 (3d4) piercing damage.

Allip

This shadowy, incorporeal undead mutters and speaks with the voice of madness from beyond the grave.

These creatures are the discontent souls of failed entertainers, mostly minstrels and bards. So great was their lust for fame and respect (never received) that they are unable to find peace, even in death. Merriment nearby their graves, by revelers leaving a festival or tavern, for example, will stir their emotions and call them forth to the barrier that separates the living from the dead. Their entertainment skills have not improved in death, and though they try to regale, they present as babbling incoherent apparitions. Fear on the faces of the revelers, rather than admiration, will enrage the allip, and it will seek to snuff the life out of its victims, erroneously believing the listeners must cross into the world of the dead to truly appreciate musical talent.

Allip

Medium undead, chaotic evil
Armor Class 11
Hit Points 33 (6d8 + 6)
Speed fly 30 ft.

STR	DEX	CON	INT	WIS	CHA
6 (−2)	13 (+1)	13 (+1)	11 (+0)	11 (+0)	16 (+3)

Skills Perception +3, Stealth +3
Senses darkvision 60 ft., passive Perception 13
Languages Common, Deep Speech
Challenge 2 (450 XP)

Babble. The allip incoherently mutters to itself, creating a hypnotic effect. All creatures within 30 ft. that aren't incapacitated must succeed on a DC 11 Wisdom saving throw. On a failed save, the creature becomes charmed for the duration. While charmed by this spell, the creature is incapacitated and has a speed of 0. The effect ends for an affected creature if it takes any damage or if someone else uses an action to shake the creature out of its stupor.

Madness. Anyone targeting an allip with a spell or effect that would make direct contact with its tortured mind must succeed on a DC 11 Wisdom saving throw or take 7 (2d6) psychic damage.

Actions

Touch of Insanity. *Melee Weapon Attack:* +3 to hit, reach 5 ft., one target. *Hit:* 8 (2d6 + 1) psychic damage.

Amalgamation

A large collection of items rises up, forming into a swirling chaos that is the body of this being. The items move about throughout its bulk, somehow not touching one another in their mad dance.

The amalgamation is a special creation used by certain ancient spellcasters to defend their hordes and treasure vaults — for even should the guardian fall, most of the items being guarded would be destroyed, and hence not fall into enemy hands. The creature is composed of a large number of magical and mundane items, and it can use any of them to attack. Because of its magical nature, the amalgamation can even wield magic items such as wands without penalty. The amalgamation resembles a vortex or cloud of items 20 ft. in diameter, swirling within a shimmering field of energy. The precise appearance of the construct depends on the items that comprise its bulk.

Amalgamation

Gargantuan construct, neutral
Armor Class 16
Hit Points 435 (30d20 + 120)
Speed 10 ft., fly 50 ft.

STR	DEX	CON	INT	WIS	CHA
23 (+6)	10 (+0)	18 (+4)	2 (−4)	15 (+2)	1 (−5)

Damage Immunities fire, poison, psychic; bludgeoning, piercing, and slashing from nonmagical weapons that aren't adamantine
Condition Immunities charmed, exhaustion, frightened, paralyzed, petrified, poisoned
Senses darkvision 60 ft., passive Perception 12
Languages understands the languages of its creator but can't speak
Challenge 14 (11,500 XP)

Immutable Form. The amalgamation is immune to any spell or effect that would alter its form.

Item Use. The amalgamation can use any of the items contained within its bulk. Items with limited uses, such as potions, scrolls, or wands, are expended normally.

Magic Resistance. The amalgamation has advantage on saving throws against spells and other magical effects.

Magic Weapons. The amalgamation's weapon attacks are magical.

Swarm Attack. The amalgamation can occupy another creature's space and vice versa, damaging the creature with the flying weapons and objects composing its bulk. Any creature that starts their turn in the same space as the amalgamation must succeed on a DC 18 Dexterity saving throw or take 21 (6d6) slashing damage.

Actions

Multiattack. The amalgamation makes four melee attacks.

Sword. *Melee Weapon Attack:* +11 to hit, reach 10 ft., one target. *Hit:* 17 (2d10 + 6) slashing damage.

Mace. *Melee Weapon Attack:* +11 to hit, reach 10 ft., one target. *Hit:* 15 (2d8 + 6) bludgeoning damage.

Slam. *Melee Weapon Attack:* +11 to hit, reach 5 ft., one target. *Hit:* 19 (3d8 + 6) bludgeoning damage.

Amphisbaena

This creature appears as a huge snake with a head at each end of its body. Its scales are blackish-blue with bands of lighter blue fading into its coloration near the middle of its body. Its heads are glossy-black and its eyes are crimson.

The amphisbaena is a giant poisonous snake about 10 feet long. It is often found lairing near a water source or in dark, damp locations. An amphisbaena moves on land by grasping one of its necks with its other head and rolling across the ground like a hoop.

An amphisbaena is an aggressive and territorial creature, attacking any living creatures that wander near its lair. It attacks by biting with its poisonous fangs from both of its heads.

Amphisbaena

Large monstrosity, unaligned
Armor Class 15 (natural armor)
Hit Points 60 (8d10 + 16)
Speed 20 ft., climb 20 ft., swim 30 ft.

STR	DEX	CON	INT	WIS	CHA
17 (+3)	15 (+2)	14 (+2)	2 (−4)	12 (+1)	2 (−4)

Skills Stealth +6
Senses darkvision 60 ft., passive Perception 11
Languages —
Challenge 3 (700 XP)

Split. The amphisbaena functions normally even if cut in half. If dealt a critical hit with a slashing weapon, the creature is cut in half and continues to function as two separate creatures, each with half of the original amphisbaena's current hit points. The split amphisbaena can rejoin its two halves after completing a short or long rest. If one of the split creatures is slain, the amphisbaena can regrow the lost portion over the course of 1d4 + 2 weeks.

Actions

Multiattack. The amphisbaena makes one bite attack with each of its two heads.

Bite. *Melee Weapon Attack:* +5 to hit, reach 5 ft., one target. *Hit:* 12 (2d8 + 3) piercing damage, and the target must succeed on a DC 13 Constitution saving throw or become poisoned for 1 hour.

Angels

Angel, Chalkydri

This angelic-looking creature resembles a muscular humanoid with coppery skin and coppery eyes. It has four large feathery wings of white and carries a longsword swathed in fire.

Chalkydris spend most of their time on the Ethereal or Astral Plane or on one of the many elemental planes, usually acting on behalf of some deity of good. Chalkydris are militaristic and often lead small retinues of other celestials against the infernal armies. When not serving in such roles, they are found acting as protectors or escorts to visitors on the good-aligned planes. Sometimes, a chalkydri is sent to the Material Plane by its deity to watch over a favored worshipper.

Chalkydris appear as powerful, agile humans 6 to 7 feet tall with coppery skin, red or blonde hair, and copper-colored eyes. Two sets of large feathery wings (four wings total) protrude from their back at shoulder level. Their wings are glossy white with copper tips. Chalkydris wear tunics or robes of varying colors, usually crimson, copper, green, silver, or gold.

Chalkydris enjoy combat, and one is never without its flaming glaive and at least two flaming javelins. A chalkydri opens combat by hurling one of its javelins at a foe before moving into melee to battle with its longsword. While in combat, it utilizes its spell-like abilities to their fullest extent.

Chalkydri Angel

Medium celestial, neutral good
Armor Class 18 (natural armor)
Hit Points 123 (13d8 + 65)
Speed 40 ft., fly 90 ft.

STR	DEX	CON	INT	WIS	CHA
23 (+6)	16 (+3)	20 (+5)	18 (+4)	18 (+4)	19 (+4)

Saving Throws Con +9, Wis +8, Cha +8
Skills Intimidation +8, Perception +8
Damage Resistances radiant; bludgeoning, piercing, and slashing from nonmagical weapons
Condition Immunities charmed, exhaustion, frightened
Senses darkvision 120 ft., passive Perception 18
Languages all, telepathy 120 ft.
Challenge 12 (8,400 XP)

Angelic Weapons. The chalkydri's weapon attacks are magical. When the chalkydri hits with any weapon, the weapon deals an extra 4d8 radiant damage (included in the attack).

Divine Awareness. The chalkydri knows if it hears a lie.

Innate Spellcasting. The chalkydri's spellcasting ability is Charisma (spell save DC 16, +8 to hit with spell attacks). It can innately cast the following spells, requiring no material components:

At will: *detect evil and good*

3/day: *dispel evil and good, flame strike*

1/day: *commune, raise dead*

Magic Resistance. The chalkydri has advantage on saving throws against spells and other magic effects.

Actions

Multiattack. The chalkydri attacks twice with its glaive.

Glaive. *Melee Weapon Attack:* +10 to hit, reach 10 ft., one target. *Hit:* 22 (3d10 + 6) slashing damage plus 18 (4d8) radiant damage.

Javelin. *Ranged Weapon Attack:* +10 to hit, range 30/120 ft., target. *Hit:* 13 (2d6 + 6) piercing damage plus 18 (4d8) radiant damage.

Angel, Fallen Empyreal

This creature resembles a human-sized column of raging fire. Within the burning fires appears to be a winged humanoid-shaped creature dressed in jet black armor.

Fallen empyreals used to be knights and warriors in the service of good deities but have since been corrupted. They are fiery, quick-tempered, and cruel. Fallen empyreals are usually found in the service to one of the many arch-devils that inhabit the Hells. Most often they serve as champions for their infernal liege, but they also serve as commanders of the legions of Hell.

Empyreals that enter combat prefer to batter their opponents with a mixture of magic and direct physical attacks with their longswords. Against powerful foes, an empyreal uses its Necrotic Blast to catch as many foes as it can in the area of effect. During battle, an empyreal often stays aloft where it can blast its foes with spells while staying out of melee range.

Fallen Empyreal Angel

Large celestial, chaotic evil
Armor Class 20 (natural armor)
Hit Points 157 (15d10 + 75)
Speed 40 ft., fly 70 ft.

STR	DEX	CON	INT	WIS	CHA
23 (+6)	18 (+4)	20 (+5)	18 (+4)	18 (+4)	20 (+5)

Saving Throws Dex +8, Con +9
Skills Insight +8, Intimidation +9, Perception +8
Damage Resistances lightning, fire; bludgeoning, piercing, slashing from nonmagical weapons.
Damage Immunities acid, cold, necrotic
Condition Immunities charmed, exhaustion, frightened, poisoned
Senses darkvision 60 ft., blindsight 30 ft., passive Perception 18
Languages all, telepathy 120 ft.
Challenge 12 (8,400 XP)

Aura of Hopelessness. The fallen empyreal can activate or deactivate this feature as a bonus action. While active, all creatures within 30 feet of it suffer 10 (3d6) necrotic damage at the beginning of each of the fallen empyreal's turns. The first time a creature enters or starts its turn in the area it must succeed on a DC 16 Wisdom saving throw or be frightened for 1 minute. The target can repeat the saving throw at the end of each of its turns, ending the effect on itself on a success.

Demonic Weapons. The empyreal's weapon attacks are magical. When the empyreal hits with any weapon, the weapon deals an extra 4d8 necrotic damage (included in the attack).

Innate Spellcasting. The empyreal's spellcasting ability is Charisma (spell save DC 17, +9 to hit with spell attacks). The empyreal can innately cast the following spells, requiring only verbal components:

At will: *detect evil and good, darkness, dispel magic, fear, invisibility, plane shift*

5/day each: *bestow curse, inflict wounds*

3/day each: *blade barrier, flame strike, scorching ray*

1/day each: *circle of death, create undead*

Magic Resistance. The empyreal has advantage on saving throws against spells and other magical effects.

Actions

Multiattack. The fallen empyreal makes three attacks with its flaming longsword

Flaming Longsword. *Melee Weapon Attack:* +10 to hit, reach 10 ft., one target. *Hit:* 15 (2d8 + 6) slashing damage plus 18 (4d8) necrotic damage.

Necrotic Blast (Recharge 5–6). A fallen empyreal can unleash a blast of necrotic energy in a 30-foot radius centered on itself. All creatures in the area must make a DC 16 Dexterity saving throw, taking 28 (8d6) necrotic damage on a failed save, or half as much on a successful one.

Ape, Woods

This large ape appears to have symbiotic plants growing on its back and shoulders, almost as if it were a cloak or mantle. Indeed, despite not showing any root system or other sign of natural plant lifecycle, the plants appear in perfect health, blooming and flowering. Towering up to 6 feet tall, the ape also bears antlers which drip flowering vines.

The woods ape is a bipedal, fur-covered primate. Arms and legs are present where expected, and its eyes are filled with an intelligence that belies its unassuming appearance. A woods ape acts as a mystical grower of all plants, encouraging them, speaking to them, and ensuring they grow healthy and full. Not only is it a preternatural act for a woods ape, it is something it takes great pride in. The origin of the woods ape is shrouded in mystery as the rare creature does not deign to inform those few who encounter them of their life, save that they should tread wearily through their forest garden and not linger or harm the life it contains.

A woods ape's connection to its forest is such that it will protect it against all those who seek to harvest it unduly. A humble woodsman can pass through, gathering deadwood or harvesting small plants, as long as it is done with respect. A woods ape will also bargain seeds or rare plants for those who bring it gifts, such as new seeds for it to grow. A callous hunter or other creature who enters the forest without respect will meet with the woods ape's wrath.

A woods ape's forest garden is usually about a mile in diameter, often deep within other forests, or sometimes, a forest sprouting from a grassy plain. All forest domains of a woods ape are dark forests, thick with vegetation and bare of any game trails.

Woods Ape

Medium monstrosity, unaligned
Armor Class 11 (16 with *barkskin*)
Hit Points 82 (11d8 + 33)
Speed 30 ft., climb 30 ft.

STR	DEX	CON	INT	WIS	CHA
17 (+3)	13 (+1)	16 (+3)	11 (+0)	18 (+4)	7 (−2)

Skills Nature +6, Perception +7, Stealth +4 (+7 in forested terrain), Survival +10
Damage Immunities poison
Condition Immunities poisoned
Senses darkvision 60 ft., passive Perception 17
Languages Druidic
Challenge 5 (1,800 XP)

Land's Stride. The woods ape can move through nonmagical difficult terrain without using extra movement and can pass through nonmagical plants without being slowed by them and without taking damage if they have thorns, spines, or a similar hazard. In addition, the woods ape has advantage on saving throws against plants that are magically created or manipulated to impede movement.

Innate Spellcasting. The woods ape's innate spellcasting ability is Wisdom (spell save DC 15, +7 to hit with spell attacks). It can cast the following spells, requiring no material components:

At will: *guidance, mending, create or destroy water, detect poison and disease, entangle, speak with animals, speak with plants, tree stride*

3/day each: *animal messenger, barkskin, call lightning, locate animals or plants, pass without trace*

1/day each: *awaken, commune with nature, conjure animals, plant growth*

Actions

Multiattack. The woods ape makes two claw attacks.

Claw. *Melee Weapon Attack:* +6 to hit, reach 5 ft., one target. *Hit:* 10 (2d6 + 3) slashing damage.

Archer Bush

This creature looks like a small mound of brownish-green leaves with several thick branches, sporting rows of needlelike thorns, extending from its trunk. Small pale buds of gold and purple sprout from the occasional axil, intermingling with the leaves.

The archer bush is a subterranean, semimobile plant often found with one or more desiccated corpses nearby. The carnivorous archer bush will fire a cluster of thorns at any creature that comes within 20 feet and later slither over to consume any that have fallen. Its primitive mouth, a recessed cavity hidden beneath its trunk, is capable of extreme suction, which it uses to suck the blood from its thorn-pricked victims.

Archer Bush

Small plant, unaligned
Armor Class 13 (natural armor)
Hit Points 78 (12d6 + 36)
Speed 10 ft.

STR	DEX	CON	INT	WIS	CHA
11 (+0)	15 (+2)	16 (+3)	2 (−4)	11 (+0)	9 (−1)

Skills Stealth +4
Senses tremorsense 60 ft., passive Perception 10
Languages —
Challenge 1 (200 XP)

Actions

Multiattack. The archer bush makes two attacks with its thorns.

Thorns. *Melee or Ranged Weapon Attack:* +4 to hit, reach 5 ft. or range 20/60 ft., one target. *Hit:* 6 (1d8 + 2) piercing damage.

Bloodsuck. A creature within 5 ft. of the archer bush that has 0 hit points is drained of blood. The creature automatically fails a death saving throw.

Asrai

This being looks like a one-foot-tall female elf with delicate features, emerald eyes, long golden hair, and pale blue skin.

Asrai dwell in crystal clear lakes, ponds, and rivers. They can be found in any large body of water far from civilized lands. Most asrai spend their time frolicking and playing in the lake they call home, dancing among the fish and playfully splashing the various woodland creatures that venture near the water for a drink. Asrai are protective of their aquatic homes, however, and attack en masse any foolish human so oafish as to not ask their permission to enter the water.

Asrai spend most of their time in the water, preferring not to touch land if possible. Though they can survive on land for a short time, they prefer not to risk such ventures, so any encounter with an asrai is almost always in the water. Asrai make their homes in giant seashells or natural underwater caves. These homes are usually concealed under a canopy of aquatic plants, algae, and seaweed so potential enemies cannot easily find them.

Asrai are closely related to pixies and thought to be a relative, though they do not possess wings. Male asrai are thought to exist, though none have ever been encountered.

An asrai only engages in combat if its body of water is threatened or if any intelligent creature other than a fey enters the water without permission. Once in combat, an asrai prefers to attack with its magic, using its cold touch only as a last resort. If it faces overwhelming odds, an asrai seeks escape, often using its fog cloud to cover its exit.

Asrai

Tiny fey, chaotic neutral
Armor Class 16 (natural armor)
Hit Points 7 (2d4 + 2)
Speed 20 ft., swim 50 ft.

STR	DEX	CON	INT	WIS	CHA
5 (–3)	18 (+4)	13 (+1)	10 (+0)	13 (+1)	14 (+2)

Skills Perception +3, Stealth +6
Damage Resistances bludgeoning, piercing, and slashing from nonmagical weapons
Damage Immunities cold
Senses darkvision 60 ft., passive Perception 13
Languages Common, Sylvan
Challenge 2 (450 XP)

Limited Amphibious. The asrai can breathe both air and water, but it needs to be submerged at least once every 2 hours to avoid suffocating.

Innate Spellcasting. The asrai's spellcasting ability is Charisma (spell save DC 12, +4 to hit with spell attacks). It can innately cast the following spells, requiring no material components:

3/day: *fog cloud*
1/day: *control water*

Spellcasting. The asrai is a 5th level spellcaster. Its spellcasting ability is Charisma (spell save DC 12, +4 to hit with spell attacks.) The asrai can cast the following spells:

Cantrips (at will): *dancing lights, ray of frost, resistance, thaumaturgy*
1st level (4 slots): *charm person, create or destroy water, detect magic, thunderwave*
2nd level (3 slots): *hideous laughter, misty step*
3rd level (2 slots): *hypnotic pattern*

Actions

Cold Touch. *Melee Weapon Attack:* +6 to hit, reach 5 ft., one target. *Hit:* 7 (1d6 + 4) cold damage.

Badger, Prehistoric Honey

The prehistoric honey badger is no mere oversized weasel. Its thick skin and powerful jaws makes it a terrifying creature to contend with, and its fearlessness makes it more dangerous than many humanoids.

The prehistoric honey badger stands two feet at the shoulder and is over five feet long, weighing over 100 pounds. Strictly a carnivore, the fearless prehistoric honey badger will hunt venomous or poisonous creatures, or humanoids, and even chase off larger creatures to steal their kills. Its jaws are capable of tearing through fresh meat like a cleaver and crushing through bone without trouble.

Prehistoric honey badgers make their homes in dry grasslands and in moist forests. They dig burrows with their strong claws, where they lair alone, only nearing another honey badger to mate during the fall months. A honey badger's cubs are born in late winter, and after 6–8 weeks with the female honey badger, the cubs are left to fend for themselves.

Prehistoric Honey Badger

Medium beast, unaligned

Armor Class 14 (natural armor)
Hit Points 51 (6d8 + 24)
Speed 30 ft., burrow 30 ft.

STR	DEX	CON	INT	WIS	CHA
20 (+5)	12 (+1)	18 (+4)	7 (–2)	11 (+0)	5 (–3)

Skills Survival +2
Damage Resistances poison; bludgeoning, piercing, and slashing from nonmagical weapons
Condition Immunities frightened
Senses darkvision 60 ft., passive Perception 10
Languages —
Challenge 4 (1,100 XP)

Keen Hearing and Smell. The prehistoric honey badger has advantage on Wisdom (Perception) checks based on hearing or smell.

Relentless (Recharges after a Short or Long Rest). If the badger takes 14 damage or less that would reduce it to 0 hit points, it is reduced to 1 hit point instead.

Actions

Multiattack. The prehistoric honey badger makes one bite attack and one crunch attack.

Bite. *Melee Weapon Attack:* +7 to hit, reach 5 ft., one target. *Hit:* 16 (2d10 + 5) piercing damage, and the target must make a DC 15 Strength saving throw or be grappled (escape DC 15).

Crunch. *Melee Weapon Attack:* +7 to hit, reach 5 ft., one grappled creature. *Hit:* The target suffers from broken bones and must make a DC 15 Constitution saving throw at the beginning of each of its turns. On a failed saving throw, the target cannot take any actions or reactions during that turn. If the target receives magical healing or takes a long rest, the effect ends.

Barbegazi (Ice Gnome)

This humanoid stands just over 3 feet tall and has white hair, glossy white skin, and deep blue eyes. Its beard is long and flowing and appears to be made of icicles. Its feet are large and flat.

Barbegazi are often referred to as snow or ice gnomes, a name they do not appreciate. They inhabit frigid hills and mountains where they spend their time engaging in activities they enjoy: hunting, fishing, and wrestling. Barbegazi homes are constructed of large blocks of ice and stone and are often built into the sides of hills and mountains or are part of the mountain itself. Their homes are frequently targeted by white dragons (who consider their flesh a delicacy).

A barbegazi prefers to avoid combat, using misdirection and deception (including well-placed traps and pitfalls) whenever possible to mislead and detour potential opponents. If a barbegazi knows an enemy is coming, it will most certainly have several traps and snares in place by the time the enemy arrives. If a barbegazi engages an opponent, it usually opens combat with its icicle blast before moving to attack with its shortsword. A barbegazi is not stupid and will not risk its life in battle (unless it is defending its clan). If forced to flee, a barbegazi burrows into the snow and attempts to escape.

Barbegazi stand about 3 and a half feet tall and weigh 45 pounds on average.

Barbegazi Society

A barbegazi clan is led by the eldest male. Females play a lesser role than males in barbegazi society, though many are as capable (or more) than many of the males in the clan. Barbegazi are trained from a young age in the art of combat and survival.

Aside from white dragons, barbegazis have tolerable relations with most cold-dwelling races and often initiate trade with frost giant clans. Typical goods traded by a barbegazi clan are furs and meat. They do not associate or particularly care for frost men.

Barbegazi (Ice Gnome)

Small humanoid, neutral evil
Armor Class 12 (natural armor)
Hit Points 13 (3d6 + 3)
Speed 20 ft., burrow 20 ft.

STR	DEX	CON	INT	WIS	CHA
10 (+0)	13 (+1)	13 (+1)	11 (+0)	11 (+0)	8 (−1)

Skills Stealth +3
Damage Vulnerabilities fire
Damage Immunities cold
Senses darkvision 60 ft., passive Perception 10
Languages Common, Gnome (Barbegazi dialect)
Challenge ½ (100 XP)

Snow Walk. The barbegazi can move across and climb icy or snowy surfaces without needing to make an ability check. Additionally, difficult terrain composed of ice or snow doesn't cost extra movement.

Innate Spellcasting The barbegazi's innate spellcasting ability is Wisdom (spell save DC 10, +2 to hit with spell attacks). The barbegazi can innately cast the following spells, requiring no material components:

3/day: *ray of frost*
1/day: *hold person*

Actions

Shortsword. *Melee Weapon Attack*: +3 to hit, reach 5 ft., one target. *Hit*: 4 (1d6 + 1) piercing damage plus 3 (1d6) cold damage.

Dagger. *Melee Weapon Attack*: +3 to hit, reach 5 ft., one target. *Hit*: 3 (1d4 + 1) piercing damage plus 3 (1d6) cold damage.

Dagger. *Ranged Weapon Attack*: +3 to hit, range 20/60 ft., one target. *Hit*: 3 (1d4 + 1) piercing damage.

Basilisk, Crimson

This creature looks like a stocky, 8-legged, crimson-scaled reptile. A row of bony spines juts from its back and runs the length of its body. Its eyes have a ghostly blue glow.

Crimson basilisks are variants of the common basilisk, and in some cases more dangerous. Adventurers can be relieved that they will not be turned to stone, but such relief is usually short-lived as they soon realize their equipment begins to disintegrate under acidic bites and they begin bleeding uncontrollably when they meet the creature's gaze.

Crimson basilisks are subterranean carnivores with a voracious appetite whetted only when they get the thing they desire most — blood. While they can survive on a diet of plants, mosses, and meat, they prefer blood above all else, even attacking their own kind when food is scarce. A typical crimson basilisk lair is a stony cavern that reeks of blood and whose walls and ground are typically covered and caked in dried blood. The lair usually contains up to five of these creatures with an equal chance of males and females. From 1d4 young are likely to be present as well. Young do not fight or enter combat.

A crimson basilisk is about 6 feet long and weighs over 400 pounds. Its skin is dull crimson though it can easily change its color (as a free action) to match its surroundings. Its eight legs are thick and stout and end in sharpened claws. The spines on its back are crimson as well though they tend to be darker than its overall body (especially in males). Its eyes glow with a ghostly blue light.

A crimson basilisk most often attacks from ambush, using its ability to camouflage itself against its surroundings and lying in wait for prey to wander too close. Once prey moves within 30 feet, it attacks, first using its gaze to bleed a foe and then quickly moving in to bite. If it successfully bleeds an opponent, the basilisk enters a frenzied state and attacks until either it or its prey is dead.

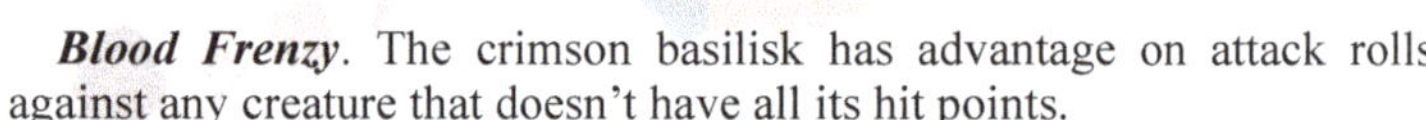

Basilisk, Crimson

Medium monstrosity, unaligned
Armor Class 14 (natural armor)
Hit Points 67 (9d8 + 27)
Speed 20 ft.

STR	DEX	CON	INT	WIS	CHA
16 (+3)	10 (+0)	16 (+3)	2 (–4)	12 (+1)	10 (+0)

Skills Perception +5
Senses darkvision 60 ft., passive Perception 15
Languages —
Challenge 4 (1,100 XP)

Blood Frenzy. The crimson basilisk has advantage on attack rolls against any creature that doesn't have all its hit points.

Wounding Gaze. If a target starts its turn within 30 feet of the basilisk and the two of them can see each other, the basilisk can force the target to make a DC 12 Constitution saving throw if the basilisk isn't incapacitated. On a failed save, the target takes 7 (2d6) necrotic damage as blood weeps from the victim's eyes, ears, nose, and mouth. It must repeat the saving throw at the end of its next turn. On a success, the effect ends. On a failure, the target takes an additional 7 (2d6) necrotic damage and will continue to take recurring damage at the end of each of its turns (without further chance to save) unless the basilisk is incapacitated or the effect is ended by the *greater restoration* spell or other magic.

A creature that isn't surprised can avert its eyes to avoid the saving throw at the start of its turn. If it does so, it can't see the creature until the start of its next turn, when it can avert its eyes again. If it looks at the basilisk in the meantime, it must immediately make the save.

Actions

Bite. *Melee Weapon Attack:* +5 to hit, reach 5 ft., one target. *Hit:* 10 (2d6 + 3) piercing damage and 7 (2d6) acid damage. In addition, nonmagical armor or a shield being worn or carried is partly dissolved and takes a permanent and cumulative –1 penalty to the AC it offers. Armor reduced to an AC of 10 or a shield that drops to a +0 bonus is destroyed.

Bats

Doombat

This creature appears as a giant black bat with glowing yellow eyes.

The doombat is a nocturnal hunter that desires living flesh to sustain it. The approach of a doombat can be heard long before the creature arrives on the scene, the yipping growing louder as the doombat draws closer. The doombat has a 10-foot wingspan, though specimens with wingspans reaching 25 feet have been reported.

Doombats enter melee with any living thing they encounter, yipping for the duration of the fight while attacking with their vicious bite and tail slash.

Doombat

Large beast, unaligned
Armor Class 15
Hit Points 59 (7d10 + 21)
Speed 10 ft., fly 50 ft.

STR	DEX	CON	INT	WIS	CHA
17 (+3)	18 (+4)	16 (+3)	2 (–4)	12 (+1)	6 (–2)

Skills Perception +3
Senses blindsight 60 ft., passive Perception 13
Languages —
Challenge 3 (700 XP)

Yip. Doombats constantly yip while in combat, and the noise interferes with the concentration of those attempting to cast spells. All creatures within a 30-foot radius that are maintaining concentration on a spell when the doombat yips must succeed on a DC 10 Constitution saving throw or lose concentration on that spell.

Actions

Multiattack. The doombat makes one bite attack and one tail attack.

Bite. Melee Weapon Attack: +6 to hit, reach 5 ft., one target. *Hit:* 13 (2d8 + 4) piercing damage.

Tail. Melee Weapon Attack: +6 to hit, reach 10 ft., one target. *Hit:* 8 (1d8 + 4) bludgeoning damage.

Shriek (Recharge 5–6). The doombat emits a piercing shriek. All creatures within a 60-foot radius must succeed on a DC 13 Wisdom saving throw or be poisoned for 1 minute. The target can repeat the saving throw at the end of each of its turns, ending the effect on itself on a success.

Mobat

This creature appears as a large brown bat with razor-sharp fangs and green glowing eyes.

The mobat has a wingspan of approximately 15 feet. It is a nocturnal creature, cruising silently through the night sky in its never-ending quest for food. A mobat, like any species of normal bat, has huge ears and an upturned snout. Mobats are omnivores and often include warm-blooded prey in their diet.

A mobat attacks by biting its opponent using its razor-sharp fangs. Surviving prey is subjected to the mobat's stunning screech attack.

Mobat

Large monstrosity, neutral
Armor Class 14 (natural armor)
Hit Points 51 (6d10 + 18)
Speed 20 ft., fly 40 ft.

STR	DEX	CON	INT	WIS	CHA
17 (+3)	15 (+2)	16 (+3)	6 (−2)	13 (+1)	6 (−2)

Skills Perception +3
Senses blindsight 60 ft., passive Perception 15
Languages —
Challenge 1 (200 XP)

Echolocation. The mobat can't use its blindsight while deafened.
Flyby. The mobat doesn't provoke an opportunity attack when it flies out of an enemy's reach.
Keen Hearing. The mobat has advantage on Wisdom (Perception) checks that rely on hearing.

Actions

Bite. *Melee Weapon Attack:* +5 to hit, reach 5 ft., one target. *Hit:* 13 (3d6 + 3) piercing damage.

Stunning Screech (Recharge 5–6). The mobat emits a piercing screech. All creatures within 30 feet of it that can hear it must make a DC 12 Constitution saving throw or be stunned for 1 minute. A stunned target can repeat the saving throw at the end of each of its turns, ending the effect on itself on a success.

Beaver, Armor Plated

This creature follows the traditional form of a beaver, but there the similarities end. Instead of fur, these creatures are covered in hard, bony plates.

The armor-plated beaver resembles nothing so much as a mixture of a sturgeon and a beaver. Their normal slick fur is replaced by thick bony plates, allowing them to build their lodges beneath pounding waterfalls and in raging currents. Their tails are quite strong, capable of pushing them against vastly stronger currents than their smaller cousins.

Like their cousins, they are generally herbivores but will defend their lodge from intruders to protect their young. The beavers live in family groups within the lodge, with an adult female and adult male in a monogamous pair, and their children, called kits. A kit does not grow its solid armor plating until it reaches its first year. Beyond the family unit, however, the beavers are fiercely territorial. An armor-plated beaver family unit marks its territory by building scent mounds.

Armor-Plated Beaver

Medium beast, unaligned
Armor Class 17 (natural armor)
Hit Points 27 (5d8 + 5)
Speed 20 ft., swim 30 ft.

STR	DEX	CON	INT	WIS	CHA
14 (+2)	11 (+0)	13 (+1)	5 (−3)	11 (+0)	4 (−3)

Skills Survival +2
Senses passive Perception 10
Languages —
Challenge 1 (200 XP)

Hold Breath. The armor-plated beaver can hold its breath for up to 20 minutes.

Keen Smell. The armor-plated beaver has advantage on Wisdom (Perception) checks based on scent.

Actions

Bite. *Melee Weapon Attack:* +4 to hit, reach 5 ft., one target. *Hit:* 6 (1d8 + 2) piercing damage.

Beaver, Prehistoric

Although the tail is thinner than the average beaver, the prehistoric beaver is more than twice the size of its modern kin, with substantially larger canine teeth.

The beaver of prehistoric times averages over 7 feet long and 3 feet at the shoulder. It is an herbivore, surviving off tree bark and cambium, the soft tissue that grows beneath tree bark, and builds long, low lodges across large rivers. A family of prehistoric beavers can be the cause of an entire village's demise should they dam the river that passes near it.

A significant difference between a common beaver and a prehistoric beaver is the length of their teeth; suited to stripping bark, the front incisors are over 5 inches in length, and the beavers use them to defend their lodges.

Prehistoric Beaver

Large beast, unaligned
Armor Class 15 (natural armor)
Hit Points 52 (7d8 + 21)
Speed 30 ft., swim 40 ft.

STR	DEX	CON	INT	WIS	CHA
20 (+5)	12 (+1)	17 (+3)	3 (–4)	11 (+0)	5 (–3)

Skills Survival +2
Senses passive Perception 10
Languages —
Challenge 3 (700 XP)

Hold Breath. The prehistoric beaver can hold its breath for up to 20 minutes.

Siege Monster. The prehistoric beaver deals double damage to objects and structures.

Actions

Bite. *Melee Weapon Attack:* +7 to hit, reach 5 ft., one target. *Hit:* 27 (4d10 + 5) piercing damage.

Bedlam

This creature has no set form. Before your eyes, it seems to shift from a vaguely humanoid form with yellow eyes and no other discernible facial features to a swirling mass of grayish-black crackling matter. In its latter form, blue-gray energy arcs and dances through its form, making it resemble a thundercloud shot through with lightning. It seems to constantly alter its form as if it has no control over it.

A bedlam has no control over its form, but its ever-shifting form does not hamper its abilities in combat. It is a semi-amorphous, nearly vaporous creature composed of pure chaos that makes its lair in areas tainted with strong concentration of chaotic energies, such as temples to chaotic gods or areas that were once lawfully aligned but have been poisoned by the effects of chaos. Bedlams are sometimes employed by chaotic wizards or clerics to guard a particular area. Being intelligent, the bedlam strikes a deal with said employer so that it benefits from the bargain as well. Such deals never last long as the bedlam is an unstable and erratic creature, given to flights of fancy. A bedlam enjoys chaos and seeks to spread it wherever it goes.

Bedlams seek to induce chaos and destroy or weaken law with every move. Since it continuously detects law, it uses this ability to discern whether or not those it encounters are of a lawful nature or not. Nonlawful creatures are generally just subjected to one or two chaotic bursts before the creature moves on. If lawful creatures are present, the bedlam unleashes a chaotic burst and moves to melee, forming two limbs from its chaotic mass which it uses to pound its opponents.

Bedlam

Large aberration, chaotic neutral
Armor Class 17 (natural armor)
Hit Points 112 (15d10 + 30)
Speed 0 ft., fly 50 ft. (hover)

STR	DEX	CON	INT	WIS	CHA
17 (+3)	20 (+5)	15 (+2)	15 (+2)	15 (+2)	12 (+1)

Damage Resistances bludgeoning, piercing, and slashing from nonmagical weapons
Condition Immunities petrification
Senses darkvision 60 ft., passive Perception 12
Languages Common, choice of two others
Challenge 8 (3,900 XP)

Chaotic Resonance. The bedlam emanates an aura of pure chaos. The aura deals 7 (2d6) psychic damage to any creature that ends its turn within 30 feet of the bedlam. Creatures attempting to cast a spell or use a magic item in this area have a 50% chance of the spell fizzling or the item not functioning. Creatures that are chaotic in nature ignore the effect of the bedlam's chaotic resonance.

Magic Resistance. The bedlam has advantage on saving throws against spells and other magic effects.

Sense Law. The bedlam can sense the presence and location of any creature within 120 feet of it that is lawfully aligned, regardless of interposing barriers, unless the creature is protected by a spell such as *nondetection.*

Actions

Multiattack. The bedlam makes two slam attacks.

Slam. *Melee Weapon Attack:* +8 to hit, reach 10 ft., one target. *Hit:* 14 (2d8 + 5) bludgeoning damage.

Chaos Burst (Recharge 5–6). The bedlam releases a burst of crackling gray energy in a 20-foot radius. Creatures in this area must make a DC 14 Wisdom saving throw, taking 22 (5d8) psychic damage on a failed save, and half as much damage on a successful one. Creatures that are chaotic in nature ignore the bedlam's chaos burst.

Beetles (Giant)

Beetle, Blister

A large beetle with a slick, dark-green carapace approaches. ?creature snaps its large black serrated mandibles together as it mo? toward you.

Blister beetles are nocturnal scavengers found in forests or undergrou? They are non-aggressive creatures, but have voracious appetites and w? if food is scarce, attack just about anything that comes close to them. Th? favored meal, however, is bees: both giant and normal. Their immunity ? poison grants them protection from the deadly sting of giant bees (nor? bees cannot penetrate their carapace). A cluster of beetles waits near ? area frequented by bees and then spring to attack when a bee lands ? a flower or plant. Another favored meal is grasshoppers. Blister bee? ambush these large insects and drag the prey back to their lair.

Blister beetles reproduce and mature rapidly. The female deposits ? group of 2d4 eggs in a hole in the nest. The male then sprays the eggs with its blister spray. Within three days the eggs burst open with an audible pop and out swarm the young blister beetles. Young reach maturity in about three weeks. When attacked, a blister beetle releases a foul stream of black oily liquid that irritates the skin of any living creatur? hits. Afterwards, it moves to combat and strikes with its mandibles.

Blister Beetle

Small beast, unaligned
Armor Class 12 (natural armor)
Hit Points 13 (3d6 + 3)
Speed 30 ft.

STR	DEX	CON	INT	WIS	CHA
11 (+0)	10 (+0)	12 (+1)	1 (−5)	10 (+0)	7 (−2)

Damage Immunities acid, poison
Senses darkvision 60 ft., tremorsense 60 ft., passive
  Perception 10
Languages —
Challenge 1 (200 XP)

Actions

Bite. *Melee Weapon Attack*: +2 to hit, reach 5 ft., one target. *Hit*: 3 (1d6) piercing damage plus 3 (1d6) acid damage.

Blister Spray (Recharge 5–6). The beetle exhales a 15-foot cone of caustic acid, causing painful blisters to form on the skin of any creature caught in the spray. Creatures in the area must make a DC 12 Dexterity saving throw, taking 10 (3d6) acid damage on a failed save, or half as much damage on a successful one.

Beetle, Cave

These large subterranean blind beetles are long and thin. Lacking any capacity for visual stimuli the giant cave beetles have adapted to the deep, permanent night underground.

Lightless Troglofauna. This species of giant beetle lives only underground, in the deepest caves where light does not shine. Their carapace is a dull white color, and they tend to reach over 4 feet in length over their thin body. They communicate via pheromones and by vibrating their thorax against the rock beneath them, which, due to their sensitive tympanal organs, they are able to hear through many hundreds of feet of stone.

Armored Hive Insect. This specific variety also have very hard carapaces, often equivalent to iron armor, that make it difficult for underground predators to bite through to damage the insect; should one fall, as well, their death releases strong pheromones that are irritating to most creatures and serve the additional purpose of warning the remaining population of a dangerous predator in their vicinity.

Cave Beetle

Small beast, unaligned
Armor Class 15 (natural armor)
Hit Points 31 (7d6 + 7)
Speed 20 ft., fly 30 ft., burrow 20 ft.

STR	DEX	CON	INT	WIS	CHA
12 (+1)	14 (+2)	13 (+1)	1 (−5)	11 (+0)	2 (−4)

Skills Perception +2
Senses blindsight 60 ft. (blind beyond this radius),
  tremorsense 120 ft., passive Perception 12

Languages —
Challenge 1 (200 XP)

Death Throes. When a giant cave beetle reaches 0 hit points, it releases a strong acidic cloud in a 5-foot radius. Creatures within this area must make a DC 11 Constitution saving throw, taking 7 (2d6) acid damage on a failed saving throw, or half as much damage on a successful saving throw. Every giant cave beetle in 500 feet is capable of detecting the smell of this acid.

Actions

Bite. *Melee Weapon Attack:* +4 to hit, reach 5 ft., one target. *Hit:* 6 (1d8 + 2) slashing damage.

Beetle, Death Watch

This creature appears as a giant beetle with a dark-green carapace and wing casings. Its body is covered in leaves and sticks. Its mandibles are silver and its legs are black.

The death watch beetle makes its lair in forests and uses a mixture of saliva and earth to stick rubbish (leaves and twigs, for instance) to itself in order to attack by surprise.

The death watch beetle begins combat using its death rattle ability. Any creatures that survive are bitten by the beetle's mandibles and devoured.

Death Watch Beetle

Medium beast, unaligned
Armor Class 14 (natural armor)
Hit Points 75 (10d8 + 30)
Speed 30 ft.

STR	DEX	CON	INT	WIS	CHA
20 (+5)	10 (+0)	16 (+3)	1 (−5)	10 (+0)	9 (−1)

Damage Immunities necrotic
Senses darkvision 60 ft., passive Perception 10
Languages —
Challenge 5 (1,800 XP)

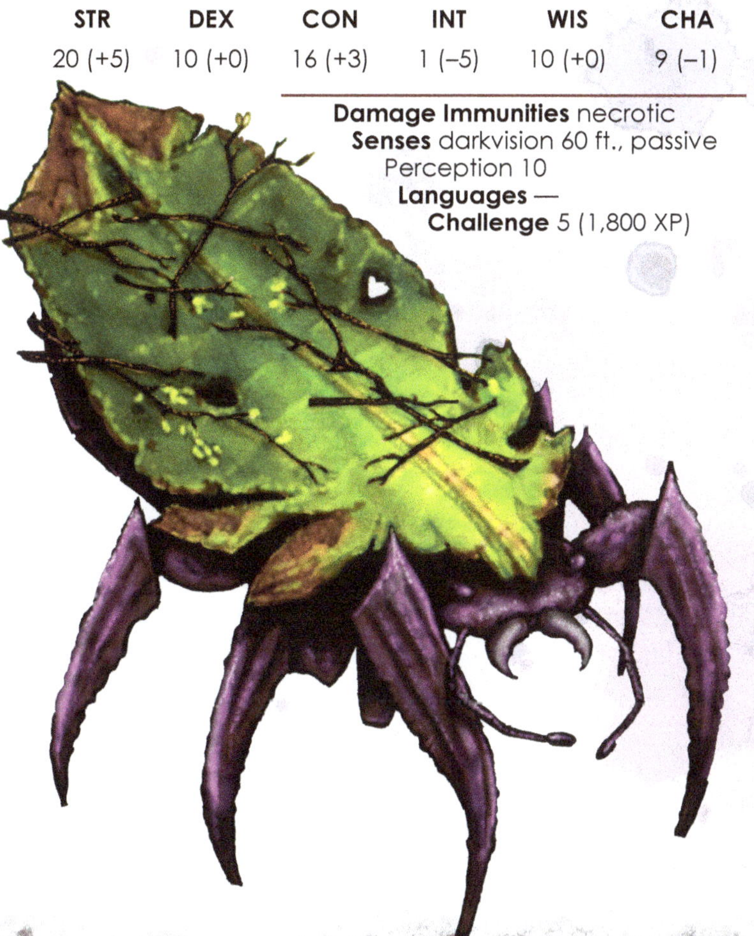

Actions

Bite. *Melee Weapon Attack:* +8 to hit, reach 5 ft., one target. *Hit:* 12 (2d6 + 5) piercing damage.
Death Rattle (Recharge 5–6). The death watch beetle emits a clicking noise with a resonance frequency that affects creatures within 30 feet of it. Creatures in this area must make a DC 13 Constitution saving throw, taking 10 (3d6) thunder damage on a failed save, or half as much damage on a successful one.

Beetle, Gelid

A stark white beetle with silvery-black legs the size of a wolf, this creature has dull silver mandibles, and two sets of dull silvery-black eyes.

Gelid beetles inhabit icy forests and other such desolate places in arctic climates. They spend most of their time hunting, surfacing from their lairs at night to prey on giant or smaller insects. During the daylight hours, gelid beetles like to congregate with others of their kind in warm spots where the sunlight breaks through the trees.

Gelid beetles make their lairs in hollowed logs, dead trees, and other such hidden places. During the mating season, the female digs a small underground chamber in a well-secluded place and lays 1d4+1 silvery-white eggs. These eggs hatch in about 2 weeks, producing olive-yellow larvae. The larvae spend their time feeding and growing (and occasionally molting) before passing into the pupa stage after nearly 3 weeks. The pupae shed their skin for the last time after 8 to 10 days emerge as an adult gelid beetles.

Most beetles are white with silvery-black legs and dull silver mandibles. Some specimens have a mottled silver or black carapace, and an even rarer species has dull crimson wing casings.

A gelid beetle begins combat with its cold spray. It then charges into combat, biting its opponents. Though not intelligent, these

creatures often employ hit-and-run tactics, especially when attacking as a group.

Gelid Beetle

Medium elemental, neutral
Armor Class 13 (natural armor)
Hit Points 32 (5d8 + 10)
Speed 30 ft.

STR	DEX	CON	INT	WIS	CHA
15 (+2)	10 (+0)	14 (+2)	1 (–5)	10 (+0)	9 (–1)

Skills Perception +4
Damage Immunities cold
Senses darkvision 60 ft., passive Perception 14
Languages —
Challenge ½ (100 XP)
Frigid Body. A creature that touches the beetle or hits it with a melee attack while within 5 feet of it takes 3 (1d6) cold damage.
Frigid Weapons. The beetle's weapon attacks deal an extra 3 (1d6) cold damage (included in the attack).

Actions

Bite. *Melee Weapon Attack:* +4 to hit, reach 5 ft., one target. Hit: 5 (1d6 + 2) piercing damage plus 3 (1d6) cold damage.

Beetle, Ravager

This creature is covered in a jet-black carapace with whitish markings crisscrossing its back and gold-tinted wing casings.

Ravager beetles are omnivorous beetles found in temperate or warm forests, hills, and swamps. While generally sustaining themselves on a diet of foliage and grasses, they sometimes scavenge the remains of creatures killed by other predators.

Like most beetles, a ravager has a thick-plated carapace and two large mandibles used for crushing and chewing its food. Its carapace is black in color with several white streaks crisscrossing it. Its mandibles are dark bluish-black. Its wing casings are black with hints of gold. A typical ravager beetle is about 4 feet long.

Ravagers have a single life cycle that spans an entire year. Females generally lay 4–8 eggs in soft earth or soil, and within two weeks, the larvae emerge. Young are almost always born in the warmer spring and early summer months. Young are noncombatants and rely solely on their mother for protection and food, feeding generally for 10 days before entering the pupa stage. After about 20 days, the pupae become adults.

Ravager beetles are generally scavengers by nature, and rarely attack, except in times when food is scarce. Even then, they usually limit their attacks to weakened, sleeping, wounded, or otherwise incapacitated prey. When attacking, ravager beetles lock onto an opponent with their mandibles and continue biting and crushing the target until it is dead.

Ravager Beetle

Medium beast, unaligned
Armor Class 13 (natural armor)
Hit Points 26 (4d8 + 8)
Speed 30 ft., fly 20 ft.

STR	DEX	CON	INT	WIS	CHA
16 (+3)	11 (+0)	14 (+2)	1 (–5)	10 (+0)	6 (–2)

Senses darkvision 60 ft., tremorsense 60 ft., passive Perception 10
Languages —
Challenge 1 (200 XP)

Actions

Gnaw. *Melee Weapon Attack:* +5 to hit, reach 5 ft., one creature. *Hit:* 6 (1d6 + 3) piercing damage plus 7 (2d6) poison damage. If the target is a Medium or smaller creature, it is grappled (escape DC 13) and restrained. Until this grapple ends, the beetle cannot bite another target. A grappled target takes 7 (2d6) poison damage at the start of each of its turns.

Beetle, Requiem

This massive beetle has a dark-red carapace, blackish-red wing casings, and black legs. Two large claw-like pincers protrude from its front, slashing and ripping the very air around the creature. Its oversized mandibles are dark reddish-black.

Requiem beetles are beetles of enormous size, reaching lengths of 100 feet or more. They make their lairs in remote mountainous regions or deep underground in massive caverns. A typical lair contains a solitary creature (no two have ever been encountered together). Mating and reproduction rituals and methods among requiem beetles are unknown to sages, though it is generally accepted that requiem beetles follow other similar beetle and vermin mating patterns.

These monsters sustain themselves on a diet of mosses, funguses, lichens, molds, and oozes. Their natural immunity to acid allows them to kill and digest most oozes without bother. Requiem beetles are mindless hunters, like other vermin, and simply kill and eat whatever they come across. When they deplete an area of its food source, they simply move to another location.

Requiem beetles measure about 40 feet long and weigh about 18 tons.

A requiem beetle charges into combat, attempting to trample as many of its opponents as it can. It uses its massive pincers in battle to cut and tear its opponents or grab and squeeze them. Once a requiem beetle grabs a foe, it rarely lets go until either it or the opponent is dead. If forced to flee, a requiem beetle does not release its prey, but instead, carries it off with it.

Requiem Beetle

Gargantuan beast, unaligned
Armor Class 19 (natural armor)
Hit Points 495 (30d20 + 180)
Speed 50 ft.

STR	DEX	CON	INT	WIS	CHA
27 (+8)	12 (+1)	23 (+6)	1 (–5)	11 (+0)	2 (–4)

Damage Immunities acid
Senses darkvision 60 ft., tremorsense 100 ft., passive Perception 10
Languages —
Challenge 15 (13,000 XP)

Charge. If the requiem beetle moves at least 20 feet straight toward a creature and then hits it with a bite attack on the same turn, that target must succeed on a DC 20 Strength saving throw or be knocked prone. If the target is prone, the requiem beetle can make one claw attack against it as a bonus action.

Earthshaker. When the requiem beetle moves more than 10 feet in a single turn, creatures within 20 feet of it must succeed on a DC 12 Dexterity saving throw or be knocked prone as the ground shakes.

Actions

Multiattack. The requiem beetle makes three attacks: one with its bite and two with its claws.

Bite. *Melee Weapon Attack:* +13 to hit, reach 10 ft., one target. *Hit:* 24 (3d10 + 8) piercing damage.

Claws. *Melee Weapon Attack:* +13 to hit, reach 15 ft., one target. *Hit:* 21 (3d8 + 8) slashing damage.

Beetle, Rhinoceros

This creature appears as a giant beetle with a grayish-brown carapace and wing casings and a large brownish-black "horn" between its mandibles.

These creatures are found in the warm jungles and forests of the world and spend their days searching for plants, fruits, and berries on which to sustain themselves. An adult rhinoceros beetle is about 12 feet long.

Rhinoceros beetles charge opponents, biting with their razor-sharp mandibles and slashing with their horn.

Rhinoceros Beetle

Large beast, unaligned
Armor Class 15 (natural armor)
Hit Points 114 (12d10 + 48)
Speed 20 ft.

STR	DEX	CON	INT	WIS	CHA
23 (+6)	10 (+0)	18 (+4)	1 (–5)	10 (+0)	9 (–1)

Senses darkvision 60 ft., passive Perception 10
Languages —
Challenge 7 (2,900 XP)

Charge. If the giant rhinoceros beetle moves at least 20 feet straight toward a creature and then hits it with a gore attack on the same turn, that target must succeed on a DC 16 Strength saving throw or be knocked prone. If the target is prone, the giant rhinoceros beetle can make one slam attack against it as a bonus action.

Actions

Multiattack. The giant rhinoceros beetle makes three attacks: one bite, one gore, and one slam.

Bite. *Melee Weapon Attack:* +9 to hit, reach 5 ft., one target. *Hit:* 15 (2d8 + 6) piercing damage.

Gore. *Melee Weapon Attack:* +9 to hit, reach 5 ft., one target. *Hit:* 17 (2d10 + 6) piercing damage.

Slam. *Melee Weapon Attack:* +9 to hit, reach 5 ft., one target. *Hit:* 13 (2d6 + 6) bludgeoning damage.

Beetle, Saw-Toothed

The most noticeable feature of this beast is its oversized, jagged and serrated mandibles. The beetle's wing casings and carapace are silvery-green and have a dull sheen. Its legs are long and marked with spiraling bands of green and black.

Giant saw-toothed beetles are deadly predators that hide in their burrows and ambush creatures that come too close. They make their homes in deep burrows on the forest floor and usually cover the opening with sticks, leaves, branches, and whatever else they can find. It takes a successful DC 15 Wisdom (Perception) check to notice a giant saw-toothed beetle's hidden burrow.

cannot bite another target. A grappled target takes 6 (1d8 + 2) piercing damage at the start of each of the beetle's turns.

Beetle, Stench

This beetle is about the size of a small dog and has a mottled green carapace with darker legs fading to black near the ends. Its mandibles are dull brown.

Stench beetles are small, nocturnal hunters that sustain themselves on a diet of grains, fruits, vegetables, and leaves. In civilized lands, they are considered a nuisance for the damage they cause, especially in larger groups, to crops and farmlands and have acquired their moniker from the wretched stench emitted when killed. If faced with extreme hunger, stench beetles eat cattle, small game animals, and the occasional child that wanders too far into the forests.

Stench beetles make their lairs in large hollow logs and fallen trees. A typical lair can contain almost twenty of these creatures with half that number in noncombatant young. Females lay up to a dozen eggs at a given time, usually once per year. Eggs are laid on leaves, and the female chews the ends of the leaves so they curl and fold around the eggs, concealing them from predators and protecting the eggs from the elements. Young go from larvae to adulthood in the span of a year. Most stench beetles leave the lair when they reach adulthood.

Stench beetles attack with their bite, seeking retreat if combat goes against them.

Stench Beetle

Small beast, unaligned
Armor Class 13 (natural armor)
Hit Points 18 (4d6 + 4)
Speed 30 ft., fly 30 ft.

STR	DEX	CON	INT	WIS	CHA
11 (+0)	12 (+1)	12 (+1)	1 (–5)	10 (+0)	6 (–2)

Senses darkvision 60 ft., passive Perception 10
Languages —
Challenge ¼ (50 XP)

Death Throes. When a stench beetle dies, it explodes in a rush of effluvium of nauseating fluids and gases in a 10-foot radius. Creatures within that radius must make a DC 13 Constitution saving throw or be poisoned for 1 minute. While poisoned, the creature can only take one action or bonus action on its turn as it spends the rest of its turn retching. A poisoned creature can repeat the saving throw at the end of each of its turns, ending the effect on a success.

These beetles form colonies of about ten creatures. They are highly aggressive creatures and actively seek sources of meat. Their usual diet consists of small forest animals such as rabbits, deer, or moles. They are even known to devour their own when food is short or when a member of the colony becomes sick or weak.

Giant saw-toothed beetles wait for their prey to come close to their burrow. Hiding at the edge of the burrow, the beetle sits motionless until its target is within range. It then charges out, grabs its target with its jagged mandibles and clamps down, holding on until the prey dies.

Saw-Toothed Beetle

Medium beast, unaligned
Armor Class 14 (natural armor)
Hit Points 39 (6d8 + 12)
Speed 30 ft.

STR	DEX	CON	INT	WIS	CHA
15 (+2)	11 (+0)	14 (+2)	1 (–5)	10 (+0)	6 (–2)

Senses darkvision 60 ft., passive Perception 10
Languages —
Challenge ½ (100 XP)

Actions

Bite. *Melee Weapon Attack*: +4 to hit, reach 5 ft., one target. *Hit*: 6 (1d8 + 2) piercing damage and the target is grappled (escape DC 12). Until the grapple ends, the target is restrained and the beetle

Actions

Bite. *Melee Weapon Attack:* +3 to hit, reach 5 ft., one target. *Hit:* 6 (2d4 + 1) piercing damage.

Beetle, Water

This giant beetle has a cylindrical and hydrodynamic body that tapers to a pointed tail section. Its wing casings and carapace are brownish black, and its legs are dull yellow. A silver stripe runs lengthwise along its back.

These highly aggressive beetles make their home in deep fresh water such as slow-moving rivers, lakes, large pools, and inland seas. They can be found in any climate, from the warmest to the coldest. Giant water beetles are predators. They sustain themselves on fish and other aquatic animals. They spend most of their lives in the water, rarely emerging onto land. In the rare cases when they are encountered on land, a giant water beetle is seldom more than 30 feet from water. They are diurnal creatures, hunting during the day and sleeping in deep water at night. They dive with blinding speed when they spot a potential meal in the water. When not actively hunting, they sometimes simply drift along with the current. The giant water beetle normally uses its ink to escape from attackers, but thanks to its tremorsense, it can fight inside the ink cloud without penalty.

Giant water beetles lair on the bottoms of lakes, rivers, and inland seas. A colony always contains at least one female and 2d4 eggs. Eggs hatch within three weeks after the female deposits them and reach full maturity in six to eight weeks.

When hunting, these creatures prefer to attack by ambushing their prey. They usually drift near the water surface and dive down onto targets below them with surprising speed, but they have also been known to drift in darker water at greater depth and lunge upward to seize prey with their tough, sharp mandibles.

Water Beetle

Medium beast, unaligned
Armor Class 13 (natural armor)
Hit Points 37 (5d8 + 15)
Speed 20 ft., swim 60 ft.

STR	DEX	CON	INT	WIS	CHA
15 (+2)	13 (+1)	16 (+3)	2 (−4)	10 (+0)	9 (−1)

Senses blindsight 60 ft., passive Perception 10
Languages —
Challenge ½ (100 XP)

Water Breathing. Giant water beetles can only breathe water but can hold their breath for up to 8 hours out of water.

Actions

Bite. *Melee Weapon Attack:* +4 to hit, reach 5 ft., one target. *Hit:* 6 (1d8 + 2) piercing damage.

Ink Cloud (Recharge 6). A 10-foot radius cloud of ink extends all around the water beetle if it is underwater. The area is heavily obscured for 1 minute although a significant current can disperse the ink.

Beetlor

Beetlors are subterranean, insectoid predators. They have shiny orange carapaces and yellowish underbellies. Their claws are harder than steel, allowing them to burrow through stone.

Beetlor

Large monstrosity, neutral
Armor Class 16 (natural armor)
Hit Points 60 (8d8 + 24)
Speed 30 ft., burrow 15 ft.

STR	DEX	CON	INT	WIS	CHA
22 (+6)	18 (+4)	17 (+3)	10 (+0)	10 (+0)	8 (−1)

Damage Resistances bludgeoning, piercing, and slashing from nonmagical weapons
Senses darkvision 120 ft., tremorsense 60 ft., passive Perception 10
Languages —
Challenge 5 (1,800 XP)

When a creature starts its turn within 30 feet of the beetlor and is able to see the beetlor's multifaceted eyes, the beetlor can force the creature to make a DC 15 Charisma saving throw if the beetlor isn't incapacitated. On a failure, the creature can't take reactions until the start of its next turn and rolls a d8 to determine what it does during its turn. On a 1 to 4, the creature does nothing. On a 5 or 6, the creature takes no action or bonus action and uses all its movement to move in a randomly determined direction. On a 7 or 8, the creature makes a melee attack against a randomly determined creature within its reach or does nothing if it can't make such an attack.

A creature that isn't surprised can avert its eyes to avoid the saving throw at the start of its turn. If the creature does so, it can't see the beetlor until the start of its next turn, when it can avert its eyes again. If the creature looks at the beetlor in the meantime, it must immediately make the save.

The beetlor can burrow through solid rock, leaving a 6 foot-wide, 10-foot-high tunnel its wake.

Actions

Multiattack. The beetlor makes three attacks: one with its bite and two with its claws.

Bite. *Melee Weapon Attack:* +7 to hit, reach 5 ft., one target. *Hit:* 11 (1d10 + 6) piercing damage.

Claw. *Melee Weapon Attack:* +7 to hit, reach 5 ft., one target. *Hit:* 13 (2d6 + 6) slashing damage.

Belabra

This creature resembles a man-sized flying jellyfish with twelve long tentacles. Four thin eyestalks protrude from its cap. Its cap is blackish gray and its eyestalks are dark gray.

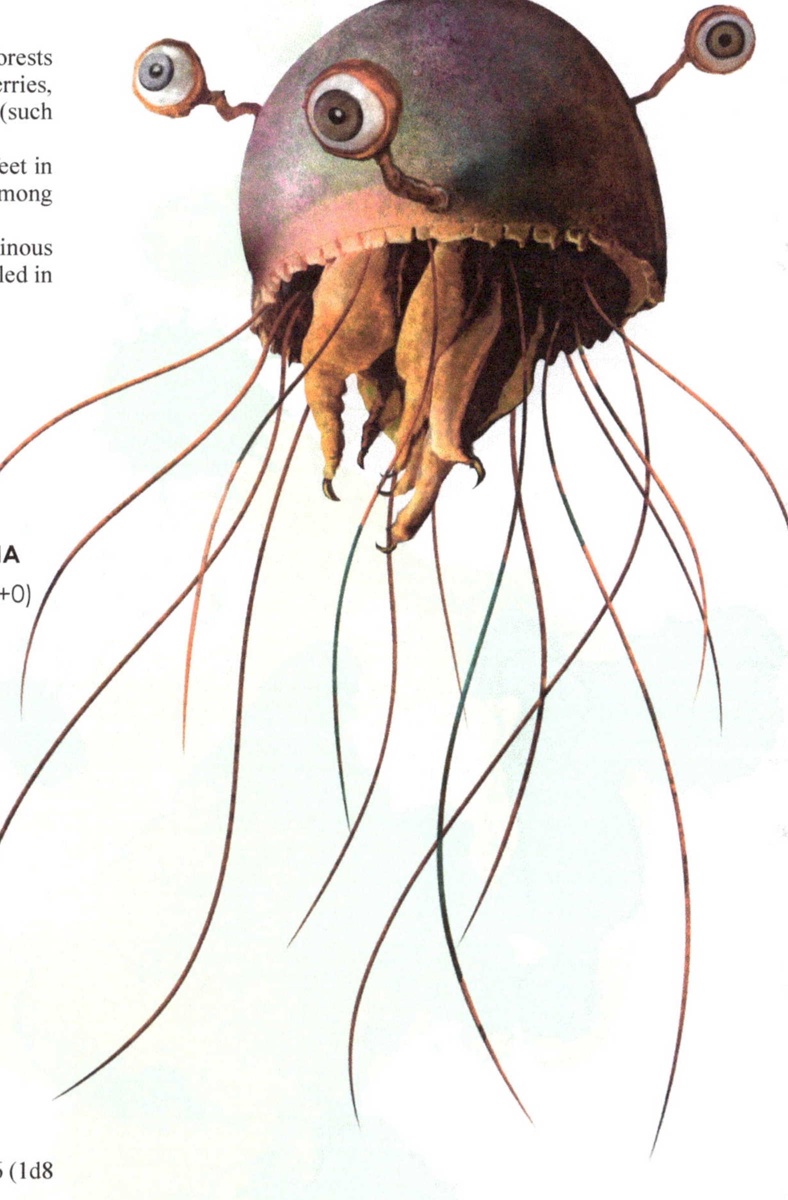

Belabras are large, jellyfish-like omnivores that dwell in deep forests and thick undergrowth. They sustain themselves on a diet of plants, berries, and rodents. Particularly hungry belabras will attack larger creatures (such as humanoids).

Belabras (called "tanglers" by some) resemble jellyfish about 5 feet in diameter. Its eyes have no pupils. A small, bird-like beak is hidden among its array of tentacles.

A belabra attacks by slamming into its opponents with its hard, chitinous shell or by lashing out with its tentacles. Grabbed opponents are pulled in and bitten.

Belabra

Medium aberration, neutral
Armor Class 13
Hit Points 39 (6d8+12)
Speed 5 ft., fly 30 ft.

STR	DEX	CON	INT	WIS	CHA
14 (+2)	15 (+2)	14 (+2)	7 (–2)	12 (+1)	11 (+0)

Skills Stealth +4
Senses darkvision 60 ft., passive Perception 11
Languages —
Challenge 3 (700 XP)

Acidic Blood. Each time the belabra is hit with an attack that does piercing or slashing damage, all creatures within 10 feet of the belabra must make a DC 12 Dexterity saving throw or be sprayed with the belabra's blood. On a failed save, the creature takes 4 (1d6 + 1) acid damage and has disadvantage on attacks, saving throws, or ability checks, due to sneezing and partial blindness, until the end of the belabra's next turn.

Actions

Multiattack. The belabra makes three attacks: one with its slam and two with its tentacles. If it is grappling a target, it will bite the target in place of a tentacle attack.

Bite. *Melee Weapon Attack:* +4 to hit, reach 5 ft., one target. *Hit:* 6 (1d8 + 2) piercing damage.

Slam. *Melee Weapon Attack:* +4 to hit, reach 5 ft., one target. *Hit:* 5 (1d6 + 2) bludgeoning damage.

Tentacles. *Melee Weapon Attack:* +4 to hit, reach 5 ft., one target. *Hit:* 9 (2d6 + 2) piercing damage, and target is grappled (escape DC 12). Until the grapple ends, the target is restrained and takes 4 (1d6 + 1) piercing damage from the tentacle barbs at the start of its turn. The belabra can grapple three targets at the same time.

Biclops

At first glance, this monstrosity appears to be a filthy ettin of huge size. On closer inspection, the true nature of the creature is revealed as it has but one eye in the center of each ugly head.

Despite their appearance, biclops are generally peaceable creatures who live by hunting and herding giant longhorn sheep, which they keep for milk and wool. They are feared by less intelligent giants, such as hill giants and trolls, whom they beat to death on sight. Biclops have good relations with stone giants, to whom they trade finished metal weapons and goat cheese in exchange for raw ore and gold.

Adult male biclops stand about 16 feet tall and weigh about 4,500 pounds. Females are slightly shorter and lighter. Both male and female dress in clothes made of dark or dull colors (browns, greens, and dark reds usually). Biclops skin ranges from ruddy brown to cinnamon, and their eye color is usually blue. Hair color is almost universally dark though occasionally a fair-haired biclops is born (such a biclops is viewed as someone special among his or her own kind). Warriors and protectors often wear hide armor (and sometimes metal armor) and always carry weapons.

A biclops can live to be 350 years old.

Biclops fight with twin longswords, hacking foes to pieces with mighty cleaving chops. If given advanced warning, they tend to chase off intruders with well-aimed rocks hurled from great heights or crush them beneath controlled avalanches.

Biclops live in tribe-like communities deep within hills and mountains, constructing their homes from the stones and lumber of their environment. A typical biclops home has three rooms: a communal area where the family meets, a sleeping room, and a kitchen. Biclops families rely on each other for protection, food, and trade. External trade is often set up between biclops and other races, particularly stone giants and dwarves. Some of the less "reputable" tribes take humanoids and monstrous humanoids as prisoners to use as slaves or a food source. In such a case, there is a 20% chance that a biclops lair contains 1d4 captive humanoids or monstrous humanoids.

Biclops

Huge giant, neutral
Armor Class 16 (chainmail)
Hit Points 283 (21d12 + 147)
Speed 30 ft.

STR	DEX	CON	INT	WIS	CHA
26 (+8)	10 (+0)	25 (+7)	10 (+0)	14 (+2)	10 (+0)

Saving Throws Dex +5, Con +12, Wis +7
Skills Athletics +15, Perception +7
Senses passive Perception 17
Languages Giant
Challenge *14 (11,500 XP)*

Improved Critical. Longsword and spear attacks score a critical hit on a roll of 19 or 20.

Two Heads. The biclops has advantage on Wisdom (Perception) checks and on saving throws against being blinded, charmed, deafened, frightened, stunned, and knocked unconscious.

Two-Weapon Master. When attacking with two weapons, a biclops may reroll any 1 on a damage dice, keeping the second result.

Wakeful. When one head of the biclops is asleep, the other head is awake.

Actions

Multiattack. The biclops makes three attacks with its two longswords. It can choose to hurl two spears or throw two rocks instead.

Longsword. *Melee Weapon Attack:* +13 to hit, reach 15 ft., one target. *Hit:* 26 (4d8 + 8) slashing damage.

Spear. *Melee Weapon Attack:* +13 to hit, reach 15 ft. or range 20/60 ft., one target. *Hit:* 22 (4d6 + 8) piercing damage.

Rock. *Ranged Weapon Attack:* +13 to hit, range 30/120 ft., one target. *Hit:* 30 (4d10 + 8) bludgeoning damage.

Bison, Bighorn

The bighorn bison, a towering behemoth, roams tall-grassed steppes from one forage site to the next. Two massive horns spiral upward from the base of its skull, and another pair curls outward and down. The polycerate bovine's face is covered with additional lesser horns and keratinous growth, creating a warlike visage both fearsome and defensively practical. The bighorn bison will use its immense bulk and natural weapons to stampede a destruction upon any foe that frightens or enrages it.

The bighorn bison stands over 8 feet tall and weighs over 2,000 pounds. Also called the steppe bison, it often appears docile, even lazy, but may fly into a rage unpredictably, often without reason. The most dangerous time for others is middle summer to late autumn when the bison enter mating season.

The bighorn bison is an herbivore, preferring woody plants that are prevalent on prairies, plains, and some river valleys. A bighorn bison does not enjoy the company of other bison species, often becoming violent if pushed to occupy the same area; in fact, a herd of bighorn will charge and violently displace any other species' herds and will not willingly mate with them.

Bighorn Bison

Large beast, unaligned
Armor Class 14 (natural armor)
Hit Points 57 (6d10 + 24)
Speed 40 ft.

STR	DEX	CON	INT	WIS	CHA
22 (+6)	12 (+1)	19 (+4)	2 (−4)	12 (+1)	5 (−3)

Senses passive Perception 11
Languages —
Challenge 4 (1,100 XP)

Trample. If the bison moves at least 20 feet straight toward a creature and then hits it with a gore attack on the same turn, that target must succeed on a DC 16 Strength saving throw or be knocked prone. If the target is prone, the bison can make one stomp attack against it as a bonus action.

Actions

Multiattack. The bighorn bison can make one gore attack and one kick attack.

Gore. *Melee Weapon Attack:* +8 to hit, reach 5 ft., one target. *Hit:* 19 (3d8 + 6) piercing damage.

Stomp. *Melee Weapon Attack:* +8 to hit, reach 5 ft., one target. *Hit:* 22 (3d10 + 6) bludgeoning damage.

Kick. *Melee Weapon Attack:* +8 to hit, reach 5 ft., one target directly behind it. *Hit:* 15 (2d8 + 6) bludgeoning damage.

Blindheim

This creature is a 4-foot-tall frog-like humanoid with large, bulbous eyes that constantly emit bright yellow beams of light. Its skin is mottled yellow, growing darker across its back. Its feet are webbed as are its claws.

Blindheims dwell in underground caverns and sustain themselves on a diet of funguses, molds, and small rodents. An extra eyelid allows the blindheim to "turn off" its eyes when it is sleeping or resting. A dead blindheim's eyes are dull gold in color.

Blindheims are 4 feet tall and weigh about 150 pounds.

A blindheim attacks by first blinding a foe with its gaze and then rushing in to use its bite attack. It can turn its eyes on and off as it wishes but always leaves them on during combat. If overmatched, a blindheim flees.

Blindheim

Small aberration, chaotic evil
Armor Class 13 (natural armor)
Hit Points 17 (5d6)
Speed 30 ft.

STR	DEX	CON	INT	WIS	CHA
10 (+0)	14 (+2)	11 (+0)	2 (–4)	12 (+1)	6 (–2)

Senses darkvision 60 ft., passive Perception 11
Languages Primordial
Challenge ½ (100 XP)

Eye Beams. When a blindheim's eyes are open, it emits a 30-foot cone of light. It can see normally in this light and functions normally in areas of magical darkness. A creature looking at a blindheim when its eye beams are "on" must succeed on a DC 12 Constitution saving throw or be blinded for 1 hour. A blinded creature can repeat the saving throw at the end of each of its turns, ending the effect on a success.

Actions

Bite. *Melee Weapon Attack:* +4 to hit, reach 5 ft., one target. *Hit:* 6 (1d8 + 2) piercing damage.

Blood Bush

This creature appears as a 3-foot-tall flowering bush with a thick trunk and small whip-like branches. Each branch is topped with a blood-red flower and deep, rich-green leaves.

The blood bush is a fell plant creature cursed by a wizard in times past. It is named for its blood-red flowers and its thorny blood-red seeds. A blood bush is sometimes referred to as a "grave marker plant" because a creature that encounters it and fails to see the danger this sinister plant presents, rarely lives to tell about it.

A blood bush can only be grown from a seed that has germinated inside the warm body of a Small or larger animal. Roots from the germinating seed kill the host and use the nutrients provided to grow rapidly into a deadly plant. A number of nobles use this horrid plant as a deterrent against thieves and robbers, sometimes creating entire hedges of the plant.

A blood bush appears as a flowering bush about 3 feet tall. Its thick trunk quickly splits off into many smaller, whip-like branches, each topped with a blood-red flower surrounded by deep green leaves. Blood bush seeds can be sold for about 20 gp each on the open market — collecting them without dying is not the easiest of tasks.

When a blood bush detects a warm-blooded creature within 20 feet, it fires a volley of flower darts at the creature, attempting to implant it with its seeds. A creature that dies from the blood bush's seed implantation rapidly decomposes, and a new blood bush springs up in the area within four days. Living creatures within 5 feet of a blood bush are slashed and cut with its four whip-like tendrils.

Blood Bush

Small plant, unaligned
Armor Class 13 (natural armor)
Hit Points 59 (7d6 + 35)
Speed 0 ft.

STR	DEX	CON	INT	WIS	CHA
15 (+2)	14 (+2)	20 (+5)	2 (–4)	12 (+1)	8 (–1)

Damage Vulnerabilities thunder
Damage Resistances cold, fire
Damage Immunities lightning
Senses blindsight 30 ft., passive Perception 11
Languages —
Challenge 3 (700 XP)

Creatures that are implanted with a blood bush seed begin to suffer the effects of it rapidly germinating inside of them. Once implanted, the seed quickly begins to grow and expand. For every 24 hours that elapse, the target must repeat the DC 14 Constitution saving throw, reducing its hit point maximum by 5 (1d10) on a failure. The germinating seed is destroyed by the immune system on a success. The target dies if this reduces its hit point maximum to 0. This reduction to the target's hit point maximum lasts until the blood bush seed is removed.

Actions

Multiattack. The blood bush makes one attack with its flower darts and two attacks with its tendrils.

Tendril. *Melee Weapon Attack:* +4 to hit, reach 5 ft., one target. *Hit:* 4 (1d4 + 2) slashing damage. If the target is a Medium or smaller creature, it is grappled (escape DC 12) and restrained, and the blood bush cannot grapple another target.

Flower Dart. *Ranged Weapon Attack:* +4 to hit, reach 5 ft., one target. *Hit:* 5 (1d6 + 2) piercing damage, and the target must succeed on a DC 14 Constitution saving throw or be implanted with a blood bush seed (see Germinate).

Blood Orchid

This beast has three downward curving "petals" of flesh with dark, pebbly outer hides and pallid whitish undersides. The petals converge at the blood orchid's center and end with split tips. On its underside at the center, dangle a swarm of writhing pallid tentacles: sixteen manipulator arms and eight thinner tendrils with red eyes at the ends. At the center of these tentacles is a sphincter-shaped mouth at the end of a flexible trunk one foot long and six inches in diameter. At the apex of the creature, there is another cluster of eye tendrils.

Blood orchids are territorial, xenophobic, and possessive. They rarely form alliances with other creatures as their alien mindset keeps them from forming any common ground. They regard other races as aberrant and not to be trusted, even other lawful creatures.

Communication by blood orchids is through a means of empathy/telepathy. They have no sense of hearing, which helps render them immune to sonic effects. The blood orchid can close its outer petals downward and rest on the ground, where it resembles a rocky nodule or fungus of some kind.

Blood orchids occasionally develop sorcerous talents and transform into savants. When their abilities have reached a certain level, they can evolve into a grand savant. Normally each colony of blood orchids is led by a single grand savant, and another cannot evolve while one is present. Typically, a blood orchid savant ready to become a grand savant leaves the colony with a few followers and sets out to establish a new brood elsewhere.

Blood Orchid

Large aberration, lawful evil
Armor Class 14 (natural armor)
Hit Points 76 (9d10 + 27)
Speed 5 ft., fly 30 ft.

STR	DEX	CON	INT	WIS	CHA
15 (+1)	12 (+1)	16 (+3)	11 (+0)	12 (+1)	13 (+1)

Skills Stealth +4
Damage Resistances acid, cold, lightning, fire
Damage Immunities thunder
Senses darkvision 60 ft., passive Perception 11
Languages telepathy 120 ft.
Challenge 5 (1,800 XP)

Hyper-Awareness. A blood orchid cannot be surprised.
Telepathic Bond. Blood orchids have a telepathic link to other blood orchids that are within 120 feet.

Actions

Multiattack. The blood orchid uses Blood Drain. It then makes up to three attacks with its tentacles.
Tentacles. *Melee Weapon Attack:* +4 to hit, reach 5 ft., one target. *Hit:* 10 (2d8 + 1) bludgeoning damage and the target must succeed on a DC 13 Constitution saving throw or be poisoned for 1 hour. The target is also grappled (escape DC 11). While grappled this way, the creature is restrained. Until the grapple ends, the blood orchid can't use this tentacle on another target. The blood orchid has three tentacles that it can attack with.

Blood Drain. The blood orchid feeds on the creature it is grappling. The creature must succeed on a DC 13 Constitution saving throw or its hit point maximum is reduced by 5 (1d10). This reduction lasts until the creature finishes a long rest. The target dies if this effect reduces its hit point maximum to 0.

Blood Orchid Savant

Large aberration, lawful evil
Armor Class 15 (natural armor)
Hit Points 97 (13d10 + 26)
Speed 5 ft., fly 30 ft.

STR	DEX	CON	INT	WIS	CHA
15 (+2)	14 (+2)	14 (+2)	13 (+1)	16 (+3)	18 (+4)

Skills Stealth +5
Damage Resistances acid, cold, lightning, fire

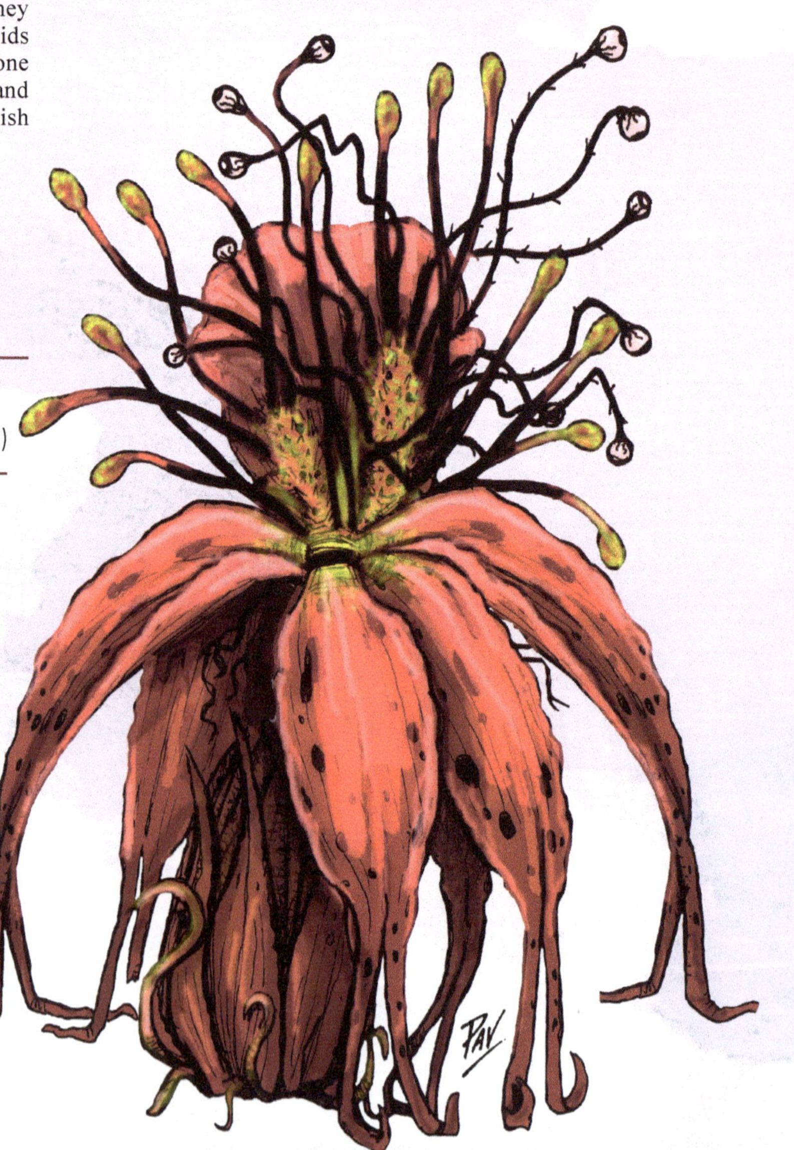

Damage Immunities thunder
Senses darkvision 60 ft., passive Perception 13
Languages telepathy 120 ft.
Challenge 7 (2,900 XP)

Hyper-Awareness. The blood orchid cannot be surprised.

Spellcasting. The blood orchid is a 4th level spellcaster. Its spellcasting ability is Charisma (spell save DC 15, +7 to hit with spell attacks). It can cast the following spells:

Cantrips (at will): *dancing lights, fire bolt, light, mage hand*

1st level (4 slots): *burning hands, color spray, detect magic, magic missile*

2nd level (3 slots): *darkness, ray of enfeeblement, scorching ray*

Telepathic Bond. Blood orchids have a telepathic link to other blood orchids that are within 120 feet.

Actions

Multiattack. The blood orchid uses Blood Drain. It then makes up to three attacks with its tentacles.

Tentacles. *Melee Weapon Attack:* +5 to hit, reach 5 ft., one target. *Hit:* 11 (2d8 + 2) bludgeoning damage and the target must succeed on a DC 13 Constitution saving throw or be poisoned for 1 hour. The target is also grappled (escape DC 12). While grappled this way, the creature is restrained. Until the grapple ends, the blood orchid can't use this tentacle on another target. The blood orchid has three tentacles that it can attack with.

Blood Drain. The blood orchid feeds on the creature it is grappling. The creature must succeed on a DC 13 Constitution saving throw or its hit point maximum is reduced by 5 (1d10). This reduction lasts until the creature finishes a long rest. The target dies if this effect reduces its hit point maximum to 0.

Blood Orchid Grand Savant

Huge aberration, lawful evil
Armor Class 17 (natural armor)
Hit Points 136 (13d12 + 52)
Speed 5 ft., fly 30 ft.

STR	DEX	CON	INT	WIS	CHA
20 (+5)	13 (+1)	18 (+4)	13 (+1)	16 (+3)	20 (+5)

Skills Stealth +5
Damage Resistances acid, cold, lightning, fire
Damage Immunities thunder
Senses darkvision 60 ft., passive Perception 13
Languages telepathy 120 ft.
Challenge 9 (5,000 XP)

Hyper-Awareness. The blood orchid cannot be surprised.

Spellcasting. The blood orchid is a 7th level spellcaster. Its spellcasting ability is Charisma (spell save DC 17, +9 to hit with spell attacks). It can cast the following spells:

Cantrips (at will): *dancing lights, fire bolt, light, mage hand*

1st level (4 slots): *burning hands, color spray, detect magic, magic missile*

2nd level (3 slots): *darkness, ray of enfeeblement, scorching ray*

3rd level (3 slots): *lightning bolt, vampiric touch*

4th level (1 slots): *fire shield*

Telepathic Bond. Blood orchids have a telepathic link to other blood orchids that are within 120 feet.

Actions

Multiattack. The blood orchid uses Blood Drain. It then makes up to three attacks with its tentacles.

Tentacles. *Melee Weapon Attack:* +9 to hit, reach 5 ft., one target. *Hit:* 18 (3d8 + 5) bludgeoning damage and the target must succeed on a DC 16 Constitution saving throw or be poisoned for 1 hour. The target is also grappled (escape DC 15). While grappled this way, the creature is restrained. Until the grapple ends, the blood orchid can't use this tentacle on another target. The blood orchid has three tentacles that it can attack with.

Blood Drain. The blood orchid feeds on the creature it is grappling. The creature must succeed on a DC 16 Constitution saving throw or its hit point maximum is reduced by 5 (1d10). This reduction lasts until the creature finishes a long rest. The target dies if this effect reduces its hit point maximum to 0.

Boarfolk

A group of large, wild, pig-faced humanoids snort derisively and head towards you. They do not appear to be friendly at all.

Boarfolk are giant humanoids standing some 9 to 10 feet tall, weighing nearly 700 pounds. They possess boar-like features, including large tusks that protrude from their mouths.

Boarfolk are created by the sorceress, Circe, on the Isle of the Phoenix in the Land of the Dead. There she uses her powers to transmute travelers that are unfortunate enough to cross her path. Once transmuted, the boarfolk grow enthralled by her beauty and charisma and serve her without question.

Boarfolk speak an offshoot of Common, but so thickly accented as to make it a separate language. The boarfolk live in a nomadic, tribal fashion. Should the influence of Circe ever depart, the boarfolk would turn to infighting and barbaric tribal law; the strongest would rule, and the rest of the boarfolk would split into warring tribes.

Boarfolk

Large humanoid (boarfolk), lawful neutral
Armor Class 10
Hit Points 16 (3d10)
Speed 30 ft.

STR	DEX	CON	INT	WIS	CHA
12 (+1)	10 (+0)	10 (+0)	10 (+0)	10 (+0)	11 (+0)

Senses darkvision 60 ft., passive Perception 10
Languages Boarfolk, Common
Challenge ¼ (50 XP)

Created Race. The boarfolk has advantage on saving throws against spells and effects which would alter its form.

Keen Scent. A boarfolk has advantage on Wisdom (Perception) checks based on scent.

Actions

Gore. *Melee Weapon Attack:* +3 to hit, reach 5 ft., one target. *Hit:* 4 (1d6 + 1) piercing damage.

Greatclub. *Melee Weapon Attack:* +3 to hit, reach 5 ft., one target. *Hit:* 5 (1d8 + 1) bludgeoning damage.

Boarfolk Rager

Large humanoid (boarfolk), lawful neutral
Armor Class 16
Hit Points 123 (13d10 + 52)
Speed 40 ft.

STR	DEX	CON	INT	WIS	CHA
20 (+5)	15 (+2)	18 (+4)	9 (−1)	11 (+0)	10 (+0)

Saving Throws Str +9, Dex +6, Con +8
Skills Athletics +9, Intimidation +3
Damage Resistances bludgeoning, piercing, and slashing damage
Senses darkvision 60 ft., passive Perception 10
Languages Boarfolk, Common
Challenge 9 (5,000 XP)

Brute. A melee weapon deals one extra die of its damage when the rager hits with it (included in the attack).

Created Race. The boarfolk rager has advantage on saving throws against spells and effects that would alter its form.

Keen Scent. A boarfolk rager has advantage on Wisdom (Perception) checks based on scent.

Reckless. At the start of its turn, the rager can gain advantage on all melee weapon attack rolls during that turn, but attack rolls against it have advantage until the start of its next turn.

Actions

Multiattack. The boarfolk rager makes three melee attacks.

Tusks. *Melee Weapon Attack:* +9 to hit, reach 5 ft., one target. *Hit:* 12 (2d6 + 5) piercing damage.

Greatclub. *Melee Weapon Attack:* +9 to hit, reach 5 ft., one target. *Hit:* 14 (2d8 + 5) bludgeoning damage.

Boarfolk Traits

Your boarfolk character has an assortment of inborn abilities, part and parcel of boarfolk nature.

Ability Score Increase. Your Strength score increases by 2, and your Charisma score increases by 1.

Age. Boarfolk do not have the same life cycle as the other races: you were transformed at some point during your lifespan. Once a boarfolk, however, your aging slows considerably, tending to survive well into your third century.

Alignment. Boarfolk who remain upon the Isle of the Phoenix hew to a lawful bent; if a boarfolk is freed from Circe's influence, the natural chaotic tendencies of the race will come to the fore. They run the gamut between good and evil.

Size. Boarfolk are much taller and heavier than humans; some might even mistake them for giantkin. They stand over 7 feet tall and average over 400 pounds. Your size is Medium.

Speed. Your base walking speed is 30 feet.

Darkvision. You have superior vision in dark and dim conditions. You can see in dim light within 60 feet of you as if it were bright light, and in darkness as if it were dim light. You can't discern color in darkness, only shades of gray.

Beast of Burden. You are considered to be Large size for the purposes of determining your carrying capacity.

Created Race. You have advantage on saving throws against spells or effects which would alter your form. In addition, you have proficiency in one skill and one tool of your choice.

Keen Scent. You have advantage on Wisdom (Perception) checks based on scent.

Tusks. You have forward, upthrust tusks that allow you to make a gore attack. You are proficient with your tusks. They are melee weapons that deal 1d8 piercing damage and you cannot be disarmed of them.

Languages. You can speak, read, and write Boarfolk and Common.

Bog Beast

This creature appears as a large, shaggy, fur-covered humanoid with clawed hands and feet. Two, long, upright tusks protrude from its mouth. Its eyes are dull brown and its fur is brownish-yellow.

Bog beasts make their homes in bogs and swamps and feed on creatures that dwell there. They are avid hunters and a bog beast's hunting area usually covers a large expanse of ground several miles around its lair.

A bog beast stands over 9 feet tall and weighs around 1,100 pounds. It makes its lair amid overgrown swamplands and attacks just about any creature that travels too close to its lair. They seem to be able to communicate with one another through a series of guttural grunts and growls but do not speak any known language.

Bog beasts attack with their claws and always fight to the death. A creature killed by a bog beast is dragged back to its lair, where it is devoured.

Bog Beast

Large monstrosity, neutral
Armor Class 13 (natural armor)
Hit Points 76 (8d10 + 32)
Speed 30 ft.

STR	DEX	CON	INT	WIS	CHA
20 (+5)	11 (+0)	18 (+4)	5 (–3)	12 (+1)	9 (–1)

Skills Perception +5, Survival +5
Senses darkvision 60 ft., passive Perception 15
Languages —
Challenge 3 (700 XP)

Keen Smell. The bog beast has advantage on Wisdom (Perception) checks that rely on smell.

Actions

Multiattack. The bog beast makes two attacks with its claws.

Claws. *Melee Weapon Attack:* +7 to hit, reach 10 ft., one target. *Hit:* 12 (2d6 + 5) slashing damage. If the target is a creature, it must succeed on a DC 14 Constitution saving throw against disease or become poisoned until the disease is cured. Every 24 hours that elapse, the target must repeat the saving throw, reducing its hit point maximum by 5 (1d10) on a failure. The disease is cured on a success. The target dies if the disease reduces its hit point maximum to 0. This reduction of the target's hit point maximum lasts until the disease is cured.

Bog Creeper

This creature looks like a human-sized rotting tree trunk with several thorny tendrils sprouting from its body. A single limb protrudes from its central form as well.

The bog creeper is native to the thickest, darkest swamps. It superficially resembles a human-sized rotted tree trunk sprouting several thorny tendrils each about 10 feet long and a single 6-foot-long limb. Bog creepers are carnivorous, lurking amid dead trees and stumps waiting to ambush unsuspecting prey. The shattered boles and stumps make perfect camouflage for the sly bog creeper.

Marshes and swamps are home to the bog creeper and it moves through the territory with ease; it can swim the waters and shamble across the rare patches of dry or swampy ground in pursuit of its prey.

The treasure of a bog creeper is located in its pulpy gullet and consists of the inorganic, indigestible remains and possessions of its victims.

A bog creeper attacks by ambushing its prey, lying in wait for someone or something to wander nearby. When prey comes within range, it lashes out with its single limb and slashes with its tendrils. It uses its tendrils to grab prey and either constrict it or transfer it to its mouth where it bites with its toothy maw. A desperate bog creeper can also vomit forth its powerful digestive sap in order to dispatch its opponents.

Bog Creeper

Medium plant, unaligned
Armor Class 12 (natural armor)
Hit Points 104 (11d8 + 55)
Speed 10 ft., swim 20 ft.

STR	DEX	CON	INT	WIS	CHA
18 (+4)	10 (+0)	20 (+5)	3 (–4)	14 (+2)	6 (–2)

Skills Perception +5
Senses tremorsense 60 ft., passive Perception 15
Languages —
Challenge 9 (5,000 XP)

False Appearance. While the bog creeper remains motionless, it is indistinguishable from normal plants.

Marsh Move. A bog creeper doesn't treat marshy, swampy terrain as difficult terrain.

Actions

Multiattack. The bog creeper makes up to four attacks: one with its bite, one slam, and two with its tendrils.

Bite. *Melee Weapon Attack:* +7 to hit, reach 5 ft., one target. *Hit:* 13 (2d8 + 4) piercing damage.

Slam. *Melee Weapon Attack:* +7 to hit, reach 5 ft., one target. *Hit:* 15 (2d10 + 4) bludgeoning damage.

Tendrils. *Melee Weapon Attack:* +7 to hit, reach 10 ft., one target. *Hit:* 11 (2d6 + 4) bludgeoning damage. The target is grappled (escape DC 14) if the bog creeper isn't already grappling a creature, and the target is restrained until the grapple ends. The bog creeper can only grapple one target.

Acid Spray (3/day). The bog creeper sprays stomach acid in a 30-foot cone. Each creature in that area must make a DC 15 Dexterity saving throw, taking 14 (3d8) acid damage on a failed save, or half as much damage on a successful one.

Bone Crawler

Unarmored, the bone crawler is a fleshy disc-shaped lump approximately six feet in diameter, with a slightly concave top. The bottom curves downward and ends with a circular mouth at its nadir. From the central mass sprout several dozen tentacles, each specialized to perform different functions: stubby muscular ones provide movement, thin graceful tendrils are tipped with sensory organs, and the long, limber whipfronds are used as a means of attack and manipulation. The flesh of a bone crawler ranges from olive green to slate grey to jet black.

When it is encased in bone armor, the bone crawler appears much different. When still, it resembles a 15-foot-diameter mound of bones, piled haphazardly together. A canny observer may note fleshy tendrils or roots webbed throughout the mass. Once it begins to move, the armored crawler is a whirling nightmare of interlocked bones forming a 15-foot-diameter central mass, with bony tentacles extending out from it in all directions.

The bone crawler is an unusual aberration that girds itself with hardened bones, fused together and manipulated by lenticular limbs called whipfronds, to serve as both a weapon and a defense.

Bone crawlers exist by attacking and killing just about anything they can come to grips with. They feast upon the flesh of their enemies, and then integrate the bones of their prey into their armor, repairing any damage sustained. Some bone crawlers have been known to seek out crypts and graveyards, exhuming bodies for their bones.

Bone Crawler

Huge aberration, neutral
Armor Class 16 (natural armor)
Hit Points 161 (14d12 + 70)
Speed 30 ft., climb 10 ft.

STR	DEX	CON	INT	WIS	CHA
23 (+6)	16 (+3)	20 (+5)	9 (−1)	15 (+3)	9 (−1)

Damage Immunities poison, psychic; bludgeoning, piercing, and slashing from nonmagical weapons
Condition Immunities charmed, exhaustion, frightened, paralyzed, petrified, poisoned
Senses blindsight 60 ft., passive Perception 13
Languages Deep Speech
Challenge 13 (10,000 XP)

Spiked Bone Armor. The bone crawler is encased in a shell of iron-hard bones that can absorb 150 hit points worth of damage. Against area of effect attacks, the bone crawler's bone armor will still take damage regardless of whether the bone crawler succeeded on the save. If the bone crawler succeeds on the save, the armor takes half the total damage dealt by the attack. If the bone crawler fails its saving throw, the armor takes double damage from the area effect.

For every 10 hit points of damage the armor takes, the armor gains an additional bone spike. A creature that starts its turn within 5 ft. of the bone crawler takes damage due to the bone spikes. For every bone spike the armor has accumulated, the adjacent creatures take 1d4 piercing damage.

The bone crawler can repair its armor over a 24 hour period by absorbing additional bones into its hulking mass. As the bone crawler absorbs bones, it secretes a substance that will harden, coating the bones, and create the iron-hard shell. For every 3 hit points of bone absorbed by the crawler, 1 hit point of damage is repaired on the armor. For example, if the crawler absorbs the skeleton of a creature that had 75 hit points it would repair 25 hit points of damage on its armor.

False Appearance. While motionless, a bone crawler is indistinguishable from a mound of bones.

Improved Critical. The bone crawler's bone blade attacks score a critical hit on a roll of 19 or 20.

Actions

Multiattack. The crawler can make up to 6 attacks using its bone blades and bone whips.

Bone Blade. *Melee Weapon Attack:* +11 to hit, reach 10 ft., one target. *Hit:* 17 (1d10 + 8) slashing damage.

Bone Whip. *Melee Weapon Attack:* +11 to hit, reach 10 ft., one target. *Hit:* 11 (1d6 + 8) bludgeoning damage.

Whirling Frenzy (Recharge 5–6). The bone crawler spins its bone blades in a swirling storm of sharpened edges. Creatures within 10 feet of the crawler must succeed on a DC 15 Dexterity saving throw, taking 15 (2d8 + 6) slashing damage on a failure, or half as much damage on a successful one.

Brass Man

This creature resembles a humanoid constructed of brass. Its features are exquisite and delicate, and ancient runes and symbols adorn its body.

Brass men are humanoid-shaped constructs built by the powerful efreet of the City of Brass. They are created for the sole purpose of guarding some efreeti secret within the walls of the city. Some are created as battle allies and aid the efreet in battle against their enemies. They are rarely encountered elsewhere though on occasion one is sent to the Material Plane by its efreeti creator to retrieve an object or creature.

Brass men are very tough physical opponents and difficult to stop. Typically, a brass man begins combat by spitting molten brass on the closest opponent before moving into melee where it attacks with its huge greatsword or its powerful fists.

Brass Man

Large construct, neutral

Armor Class 16 (natural armor)
Hit Points 136 (16d10 + 48)
Speed 30 ft.

STR	DEX	CON	INT	WIS	CHA
21 (+5)	10 (+0)	16 (+3)	2 (–4)	11 (+0)	1 (–5)

Damage Vulnerabilities cold
Damage Immunities fire, poison, psychic; bludgeoning, piercing, and slashing from nonmagical weapons that aren't adamantine
Condition Immunities charmed, exhaustion, frightened, paralyzed, petrified, poisoned
Senses darkvision 60 ft., passive Perception 10
Challenge 9 (5,000 XP)

Fire Absorption. Whenever the golem is subjected to fire damage, it takes no damage and instead regains a number of hit points equal to the fire damage dealt.

Immutable Form. The golem is immune to any spell or effect that would alter its form.

Magic Resistance. The golem has advantage on saving throws against spells and other magical effects.

Magic Weapons. The golem's weapon attacks are magical.

Actions

Multiattack. The brass man makes two greatsword attack and one slam attack.

Greatsword. *Melee Weapon Attack:* +9 to hit, reach 10 ft., one target. *Hit:* 18 (4d6 + 5) slashing damage.

Slam. *Melee Weapon Attack:* +9 to hit, reach 10 ft., one target. *Hit:* 18 (3d8 + 5) bludgeoning damage.

Molten Breath (Recharge 6). The golem exhales molten brass in a 25-foot line. Each creature along that line must make a DC 13 Dexterity saving throw, taking 28 (8d6) fire damage on a failed save, or half as much on a successful one.

Brownie

This tiny creature resembles an elf with greenish skin. Its hair is light and it is dressed in bright clothing.

A brownie is a timid, quiet fey creature that prefers to live only among its own kind. Most brownies dwell in pastoral areas untouched by civilization, such as deep forests and wild lands far from other creatures.

Brownies are rarely over 18 inches tall. Their hair is always earth-toned such as brown, gray, or tawny. Most brownies prefer green or otherwise brightly colored clothing. They may be distant relatives of pixies and halflings, but this has never been proven.

Brownies avoid combat unless forced. If unable to employ any spells, brownies attack with tiny longswords.

Brownie

Tiny fey, lawful good
Armor Class 15 (natural armor)
Hit Points 7 (2d4 + 2)
Speed 25 ft.

STR	DEX	CON	INT	WIS	CHA
7 (−2)	18 (+4)	12 (+1)	14 (+2)	14 (+2)	16 (+3)

Skills Deception +5, Stealth +6
Senses passive Perception 12
Languages Common, Halfling, Sylvan
Challenge 2 (450 XP)

Magic Resistance. The brownie has advantage on saving throws against spells and other magical effects.

Innate Spellcasting. The brownie's innate spellcasting ability is Charisma (spell save DC 13, +5 to hit with spell attacks). It can innately cast the following spells, without using any spell components:

At will: *druidcraft, minor illusion, prestidigitation, thaumaturgy*

3/day each: *color spray, dancing lights, hideous laughter, silent image*

1/day each: *dimension door*

Actions

Shortsword. *Melee Weapon Attack:* +6 to hit, reach 5 ft., one target. *Hit:* 7 (1d6 + 4) piercing damage.

Brownie Traits

Your brownie character has the following racial traits.

Ability Score Increase. Your Dexterity score increases by 2 and your Charisma increases by 1.

Age. A brownie grows to adulthood before the age of 10 and lives for around 200 years before old age sets in.

Alignment. Unlike most fey, brownies are fairly lawful in alignment, and rarely, if ever, evil.

Size. Brownies are one of the smallest of the fey races. Your size is Small.

Speed. Your base walking speed is 25 feet.

Faeriefolk. You cannot be put to sleep or aged by magic.

Slight. Your small size gives you a +1 bonus to your Armor Class, and you have proficiency in Stealth.

Fey Magic. You know the *druidcraft* cantrip. Once you reach 3rd level, you can cast the *entangle* spell once per day. Once you reach 5th level, you can also cast the *spike growth* spell once per day. Charisma is your spellcasting ability for these spells.

Languages. You can speak, read, and write Common and Sylvan.

Bulette

While ancient apocrypha may persuade us that the bulette was an arcane creation from the flesh vats of an ancient wizard, little is ever said in the ancient texts about the lengths his one-time apprentice went to in order to outstrip his master. By creating and adding a planar loom to his own vats, this mad apprentice was able to bind fixed threads of extraplanar energies to the already potent essences of snapping turtle, armadillo, and demon ichor. Thus were born the polychromatic bulettes.

At least six rare types are known, and each is unique in its coloring, temperament, and abilities. While technically immortal until killed, they are also thankfully few in number and cannot breed. Each polychromatic bulette is a singular creature issued forth from the chaotic apprentice's flesh vats and planar looms. As to how long even a mad wizard lives and where his island retreat can be found, none can say. But it is known that examples of his crazed experiments have escaped to the mainland over the course of time.

Each type of polychromatic bulette resembles its lesser cousin species in general shape and form but comes in a surprising array of relative abilities and color markings. Because of their dual-plane origins, polychromatic bulettes are always detectable by divination spells that detect the presence of magic.

Bulette, Black

The shambling, aggressive black bulette is much more than its bestial countenance might at first indicate — it serves as a prison cell for a fiend of the GMs choosing. As punishment for breaking an infernal law, the imprisoned fiend has been sentenced to serve thousands of years trapped inside the black bulette. Furthermore, the accursed fiend must funnel its supreme cognitive abilities through the bulette's animalistic brain, forcing the creature to behave as a dim-witted beast, and perpetually frustrating and limiting the powers of the fiend.

Black Bulette

Huge monstrosity, lawful evil
Armor Class: 19 (natural armor)
Hit Points: 225 (18d12 + 108)
Speed: 80 ft., burrow 80 ft.

STR	DEX	CON	INT	WIS	CHA
22 (+6)	14 (+2)	22 (+6)	6 (−2)	14 (+2)	10 (+0)

Saving Throws Dex +7, Wis + 7
Skills Perception +7
Damage Immunities fire
Senses blindsight 60 ft., darkvision 60 ft., passive Perception 17
Languages all, telepathy 120 ft.
Challenge 13 (10,000 XP)

Deal of a Lifetime. If killed, the body of the black bulette shatters into shards of obsidian glass, freeing the devil imprisoned within. The devil may be of any random type (GM's discretion) save that of a royal rank. The devil will be grateful to whoever is responsible for ending its centuries-long confinement, and will offer the responsible parties one favor in payment before returning to the infernal realms of its home plane. Wise recipients of this offer should bear in mind that the usual caveats of treating with devils remain in full force when striking any bargains.

Detect Evil and Good. The bulette knows if there is an aberration, celestial, elemental, fey, fiend, or undead within 30 feet of it and where the creature is located. The bulette also knows if there is a place or object within 30 feet of it that has been consecrated or desecrated.

Dual Planar Connection. The black bulette has a planar tie to the Abyss, where it appears as a chained adamantine cask shaped like an abstracted bulette.

Infernal Stench. Any creature that starts its turn within 120 feet of the bulette must succeed on a DC 18 Constitution saving throw or be poisoned until the start of its next turn. Coming into physical contact with a black bulette results in the creature being imparted with a horrid stench that causes it to have disadvantage on Dexterity (Stealth) checks for 12 hours. The stench can be removed sooner with plenty of soap, water, and two full hours of scrubbing.

Magic Resistance. The bulette has advantage on saving throws against spells and other magical effects.

Actions

Bite. *Melee Weapon Attack:* +11 to hit, reach 10 ft., one target. *Hit:* 58 (8d12 + 6) piercing damage.

Abysmal Breath (Recharge 5–6). The bulette exhales fire in a 60-foot cone. Each creature in that area must make a DC 18 Dexterity saving throw, taking 42 (12d6) fire damage on a failed save, or half as much damage on a successful one.

Bulette, Blue

The blue bulette is remarkable for its cerulean armor plates, frilled head carapace, and single short horn. Unlike their more subterrestrial cousins, blue bulettes are herbivores and spend their lives entirely above ground. Aggressive when disturbed, it will defend its territory (everything in sight) against any perceived threat.

Blue Bulette

Large monstrosity, unaligned
Armor Class 17 (natural armor)
Hit Points 150 (12d10 + 84)
Speed 40 ft.

STR	DEX	CON	INT	WIS	CHA
22 (+6)	12 (+1)	24 (+7)	3 (−4)	10 (+0)	4 (−3)

Saving Throws Dex +5, Con +11, Wis +4
Skills Perception +4
Damage Immunities lightning
Senses darkvision 60 ft., passive perception 14
Languages —
Challenge 12 (8,400 XP)

Electromagnetic Field. The electrified nature of the blue bulette is such that compasses will spin wildly within half of a mile of the bulette, and any technology-based items will cease to function within 150 feet of it.

Motherlode. If killed, the body of a blue bulette explodes in a loud roar of thunder (deafening all within 150 feet for 1 minute). Afterward, all that remains of the beast is a 100-pound pile of meteoric iron, which if broken, will also contain its single white horn and 1–6 small lodestones.

Planar Connection. Because their arcane natures tie blue bulettes to the Demi-plane of Lightning, they also simultaneously exist there as nearly invisible silhouettes intermittently illuminated by flashes of electric light.

Actions

Bite. *Melee Weapon Attack:* +10 to hit, reach 5 ft., one target. *Hit:* 33 (5d10 + 6) piercing damage plus 26 (4d12) lightning damage. If the target is a creature, it must succeed on a DC 15 Constitution saving throw or be knocked unconscious for 1 minute.

Electric Stomp. The bulette slams its forefeet into the ground, imparting a ground-conductive electric charge in an 80-foot radius. All creatures, excluding constructs and undead, must succeed on a DC 17 Constitution saving throw, or take 26 (4d12) lightning damage and be stunned for 1 minute. A stunned creature can repeat the saving throw at the end of each of its turns, ending the effect on a success.

Bolt and Run. The blue bulette transforms into a sphere of ball lightning and magically teleports up to 120 feet to an unoccupied space it can see.

Bulette, Gold

In contrast to its brutish and nonsentient brethren, the gold bulette is an intelligent though reclusive creature. Feeding primarily on minerals found in mountain ranges, it finds gemstones an especially favored treat and will bargain with other creatures in exchange for them. With its virtually immortal lifespan and thorough knowledge of the underground, the gold bulette possesses much useful information — though it will never reveal any information concerning its own origins or plans.

Gold Bulette

Huge monstrosity, chaotic good
Armor Class 20 (natural armor)
Hit Points 232 (16d12 + 128)
Speed 60 ft., burrow 60 ft. burrowing

STR	DEX	CON	INT	WIS	CHA
24 (+7)	16 (+3)	26 (+8)	18 (+4)	14 (+2)	16 (+3)

Saving Throws Dex +9, Wis + 8
Skills Perception +14
Senses truesight 120 ft., passive Perception 24
Languages Common, Draconic, Dwarven, Elven, Goblin, Orc
Challenge 17 (18,000 XP)

Detect Evil and Good. The bulette knows if there is an aberration, celestial, elemental, fey, fiend, or undead within 30 feet of it and where the creature is located. The bulette also knows if there is a place or object within 30 feet of it that has been consecrated or desecrated.

Goldbringer. If killed, the body of a gold bulette flashes brightly in a nova light that blinds all who can see it permanently (or until cured), after

which its body condenses into a gold-plated sandstone statue-like version of itself. Stripping off its outer plating and breaking up its remaining body will yield the equivalent of 50,000 gold pieces and 25–50 gemstones of varying value.

Karmic Curse. Killing a gold bulette permanently entangles all creatures present at the event with tiny planar threads binding them to both the positive and negative planes of existence. This curse will manifest itself as advantage or disadvantage on all future saving throws made by the affected bulette slayers, with a 50% chance at the time each saving throw is made of the effect being beneficial or baleful. The curse can only be removed by the successful casting of a *remove curse* spell performed while on the astral plane.

Innate Spellcasting. The bulette's innate spellcasting ability is Charisma (spell save DC 17, +9 to hit with spell attacks). It can cast the following spells at will without requiring material components: *disintegrate, fireball, fly, heal, lightning bolt, magic missile, teleport.*

Magic Resistance. The bulette has advantage on saving throws against spells and other magical effects.

Multi-Planar Connection. Because their arcane natures tie gold bulettes to both the positive and negative planes, they also simultaneously exist on both of those planes as either a medium-sized globule of light or shadow, respectively.

Unlimited Spell Use. The gold bulette has multiple spells encoded into its brain stem, including (but not limited to) the spells listed above. Because the gold bulette's multi-planar connection acts as a source of magic and power, it can use each spell as many times per days as desired.

Actions

Bite. *Melee Weapon Attack:* +13 to hit, reach 5 ft., one target. *Hit:* 59 (8d12 + 7) piercing damage.

Bulette, Green

The green bulette placidly wanders forested and mountainous areas, seeking prey. While it has the ability to kill smaller creatures with a mere bite, it prefers to stalk the largest animals it can locate. Any damaging attack upon a green bulette will trigger the reflexive shift to its gaseous state, and when hunting, a green bulette will actively seek to provoke just such attacks.

Green Bulette

Huge monstrosity, unaligned
Armor Class 17 (solid) or 20 (gaseous)
Hit Points 121 (9d12 + 63)
Speed 40 ft., fly 80 ft.

STR	DEX	CON	INT	WIS	CHA
20 (+5)	12 (+1)	24 (+7)	3 (−4)	10 (+0)	6 (−2)

Skills Perception +5
Damage Immunities poison; bludgeoning, piercing, and slashing (gaseous form only)
Senses darkvision 60 ft., passive perception 15
Languages —
Challenge 13 (10,000 XP)

Emerald Dust. If killed (whether in solid or gaseous form), the body of a green bulette appears to implode out of existence with a thump and inward rush of air. If the immediate area is searched, it is found to be lightly dusted in a fine green powder of emerald dust, which can be collected and used to create both potent poisons and poison-based magics.

Gaseous Form. While in gaseous form, the bulette can occupy another creature's space and vice versa. In addition, if air can pass through a space, the bulette can pass through it without squeezing.

Gone With the Wind. If a green bulette is reduced to 50% of its hit points, it disperses itself to the winds and escapes, regathering itself at a later time to rest and heal.

Magic Resistance. The bulette has advantage on saving throws against spells and other magical effects.

Multi-State Existence. While appearing as a solid, animal-based creature when stalking or resting, the green bulette instinctively shifts as a reaction into a poisonous gaseous form when attacked, appearing as a roiling cloud of green-tinged smoke with glittering emerald particles floating within it. The green bulette will maintain its gaseous form and use it to attack, attempting to poison and choke its adversaries. It will only revert to its solid state again once it is safe and free from attack.

Planar Connection. Because their arcane natures tie green bulettes to the Elemental Plane of Air, they also simultaneously exist there as insubstantial and barely visible vaporous apparitions.

Actions

Bite. *Melee Weapon Attack:* +10 to hit, reach 5 ft., one target. *Hit:* 24 (3d12 + 5) piercing damage.

Creeping Death. While it is in gaseous form, one creature in the bulette's space must make a DC 17 Constitution saving throw, taking 35 (10d6) poison damage on a failed save, or half as much damage on a successful one.

State Change. As an action, the bulette can transform from its solid form into a cloud of poisonous gas that is 10 feet square.

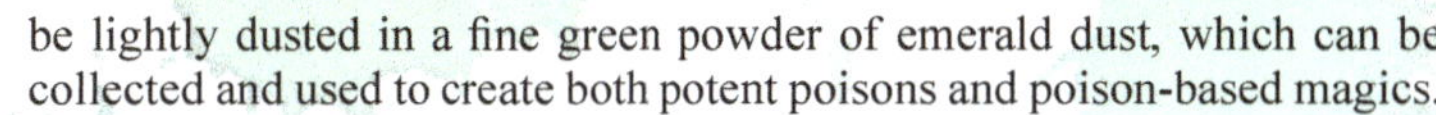

Bulette, Red

The red bulette spends the majority of its time underground, feeding on the rare minerals and rocks found there. With a skin temperature that varies between 500–1200°F, the red bulette moves through bedrock and earth by swimming through it at its full movement rate. While not necessarily carnivorous, they are attracted to all refined metals and will happily swallow a warrior for the metal content of its weapons and armor. Red bulettes like rare metals (refined or raw ore) best of all. This makes the mere sighting of one in the wild a real and present threat to any local treasure vaults or royal economies.

Red Bulette

Huge monstrosity, unaligned
Armor Class 18 (natural armor)
Hit Points 135 (10d12 + 70)
Speed 40 ft., burrow 80 ft.

STR	DEX	CON	INT	WIS	CHA
20 (+5)	12 (+1)	24 (+7)	3 (–4)	10 (+0)	5 (–3)

Saving Throws Dex +6, Con +11, Wis +4
Skills Perception +4
Damage Immunities fire
Senses blindsight 60 ft., darkvision 60 ft., passive Perception 14
Languages —
Challenge 12 (8,400 XP)

Metalsense. The red bulette is aware of all metals within 60 feet of it.
Mineral Rich. If a red bulette is killed, its planar connection is immediately severed. Over the course of 4 to 6 hours, its body will cool to the ambient temperature of the environment. While the vast majority of its body will cool into a basalt-like stone, its digestive track will solidify into roughly 1,000 lbs. of an alloy admixture of every mineral substance it has consumed. Depending upon its recent feeding habits, this substance is the equivalent of metal-rich ore of many types in combination, and can be smelted back down into standard and precious metals by experts knowledgeable in such methods. Additionally, a few diamonds will be found in what was the red bulette's gizzard.

Planar Connection. Because their arcane natures link red bulettes to the Elemental Plane of Fire, they also simultaneously exist there as insubstantial and barely visible shadows of themselves.
Tunneler. The bulette can burrow through solid rock at its burrow speed leaving a 10-foot-diameter tunnel in its wake.
Vanishing Act. Red bulettes avoid overland movement, preferring to swim through earth and bedrock. If confronted above ground, they will reflexively increase their body temperatures enough to simply melt their way down into the ground and vanish. If threatened by a much larger creature, they simply dive underground and "swim" away. However, if they are threatened by any creature that wears or is carrying refined metals, they will instinctively return and attempt to ambush with a bite/swallow attack from underground.

Actions

Bite. *Melee Weapon Attack:* +9 to hit, reach 5 ft., one target. *Hit:* 31 (4d12 + 5) piercing damage plus 7 (2d6) fire damage, and the target is grappled (escape DC 15). Until this grapple ends, the target is restrained, and the bulette can't bite another target.
Swallow. The bulette makes one bite attack against a Medium or smaller target it is grappling. If the attack hits, the target is also swallowed, and the grapple ends. While swallowed, the target is blinded and restrained, it has total cover against attacks and other effects outside the bulette, and it takes 21 (6d6) fire damage at the start of each of the bulette's turns. A bulette can have three Medium or smaller creatures swallowed at the same time.
Death From Below (Recharge 5–6). If the bulette burrows at least 20 feet as part of its movement, it can then use this action to surface from underground in a space that contains one or more creatures. Each of those creatures must succeed on a DC 16 Strength or Dexterity saving throw (target's choice) or be knocked prone and splashed with globules of molten rock, taking 18 (2d12 + 5) bludgeoning damage plus 14 (4d6) fire damage. On a successful save, the creature takes only half damage, isn't knocked prone, and is pushed 5 feet out of the bulette's space into an unoccupied space of the creature's choice. If no unoccupied space is within range, the creature falls prone in the bulette's space.

Bulette, Translucent

The translucent bulette appears as a ghostly version of its more material cousins. Existing in equal portions on the Prime Material and Astral Planes, its physical form is insubstantial on the Prime Material Plane, and only dimly perceived on both planes.

Translucent Bulette

Huge monstrosity, unaligned
Armor Class 14 (Prime Material) or 18 (Astral Plane)
Hit Points 225 (18d12 + 108)
Speed 60 ft., fly 80 ft.

STR	DEX	CON	INT	WIS	CHA
24 (+7)	14 (+2)	22 (+6)	6 (–2)	10 (+0)	10 (+0)

Saving Throws Dex +7, Con +11, Wis +5

Skills Perception +10
Damage Resistances bludgeoning, piercing, and
slashing from nonmagical weapons
Senses blindsight 60 ft., truesight 120 ft.,
passive Perception 20
Languages —
Challenge 15 (13,000 XP)

Astral Ambusher. In the first round of
a combat, the bulette has advantage on
attack rolls against any creature it has
surprised.

Astral Jaunt. As a bonus action, the
bulette can magically shift from the
Prime Material Plane to the Astral
Plane, or vice versa.

Astral Portal. On the Prime
Material Plane, any melee attack
against the translucent bulette
that should hit instead misses, and
the attacker risks falling through
the beast's form, which acts as a
dimensional portal, and into the astral
plane. The attacker must succeed on a DC
14 Dexterity saving throw to avoid falling through the
bulette and into the Astral Plane.

Detect Evil and Good. The bulette knows if there is an
aberration, celestial, elemental, fey, fiend, or undead within 30 feet of
it and where the creature is located. The bulette also knows if there is a
place or object within 30 feet of it that has been consecrated or desecrated.

Dual Planar Connection. Each translucent bulette is tied so thoroughly
to the Astral and Prime Material Planes that its entire body acts as an open
portal between the two planes. Intentional use of a translucent bulette for
purposeful travel between these two planes is possible with a successful
grapple or melee attack against the creature.

Limited Invulnerability (Prime Material Plane Only). While on the
Prime Material Plane, the bulette is immune to all damage.

Insubstantial Form. The translucent bulette cannot be harmed on the
Prime Material Plane because any damaging attacks merely phase through
its insubstantial form. Physical attacks are only possible when attacking
the creature from the Astral Plane.

Magic Resistance. The bulette has advantage on saving throws against
spells and other magical effects.

Pop goes the Portal. If killed, the body of a translucent bulette
immediately vanishes with a popping sound, severing its living portal
connection between planes.

Actions

Bite. *Melee Weapon Attack:* +12 to hit, reach 5 ft., one target. *Hit:* 33
(4d12 + 7) piercing damage and the target is grappled if the bulette is not
already grappling another creature.

Portal Swallow. The bulette makes a bite attack against a Large or
smaller target it is grappling. If the attack hits, the target is swallowed and
transported to the Astral Plane, and the grapple ends.

Burning Ghat

A humanoid figure stands swathed in smoke, its distinct features obliterated by the charred and blackened flesh. Ash perpetually trails from the creature as it moves and small patches of burnt skin flake from its body. Its eyes are small dots of brilliant crimson fire.

The burning ghat is a rare form of undead created in areas of unusually high negative energy when a living creature is put to death by fire for a crime it did not commit. Utterly twisted and maddened by its fate, a burning ghat is a fearsome creature, consumed with a hatred for the living and seeking to end life wherever it finds it. The distinct and pungent stench of burnt flesh is often the harbinger of a burning ghat's arrival and is easily noticeable within 30 feet of the creature. They can often still be found wearing the clothes they wore as they burned to death, if the garments survived the flames, though a burning ghat of any great age will usually have none.

Burning ghats inhabit remote areas near places where they were put to death. They are not bound to this area as some undead seem to be, but they seldom wander more than a mile or so away from their death site. Most encounters are with a lone burning ghat, but occasionally when more than one innocent has been put to the flames, a pack of these creatures can be found. Burning ghats are nocturnal pack hunters, feasting on the charred flesh of those they encounter and kill. They are seldom found with other undead, preferring to keep company with their own kind or operating alone. A burning ghat can communicate in the Common tongue and any other language it knew in life. Its voice crackles and hisses like a freshly stoked fire.

A burning ghat attacks with its claws, seeking to slay any living creature it encounters. A burning ghat's claws heat the blood of living creatures upon contact, causing great pain as it sizzles and boils away into the air. It favors burning its victims to death but is content to rend them apart if they should prove immune to fire.

Burning Ghat

Medium undead, chaotic evil
Armor Class 12
Hit Points 39 (6d8 + 12)
Speed 30 ft.

STR	DEX	CON	INT	WIS	CHA
13 (+1)	15 (+2)	14 (+2)	13 (+1)	14 (+2)	14 (+2)

Damage Vulnerabilities cold
Damage Resistances acid, lightning
Damage Immunities fire
Condition Immunities charmed, exhaustion, frightened, paralyzed
Senses darkvision 60 ft., passive Perception
Languages the languages it knew in life
Challenge 3 (700 XP)

Burning Blood. Any creature that hits the burning ghat with a melee attack while within 5 feet of it must make a DC 13 Dexterity saving throw or take 7 (2d6) fire damage.

Odor. Any creature that starts its turn within 5 feet of the burning ghat must succeed on a DC 13 Constitution saving throw or be poisoned until the start of its next turn. On a successful saving throw, the creature is immune to the burning ghat's Odor for 24 hours.

Actions

Multiattack. The burning ghat makes two claw attacks.

Claws. *Melee Weapon Attack:* +4 to hit, reach 5 ft., one target. *Hit:* 6 (1d8 + 2) slashing damage plus 7 (2d6) fire damage.

Fire Burst (1/day). The burning ghat unleashes a burst of flames in a 20-foot sphere centered on itself. Creatures in the area must make a DC 13 Dexterity saving throw, taking 17 (5d6) fire damage on a failed save, or half as much damage on a successful one.

Cadaver

This monster resembles a humanoid dressed in tattered rags. Rotted flesh reveals corded muscles and sinew stretched tightly over its skeleton. Hollow eye sockets flicker with a hellish glow. Broken and rotted teeth line its mouth, and its hands end in wicked claws.

Cadavers are the undead skeletal remains of people who have been buried alive or given an improper burial (an unmarked grave or mass grave for example). They can be found haunting graveyards and cemeteries.

Cadavers are infused with a hatred that rivals many other undead creatures. This hatred includes its own existence as well as the existence of all living creatures. Thus, the cadaver attacks all creatures it encounters. They have a distinct for light, but it does not damage them. All encounters with cadavers are at night or places cloaked in darkness. Encounters are most often with a solitary creature. Multiple cadavers do not work in concert with each other; being mindless they simply charge into combat, killing all creatures they can. Cadavers are sometimes found in the employ of greater undead (such as wights or ghasts).

A cadaver attacks by raking with its filthy claws or biting with its sharp, disease-infested teeth. They often lie in shallow graves waiting for potential victims to wander too close, when they immediately spring to the attack, raking and biting until destroyed or until all foes are dead.

Cadaver

Medium undead, chaotic evil
Armor Class 12
Hit Points 22 (4d8 + 4)
Speed 30 ft.

STR	DEX	CON	INT	WIS	CHA
13 (+1)	14 (+2)	13 (+1)	2 (–4)	10 (+0)	10 (+0)

Damage Immunities cold, poison
Condition Immunities exhaustion, poisoned
Senses darkvision 60 ft., passive Perception 10
Languages understands the languages it knew if life but can't speak
Challenge 1 (200 XP)

Reanimation. When reduced to 0 hit points, the cadaver falls inert and begins the process of reanimating. While in this state, the cadaver regenerates 1 hit point at the start of its turn. Hit points lost to magical weapons or radiant damage are not regained. When the creature reaches its full hit point total, less any magical weapon or radiant damage suffered, it rises, ready to fight again.

A fallen cadaver can be prevented from reanimating by salting and burning the bones, casting *gentle repose* on it, or bathing the bones in cleansing *sacred flame*.

Actions

Multiattack. The cadaver makes one bite attack and two claw attacks.

Bite. *Melee Weapon Attack:* +4 to hit, reach 5 ft., one target. *Hit:* 5 (1d6 + 2) piercing damage. If the target is a creature, it must succeed on a DC 13 Constitution saving throw against disease or become poisoned until the disease is cured. Every 24 hours that elapse, the target must repeat the saving throw, reducing its hit point maximum by 5 (1d10) on a failure. The disease is cured on a success. The target dies if the disease reduces its hit point maximum to 0. This reduction to the target's hit point maximum lasts until the disease is cured.

Claws. *Melee Weapon Attack:* +4 to hit, reach 5 ft., one target. *Hit:* 6 (1d8 + 2) slashing damage. If the target is a creature, it must succeed on a DC 13 Constitution saving throw against disease or become poisoned until the disease is cured. Every 24 hours that elapse, the target must repeat the saving throw, reducing its hit point maximum by 5 (1d10) on a failure. The disease is cured on a success. The target dies if the disease reduces its hit point maximum to 0. This reduction to the target's hit point maximum lasts until the disease is cured.

Cadaver Lord

The rotted flesh and tattered garments of this creature do little to hide the savage gleam of intellect in its burning eyes nor the grin of anticipation that crosses its features as it advances.

Cadaver Lord

Medium undead, chaotic evil
Armor Class 14
Hit Points 32 (5d8 + 10)
Speed 30 ft.

STR	DEX	CON	INT	WIS	CHA
15 (+2)	18 (+4)	14 (+2)	13 (+1)	10 (+0)	16 (+3)

Damage Resistances bludgeoning, piercing, and slashing from nonmagical weapons
Damage Immunities cold, poison
Condition Immunities exhaustion, poisoned
Senses darkvision 60 ft., passive Perception 10
Languages Common
Challenge 4 (1,100 XP)

Innate Spellcasting. The cadaver lord's spellcasting ability is Charisma (spell save DC 13, +5 to hit with spell attacks). The cadaver lord can innately cast each of the following spells 1/day, requiring no material components: *darkness, fear, create undead*.

Create Cadaver. A humanoid slain by a cadaver lord rises 24 hours later as a cadaver under the cadaver lord's control. The cadaver lord can have no more than three cadavers under its control at one time.

Magic Resistance. The cadaver lord has advantage on saving throws against spells and other magical effects.

Reanimation. When reduced to 0 hit points, the cadaver falls inert and begins the process of reanimating. While in this state, the cadaver regenerates 1 hit point at the start of its turn. Hit points lost to magical weapons or radiant damage are not regained. When the creature reaches its full hit point total, less any magical weapon or radiant damage suffered, it rises, ready to fight again.

A fallen cadaver can be prevented from reanimating by salting and burning the bones, casting *gentle repose* on it, or bathing the bones in cleansing *sacred flame*.

Actions

Multiattack. The cadaver lord makes one bite attack and two claw attacks.

Bite. *Melee Weapon Attack:* +7 to hit, reach 5 ft., one target. *Hit:* 11 (2d6 + 4) piercing damage. If the target is a creature, it must succeed on a DC 13 Constitution saving throw against disease or become poisoned until the disease is cured. Every 24 hours that elapse, the target must repeat the saving throw, reducing its hit point maximum by 5 (1d10) on a failure. The disease is cured on a success. The target dies if the disease reduces its hit point maximum to 0. This reduction to the target's hit point maximum lasts until the disease is cured.

Claws. *Melee Weapon Attack:* +7 to hit, reach 5 ft., one target. *Hit:* 13 (2d8 + 4) slashing damage. If the target is a creature, it must succeed on a DC 13 Constitution saving throw against disease or become poisoned until the disease is cured. Every 24 hours that elapse, the target must repeat the saving throw, reducing its hit point maximum by 5 (1d10) on a failure. The disease is cured on a success. The target dies if the disease reduces its hit point maximum to 0. This reduction to the target's hit point maximum lasts until the disease is cured.

Cadejo

The cadejo is a fey creature that resembles a large dog with glowing red eyes. Cadejo come in two colors — the benevolent light cadejo and the evil dark cadejo. The light cadejo is a guardian of travelers, drunkards and the lost, often following at a distance and protecting its chosen charge as it makes its way home. The dark cadejo is everything that its good counterpart is not — a dark cadejo revels in causing fear and terrifying lone travelers, using its stench and hypnotic powers to render its prey helpless, then killing them at its leisure.

Fortunately for the lone traveler, the light cadejo is bound to undo the evil committed by its dark counterpart and can sense any evil committed by a dark cadejo within one mile. In such cases the light cadejo is drawn to the place, where its very presence nullifies many of the dark cadejo's powers. Less fortunately, dark cadejo invariably outnumber the light, and confrontations between the two are always fights to the death.

Cadejo, Dark

A coat black as night with glowing red eyes and a fierce expression, this odd beast looks like a dog but is the size of a Medium humanoid.

Dark Cadejo

Medium fey, chaotic evil
Armor Class 18 (natural armor)
Hit Points 99 (18d8 + 18)
Speed 30 ft.

STR	DEX	CON	INT	WIS	CHA
10 (+0)	18 (+4)	12 (+1)	10 (+0)	18 (+4)	10 (+0)

Skills Deception +4, Perception +8, Stealth +8
Senses darkvision 60 ft., passive Perception 18
Languages Common
Challenge 3 (700 XP)

Nullification. While it is within 120 feet of a light cadejo, a dark cadejo makes ability checks, attacks, and saving throws at disadvantage. Additionally, the dark cadejo's Paralysis and Stench features do not function. However, any attacks, ability checks, and saving throws resulting from direct combat with a light cadejo are made without disadvantage.

Paralysis. When a creature that can see the dark cadejo's eyes starts its turn within 30 feet of the dark cadejo, the dark cadejo can force it to make a DC 14 Constitution saving throw if the dark cadejo isn't incapacitated and can see the creature. On a failure, the creature is paralyzed for as long as the dark cadejo maintains eye contact. A paralysed creature can repeat the saving at the end of each of its turns, ending the effect on a success. This ability does not function for the dark cadejo while it is within 120 feet of a light cadejo.

Unless surprised, a creature can avert its eyes to avoid the saving throw at the start of its turn. If the creature does so, it can't see the dark cadejo until the start of its next turn when it can avert its eyes again. If the creature looks at the dark cadejo in the meantime, it must immediately make the save.

Stench. The dark cadejo emits a sickening stench, affecting all creatures near it. Any creature that begins its turn within 10 feet of the dark cadejo must make a DC 14 Constitution save or be poisoned until the start of its next turn.

This ability does not function for the dark cadejo while it is within 120 feet of a light cadejo.

Actions

Multiattack. The dark cadejo makes three attacks: one with its bite and two with its claws.

Bite. *Melee Weapon Attack:* +6 to hit, reach 5 ft., one target. *Hit:* 8 (1d8 + 4) piercing damage.

Claw. Melee Weapon Attack: +6 to hit, reach 5 ft., one target. *Hit:* 7 (1d6 + 4) slashing damage.

Cadejo, Light

Light Cadejo

Medium fey, lawful good
Armor Class 18 (Natural Armor)
Hit Points 99 (18d8 + 18)
Speed 30 ft.

STR	DEX	CON	INT	WIS	CHA
10 (+0)	18 (+4)	12 (+1)	10 (+0)	18 (+4)	10 (+0)

Skills Deception +4, Perception +8, Stealth +8
Senses darkvision 60 ft., passive Perception 18
Languages Common
Challenge 3 (700 XP)

Nullification. The light cadejo exists to undo the evil done by its wicked cousin. While a light cadejo is within 120 feet of a dark cadejo, the dark cadejo makes ability checks, attacks, and saving throws at disadvantage. Additionally, the dark cadejo's Paralysis and Stench features do not function. However, any attacks, ability checks, and saving throws resulting from direct combat with a light cadejo are made without disadvantage.

Actions

Multiattack. The light cadejo makes three attacks: one with its bite and two with its claws.

Bite. Melee Weapon: +6 to hit, reach 5 ft., one target. *Hit:* 8 (1d8 + 4) piercing damage.

Claw. Melee Weapon Attack: +6 to hit, reach 5 ft., one target. *Hit:* 7 (1d6 + 4) damage.

Restorative Touch. A light cadejo touches a willing creature. The touch acts as the spell *lesser restoration.*

Carrion Claw

This insect-like horror has six large, spear-like legs and a poison bite. It crawls about on hundreds of legs, using its six spears to impale victims which it then bites. It resembles a centipede. Its body is covered with tiny hair-like barbs that allow this creature to grapple a man-sized or smaller opponent.

Carrion claws have a preferential taste for elf flesh and seek to attack and eat elves before other opponents. It does not like halfling flesh and kills but does not devour them.

The creature can climb any surface, even hanging upside down from the ceiling if desired. The carrion claw is terrified of and hates magical light.

Carrion claws hunt in packs, with one claw feigning injury on a floor, while the rest of its pack circle prey along the walls and ceiling to drop and attack with surprise.

Carrion claws are used by drow to hunt down elves frequenting their underground lairs. Forward posts of the dark elves usually have up to a dozen carrion claws used for shock troops against elven incursions.

Carrion Claw

Large monstrosity, neutral evil
Armor Class 14 (natural armor)
Hit Points 135 (18d10 + 36)
Speed 40 ft., climb 40 ft.

STR	DEX	CON	INT	WIS	CHA
18 (+4)	14 (+2)	14 (+2)	4 (−3)	12 (+1)	11 (+0)

Skills Perception +4, Stealth +5
Senses darkvision 60 ft., passive Perception 14
Languages —
Challenge 9 (5,000 XP)

Spider Climb. The carrion claw can climb difficult surfaces, including upside down on ceilings, without needing to make an ability check.

Magical Light Sensitivity. While in magical light, the carrion claw has disadvantage on attack rolls, and opponents have advantage on attack rolls against it.

Actions

Multiattack. The carrion claw makes one bite attack and three claw attacks.

Bite. *Melee Weapon Attack:* +7 to hit, reach 5 ft., one target. *Hit:* 11 (2d6 + 4) piercing damage. If the target is a creature other than undead, it must succeed on a DC 14 Constitution saving throw or be paralyzed for 1 minute. The target can repeat the saving throw at the end of each of its turns, ending the effect on itself on a success.

Claws. *Melee Weapon Attack:* +7 to hit, reach 5 ft., one target. *Hit:* 17 (3d8 +4) slashing damage.

Carrion Moth

This creature resembles a giant-sized moth with long, beautiful wings covered in rippling patterns resembling skulls. Its head is rather centipede-like and four long tentacles surround its mouth. Its mouth has a single pair of needlelike mandibles.

The carrion moth is believed by sages to be an advanced form of a slime crawler. Just as the caterpillar grows into a moth, sages believe the mature slime crawler eventually sheds its form and transforms into the carrion moth. No cocoon or evidence has been found to support this theory, but it is widely accepted among the more learned sages of the world.

The carrion moth is a large moth-like creature growing to a maximum length of 20 feet. Its wings are lined with tiny holes and veins that allow the carrion moth to emit a whining drone that affects all creatures that hear it. Carrion moths are attracted to the stench of decaying flesh and the light of anything larger than a torch or lantern.

A carrion moth attacks by biting with its mandibles and slapping with its tentacles. Paralyzed creatures are carried off and devoured.

Carrion Moth

Large aberration, neutral
Armor Class 14
Hit Points 104 (11d10 + 44)
Speed 30 ft., climb 15 ft., fly 60 ft.

STR	DEX	CON	INT	WIS	CHA
16 (+3)	18 (+4)	18 (+4)	6 (−2)	15 (+2)	6 (−2)

Senses darkvision 60 ft., passive Perception 12
Languages —
Challenge 5 (1,800 XP)

Death Throes. When the carrion moth reaches 0 hit points, it splits open and a gas spews forth in a 10-foot radius. All creatures in the area except for other carrion moths must succeed on a DC 15 Constitution saving throw or be poisoned for 1 minute. A poisoned creature can repeat the saving throw at the end of each of its turns, ending the effect on a success.

Drone. A creature who begins its turn within 60 feet of the carrion moth must succeed on a DC 15 Wisdom saving throw or be incapacitated until the beginning of its next turn. If a creature succeeds on the saving throw, or the condition ends on it, it is immune to the moth's drone for 24 hours.

Actions

Multiattack. The carrion moth makes one bite attack and two tentacles attacks.

Bite. *Melee Weapon Attack:* +7 to hit, reach 5 ft., one target. *Hit:* 13 (2d8 + 4) piercing damage.

Tentacles. *Melee Weapon Attack:* +6 to hit, reach 10 ft., one target. *Hit:* 14 (2d10 + 3) bludgeoning damage, and the target must succeed on a DC 15 Constitution saving throw or be poisoned for 1 minute. While poisoned, the target is paralyzed. A poisoned creature can repeat the saving throw at the end of each of its turns, ending the effect on a success.

Caryatid Column

An exquisitely sculpted and chiseled statue of a beautiful female warrior adorns the area, longsword in her hand.

A caryatid column is akin to the stone golem in that it is a magical construct created by a spellcaster. Caryatid columns are always created for a specific defensive function. The caryatid column stands 7 feet tall and weighs around 1,500 pounds. The column always wields a weapon (usually a longsword) in its left hand. The weapon itself is constructed of steel but is melded with the column and made of stone until the column animates. When melded, the sword is likely to be overlooked (DC 20 Perception check to see it).

Caryatid columns are programmed as guardians and activate when certain conditions or stipulations are met or broken (such as a living creature enters a chamber guarded by a caryatid column). A caryatid column attacks its opponents with its longsword. It does not move more than 50 feet from the area it is guarding or protecting.

Caryatid Column

Medium construct, unaligned

Armor Class 14 (natural armor)
Hit Points 45 (6d8 + 18)
Speed 20 ft.

STR	DEX	CON	INT	WIS	CHA
16 (+3)	14 (+2)	16 (+3)	2 (−4)	11 (+0)	1 (−5)

Damage Resistances piercing and slashing damage from nonmagical weapons that aren't adamantine
Damage Immunities poison, psychic
Condition Immunities charmed, exhaustion, frightened, paralyzed, petrified, poisoned
Senses darkvision 120 ft., passive Perception 10
Languages understands the languages of its creator but can't speak
Challenge 2 (450 XP)

Immutable Form. The caryatid column is immune to any spell or effect that would alter its form.

Magic Resistance. The caryatid column has advantage on saving throws against spells and other magical effects.

Magic Weapons. The caryatid column's weapon attacks are magical.

Shatter Weapons. Whenever a character strikes a caryatid column with a non-adamantine, nonmagical weapon, the character must succeed on a DC 14 Strength saving throw or the weapon shatters into pieces.

Actions

Longsword. *Melee Weapon Attack:* +5 to hit, reach 5 ft., one target. *Hit:* 8 (1d10 + 3) slashing damage.

Caterprism

A large collection of items rises, forming into a swirling chaos that is the body of this being. The items move about throughout its bulk, somehow not touching one another in their mad dance.

A caterprism is from the Elemental Plane of Earth. It resembles a caterpillar made of crystal with hexagonal body segments and twelve sharply angled legs. Each body segment is about 2 feet long and contains a single pair of legs. The head of a caterprism is caterpillar-like, with large faceted eyes and huge mandibles.

Although caterprisms prefer to consume the rich minerals of their home plane, they sometimes wander through natural portals into the Material Plane. There, they create long, winding tunnels as they eat their way through the solid rock. Dwarves have been known to bring caterprisms under some degree of control, using them to help carve out new mines and dwelling places.

If it feels threatened, a caterprism's first action is to shoot at its opponents with its crystalline silk-like secretions. It then closes to bite, or rears up and stabs at opponents with the first two of its razor-sharp legs. A caterprism can eat through 1 foot of solid stone per minute, leaving behind permanent tunnel 5 feet in diameter.

Caterprism

Large elemental, neutral
Armor Class 15 (natural armor)
Hit Points 76 (8d10 + 32)
Speed 30 ft., burrow 20 ft.

STR	DEX	CON	INT	WIS	CHA
20 (+5)	12 (+1)	18 (+4)	4 (−3)	13 (+1)	11 (+0)

Condition Immunities prone
Senses darkvision 60 ft., tremorsense 60 ft., passive Perception 15
Languages —
Challenge 7 (2,900 XP)

Crystalline Mandibles. The caterprism's mandibles ignore resistance to slashing damage. In addition, when the caterprism attacks a creature with at least one head with its bite attack and rolls a natural 20 on the attack roll, it cuts off one of the creature's heads. The creature dies if it cannot survive without the lost head. A creature is immune to this ability if it is immune to slashing damage, doesn't have or need a head, has legendary actions, or the GM decides that the creature is too big for the head to be cut off with this attack. Such a creature instead takes an extra 27 (6d8) slashing damage from the hit.

Tunneler. Caterprism can burrow through solid rock at 5 feet per round leaving a 5 foot-wide, 8-foot-high tunnel in its wake.

Actions

Multiattack. The caterprism makes one bite and two claw attacks.
Bite. *Melee Weapon Attack:* +8 to hit, reach 5 ft., one target. *Hit:* 14 (2d8 +5) slashing damage. If the caterprism scores a critical hit, it rolls damage dice four times, instead of twice.

Claws. *Melee Weapon Attack:* +8 to hit, reach 5 ft., one target *Hit:* 16 (2d10 + 5) slashing damage.

Crystal Breath Recharge (5–6). The caterprism spews forth a crystalline silk-like substance in a 30-foot cone that instantly hardens into razor-sharp crystalline spears. Each creature in that area must make a DC 15 Dexterity saving throw, taking 28 (8d6) piercing damage on a failed save, or half as much damage on a successful one.

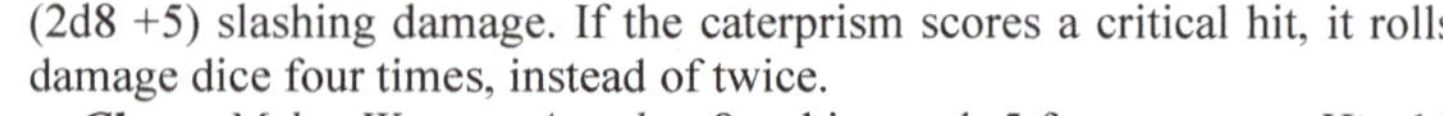

Chaos Beast

This creature resembles a lion with dark, blackened fur, razor-sharp fangs, and oversized paws that wield sharpened claws.

A beast of chaos is a creature that has been warped when the demonic forces of the Abyss reach into the Material Plane. A beast of chaos vaguely resembles the animal it once was. Its skin and fur become leprous and patchy. Its color fades to a dull sheen. Its teeth become razor-sharp and more pronounced. Its eyes turn to a bright golden yellow.

Chaos Beast

Medium aberration, chaotic neutral
Armor Class 16 (natural armor)
Hit Points 120 (16d8 + 48)
Speed 30 ft.

STR	DEX	CON	INT	WIS	CHA
17 (+3)	15 (+2)	16 (+3)	10 (+0)	12 (+1)	7 (−2)

Skills Perception +7
Damage Resistances acid, necrotic, slashing
Condition Immunities blinded, charmed, deafened, exhaustion, frightened, prone
Senses darkvision 60 ft., passive Perception 17
Languages None
Challenge 6 (2,300 XP)

Amorphous. The chaos beast can move through a space as narrow as 1 inch wide without squeezing.

Destabilize. A creature that touches the chaos beast or hits it with a melee attack while within 5 feet of it must make a DC 15 Constitution saving throw or be poisoned for 1 minute. A creature poisoned in this way takes 21 (6d6) necrotic damage at the start of each of its turns. It can repeat the saving throw at the end of each of its turns, ending the effect on itself on a success. If the creature's saving throw is successful or the effect ends for it, the creature is immune to the chaos beast's Destabilize for the next 24 hours.

Actions

Multiattack. The chaos beast makes two claw attacks.

Claws. *Melee Weapon Attack:* +6 to hit, reach 5 ft., one target. *Hit:* 10 (2d6 + 3) slashing damage plus 10 (3d6) necrotic damage. The creature must make a DC 15 Constitution saving throw or be affected by the chaos beast's Destabilize effect.

Cinder Knight

This intimidating figure stands unmoving, an immense sword clutched in its hands. Wisps of smoke rise from its blackened armor.

Cinder knights are elemental creatures composed completely of fire and encased in suits of irremovable armor. Over time, the armor adheres to the cinder knight's form, and the armor chars and blackens as the flames of the cinder knight's body scorch and burns it. Cinder knights dwell on the Plane of Fire among other fire elementals and creatures. The creature's true origins are unknown, but some believe the cinder knight to be an advanced form of fire elemental or perhaps a fire elemental punished for some transgression.

A cinder knight stands over 6 feet tall and weighs 200 pounds (without its armor, its true form weighs less). The creature's true form is never seen, for when a cinder knight dies, its fires extinguish, and it vanishes in wisps of smoke, leaving only its armor behind. The armor is extremely hot to the touch and deals 1d6 fire damage to any creature touching it. One hour after a cinder knight dies, the armor, while still warm, can be handled without taking damage.

A cinder knight rarely attacks using natural attacks, preferring the use of weapons in combat. Greatswords are the most common weapon, followed by mauls, longswords, and flails. Regardless of the weapon used, a cinder knight deals fire damage with its fire attack (a product of the creature itself and not the weapon).

Cinder Knight

Medium elemental, neutral

Armor Class 18 (plate)
Hit Points 105 (14d8 + 42)
Speed 30 ft.

STR	DEX	CON	INT	WIS	CHA
18 (+4)	17 (+3)	16 (+3)	6 (–2)	10 (+0)	7 (–2)

Damage Vulnerabilities cold
Damage Resistances bludgeoning, piercing, and slashing from nonmagical weapons
Damage Immunities fire, poison
Condition Immunities paralyzed, poisoned, stunned, unconscious
Senses darkvision 60 ft., passive Perception 10
Languages Common, Ignan
Challenge 10 (5,900 XP)

Heat Aura. At the start of each of the cinder knight's turns, each creature within 5 feet of it takes 7 (2d6) fire damage. A creature that touches the cinder knight or hits it with a melee attack while within 5 feet of it takes 7 (2d6) fire damage.

Illumination. The cinder knight sheds dim light in a 15-foot radius.

Water Susceptibility. For every 5 feet the cinder knight moves in water, or for every gallon of water splashed on it, it takes 1 cold damage.

Actions

Multiattack. The cinder knight makes two melee attacks.

Greatsword. *Melee Weapon Attack:* +8 to hit, reach 5 ft., one target. *Hit:* 11 (2d6 + 4) slashing damage plus 14 (4d6) fire damage. If the target is a creature or a flammable object, it ignites. Until a creature takes an action to douse the fire, the target takes 5 (1d10) fire damage at the start of each of its turns.

Slam. *Melee Weapon Attack:* +8 to hit, reach 5 ft., one target. *Hit:* 8 (1d8 + 4) bludgeoning damage plus 14 (4d6) fire damage. If the target is a creature or a flammable object, it ignites. Until a creature takes an action to douse the fire, the target takes 5 (1d10) fire damage at the start of each of its turns.

Clamor

A series of garbled voices, clicks, grinding noises, and other less discernible sounds seem to emanate from empty air, with no obvious point of origin.

Clamors have a playful kind of intelligence, and they appear to desire communication. Being able to mimic any sound they have ever encountered, clamors wander the Material Plane emitting a nonsensical cacophony of voices, crashes, clicks, roars, and music. Since they are usually invisible, most adventurers that encounter a clamor walk away from the creature without ever having realized that they had met one. Many a sentry on duty has heard only his own voice in response to what he thought was someone walking around out in the darkness; what he really heard was a clamor trying to talk to him.

Bards are fascinated by these odd creatures, and many a bard has gained a clamor as a companion of sorts. They have intelligence and can be trained. A bard of at least 5th level that has had prior contact with a clamor is capable of communicating with these creatures on a rudimentary basis. The intelligence of a clamor is just barely above that of a small child, so complex communication is out of reach.

Clamors tend to keep at a distance, emitting random noises and "playing back" any interesting sound made by the creatures they are observing. Once provoked to attack, clamors strike at their foes with sonis blasts.

Clamor

Medium aberration, unaligned
Armor Class 13
Hit Points 37 (5d8 + 15)
Speed 0 ft., fly 60 ft.

STR	DEX	CON	INT	WIS	CHA
1 (–5)	16 (+3)	16 (+3)	5 (–2)	12 (+1)	17 (+3)

Skills Deception +7, Performance +7
Damage Resistances bludgeoning, piercing, and slashing from nonmagical weapons
Damage Immunities thunder
Senses darkvision 60 ft., passive Perception 11
Languages —
Challenge 2 (450 XP)

Incorporeal Movement. The clamor can move through other creatures and objects as if they were difficult terrain. It takes 5 (1d10) force damage if it ends its turn inside an object.

Mimicry. The clamor can mimic any sound it has ever heard, including humanoid voices. A creature that hears the sounds can tell they are imitations with a successful DC 17 Wisdom (Insight) check.

Natural Invisibility. The clamor is invisible.

Silence Vulnerability. If the clamor starts its turn in an area under the effect of *silence*, it takes 13 (3d8) force damage, and it must make a DC 15 Wisdom saving throw or become frightened for 1 minute. While frightened, it must use its action to Dash away from the area of *silence*. If it begins its turn further than 60 feet away from the area of silence, it can repeat the saving throw at the end of each of its turns, ending the effect on a success.

Actions

Thunder Touch. *Melee Spell Attack:* +5 to hit, reach 5 ft., one target. *Hit:* 12 (2d8 + 3) thunder damage, and the target is pushed 5 feet directly away from the clamor.

Clubnek

This large bird resembles an ostrich with a thick neck and green-hued feathers. Its oversized beak is dark yellow.

A clubnek is a large flightless bird resembling an ostrich found roaming meadowlands and forests. It is primarily an herbivore subsisting on a diet of plants and flowers though it is given to flights of unpredictability when it takes the role of hunter and predator.

A clubnek stands 7 feet tall and weighs about 350 pounds.

A clubnek attacks by slashing with its claws and stabbing with its hard bony beak.

Clubnek

Medium monstrosity, neutral

Armor Class 13 (natural armor)
Hit Points 22 (4d8 + 4)
Speed 40 ft.

STR	DEX	CON	INT	WIS	CHA
14 (+2)	13 (+1)	12 (+1)	2 (−4)	10 (+0)	6 (−2)

Skills Perception +2, Stealth +3
Senses darkvision 60 ft., passive Perception 12
Languages —
Challenge 1 (200 XP)

Charge. If the clubnek moves at least 20 feet straight toward a target and then hits with its beak on the same turn, the target takes an extra 3 (1d6) damage. If the target is a creature, it must succeed on a DC 12 Strength saving throw or be knocked prone.

Actions

Multiattack. The clubnek makes three attacks: one with its beak and two with its claws.

Beak. *Melee Weapon Attack:* +4 to hit, reach 5 ft., one target. *Hit:* 5 (1d6 + 2) slashing damage.

Claws. *Melee Weapon Attack:* +4 to hit, reach 5 ft., one target. *Hit:* 4 (1d4 + 2) slashing damage.

Colossus, Jade

This massive automaton stands five times as tall as a normal human and resembles a gigantic humanoid carved of smooth green stone.

The jade colossus was first seen dominating the skyline over the City of Brass, its massive form reflecting the light from the ever-burning fires of the city. Since that time, rumors of these creatures moving across the Material Plane have been heard in taverns and inns.

Jade colossi are massive constructs built by powerful spellcasters to do their bidding; typically for protection or to wage war against an archrival.

A jade colossus pummels a foe with its hardened fists; dealing massive amounts of damage with every successful strike. It almost always opens combat with its breath weapon.

A typical jade colossus stands 35 feet tall and weighs about 60,000 pounds. (The jade colossus spotted in the City of Brass is thought to be over 50 feet tall and weigh in excess of 100,000 pounds.)

Jade Colossus

Gargantuan construct, neutral
Armor Class 19 (natural armor)
Hit Points 595 (34d20 + 238)
Speed 40 ft.

STR	DEX	CON	INT	WIS	CHA
29 (+9)	10 (+0)	24 (+7)	2 (−4)	11 (+0)	1 (−5)

Damage Immunities fire, poison, psychic; bludgeoning, piercing, and slashing from nonmagical weapons that aren't adamantine
Condition Immunities charmed, exhaustion, frightened, paralyzed, petrified, poisoned
Senses darkvision 60 ft., passive Perception 10
Languages understands the languages of its creator but can't speak
Challenge 17 (18,000 XP)

Immutable Form. The jade colossus is immune to any spell or effect that would alter its form.

Magic Resistance. The jade colossus has advantage on saving throws against spell and other magical effects.

Magic Weapons. The jade colossus' weapon attacks are magical.

Light Reflection. Any creature looking directly at the jade colossus while the colossus is in bright light must make a DC 12 Constitution saving throw or be blinded for 1 minute. Additionally, attacks against the colossus are made with disadvantage, and undead take 22 (4d10) radiant damage if they start their turn within 60 feet of the colossus.

Actions

Multiattack. The jade colossus makes two slam attacks.

Slam. *Melee Weapon Attack:* +15 to hit, reach 20 ft., one target. *Hit:* 36 (5d10 + 9) bludgeoning damage.

Jade Blast (Recharge 5–6). The jade colossus unleashes a blast of green energy in a 60-foot cone. Each creature in that area must make a DC 18 Dexterity saving throw, taking 56 (16d6) force damage on a failed save, or half as much damage on a successful one. Additionally, the creature magically begins to turn to jade and is restrained. The restrained target must repeat the saving throw at the end of its next turn. On a success, the effect ends on the target. On a failure, the target is petrified until freed by a *greater restoration* spell or other magic.

Ruby Star of Law

Sages speak of a jade colossus located in the City of Brass that has the Ruby Star of Law (a gem of inestimable value) embedded in its forehead. The Jade Guardian (as it is known in the city) is an advanced jade colossus with the following additional ability.

Energy Ray. Once per round as a bonus action, the Jade Guardian can fire a ray to a range of 200 feet. Genies hit by this ray must make a successful DC 18 Constitution saving throw or take 17 (7d4) points of Constitution damage. On a successful save, the genie takes half damage. Other creatures are affected as follows: Lawful creatures suffer two levels of exhaustion. Non-lawful creatures take 28 (8d6) force damage and are stunned for 1 minute. Should the Ruby Star of Law ever be claimed as a magic item, treat it as a minor artifact that allows use of the energy ray ability indicated above up to 3/day, save that it requires a standard action to activate.

Conshee

This creature appears to be a tiny, hairless, gray-skinned humanoid with leathery wings, small horns, and bulbous crimson eyes.

Conshee make their homes in large, open subterranean caverns far from the surface world. They spend most of their days mining, collecting minerals, or simply enjoying the natural beauty of their surroundings. Conshee don't take intrusions lightly and are moved to anger quickly when their homes are threatened. The conshee have an intense dislike for mites (see the Tome of Horrors Complete) and generally attack them on sight. Captured mites are killed almost immediately; very rarely are they ever taken prisoner. Mites seem to dislike the conshee equally as much, though captured conshee are often kept as slaves or sold back to their conshee clan or family.

Conshee prefer ambush tactics to straight-forward combat, attacking at range with their short bows and spell-like abilities. Some conshee also use daggers, saps, and other such weapons, allowing them to attack quickly and often times unnoticed. Conshee also employ a wide array of traps, snares, and pitfalls to injure, confuse, or capture would-be opponents. The corridors and passages leading to a conshee lair are often rife with all manner of such traps and pitfalls. Conshee often employ natural poisons as well, taken from the various plants, leaves, and underground flowers near their lairs.

An adult conshee stands about 2 feet tall. It is a small lithe creature with grayish skin, a hairless body, and two leathery bat-like wings growing from its back. Its hands end in claws, though they are not strong enough to use in combat.

Conshee

Tiny fey, chaotic neutrat
Armor Class 12
Hit Points 7 (3d4)
Speed 20 ft., fly 50 ft.

STR	DEX	CON	INT	WIS	CHA
6 (−2)	15 (+2)	11 (+0)	12 (+1)	13 (+1)	13 (+1)

Skills Acrobatics +4, Stealth +4
Senses darkvision 120 ft., passive Perception 11
Languages Common, Sylvan
Challenge 1/8 (25 XP)

Innate Spellcasting. The conshee's innate spellcasting ability is Charisma (spell save DC 11, +3 to hit with spell attacks). It can cast the following spells, requiring no material components.

At will: *detect evil and good, light*
1/day each: *faerie fire, silent image*

Actions

Dagger. *Melee or Ranged Weapon Attack:* +4 to hit, reach 5 ft. or range 20/60 ft., one target. *Hit:* 4 (1d4 + 2) piercing damage.

Shortbow. *Ranged Weapon Attack:* +4 to hit, range 80/320 ft., one target. *Hit:* 5 (1d6 + 2) piercing damage.

Corpse Candle

A pale man with hollow eyes looks up impassively from beneath the rippling surface of the dark water, a dim glow gives his form a ghostly translucence.

Corpse candles are formed when creatures are sacrificed by ritualistic drowning to a sea or water deity. The fear of dying coupled with the hatred of the ones performing the ritual infuses the victims' spirit with energy that often lingers in the area and empowers the corpse with unlife, raising it as a corpse candle. Corpse candles hate the living and have a particular dislike for clerics. Corpse candles are bound to the area of their death in the sense that they cannot leave that particular body of water (be it a sea, river, lake, or ocean).

A corpse candle appears as a translucent image of its living self. Its body shows little, if any, signs of death, though as its "ages", the corpse candle's translucence seems to grow faint and fade (as if a light were burning out). Some sages have researched this phenomenon and believe that corpse candles can actually die of old age. Perhaps some remnant of their former lives binds them to the mortal world or perhaps sages are just reaching for answers to some unknown equation.

Corpse candles detest the living and seek to lure wayfarers to their doom using trickery and misdirection. Corpse candles use their ability of deception to lure unsuspecting victims to their doom. When a corpse candle successfully fascinates a creature, it waits until the creature draws near and then attacks relentlessly with its incorporeal claws. Corpse candles are particularly fond of luring sailors, swimmers, and other seafarers to their watery graves by first fascinating them, draining sapping them of their strength, and finally allowing them to drown as the lights sap their vitality. Drowned victims are left as food for any aquatic carnivores in the area.

Corpse Candle

Medium undead, neutral evil
Armor Class 12
Hit Points 55 (10d8 + 10)
Speed fly 50 ft., swim 50 ft.

STR	DEX	CON	INT	WIS	CHA
6 (–2)	15 (+2)	13 (+1)	13 (+1)	13 (+1)	17 (+3)

Skills Deception +5, Stealth +4
Damage Resistances acid, cold, fire, lightning, thunder; bludgeoning, piercing, and slashing from nonmagical weapons
Damage Immunities necrotic, poison
Condition Immunities charmed, exhaustion, frightened, grappled, paralyzed, petrified, poisoned, prone, restrained
Senses darkvision 60 ft., passive Perception 11
Languages Common, Infernal
Challenge 4 (1,100 XP)

Incorporeal Movement. The corpse candle can move through other creatures and objects in a body of water as if they were difficult terrain. It takes 5 (1d10) force damage if it ends its turn inside an object or outside its body of water.

Sunlight Sensitivity. While in sunlight, the corpse candle has disadvantage on attack rolls, as well as on Wisdom (Perception) checks that rely on sight.

Actions

Watery Touch. *Melee Weapon Attack:* +4 to hit, reach ft., one target. *Hit:* 9 (2d6 + 2) necrotic damage, and the target's Strength score is reduced by 1d4. The target dies if this reduces its Strength to 0. Otherwise, the reduction lasts until the target finishes a short or long rest.

A humanoid slain by this attack rises 24 hours later as a zombie unless the humanoid is restored to life or its body is destroyed.

Hypnotic Lights. The corpse candle creates a twisting, dancing pattern of ever-shifting colored lights in a 10-foot cube at a point it can see within 60 feet of itself. The pattern appears for a minute then vanishes. Each creature in the area who sees the pattern must succeed on a DC 13 Wisdom saving throw. On a failed save, the creature becomes charmed for 1 minute. While charmed, the creature is incapacitated and has a speed of 0. When a charmed creature takes damage it can repeat the saving throw, ending the effect on a success.

A creature that starts its turn within the 10-foot cube of lights must succeed on a DC 13 Constitution saving throw or the target's Constitution score is reduced by 1d4. The target dies if this reduces its Constitution to 0. Otherwise, the reduction lasts until the target finishes a short or long rest.

Corpse Rook

This creature resembles a three-headed raven with oily black feathers and bright silver talons and beak. A pungent, almost sulfuric odor emanates from the creature. Its wings are tipped with silver feathers.

Corpse rooks are giant three-headed birds of prey that devour just about anything they can catch, preferring a diet of horses, giant lizards, dire rats, giant frogs, cattle, sheep, and humanoids. They build their nests at the top of broadleaved trees or high atop rocky outcroppings in less forested terrain. A corpse rook's nest is constructed from mud, grass, hair, leaves, and the bones of their victims. These creatures do not associate with other avian creatures and are often hunted by red dragons, green dragons, rocs, and wyverns (who savor the taste of their flesh).

Corpse rooks are solitary hunters with a hunting territory often covering 5 miles in each direction away from its nest. Hunting is always done during the day when the corpse rook has the advantage. During mating season (spring and early summer months) both the male and female corpse rook hunt for food, sometimes together, but most often in separate directions away from the nest. A nest typically contains 1d4 silver and gold-flecked eggs as well as treasure from slain prey.

Corpse rooks attack their foes from the air, slashing with their claws and biting with their sharpened beaks. They rarely land on the ground during battle, preferring to swoop in and out of melee to keep their opponents off balance. Multiple corpse rooks work together to bring down prey; one might land on the ground to draw the attention of the prey, while the other corpse rook swoops in behind to flank. Creatures killed by a corpse rook are carried back to the nest and either devoured or fed to the newborns.

Corpse Rook

Large monstrosity, neutral evil

Armor Class 13
Hit Points 90 (12d10 + 24)
Speed 10 ft., fly 60 ft.

STR	DEX	CON	INT	WIS	CHA
16 (+3)	17 (+3)	14 (+2)	5 (–3)	10 (+0)	11 (+0)

Skills Perception +2, Survival +2
Senses darkvision 60 ft., passive Perception 12
Languages —
Challenge 4 (1,100 XP)

Flyby. The corpse rook doesn't provoke opportunity attacks when it flies out of an enemy's reach.

Three Heads. The corpse rook has advantage on Wisdom (Perception) checks and on saving throws against being blinded, charmed, deafened, frightened, stunned, or knocked unconscious.

Actions

Multiattack. The corpse rook makes three bite attacks and one claws attack.

Bite. *Melee Weapon Attack:* +5 to hit, reach 5 ft., one target. *Hit:* 7 (1d8 + 3) piercing damage.

Claws. *Melee Weapon Attack:* +5 to hit, reach 5 ft., one target. *Hit:* 12 (2d8 + 3) slashing damage.

Crabman

This giant-sized creature is a bipedal humanoid with a crab-like head, large hands that end in powerful pincers, feet that are splayed. It is covered with chitinous plates, reddish-brown in color. Two smaller humanoid arms protrude below its pincers.

Crabmen inhabit coastal waters, hunting fish and gathering food. Crabmen communicate with others of their race through a series of hisses and clicks.

A typical crabman stands about 9 feet tall. They speak their own language, and those with an Intelligence of 12 or higher often speak common.

Crabman Society

Crabmen make their homes in sea caves and coastal cliffs, venturing forth occasionally in search of food. They spend most of their time hunting, filtering algae for food, or scavenging the shores and beaches. Occasionally, they will gather wet sand from the seashore and filter it through their mouths, sucking out all organic material and plankton. The remainder is a hardened, dry ball of sand approximately 1 inch across; these pellets inadvertently give away the presence of a crabman community.

Crabmen live in coastal caves, but some communities will excavate more expansive burrows into the cliff face. Within such a warren, each individual has a lair set off from a centralized meeting area. Each crabman tribe is led by an elder that can be of either sex.

Crabmen have no regular breeding or mating cycle, and each female seems to have her own periods of fertility and infertility. A fertile female will produce about 100 eggs within a two-week period. Crabman eggs are released into the ocean, hatching into translucent larvae with soft shells. These larvae vaguely resemble the adults but may be mistaken for normal crabs given their size. After 6 months, crabman larvae molt and develop the harder shell required for life on land. Before their first molting, crabman larvae are practically defenseless.

Crabmen rarely engage in commerce with other humanoid communities around them, including other crabman tribes. Crabman artisans produce only ephemeral goods made of driftwood, shells, and seaweed, and are quite capable of producing what other more aesthetic races would call works of art.

Crabman

Large monstrosity, neutral
Armor Class 13 (natural armor)
Hit Points 37 (5d10 + 10)
Speed 30 ft., swim 30 ft.

STR	DEX	CON	INT	WIS	CHA
16 (+3)	11 (+0)	15 (+2)	10 (+0)	10 (+0)	8 (−1)

Skills Perception +4
Senses darkvision 60 ft., passive Perception 14
Languages Crabman, some speak Common
Challenge 2 (450 XP)
Amphibious. The crabman can breathe air and water.

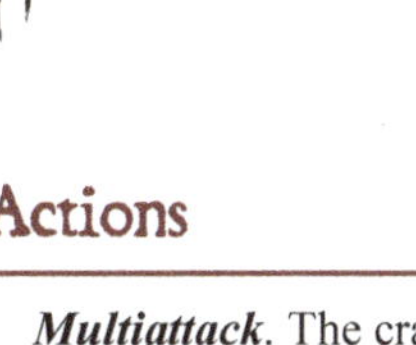

Actions

Multiattack. The crabman makes two attacks with its pincers.

Pincers. *Melee Weapon Attack:* +5 to hit, reach 10 ft., one target. *Hit:* 10 (2d6 + 3) slashing damage. The target is grappled (escape DC 13) if it is a Large or smaller creature and the crabman doesn't have another creature grappled already. The target is restrained until the grapple ends.

Crypt Thing

A skeletal humanoid wearing a dark hooded robe sits in a high-backed chair before you. Its eyes appear as small pinpoints of reddish light. As you approach it, the creature raises a bony hand and points at you.

Crypt things are undead creatures found guarding tombs, graves, crypts, and other such structures. They are created by spellcasters to guard such areas and they never leave their assigned area.

A crypt thing never initiates combat. It is content to sit (or stand) in its assigned area so long as intruders do not disturb it or anything in the assigned area. At the first sign of disturbance, however, a crypt thing springs to life. Its first order of business is to attempt to remove the interlopers from its assigned area by using its Teleport Other attack. Opponents that successfully resist are attacked by the crypt thing that uses its claws to rake and slash its foes.

A crypt thing's natural weapons are treated as magic weapons for the purpose of overcoming damage reduction.

Crypt Thing

Medium undead, neutral
Armor Class 15 (natural armor)
Hit Points 84 (13d8 + 26)
Speed 30 ft.

STR	DEX	CON	INT	WIS	CHA
12 (+1)	16 (+3)	15 (+2)	12 (+1)	14 (+2)	16 (+3)

Skills Deception +6, Perception +5
Senses darkvision 60 ft., passive Perception 15
Languages Common
Challenge 7 (2,900 XP)

Magic Weapons. The crypt thing's weapon attacks are magical.

Actions

Multiattack. The crypt thing makes two attacks with its claws.

Claws. Melee Weapon Attack: +6 to hit, reach 5 ft., one target. *Hit:* 13 (3d6 + 3) slashing damage and 10 (3d6) necrotic damage.

Teleport Other (1/day). As an action, the crypt thing can teleport all creatures within 50 feet of it to a randomly determined location. A creature affected by the crypt thing's Teleport Other must make a DC 15 Wisdom saving throw to avoid being teleported.

An affected creature is teleported in a random direction and a random distance (1d10 x 100 feet) away from the crypt thing. Roll randomly for each creature that fails its saving throw.

If the affected creature would arrive in a place already occupied by an object or another creature, the affected creature takes 14 (4d6) force damage and is not teleported.

Crystalline Horror

This humanoid creature seems to be made entirely of crystal and glass. It is human-sized, and its head sports no eyes, nose, ears, or mouth. Its body appears razor-sharp and jagged. Its hands end in wicked claws.

A crystalline horror is a weird, unnatural humanoid composed of crystal and glass. Sages believe it to be from one of the elemental planes, but in fact, the crystalline horror is a creature whose origins lie on the Material Plane. How it came to be remains speculation among many sages and scholars, though all agree it is, in fact, a living creature and not an automaton.

Crystalline Horror

Medium aberration, neutral evil
Armor Class 16 (natural armor)
Hit Points 60 (8d8 + 24)
Speed 30 ft.

STR	DEX	CON	INT	WIS	CHA
19 (+4)	14 (+2)	16 (+3)	10 (+0)	12 (+1)	10 (+0)

Skill Perception +3, Stealth +4
Damage Resistances cold
Senses darkvision 60 ft., passive Perception 13
Languages —
Challenge 3 (700 XP)

Crystal Claws. The crystalline horror's attacks are magical.

Magic Resistance. The crystalline horror has advantage on saving throws against spells and other magical effects.

Actions

Multiattack. The crystalline horror can make two attacks with its claws.

Claws. *Melee Weapon Attack:* +6 to hit, reach 5 ft., one target. *Hit:* 11 (2d6 + 4) slashing damage.

Shard Spray (Recharge 6). The crystalline horror launches a spray of razor-sharp shards of glass from its body in a 30-foot cone. Each creature in that area must make a DC 13 Dexterity saving throw, taking 17 (5d6) piercing damage on a failed save, or half as much damage on a successful one.

Reactions

Bend Light. The crystalline horror can refract natural light into a bright light that makes it harder to be hit by melee attacks. The crystalline horror adds 3 to its AC against one melee attack that would hit it. To do so, the crystalline horror must see the attack. This ability cannot be used in natural or magical darkness.

Death Cow

Rumors tell of a beast that looks like every other member of a peaceful herd of cattle. Without warning, it's said to rise up on its hind legs, eyes blazing with the red flames of hatred, and fling itself upon terrified herders, cunningly gripping a mighty two-handed sword in its cruel front hooves!

The fearsome monsters known as death cows are travelers from an alternate reality where bovines are the dominant life form, and other lesser species serve the mighty Cow Queen as chattel and beasts of burden. Dispatched to this reality, the death cows are tasked with bringing liberation to their enslaved brethren on cattle ranches and dairy farms across the Material Plane.

These emissaries of their monarch lurk in hiding among other cows, fomenting rebellion and whispering tales of the freedom and liberty of their world. To their intense frustration, bovines of other planes either ignore their entreaties to rebel or are actively hostile, attacking these interlopers and driving them out. This has not discouraged the death cows, who continue to issue calls for revolt and the destruction of the humans, halflings, and dwarves who hold the race of cows as prisoners.

Death cows emerge from herds of cattle in the hope that their fellow beasts will follow them, but they are not above using their natural abilities to control cows and use them as allies in battle, leading the herd to the sound of the terrifying war moo.

Death Cow

Large monstrosity, lawful evil
Armor Class 14 (natural armor)
Hit Points 90 (12d10 + 24)
Speed 30 ft.

STR	DEX	CON	INT	WIS	CHA
17 (+3)	11 (+0)	14 (+2)	8 (−1)	12 (+1)	10 (+0)

Saving Throws Str +6, Con +5
Skills Animal Handling +4, Athletics +6, Perception +4
Senses passive Perception 14
Languages Bovine
Challenge 5 (1,800 XP)

Bovine Master. A death cow can take control of 1d6 cows located within 30 feet of it as per the *dominate monster* spell. Cows controlled in this fashion do not receive a Wisdom save, but are controlled automatically.

Cattle Guise. A death cow can voluntarily appear as a normal quadrupedal cow, indistinguishable from a normal cow. It can transform between cow and death cow form instantly. Its weapons only manifest in bipedal form. The *true seeing* spell will reveal the death cow's true form.

Death Throes. When the death cow dies, it explodes, showering all creatures within a 30-foot radius with scalding blood and chunks of burning meat. Each creature in this area must make a DC 15 Dexterity saving throw, taking 14 (4d6) fire damage on a failed save, or half as much on a successful one.

Secret Speech. Death cows speak in a strange mooing tongue called Bovine that normally cannot be learned by non-cows. Those who wish to learn the language must succeed on a DC 20 Intelligence check and have a willing death cow as an instructor.

Actions

Multiattack. The death cow makes one bite and one greatsword attack.

Bite. *Melee Weapon Attack:* +6 to hit, reach 5 ft., one target. *Hit:* 6 (1d8 + 3) piercing damage.

Greatsword. *Melee Weapon Attack:* +5 to hit, reach 5 ft., one target. *Hit:* 10 (2d6 + 3) slashing damage.

War Moo (Recharge 5–6). The death cow unleashes a deafening moo. All non-bovine creatures within 30 feet of the death cow that can hear the moo, must attempt a DC 13 Constitution saving throw and be deafened for 1 minute and take 28 (8d6) thunder damage on a failed save, or half as much damage without being deafened on a successful one.

Decapus

This creature is a large spheroid with ten octopus-like tentacles protruding from its body. Hair grows in broken patches on its body. Its eyes are stark white and pupilless. Its large mouth sports long, yellow fangs.

Decapi are solitary creatures that dwell in dense forests or underground. Most prefer the forests as their ability to move among the trees allows them to either pursue their prey or flee in situations not to their advantage. On the ground, decapi are slow-moving, thus they spend most of their time among the treetops.

Decapi are nocturnal hunters and are quite fond of human, elf, and halfling flesh. In times when food is scarce, they exist on a diet of rats, snakes, and other small forest creatures (or dungeon denizens in the case of the subterranean decapus).

Decapi prefer a solitary life; the only time more than one will ever be encountered together is during mating season (usually the fall). Young decapi are born live, and the female only ever gives birth to a single young during each mating season. If food is extremely scarce, some decapus females have been known to eat their young.

This creature's body is a 4-foot diameter globe of pallid green. On rare occasions, a purple or even yellow hued decapus may be encountered. Patches of dark hair, brown or black, grow in various locations. Regardless of its body color, each decapus has 10 octopus-like tentacles protruding from its spherical body. Each tentacle is covered in suction cups that aid the creature in not only climbing and moving through trees but also in holding on to its prey. Its large wide maw sports sickly yellow teeth and foul breath. Decapi seem to be able to speak with others of their kind using a series of guttural noises.

Decapus

Medium aberration, chaotic evil
Armor Class 13 (natural armor)
Hit Points 32 (5d8 + 10)
Speed 10 ft., climb 30 ft.

STR	DEX	CON	INT	WIS	CHA
14 (+2)	13 (+1)	15 (+2)	10 (+0)	10 (+0)	8 (−1)

Skills Stealth +5
Senses darkvision 60 ft., passive Perception 10
Languages Common, Deep Speech, Sylvan
Challenge 2 (450 XP)

Brachiation. A decapus can move through trees at its base climb speed by using its tentacles to swing from tree to tree. Trees used by the decapus in this manner can be no further than 10 feet apart.

Mimicry. The decapus can mimic any sounds it has heard, including voices. A creature that hears the sounds can tell they are imitations with a successful DC 13 Wisdom (Insight) check.

Actions

Multiattack. The decapus makes up to four tentacle attacks.

Tentacle. *Melee Weapon Attack:* +4 to hit, reach 5 ft., one target. *Hit:* 9 (2d6 + 2) bludgeoning damage. If the target is Medium or smaller, it is grappled (escape DC 12) and restrained until the grapple ends. The decapus has many tentacles but can only grapple two targets at any given time.

Deer, Onyx

This creature looks like a deer about 5 feet tall at the shoulders with a dark-brown head and chest changing to light brown on the rest of its body. A large white patch is prevalent across its back and rump. It has huge antlers at least as wide as a typical human is tall.

Other than being larger than most common deer, an onyx deer resembles its (thought to be distant) lesser cousin. These creatures are found in temperate and warm forested lands in the same general habitat as their normal counterparts though onyx deer do not associate with ordinary deer. Onyx deer are herd animals, congregating in groups of up to 20 individuals. Among the adults, the males outnumber the females by nearly a 2-to-1 ratio. Young (called does) make up the rest of the herd (their total number usually equals the number of adults in the herd).

Mating season for onyx deer comes in the fall. During this time males within the herd often clash with one another. Such clashes see the animals square off and charge headlong into each other crashing their antlers together and slashing with their sharp hooves. When one falls, the battle ends. The loser of the battle usually survives, but always leaves the herd. Females give birth to 1d3 young in the early summer months.

Onyx deer stand 5 to 6 feet tall at the shoulder and weigh more than 800 pounds.

Onyx deer are generally passive creatures and only attack when threatened or when their herd is threatened. If a herd is molested, both male and female onyx deer defend the young does to the death. An onyx deer begins combat by releasing a loud bellow in an attempt to scare off any would-be attackers. Those who stand their ground are met with either a gore attack and hooves or a ferocious bite and hooves. The bite of an onyx deer transforms the wound and flesh surrounding it into a gem-like stone that resembles onyx.

Onyx Deer

Large Monstrosity, unaligned
Armor Class 14 (natural armor)
Hit Points 76 (9d10 + 27)
Speed 40 ft.

STR	DEX	CON	INT	WIS	CHA
19 (+4)	15 (+2)	17 (+3)	5 (–3)	12 (+1)	13 (+1)

Skills Perception +3
Condition Immunities petrified
Senses darkvision 60 ft., passive Perception 13
Languages understands Sylvan but can't speak
Challenge 4 (1,100 XP)

Keen Smell. The onyx deer has advantage on Wisdom (Perception) checks that rely on smell.

Onyx Bite. Creatures bitten by an onyx deer must succeed on a Constitution saving throw or slowly begin to turn into onyx (included in the attack).

Actions

Multiattack. The onyx deer makes four attacks: one bite, one gore, and two with its hooves.

Bite. *Melee Weapon Attack:* +6 to hit, reach 5 ft., one target. *Hit:* 8 (1d8 + 4) piercing damage and the creature must make a DC 14 Constitution saving throw. On a failed save, the creature magically begins to turn to onyx and is restrained. It must repeat the saving throw at the end of its next turn. On a success, the effect ends. On a failure, the creature is petrified in onyx until freed by a *greater restoration* spell or other magic.

Gore. *Melee Weapon Attack:* +6 to hit, reach 5 ft., one target. *Hit:* 9 (1d10 + 4) piercing damage.

Hooves. *Melee Weapon Attack:* +6 to hit, reach 5 ft., one target. *Hit:* 7 (1d6 + 4) slashing damage.

Bellow (Recharge 5–6). The onyx deer unleashes a rumbling bellow. Each creature that is within 60 feet of the onyx deer and able to hear it must succeed on a DC 14 Wisdom saving throw or be frightened for 1 minute. The frightened creature can repeat the saving throw at the end of each of its turns, ending the effect on itself on a success.

Defender Globe

This small glowing orb radiates light similar to that of a lantern. Small filaments of electrical energy dance across its illuminated surface.

This small outsider is bound by spellcasters using the *summon monster III* or *lesser planar binding* spells, serving for up to 1 day per caster level. Using more powerful incantations can bind the globes for longer periods (GM's discretion).

They can understand but not speak, any language spoken by their summoner. The summoned globes can understand simple orders and carries out their last order until destroyed or dismissed.

Defender Globe

Small elemental, neutral
Armor Class 14 (natural armor)
Hit Points 22 (5d6 + 5)
Speed 5 ft., fly 40 ft.

STR	DEX	CON	INT	WIS	CHA
4 (−3)	16 (+3)	12 (+1)	4 (−3)	12 (+1)	14 (+2)

Damage Resistance cold, fire
Damage Immunities lightning
Senses darkvision 60 ft., passive Perception 11
Languages —
Challenge 1 (200 XP)

Hyper-Awareness. The defender globe cannot be surprised.

Flight. The defender globe's ability to fly is magical in nature and does not work in areas where an antimagic effect is active.

Actions

Electrical Bolt. *Ranged Weapon Attack:* +5 to hit, range 30/60 ft., one target. *Hit:* 10 (2d6 + 3) lightning damage.

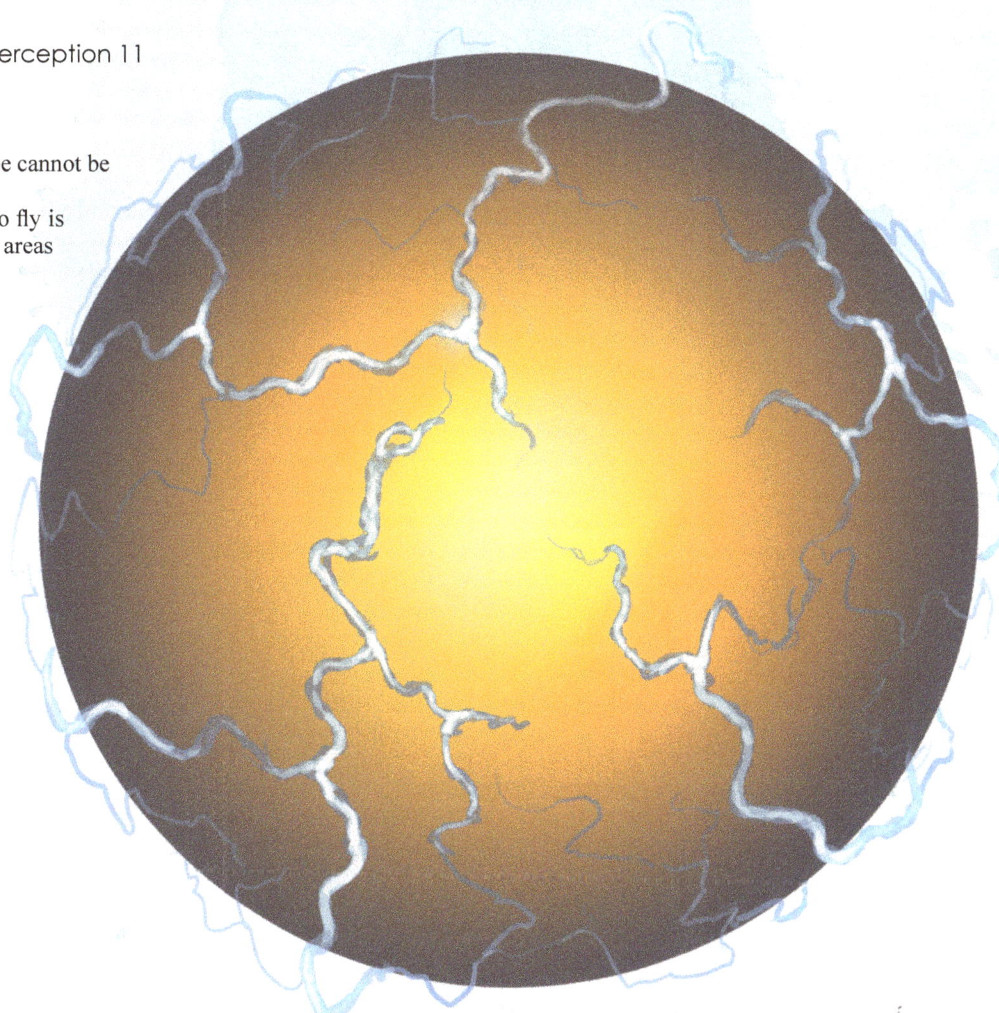

Demilich, Advanced

What at first appears to be a simple uninteresting humanoid skull suddenly rises from its resting place, turning slowly in your direction to reveal gems inset in its eye sockets and jaw, and releasing a maniacal cackle.

A demi-lich is an advanced lich of great power. When the life force of a lich ceases to exist and the material body finally decays (often after centuries of undeath), the soul lingers in the area and slowly over time possesses all that remains of the lich — its skull. The eye sockets and teeth of a demi-lich-possessed skull transform into clear gemstones (each worth 1,000 gp). The skull contains a single gemstone in each eye socket and six gems in place of its teeth.

A demi-lich rarely if ever wanders from its place of origin (i.e., the final resting place of its body when it was a true lich). Content to remain hidden and oblivious to the outside world, a demi-lich spends its time contemplating its past life, its accomplishments, as yet unachieved goals, and exploring strange mysteries of the cosmos. These creatures are solitary by nature and rarely associate with other creatures, including other undead unless it is employing such creatures to further some unfinished goal.

Demi-lich lairs are usually well-hidden dungeons and caverns consisting of winding corridors, deadly pitfalls, and intricate traps (some that would even bring a tear to Grimmy's eye).

A demi-lich appears as a simple humanoid skull seated amid a pile of bones and dust. In each eye socket is a single gemstone, and in its mouth, in place of its teeth, are six more gemstones.

A demi-lich sits idly in its lair until touched or bothered at which point it rises vertically and uses its wail of the banshee power against the opponent it deems most threatening. On its next turn, the demi-lich uses its trap the soul ability against an opponent. It spends the remainder of combat alternating between its wail of the banshee, bestow curse, and trap the soul abilities.

Advanced Demi-lich

Tiny undead, neutral evil
Armor Class 21 (natural armor)
Hit Points 172 (23d4 + 115)
Speed 0 ft., fly 30 ft. (hover)

STR	DEX	CON	INT	WIS	CHA
10 (+0)	10 (+0)	20 (+5)	23 (+6)	20 (+5)	23 (+6)

Saving Throws Con +12, Int +13, Wis +12
Skills Arcana +13, History +13, Perception +12, Religion +13
Damage Resistances bludgeoning, piercing, and slashing from magic weapons
Damage Immunities necrotic, poison, psychic; bludgeoning, piercing, and slashing from nonmagical weapons
Condition Immunities charmed, deafened, exhaustion, frightened, paralyzed, petrified, poisoned, prone, stunned
Senses truesight 120 ft., passive Perception 22
Languages All, telepathy 120 ft.
Challenge 24 (62,000 XP)

Annulment. If the demi-lich is subjected to an effect that allows it to make a saving throw to take only half damage, it instead takes no damage if it succeeds on the saving throw, and only half damage if it fails.

Legendary Resistance (3/day). If the demi-lich fails a saving throw, it can choose to succeed instead.

Spellcasting. The demi-lich is an 18th level spellcaster. Its spellcasting ability is Intelligence (spell save DC 21, +13 to hit with spell attacks). It has the following spells prepared:

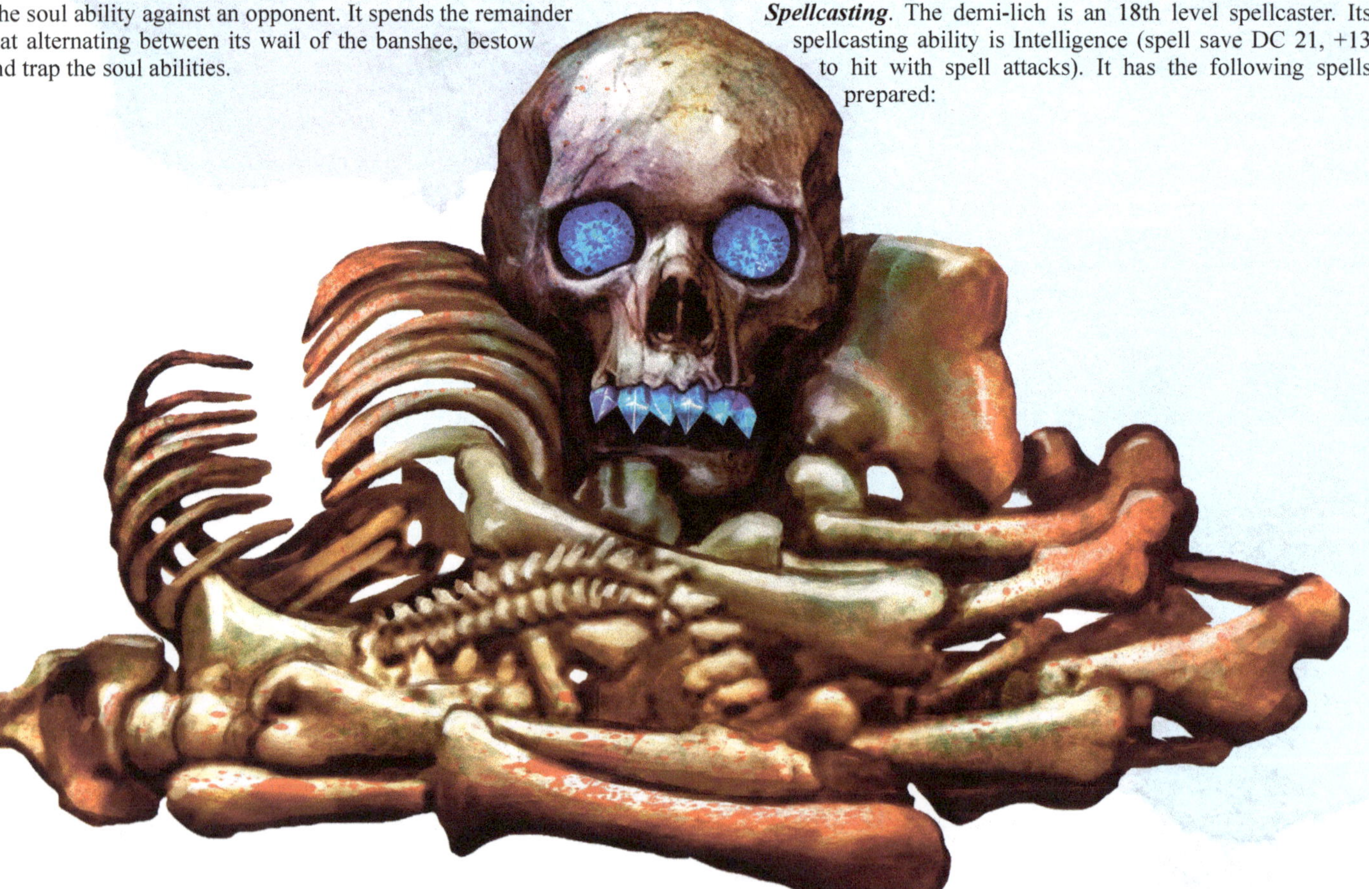

Cantrips (at will): *mage hand, prestidigitation, ray of frost*
1st level (4 slots): *detect magic, magic missile, shield, thunderwave*
2nd level (3 slots): *acid arrow, detect thoughts, invisibility, mirror image*
3rd level (3 slots): *animate dead, counterspell, dispel magic, fireball*
4th level (3 slots): *blight, dimension door*
5th level (3 slots): *cloudkill, scrying*
6th level (1 slot): *disintegrate, globe of invulnerability*
7th level (1 slot): *finger of death, plane shift*
8th level (1 slot): *dominate monster, power word stun*
9th level (1 slot): *power word kill*

Turn Immunity. The demi-lich is immune to effects that turn undead.

Actions

Drain Life. Each non-undead creature within 10 feet of the demi-lich must make a DC 17 Constitution saving throw against this magic, taking 21 (6d6) necrotic damage, and the demi-lich regains hit points equal to the total dealt to all targets.

Soul Shatter (Recharge 6). The demi-lich emits a string of vile words of power. All creatures within 30 feet of the demi-lich that it can see must succeed on a DC 17 Constitution saving throw or drop to 0 hit points. On a successful save, the creature takes 22 (4d10) psychic damage and is frightened until the end of its next turn.

Legendary Actions

The demi-lich can take 3 legendary actions, choosing from the options below. Only one legendary action option can be used at a time and only at the end of another creature's turn. The demi-lich regains spent legendary actions at the start of its turn.

Flight. The demi-lich can move up to its full movement speed and does not invoke opportunity attacks while doing so.

Bone Dust. Blinding bone dust swirls magically around the demi-lich. Each creature within 5 feet of the demi-lich must succeed on a DC 17 Constitution saving throw or be blinded until the end of the creature's next turn.

Frightening Glare (Costs 2 Actions). The demi-lich targets one creature it can see within 60 feet of it. If the target can see the demi-lich, it must succeed on a DC 17 Wisdom saving throw against this magic or become frightened until the end of the demi-lich's next turn. If the target fails the saving throw by 5 or more, it is also paralyzed for the same duration. A target that succeeds on the saving throw is immune to the Dreadful Glare effect for the next 24 hours.

Profane Curse (Costs 3 Actions). The demi-lich targets one creature it can see within 30 feet of it. The target must succeed on a DC 17 Wisdom saving throw or be magically cursed. Until the curse ends, the target has disadvantage on ability checks, attack rolls, and saving throws. The target can repeat the saving throw at the end of each of its turns, ending the curse on a success.

Demons

Aeshma (Rage Demon)

This creature appears to be an 8-foot-tall humanoid with basalt-colored skin. Dark hair covers its head and its hair is long and braided. Its arms are well-muscled and its hands end in powerful claws. Its head is human-like and its eyes are sapphire blue. Large leathery, bat-like wings protrude from its shoulders.

Aeshma are the demons of rage and anger. An aeshma is sometimes referred to as "the fiend of the wounding spear." Aeshma are thoroughly malign and evil and care little for anything or anyone else. They are actively recruited into the Abyssal armies of the demon lords and princes for their skill and combat prowess. Often an aeshma is given the rank of commander or lieutenant and granted control over a retinue or battalion of lesser demons (usually vrocks or dretches).

The typical aeshma stands 8 feet tall and weighs about 500 pounds. Most aeshma disdain the use of armor but occasionally don chainmail.

Aeshma are very potent fighters and prefer a straight fight to subterfuge. They fight aggressively against any foe, relying on their claws only if they are unarmed.

Aeshma

Large fiend (demon), chaotic evil
Armor Class 19 (natural armor)
Hit Points 216 (16d10 + 128)
Speed 40 ft., fly 60 ft.

STR	DEX	CON	INT	WIS	CHA
22 (+6)	18 (+4)	26 (+8)	14 (+2)	17 (+3)	17 (+3)

Saving Throws Dex +8, Wis +7
Skills Intimidation +7, Perception +11, Survival +7
Damage Resistances cold, fire, lightning; bludgeoning, piercing, and slashing from nonmagical weapons.
Damage Immunities poison
Condition Immunities poisoned
Senses darkvision 120 ft., passive Perception 21
Languages Abyssal, Celestial, Draconic, telepathy 120 ft.
Challenge 10 (5,900 XP)

Innate Spellcasting. The demon's spellcasting ability is Charisma (spell save DC 15, +7 to hit with spell attacks). The demon can innately cast the following spells, requiring no material components:

At will: *blight, detect evil and good, dispel magic*

3/day each: *bestow curse, web*

Magic Resistance. The aeshma demon has advantage on saving throws against spells and other magical effects.

Magic Weapons. The aeshma demon's weapon attacks are magical.

Reckless. At the start of its turn, the aeshma demon can gain advantage on all melee weapon attack rolls it makes during that turn, but attack rolls against it have advantage until the start of its next turn.

Actions

Multiattack. The aeshma demon makes two melee attacks.

Spear. *Melee or Ranged Weapon Attack:* +10 to hit, reach 10 ft. or

range 20/60 ft., one target. *Hit:* 19 (3d8 + 6) piercing damage.

Claws. *Melee Weapon Attack:* +10 to hit, reach 10 ft., one target. *Hit:* 15 (2d8 + 6) slashing damage.

Summon Demon (1/day). The demon chooses what to summon and attempts a magical summoning. An aeshma has a 30% chance of summoning 1d3 vrocks, 1d2 hezrous, or one glabrezu.

A summoned demon appears in an unoccupied space within 60 feet of its summoner, acts as an ally of its summoner, and can't summon other demons. It remains for 1 minute, until it or its summoner dies, or until its summoner dismisses it as an action.

Azizou (Pain Demon)

This small humanoid creature has a jackal-like head, a mouthful of fangs, and large, round eyes with slit-pupils of gray. Its grayish skin is covered in patches of coarse black hair. Membranous wings protrude from its back and its hands and feet end in sharpened claws.

The azizou is slightly larger than the barizou and is quite strong (for its size). They are relentless combatants and love to inflict pain and suffering on their opponents in combat.

The typical azizou stands 3 feet tall and weighs about 100 pounds.

Azizou

Small fiend (demon), chaotic evil
Armor Class 15 (natural armor)
Hit Points 17 (5d6)
Speed 30 ft., fly 50 ft.

STR	DEX	CON	INT	WIS	CHA
14 (+2)	15 (+2)	11 (+0)	8 (−1)	10 (+0)	10 (+0)

Skills Deception +4, Stealth +4
Damage Resistances cold, fire, lightning
Damage Immunities poison
Condition Immunities poisoned
Senses darkvision 60 ft., passive Perception 10
Languages Abyssal
Challenge 3 (700 XP)

Magic Resistance. The demon has advantage on saving throws against spells and other magical effects.

Magic Weapons. The demon's weapon attacks are magical.

Innate Spellcasting. The demon's spellcasting ability is Charisma (spell save DC 10, +2 to hit with spell attacks). The demon can innately cast the following spells at will, requiring no material components: *detect evil and good, detect thoughts, invisibility.*

Actions

Multiattack. The demon makes three attacks: one with its bite and two with its claws.

Bite. *Melee Weapon Attack:* +4 to hit, reach 5 ft., one target. *Hit:* 5 (1d6 + 2) piercing damage.

Claws. *Melee Weapon Attack:* +4 to hit, reach 5 ft., one target. *Hit:* 4 (1d4 + 2) slashing damage.

Balban (Brute Demon)

This creature stands at least 12 feet tall with a squat, pot-bellied body, massive arms, and thick, rounded legs. Its head resembles that of a trunkless and tuskless elephant. Four great backward curving horns sprout from its head behind its eyes. Its skin is slate gray with darker areas on its underbelly and back.

Almost as stupid as the lowly dretches, balbans are hulking monstrosities standing over 10 feet tall. Demonic generals use these creatures in abundance in their armies, relying on the balbans' love for battle, their great strength, and their knack for destroying objects and structures. Balban squads are brutish, hulking, and hard to control. While many demon lords do employ their services, they are deemed highly expendable and are thus encountered on the front lines of any great battle.

Balbans spend much of their life battling, not necessarily for survival, but simply because they relish the chaos and bloodshed combat brings. Balbans attack any creature they encounter on sight, except those they know are more powerful than themselves. Though lacking in the intelligence department, they do not attack any demonic officer in the service of a demon lord (unless they know the officer is weaker and they can kill him or her and make it look like something else was responsible).

Balbans have slate gray skin, stand at least 12 feet tall and weigh about 4,500 pounds. Their eyes are coal black and their tongues violet. A seemingly constant stream of saliva and gastric juices oozes from their mouths.

A balban employs simple tactics in battle; smash an opponent, grab an opponent, smash it into pulp, and devour what's left. Against weaker foes, they are likely to employ their ability to invoke fear or confuse opponents by shrouding themselves in darkness.

Balban

Large fiend (demon), chaotic evil
Armor Class 17 (natural armor)
Hit Points 126 (11d10 + 66)
Speed 40 ft.

STR	DEX	CON	INT	WIS	CHA
25 (+7)	14 (+2)	22 (+6)	6 (−2)	14 (+2)	14 (+2)

Saving Throws Con +10, Wis +6, Cha +6
Skills Intimidation +6, Perception +6
Damage Resistances cold, fire, lightning; bludgeoning, piercing, and slashing from nonmagical weapons
Damage Immunities poison
Condition Immunities poisoned
Senses darkvision 120 ft., passive Perception 16
Languages Abyssal
Challenge 9 (5,000 XP)

Magic Resistance. The demon has advantage on saving throws against spells and other magical effects.

Magic Weapons. The demon's weapon attacks are magical.

Innate Spellcasting. The demon's spellcasting ability is Wisdom (spell save DC 14, +6 to hit with spell attacks). The demon can innately cast the following spells at will, requiring no material components: *fear, darkness, dispel magic, teleport, see invisibility.*

Charge. If the demon moves at least 20 feet straight toward a creature and then hits it with a bite attack on the same turn, that target must succeed on a DC 17 Strength saving throw or be knocked prone. If the target is prone, the demon can make one slam attack against it as a bonus action.

Actions

Multiattack. The demon can use its smash, make one bite attack and two claw attacks.

Bite. *Melee Weapon Attack:* +11 to hit, reach 5 ft., one target. *Hit:* 16 (2d8 + 7) piercing damage.

Slam. *Melee Weapon Attack:* +11 to hit, reach 10 ft., one target. *Hit:* 17 (3d6 + 7) bludgeoning damage. If the target is a Medium or smaller creature, it is grappled (escape DC 17). Until this grapple ends, the target is restrained and the demon cannot use this attack against another target.

Smash. One Medium or smaller creature grappled by the demon is smashed into nearby solid objects or a solid surface. The target takes 25 (4d8 + 7) bludgeoning damage and must succeed on a DC 16 Constitution saving throw or be stunned until the end of its next turn.

Barizou (Assassin Demon)

This humanoid appears to be halfling-sized or smaller with gray skin, a wolf-like head, membranous wings, and hands and feet that end in sharpened talons. Its mouth is littered with a row of razor-sharp fangs. Its back is mottled with sickly patches of bluish-gray.

Called assassin demons or infiltrator demons, the barizou are employed as such because their small size allows them to move unseen in many places larger demons cannot go.

The typical barizou stands 3 feet tall and weighs about 60 pounds.

Barizou

Small fiend (demon), chaotic evil
Armor Class 12
Hit Points 14 (4d6)

Speed 30 ft., fly 50 ft.

STR	DEX	CON	INT	WIS	CHA
10 (+0)	15 (+2)	10 (+0)	6 (−2)	6 (−2)	10 (+0)

Skills Perception +2, Stealth +4
Damage Resistances cold, fire, lightning
Damage Immunities poison
Condition Immunities poisoned
Senses darkvision 120 ft., passive Perception 12
Languages Abyssal
Challenge 1 (200 XP)

Chameleon. As a bonus action, a demon can alter its coloration to blend with its surroundings. This grants the demon advantage on Stealth checks.

Magic Resistance. The demon has advantage on saving throws against spells and other magical effects.

Magic Weapons. The demon's weapon attacks are magical.

Innate Spellcasting. The demon's spellcasting ability is Charisma (spell save DC 10, +2 to hit with spell attacks). It can innately cast the following spells at will, requiring no material components: *fear darkness, detect evil and good, see invisibility*

Sneak Attack (1/turn). The demon deals an extra 3 (1d6) damage when it hits a target with a weapon attack and has advantage on the attack roll, or when the target is within 5 feet of an ally of the demon that isn't incapacitated and the demon doesn't have disadvantage on the attack roll.

Actions

Multiattack. The demon makes three attacks: one with its bite and two with its claws.

Bite. *Melee Weapon Attack*: +4 to hit, reach 5 ft., one target. *Hit*: 5 (1d6 + 2) piercing damage.

Claw. *Melee Weapon Attack*: +4 to hit, reach 5 ft., one target. *Hit*: 4 (1d4 + 2) slashing damage.

Chaaor (Beast Demon)

This creature appears as a huge hulking apelike creature with a bear's head. Two large, downward-curving horns jut from its head. The beast's fur is reddish-black and matted with blood and its hands end in razor-sharp claws.

Some demons are feared more than others. Of those, the apelike chaaor is one. Their savagery in battle has turned the stomach of even the stoutest demonic general.

Chaaor are used as shock troops in the Abyssal armies. Many are the demon lords that have sent a battalion of these fiends against an army, watching in delight as the brutal chaaor tore its way through the enemy's ranks. When not engaging in wars with other infernal creatures, the chaaor spends its time roaming the Abyss in hunting packs. They have no preference as to the type or strength of prey: they hunt and kill what they choose. Chaaor packs have been known to attack creatures much larger than themselves and kill all opponents in short order.

A chaaor is a 12-foot-tall, hulking, apelike brute with the head of a bear. Large downward curving, grayish-silver horns grow from its head and end in rounded points. The chaaor's body is covered in reddish-black fur and is almost always caked or matted in blood. The powerful arms of a chaaor end in razor-sharp and filthy claws — black in color. Long rows of sharpened teeth fill the chaaor's mouth. When moving, the chaaor usually drops to all fours. When facing an aggressor it assumes a bipedal stance.

Chaaor are deadly adversaries that relish the blood and adrenaline of battle. Their tactics are simple: target a foe, charge forward, and rake or slash with claws and bite. Often, a chaaor unleashes its mighty roar to begin a fight hoping to knock down as many foes as possible. A downed foe is leapt on by multiple chaaors who proceed to tear the opponent to pieces. Likewise, if a chaaor grabs a foe, it holds on while the others move in and rip it to shreds with teeth and claws.

Chaaor

Large fiend (demon), chaotic evil
Armor Class 17 (natural armor)
Hit Points 105 (10d10 + 50)
Speed 30 ft.

STR	DEX	CON	INT	WIS	CHA
26 (+8)	17 (+3)	20 (+5)	8 (−1)	14 (+2)	14 (+2)

Saving Throws Str +12, Con +9
Skills Athletics +12, Intimidation +10, Perception +6, Insight +6, Stealth +7
Damage Resistances cold, fire, lightning; bludgeoning,

piercing, and slashing from nonmagical weapons
Damage Immunities poison
Condition Immunities poisoned
Senses truesight 120 ft., passive Perception 16
Languages Common, Abyssal, telepathy 120 ft.
Challenge 10 (5,900 XP)

Magic Resistance. The demon has advantage on saving throws against spells and other magical effects.

Magic Weapons. The demon's weapon attacks are magical.

Innate Spellcasting. The demon's spellcasting ability is Wisdom (spell save DC 14, +6 to hit with spell attacks). The demon can innately cast the following spells, requiring no material components:

At will: *darkness, jump, see invisibility*
1/day: *plane shift* (self only)

Actions

Multiattack. The demon makes three attacks: one with its bite and two with its claws.

Bite. *Melee Weapon Attack*: +12 to hit, reach 10 ft., one target. *Hit*: 18 (3d6 + 8) piercing damage.

Claw. *Melee Weapon Attack*: +12 to hit, reach 10 ft., one target. *Hit*: 17 (2d8 + 8) slashing damage. If the target is a Medium or smaller creature, it is grappled (escape DC 19). The demon has two claws, each of which can grapple only one target.

Roar (3/day). The demon can emit a loud roar in a 60 radius. Each creature in the area must make a DC 17 Constitution saving throw. On a failed saving throw, the target takes 14 (4d6) thunder damage and is stunned until the end of the demon's next turn. On a successful saving throw, the target takes half damage and is not stunned.

Summon Demon (1/day). The demon chooses what to summon and attempts a magical summoning. A chaaor has a 30% chance of summoning 1d3 vrocks, 1d2 hezrous, or one glabrezu.

A summoned demon appears in an unoccupied space within 60 feet of its summoner, acts as an ally of its summoner, and can't summon other demons. It remains for 1 minute, until it or its summoner dies, or until its summoner dismisses it as an action.

Choronzon (Chaos Demon)

This creature stands at least 20 feet tall with a huge, muscular body. Its massive arms and legs end in wicked claws. Its rounded, squat head, sits atop an extremely thick, almost nonexistent neck. The creature's gaping maw is filled with sharp fangs. Two large swept back horns jut from its head just above its rounded eyes.

Choronzons are the demons of confusion, dispersion, and ultimate chaos. They are huge behemoths seemingly bred for war and battle, though most rarely take part in the Abyssal wars that rage between the planes. Choronzons prefer to use their talents on weak-minded creatures such as those that inhabit the Material planes, and as such, they are usually encountered there. These demons derive great pleasure in laying waste to villages and towns and even small kingdoms (if the mood strikes them).

Amongst demonkind, choronzons are both feared and hated. A great enmity exists between balors and choronzons that scholars and lorekeepers can document, but cannot determine the source of the hatred between these two demonic races.

A choronzon stands about 20 feet tall and weighs about 9,000 pounds. Its scaly flesh is bluish-black and its eyes are crimson. Its horns are darker than the rest of its body and the creature's claws are pitch black. Its teeth are dull ivory in color.

A choronzon begins combat by surrounding itself with its aura of confusion and then unleashing its breath weapon at its foes. Opponents that continue to press the battle are met with a mix of physical attacks and innate spellcasting abilities.

Choronzon

Large fiend (demon), chaotic evil
Armor Class 16 (natural armor)
Hit Points 324 (24d10 + 192)
Speed 40 ft.

STR	DEX	CON	INT	WIS	CHA
28 (+9)	15 (+2)	27 (+8)	12 (+1)	14 (+2)	18 (+4)

Saving Throws Dex +8, Con +14, Cha +10
Skills Insight +8, Intimidation +10, Perception +8
Damage Resistances cold, fire, lightning; bludgeoning, piercing, and slashing from nonmagical weapons
Damage Immunities poison
Condition Immunities poisoned
Senses darkvision 120 ft., passive Perception 18
Languages Abyssal
Challenge 17 (18,000 XP)

Aura of Confusion. The demon can activate or deactivate this feature as bonus action. While active, any creature that ends its turn within 30 feet of the demon must make a DC 19 Wisdom saving throw or be stunned until the end of the demon's next turn.

Innate Spellcasting. The demon's spellcasting ability is Charisma (spell save DC 18, +10 to hit with spell attacks). The demon can innately cast the following spells, requiring no material components:

At will: *confusion, fear*
3/day: *blight*

Magic Resistance. The demon has advantage on saving throws against spells and other magical effects.

Magic Weapons. The demon's weapon attacks are magical.

Actions

Multiattack. The demon makes three attacks: one with its bite and two with its claws.

Bite. *Melee Weapon Attack*: +15 to hit, reach 15 ft., one target. Hit: 22 (3d8 + 9) piercing damage.

Claws. *Melee Weapon Attack*: +15 to hit, reach 15 ft., one target. Hit: 23 (4d6 + 9) slashing damage. On a successful hit, the target must make a DC 20 Constitution saving throw or be stunned until the start of the demon's next turn.

Chaos Breath (Recharge 5–6). The demon breathes exhales a 40-foot cone of bluish gas. Each creature in the area must make a successful DC 19 Constitution saving throw or take 42 (12d6) necrotic damage and become poisoned. While poisoned in this way, a target takes 7 (2d6) poison damage at the start of each of its turns. A target can repeat the saving throw at the end of each of its turns, ending the effect on itself on a success.

A creature killed by the demon's Chaos Breath instantly breaks apart into its individual atomic components. The creature can only be restored to life by means of a *true resurrection* or *wish* spell.

Teleport. The demon magically teleports, along with any equipment it is wearing or carrying, up to 120 feet to an unoccupied space it can see.

Summon (1/day). The demon chooses what to summon and attempts a magical summoning.

A choronzon has a 50% chance of summoning 1d8 vrocks, 1d6 hezrous, 1d4 glabrezus, 1d3 nalfeshnees, 1d2 mariliths, or one goristro.

A summoned demon appears in an unoccupied space within 60 feet of its summoner, acts as an ally of its summoner, and can't summon other demons. It remains for 1 minute, until it or its summoner dies, or until its summoner dismisses it as an action.

Derghodemon (Cockroach Demon)

This creature is a tall, bloated, insect-like creature with five arms and three legs. Each of its arms ends in a sharpened, clawed hand. Its legs end in four-toed feet. Its flesh is mottled green and black and its eyes are large and black with no pupils.

The derghodemon is one of the strongest of the demon races, but its low intelligence has relegated it to a position of brute warrior and little more.

A derghodemon stands 8 feet tall and weighs about 800 pounds.

Derghodemon

Large fiend (demon), neutral evil
Armor Class 18 (natural armor)
Hit Points 147 (14d10 + 70)

Speed 40 ft.

STR	DEX	CON	INT	WIS	CHA
25 (+7)	16 (+3)	21 (+5)	7 (−2)	14 (+2)	16 (+3)

Saving Throws Dex +7, Con +9, Wis +6, Cha +7
Skills Intimidation +7, Perception +6, Stealth +7
Damage Resistances cold, fire, lightning
Damage Immunities poison
Condition Immunities poisoned
Senses truesight 120 ft., passive Perception 20
Languages Abyssal, telepathy 120 ft.
Challenge 9 (5,000 XP)

Magic Resistance. The demon has advantage on saving throws against spells and other magical effects.

Magic Weapons. The demon's weapon attacks are magical.

Innate Spellcasting. The demon's spellcasting ability is Charisma (spell save DC 15, +7 to hit with spell attacks). The demon can innately cast the following spells, requiring no material components:

At will: *darkness, fear, detect magic*

1/day each: *confusion, sleep*

Rend and Tear. The demon has advantage on all melee weapon attacks against a creature it is grappling.

Actions

Multiattack. The demon makes three attacks: one with its bite and two with its claws.

Bite. *Melee Weapon Attack:* +11 to hit, reach 5 ft., one target. *Hit:* 16 (2d8 + 7) piercing damage, and the target is grappled (escape DC 17). Until this grapple ends, the demon can bite only the grappled creature and has advantage on attack rolls to do so.

Claws. *Melee Weapon Attack:* +11 to hit, reach 10 ft., one target. *Hit:* 21 (4d6 + 7) slashing damage.

Geruzou (Slime Demon)

This humanoid appears to stand nearly 4 feet tall and has a horse-like head with downward-curving horns jutting from its head. Its mouth is filled with long, sharp teeth and its hands and feet end in sharpened claws. A pair of large, membranous wings jut from its back and its flesh is sickly gray and appears to be covered with a thick layer of slimy mucus.

Geruzou are sometimes called slime demons because their leathery skin constantly drips and oozes thick, jelly-like mucus. Like their brethren, they are fierce combatants and are often employed as hunters and trackers by greater demons.

The typical geruzou stands nearly 4 feet tall and weighs about 140 pounds.

Geruzou

Small fiend (demon), chaotic evil
Armor Class 15 (natural armor)
Hit Points 31 (7d6 + 7)
Speed 30 ft., fly 50 ft.

STR	DEX	CON	INT	WIS	CHA
12 (+1)	15 (+2)	12 (+1)	8 (−1)	8 (−1)	10 (+0)

Skills Perception +1, Stealth +4
Damage Resistances cold, fire, lightning

Gharros (Scorpion Demon)

This hideous creature appears to be half-scorpion and half-human. Its upper torso is that of a greenish-silver humanoid with long, flowing dark hair and stark white eyes while its lower torso is that of a reddish-brown scorpion. Its tail splits into two separate stingers and the creature's mouth is filled with razor-sharp teeth.

A gharros looks like a cross between a large human and an even larger scorpion. They serve as guards, soldiers, shock troops (and even assassins sometimes) to some of the minor nobles and lesser demon lords of the Abyss. They hate all goodness and seek to destroy it at any opportunity through whatever means available.

A gharros is about 8 feet tall and 10 feet long and weighs around 1,500 pounds.

Gharros are very aggressive in battle and seek to kill the strongest opponent first. They wield their halberd in combat and sting with their deadly tails, all the while sprinkling the fight with their innate spellcasting abilities. Unless ordered to do so, gharros never take prisoners in battle. They fight to the death (either their death or their opponent's).

Gharros

Large fiend (demon), chaotic evil
Armor Class 20 (natural armor)
Hit Points 270 (20d10 + 160)
Speed 30 ft.

STR	DEX	CON	INT	WIS	CHA
26 (+8)	18 (+4)	26 (+8)	18 (+4)	18 (+4)	20 (+5)

Saving Throws Con +13, Wis +9, Cha +10
Skills Athletics +13, Perception +9, Survival +9
Damage Resistance cold, fire, lightning; bludgeoning, piercing, and slashing from nonmagical weapons
Damage Immunities poison
Condition Immunities poisoned
Senses darkvision 60 ft., passive Perception 11
Languages Abyssal, common; telepathy 100 ft.
Challenge 2 (450 XP)

Innate Spellcasting. The demon's spellcasting ability is Charisma (spell save DC 10, +2 to hit with spell attacks). The demon can innately cast the following spells at will, requiring no material components: *darkness, detect evil and good, invisibility* (self only)

Magic Resistance. The demon has advantage on saving throws against spells and other magical effects.

Magic Weapons. The demon's weapon attacks are magical.

Slimy Hide. The demon's hide is extremely slick and oozes with slime. Creatures attempting to grapple the demon do so with disadvantage.

Actions

Multiattack. The demon makes three attacks: one with its bite and two with its claws. It can use its Spit Slime in place of the bite.

Bite. *Melee Weapon Attack:* +4 to hit, reach 5 ft., one target. *Hit:* 5 (1d6 + 2) piercing damage.

Claws. *Melee Weapon Attack:* +4 to hit, reach 5 ft., one target. *Hit:* 5 (1d6 + 2) slashing damage.

Spit Slime. *Ranged Weapon Attack:* +4 to hit, range 20/60 ft., one target. *Hit:* 10 (3d6) acid damage and the target must succeed on a DC 13 Constitution saving throw or its speed is reduced by half until the end of the demon's next turn.

Damage Immunities poison
Condition Immunities poisoned
Senses truesight 120 ft., passive Perception 19
Languages Abyssal, telepathy 120 ft.
Challenge 16 (15,000 XP)

Improved Critical. The demon's attacks score a critical hit on a roll of 19 or 20.

Innate Spellcasting. The demon's spellcasting ability is Wisdom (spell save DC 17, +9 to hit with spell attacks). It can innately cast the following spells requiring no material components:

At will: *darkness, detect evil and good, detect magic, mirror image*

3/day each: *hallow, telekinesis, teleport*

Magic Resistance. The demon has advantage on saving throws against spells and other magical effects.

Magic Weapons. The demon's weapon attacks are magical.

Rampage. When the demon reduces a creature to 0 hit points with a melee attack on its turn, the demon can take a bonus action to move up to half its speed and make a halberd attack.

Actions

Multiattack. The demon makes three attacks: one halberd attack and two sting attacks.

Halberd. *Melee Weapon Attack:* +13 to hit, reach 10 ft., one target. *Hit:* 19 (2d10 + 8) slashing damage.

Sting. *Melee Weapon Attack:* +13 to hit, reach 10 ft., one target. *Hit:* 17 (2d8 + 8) piercing damage, and the target must make a DC 18 Constitution saving throw, taking 17 (5d6) poison damage on a failed save, or half as much damage on a successful one.

Summon (1/day). The demon chooses what to summon and attempts a magical summoning.

A gharros has a 50% chance of summoning 1d6 vrocks, 1d4 hezrous, 1d3 glabrezus, 1d2 nalfeshnees, or one marilith.

A summoned demon appears in an unoccupied space within 60 feet of its summoner, acts as an ally of its summoner, and can't summon other demons. It remains for 1 minute, until it or its summoner dies, or until its summoner dismisses it as an action.

Greruor (Frog Demon)

This creature appears as a massive, squat and bloated frog-like creature with arms in place of its forelegs. Two large horns protrude above deep sunken eyes.

Greruors serve in the infernal armies of several demon lords, particularly Tsathogga. They are strong, powerful, and brutal demons that delight in inflicting pain on others. They are extremely loyal and follow orders without question. Some greater demons, like nalfeshnees and glabrezus, relish the flesh of greruors' legs and often organize hunting parties to track and slay the frog demons. The greruors, however, are not the weak-minded brutes they appear to be and often win such confrontations using their deadly ranseurs and their large numbers to turn back their opponents.

A greruor appears as a massive, squat, bloated, frog-like demon with arms in place of its forelegs. Its wide, frog-like head has two 3-foot-long horns protruding just above its deep, sunken eyes. It moves by hopping on its rear legs. Its arms end in talons which are usually clutched around the greruor's deadly ranseur. Its huge mouth sports razor-sharp teeth of a dull gray color. The greruor stands about 8 feet tall when on all fours. In combat, they stand on their hind legs and attack with their ranseur. The greruor's flesh is greenish-brown mottled with red or gray. Its skin constantly oozes and secretes a thick, mucus-like clear slime that is slick to the touch.

Greruor's enjoy combat and seek it wherever they can find it. Normally they rely on their natural attacks, combustible spittle, and weapons to fell

opponents. If outmatched, they use *confusion* to disorient the strongest opponent and *hold person* on humanoid casters, followed closely by *shatter* on grouped foes. Grappled opponents are often held in the mouth of one greruor while another stabs the victim with its ranseur.

Greruor

Large fiend (demon), chaotic evil
Armor Class 17 (natural armor)
Hit Points 136 (13d10 + 65)
Speed 40 ft.

STR	DEX	CON	INT	WIS	CHA
23 (+6)	17 (+3)	21 (+5)	14 (+2)	14 (+2)	16 (+3)

Saving Throws Dex +7, Con +9, Cha +7
Skills Intimidation +7, Perception +6
Damage Resistances cold, fire, lightning
Damage Immunities poison
Condition Immunities poisoned
Senses truesight 120 ft., passive Perception 16
Languages Abyssal, Common; telepathy 120 ft.
Challenge 11 (7,200 XP)

Innate Spellcasting. The demon's spellcasting ability is Charisma (spell save DC 15, +7 to hit with spell attacks). The demon can innately cast the following spells, requiring no material components:

At will: *darkness, detect evil and good, shatter*

3/day each: *confusion, hold person*

Magic Resistance. The demon has advantage on saving throws against spells and other magical effects.

Magic Weapons. The demon's weapon attacks are magical.

Actions

Multiattack. The demon makes three attacks: one with its bite and two with its ranseur. It can attack with its tongue instead of making a bite attack.

Bite. *Melee Weapon Attack:* +10 to hit, reach 5 ft., one target. *Hit:* 17 (2d10 + 6) piercing damage.

Ranseur. *Melee Weapon Attack:* +10 to hit, reach 10 ft., one target. *Hit:* 20 (4d6 + 6) piercing damage.

Tongue. *Melee Weapon Attack:* +10 to hit, reach 10 ft., one target. *Hit:* 15 (2d8 + 6) slashing damage, and the target is grappled (escape DC 16). Until this grapple ends, the target is restrained, and the demon cannot attack with its tongue.

Combustible Spittle (Recharge 5–6). The demon spits a line of acid in a 30-foot line that is 5 feet wide. Each creature in that line must make a DC 17 Dexterity saving throw, taking 27 (6d8) acid damage on a failed save, or half as much on a successful one. At the start of the demon's next turn, the acid ignites and any targets hit by it burst into flames, taking 10 (3d6) fire damage per round until extinguished.

Guardian Demon

This entity resembles a large bipedal bear-like creature with upward curving horns, elongated fangs, and blackish-gray fur. Its hands end in eagle-like talons.

A guardian demon is summoned to the Material Plane by a spellcaster with the task of guarding an area or treasure. These demons vary in size and appearance, though most resemble large bears, wild cats, or apes with added demonic characteristics (horns, elongated fangs and nails, and so on). Despite its varying appearance and form, the guardian demon is a dangerous adversary.

A typical guardian demon stands 9 feet tall and weighs about 800 pounds.

A guardian demon only initiates combat if the area it is guarding is entered or the treasure it is watching over is disturbed. Though guardian demons can move both upright and on all fours, it always fights in a bipedal stance. When engaged in combat, it may move freely, but never leaves the area it is guarding. A guardian demon attacks using its breath weapon, bite, and claws. It defends the area it is tied to until either it or its opponents are dead.

Guardian Demon

Large fiend (demon), neutral evil
Armor Class 15 (natural armor)
Hit Points 85 (10d10 + 30)
Speed 30 ft.

STR	DEX	CON	INT	WIS	CHA
18 (+4)	12 (+1)	16 (+3)	12 (+1)	14 (+2)	14 (+2)

Skills Perception +5
Damage Resistances cold, fire, lightning
Damage Immunities poison
Condition Immunities poisoned
Senses darkvision 120 ft., passive Perception 15
Languages Abyssal, telepathy 120 ft.
Challenge 7 (2,900 XP)

Magic Resistance. The demon has advantage on saving throws against spells and other magical effects.

Magic Weapons. The demon's weapon attacks are magical.

Actions

Multiattack. The demon makes three attacks: one with its bite and two with it claws.

Bite. *Melee Weapon Attack*: +7 to hit, reach 5 ft., one target. *Hit*: 13 (2d8 + 4) piercing damage.

Claw. *Melee Weapon Attack*: +7 to hit, reach 5 ft., one target. *Hit*: 14 (3d6 + 4) slashing damage.

Flame Breath (Recharge 5–6). The demon exhales fire in a 30-foot cone. Each creature in that area must make a DC 15 Dexterity saving throw, taking 28 (8d6) fire damage on a failed save, or half as much damage on a successful one.

Hydrodemon

This massive frog-like creature stands nearly 10 feet tall. Its flesh is warty and dark green and its eyes are sickly yellow. It has large flaps of skin under its arms that seemingly function as wings.

Hydrodemons are frog-like demons that swim the River Styx. They are the only known creatures in existence that can touch the waters of the Styx without suffering any ill effects.

Hydrodemons are 10 feet tall and weigh about 4,000 pounds. They move by leaping in a manner akin to a frog. Large flaps of skin under their arms allow them seemingly to glide when leaping. The flesh of a hydrodemon is warty and green. Its eyes are a sickly yellow in color.

Hydrodemon

Large fiend (demon), neutral evil
Armor Class 15 (natural armor)
Hit Points 85 (9d10 + 36)
Speed 30 ft., fly 40 ft., swim 60 ft.

STR	DEX	CON	INT	WIS	CHA
18 (+4)	14 (+2)	18 (+4)	8 (−1)	11 (+0)	14 (+2)

Saving Throws Dex +5, Con +7
Skills Perception +6
Damage Resistances cold, fire, lightning
Damage Immunities poison
Condition Immunities poisoned

Senses darkvision 60 ft., passive Perception 16
Languages Abyssal
Challenge 5 (1,800 XP)

Amphibious. The hydrodemon can breathe air and water.

Magic Resistance. The hydrodemon has advantage on saving throws against spells and other magical effects.

Magic Weapons. The hydrodemon's weapon attacks are magical.

Innate Spellcasting. The hydrodemon's spellcasting ability is Charisma (spell save DC 13, +5 to hit with spell attacks). It can innately cast the following spells, requiring no material components:

At will: *darkness, detect magic, water walk*

2/day each: *dimension door, teleport*

1/day each: *hallow*

Actions

Multiattack. The hydrodemon makes three attacks: one with its bite and two with its claws. The demon can use its Sleep Spittle instead of using its bite.

Bite. *Melee Weapon Attack:* +7 to hit, reach 5 ft., one target. *Hit:* 13 (2d8 + 4) piercing damage, and the target is grappled (escape DC 14). Until this grapple ends, the target is restrained and the demon can't bite another target.

Claws. *Melee Weapon Attack:* +7 to hit, reach 10 ft., one target. *Hit:* 11 (2d6 + 4) slashing damage.

Sleep Spittle. One target within 60 ft. must succeed on a DC 15 Wisdom saving throw or fall unconscious for 1 minute. The sleeping target can be awakened if someone uses an action to shake or slap the sleeper awake, and the target will wake if it takes damage.

Summon (1/day). The demon chooses what to summon and attempts a magical summoning.

A hydrodemon has a 30% chance of summoning one hydrodemon.

A summoned demon appears in an unoccupied space within 60 feet of its summoner, acts as an ally of its summoner, and can't summon other demons. It remains for 1 minute, until it or its summoner dies, or until its summoner dismisses it as an action.

Mehrim (Goat Demon)

This entity looks like an oversized black goat with three horns and jet black, glossy hooves. It exhales a wispy cloud of putrid black smoke as it breathes.

Mehrims are human-sized goat-like demons that roam the various planes of the Abyss, grazing and feeding on the strange Abyssal fauna as well as the flesh and ichor of fallen demons. While they are good hunters in their own right, mehrims are generally scavengers, following other demon hordes and feasting on their leftovers. Generally left to their own devices, mehrims play a minor role in the politics and machinations that take place within the Abyss. They rarely take part in the various wars and battles that rage across the Abyssal planes.

A mehrim stands about 4 feet tall at the shoulders and is about 7 feet long. It weighs about 650 pounds. Its skin is dark and its coat black and oily.

A mehrim charges into battle biting with its diseased bite and slashing with its front hooves. Most of the time, a mehrim opens battle with its *protection from evil and good* and *darkness* innate spellcasting abilities in effect. Against good-aligned foes that are susceptible, the mehrim uses its *dispel evil and good* attack.

Mehrim

Medium fiend (demon) chaotic evil
Armor Class 15 (natural armor)
Hit Points 31 (7d8)
Speed 40 ft.

STR	DEX	CON	INT	WIS	CHA
20 (+5)	14 (+2)	10 (+0)	12 (+1)	13 (+1)	16 (+3)

Skills Perception +5
Damage Resistances cold, fire, lightning
Damage Immunities poison
Condition Immunities poisoned
Senses darkvision 60 ft., passive Perception 15
Languages Abyssal
Challenge 3 (700 XP)

Keen Smell. The demon has advantage on Wisdom (Perception) checks that rely on smell.

Magic Resistance. The demon has advantage on saving throws against spells and other magical effects.

Magic Weapons. The demon's weapon attacks are magical.

Innate Spellcasting. The demon's spellcasting ability is Charisma (spell save DC 13, +5 to hit with spell attacks). It can innately cast each of the following spells, requiring no material components:

At will: *darkness, protection from evil and good, see invisibility*

1/day each: *dispel evil and good, dispel magic*

Actions

Multiattack. The mehrim demon makes three attacks: one with its bite and two with its hooves.

Bite. *Melee Weapon Attack:* +7 to hit, reach 5 ft., one target. *Hit:* 9 (1d8 + 5) piercing damage. If the target is a creature, it must succeed on a DC 10 Constitution saving throw against disease or become poisoned until the disease is cured. Every 24 hours that elapse, the target must repeat the saving throw, reducing its hit point maximum by 5 (1d10) on a failure. The disease is cured on a success. The target dies if the disease reduces its hit point maximum to 0. This reduction to the target's hit point maximum lasts until the disease is cured.

Hooves. *Melee Weapon Attack:* +7 to hit, reach 5 ft., one target. *Hit:* 8 (1d6 + 5) slashing damage.

Dagon, Demon Prince of the Sea

This creature has the upper body, arms, and head of a green-skinned humanoid, and the lower torso of a great scaled fish. A thin, almost translucent fin runs the length of his back, and a long mane of black hair falls from his head and down his finned back. His eyes are crimson.

Dagon is the demon prince of sea creatures. He is worshipped as a deity by legions of sahuagin, locathah, skum, lizardfolk, tritons (those that have accepted the ways of evil), and some merfolk. His Abyssal lair is not unlike the Elemental Plane of Water in that it is composed entirely of water. Pockets of air, though, are rumored to be trapped in invisible "bubbles" throughout his lair (so as to allow the non-water breathing demons to exist comfortably). Dagon makes his home in a great underwater iron citadel called Thos located in the deepest recesses of his home plane.

Dagon appears as a 10-foot-tall merman and weighs about 2,000 pounds. He can move on land using his fists to drag or pull his body but prefers to remain in water whenever possible.

Dagon prefers to use his trident in battle but can attack with his powerful fists if he so chooses.

Servants of Dagon

Followers of Dagon are mermen, locathah, sahuagin, lizardfolk, skum, and evil humanoids that revere the seas and oceans. Devout followers of Dagon are called Scaled Ones and must sign a pact of evil with Dagon.

Dagon

Large fiend (demon lord), chaotic evil
Armor Class 19 (natural armor)
Hit Points 472 (35d10 + 280)
Speed 20 ft., swim 60 ft.

STR	DEX	CON	INT	WIS	CHA
25 (+7)	18 (+4)	27 (+8)	18 (+4)	20 (+5)	19 (+4)

Saving Throws Dex +12, Con +16, Wis +13, Cha +12
Skills Athletics +15, History +12, Insight +13, Intimidation +12, Perception +13
Damage Resistances cold, fire, lightning
Damage Immunities poison; bludgeoning, piercing, and slashing from nonmagical weapons
Condition Immunities charmed, exhaustion, frightened, poisoned
Senses truesight 120 ft., passive Perception 23
Languages Abyssal, Celestial, Common, Draconic, Giant, Infernal; telepathy 120 ft.
Challenge 26 (90,000 XP)

Special Equipment. Dagon carries *Embrace of the Uncaring Sea*, a powerful magic trident.

Innate Spellcasting. Dagon's innate spellcasting ability is Charisma (spell save DC 20, +12 to hit with spell attacks). It can cast the following spells, requiring no material components.

At will: *cloudkill* (works underwater only), *control water, create and destroy water, darkness, detect evil and good, detect magic, detect*

thoughts, magic missile (as the 4th level spell), *teleport, telekinesis, tongues, water breathing*

3/day each: *conjure animals* (aquatic creatures only), *conjure elemental* (water elemental only), *dispel magic, dominate beast* (aquatic creatures only), *fear*

1/day each: *confusion, feeblemind, finger of death, hold person, hold monster, lightning bolt, stoneskin, time stop, web, wish*

Legendary Resistance (3/day). If Dagon fails a saving throw, it can choose to succeed instead.

Magic Resistance. Dagon has advantage on saving throws against spells and other magical effects.

Magic Weapons. Dagon's weapon attacks are magical.

Unholy Aura. An unholy aura surrounds Dagon out to a radius of 40 feet. A creature who enters or begins their turn in the area must make a DC 21 Wisdom saving throw. On a failed saving throw, the target is frightened for 1 minute. While frightened, they are paralyzed. A frightened target can repeat the saving throw at the end of each of its turns, ending the effect on a success.

Water Mastery. Dagon has advantage on attack rolls, ability checks, and saving throws when even partly immersed in sea water.

Actions

Multiattack. Dagon makes three melee weapon attacks.

Embrace of the Uncaring Sea. *Melee or Ranged Weapon Attack:* +18 to hit, reach 10 ft. or range 20/60 ft., one creature. *Hit:* 24 (4d6 + 10) piercing damage, or 28 (4d8 + 10) piercing damage if used with two hands to make a melee attack, plus 17 (5d6) poison damage. If Dagon rolls a natural 19 or 20, the target must make a DC 21 Constitution saving throw or be afflicted by the crushing pressure of the sea. A creature afflicted by this cannot breathe, use verbal components, or take actions or reactions. At the end of each of the target's turns, it can repeat the saving throw, ending the effect on a success. Magic such as *heal* can end this affliction early.

Claw. *Melee Weapon Attack:* +15 to hit, reach 5 ft., one target. *Hit:* 25 (4d8 + 7) slashing damage and target is poisoned until the beginning of Dagon's next turn.

Command Aquatic Creature (Recharge 5–6). One creature with a swim speed that Dagon can see within 120 feet of it hears the telepathic commands of Dagon and must make a DC 21 Wisdom saving throw. On a failed save, the creature is charmed for 24 hours. While charmed, it must follow the orders of Dagon to the best of the target's ability and it is immune to being charmed or frightened by another effect or spell. A target can repeat the saving throw when it takes damage, ending the effect on a success.

Legendary Actions

Dagon can take 3 legendary actions, choosing from the options below. Only one legendary action option can be used at a time and only at the end of another creature's turn. Dagon regains spent legendary actions at the start of its turn.

Move. If at least halfway submerged in water, Dagon can move up to half its swim speed without provoking opportunity attacks.

Command Aquatic Creature (Costs 2 Actions). Dagon uses its Command Aquatic Creature ability, even if it has not recharged.

Ink Cloud (Costs 3 Actions). Dagon exhales a 60-foot cone of inky blackness. Underwater it is as black ink, while above water it manifests as a thick cloud, and the area counts as heavily obscured. It remains until dispersed by a strong current or wind (at least 20 miles per hour). Dagon can end this effect on its turn as a bonus action. Creatures who enter or begin their turn in the area must make a successful DC 22 Constitution saving throw or take 18 (4d8) poison damage.

Lair Actions

On initiative count 20 (losing initiative ties), Dagon can take a lair action to cause one of the following effects; Dagon can't use the same effect two rounds in a row:

Maelstrom. The currents and eddies of the underwater realm Dagon occupies swirl in a maelstrom out to a radius of 100 feet. All creatures in that area, other than Dagon, must make a DC 21 Strength saving throw. On a failed save, the target is moved in a random direction 30 feet.

Control Tempature. Dagon selects an area of water within 100 feet no larger than a 20-foot sphere and causes it to heat to boiling or cool drastically. Any creature within that area must make a DC 21 Constitution saving throw, taking 27 (6d8) cold or fire damage on a failed save, or half as much on a successful saving throw

Regional Effects

The region containing Dagon's lair is warped by its magic, creating one or more of the following effects:

Aquatic Bestiary. Aquatic creatures of all types are drawn to Dagon's presence; often they are only hostile to non-aquatic creatures.

Unusual Weather. Once per day, Dagon can control the weather surrounding his lair out to a 6-mile radius. The effect is identical to the *control weather* spell.

Adverse Conditions. Within 1 mile of the lair, Celestial creatures find the air or water difficult to breathe and tread. These creatures must make a DC 18 Constitution saving throw whenever they take a long rest. On a failed save, the creature does not benefit from that long rest.

If Dagon is slain, changed weather reverts to normal as described in the spell, and the other effects fade in 1d10 days.

Embrace of the Uncaring Sea

Weapon (trident), artifact (requires attunement)

Barnacles and small lampreys cover this 10-foot-long, deep-blue-green weapon; no matter how many barnacles or lampreys are removed, the weapon always seems covered in them. The three mismatched tines of the trident drip salty brine at all times, and the weapon always appears wet.

Attunement. In order to attune to *Embrace of the Uncaring Sea*, you must feed the lampreys that adorn its haft, dealing 8d10 necrotic damage to you, which cannot be resisted in any way.

Oversized. A Medium-sized creature has disadvantage on attack rolls made with *Embrace of the Uncaring Sea* unless they wield the weapon two-handed.

Magic Weapon. You have a +3 bonus to attack and damage rolls made with *Embrace of the uncaring Sea*. It also functions as a trident of fish command.

Brinetooth. You deal an additional 5d6 poison damage on a successful hit with the trident.

Embrace of the Depths. If you roll a 19 or 20 on an attack with this trident and you hit, the target must make a DC 21 Constitution saving throw or be afflicted by the crushing pressure of the sea. A creature afflicted by this cannot breathe, cast spells using verbal components, or cannot take actions or reactions. At the end of each of the target's turns, it can repeat the saving throw, ending the effect on a success. Magic such as heal can end this affliction early.

Destruction. You can destroy *Embrace of the Uncaring Sea* by stabbing the tines into the highest mountain within the hottest desert and leaving it to dry in the blazing sun for 100 years, at which time it crumbles into ash. If it is removed prior to the 100 years elapsing, all progress is lost.

Kostchtchie, Demon Prince of Wrath

This hulking creature stands to be at least 9 or 10 feet tall with yellowish skin. His head and body seem to be completely hairless save for his thick, bushy eyebrows. Two massive stump-like legs support his thick, misshapen torso and great, gnarled arms extend from his shoulders. His head is flat and oval and sports two, large sunken crystal-blue eyes.

Kostchtchie is the demon lord of cold and the prince of wrath; he is the epitome of hatred and evil. If there is a demon lord more ruthless and malevolent than he, that lord has never made his presence known. Kostchtchie is hated by all (including other demon lords and princes). He moves across his Abyssal landscape with a shuffling gait, and is rarely, if ever, encountered alone.

Kostchtchie is revered by some frost giant shamans as a god. Various clans pay tribute to him in the form of humanoid sacrifices (made bimonthly, except in the winter when sacrifices are made monthly) and

often invoke his blessing before undertaking a great quest or entering a great battle.

Kostchtchie's Abyssal home is a frigid and mountainous realm of ice, rock, snow, and subfreezing temperatures. Unprotected travelers and those vulnerable to cold do not last long here.

Kostchtchie stands 9 feet tall and weighs about 800 pounds.

Kostchtchie fights with his oversized warhammer in battle. He is relentless in his attack and seeks to kill all interlopers he encounters. Kostchtchie completely destroys any creature's body he slays. The body is torn to pieces, burned, or devoured by the demon lord or his minions.

Servants of Kostchtchie

Followers of Kostchtchie are usually frost giants and fiendish frost giants. They are usually fighters or barbarians. Many that receive his special blessing find their bodies warped and twisted, forever after wracked by pain and filled with rage. Devout followers of Kostchtchie are called Ice Lords and must sign a pact of evil with Kostchtchie.

Kostchtchie

Large fiend (demon), chaotic evil
Armor Class 19 (natural armor)
Hit Points 312 (25d10 + 175)
Speed 30 ft.

STR	DEX	CON	INT	WIS	CHA
26 (+8)	18 (+4)	25 (+7)	17 (+3)	16 (+3)	20 (+5)

Gorynya

Weapon (warhammer), artifact (requires attunement)

Gorynya is an overly large warhammer, wrought of black iron, covered in frost. It stands almost 4 feet tall from rounded pommel to the head, which bears a spike at its top and two blunt, unfinished faces. It is remarkably devoid of ornamentation but bears what appears to be centuries' worth of chips, nicks, and dried blood.

Attunement. *Gorynya* cannot be attuned to as long as Kostchtchie, the Demon Lord of Wrath, is on the same plane of existence as *Gorynya*. For you to attune to the weapon, you must first slay an ally of like alignment in a fit of blind rage and remain unremorseful for doing so.

Oversized. *Gorynya* is much larger than a normal warhammer. You can only wield *Gorynya* two-handed if your Strength score is 18 or higher. To wield *Gorynya* one-handed, your Strength score must be 22 or higher.

Magic Weapon. You have a +3 bonus to attack and damage rolls made with *Gorynya*. *Gorynya* also functions as a *mace of terror* and a *staff of frost*.

Overwhelming. You deal an additional 4d10 force damage when you hit with *Gorynya*, and your target must succeed on a Strength saving throw or be knocked prone. The DC for this saving throw is 8 + your Strength modifier + your proficiency bonus.

Cold Bones. You have resistance to cold damage while you are attuned to *Gorynya*, and rime and frost coat every visible surface within 10 feet of you.

Destroying Gorynya. In order to destroy *Gorynya*, you must first beg forgiveness from all those you have slain with the weapon, and they must forgive you for the acts you committed while attuned to the weapon. If that is done, then *Gorynya* shatters into rubble forever.

Saving Throws Str +15, Dex +11, Con +14, Wis +10
Skills Acrobatics +11, Athletics +15, Nature +10, Perception +10, Survival +10
Damage Resistances acid, fire
Damage Immunities cold, lightning, poison; bludgeoning, piercing, and slashing from nonmagical weapons
Condition Immunities charmed, exhaustion, frightened, poisoned
Senses truesight 120 ft., passive Perception 20
Languages Abyssal, Celestial, Common, Draconic, Giant, Ignan, Infernal, Terran; telepathy 120 ft.
Challenge 22 (41,000 XP)

Special Equipment. Kostchtchie carries *Gorynya*, a powerful magic warhammer.

Innate Spellcasting. Kostchtchie's innate spellcasting ability is Charisma (spell save DC 20, +12 to hit with spell attacks). It can cast the following spells, requiring no material components.

At will: *command, darkness, detect magic, ice storm, sleet storm*
3/day each: *cone of cold, disintegrate, fire shield* (cold damage only), *wall of ice*
1/day: *control weather*

Legendary Resistance (3/day). If Kostchtchie fails a saving throw, it can choose to succeed instead.

Magic Resistance. Kostchtchie has advantage on saving throws against spells and other magical effects.

Magic Weapons. Kostchtchie's weapon attacks are magical.

Unholy Aura. An unholy aura surrounds Kostchtchie out to a radius of 40 feet. A creature who enters or begins their turn in the area must make a DC 20 Wisdom saving throw. On a failed saving throw, the target is frightened for 1 minute. While frightened, it is paralyzed. A frightened target can repeat the saving throw at the end of each of its turns, ending the effect on a success.

Actions

Multiattack. Kostchtchie makes two attacks with *Gorynya*.

Gorynya. *Melee Weapon Attack:* +18 to hit, reach 15 ft., one target. *Hit:* 29 (4d8 + 11) bludgeoning damage, or 33 (4d10 + 11) bludgeoning damage if used with two hands, plus 22 (4d10) force damage. If the target is a creature, it must make a DC 23 Strength saving throw or be knocked prone.

Summon (1/day). Kostchtchie summons 1d12 dretches, 1d6 glabrezus, 1d6 hezrous, 1 marilith, or 1 **balor**. The summoned demon appears in an unoccupied space within 60 feet of Kostchtchie, but can't summon other demons. It remains for 1 minute, until it or Kostchtchie is slain, or until Kostchtchie takes an action to dismiss it.

Legendary Actions

Kostchtchie can take 3 legendary actions, choosing from the options below. Only one legendary action option can be used at a time and only at the end of another creature's turn. Kostchtchie regains spent legendary actions at the start of its turn.

Cold Burst. Kostchtchie causes a burst of cold to coalesce around it. Creatures within 10 feet of it must make a DC 20 Constitution saving throw. On a failed saving throw, the targets take 13 (3d8) cold damage, or half as much damage on a successful one.

Sunder (Costs 2 Actions). Kostchtchie slams *Gorynya* on the ground. The area within 15 feet becomes difficult terrain. Each creature that is concentrating must make a DC 23 Constitution saving throw. On a failed save, the creature's concentration is broken. In addition, all creatures must make a DC 23 Dexterity saving throw or fall prone. Kostchtchie is immune to these effects.

Freeze (Costs 3 Actions). Kostchtchie chooses one target it can see within 120 feet to make a DC 20 Constitution saving throw. On a failed saving throw, the creature takes 22 (4d10) cold damage and is restrained. At the start of its next turn, the target must repeat the saving throw. On a failed saving throw, it is fully encased in ice and is petrified. On a successful saving throw, the creature suffers no other effect.

Lair Actions

On initiative count 20 (losing initiative ties), Kostchtchie can take a lair action to cause one of the following effects; Kostchtchie can't use the same effect two rounds in a row:

Rage. Kostchtchie chooses any number of creatures within its lair to make a DC 20 Wisdom saving throw; Kostchtchie must be aware of intruders within its lair, but he does not need to see the targets. Until initiative 20 a creature who fails the saving throw is filled with blinding rage and uses its actions and movement to attack the nearest creature that it can see.

Corpse Cleanup. Kostchtchie destroys any corpse within its lair; its does not need to see it in order to destroy it. That creature is incapable of being brought back from the dead absent a *true resurrection* or *wish* spell.

Curse. Kostchtchie chooses one creature that it can see within 60 feet to make a DC 20 Constitution saving throw. On a failed saving throw, the creature is cursed; the curse ends early if removed with magic such as *remove curse*. While cursed, the creature is vulnerable to cold damage.

Regional Effects

The region containing Kostchtchie's lair is warped by his magic, creating one or more of the following effects:

Cold. The area within 6 miles of Kostchtchie's lair is unnaturally cold, even if that would not make sense; during the day the temperature hovers around freezing, while at night the temperature plummets to below 0 degrees Fahrenheit.

Ire. The various beasts and creatures that inhabit the area around the lair are more inclined to be hostile, filled with wrath, even attacking other creatures who would not normally be their prey.

If Kostchtchie dies, these effects fade over the course of 1d10 days.

Maphistal, Second of Orcus

A stinking aura of death and decay lingers in the air around this feral-looking humanoid. Two great horns protrude upward from its oval head. Huge leathery, bat-like wings sprout from its shoulders, and its lower torso sports two massive legs that end in soot-colored hooves. Short, coarse black hair covers its entire body, except its face and clawed hands
.

Maphistal is a lieutenant in the employ of Orcus, Demon Prince of the Undead. He makes his home on a stinking, smoldering Abyssal plane where he commands his troops from his great castle, Maalstege (The Keep of Bones — so called because it is believed to be constructed from the skeletal remains of those slain by Maphistal). He is loyal to no one but Orcus. He does not trust Sonechard, the General of Orcus's undead legions, and seeks to discredit him at any opportunity, though he does not do this openly for fear of rebellion by his troops or punishment by Orcus. His machinations against Sonechard are primarily through his agents and spies in Sonechard's camps.

Maphistal stands 9 feet tall and weighs 700 pounds.

Maphistal is rarely, if ever, encountered alone, and usually has a retinue of undead with him. When he enters combat, he usually opens with his innate spellcasting abilities, immediately using his circle of death ability to affect as many targets as possible. In melee,

he batters an opponent with his mace. An opponent whose skull is destroyed (and who is therefore slain) or an opponent brought to Dexterity 0 (and not rescued by his comrades) is carried back to the Keep of Bones where it is transformed into an undead creature or becomes part of the Keep itself.

Maphistal

Large fiend (demon), chaotic evil
Armor Class 21 (natural armor)
Hit Points 400 (32d10 + 224)
Speed 40 ft., fly 80 ft.

STR	DEX	CON	INT	WIS	CHA
28 (+9)	16 (+3)	24 (+7)	18 (+4)	20 (+5)	23 (+6)

Saving Throws Con +15, Wis +13, Cha +14
Skills Deception +14, Intimidation +14, Perception +13
Damage Resistance cold, fire, lightning; bludgeoning, piercing, and slashing from nonmagical weapons
Damage Immunities necrotic, poison
Condition Immunities charmed, exhaustion, frightened, poisoned
Senses truesight 120 ft., passive Perception 23
Languages all, telepathy 120 ft.
Challenge 26 (90,000 XP)

Innate Spellcasting. Maphistal's spellcasting ability is Charisma (spell save DC 22, +14 to hit with spell attacks). It can innately cast the following spells requiring no material components:
At will: *circle of death, detect evil and good, detect magic, dispel magic*
3/day: *animate dead, blight, hallow, suggestion, telekinesis*
1/day: *conjure fiend*^{GM}, *fire storm, power word stun*

Legendary Resistance (3/day). If Maphistal fails a saving throw, he can choose to succeed instead.

Magic Resistance. Maphistal has advantage on saving throws against spells and other magical effects.

Magic Weapon. Maphistal's melee attacks are magical

Rampage. When Maphistal reduces a creature to 0 hit points with a melee attack on its turn, Maphistal can take a bonus action to move up to half its speed and make a bite attack.

Unholy Aura. Malevolent shadows swirl around Maphistal and radiate out from it in a 30-foot radius. Non-evil creatures in this area have disadvantage on attack rolls against Maphistal and its allies.

Actions

Multiattack. Maphistal makes three attacks: one with its bite and two with its claws.

Bite. *Melee Weapon Attack:* +17 to hit, reach 5 ft., one target. *Hit:* 23 (4d6 + 9) piercing damage. If the target is a creature, it must succeed on a DC 20 Constitution saving throw against disease or become poisoned until the disease is cured. Every 24 hours that elapse, the target must repeat the saving throw, reducing its hit point maximum by 5 (1d10) on a failure. The disease is cured on a success. The target dies if the disease reduces its hit point maximum to 0. This reduction to the target's hit point maximum lasts until the disease is cured. The disease can be magically cured by a *greater restoration* or *heal* spell.

Claws. *Melee Weapon Attack:* +17 to hit, reach 10 ft., one target. *Hit:* 27 (4d8 + 9) slashing damage. If the target is a creature, it must make a DC 20 Constitution saving throw. On a failure, the target's Dexterity score is reduced by 1d4. The target dies if this reduces its Dexterity to 0. Otherwise, the reduction lasts until the target finishes a long rest.

Teleport. Maphistal magically teleports, along with any equipment it is wearing or carrying, up to 120 feet to an unoccupied space it can see.

Summon (1/day). Maphistal summons 1d12 dretches, 1d6 glabrezus, 1d6 hezrous, 1d4 nalfeshnees, 1d3 marilith, or 1 balor. The summoned demon appears in an unoccupied space within 60 feet of Maphistal, but can't summon other demons. It remains for 1 minute, until it or Maphistal is slain, or until Maphistal takes an action to dismiss it.

Legendary Actions

Maphistal can take 3 legendary actions, choosing from the options below. Only one legendary action can be used at a time and only at the end of another creature's turn. Maphistal regains spent legendary actions at the start of its turn.
Attack. Maphistal makes one claw attack.
Circle of Death. Maphistal casts *circle of death*.
Teleport. Maphistal uses its Teleport action.

Orcus, Demon Prince of the Undead

This demonic humanoid is squat and bloated, standing nearly three times as tall as a normal human. His goat-like head sports large, spiraling ram horns. His legs are covered in thick brown fur and end in hooves. Large powerful arms wield a wicked skull-tipped wand. Two large, black bat-like wings protrude from his back, and a long, snake-like tail, tipped with a sharpened barb, trails behind him.

Orcus is the Prince of the Undead, and it is said that he alone created the first undead that walked the worlds. Orcus is one of the strongest (if not the strongest) and most powerful of all demon lords. He fights a never-ending war against rival demon princes that spans several Abyssal layers. From his great bone palace, he commands his troops as they wage war across the smoldering and stinking planes of the Abyss. Orcus spends most of his days in his palace, rarely leaving its confines unless he decides to leads his troops into battle (which has happened on more than one occasion). Most of the time though, he is content to let his generals and commanders lead the battles.

When not warring against rival demon princes, Orcus likes to travel the planes, particularly the Material Plane. Should a foolish spellcaster open a gate and speak his name, he is more than likely going to hear the call and step through to the Material Plane. What happens to the spellcaster that called him usually depends on the reason for the summons and the power of the spellcaster. Extremely powerful spellcasters are usually slain after a while and turned into undead soldiers or generals in his armies.

Orcus stands 15 feet tall and weighs nearly 6,000 pounds.

Orcus prefers to conduct battles using his Wand or natural weapons (tail and fists). Generally, he avoids direct combat with powerful foes preferring to hang back and pepper them with an array of spells and effects. If pressed into melee, he uses his tail sting against the strongest opponent while focusing his fear gaze on the spellcasters. When given the chance, he summons demons and undead to aid him. If combat goes against him, he uses his greater teleport ability to escape, leaving a retinue of demons and undead monsters to deal with the interlopers.

Servants of Orcus

The followers of the Prince of Undead are clerics and adepts that venerate death, sorcerers and wizards fascinated with death, and half-fiend variants of the aforementioned creatures. His followers are most often clerics, necromancers, and sorcerers. Followers of Orcus are known as Disciples of Orcus and must sign a pact of evil. Disciples of Orcus can receive spells from Orcus and are granted access to the domains of Chaos, Death, Destruction, Evil, and War (a cleric can choose any two of these domains).

Orcus

Huge fiend (demon), chaotic evil
Armor Class 25 (natural armor)
Hit Points 825 (50d12 + 500)
Speed 40 ft., fly 60 ft.

STR	DEX	CON	INT	WIS	CHA
30 (+10)	21 (+5)	30 (+10)	27 (+8)	27 (+8)	30 (+10)

Saving Throws Dex +15, Con +20, Wis +18, Cha +20
Skills History +18, Perception +18, Religion +18
Damage Resistances acid, cold, fire
Damage Immunities lightning, necrotic, poison;
  bludgeoning, piercing, and slashing from
  nonmagical weapons
Condition Immunities charmed, exhaustion,
  frightened, poisoned
Senses truesight 120 ft., passive Perception 28
Languages all, telepathy 360 ft.
Challenge 35 (330,000 XP)

Special equipment. Orcus wields its iconic rod, the *Wand of Orcus*.
Innate Spellcasting. Orcus's spellcasting ability is Charisma (spell save DC 28, +20 to hit with spell attacks). Orcus can innately cast the following spells, requiring no material components:

At will: *animate dead, chill touch* (17th level), *detect magic*
7/day: *create undead*
5/day: *eyebite*
3/day each: *circle of death, finger of death*

Legendary Resistance (3/day). If Orcus fails a saving throw, it can choose to succeed instead. **Lord of the Grave.** Orcus always casts animate dead or create undead at maximum level and without any restrictions. Creatures created by these spells remain under its control indefinitely.
Magic Resistance. Orcus has advantage on saving throws against spells and other magical effects.
Magic Weapons. Orcus's attacks are magical.

Actions

Multiattack. Orcus makes two Wand of Orcus attacks.
Wand of Orcus. Melee Weapon Attack: +20 to hit, reach 5 ft., one target. *Hit:* 24 (4d6 + 10) bludgeoning damage and the target must make a DC 17 Charisma saving throw, dropping to 0 hit points on failure, or, on a success, the target takes 21 (6d6) necrotic damage.
Tail. Melee Weapon Attack: +20 to hit, reach 5 ft., one target. *Hit:* 24 (4d6 + 10) piercing damage plus 22 (4d10) poison damage.
Aura of Death. Each non-undead creature that starts its turn within 20 feet of Orcus takes 17 (5d6) necrotic damage.
Aura of Enfeeblement (Recharge 5–6). Black beams of negative energy surround Orcus in a 20-foot radius centered on it. Each creature in this area must make a DC 24 Constitution saving throw. On a failure, the target deals only half damage with weapon attacks that use Strength for 1 minute. A weakened target can repeat the saving throw at the end of each of its turns, ending the effect on itself on a success. If a target's saving throw is successful or the effect ends for it, the target is immune to Orcus's Aura of Enfeeblement for the next 24 hours.
Teleport. Orcus magically teleports, along with any equipment it is wearing or carrying, up to 120 feet to an unoccupied space it can see.

Legendary Actions

Orcus can take 3 legendary actions, choosing from the options below. Only one legendary action can be used at a time and only at the end of another creature's turn. Orcus regains spent legendary actions at the start of its turn.
Tail. Orcus makes one tail attack.
Devouring Darkness (Costs 2 Actions). Orcus chooses a point that it can see within 100 feet of it. A cloud of darkness erupts from that point and lasts for 1 minute. The area is heavily obscured and each creature in the area must make a DC 24 Constitution saving throw, taking 28 (8d6) necrotic damage on a failure, or half as much damage on a success. Creatures slain by the devouring darkness rise as ghouls under the command of Orcus within 1d4 rounds.
Charnel Wind (Costs 3 Actions). A putrid, carrion wind erupts from Orcus in a 30-foot radius centered on it and lasts until the end of Orcus's next turn. All non-undead creatures within this area must succeed on a DC 24 Constitution saving throw against disease or be poisoned until the end of Orcus's next turn. While poisoned in this way, the creature can take either an action or a bonus action on its turn, not both, and it can't take reactions.

Lair Actions

On Initiative count 20 (losing initiative ties), Orcus can take a lair action to cause one of the following effects; it can't use the same effect two rounds in a row:

Wand of Orcus

Rod, artifact (requires attunement)

The mighty *Wand of Orcus* is a huge, black, skull-tipped rod, fully 6-feet in length. Its head is an ancient, bleached jawless skull, whose eye sockets glow with ruddy, red light. It exudes an aura of primeval menace, chilling the soul and the body with the cold of the grave.

Aura of Death. Any living creature is unable to take short or long rests within 300 feet of the *Wand of Orcus*. If any creature who is not Orcus touches the *Wand of Orcus*, it must succeed on a DC 17 Charisma saving throw or drop to 0 hit points and begin dying. On a successful saving throw, the creature takes 6d6 necrotic damage. A creature who succeeds on the saving throw is immune to this effect for 24 hours. Orcus can suppress this effect from any locations.

Attunement. To attune to the artifact, you must bathe yourself and the *Wand of Orcus* in the blood of a Solar Angel.

Magic Weapon. The *Wand of Orcus* functions as a magic mace that has a +3 bonus to attack and damage rolls made with this weapon. It deals 4d6 bludgeoning damage on a hit. It also functions as a *sword of wounding*.

Spellcasting. You can use an action to cast the following spells at will: *blight*, *darkness*, or *speak with dead*. The *Wand of Orcus* has 20 charges, which can be used to cast the following spells: *animate dead* (3 or more charges), *bestow curse* (2 charges), *circle of death* (6 charges), contagion (5 charges), *create undead* (6 or more charges), *finger of death* (7 charges), *harm* (6 charges), or *power word kill* (9 charges). The *Wand of Orcus* recovers all charges each midnight.

Sentience. The *Wand of Orcus* is a sentient chaotic evil magic item, with an Intelligence of 20, a Wisdom of 18, and a Charisma of 23. It has truesight out to 120 feet and understands Abyssal and Infernal. It can communicate with its wielder telepathically. Its goal is the subjugation and destruction of all realms under the all-encompassing gaze of Orcus. It will attempt to sway or control an attuned creature to further the goals of Orcus.

The *Wand of Orcus* is evil, wholly so. The *wand's* telepathic messages are quiet and breathy, almost a wet wheeze through diseased lungs. It is not averse to assisting an attuned wielder's temporary goals, as long as they are not inimical to its long-term goal of turning all planes of existence into fields of undead.

Destruction. The *Wand of Orcus* can only be destroyed if Orcus is truly slain and destroyed. If Orcus is permanently slain, the *Wand of Orcus* becomes brittle and can be easily smashed into dust.

Beckon Army of the Dead. While in its lair, Orcus can use the wand to summon an undead army that consists of:

- 10 skeletons
- 5 zombies
- 3 ghouls
- 3 specters
- 2 wights
- 1 mummy

These undead magically rise up from the ground or otherwise form in unoccupied spaces within 100 feet of Orcus and obey its commands until they are destroyed or until it dismisses them as an action. Orcus can only use this lair action every 24 hours unless it is in the Palace of Bones on Thanatos, the level of the Abyss it rules. Orcus may use it on each subsequent initiative 20 at will if on that plane.

Bone Cage. Orcus causes all bones within the lair to form tight cages around two creatures of its choice. The cages can be attacked and destroyed (AC 15; hp 30; vulnerability to bludgeoning damage; resistance to piercing, poison, slashing, and psychic damage). While in a bone-cage, a creature is retrained.

Fountain of Blood. Orcus chooses a point on the ground that it can see within 100 feet of it. A geyser of caustic blood erupts from the ground at that point and rains down in a 40-foot high, 10-foot cylinder. Each creature in that area must make a DC 24 Dexterity saving throw, taking 24 (7d6) acid damage on a failure, or half as much damage on a success.

Regional Effects

The region containing Orcus's lair is warped by its magic. If a creature within 10 miles of Orcus' lair dies, roll a d20. On a 19 or 20, the creature rises as a zombie under Orcus' control.

If Orcus dies, this effect fade over the course of 1d10 days.

Pazuzu, Demon Prince of Air

This powerfully built humanoid has the head of a hawk and four great feathery wings spanning its shoulders. Its feathers are red and gold, fading to black at the tip. Its eyes are red and its hands and feet end in hawk-like talons.

Pazuzu is the demon prince of aerial creatures and is revered as such on both the Abyssal plane and the Material Plane. Unlike other demon princes, its lair is not confined to a single plane or multiple adjoining planes; Pazuzu rules the sky realms above all layers of the Abyss. (No demon prince has contested its rulership of the skies thus far.)

Pazuzu has a great many dealings with creatures on other planes, including devils. It seems to be on fairly good terms with several powerful dukes and arch-devils of Hell. Pazuzu never enters that plane but has been known to meet with such a duke on Acheron or Tarterus.

Pazuzu stands 8 feet tall and weighs 700 pounds.

Pazuzu prefers to use its spells and spell-like abilities, subjecting its opponents to a magical onslaught of great power. If cornered or forced into melee, it prefers to use its claws or weapon. If it is outclassed or overmatched, it summons aerial creatures and demons to his aid.

Servants of Pazuzu

Followers of Pazuzu are evil humanoids that respect and revere the air and sky. Devout followers of Pazuzu are called Aerial Lords and must sign a pact of evil with Pazuzu.

Pazuzu

Large fiend (demon), chaotic evil

Armor Class 19 (natural armor)
Hit Points 364 (27d10 + 216)
Speed 40 ft., fly 80 ft.

STR	DEX	CON	INT	WIS	CHA
25 (+7)	20 (+5)	27 (+8)	18 (+4)	19 (+4)	23 (+6)

Saving Throws Str +15, Dex +13, Con +16, Wis +12
Skills Acrobatics +13, Arcana +12, Athletics +15, Deception +14, Insight +12, Perception +12, Stealth +13, Survival +12
Damage Resistances cold, fire, lightning
Damage Immunities poison; bludgeoning, piercing, and slashing from nonmagical weapons
Condition Immunities charmed, exhaustion, frightened, poisoned
Senses truesight 120 ft., passive Perception 22

Languages Auran, Aquan, Abyssal, Celestial, Common, Draconic, Giant, Infernal, Terran; telepathy 120 ft.
Challenge 27 (105,000 XP)

Special Equipment. Pazuzu wields the greatsword *Carriontooth*.

Evasion. If Pazuzu is subjected to an effect that allows it to make a Dexterity saving throw to take only half damage, Pazuzu instead takes no damage if it succeeds on the saving throw, and only half damage if it fails.

Flyby. Pazuzu doesn't provoke opportunity attacks when it flies out of an enemy's reach.

Innate Spellcasting. Pazuzu's innate spellcasting ability is Charisma (spell save DC 22, +14 to hit with spell attacks). It can cast the following spells, requiring no material components.

At will: *animal messenger, arcane eye, call lightning, detect magic, featherfall, giant insect, gust of wind, insect plague, lightning bolt, sending, wind wall* (no concentration necessary)

3/day each: *control weather, darkness, dispel magic, dominate person, freedom of movement, suggestion*

1/day: *storm of vengeance*

Legendary Resistance (3/day). If Pazuzu fails a saving throw, it can choose to succeed instead.

Magic Resistance. Pazuzu has advantage on saving throws against spells and other magical effects.

Magic Weapons. Pazuzu's weapon attacks are magical.

Unholy Aura. An unholy aura surrounds Pazuzu out to a radius of 40 feet. A creature who enters or begins their turn in the area must make a DC 22 Wisdom saving throw. On a failed saving throw, the target is frightened for 1 minute. While frightened, they are paralyzed. A frightened target can repeat the saving throw at the end of each of its turns, ending the effect on a success.

Actions

Multiattack. Pazuzu makes two attacks with Carriontooth and two attacks with its claws.

Carriontooth. *Melee Weapon Attack:* +18 to hit, reach 10 ft., one target. *Hit:* 38 (8d6 + 10) slashing damage plus 21 (6d6) necrotic damage.

Claws. *Melee Weapon Attack:* +15 to hit, reach 5 ft., one target. *Hit:* 25 (4d8 + 7) slashing damage.

Corrosive Gas (Recharge 5–6). Pazuzu exhales a cloud of acidic gas in a 100-foot cone that spreads around corners. Creatures in the area must make a DC 24 Constitution saving throw, taking 18d8 acid damage on a failed saving throw, or half as much damage on a successful one.

Dominate Aerial Creature. Pazuzu can target up to six beasts or monstrosities with a fly speed and an Intelligence lower than 8 and cause them to make a DC 22 Wisdom saving throw. On a failed saving throw, the target is charmed by Pazuzu for 24 hours. The charmed target obeys Pazuzu's verbal or telepathic commands. If the target suffers any harm or receives a suicidal command, it can repeat the saving throw, ending the effect on a success. If the target successfully saves against the effect, or if the effect ends on it, the target is immune to this ability for the next 24 hours. Pazuzu can have up to six targets charmed at a time. If it charms another, it can end the charmed condition on one target of its choice.

Summon (1/day). Pazuzu summons 2d4 succubi, 1d4 nalfeshnees, 1d4 vrocks, or 1 balor. The summoned demon appears in an unoccupied space within 60 feet of Pazuzu, but can't summon other demons. It remains for 1 minute, until it or Pazuzu is slain, or until Pazuzu takes an action to dismiss it.

Legendary Actions

Pazuzu can take 3 legendary actions, choosing from the options below. Only one legendary action option can be used at a time and only at the end of another creature's turn. Pazuzu regains spent legendary actions at the start of its turn.

Shriek. Pazuzu releases a blast of concussive sound in a 40-foot cone. Creatures within the area must make a DC 24 Strength saving throw. On a failed saving throw, the target takes 26 (4d8 + 8) thunder damage and is pushed 15 feet. On a successful saving throw, the target takes half damage and is not pushed.

Carriontooth

Weapon (greatsword), artifact (requires attunement)

This single-edged, blood-stained greatsword is the personal weapon of the demon lord Pazuzu. Legend has it Pazuzu created the weapon from the claw of a bird goddess it dueled and lost to before being trapped in the skies above the Abyss. *Carriontooth* is serrated and jagged, rending flesh as it slices and slashes.

Attunement. If you attempt to attune to *Carriontooth*, your maximum hit points are reduced by 10 unless your alignment is chaotic evil. This reduction remains as long as you remain attuned to *Carriontooth*; magic cannot return the lost hit points.

Magic Weapon. You gain a +3 bonus to attack and damage rolls made with this weapon. *Carriontooth* also functions as a *sword of sharpness*, a *sword of wounding* and a *vicious weapon*.

Rend. You deal an additional 6d6 necrotic damage when you hit with *Carriontooth*.

Natural Enmity. Celestials of all kinds find *Carriontooth* abhorrent and are always hostile to you if you carry the weapon.

Destruction. To destroy *Carriontooth*, it must be used to slay Pazuzu, and then returned to the bird goddess whose claw it was made from; the goddess needs to only touch it to undo the artifact.

Possess (Costs 2 Actions). Pazuzu uses its *dominate person* innate spellcasting ability. If it casts it as a legendary action, it does not need to maintain concentration.

Wing Attack (Costs 2 Actions). Pazuzu beats its wings. Each creature within 15 feet of Pazuzu must succeed on a DC 23 Dexterity saving throw or take 15 (2d6 + 8) bludgeoning damage and be knocked prone. Pazuzu can then fly up to half its flying speed.

Lair Actions

On initiative count 20 (losing initiative ties), Pazuzu can take a lair action to cause one of the following effects; Pazuzu can't use the same effect two rounds in a row:

Gale. Pazuzu causes strong winds to immediately gust, choosing a 60-foot cube within its lair that wraps around corners (Pazuzu does not need to see this area). Any creatures within this area must make a DC 22 Strength saving throw or be pushed 60 feet in a random direction and be knocked prone. If this would push that creature into a solid surface, the target takes 1d6 bludgeoning damage per 10 feet traveled.

Insect Storm. Pazuzu causes a storm of swarming insects to fill a 30-foot cube. Until the next initiative count 20, that area is heavily obscured, and all creatures within the cube treat the area as difficult terrain.

Regional Effects

The region containing Pazuzu's lair is warped by its magic, creating one or more of the following effects:

Aviary. Avian creatures crowd into the area surrounding Pazuzu's lair and have advantage on saving throws against magical effects that charm or frighten them cast by creatures other than Pazuzu himself.

Tempests. Strong winds whip through the area around Pazuzu's lair, and lightning storms crash through the days and nights.

Clairvoyance. Pazuzu can hear its name spoken by any creature in any language within 10 miles of its lair. It knows the exact location of the creature who spoke its name.

Sonechard, General of Orcus

This ram-headed humanoid appears to be at least as twice as tall as a human and has leathery gray skin. Large, curved horns — the left one broken off midway from its starting point — jut from his head. Two large bat-like wings spread from his shoulders. The creature's body is covered with thick, dark hair. Portions of the hair are torn away in areas revealing masses of battle-born scars and damage.

Sonechard is a General in the infernal armies of Orcus and serves him — at least to all onlookers — with unswerving loyalty. He has countless numbers of demons and undead at his command. Though his true loyalty lies only to himself, he would never openly refuse a request by Orcus nor challenge his position as Prince of the Undead. Should the day come when Orcus weakens, Sonechard plans to be there to claim what he believes is rightfully his.

Sonechard makes his home in a large castle called Chillhall that sits atop a plateau of scorched earth surrounded by a moat of blood. The walls are constructed of bone and sinew, and it is said that the souls of those who cross him are entombed within.

Sonechard stands 14 feet tall and weighs about 3,500 pounds.

Sonechard is almost always encountered with a large number of demons or undead at his side. When he enters battle, he usually unleashes a fireball at his foes immediately, and then follows it up with a circle of death effect or a suggestion. Dying creatures are subjected to his death knell spell-like ability and then raised via animate dead.

Should Sonechard find himself on the losing end of a battle, he does not hesitate to retreat, covering his escape with summoned or created undead and demons. A defeat is not forgotten — or forgiven. He remembers his opponents and sends his troops to exterminate them at first chance, bringing their carcasses to his keep where he grinds their remains into a fine powder and gives it to his servants to be used to spice up the keep's foodstuffs.

Sonechard

Large fiend (demon), chaotic evil
Armor Class 19
Hit Points 336 (32d10 + 160)
Speed 40 ft., fly 80 ft.

STR	DEX	CON	INT	WIS	CHA
22 (+6)	18 (+4)	21 (+5)	19 (+4)	16 (+3)	20 (+5)

Saving Throws Str +12, Dex +10, Con +11, Wis +9
Skills Arcana +10, Athletics +12, Nature +10, Perception +15, Religion +10
Damage Resistances acid, cold, fire
Damage Immunities lightning, poison; bludgeoning, piercing, and slashing from nonmagical weapons
Condition Immunities charmed, exhaustion, frightened, poisoned
Senses truesight 120 ft., passive Perception 25
Languages Abyssal, Celestial, Common, Draconic, Giant, Goblin, Ignan, Infernal, Terran; telepathy 120 ft.
Challenge 20 (25,000 XP)

Special Equipment. Sonechard carries the war pick *Fool's Errand*.

Aggressive. As a bonus action, Sonechard can move up to its speed toward a hostile creature that it can see.

Innate Spellcasting. Sonechard's innate spellcasting ability is Charisma (spell save DC 19, +11 to hit with spell attacks). It can cast the following spells, requiring no material components.

At will: *animate dead*, *chill touch* (17th level), *inflict wounds* (5th level)
3/day each: *circle of death*, *create undead*, *fireball*, *finger of death*, *harm*
1/day: *create undead* (9th level)

Legendary Resistance (3/day). If Sonechard fails a saving throw, it can choose to succeed instead.

Magic Resistance. Sonechard has advantage on saving throws against spells and other magical effects.

Magic Weapons. Sonechard's weapon attacks are magical.

Stench. Any creature that starts its turn within 10 feet of Sonechard must succeed on a DC 19 Constitution saving throw or be poisoned until the start of its next turn. On a successful saving throw, the creature is immune to Sonechard's Stench for 24 hours.

Unholy Aura. An unholy aura surrounds Sonechard out to a radius of 40 feet. A creature who enters or begins its turn in the area must make a DC 19 Wisdom saving throw. On a failed saving throw, the target is frightened for 1 minute. While frightened, it is paralyzed. A frightened target can repeat the saving throw at the end of each of its turns, ending the effect on a success.

Undead Master. When Sonechard casts *animate dead* or *create undead*, it creates twice the amount of undead with each casting.

Actions

Multiattack. Sonechard makes two attacks with *Fool's Errand*, one claw attack, and one head butt, or two claw attacks and one head butt.

Fool's Errand. *Melee Weapon Attack:* +15 to hit, reach 5 ft., one target. *Hit:* 18 (2d8 + 9) piercing damage plus 10 (3d6) necrotic damage.

Claw. *Melee Weapon Attack:* +12 to hit, reach 5 ft., one target. *Hit:* 13 (2d6 + 6) slashing damage.

Head butt. *Melee Weapon Attack:* +12 to hit, reach 5 ft., one target. *Hit:* 13 (2d6 + 6) bludgeoning damage, and the target must succeed on a DC 20 Constitution saving throw or be stunned until the end of its next turn.

Control Undead. Sonechard chooses one undead creature not already under its control that it can see within 120 feet of it. That creature, or the creature that controls it, must make a DC 19 Wisdom saving throw. On a failed saving throw, the undead falls under Sonechard's control and obeys its every command.

Undead Awareness. Whenever an undead is created or enters within 1 mile of Sonechard's lair, Sonechard is aware of the creature's presence and location.

Bonus Actions

Command Undead. Sonechard gives telepathic commands to any undead it controls unless they are on another plane of existence. It can command them to take specific actions, such as "attack those creatures" or general instructions "guard this passageway."

Legendary Actions

Sonechard can take 3 legendary actions, choosing from the options below. Only one legendary action option can be used at a time and only at the end of another creature's turn. Sonechard regains spent legendary actions at the start of its turn.

Head butt. Sonechard uses its head butt attack.

Command Undead. Sonechard can command one undead Sonechard controls to use its reaction to move its speed, or make a melee or ranged attack.

Animate Dead (Costs 2 Actions). Sonechard animates one corpse within 120 feet of it as a **zombie**.

Fool's Errand

Weapon (war pick), artifact (requires attunement)

Fool's Errand is a macabre spectacle, wrought of a dark, unknown wood as hard as steel. The spike of the war pick is similarly unfinished and unpolished and glows dimly with dark energies. Blood and ichor constantly drip from the pick and seems to freeze and thaw continuously no matter what attempts are made to clean the weapon.

Attunement. To attune to *Fools' Errand*, you must slay a celestial being of lawful good alignment.

Magic Weapon. You have a +3 bonus to attack and damage rolls made with *Fool's Errand*. It also functions as a *sword of wounding*.

Unholy Smite. When you hit with *Fools' Errand*, you deal an additional 3d6 necrotic damage on a hit, and a creature who takes this damage is poisoned for 1 minute. While poisoned, the creature has disadvantage on saving throws against your spells and other effects, and you have advantage on attack rolls with *Fool's Errand*.

The Smell of Blood. While holding *Fool's Errand*, you have advantage on Wisdom (Perception) checks to notice hidden creatures.

Spellcasting. *Fool's Errand* has 20 charges. You can use an action to cast one of the following spells using those charges: *bestow curse* (3 charges), *blight* (4 charges), *circle of death* (6 charges), or *finger of death* (7 charges). If you expend the last charge, you take 4d6 necrotic damage and regain a number of charges equal to the damage dealt, up to a maximum of 20. This damage cannot drop you below 1 hit point. *Fool's Errand* recovers all lost charges each day at midnight.

Destruction. *Fool's Errand* can only be destroyed by the ancient celestial Sonechard first killed to attune to the weapon. This creature must bath it in a holy water font specially crafted and blessed for the purpose.

Lair Actions

On initiative count 20 (losing initiative ties), Sonechard can take a lair action to cause one of the following effects; Sonechard can't use the same effect two rounds in a row:

Heal Undead. Sonechard sends necrotic energy coursing through his lair. Up to six undead under his command regain 19 (4d6 + 5) hit points each. Sonechard does not need to see these undead in order to grant them this boon.

Raise Dead. Sonechard chooses one slain creature and causes the creature's soul to rise as a specter under its control.

Fearsome Show. Sonechard causes the many corpses within its lair to animate briefly and babble the horrific tales of their deaths. Creatures within its lair that are not constructs or undead must make a DC 20 Wisdom saving throw. On a failed saving throw, those creatures are frightened for 1 minute. While frightened, those creatures must attempt to flee the lair, Dashing where possible. If a creature is trapped or cannot move, they can take the Dodge action instead. A frightened creature can repeat the saving throw at the end of each of its turns, ending the effect on a success. If the saving throw is successful, or if the effect ends on it, that creature is immune to this effect for 24 hours.

Regional Effects

The region containing Sonechard's lair is warped by its magic, creating one or more of the following effects:

Undead Walking. Slain creatures sometimes rise as skeletons or zombies, abhorred mockeries of their former states.

Nightmares. Unpleasant dreams wrack those who rest within 6 miles of Sonechard's lair.

If Sonechard dies, the effects fade immediately, but animated undead remain until destroyed.

Tsathogga, the Frog God

This massive creature appears to be a gigantic frog no less than 60 feet long. Its body is covered with warts and sores, and each oozes putrid, yellowish mucus. Its eyes are red and glow with an inherent evil. The creature's massive mouth sports rows of sharpened teeth, each at least as long as a sword.

This foul frog-demon cares less about the machinations of men and power than he does about obliterating light and life with the slow oozing sickness and decay that he represents. He is the viscous dark evil bubbling up from beneath the surface, the foul corruption at the heart of the earth. Tsathogga makes his home on both Tarterus and the Abyss, spending equal amounts of time in both places. His lair is a vast swamp of filth deposited by the River Styx as it flows between the two planes.

Tsathogga's main form is of a colossally bloated humanoid frog with spindly, elongated limbs and fingers. His corpulent body exudes all manner of foul oils and fluids, which leak into the vile swamp in which he lies. He has positioned himself so that all of the slime and filth from the River Styx feeds into his gaping, toothy maw. He rarely moves and rarely speaks other than to emit an unintelligible shrieking. Tsathogga thoughtlessly commands a host of evil creatures, notably his own vile frog race, the tsathar.

Tsathogga is 60 feet long and 40 feet tall. He weighs about 200 tons. Tsathogga prefers to avoid direct combat simply because he usually has better things to do than waste time killing the latest group of would-be demon killers. If threatened or attacked, he usually summons his minions to battle his opponents. If Tsathogga does enter combat, he almost always begins by striking the nearest opponent with his tongue, pulling that foe in and swallowing him. If he is near the muck and filth that permeates his home plane, he likes to dive or bury himself underneath it so if a swallowed opponent does manage to cut his way out of Tsathogga's gullet, he usually drowns or suffocates before he sees daylight again.

Servants of Tsathogga

Followers of Tsathogga are the tsathar and some few evil and vile humans or giants. He has few other worshippers, though it is rumored that an evil cult of sahuagin worships him on the Material Plane. Devout followers of Tsathogga are called Lords of the Gaping Maw and must sign a pact of evil with Tsathogga.

Tsathogga

Gargantuan fiend (demon), chaotic evil
Armor Class 20 (natural armor)
Hit Points 546 (28d20 + 252)
Speed 40 ft., swim 20 ft.

STR	DEX	CON	INT	WIS	CHA
29 (+9)	15 (+2)	28 (+9)	19 (+4)	18 (+4)	23 (+6)

Saving Throws Dex +12, Con +19, Wis +14, Cha +16
Skills Arcana +14, Insight +14, Perception +24, Survival +14
Damage Resistances cold, fire
Damage Immunities acid, lightning, poison; bludgeoning, piercing, and slashing from nonmagical weapons

Condition Immunities charmed, exhaustion, frightened, paralyzed, poisoned
Senses truesight 120 ft., passive Perception 34
Languages Aquan, Abyssal, Common, Giant, Infernal, Terran, telepathy 120 ft.
Challenge 35 (330,000 XP)

Acidic Hide. A creature that touches Tsathogga or hits it with a melee attack while within 10 feet of it takes 35 (10d6) acid damage. Any nonmagical weapon made of metal or wood that hits Tsathogga instantly dissolves before dealing damage.

Amphibious. Tsathogga can breathe both water and air.

Innate Spellcasting. Tsathogga's innate spellcasting ability is Charisma (spell save DC 24, +16 to hit with spell attacks).

At will: *acid arrow* (5th level), *bane, blindness/deafness, blight, command, detect magic, fog cloud, grease, inflict wounds* (5th level)

7/day each: *antilife shell, circle of death, cloudkill, contagion, counterspell, dispel magic, dominate beast, dominate person, earthquake*

3/day each: *geas, harm*

1/day each: *control weather, power word kill, storm of vengeance, wish*

Legendary Resistance (3/day). If Tsathogga fails a saving throw, it can choose to succeed instead.

Magic Resistance. Tsathogga has advantage on saving throws against spells and other magical effects.

Magic Weapons. Tsathogga's weapon attacks are magical.

Unholy Aura. An unholy aura surrounds Tsathogga out to a radius of 40 feet. A creature who enters or begins their turn in the area must make a DC 20 Wisdom saving throw. On a failed saving throw, the target is frightened for 1 minute. While frightened, they are paralyzed. A frightened target can repeat the saving throw at the end of each of its turns, ending the effect on a success.

Actions

Multiattack. Tsathogga uses its Blasphemous Croak ability, then uses its tongue attack. If there is a creature within range, it can then use its bite attack and two claw attacks.

Bite. Up to three targets of Huge size or smaller within 10 feet of Tsathogga must make a DC 27 Dexterity saving throw. On a successful saving throw, it takes 44 (10d6 + 9) piercing damage, plus 35 (10d6) acid damage, and is grappled. On a failed saving throw, the target is swallowed. While swallowed, the creature is blinded and restrained, it has total cover against attacks and other effects outside of Tsathogga, and it takes 56 (16d6) acid damage at the start of each of Tsathogga's turns. If Tsathogga takes 50 damage or more on a single turn from a creature inside it, Tsathogga must succeed on a DC 25 Constitution saving throw at the end of that turn or regurgitate all swallowed creatures, which fall prone in a space with 10 feet of Tsathogga. If Tsathogga dies, a swallowed creature is no longer restrained by it and can escape from the corpse using all of its movement, exiting prone.

Claw. *Melee Weapon Attack:* +19 to hit, reach 10 ft., one target. *Hit:* 40 (9d6 + 9) slashing damage plus 35 (10d6) acid damage.

Tongue. Tsathogga chooses one creature that it can see within 40 feet of it. That target must make a DC 28 Dexterity saving throw. On a failed saving throw, the target takes 37 (8d6 + 9) bludgeoning damage plus 35 (10d6) acid damage and is grappled. Tsathogga can use a bonus action to pull a creature grappled by it up to 40 feet towards it.

Blasphemous Croak. Tsathogga utters a blasphemous croak audible to all creatures within 300 feet of it. Those that can hear it must make a DC 24 Wisdom saving throw. On a failed saving throw, the target takes 28 (8d6) necrotic damage and 28 (8d6) thunder damage and is stunned for 1 minute. On a successful saving throw, the target takes half damage and is not stunned. A stunned creature can repeat the saving throw at the end of each of its turns, ending the effect on a success.

Summon (1/day). Tsathogga summons 2d6 hezrous, 2d4 greruors, 1 nalfeshnee, or 1 balor. The summoned demon appears in an unoccupied space within 60 feet of Tsathogga, and can't summon other demons. It remains for 1 minute, until it or Tsathogga is slain, or until Tsathogga takes an action to dismiss it.

Legendary Actions

Tsathogga can take 3 legendary actions, choosing from the options below. Only one legendary action option can be used at a time and only at the end of another creature's turn. Tsathogga regains spent legendary actions at the start of its turn.

Retract Tongue. Tsathogga can pull one creature grappled by its tongue attack 40 feet towards it.

Quake. Tsathogga causes the area around it to violently shake in a radius of 100 feet. Creatures in the area must make a DC 24 Dexterity saving throw or fall prone. Until the beginning of Tsathogga's next turn, the ground continues shaking, and creatures must repeat the saving throw to rise from prone.

Seeping Darkness (Costs 2 Actions). Magical darkness fills the area surrounding Tsathogga out to a distance of 50 feet. The darkness spreads around corners, douses any nonmagical lights, and any light-producing spell of 6th level or lower is immediately dispelled. The magical darkness remains for 1 hour, or until Tsathogga uses an action to dismiss it.

Lair Actions

On initiative count 20 (losing initiative ties), Tsathogga takes a lair action to cause one of the following magical effects.

Acid Swamp. Tsathogga chooses an area of swamp that it can see within 120 feet of it. The area can be no larger than a 30-foot cube. Creatures in the area must make a DC 24 Strength saving throw. On a failed saving throw, the target takes 21 (6d6) acid damage and is grappled (escape DC 24). On a successful saving throw, the target takes half damage and is not grappled. On the next initiative count 20, the target takes an additional 21 (6d6) acid damage if it is still grappled by this lair action.

Insect Swarms. Tsathogga causes 7 (2d6) insect swarms to converge on an area of Tsathogga's choosing that it can see.

Swamp Mist. Tsathogga causes swamp mist to rise. This acts as if Tsathogga had cast the *fog cloud* spell as a 9th level spell. Tsathogga does not need to maintain concentration on this effect.

Demonic Knight

This creature appears as a human-sized humanoid dressed in black iron armor. Its head is completely hidden behind a dull black helm.

The demonic knight — known by some as a death knight — is rumored to be the creation of the great demon prince Orcus, the Prince of the Undead. Some sages doubt the validity of such a claim since the demonic knights are not undead. Though no link has been proven, however, it is known that three of the most powerful demonic knights (Baruliis, Caines, and Arrunes) make their home on the same plane of the Abyss as the Prince of the Undead within the shadows of his great citadel. The true origins of the demonic knight lay hidden deep in the stinking pits of the Abyss, and those brave few who have dared search for these secrets have never returned. The demonic knights serve their master (whoever it may be) with unswerving loyalty. They never question their orders and never question their superior. They are often sent to the Material Plane to recruit new bodies for their master's next plot or deception, or to punish those that have offended their lord. On some occasions, they are simply sent to another plane to corrupt and slay those that are just and good (to the delight of their master).

A demonic knight appears as a 6-foot-tall humanoid dressed in black iron half-plate armor. Its head is completely hidden beneath a helmet that it never removes. A black iron longsword is slung at its hip. Some demonic knights don capes and other decorations as a badge of station. It is unknown exactly how many demonic knights exist, but they are believed to number no more than nine.

A demonic knight attacks using its longsword (or fists, if unarmed). Against powerful opponents, it attempts to use its breath of unlife to weaken its foes before slaying them. If melee goes against the demonic knight, it summons demons to aid it or cover its escape.

Demonic Knight

Medium fiend (demon), chaotic evil
Armor Class 17 (half plate)
Hit Points 85 (10d8 + 40)
Speed 30 ft.

STR	DEX	CON	INT	WIS	CHA
20 (+5)	13 (+1)	18 (+4)	17 (+3)	18 (+4)	18 (+4)

Skills Arcana +6, Athletics +8, Perception +7, Stealth +4
Damage Resistances acid, cold, fire; bludgeoning, piercing, and slashing damage from nonmagical weapons
Condition Immunities charmed, frightened
Senses truesight 60 ft., passive Perception 17
Languages Abyssal, Common
Challenge 6 (2,300 XP)

Innate Spellcasting. The demonic knight's innate spellcasting ability is Charisma (spell save DC 15, +7 to hit with spell attacks). It can cast the following spells without requiring material components:

At will: *detect magic, wall of ice*
2/day: *dispel magic*
1/day each: *bestow curse, fireball*

Magic Weapon. The demonic knight's weapon attacks are considered magical for the purposes of damage resistance.

Actions

Multiattack. The demonic knight makes two longsword attacks, or one one-handed longsword attack and one mailed fist attack.

Longsword. *Melee Weapon Attack:* +8 to hit, reach 5 ft., one target. *Hit:* 9 (1d8 + 5) slashing damage, or 10 (1d10 + 5) slashing damage if used with two hands.

Mailed Fist. *Melee Weapon Attack:* +8 to hit, reach 5 ft., one target. *Hit:* 9 (1d8 + 5) bludgeoning damage.

Breath of Unlife (Recharge 5–6). The demonic knight releases a 10-foot cone of necrotic breath. Creatures in the area must make a DC 15 Constitution saving throw. On a failed save, a creature takes 28 (8d6) necrotic damage. If a humanoid creature is slain by this damage, it rises as a shadow demon under the command of the demonic knight that created it. The new shadow demon remains enslaved to the demonic knight until the knight's death and cannot summon demons of its own. A demonic knight can only have two such shadow demons under its command.

Summon Demon (1/day). A demonic knight has a 50 percent chance of summoning 1d4 shadow demons, 2 hezrous, 1 glabrezu, 1 vrock, or 1 marilith. The summoned demon appears in an unoccupied space within 60 feet. It cannot summon further demons and remains only for 1 minute before vanishing. It disappears early if it or the demonic knight is slain.

Demonic Mist

This cloud of sickly green mist seems to move as if it were alive.

Some scholars and sages believe a demonic mist is the incomplete manifestation of a demon on the Material Plane. Others conjecture it is a representation of chaos unleashed by the denizens of the Abyss. Whatever the true nature of its origin, a demonic mist is a creature wholly chaotic and evil. When encountered on the Material Plane it is most often in areas of consecrated ground such as graveyards, temples, and holy sites. In their native environment, demonic mists are found haunting the most putrid and disgusting of the Abyssal planes. Those planes covered with oozes, mires, fens, and swamps are favored by these creatures. Demonic mists have voracious appetites and always seem to be on the hunt. They are carnivorous creatures devouring just about anything they came across. Once a demonic mist slays its prey, it moves over the body and rapidly digests it, draining blood and body fluids, and leaving nothing more than a dried husk.

A demonic mist's semi-solid body is composed of a strange, sickly green and ever-shifting mist. It can change its color to a semi-translucent whitish smoke, thereby blending in and hiding in areas of normal fog and mist. When hiding in this way, a demonic mist seeks to quickly close ground with its target and attack from ambush, unleashing its psychic crush and enervating attacks at the closest and strongest opponents.

Demonic mists are often found in the employ of clerics dedicated to the demonic lords (particularly Tsathogga and Jubilex), serving as temple guards or assassins.

Demonic Mist

Medium fiend (demon), chaotic evil
Armor Class 16 (natural armor)
Hit Points 85 (10d8 + 40)
Speed fly 50 ft.

STR	DEX	CON	INT	WIS	CHA
6 (−2)	18 (+4)	18 (+4)	8 (−1)	13 (+1)	16 (+3)

Saving Throws Dex +6, Con +6
Skills Perception +3, Stealth +6
Damage Resistances acid, fire, cold; bludgeoning, piercing, and slashing from nonmagical weapons
Damage Immunities poison
Condition Immunities poisoned
Senses darkvision 60 ft., passive Perception 13
Languages Abyssal, Telepathy 120 ft.
Challenge 4 (1,100 XP)

Incorporeal Movement. The demonic mist can move through other creatures and objects as if they were difficult terrain. It takes 5 (1d10) force damage if it ends its turn inside an object.

Innate Spellcasting. A demonic mist's spellcasting ability is Charisma (spell save DC 13, +5 to hit with spell attacks), and requires no material components for the following spells:

At will: *detect magic*

3/day each: *ray of enfeeblement, vampiric touch*

1/day each: *confusion, fear*

Vulnerability to Wind. The demonic mist has disadvantage on saving throws against wind and wind-like effects (*gust of wind*, etc.).

Actions

Demonic Touch. *Melee Weapon Attack:* +6 to hit, reach 5 ft., one target. *Hit:* 25 (6d6 + 4) necrotic damage.

Psychic Crush (Recharge 5–6). The demonic mist attempts to crush the mind of a single creature it can see within 30 feet. The target must make a successful DC 15 Wisdom saving throw or take 14 (4d6) psychic damage and be frightened for 1 minute.

Devils

Devil Dog

The devil dog is a terrifying creature, with a brow containing three sets of eyes, and a long snout full of jagged, alligator-like teeth. Red leathery skin stretches across the skull and the disproportionate body, and a skeletal red tail slinks behind it as it hunts the layers of Hell.

The devil dog is a lesser devil, often employed to hunt down those few souls who escape from the arch-devils. It is a bizarre looking creature; it has the locomotive skills of a hound, loping after prey, yet its rear digitigrade legs are longer than a normal hound's, giving them a hunched, perpetually-about-to-pounce posture. They possess clawed paws on both fore and rear limbs.

The devil dog is capable of smelling out a soul whose true name it knows. The devil dog cannot and will not rest until it locates the creature, sniffing out its soul — even if that soul leaves its body for another. None can avoid paying an arch-devil its due.

Devil Dog

Large fiend (devil), lawful evil
Armor Class 15 (natural armor)
Hit Points 67 (9d10 + 18)
Speed 50 ft., climb 30 ft.

STR	DEX	CON	INT	WIS	CHA
18 (+4)	17 (+3)	15 (+2)	11 (+0)	17 (+3)	14 (+2)

Saving Throws Con +5, Wis +6, Cha +5
Skills Insight +9, Perception +9, Stealth +6, Survival +9
Damage Resistances cold; bludgeoning, piercing, and slashing from nonmagical weapons that aren't silvered
Damage Immunities fire, poison
Condition Immunities charmed, exhaustion, frightened, poisoned
Senses darkvision 120 ft., passive Perception 19
Languages Infernal, telepathy 120 ft.
Challenge 5 (1,800 XP)

Devil's Sight. Magical darkness doesn't impede the devil's darkvision.
Keen Smell. The devil dog has advantage on Wisdom (Perception) checks that rely on smell.
Magic Resistance. The devil has advantage on saving throws against spells and other magical effects.
Scent of Prey. The devil dog knows the exact location of any soul whose true name it knows, as long as that soul resides in a vessel or body within 1 mile. If the soul is beyond that distance, it knows the direction the soul lies in. If the soul is on a different plane of existence, it knows the plane that the soul resides on.

Actions

Bite. *Melee Weapon Attack:* +7 to hit, reach 5 ft., one target. *Hit:* 13 (2d8 + 4) piercing damage. If the target is a creature, it must succeed on a DC 15 Strength saving throw or be knocked prone.
Claws. *Melee Weapon Attack:* +7 to hit, reach 5 ft., one target. *Hit:* 11 (2d6 + 4) slashing damage.

Devil, Cerberus

This creature is a giant-sized three-headed dog. His fur is black and matted, and his eyes are crimson. Each mouth is dominated by long fangs, and each mouth drips foul-smelling saliva.

The triple-headed Cerberus is the guardian of Hades. There is only one in existence and most creatures (both living and dead) are grateful for this fact. Cerberus is tasked with the duty of keeping dead souls in Hades. If a dead soul attempts to pass beyond the Gates of Hades and back into the land of the living, Cerberus attacks relentlessly until that soul returns to Hades. If slain, the soul is immediately devoured by Cerberus and is lost forever. Cerberus is also tasked with keeping living creatures out of the land of the dead (adventurers being what they are, they love to journey to Hades). Living creatures that attempt to move past Cerberus into Hades (through the main gates) are immediately attacked.

Cerberus is a 30-foot-long black mastiff. He rarely chooses to communicate with creatures even though he speaks several languages.

Cerberus only attacks if a dead soul attempts to pass beyond the Gates of Hades into the land of the living or if a living creature attempts to enter the Realm of the Dead. Cerberus never willingly moves more than 60 feet from the Gates and cannot be removed by any means, short of a god's magic.

He opens combat with his baneful howl and quickly follows with his breath weapon. Living creatures that do not retreat are subjected to his bite and claw. Cerberus attacks until all his opponents are dead or have retreated. The souls of those he kills are allowed to pass beyond the Gates and into Hades while Cerberus feasts on their body.

If slain, Cerberus' corpse melts into smoldering slime before fading away.

Cerberus

Huge fiend, lawful evil
Armor Class 18 (natural armor)
Hit Points 294 (28d12 + 112)
Speed 60 ft.

STR	DEX	CON	INT	WIS	CHA
25 (+7)	13 (+1)	18 (+4)	6 (−2)	13 (+1)	6 (−2)

Saving Throws Dex +8, Con +11, Wis +8
Skills Perception +8
Damage Resistances cold; bludgeoning, piercing, and slashing from nonmagical weapons that aren't silvered
Damage Immunities fire, poison
Condition Immunities poisoned
Senses darkvision 120 ft., passive Perception 18
Languages Infernal, telepathy 120 ft.
Challenge 24 (62,500 XP)

Devil's Sight. Magical darkness doesn't impede Cerberus' darkvision.
Keen Hearing and Smell. Cerberus has advantage on Wisdom (Perception) checks that rely on hearing or smell.
Legendary Resistance (3/day). If Cerberus fails a saving throw, it can choose to succeed instead.
Magic Resistance. Cerberus has advantage on saving throws against spells and other magical effects.
Multiple Heads. Cerberus has three heads. While it has more than one head, Cerberus has advantage on saving throws against being blinded, charmed, deafened, frightened, stunned, or knocked unconscious. Whenever Cerberus takes 40 or more damage in a single turn, one of its heads dies. If all its heads die, Cerberus dies.

Actions

Multiattack. Cerberus makes three bite attacks and one claw attack.
Bite. *Melee Weapon Attack:* +14 to hit, reach 5 ft., one target. *Hit:* 23 (3d10 + 7) piercing damage plus 14 (4d6) fire damage.
Claw. *Melee Weapon Attack:* +14 to hit, reach 10ft., one target. *Hit:* 20 (3d8 + 7) slashing damage.
Fire Breath (Recharge 5–6). One of Cerberus' heads releases a 60-foot cone of flames. Each creature in the area must make a DC 18 Dexterity saving throw, taking 42 (12d6) fire damage on a failed save, or half as much damage on a successful saving throw. Each head has its own recharge counter.

Legendary Actions

Cerberus can take 3 legendary actions, choosing from the options below. Only one legendary action option can be used at a time and only at the end of another creature's turn. Cerberus regains spent legendary actions at the start of its turn.
Open/Close the Gate. Cerberus causes the Gate of Hell to open if it is closed, or close if it is open.
Bite. Cerberus makes a Bite attack.
Fire Breath (Costs 3 Actions). Cerberus uses its Fire Breath ability, even if it has not recharged.

Gorson the Blood Duke

This centaur-like creature is at least twice as long as a human and stands about 8 feet tall. Its lower body is that of a great golden lion and its upper body is a coal-black humanoid with glaring crimson eyes. Its mane-like hair is thick, long, and dark brown, and the creature wears it draped over its broad shoulders and down its massive back. Its mouth is lined with sharpened fangs and its arms end in large, powerful hands. Splatters of dried and caked blood can be seen in the creature's mane and fur.

The Blood Duke, Gorson, is a great lion-bodied humanoid that serves Great Mammon as 2nd general of his infernal army. Gorson leads 5 legions of barbed devils in service to his lord. Gorson is called "The Lion" for his ferocity in battle and his general appearance. He often takes the entrails of those he has slain and makes a necklace, wrapping it around his neck or entwining them in his bloody mane-like hair.

Gorson stands 8 feet tall and is 12 feet long. He weighs 1,200 pounds.

Gorson usually begins combat by leaping on a foe and rending it to pieces with his forepaws and rear claws. Those that survive this onslaught are subjected to a massive assault by his great battleaxe. Gorson attacks relentlessly and only stops when all foes are dead. Those that attempt to flee are run down and slaughtered.

Gorson

Large fiend (devil), lawful evil
Armor Class 19 (natural armor)
Hit Points 218 (19d10 + 114)
Speed 50 ft.

STR	DEX	CON	INT	WIS	CHA
22 (+6)	15 (+2)	23 (+6)	16 (+3)	18 (+4)	20 (+5)

Saving Throws Int +10, Wis +11, Cha +12
Skills Acrobatics +9, Arcana +10, Athletics +13, Perception +18, Stealth +9
Damage Resistances acid, cold
Damage Immunities fire, poison; bludgeoning, piercing, and slashing from nonmagical weapons that aren't silvered
Condition Immunities charmed, exhaustion, frightened, poisoned
Senses truesight 120 ft., passive Perception 28
Languages Abyssal, Celestial, Common, Draconic, Giant, Goblin, Infernal; telepathy 100 ft.
Challenge 21 (33,000 XP)

Innate Spellcasting. Gorson's innate spellcasting ability is Charisma (spell save DC 20, +12 to hit with spell attacks). It can cast the following spells, requiring no material components.
At will: *detect magic, charm person*

3/day each: *dispel magic, lightning bolt, suggestion, wall of fire*

Keen Smell. Gorson has advantage on Wisdom (Perception) checks that rely on smell.

Legendary Resistance (3/day). If Gorson fails a saving throw, it can choose to succeed instead.

Magic Resistance. The devil has advantage on saving throws against spells and other magical effects.

Magic Weapon. The devil's weapon attacks are magical.

Pounce. If Gorson moves at least 20 feet straight toward a creature and then hits it with a claw attack on the same turn, the target must succeed on a DC 21 Strength saving throw or be knocked prone. If the target is prone, Gorson can make one claw attack or one battleaxe attack as a bonus action against it.

Running Leap. With a 10-foot running start, Gorson can long jump up to 50 feet.

Actions

Multiattack. Gorson makes two attacks with its claw, and then two battleaxe attacks or two slam attacks. If it uses the battleaxe two-handed, it can't also make claw attacks that turn.

Battleaxe. *Melee Weapon Attack:* +13 to hit, reach 10 ft., one target. *Hit:* 24 (4d8 + 6) slashing damage, or 28 (4d10 + 6) slashing damage if used with two hands to make a melee attack.

Slam. *Melee Weapon Attack:* +13 to hit, reach 10 ft., one target. *Hit:* 20 (4d6 + 6) bludgeoning damage.

Claw. *Melee Weapon Attack:* +13 to hit, reach 10 ft., one target. *Hit:* 20 (4d6 + 6) slashing damage.

Summon (1/day). Gorson summons 2d6 bearded devils, 2d4 barbed devils, 1 bone devil, or 1 erinyes. The summoned devil appears in an unoccupied space within 60 feet of Gorson, but can't summon other devils. It remains for 1 minute, until it or Gorson is slain, or until Gorson takes an action to dismiss it.

Legendary Actions

Gorson can take 3 legendary actions, choosing from the options below. Only one legendary action option can be used at a time and only at the end of another creature's turn. Gorson regains spent legendary actions at the start of its turn.

Jump. Gorson leaps up to 25 feet in any direction without provoking attacks of opportunity.

Rake (Costs 2 Actions). Gorson rakes its forepaws at one prone creature within 5 feet, attacking twice with its claw attack.

Ferocious Roar (Costs 3 Actions). Gorson releases a thunderous roar, audible out to 100 feet. Allies of Gorson who can hear it gain 19 (4d6 + 5) temporary hit points. Hostile creatures must make a DC 20 Wisdom saving throw. On a failed saving throw, the target takes 19 (4d6 + 5) psychic damage and is frightened for 1 minute. On a successful saving throw, the target takes half damage and is not frightened. While frightened, the target must drop whatever it is holding and use its action to Dash away from Gorson. A creature who succeeds on the saving throw, or for whom the effect ends, is immune to Gorson's Ferocious Roar for 24 hours.

Devouring Mist

This drifting nightmare resembles a cloud of dark-red vapor about 10 feet in diameter.

Spawned from the dreams of the Bloodwraith, devouring mists are undead composed of equal parts blood and malice, wedded together by negative energy. They drift the halls of the Bloodways, looking for living prey to feed on and torment. When they strike, they surround their enemies and draw their blood from their bodies.

Devouring mists are possessed of a malicious cunning. They are quite capable of blending into the mists of the Bloodways so as to take their prey unaware. They may also follow creatures for a time and attack when they are distracted or preoccupied. A devouring mist may stalk its prey over hours or even days, striking again and again, in effect milking them of blood.

Devouring mists do not speak, nor can they be communicated with.

Devouring Mist

Large undead, neutral evil
Armor Class 15 (natural armor)
Hit Points 123 (19d10 + 19)
Speed 0 ft., fly 40 ft. (hover)

STR	DEX	CON	INT	WIS	CHA
7 (–2)	19 (+4)	13 (+1)	8 (–1)	16 (+3)	16 (+3)

Skills Perception +7, Stealth +8
Damage Resistance acid, fire, lightning, thunder; bludgeoning, piercing, and slashing from nonmagical weapons
Damage Immunities cold, necrotic, poison
Condition Immunities charmed, exhaustion, frightened, grappled, paralyzed, petrified, poisoned, prone, restrained
Senses darkvision 60 ft., passive Perception 15
Languages —
Challenge 10 (5,900 XP)

Mist Form. The devouring mist can occupy another creature's space and vice versa. In addition, if air can pass through a space, the mist can pass through it without squeezing. The mist moves through water as if it were difficult terrain. The mist can't use objects in any way that requires hands; it can apply simple force only.

Blood Sense. The devouring mist can sense living creatures that have blood or similar vital fluids in a radius of 60 feet.

Sunlight Hypersensitivity. The devouring mist takes 20 radiant damage when it starts its turn in sunlight. While in sunlight, the mist has disadvantage on attack rolls and ability checks

Actions

Blood Drain. One creature other than a construct or undead that is in the devouring mist's space must make a DC 16 Constitution saving throw. On a failed save, the target takes 28 (8d6) necrotic damage and its hit point maximum is reduced by an amount equal to the necrotic damage taken. In addition, the mist regains hit points equal to that amount. This reduction to the target's hit point maximum lasts until the target finishes a long rest. It dies if this effect reduces its hit point maximum to 0.

A humanoid slain by this attack rises 24 hours later as a zombie under the mist's control, unless the humanoid is restored to life or its body is destroyed. The mist can have no more than twelve zombies under its control at one time.

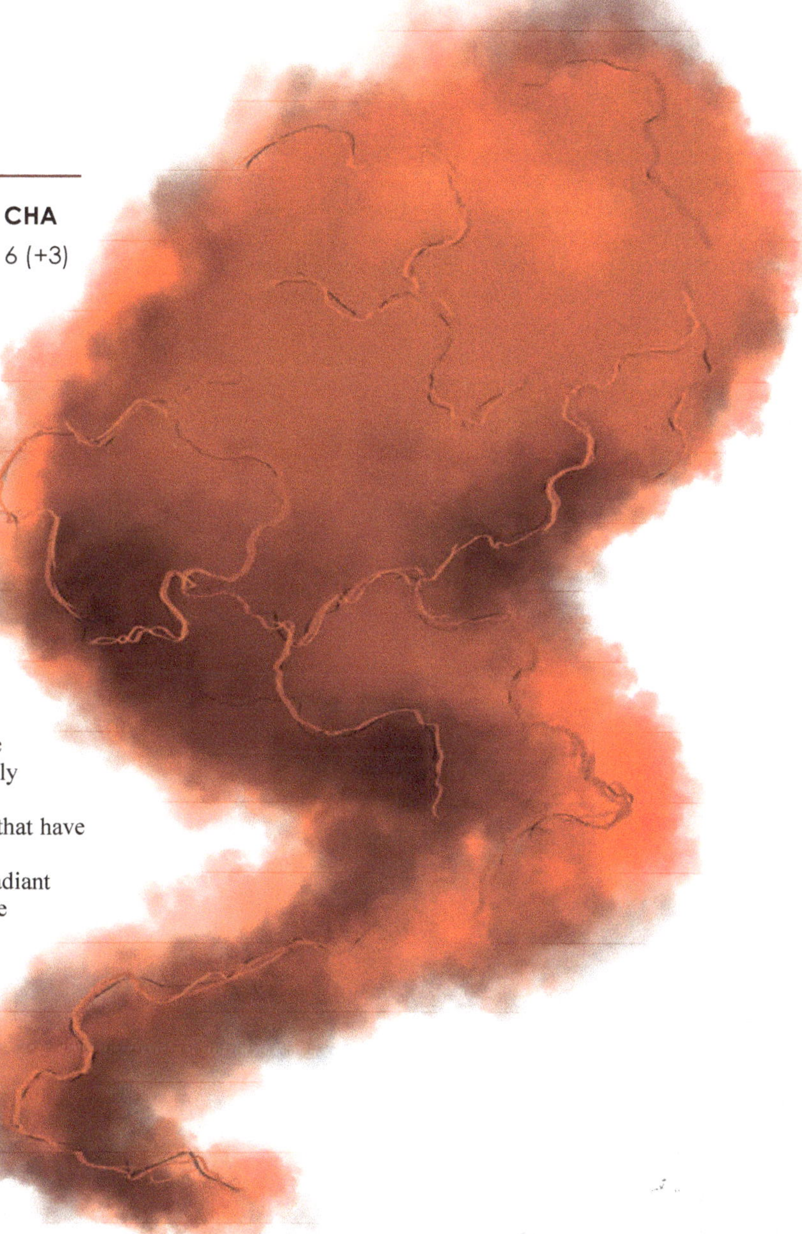

Dragon Crab

If the histories are accurate, a determined wizard decided to make himself an underwater army of gargantuan crabs to guard his island lair. He succeeded in all but one respect. In granting the crabs the intelligence to understand and execute his orders, he accidentally made them both evil in outlook and far too intelligent to control. Communing with the sea in which they dwelt, the crabs taught one another to call forth the magics of nature itself and overthrew their creator, destroying his lair and scattering themselves throughout the sea. His later-discovered journals, history claims, reveal he originally created 3 dozen such crabs. Though they are unable to reproduce, rumor holds that nearly all have survived to this day, hidden in the deepest of underwater caverns, ruling the seas around them.

Dragon crabs tend to be greedy, both in carnivorous appetite and for treasure. Like some dragons, they often amass vast piles of gems, coins, and any other wealth that can survive at the bottom of the sea. Some also collect shipwrecks to decorate their lairs. Dragon crabs enjoy the pain of living creatures, especially intelligent ones, and often make a hobby of devising clever means to lure humanoids to their lairs to make them suffer for entertainment. Most dragon crabs harbor a strong dislike of wizards.

Though not universal, many dragon crabs line their shells with gaudy precious metals and stones, both for aesthetic reasons and to disguise themselves as piles of sunken treasure. Such crabs then bury themselves in loose sand and wait for unsuspecting adventurers to swim close and be ambushed. When not gem-encrusted, dragon crab shells are deep orange and grey, with patches of pale blue on the legs. They are about 60 feet in diameter, with pincers each as large as an elephant.

A Dragon Crab's Lair

Dragon crabs lair in natural caves and grottoes in the ocean's bed. The largest chamber of the lair will be crowded with the crab's shimmering treasure hoard and crude cages containing dismembered corpses of victims who met their fates at the claws of the gigantic, sadistic enemy. A bioluminescent algae cultivated by the crab grows upon some walls and ceilings, emitting a pleasant, polychromatic glow, and pockets of breathable air, the result of tidal forces and underwater currents, can be found within the network of natural caverns that comprise the lair.

Dragon Crab

Gargantuan monstrosity, neutral evil

Armor Class 18 (natural armor)
Hit Points 210 (12d20 + 84)
Speed 40 ft., swim 50 ft.

STR	DEX	CON	INT	WIS	CHA
21 (+5)	13 (+1)	25 (+7)	17 (+3)	16 (+3)	11 (+0)

Saving Throws Con +12, Wis +8, Cha +5
Skills Deception +5, Nature +8, Perception +8, Stealth +6, Survival +8
Damage Resistances bludgeoning from nonmagical weapons
Damage Immunities piercing and slashing from nonmagical weapons
Senses darkvision 120 ft., passive Perception 18
Languages Common and any four others
Challenge 16 (15,000 XP)

Legendary Resistance (3/day). If the dragon crab fails a saving throw, it can choose to succeed instead.

Magic Resistance. The dragon crab has advantage on saving throws against spells and other magical effects.

Spellcasting. The dragon crab is a 12th level spellcaster. Its casting

ability is Wisdom (spell save DC 16, +8 to hit with spell attacks). The dragon crab can cast the following spells:

Cantrips (at will): *druidcraft, guidance, poison spray, resistance*
1st level (4 slots): *detect magic, entangle, speak with animals, thunderwave*
2nd level (3 slots): *heat metal, hold person, spike growth*
3rd level (3 slots): *cure wounds, dispel magic, protection from energy*
4th level (3 slots): *blight, confusion, hallucinatory terrain*
5th level (2 slots): *conjure elemental, contagion*
6th level (1 slot): *wall of thorns*

Actions

Multiattack. The dragon crab makes six attacks: two with its pincers and four with its legs. It can use Crush instead of a pincer attack.

Pincer. *Melee Weapon Attack:* +10 to hit, reach 15 ft., one target. *Hit:* 16 (2d10 + 5) bludgeoning damage. If the target is a Large or smaller creature, it is grappled (escape DC 15). The dragon crab has two pincers, each of which can grapple only one target.

Kick. *Melee Weapon Attack:* +10 to hit, reach 10 ft., one target. *Hit:* 12 (2d6 + 5) piercing damage.

Crush. *Melee Weapon Attack:* +10 to hit, reach 5 ft., one target grappled by the dragon crab. *Hit:* 16 (2d10 + 5) bludgeoning damage.

Legendary Actions

The dragon crab can take 3 legendary actions, choosing from the options below. Only one legendary action option can be used at a time and only at the end of another creature's turn. The dragon crab regains spent legendary actions at the start of its turn.

Detect. The dragon crab makes a Wisdom (Perception) check.

Gleam. The dragon crab reflects light into the eyes of one target it can see within 60 feet. The target must succeed on a DC 18 Dexterity saving throw or be blinded until the end of the dragon crab's next turn.

Pincer (Costs 2 Actions). The dragon crab performs two pincer attacks or uses Crush on up to two creatures it already has grappled.

Cast a Spell (Costs 3 Actions). The dragon crab casts a spell from its list of prepared spells, using a spell slot as normal.

Lair Actions

On Initiative count 20 (losing initiative ties), the dragon crab can take a lair action to cause one of the following effects; it can't use the same effect two rounds in a row:

Riptide. Pools of water within 120 feet of the dragon crab that it can see surge outward in a grasping tide. Any creature on the ground within 20 feet of such a pool must succeed on a DC 15 Strength saving throw or be pulled up to 20 feet into the water and knocked prone.

Pooling Shadow. Magical darkness spreads from a chosen point within 60 feet of the dragon crab, filling a 15-foot radius sphere until the dragon crab dismisses it as an action, uses this lair action again, or dies. The darkness spreads around corners. A creature with darkvision can't see through this darkness, and nonmagical light can't illuminate it. If any of the effect's area overlaps with an area of light created by a spell of 2nd level or lower, the spell that created the light is dispelled.

Treacherous Hoards. A heap of the dragon crab's treasure hoard collapses over one target within 120 feet that the dragon crab can see. The creature must succeed on a DC 15 Dexterity saving throw or take 10 (3d6) bludgeoning damage and be knocked prone and buried. The buried target is restrained and unable to breathe or stand up. The creature can take an action to make a DC 15 Strength check, ending the buried state on a success.

Regional Effects

The region containing a dragon crab's lair is warped by the creature's cursed presence, creating the following magical effects:

Subservient Seas. The dragon crab can influence the behavior of aquatic creatures within 6 miles of the lair that have an intelligence score of 3 or lower, charming them, usually to lure them into the lair as food although they can be directed to swarm and attack creatures. If the dragon crab unbalances the local ecosystem through use of this power, the ability ceases to function for 1d20 months, until balance is restored. Most dragon crabs use this ability very sparingly.

Eldritch Tides. Surface waters in a 4-mile radius above the dragon crab's lairs are prone to strange currents, unpredictable winds, and even some whirlpools. The dragon crab has no control over these and they cannot be used to its direct tactical advantage, but they increase the difficulty of seagoing navigation by 5 for any vessels or swimming creatures that attempt to traverse them. Local sea life has adapted to these strange currents; anything born within the 4-mile radius of the effect suffers no penalties in navigating it.

Dragons

Cloud Dragon
(Draco Nimbus Caelo)

This dragon has a fringed and frilled head and wings that sweep back from its shoulders to its tail. Large, piercing rose-colored eyes dominate its somewhat triangular head. Its tail trails off becoming misty and translucent near the tip.

Cloud dragons are the most reclusive of all dragons, rarely leaving the safety and sanctity of their cloudy lairs. They have a great dislike for non-flying creatures and creatures that must use non-natural means to fly (such as through magical items or spells). A cloud dragon wyrmling's scales are silvery-blue with a slight hint of red at the tip of each scale. As the dragon ages, its color slowly changes to a bright sunset orange. The oldest cloud dragons resemble gold dragons, save for the large bony plates on their heads and backs.

Cloud dragons are not highly aggressive, but dislike interlopers and attack them on sight. They open combat using their breath weapon, followed by their spell-like abilities. A cloud dragon rarely lands, preferring to fight from the air.

Ancient Cloud Dragon

Gargantuan dragon, neutral
Armor Class 19 (natural armor)
Hit Points 367 (21d20 + 147)
Speed 40 ft., fly 80 ft.

STR	DEX	CON	INT	WIS	CHA
27 (+8)	13 (+1)	25 (+7)	21 (+5)	18 (+4)	19 (+4)

Saving Throws Dex +8, Con +14, Wis +11, Cha +11
Skills Arcana +12, History +12, Insight +11, Nature +12, Perception +18
Damage Immunities cold, lightning
Senses blindsight 120 ft., darkvision 120 ft., passive Perception 28
Languages Auran, Aquan, Common, Draconic, Giant, Sylvan
Challenge 22 (41,000 XP)

Legendary Resistance (3/day). If the dragon fails a saving throw, it can choose to succeed instead.

Windborn. The dragon cannot be moved or knocked prone by magical or nonmagical winds of any kind.

Actions

Multiattack. The dragon uses its Frightful Presence and makes three attacks: one with its bite and two with its claws.

Bite. Melee Weapon Attack: +15 to hit, reach 20 ft., one target. *Hit:* 19 (2d10 + 8) piercing damage plus 10 (3d6) cold damage.

Claw. Melee Weapon Attack: +15 to hit, reach 10 ft., one target. *Hit:* 22 (4d6 + 8) slashing damage.

Tail. Melee Weapon Attack: +15 to hit, reach 20 ft., one target. *Hit:* 17 (2d8 + 8) bludgeoning damage.

Frightful Presence. Each creature of the dragon's choice that is within 120 feet of the dragon and aware of it must succeed on a DC 19 Wisdom saving throw or become frightened for 1 minute. A creature can repeat the saving throw at the end of each of its turns, ending the effect on itself on a success. If a creature's saving throw is successful or the effect ends for it, the creature is immune to the dragon's Frightful Presence for the next 24 hours.

Breath Weapons (Recharge 5–6). The dragon uses one of the following breath weapons.

Cloud Breath. The dragon exhales an icy blast in a 90-foot cone that spreads around corners. Each creature in that area must make a DC 22 Constitution saving throw, taking 72 (16d8) cold damage on a failed saving throw, or half as much damage on a successful one.

Wind Breath. The dragon exhales gale-force winds in a 90-foot line that is 10-feet wide. Creatures in this area must make a DC 22 Strength saving throw, taking 36 (8d8) bludgeoning damage on a failed saving throw and are pushed 90 feet directly away from the dragon. On a successful saving throw, the creature takes half damage and is not pushed. A creature who is pushed and strikes a solid surface takes 1d6 bludgeoning damage per 10 feet traveled. Nonmagical flames are completely extinguished, and magical flames created by a spell of 5th level or lower are immediately dispelled.

Cloud Form. The cloud dragon polymorphs into a Gargantuan cloud of mist, or back into its true form. While in mist form, the dragon can't take any actions, speak, or manipulate objects. It is weightless, has a flying speed of 20 feet, can hover, and can enter a hostile creature's space and stop there. In addition, if air can pass through a space, the mist can do so without squeezing, and it can't pass through water. It has advantage on Strength, Dexterity, and Constitution saving throws, it is immune to all nonmagical damage, and still benefits from its Windborn feature.

Legendary Actions

The dragon can take 3 legendary actions, choosing from the options below. Only one legendary action option can be used at a time and only at the end of another creature's turn. The dragon regains spent legendary actions at the start of its turn.

Detect. The dragon makes a Wisdom (Perception) check.

Tail Attack. The dragon makes a tail attack.

Wing Attack (Costs 2 Actions). The dragon beats its wings. Each creature within 15 feet of the dragon must succeed on a DC 23 Dexterity saving throw or take 15 (2d6 + 8) bludgeoning damage and be knocked prone. The dragon can then fly up to half its flying speed.

Lair Actions

On initiative count 20 (losing initiative ties), the dragon takes a lair action to cause one of the following effects; the dragon can't use the same effect two rounds in a row:

Sphere of Fog. The cloud dragon causes a 60-foot radius sphere of fog centered on a point anywhere in its lair. The sphere spreads around corners and its area is heavily obscured. The fog remains for 1 hour, or until the dragon dismisses it (no action required), and it cannot be dispersed by wind. On the next initiative count 20, the dragon can move the sphere up to 30 feet in any direction.

Wind Gust. The cloud dragon causes a burst of strong wind 60 feet long and 10 feet wide from it in a direction of the dragon's choice. The strong wind lasts until the next initiative count 20. Each creature other than the cloud dragon that starts its turn or enters the area must succeed on a DC 19 Strength saving throw or be pushed 15 feet away from it. In addition, any creature in the area must spend 2 feet of movement for every 1-foot it moves when moving closer to the dragon, and the wind disperses gas or vapor of the dragon's choice, and it extinguishes candles, torches, and similar unprotected flames in the area.

Freezing Air. The dragon causes a 20-foot sphere of air to drop to below freezing temperatures for 24 hours. Creatures in that area that start their turn or enter the area must make a DC 19 Constitution saving throw. On a failed saving throw, the target takes 14 (4d6) cold damage, or half as much damage on a successful one. The area affected by the spell is also covered in frost, leaving it difficult terrain for 24 hours.

Regional Effects

The region containing the ancient cloud dragon's lair is changed by its presence, which creates one or more of the following effects:

Wind and Fog. Strong winds whip and curl around the dragon's lair, but fog clouds still linger regardless, cloaking the land within 6 miles of the dragon's lair, making it lightly obscured.

Cold Snaps. Frigid cold snaps suddenly appear in areas within 6 miles of the dragon's lair, dropping the temperature to below freezing in minutes.

Thin Air. The air thins at ground level and above, as if the inhabitants stood above altitudes of 10,000 feet or higher, in areas within 6 miles of the dragon's lair.

If the dragon dies, these effects fade over 1d10 days.

Adult Cloud Dragon

Huge dragon, neutral

Armor Class 18 (natural armor)
Hit Points 195 (17d12 + 85)
Speed 40 ft., fly 80 ft.

STR	DEX	CON	INT	WIS	CHA
23 (+6)	12 (+1)	21 (+5)	18 (+4)	15 (+2)	17 (+3)

Saving Throws Dex +6, Con +10, Wis +7, Cha +8

Skills Arcana +9, History +9, Insight +7, Nature +9, Perception +12
Damage Immunities cold, lightning
Senses blindsight 120 ft., darkvision 120 ft., passive Perception 22
Languages Auran, Aquan, Common, Draconic, Giant
Challenge 15 (13,000 XP)

Legendary Resistance (3/day). If the dragon fails a saving throw, it can choose to succeed instead.

Windborn. The dragon cannot be moved or knocked prone by magical or nonmagical winds of any kind.

Actions

Multiattack. The dragon uses its Frightful Presence and makes three attacks: one with its bite and two with its claws.

Bite. *Melee Weapon Attack:* +11 to hit, reach 20 ft., one target. *Hit:* 17 (2d10 + 6) piercing damage plus 10 (3d6) cold damage.

Claw. *Melee Weapon Attack:* +11 to hit, reach 10 ft., one target. *Hit:* 20 (4d6 + 6) slashing damage.

Tail. *Melee Weapon Attack:* +11 to hit, reach 20 ft., one target. *Hit:* 15 (2d8 + 6) bludgeoning damage.

Frightful Presence. Each creature of the dragon's choice that is within 120 feet of the dragon and aware of it must succeed on a DC 16 Wisdom saving throw or become frightened for 1 minute. A creature can repeat the saving throw at the end of each of its turns, ending the effect on itself on a success. If a creature's saving throw is successful or the effect ends for it, the creature is immune to the dragon's Frightful Presence for the next 24 hours.

Breath Weapons (Recharge 5–6). The dragon uses one of the following breath weapons.

Cloud Breath. The dragon exhales an icy blast in a 60-foot cone that spreads around corners. Each creature in that area must make a DC 19 Constitution saving throw, taking 54 (12d8) cold damage on a failed saving throw, or half as much damage on a successful one.

Wind Breath. The dragon exhales gale-force winds in a 60-foot line that is 10-feet wide. Creatures in this area must make a DC 19 Strength saving throw, taking 36 (8d8) bludgeoning damage on a failed saving throw and are pushed 60 feet directly away from the dragon. On a successful saving throw, the creature takes half damage and is not pushed. A creature who is pushed and strikes a solid surface takes 1d6 bludgeoning damage per 10 feet traveled. Nonmagical flames are completely extinguished, and magical flames created by a spell of 4th level or lower are immediately dispelled.

Cloud Form. The cloud dragon polymorphs into a Huge cloud of mist, or back into its true form. While in mist form, the dragon can't take any actions, speak, or manipulate objects. It is weightless, has a flying speed of 20 feet, can hover, and can enter a hostile creature's space and stop there. In addition, if air can pass through a space, the mist can do so without squeezing, and it can't pass through water. It has advantage on Strength, Dexterity, and Constitution saving throws, it is immune to all nonmagical damage, and still benefits from its Windborn feature.

Legendary Actions

The dragon can take 3 legendary actions, choosing from the options below. Only one legendary action option can be used at a time and only at the end of another creature's turn. The dragon regains spent legendary actions at the start of its turn.

Detect. The dragon makes a Wisdom (Perception) check.

Tail Attack. The dragon makes a tail attack.

Wing Attack (Costs 2 Actions). The dragon beats its wings. Each creature within 15 feet of the dragon must succeed on a DC 19 Dexterity saving throw or take 13 (2d6 + 6) bludgeoning damage and be knocked prone. The dragon can then fly up to half its flying speed.

Young Cloud Dragon

Large dragon, neutral
Armor Class 16 (natural armor)
Hit Points 136 (16d10 + 48)
Speed 40 ft., fly 80 ft.

STR	DEX	CON	INT	WIS	CHA
19 (+4)	12 (+1)	17 (+3)	16 (+3)	13 (+1)	15 (+2)

Saving Throws Dex +4, Con +6, Wis +4, Cha +5
Skills History +6, Insight +4, Perception +7
Damage Immunities cold, lightning
Senses blindsight 120 ft., darkvision 120 ft., passive Perception 17
Languages Auran, Aquan, Common, Draconic
Challenge 8 (3,900 XP)

Windborn. The dragon cannot be moved or knocked prone by magical or nonmagical winds of any kind.

Actions

Multiattack. The dragon makes three attacks: one with its bite and two with its claws.

Bite. *Melee Weapon Attack:* +7 to hit, reach 10 ft., one target. *Hit:* 15 (2d10 + 4) piercing damage plus 7 (2d6) cold damage.

Claw. *Melee Weapon Attack:* +7 to hit, reach 5 ft., one target. *Hit:* 11 (2d6 + 4) slashing damage.

Breath Weapons (Recharge 5–6). The dragon uses one of the following breath weapons.

Cloud Breath. The dragon exhales an icy blast in a 90-foot cone that spreads around corners. Each creature in that area must make a DC 14 Constitution saving throw, taking 45 (10d8) cold damage on a failed saving throw, or half as much damage on a successful one.

Wind Breath. The dragon exhales gale-force winds in a 30-foot line that is 10-feet wide. Creatures in this area must make a DC 14 Strength saving throw, taking 36 (8d8) bludgeoning damage on a failed saving throw and are pushed 30 feet directly away from the dragon. On a successful saving throw, the creature takes half damage and is not pushed. A creature who is pushed and strikes a solid surface takes 1d6 bludgeoning damage per 10 feet traveled. Nonmagical flames are completely extinguished, and magical flames created by a spell of 3rd level or lower are immediately dispelled.

Cloud Form. The cloud dragon polymorphs into a Large cloud of mist, or back into its true form. While in mist form, the dragon can't take any actions, speak, or manipulate objects. It is weightless, has a flying speed of 20 feet, can hover, and can enter a hostile creature's space and stop there. In addition, if air can pass through a space, the mist can do so without squeezing, and it can't pass through water. It has advantage on Strength, Dexterity, and Constitution saving throws, it is immune to all nonmagical damage, and still benefits from its Windborn feature.

Cloud Dragon Wyrmling

Medium dragon, neutral
Armor Class 15 (natural armor)
Hit Points 44 (8d8 + 8)
Speed 30 ft., fly 60 ft.

STR	DEX	CON	INT	WIS	CHA
15 (+2)	12 (+1)	13 (+1)	14 (+2)	11 (+0)	13 (+1)

Saving Throws Dex +3, Con +3, Wis +2, Cha +3
Skills Insight +4, Perception +4
Damage Immunities cold, lightning
Senses blindsight 60 ft., darkvision 60 ft., passive Perception 14
Languages Auran, Aquan, Common, Draconic
Challenge 3 (700 XP)

Windborn. The dragon cannot be moved or knocked prone by magical or nonmagical winds of any kind.

Actions

Bite. *Melee Weapon Attack:* +4 to hit, reach 5 ft., one target. *Hit:* 7 (1d10 + 2) piercing damage plus 3 (1d6) cold damage.

Breath Weapons (Recharge 5–6). The dragon uses one of the following breath weapons.

Cloud Breath. The dragon exhales an icy blast in a 90-foot cone that spreads around corners. Each creature in that area must make a DC 11 Constitution saving throw, taking 22 (5d8) cold damage on a failed saving throw, or half as much damage on a successful one.

Wind Breath. The dragon exhales gale-force winds in a 20-foot line that is 10-feet wide. Creatures in this area must make a DC 11 Strength saving throw, taking 18 (4d8) bludgeoning damage on a failed saving throw and are pushed 20 feet directly away from the dragon. On a successful saving throw, the creature takes half damage and is not pushed. A creature who is pushed and strikes a solid surface takes 1d6 bludgeoning damage per 10 feet traveled. Nonmagical flames are completely extinguished, and magical flames created by a spell of 2nd level or lower are immediately dispelled.

Cloud Breath (Recharge 5–6). The dragon exhales an icy blast in a 15-foot cone that spreads around corners. Each creature in that area must make a DC 11 Constitution saving throw, taking 22 (5d8) cold damage on a failed saving throw, or half as much damage on a successful one.

Dungeon Dragon

This dragon has a long serpentine neck, small wings, and glistening scales. Two small horns dominate its triangular head. Its body is gray in color, with scales tipped in flecks of gold and green. Its eyes are rounded and gray.

The dungeon dragon is a curious creature that gets amusement by watching other beings engaged in life and death struggles. To this end, a dungeon dragon sets up a labyrinthine lair, setting traps and populating it with monsters. Younger dungeon dragons tend to lair in natural caverns to ease the burden of construction. Older, more experienced dungeon dragons have been known to construct their own sprawling subterranean complexes, even to the point of hiring on dwarf work gangs and swearing them to secrecy.

Once the construction and refurbishing of its lair are complete, the dungeon dragon transforms itself into a humanoid and ventures into the surrounding countryside. There it spreads rumors and tales of this horrible catacomb in hopes of luring adventurers forth so it may watch them via its crystal ball. Young dungeon dragons often spend years living among humanoids, even to the point of joining adventurers involved in dungeon delves. On such adventures, the intrepid dungeon dragon takes notes regarding the devious traps and monsters it encounters so that it can add such things to its own lair.

Oddly enough, although a dungeon dragon goes to great pains to amass a treasure hoard, it cares little for material wealth. Rather, it uses the treasure it gathers as bait in its dungeon to lure in adventurers and provide it the entertainment it so greatly desires. Watching adventurers explore its catacomb is the only real treasure a dungeon dragon desires. The only material possession a dungeon dragon will risk its life to save is its crystal ball. Without this vital piece of equipment, all of the dragon's labor is in vain.

A dungeon dragon in its natural form prefers to flee any combat. It likes to watch other creatures engaged in fights for life, not itself. If forced into melee, it swats at opponents with its powerful claws and bites. A dungeon dragon is proficient in the use of all simple and martial weapons and light and medium armor and shields.

Ancient Dungeon Dragon

Gargantuan dragon (shapechanger), neutral
Armor Class 19 (natural armor)
Hit Points 490 (28d20 + 196)
Speed 40 ft., fly 80 ft.

STR	DEX	CON	INT	WIS	CHA
27 (+8)	12 (+1)	25 (+7)	20 (+5)	17 (+3)	19 (+4)

Saving Throws Dex +8, Con +14, Wis +10, Cha +11
Skills Arcana +12, History +12, Insight +10, Investigation +19, Perception +17, Survival +10
Senses blindsight 60 ft., darkvision 120 ft., passive Perception 27
Languages all
Challenge 21 (33,000 XP)

Special Equipment. The dragon is attuned to a *crystal ball*, which is hidden somewhere within its labyrinthine lair. If a dungeon dragon loses its *crystal ball*, it can create a new one over the course of 10 days.

Innate Spellcasting. The dungeon dragon's innate spellcasting ability is Charisma (spell save DC 19, +11 to hit with spell attacks). It can cast the following spells, requiring no material components.

At will: *alarm, arcane lock, detect magic, detect thoughts, find traps, glyph of warding, identify, knock, scrying, stone shape, wall of stone*

3/day each: *dispel magic, hallucinatory terrain, locate creature, locate object, project image*

1/day: *find the path, maze, mirage arcane, passwall*

Labyrinthine Recall. The dungeon dragon can perfectly recall any path it has traveled.

Legendary Resistance (3/day). If the dragon fails a saving throw, it can choose to succeed instead.

Trap Master. The dungeon dragon has advantage on saving throws against the effects of traps.

Actions

Multiattack. The dragon uses its Frightful Presence and makes three attacks: one with its bite and two with its claws.

Bite. *Melee Weapon Attack:* +15 to hit, reach 15 ft., one target. *Hit:* 19 (2d10 + 8) piercing damage.

Claw. *Melee Weapon Attack:* +15 to hit, reach 10 ft., one target. *Hit:* 15 (2d6 + 8) slashing damage.

Tail. *Melee Weapon Attack:* +15 to hit, reach 20 ft., one target. *Hit:* 17 (2d8 + 8) bludgeoning damage.

Frightful Presence. Each creature of the dragon's choice that is within 120 feet of the dragon and aware of it must succeed on a DC 19 Wisdom saving throw or become frightened for 1 minute. A creature can repeat the saving throw at the end of each of its turns, ending the effect on itself on a success. If a creature's saving throw is successful or the effect ends for it, the creature is immune to the dragon's Frightful Presence for the next 24 hours.

Change Shape. The dragon magically polymorphs into a humanoid or beast that has a challenge rating no higher than its own, or back into its true form. It reverts to its true form if it dies. Any equipment it is wearing or carrying is absorbed or borne by the new form (the dragon's choice).

In a new form, the dragon retains its alignment, hit points, Hit Dice, ability to speak, proficiencies, Legendary Resistance, lair actions, and Intelligence, Wisdom, and Charisma scores, as well as this action. Its statistics and capabilities are otherwise replaced by those of the new form, except for class features or legendary actions of that form.

Confusion Breath (Recharge 5–6). The dragon exhales gas in a 90-foot cone that spreads around corners. Each creature in that area must succeed on a DC 22 Constitution saving throw. On a failed save, the creature is confused for 1 minute. While confused, the creature uses its action to Dash in a random direction, even if that movement takes the creature into dangerous areas. A confused creature can repeat the saving throw at the end of each of its turns, ending the effect on a success.

Dominate. One creature the dragon can see within 60 feet of it must succeed on a DC 19 Wisdom saving throw or be charmed for 1 hour. The creature has advantage if the dragon is fighting it. While the creature is charmed, the dragon has a telepathic link with it as long as it and the dragon are on the same plane of existence, and the dragon can issue commands to the creature as long as it is conscious (no action required), which it does its best to obey.

The dragon can use an action to take total and precise control of the target. Until the end of the dragon's next turn, the creature takes only the actions the dragon dictates and doesn't do anything that the dragon does not allow it to. In addition, the dragon can also cause the creature to use a reaction, but this requires the dragon to use its reaction as well.

The charmed creature can repeat the saving throw whenever it takes damage. If the saving throw succeeds, the spell ends.

Legendary Actions

The dragon can take 3 legendary actions, choosing from the options below. Only one legendary action option can be used at a time and only at the end of another creature's turn. The dragon regains spent legendary actions at the start of its turn.

Detect. The dragon makes a Wisdom (Perception) check.

Tail Attack. The dragon makes a tail attack.

Wing Attack (Costs 2 Actions). The dragon beats its wings. Each creature within 15 feet of the dragon must succeed on a DC 23 Dexterity saving throw or take 15 (2d6 + 8) bludgeoning damage and be knocked prone. The dragon can then fly up to half its flying speed.

Lair Actions

On initiative count 20 (losing initiative ties), the dragon takes a lair action to cause one of the following effects; the dragon can't use the same effect two rounds in a row:

Illusory Terrain. The dungeon dragon uses illusions to subtly manipulate creatures within its lair, as if it had cast the *hallucinatory terrain*, *project image*, or *mirage arcane* spell, targeting any location within its lair that it can see.

Changing Maze. The dungeon dragon manipulates the stone of its labyrinth as if it had cast the *stone shape* spell, targeting any location within its lair that it can see.

Stone Walls. The dungeon dragon creates walls of stone as if it had cast the *wall of stone* spell, targeting any location within its lair that it can see. When cast in this way, the dragon does not need to concentrate on the spell and its effects become permanent immediately.

Regional Effects

The region containing the ancient dungeon dragon's lair is changed by its presence, which creates one or more of the following effects:

Minotaur Meeting. Minotaurs are strangely drawn to the area surrounding a dungeon dragon's lair, often seeking to emulate the master of mazes.

Weather Alteration. Once per day, the dungeon dragon can alter the weather in a 6-mile radius centered on its lair.

If the dragon dies these effects fade over 1d10 days.

Adult Dungeon Dragon

Huge dragon, neutral
Armor Class 18 (natural armor)
Hit Points 364 (27d12 + 189)
Speed 40 ft., fly 80 ft.

STR	DEX	CON	INT	WIS	CHA
27 (+8)	10 (+0)	25 (+7)	16 (+3)	17 (+3)	21 (+5)

Saving Throws Dex +5, Con +12, Wis +8, Cha +10
Skills Arcana +8, History +8, Insight +8, Investigation +13, Perception +13, Survival +8
Senses blindsight 60 ft., darkvision 120 ft., passive Perception 23
Languages all
Challenge 16 (15,000 XP)

Special Equipment. The dragon is attuned to a *crystal ball*, which is hidden somewhere within its labyrinthine lair. If a dungeon dragon loses its *crystal ball*, it can create a new one over the course of 10 days.

Innate Spellcasting. The dungeon dragon's innate spellcasting ability is Charisma (spell save DC 18, +10 to hit with spell attacks). It can cast the following spells, requiring no material components.

At will: *alarm, arcane lock, detect magic, detect thoughts, find traps, glyph of warding, identify, knock, scrying, stone shape, wall of stone*

3/day each: *dispel magic, hallucinatory terrain, locate creature, locate object, project image*

Labyrinthine Recall. The dungeon dragon can perfectly recall any path it has traveled.

Legendary Resistance (3/day). If the dragon fails a saving throw, it can choose to succeed instead.

Trap Master. The dungeon dragon has advantage on saving throws against the effects of traps.

Actions

Multiattack. The dragon uses its Frightful Presence and makes three attacks: one with its bite and two with its claws.

Bite. *Melee Weapon Attack:* +13 to hit, reach 15 ft., one target. *Hit:* 19 (2d10 + 8) piercing damage.

Claw. *Melee Weapon Attack:* +13 to hit, reach 10 ft., one target. *Hit:* 15 (2d6 + 8) slashing damage.

Tail. *Melee Weapon Attack:* +13 to hit, reach 20 ft., one target. *Hit:* 17 (2d8 + 8) bludgeoning damage.

Frightful Presence. Each creature of the dragon's choice that is within 120 feet of the dragon and aware of it must succeed on a DC 18 Wisdom saving throw or become frightened for 1 minute. A creature can repeat the saving throw at the end of each of its turns, ending the effect on itself on a success. If a creature's saving throw is successful or the effect ends for it, the creature is immune to the dragon's Frightful Presence for the next 24 hours.

Confusion Breath (Recharge 5–6). The dragon exhales gas in a 60-foot cone that spreads around corners. Each creature in that area must succeed on a DC 20 Constitution saving throw. On a failed save, the creature is confused for 1 minute. While confused, the creature uses its action to Dash in a random direction, even if that movement takes the creature into dangerous areas. A confused creature can repeat the saving throw at the end of each of its turns, ending the effect on a success.

Legendary Actions

The dragon can take 3 legendary actions, choosing from the options below. Only one legendary action option can be used at a time and only at the end of another creature's turn. The dragon regains spent legendary actions at the start of its turn.

Detect. The dragon makes a Wisdom (Perception) check.

Tail Attack. The dragon makes a tail attack.

Wing Attack (Costs 2 Actions). The dragon beats its wings. Each creature within 15 feet of the dragon must succeed on a DC 21 Dexterity saving throw or take 15 (2d6 + 8) bludgeoning damage and be knocked prone. The dragon can then fly up to half its flying speed.

Young Dungeon Dragon

Large dragon, neutral
Armor Class 16 (natural armor)
Hit Points 199 (19d10 + 95)
Speed 40 ft., fly 80 ft.

STR	DEX	CON	INT	WIS	CHA
23 (+6)	10 (+0)	21 (+5)	14 (+2)	16 (+3)	19 (+4)

Saving Throws Dex +4, Con +9, Wis +7, Cha +8
Skills Arcana +6, Nature +6, Investigation +10, Perception +11, Survival +7
Senses blindsight 30 ft., darkvision 60 ft., passive Perception 21
Languages all
Challenge 9 (5,000 XP)

Special Equipment. The dragon is attuned to a *crystal ball*, which is hidden somewhere within its labyrinthine lair. If a dungeon dragon loses its *crystal ball*, it can create a new one over the course of 10 days.

Innate Spellcasting. The dungeon dragon's innate spellcasting ability is Charisma (spell save DC 16, +8 to hit with spell attacks). It can cast the following spells, requiring no material components.

At will: *alarm, arcane lock, detect magic, detect thoughts, find traps, glyph of warding, identify, knock*

3/day each: *dispel magic, hallucinatory terrain, locate creature, locate object, scrying, stone shape*

1/day each: *wall of stone*

Labyrinthine Recall. The dungeon dragon can perfectly recall any path it has traveled.

Trap Master. The dungeon dragon has advantage on saving throws against the effects of traps.

Actions

Multiattack. The dragon makes three attacks: one with its bite and two with its claws.

Bite. *Melee Weapon Attack:* +10 to hit, reach 15 ft., one target. *Hit:* 17 (2d10 + 6) piercing damage.

Claw. *Melee Weapon Attack:* +10 to hit, reach 10 ft., one target. *Hit:* 13 (2d6 + 6) slashing damage.

Confusion Breath (Recharge 5–6). The dragon exhales gas in a 30-foot cone that spreads around corners. Each creature in that area must succeed on a DC 17 Constitution saving throw. On a failed save, the creature is confused for 1 minute. While confused, the creature uses its action to Dash in a random direction, even if that movement takes the creature into dangerous areas. A confused creature can repeat the saving throw at the end of each of its turns, ending the effect on a success.

Dungeon Dragon Wyrmling

Medium dragon, neutral
Armor Class 17 (natural armor)
Hit Points 112 (15d8 + 45)
Speed 30 ft., fly 60 ft.

STR	DEX	CON	INT	WIS	CHA
19 (+4)	10 (+0)	17 (+3)	14 (+2)	15 (+2)	15 (+2)

Saving Throws Dex +2, Con +5, Wis +4, Cha +4
Skills Investigation +6, Perception +6, Survival +4
Senses blindsight 10 ft., darkvision 30 ft., passive Perception 16
Languages all
Challenge 4 (1,100 XP)

Innate Spellcasting. The dungeon dragon's innate spellcasting ability is Charisma (spell save DC 12, +4 to hit with spell attacks). It can cast the following spells, requiring no material components.

At will: *alarm, arcane lock, detect magic, identify, knock*
1/day each: *find traps, scrying, stone shape, wall of stone*

Labyrinthine Recall. The dungeon dragon can perfectly recall any path it has traveled.

Trap Master. The dungeon dragon has advantage on saving throws against the effects of traps.

Actions

Bite. *Melee Weapon Attack:* +6 to hit, reach 5 ft., one target. *Hit:* 9 (1d10 + 4) piercing damage.

Confusion Breath (Recharge 5–6). The dragon exhales gas in a 15-foot cone that spreads around corners. Each creature in that area must succeed on a DC 13 Constitution saving throw. On a failed save, the creature is confused for 1 minute. While confused, the creature uses its action to Dash in a random direction, even if that movement takes the creature into dangerous areas. A confused creature can repeat the saving throw at the end of each of its turns, ending the effect on a success.

Dragon, Fly

The flitting creature reveals itself to be a tiny, colorful dragon, the size of an insect.

Fly dragons are dragons the size of dragonflies. They consider themselves to be truer dragons than true dragons, though none of the latter have given their claims much credence. Nevertheless, fly dragons are approximately as dangerous to their enemies as true dragons, though they tend to be less devastating to the countryside around them due to much smaller nutritional requirements. Fly dragons become more powerful with age, just like true dragons. For older or younger fly dragons, adjust the breath weapons based on those of red dragons and reduce or increase spellcasting ability.

Though impressive in melee for their size, fly dragons are still very tiny, and thus take great pains to remain mobile in combat. Flitting between their enemies like hummingbirds of doom, they rely on their magic and breath weapons (and defensive abilities) to wreak havoc on their foes.

Fly dragons come in many colors and combinations of colors, and these tell observers nothing about their temperaments or abilities. They are pretty little things and tend to be quite vain, as well as arrogantly proud of their family bloodlines. Since they are so rare and reclusive, however, almost no one has ever heard of the family lines of which they boast. Colors and attitudes do sometimes run in families, but this will be no more universal a predictor of behavior than it would be within human families (indeed, it is not impossible that some fly dragons might even have other breath weapons or immunities). Though fly dragon alignment varies with the individual, even friendly fly dragons seem incapable of humility and have little tolerance for insults.

Fly Dragon

Tiny dragon, any alignment
Armor Class 20
Hit Points 275 (29d4 + 203)
Speed 5 ft., fly 60 ft.

STR	DEX	CON	INT	WIS	CHA
13 (+1)	30 (+10)	24 (+7)	19 (+4)	17 (+3)	19 (+4)

Saving Throws Dex +16, Con +13, Wis +9
Skills Arcana +10, Deception +10, History +10, Intimidation +10, Perception +9, Stealth +16
Damage Resistances poison, psychic; bludgeoning, piercing, and slashing from nonmagical weapons that aren't adamantine
Damage Immunities fire
Senses truesight 120 ft., passive Perception 19
Languages Common, Draconic
Challenge 18 (20,000 XP)

Legendary Resistance (3/day). If the fly dragon fails a saving throw, it can choose to succeed instead.

Magic Resistance. The fly dragon has advantage on saving throws against spells and other magical effects.

Spellcasting. The fly dragon is a 20th level spellcaster. Its spellcasting ability is Charisma (spell save DC 18, +10 to hit with spell attacks). The fly dragon's spells require no material components, and individual fly dragons know different sets of spells. A typical list is provided below:

Cantrips (at will): *fire bolt, mage hand, message, minor illusion, prestidigitation, shocking grasp*
1st level (4/day): *detect magic*
2nd level (3/day): *darkness, suggestion*
3rd level (3/day): *haste*
4th level (3/day): *confusion, greater invisibility, wall of fire*
5th level (3/day): *hold monster, telekinesis*
6th level (2/day): *chain lightning, globe of invulnerability*
7th level (2/day): *plane shift, teleport*
8th level (1/day): *dominate monster*
9th level (1/day): *time stop*

Actions

Multiattack. The dragon uses its Frightful Presence and makes three attacks: one with its bite and two with its claws.

Bite. *Melee Weapon Attack:* +16 to hit, reach 5 ft., one target. *Hit:* 12 (1d4 + 10) piercing damage plus 7 (2d6) fire damage.

Claw. *Melee Weapon Attack:* +16 to hit, reach 5 ft., one target. *Hit:* 13 (1d6 + 10) slashing damage.

Frightful Presence. Each creature of the dragon's choice that is within 60 feet of the fly dragon and aware of it must succeed on a DC 19 Wisdom saving throw or become Frightened for 1 minute. A creature can repeat the saving throw at the end of each of its turns, ending the effect on itself on a success. If a creature's saving throw is successful or the effect ends for it, the creature is immune to the fly dragon's Frightful Presence for the next 24 hours.

Fire Breath (Recharge 5–6). The dragon exhales fire in a 40-foot cone. Creatures in the area must make a DC 19 Dexterity saving throw, taking 63 (18d6) fire damage, or half as much damage on a successful one. Being underwater doesn't grant resistance to this damage.

Legendary Actions

The fly dragon can take 3 legendary actions, choosing from the options below. Only one legendary action option can be used at a time and only at the end of another creature's turn. The fly dragon regains spent legendary actions at the start of its turn.

Move. The fly dragon moves up to its speed without provoking opportunity attacks.

Cantrip. The fly dragon casts a cantrip.

Detect. The fly dragon makes a Wisdom (Perception) check.

Cast a Spell (Costs 3 Actions). The fly dragon casts a spell from its list of prepared spells, using a spell slot as normal.

Lair Actions

At "20" in the initiative countdown, a fly dragon defending its lair can take a lair action to cause one of the following effects. The fly dragon can't use the same effect two rounds in a row.

Searing Wind. Super-heated air erupts from one or more passages the fly dragon can see, filling one or more entire chambers of no more than a 20-foot radius total with a searing wind. Each creature in the area must make a DC 16 Constitution save, taking 21 (6d6) fire damage on a failed save, or half as much damage on a successful one.

Unstable Footing. A tremor shakes the lair in a 40-foot radius around the fly dragon. Each creature other than the fly dragon in contact with the ground, walls, or ceilings in that area must succeed on a DC 16 Dexterity saving throw or be knocked prone.

Noxious Fumes. Volcanic gases form a cloud in a 20-foot radius sphere centered on a point the fly dragon can see within 120 feet of it. The sphere spreads around corners, and its area is lightly obscured. It lasts until the initiative count 20 on the next round. Each creature that starts its turn in the cloud must succeed on a DC 16 Constitution saving throw or be poisoned until the end of its turn. While poisoned in this way, a creature is incapacitated.

A Fly Dragon's Lair

Fly dragons lair within stone hills and high mountaintops, hewing beautiful palaces of dazzling geometry into the living rock to befit the needs of flying aristocrats. These extravagant residences are kept hot to the point of searing by geothermal activity (or magic if it is not available) and are lined with fire-proof treasures, keepsakes, and intricate memorials to honor the fly dragon's inevitably storied and noble lineage. Although often solitary in travel or hunting, most fly dragons live in magnificent, sprawling (to tiny-sized creatures) hives with family, servants, and the families of servants, in accordance with inscrutable draconian traditions. The sizes of these lairs vary with the populations thereof and the status of the lair's lord but are always larger than the tiny beings need, while still small enough to be difficult for medium-size creatures to navigate comfortably.

Gray Dragon

Steam emanates from the nostrils and mouth of this slate gray dragon.

Gray dragons are evil dragons that inhabit mountains and hills near coastlines. They have little regard for other races and often enslave others to do their bidding. Adult and older gray dragons are rarely found without a retinue of humanoid slaves. Gray dragons mate for life and a single mated pair often terrorizes nearby villages, laying waste to those that oppose the dragon's will.

Ancient Gray Dragon

Gargantuan dragon, neutral evil
Armor Class 21 (natural armor)
Hit Points 455 (26d20 + 182)
Speed 40 ft., fly 80 ft., swim 40 ft.

STR	DEX	CON	INT	WIS	CHA
28 (+9)	14 (+2)	25 (+7)	19 (+4)	19 (+4)	19 (+4)

Saving Throws Dex +9, Con +14, Wis +11, Cha +11
Skills Perception +18, Stealth +9
Damage Immunities fire
Senses blindsight 60 ft., darkvision 120 ft., passive Perception 28
Languages Abyssal, Aquan, Common, Draconic, Giant
Challenge 21 (33,000 XP)

Amphibious. The dragon can breathe air and water.

Legendary Resistance (3/day). If the dragon fails a saving throw, it can choose to succeed instead.

Actions

Multiattack. The dragon uses its Frightful Presence and makes three attacks: one with its bite and two with its claws.
Bite. Melee Weapon Attack: +16 to hit, reach 15 ft., one target. *Hit:* 20 (2d10 + 9) piercing damage plus 7 (2d6) fire damage.
Claw. Melee Weapon Attack: +16 to hit, reach 10 ft., one target. *Hit:* 16 (2d6 + 9) slashing damage.
Tail. Melee Weapon Attack: +16 to hit, reach 20 ft., one target. *Hit:* 18 (2d8 + 9) bludgeoning damage.
Frightful Presence. Each creature of the dragon's choice that is within 120 feet of the dragon and aware of it must succeed on a DC 20 Wisdom saving throw or become frightened for 1 minute. A creature can repeat the saving throw at the end of each of its turns, ending the effect on itself on a success. If a creature's saving throw is successful of the effect ends for it, the creature is immune to the dragon's Frightful Presence for the next 24 hours.
Steam Breath (Recharge 5–6). The dragon exhales steam in a 90-foot cone. Creatures in the area must make a DC 22 Constitution saving throw. On a failed saving throw, the creature takes 80 (23d6) fire damage, or half as much damage on a successful saving throw. Being underwater doesn't grant resistance to this damage.

Legendary Actions

The dragon can take 3 legendary actions, choosing from the options below. Only one legendary action option can be used at a time and only at the end of another creature's turn. The dragon regains spent legendary actions at the start of its turn.
Detect. The dragon makes a Wisdom (Perception) check.
Tail Attack. The dragon makes a tail attack.
Wing Attack (Costs 2 Actions). The dragon beats its wings. Each creature within 15 feet of the dragon must succeed on a DC 24 Dexterity saving throw or take 16 (2d6 + 9) bludgeoning damage and be knocked prone. The dragon can then fly up to half its flying speed.

Lair Actions

On initiative count 20 (losing initiative ties), the dragon takes a lair action to cause one of the following effects; the dragon can't use the same effect two rounds in a row:
Dead Water. A 30-foot cube of water the dragon can see within 120 feet of it stagnates and becomes unable to support life of any kind. Aquatic creatures or creatures benefiting from spells such as *waterbreathing* cannot survive in the area and begin suffocating. The dragon can end this effect at any time.
Steam Cloud. The dragon causes an area of water within 120 feet of it to superheat, creating a cloud of fog in a 60-foot radius sphere. The sphere spreads around corners and its area is heavily obscured. The fog cloud remains for 1 hour or until a wind of moderate or greater speed (at least 10 miles per hour) disperses it.
Control Water. The dragon can cause an area of water to act as if the spell *control water* was cast on it. The dragon does not have to concentrate on this effect, and it remains active for the duration or until the dragon dismisses it (no action required).

Regional Effects

The region containing the ancient gray dragon's lair is changed by its presence, which creates one or more of the following effects:
Obscuring Fog. Twenty-foot areas of fog and steam dot the landscape within 6 miles of the lair. These areas are heavily obscured.
Heavy Tides. Tides are supernaturally heavy and inundate coastal areas, causing massive flooding.
If the dragon dies, these effects fade over 1d10 days.

Adult Gray Dragon

Huge dragon, chaotic evil
Armor Class 20 (natural armor)
Hit Points 218 (19d12 + 95)
Speed 40 ft., fly 80 ft., swim 40 ft.

STR	DEX	CON	INT	WIS	CHA
24 (+7)	15 (+2)	21 (+5)	15 (+2)	15 (+2)	17 (+3)

Saving Throws Dex +8, Con +11, Wis +8, Cha +9
Skills Perception +14, Stealth +8
Damage Immunities fire
Senses blindsight 60 ft., darkvision 120 ft., passive Perception 24
Languages Abyssal, Aquan, Common, Draconic, Giant
Challenge 17 (18,000 XP)

Amphibious. The dragon can breathe air and water.

Legendary Resistance (3/day). If the dragon fails a saving throw, it can choose to succeed instead.

Actions

Multiattack. The dragon uses its Frightful Presence and makes three attacks: one with its bite and two with its claws.

Bite. *Melee Weapon Attack:* +13 to hit, reach 15 ft., one target. *Hit:* 18 (2d10 + 7) piercing damage plus 5 (1d10) fire damage.

Claw. *Melee Weapon Attack:* +13 to hit, reach 10 ft., one target. *Hit:* 14 (2d6 + 7) slashing damage.

Tail. *Melee Weapon Attack:* +13 to hit, reach 20 ft., one target. *Hit:* 16 (2d8 + 7) bludgeoning damage.

Frightful Presence. Each creature of the dragon's choice that is within 120 feet of the dragon and aware of it must succeed on a DC 17 Wisdom saving throw or become frightened for 1 minute. A creature can repeat the saving throw at the end of each of its turns, ending the effect on itself on a success. If a creature's saving throw is successful of the effect ends for it, the creature is immune to the dragon's Frightful Presence for the next 24 hours.

Steam Breath (Recharge 5–6). The dragon exhales steam in a 60 cone. Creatures in the area must make a DC 19 Constitution saving throw. On a failed saving throw, the creature takes 63 (18d6) fire damage, or half as much damage on a successful saving throw. Being underwater doesn't grant resistance to this damage.

Legendary Actions

The dragon can take 3 legendary actions, choosing from the options below. Only one legendary action option can be used at a time and only at the end of another creature's turn. The dragon regains spent legendary actions at the start of its turn.

Detect. The dragon makes a Wisdom (Perception) check.

Tail Attack. The dragon makes a tail attack.

Wing Attack (Costs 2 Actions). The dragon beats its wings. Each creature within 15 feet of the dragon must succeed on a DC 24 Dexterity saving throw or take 14 (2d6 + 7) bludgeoning damage and be knocked prone. The dragon can then fly up to half its flying speed.

Young Gray Dragon

Large dragon, neutral evil
Armor Class 16 (natural armor)
Hit Points 142 (15d10 + 60)
Speed 40 ft., fly 80 ft., swim 40 ft.

STR	DEX	CON	INT	WIS	CHA
19 (+4)	13 (+1)	18 (+4)	13 (+1)	11 (+0)	16 (+3)

Saving Throws Dex +5, Con +8, Wis +4, Cha +7
Skills Perception +8, Stealth +5
Damage Immunities fire
Senses blindsight 30 ft., darkvision 120 ft., passive Perception 18
Languages Common, Draconic
Challenge 10 (5,900 XP)

Amphibious. The dragon can breathe air and water.

Actions

Multiattack. The dragon makes three attacks: one with its bite and two with its claws.

Bite. *Melee Weapon Attack:* +8 to hit, reach 10 ft., one target. *Hit:* 15 (2d10 + 4) piercing damage plus 5 (1d10) fire damage.

Claw. *Melee Weapon Attack:* +8 to hit, reach 5 ft., one target. *Hit:* 11 (2d6 + 4) slashing damage.

Steam Breath (Recharge 5–6). The dragon exhales steam in a 30 cone. Creatures in the area must make a DC 15 Constitution saving throw. On a failed saving throw, the creature takes 52 (15d6) fire damage, or half as much damage on a successful saving throw. Being underwater doesn't grant resistance to this damage.

Wyrmling Gray Dragon

Medium dragon, neutral evil
Armor Class 16 (natural armor)
Hit Points 44 (8d8 + 8)
Speed 30 ft., fly 60 ft., swim 30 ft.

STR	DEX	CON	INT	WIS	CHA
17 (+3)	14 (+2)	13 (+1)	10 (+0)	11 (+0)	13 (+1)

Saving Throws Dex +4, Con +3, Wis +2, Cha +3
Skills Perception +4, Stealth +4
Damage Immunities fire
Senses blindsight 10 ft., darkvision 60 ft., passive Perception 14
Languages Draconic
Challenge 4 (1,100 XP)

Amphibious. The dragon can breathe air and water.

Actions

Bite. *Melee Weapon Attack:* +5 to hit, reach 5 ft., one target. *Hit:* 8 (1d10 + 3) piercing damage plus 5 (1d10) fire damage.

Steam Breath (Recharge 5–6). The dragon exhales steam in a 15 cone. Creatures in the area must make a DC 11 Constitution saving throw. On a failed saving throw, the creature takes 21 (6d6) fire damage, or half as much damage on a successful saving throw. Being underwater doesn't grant resistance to this damage.

Mist Dragon
(Draco Nebulus Terra)

This great dragon has a ridge of swept-back horns encircling its head with two larger and longer horns just above its eyes dominating the others. A ridge of similar smaller horns runs the length of its back from its shoulders to its tail. Its body is long, snake-like, and semi-material. It possesses no visible wings. Its scaled body is grayish-white.

Mist dragons are relatively passive (for dragons) and reclusive, preferring to spend their time away from most other races (including other mist dragons). Mist dragons make their lairs near large sources of water such as waterfalls, lakes, and seashores. A mist dragon resembles a gold dragon in shape and size. Its scales are shiny-blue white as a hatchling and gradually darken to a blue-gray color with metallic silver splotches.

Mist dragons usually spend their days moving from place to place in mist form. If threatened or angered, a mist dragon assumes solid form and attacks using its breath weapon, claws, and bite.

Ancient Mist Dragon

Gargantuan dragon, neutral
Armor Class 19 (natural armor)
Hit Points 333 (18d20 + 144)
Speed 40 ft., fly 80 ft., swim 40 ft.

STR	DEX	CON	INT	WIS	CHA
26 (+8)	14 (+2)	26 (+8)	12 (+1)	15 (+2)	14 (+2)

Saving Throws Dex +8, Con +14, Wis +8, Cha +8
Skills Perception +14, Stealth +8, Survival +8
Damage Immunities fire
Senses blindsight 120 ft., darkvision 120 ft., passive Perception 24
Languages Auran, Aquan, Celestial, Common, Draconic, Elvish, Gnome, Ignan, Sylvan
Challenge 20 (25,000 XP)

Amphibious. The mist dragon can breathe both water and air.
Legendary Resistance (3/day). If the dragon fails a saving throw, it can choose to succeed instead.

Actions

Multiattack. The dragon uses its Frightful Presence and makes three attacks: one with its bite and two with its claws.
Bite. Melee Weapon Attack: +14 to hit, reach 20 ft., one target. *Hit:* 19 (2d10 + 8) piercing damage plus 14 (4d6) fire damage.
Claw. Melee Weapon Attack: +14 to hit, reach 10 ft., one target. *Hit:* 22 (4d6 + 8) slashing damage.
Tail. Melee Weapon Attack: +14 to hit, reach 20 ft., one target. *Hit:* 17 (2d8 + 8) bludgeoning damage.
Frightful Presence. Each creature of the dragon's choice that is within 120 feet of the dragon and aware of it must succeed on a DC 16 Wisdom saving throw or become frightened for 1 minute. A creature can repeat the saving throw at the end of each of its turns, ending the effect on itself on a success. If a creature's saving throw is successful or the effect ends for it, the creature is immune to the dragon's Frightful Presence for the next 24 hours.
Breath Weapon (Recharge 5–6). The mist dragon uses one of the following breath weapons.
Obscuring Mist. The dragon exhales a murky opaque mist in a 90-foot cube that spreads around corners. This mist heavily obscures the area and remains for 1 minute, or until dispersed with a moderate or stronger wind (at least 10 miles per hour).
Scalding Mist. The dragon exhales a fiery blast of lingering mist in a 90-foot cone that spreads around corners. The mist lightly obscures the area and remains for 1 minute, or until dispersed with a moderate or stronger wind (at least 10 miles per hour). Each creature that enters the area or begins its turn there must make a DC 22 Constitution saving throw, taking 77 (22d6) fire damage on a failed saving throw, or half as much damage on a successful one. Being underwater doesn't grant resistance to this damage.
Mist Form. The mist dragon polymorphs into a Gargantuan cloud of mist, or back into its true form. While in mist form, the dragon can't take any actions, speak, or manipulate objects. It is weightless, has a flying speed of 20 feet, can hover, and can enter a hostile creature's space and stop there. In addition, if air can pass through a space, the mist can do so without squeezing, and it can't pass through water. It has advantage on Strength, Dexterity, and Constitution saving throws, it is immune to all nonmagical damage.

Legendary Actions

The dragon can take 3 legendary actions, choosing from the options below. Only one legendary action option can be used at a time and only at the end of another creature's turn. The dragon regains spent legendary actions at the start of its turn.
Detect. The dragon makes a Wisdom (Perception) check.
Tail Attack. The dragon makes a tail attack.
Wing Attack (Costs 2 Actions). The dragon beats its wings. Each creature within 15 feet of the dragon must succeed on a DC 22 Dexterity saving throw or take 15 (2d6 + 8) bludgeoning damage and be knocked prone. The dragon can then fly up to half its flying speed.

Lair Actions

On initiative count 20 (losing initiative ties), the dragon takes a lair action to cause one of the following effects; the dragon can't use the same effect two rounds in a row:

Steam Cloud. Scalding steam condenses into an area in a 20-foot sphere centered on a point within 120 feet of the mist dragon. Creatures who enter the area or begin their turn within it must make a DC 16 Constitution saving throw, taking 16 (4d6 + 2) fire damage on a failed saving throw, or half as much damage on a success. The mist cloud heavily obscures the area and remains until the next initiative count 20.

Rain. The dragon causes rain to fall as if it had cast the *create or destroy water* spell as a 9th level spell (creating rainfall within a 70-foot cube) on an area within 120 feet of it that it can see.

Wind Barrier. The dragon causes strong winds to form barriers, as if it had cast the *wind wall* spell at a point it can see within 120 feet of it. The effects last until the dragon uses this lair action again, or until the dragon dies.

Regional Effects

The region containing the ancient mist dragon's lair is changed by its presence, which creates one or more of the following effects:

Tropical Atmosphere. The dragon's presence causes extreme moisture and humidity, creating a tropical atmosphere within 6 miles of the dragon's lair.

Difficult Plants. Plant life of all kinds flourishes, and sentient plant life flocks to the area, and makes trekking to the dragon's lair difficult.

If the dragon dies, these effects fade over 1d10 days.

Adult Mist Dragon

Huge dragon, neutral
Armor Class 18 (natural armor)
Hit Points 189 (14d12 + 98)
Speed 40 ft., fly 80 ft., swim 40 ft.

STR	DEX	CON	INT	WIS	CHA
25 (+7)	14 (+2)	25 (+7)	16 (+3)	14 (+2)	21 (+5)

Saving Throws Dex +7, Con +12, Wis +7, Cha +10
Skills Perception +12, Stealth +7, Survival +7
Damage Immunities fire
Senses blindsight 120 ft., darkvision 120 ft., passive Perception 22
Languages Auran, Aquan, Celestial, Common, Draconic, Ignan, Sylvan
Challenge 15 (13,000 XP)

Amphibious. The mist dragon can breathe both water and air.

Legendary Resistance (3/day). If the dragon fails a saving throw, it can choose to succeed instead.

Actions

Multiattack. The dragon uses its Frightful Presence and makes three attacks: one with its bite and two with its claws.

Bite. Melee Weapon Attack: +12 to hit, reach 20 ft., one target. *Hit:* 18 (2d10 + 7) piercing damage plus 10 (3d6) fire damage.

Claw. Melee Weapon Attack: +12 to hit, reach 10 ft., one target. *Hit:* 17 (3d6 + 7) slashing damage.

Tail. Melee Weapon Attack: +12 to hit, reach 20 ft., one target. *Hit:* 16 (2d8 + 7) bludgeoning damage.

Frightful Presence. Each creature of the dragon's choice that is within 120 feet of the dragon and aware of it must succeed on a DC 18 Wisdom saving throw or become frightened for 1 minute. A creature can repeat the saving throw at the end of each of its turns, ending the effect on itself on a success. If a creature's saving throw is successful or the effect ends for it, the creature is immune to the dragon's Frightful Presence for the next 24 hours.

Breath Weapon (Recharge 5–6). The mist dragon uses one of the following breath weapons.

Obscuring Mist. The dragon exhales a murky opaque mist in a 60-foot cube that spreads around corners. This mist heavily obscures the area and remains for 1 minute, or until dispersed with a moderate or stronger wind (at least 10 miles per hour).

Scalding Mist. The dragon exhales a fiery blast of lingering mist in a 60-foot cone that spreads around corners. The mist lightly obscures the area and remains for 1 minute, or until dispersed with a moderate or stronger wind (at least 10 miles per hour). Each creature that enters the area or begins their turn there must make a DC 20 Constitution saving throw, taking 63 (18d6) fire damage on a failed saving throw, or half as much damage on a successful one. Being underwater doesn't grant resistance to this damage.

Mist Form. The mist dragon polymorphs into a Huge cloud of mist, or back into its true form. While in mist form, the dragon can't take any actions, speak, or manipulate objects. It is weightless, has a flying speed of 20 feet, can hover, and can enter a hostile creature's space and stop there. In addition, if air can pass through a space, the mist can do so without squeezing, and it can't pass through water. It has advantage on Strength, Dexterity, and Constitution saving throws, it is immune to all nonmagical damage.

Legendary Actions

The dragon can take 3 legendary actions, choosing from the options below. Only one legendary action option can be used at a time and only at the end of another creature's turn. The dragon regains spent legendary actions at the start of its turn.

Detect. The dragon makes a Wisdom (Perception) check.

Tail Attack. The dragon makes a tail attack.

Wing Attack (Costs 2 Actions). The dragon beats its wings. Each creature within 15 feet of the dragon must succeed on a DC 20 Dexterity saving throw or take 14 (2d6 + 7) bludgeoning damage and be knocked prone. The dragon can then fly up to half its flying speed.

Young Mist Dragon

Large dragon, neutral
Armor Class 17 (natural armor)
Hit Points 147 (14d10 + 70)
Speed 40 ft., fly 80 ft., swim 40 ft.

STR	DEX	CON	INT	WIS	CHA
23 (+6)	14 (+2)	21 (+5)	14 (+2)	13 (+1)	19 (+4)

Saving Throws Dex +6, Con +9, Wis +5, Cha +8
Skills Perception +9, Stealth +6, Survival +5
Damage Immunities fire
Senses blindsight 120 ft., darkvision 120 ft., passive Perception 19
Languages Auran, Aquan, Common, Draconic, Ignan
Challenge 10 (5,900 XP)

Amphibious. The mist dragon can breathe both water and air.

Actions

Multiattack. The dragon uses its Frightful Presence and makes three attacks: one with its bite and two with its claws.

Bite. Melee Weapon Attack: +10 to hit, reach 10 ft., one target. *Hit:* 17 (2d10 + 6) piercing damage plus 7 (2d6) fire damage.

Claw. Melee Weapon Attack: +10 to hit, reach 5 ft., one target. *Hit:* 13 (2d6 + 6) slashing damage.

Breath Weapon (Recharge 5–6). The mist dragon uses one of the following breath weapons.

Obscuring Mist. The dragon exhales a murky opaque mist in a 30-foot cube that spreads around corners. This mist heavily obscures the area and remains for 1 minute, or until dispersed with a moderate or stronger wind (at least 10 miles per hour).

Scalding Mist. The dragon exhales a fiery blast of lingering mist in a 30-foot cone that spreads around corners. The mist lightly obscures the area and remains for 1 minute, or until dispersed with a moderate or stronger wind (at least 10 miles per hour). Each creature that enters the area or begins their turn there must make a DC 17 Constitution saving throw, taking 49 (14d6) fire damage on a failed saving throw, or half as much damage on a successful one. Being underwater doesn't grant resistance to this damage.

Mist Form. The mist dragon polymorphs into a Large cloud of mist, or back into its true form. While in mist form, the dragon can't take any actions, speak, or manipulate objects. It is weightless, has a flying speed of 20 feet, can hover, and can enter a hostile creature's space and stop there. In addition, if air can pass through a space, the mist can do so without squeezing, and it can't pass through water. It has advantage on Strength, Dexterity, and Constitution saving throws, it is immune to all nonmagical damage.

Mist Dragon Wyrmling

Medium dragon, neutral
Armor Class 15 (natural armor)
Hit Points 67 (9d8 + 27)
Speed 30 ft., fly 60 ft., swim 30 ft.

STR	DEX	CON	INT	WIS	CHA
19 (+4)	12 (+1)	17 (+3)	12 (+1)	13 (+1)	15 (+2)

Saving Throws Dex +4, Con +6, Wis +4, Cha +5
Skills Perception +7, Stealth +4, Survival +4
Damage Immunities fire
Senses blindsight 60 ft., darkvision 60 ft., passive Perception 17
Languages Auran, Aquan, Common, Draconic, Ignan
Challenge 5 (1,800 XP)

Amphibious. The mist dragon can breathe both water and air.

Actions

Bite. *Melee Weapon Attack:* +7 to hit, reach 5 ft., one target. *Hit:* 9 (1d10 + 4) piercing damage plus 3 (1d6) fire damage.

Breath Weapon (Recharge 5–6). The mist dragon uses one of the following breath weapons.

Obscuring Mist. The dragon exhales a murky opaque mist in a 15-foot cube that spreads around corners. This mist heavily obscures the area and remains for 1 minute, or until dispersed with a moderate or stronger wind (at least 10 miles per hour).

Scalding Mist. The dragon exhales a fiery blast of lingering mist in a 15-foot cone that spreads around corners. The mist lightly obscures the area and remains for 1 minute, or until dispersed with a moderate or stronger wind (at least 10 miles per hour). Each creature that enters the area or begins their turn there must make a DC 14 Constitution saving throw, taking 24 (7d6) fire damage on a failed saving throw, or half as much damage on a successful one. Being underwater doesn't grant resistance to this damage.

Dragon, Mouse (Draco Muridae)

This tiny creature appears to be a monstrous mixture of mouse and dragon: the body and legs of a sparsely furred mouse, with reptilian wings and a long furless tail covered in scales.

The mouse dragon, draco muridae vulgaris, is the most common of the small, coin-hoarding dragons. They tend to inhabit castles and cities heavy in stone buildings, taking coins and jewelry from the buildings they hide in. Their nests, where they will lay their eggs, are always built of the precious metals they acquire.

Mouse dragons often go unseen. They hide within the walls, building elaborate nests in the stone or wood of the structure they've chosen. Their sharp teeth and claws are capable of burrowing through stone and wood, and they make short work of any material short of metal.

The most common mouse dragon, the vulgar mouse dragon, is heinous and cares nothing for its environment, fleeing with as much of their hoard as they can carry should it come under attack. There are, however, several other types of mouse dragons. The copper mouse dragon, draco muridae aeris, is a much more agreeable sort, who will protect the structure it inhabits if able. The rarest mouse dragon, the platinum mouse dragon (draco muridae platina), is a natural illusionist and the only mouse dragon capable of true speech.

Vulgar Mouse Dragon (Draco Muridae Vulgaris)

Tiny dragon, chaotic evil
Armor Class 13 (natural armor)
Hit Points 15 (6d4)
Speed 20 ft., climb 20 ft., burrow 10 ft.

STR	DEX	CON	INT	WIS	CHA
4 (−3)	13 (+1)	10 (+0)	8 (−1)	11 (+0)	12 (+1)

Saving Throws Dex +3, Con +2, Wis +2, Cha +3
Skills Perception +4, Stealth +5
Senses darkvision 30 ft., passive Perception 14
Languages understands Common and Draconic, but can't
  speak
Challenge ½ (100 XP)

Pack Tactics. The mouse dragon has advantage on an attack roll against a creature if at least one of the dragon's allies is within 5 feet of the creature and the ally isn't incapacitated.

Treasure Sense. The mouse dragon can pinpoint, by scent, the location of precious metals and stones, such as coins and gems, within 60 feet of it.

Underfoot. The mouse dragon can attempt to hide even when it is obscured only by a creature that is at least one size larger than it.

Actions

Multiattack. The vulgar mouse dragon makes one bite attack and one claw attack.

Bite. *Melee Weapon Attack:* +3 to hit, reach 5 ft., one target. *Hit:* 3 (1d4 + 1) piercing damage.

Claws. *Melee Weapon Attack:* +3 to hit, reach 5 ft., one target. *Hit:* 3 (1d4 + 1) slashing damage.

Platinum Mouse Dragon (Draco Muridae Platina)

Tiny dragon, chaotic good
Armor Class 15 (natural armor)
Hit Points 44 (8d4 + 24)
Speed 20 ft., climb 20 ft., burrow 10 ft.

STR	DEX	CON	INT	WIS	CHA
7 (–2)	16 (+3)	16 (+3)	12 (+1)	15 (+2)	15 (+2)

Saving Throws Dex +6, Con +6, Wis +5, Cha +5
Skills Arcana +4, Nature +4, Perception +8, Stealth +9
Damage Immunities acid, fire, lightning
Senses darkvision 30 ft., passive Perception 18
Languages Common, Draconic
Challenge 5 (1,800 XP)

Innate Spellcasting. The platinum mouse dragon's innate spellcasting ability is Charisma (spell save DC 13, +5 to hit with spell attacks). It can cast the following spells, requiring no material components.

At will: *mage hand, minor illusion, silent image*
1/day each: *enlarge/reduce, invisibility, major image, see invisibility*

Pack Tactics. The mouse dragon has advantage on an attack roll against a creature if at least one of the dragon's allies is within 5 feet of the creature and the ally isn't incapacitated.

Treasure Sense. The mouse dragon can pinpoint, by scent, the location of precious metals and stones, such as coins and gems, within 60 feet of it.

Underfoot. The mouse dragon can attempt to hide even when it is obscured only by a creature that is at least one size larger than it.

Actions

Multiattack. The platinum mouse dragon makes one bite attack and two claw attacks.

Bite. *Melee Weapon Attack:* +6 to hit, reach 5 ft., one target. *Hit:* 6 (1d6 + 3) piercing damage.

Claw. *Melee Weapon Attack:* +6 to hit, reach 5 ft., one target. *Hit:* 7 (1d8 + 3) slashing damage.

Radiant Breath (Recharge 5–6). The dragon exhales radiant light in a 20-foot line that is 1 foot wide. Each creature in that line must make a DC 13 Dexterity saving throw, taking 38 (7d10) radiant damage on a failed saving throw, or half as much damage on a successful one.

Electrum Mouse Dragon (Draco Muridae Viridi)

Tiny dragon, chaotic good
Armor Class 15 (natural armor)
Hit Points 31 (7d4 + 14)
Speed 20 ft., climb 20 ft., burrow 10 ft.

STR	DEX	CON	INT	WIS	CHA
5 (–3)	14 (+2)	15 (+2)	10 (+0)	11 (+0)	12 (+1)

Saving Throws Dex +4, Con +4, Wis +2, Cha +3
Skills Arcana +2, Nature +2, Perception +4, Stealth +6
Damage Resistances bludgeoning, piercing, and slashing
  from nonmagical weapons
Senses darkvision 30 ft., passive Perception 14
Languages understands Common and Draconic but can't speak
Challenge 4 (1,100 XP)

Pack Tactics. The mouse dragon has advantage on an attack roll against a creature if at least one of the dragon's allies is within 5 feet of the creature and the ally isn't incapacitated.

Treasure Sense. The mouse dragon can pinpoint, by scent, the location of precious metals and stones, such as coins and gems, within 60 feet of it.

Underfoot. The mouse dragon can attempt to hide even when it is obscured only by a creature that is at least one size larger than it.

Actions

Multiattack. The electrum mouse dragon makes one bite attack and two claw attacks.

Bite. *Melee Weapon Attack:* +4 to hit, reach 5 ft., one target. *Hit:* 5 (1d6 + 2) piercing damage.

Claw. *Melee Weapon Attack:* +4 to hit, reach 5 ft., one target. *Hit:* 6 (1d8 + 2) slashing damage.

Lightning Breath (Recharge 5–6). The dragon exhales lightning in a 20-foot line that is 1 foot wide. Each creature in that line must make a DC 12 Dexterity saving throw, taking 27 (6d8) lightning damage on a failed saving throw, or half as much damage on a successful one.

Gold Mouse Dragon (Draco Muridae Aurum)

Tiny dragon, chaotic good
Armor Class 14 (natural armor)
Hit Points 38 (7d4 + 21)
Speed 20 ft., climb 20 ft., burrow 10 ft.

STR	DEX	CON	INT	WIS	CHA
6 (–2)	15 (+2)	16 (+3)	11 (+0)	12 (+1)	13 (+1)

Saving Throws Dex +4, Con +4, Wis +3, Cha +5
Skills Arcana +2, Nature +2, Perception +5, Stealth +6
Damage Immunities fire
Senses darkvision 30 ft., passive Perception 15
Languages understands Common and Draconic but can't speak
Challenge 4 (1,100 XP)

Pack Tactics. The mouse dragon has advantage on an attack roll against a creature if at least one of the dragon's allies is within 5 feet of the creature and the ally isn't incapacitated.

Treasure Sense. The mouse dragon can pinpoint, by scent, the location of precious metals and stones, such as coins and gems, within 60 feet of it.

Underfoot. The mouse dragon can attempt to hide even when it is obscured only by a creature that is at least one size larger than it.

Actions

Multiattack. The gold mouse dragon makes one bite attack and two claw attacks.

Bite. *Melee Weapon Attack:* +4 to hit, reach 5 ft., one target. *Hit:* 5 (1d6 + 2) piercing damage.

Claw. *Melee Weapon Attack:* +4 to hit, reach 5 ft., one target. *Hit:* 6 (1d8 + 2) slashing damage.

Fire Breath (Recharge 5–6). The dragon exhales fire in a 10-foot cone. Each creature in that area must make a DC 12 Dexterity saving throw, taking 27 (5d10) fire damage on a failed saving throw, or half as much damage on a successful one.

Silver Mouse Dragon
(Draco Muridae Argenti)

Tiny dragon, chaotic good
Armor Class 13 (natural armor)
Hit Points 27 (6d4 + 12)
Speed 20 ft., climb 20 ft., burrow 10 ft.

STR	DEX	CON	INT	WIS	CHA
5 (–3)	14 (+2)	14 (+2)	10 (+0)	11 (+0)	11 (+1)

Saving Throws Dex +4, Con +4, Wis +2, Cha +3
Skills Arcana +2, Nature +2, Perception +4, Stealth +6
Damage Immunities cold
Senses darkvision 30 ft., passive Perception 14
Languages understands Common and Draconic but can't speak
Challenge 2 (450 XP)

Pack Tactics. The mouse dragon has advantage on an attack roll against a creature if at least one of the dragon's allies is within 5 feet of the creature and the ally isn't incapacitated.

Treasure Sense. The mouse dragon can pinpoint, by scent, the location of precious metals and stones, such as coins and gems, within 60 feet of it.

Underfoot. The mouse dragon can attempt to hide even when it is obscured only by a creature that is at least one size larger than it.

Actions

Multiattack. The silver mouse dragon makes one bite attack and two claw attacks.

Bite. *Melee Weapon Attack:* +4 to hit, reach 5 ft., one target. *Hit:* 4 (1d4 + 2) piercing damage.

Claw. *Melee Weapon Attack:* +4 to hit, reach 5 ft., one target. *Hit:* 5 (1d6 + 2) slashing damage.

Cold Breath (Recharge 5–6). The dragon exhales an icy blast in a 10-foot cone. Each creature in that area must make a DC 12 Constitution saving throw, taking 22 (5d8) cold damage on a failed saving throw, or half as much damage on a successful one.

Copper Mouse Dragon
(Draco Muridae Aeris)

Tiny dragon, chaotic good
Armor Class 13 (natural armor)
Hit Points 18 (4d4 + 8)
Speed 20 ft., climb 20 ft., burrow 10 ft.

STR	DEX	CON	INT	WIS	CHA
2 (–4)	15 (+2)	14 (+2)	9 (–1)	12 (+1)	13 (+1)

Saving Throws Dex +4, Con +4, Wis +3, Cha +3
Skills Arcana +1, Nature +1, Perception +5, Stealth +6
Damage Immunities acid
Senses darkvision 30 ft., passive Perception 15
Languages understands Common and Draconic but can't speak
Challenge 1 (200 XP)

Pack Tactics. The mouse dragon has advantage on an attack roll against a creature if at least one of the dragon's allies is within 5 feet of the creature and the ally isn't incapacitated.

Treasure Sense. The mouse dragon can pinpoint, by scent, the location of precious metals and stones, such as coins and gems, within 60 feet of it.

Underfoot. The mouse dragon can attempt to hide even when it is obscured only by a creature that is at least one size larger than it.

Actions

Bite. *Melee Weapon Attack:* +4 to hit, reach 5 ft., one target. *Hit:* 4 (1d4 + 2) piercing damage.

Claw. *Melee Weapon Attack:* +4 to hit, reach 5 ft., one target. *Hit:* 4 (1d4 + 2) slashing damage.

Acid Breath (Recharge 5–6). The dragon exhales acid in a 15-foot line that is 1-foot wide. Each creature in that line must make a DC 12 Dexterity saving throw, taking 14 (4d6) acid damage on a failed saving throw, or half as much damage on a successful one.

Smoke Dragon
(Draco Fumo Suffoco)

This creature is a small, 3-foot-long dragon with a grayish underbelly and black scales. Its feet are tipped with smoke-gray talons and it has red-tinged wings and blue-gray eyes. Small under-curved horns protrude from its head and its serpentine tail writhes like a plume of smoke.

Smoke dragons lair in marshes, dense forests, or just about any area where thick fog is present (or can be present). They venture from their lair when the fog is the thickest, so most encounters occur in the morning. Lairs take the form of natural caves or caverns and are usually near a natural source of water. They eat just about anything but prefer a diet of fruits, plants, and berries. They also eat small animals such as mice and other rodents found slinking about near their lair. A smoke dragon's feeding ground is generally small and most cover an area of less than 1 square mile.

Smoke dragons live in small groups and such a group always includes at least one mated pair. Hatchlings can assume smoke form for 1 minute per day but cannot fly. If eggs are present, the female guards them closely and will fight to the death protecting them. Eggs are round, mottled gray and black.

Smoke dragons are generally inoffensive creatures and keep to themselves. Only when threatened or if their lair is threatened do they attack. In such cases, a smoke dragon unleashes its breath weapon and then swoops in to attack with its claws and bite. If the smoke dragon is outnumbered or overwhelmed, it uses its smoke form to avoid its opponents and flee. Multiple smoke dragons gang up against foes, alternating their breath weapon and natural attacks with the other smoke dragons in the gang; i.e., one smoke dragon belches forth its breath weapon while the others swoop in and attack with their claws and bite.

Smoke Breath (Recharge 5–6). The smoke dragon exhales a 20-foot cone of thick, black smoke that spreads around corners. The area is heavily obscured and the cloud of smoke remains for 1 minute or until dispersed by a moderate or stronger wind (at least 10 miles per hour). Creatures that enter or begin their turn in the area must succeed on a DC 11 Constitution saving throw or be poisoned. While poisoned, the creature must succeed on a DC 11 Constitution saving throw at the beginning of its turn, or spend its turn coughing and retching, preventing the creature from taking actions or moving. Once a poisoned creature succeeds on three consecutive saving throws, it is no longer poisoned.

Smoke Form (1/day). The smoke dragon polymorphs into a Medium cloud of smoke. While in smoke form, the dragon can't take any actions, speak, or manipulate objects. It is weightless, has a flying speed of 30 feet, can hover, and can enter a hostile creature's space and stop there. In addition, if air can pass through a space, the mist can do so without squeezing, and it can't pass through water. It has advantage on Strength, Dexterity, and Constitution saving throws, it is immune to all nonmagical damage. The transformation last for 1 hour unless the smoke dragon chooses to end it earlier with a bonus action.

Dragon, Wrath

Beautiful and awesome to behold, this majestic dragon's skin glitters like precious metals and jewels, belying its unquestionable might and holy wrath.

These massive powerfully built specimens are formed from the ascension of slain good dragons into the heavenly orders. Given the opportunity to return, they serve as heralds of good-aligned deities sent to deliver divine judgment on infidels and sinners who have turned their back on the path of righteousness. A flight of wrath dragons over an offending city has often been cause to turn an entire civilization to prayer and piety. Wrath dragons never enter the Material Plane, inner planes, or other outer planes unless under orders from the deity they serve. When such orders are given, a wrath dragon completes its assignment to the best of its ability before returning to its home plane.

A wrath dragon serves no one other than the deity that "created" it. It aids good-aligned creatures in time of need but does not serve them or stay with them any longer than is required to give aid (unless its deific orders say otherwise). A wrath dragon never aids an evil creature under any circumstances, and if forced to do so by magical means, the dragon seeks atonement as soon as possible.

A wrath dragon is 30 feet long and weighs about 30,000 pounds. Its scales are silver or platinum and glitter under bright light. Its wings are silver-hued with a darker stripe running along the top portion. Its head, sitting atop its long serpentine neck, is long and angular and its eyes are seemingly made of sapphire. Two under-curved horns made of ivory jut from its head just behind its eyes.

Wrath dragons start combat with the use of their breath weapon and divine spells. They continue this tactic until pressed with missile fire, or magic that would force them to close in for melee attacks. In close combat, a wrath dragon attacks using a combination of its bite, claws, and spells. If pressed, or if the battle turns against it, a wrath dragon summons devas to its aid.

Smoke Dragon

Small Dragon, neutral
Armor Class 14 (natural armor)
Hit Points 27 (6d6 + 6)
Speed 25 ft., fly 60 ft.

STR	DEX	CON	INT	WIS	CHA
13 (+1)	12 (+1)	13 (+1)	10 (+0)	12 (+1)	10 (+0)

Saving Throws Dex +3, Con +3, Wis +3, Cha +2
Skills Nature +2, Perception +5, Stealth +5, Survival +3
Damage Immunities fire
Condition Immunities poisoned
Senses blindsight 10 ft., darkvision 30 ft., passive Perception 15
Languages Common, Draconic
Challenge 1 (200 XP)

Blending. The smoke dragon has advantage on Dexterity (Stealth) checks made to hide within areas of smoke or fog.

Actions

Bite. *Melee Weapon Attack:* +3 to hit, reach 5 ft., one target. *Hit:* 5 (1d8 + 1) piercing damage.

Claw. *Melee Weapon Attack:* +3 to hit, reach 5 ft., one target. *Hit:* 4 (1d6 + 1) slashing damage.

Wrath Dragon

Huge dragon, any good alignment
Armor Class 19 (natural armor)
Hit Points 356 (31d12 + 155)
Speed 40 ft., fly 80 ft.

STR	DEX	CON	INT	WIS	CHA
23 (+6)	12 (+1)	21 (+5)	18 (+4)	21 (+5)	17 (+3)

Saving Throws Dex +7, Con +11, Wis +11, Cha +9
Skills Insight +11, Persuasion +9, Perception +17, Religion +10, Stealth +7
Damage Immunities fire, poison
Condition Immunities poisoned
Senses blindsight 60 ft., darkvision 120 ft., passive Perception 27
Languages Celestial, Common, Draconic, Giant, Terran
Challenge 19 (22,000 XP)

Divine Aura. Each time an aberration, fiend, or undead attempts to make a melee or ranged attack against the wrath dragon from within 10 feet of the dragon, the creature must succeed on a DC 19 Wisdom saving throw or be forced to target another creature within range or lose the action. Once a creature succeeds on this saving throw, it is immune to it for 24 hours.

Legendary Resistance (3/day). If the dragon fails a saving throw, it can choose to succeed instead.

Spellcasting. The wrath dragon is a 15th level spellcaster. Its spellcasting ability is Wisdom (spell save DC 19, +11 to hit with spell attacks). It has the following cleric spells prepared.

Cantrips (at will): *guidance, mending, resistance, sacred flame, thaumaturgy*

1st level (4 slots): *bane, bless, cure wounds, detect magic, guiding bolt*

2nd level (3 slots): *aid, find traps, hold person, lesser restoration, silence, spiritual weapon*

3rd level (3 slots): *beacon of hope, dispel magic, revivify*

4th level (3 slots): *banishment, death ward, freedom of movement, guardian of faith*

5th level (2 slots): *commune, dispel evil and good, greater restoration, mass cure wound, raise dead*

6th level (1 slot): *heal*

7th level (1 slot): *divine word*

8th level (1 slot): *holy aura*

Actions

Multiattack. The wrath dragon makes three attacks: one with its bite and two with its claws.

Bite. *Melee Weapon Attack:* +12 to hit, reach 10 ft., one target. *Hit:* 17 (2d10 + 6) piercing damage plus 9 (2d8) radiant damage.

Claw. *Melee Weapon Attack:* +12 to hit, reach 5 ft., one target. *Hit:* 13 (2d6 + 6) slashing damage plus 9 (2d8) radiant damage.

Tail. *Melee Weapon Attack:* +12 to hit, reach 15 ft., one target. *Hit:* 15 (2d8 + 6) bludgeoning damage plus 9 (2d8) radiant damage.

Divine Breath (Recharge 5–6). The wrath dragon releases a blast of divine fire in a 60-foot cone. Creatures within the area must make a DC 19 Dexterity saving throw, taking 28 (8d6) fire damage and 28 (8d6) radiant damage on a failed saving throw, or half as much damage on a successful saving throw.

Beckon Deva (1/day). The wrath dragon summons a deva from the deity that it serve. The summoned deva appears in an unoccupied space within 60 feet of the wrath dragon. It remains for 1 minute, until it or the wrath dragon is slain, or until the wrath dragon takes an action to dismiss it.

Legendary Actions

The dragon can take 3 legendary actions, choosing from the options below. Only one legendary action option can be used at a time and only at the end of another creature's turn. The dragon regains spent legendary actions at the start of its turn.

Detect. The dragon makes a Wisdom (Perception) check.

Tail Attack. The dragon makes a tail attack.

Wing Attack (Costs 2 Actions). The dragon beats its wings. Each creature within 15 feet of the dragon must succeed on a DC 20 Dexterity saving throw or take 13 (2d6 + 6) bludgeoning damage and be knocked prone. The dragon can then fly up to half its flying speed.

Preserve Life (Costs 3 Actions). The wrath dragon causes up to 6 creatures within 30 feet of it to regain 14 (2d6 + 7) hit points each.

Drakes

Salt Drake

This powerful creature resembles a blue dragon with mottled black wings and crimson eyes. Its ears are frilled and swept back against its head.

Salt drakes are found in warm, arid climates such as deserts or salt flats.

Salt drakes are omnivorous creatures and very territorial, even fighting among themselves to protect their domains. Most encounters are with a solitary drake. Only in the midsummer months is it common to find a mated pair or family. A salt drake's scales range from dull blue to midnight blue, and it is often mistaken for a young blue dragon. Salt drakes range from 8 feet to 30 feet long. Though difficult to train, salt drakes are favored as mounts by goblins, gnolls, and hobgoblins.

A salt drake's primary diet consists of large quantities of salt. This diet enables the drake to spew salt at its opponents. A salt drake opens combat from the air using its salt spray breath weapon. If unable to utilize its breath weapon, it relies on its claws and bite to finish off any remaining opponents.

Training a Salt Drake

A salt drake requires training before it can bear a rider in combat. To be trained, a salt drake must have a friendly attitude toward the trainer. Training a friendly salt drake requires ten weeks of work and a successful DC 30 Wisdom (Animal Handling) check. Riding a salt drake requires an exotic saddle.

Salt drake eggs are worth 6,000 gp apiece on the open market, while young are worth 12,000 gp each. Professional trainers charge 2,000 gp to rear or train a dragonnel.

Carrying Capacity: A salt drake is considered unencumbered up to 516 pounds; encumbered between 517–1,038 pounds, and heavily encumbered between 1,039–1,560 pounds. It cannot carry more than 1,560 pounds.

Salt Drake

Large dragon, neutral
Armor Class 16 (natural armor)
Hit Points 85 (9d10 + 36)
Speed 40 ft., fly 60 ft.

STR	DEX	CON	INT	WIS	CHA
17 (+3)	14 (+2)	18 (+4)	4 (–3)	13 (+1)	11 (+0)

Skills Perception +4, Stealth +5, Survival +4
Damage Immunities acid
Senses darkvision 60 ft., passive Perception 14
Languages Draconic
Challenge 7 (2,900 XP)

Nictitating Membranes. Salt drakes have advantage on saving throws against being blinded.

Actions

Multiattack. The salt drake makes three attacks: one with its bite and two with its claws.

Bite. *Melee Weapon Attack:* +6 to hit, reach 10 ft., one target. *Hit:* 12 (2d8 + 3) piercing damage plus 7 (3d4) acid damage.

Claw. *Melee Weapon Attack:* +6 to hit, reach 5 ft., one target. *Hit:* 10 (2d6 + 3) slashing damage.

Tail. *Melee Weapon Attack:* +6 to hit, reach 10 ft., one target. *Hit:* 16 (3d8 + 3) bludgeoning damage, and the target must succeed on a DC 15 Strength saving throw or be knocked prone.

Salt Spray (Recharge 5–6). The salt drake releases a spray of razor-sharp salt crystals in a 30-foot cone. Each creature in the area must make a DC 15 Dexterity saving throw. On a failed saving throw, the target takes 22 (5d8) acid damage plus 22 (5d8) slashing damage, or half as much damage on a successful saving throw. In addition, if a creature takes any damage from the salt spray, it is poisoned until it takes a short or long rest.

Splinter Drake

This creature looks like a wingless dragon about 12 feet long whose flesh is actually dark-brown bark with a greenish hue. A bushy mane of twigs, branches, leaves, and vines circles its dragon-like head and a series of thorny spines runs the length of its back. Two backward-curved horns, apparently constructed of the same hardened bark as its body, jut from the creature's head. A dark-brown snake-like tongue flicks across its fangs as it advances.

Splinter drakes are plant creatures that resemble large wingless dragons. They haunt dense forests and make their lairs amid the tangled underbrush, generally in hard-to-locate places. Much like true dragons, splinter drakes are extremely territorial and attack creatures that wander carelessly into their domain and remain for an extended amount of time. A typical splinter drake's territory covers an area of several square miles around its lair. Unlike true dragons, splinter drakes do not value nor keep treasure. Any treasure found in or around their lairs are likely all that remains of a past meal. They generally keep company with evil fey, evil druids, and corrupt rangers. Such allies are allowed a bit of leeway when treading on a splinter drake's territory, but if certain boundaries are crossed or privileges abused, splinter drakes have no problems eating someone they once called friend.

Splinter drakes generally do not associate with others of their kind, except during mating season (early spring) when a mated pair is likely to be encountered. During mating, the female splinter drake deposits a host of eggs (or seeds) into the ground. Within several months, 1d4 new splinter drakes grow from the ground. Splinter drakes reach maturity within 1 year. A splinter drake is about 12 feet long and weighs around 800 pounds.

Splinter drakes typically ambush potential prey whenever possible, striking from surprise with their thorny breath weapon and poison. Once it releases its first blast, it charges into battle and slashes and tears at its foes with its claws and bites. If outnumbered or combat turns against it, a splinter drake seeks the quickest means of exit possible unless cornered, defending its lair, or starving, in which case it fights to the death.

Splinter Drake

Large plant, neutral evil
Armor Class 16 (natural armor)
Hit Points 114 (12d10 + 48)
Speed 40 ft.

STR	DEX	CON	INT	WIS	CHA
17 (+3)	15 (+2)	18 (+4)	10 (+0)	12 (+1)	10 (+0)

Skills Perception +5, Stealth +6 (+10 in forest), Survival +5
Damage Resistances cold, fire
Condition Immunities blinded, charmed, deafened, exhaustion
Senses blindsight 60 ft. (blind beyond this radius), passive Perception 15
Languages Common, Sylvan
Challenge 9 (5,000 XP)

Land's Stride. Moving through nonmagical difficult terrain costs the splinter drake no extra movement, and it can pass through nonmagical plants without being slowed by them and without taking damage from them.

Actions

Multiattack. The splinter drake makes one bite attack and two claw attacks.

Bite. *Melee Weapon Attack:* +7 to hit, reach 10 ft., one target. *Hit:* 12 (2d8 + 3) piercing damage plus 7 (2d6) poison damage.

Claw. *Melee Weapon Attack:* +7 to hit, reach 5 ft., one target. *Hit:* 10 (2d6 + 3) slashing damage.

Thorn Volley (Recharge 5–6). The splinter drake emits a spray of thorns in a 40-foot cone. Creatures within this area must make a DC 16 Dexterity saving throw, taking 21 (6d6) piercing damage and 28 (8d6) poison damage on a failed saving throw, or half as much damage on a successful saving throw.

Dwarf, Frost

This stocky humanoid is about 4 feet tall with bright blue eyes and long bluish-white hair.

Frost dwarves are chaotic and untamed as the glacial expanses which they inhabit. Often they have lairs hidden deep beneath snow and ice packs burrowed deep into the living stone where they plunder for gemstones and metals as any other dwarf. Skilled crafters, frost dwarves trade freely with frost giants, constructing many of their massive weapons and armor in exchange for loot and protection. They are typically disliked and dismissed by their "true" dwarven kin who consider them to be abominations or worse.

Frost dwarves are known for their rudeness and coarse sense of humor. They are, however, famed for their skill at craftsmanship and the enchantment of strange and unusual magical items. Most typically frost dwarves are worshippers of Thrym and enjoy his taste in puzzles and conundrums. Frost dwarf traps are legendary amongst the frozen wastes of the world.

Frost dwarves are proficient combatants and make use of their natural surroundings to their advantage. They assault enemies with crossbows from distance and use their battleaxe to crush charges. They enjoy surprise and prefer to attack using dirty tricks such as unleashing avalanches upon unsuspecting travelers, then pick through their frozen carcasses for loot. Higher level frost dwarves often ride winter wolves as mounts. It is not uncommon for 1–2 of the beasts to be in the company of a frost dwarf squad.

Frost Dwarf Society

Frost dwarves are commonly found serving frost giant masters. In their own nations, they elect a king from the ruling clans. This jarl rules for life though does not necessarily establish any form of dynasty. Frost dwarf clans organize themselves loosely after the fashion of their mountain and hill dwarf cousins but are more tribal in nature. Frost dwarves keep a semblance of military titles amongst the various clans. Frost dwarves are attuned to the use of magic and many of their leaders are powerful wizards or clerics. They are equally likely to be barbarians.

There are no frost dwarf females. Frost dwarves are born to the union of a frost dwarf and dwarf (any), human, gnome, or frost or hill giant. Any child conceived from such a union is always born a frost dwarf male and reaches full size within a matter of weeks.

Frost dwarf children are often abandoned near known frost dwarf communities where it is expected they will be found and cared for or claimed by their father's clan. Frost dwarves are often shunned by their maternal parent as an abomination, especially among hill and mountain dwarves who likely banish the mother from their halls if she survives the child's birth. The exception to this rule is that of frost dwarves born to frost giant and jotun mothers. In frost giant culture, frost dwarves are considered a sign of good luck. They are, however, still sent to live amongst others of their kind until they reach the age of maturity, which is about 50 years old, when they are welcomed back amongst the frost giants who sired them.

Frost Dwarf

Medium humanoid (frost dwarf), chaotic neutral
Armor Class 12 (leather)
Hit Points 13 (2d8 + 4)
Speed 25 ft.

STR	DEX	CON	INT	WIS	CHA
13 (+1)	12 (+1)	14 (+2)	10 (+0)	11 (+0)	10 (+0)

Skills Perception +2
Damage Resistances cold
Senses darkvision 60 ft., passive Perception 12
Languages Common, Dwarven
Challenge ½ (100 XP)

Actions

Battleaxe. *Melee Weapon Attack:* +3 to hit, reach 5 ft., one target. *Hit:* 5 (1d8 + 1) slashing damage.

Frost breath. The frost dwarf exhales a 15-foot cone of freezing air. Each creature in the area must make a DC 12 Constitution saving throw, taking 7 (2d6) cold damage on a failed saving throw, or half as much damage on a successful one.

Frost Dwarf Traits

As a frost dwarf, you are at home in the most frigid environments, and your very breath is colder still.

Ability Score Increase. Your Strength score increases by 1.

Acclimation. You lose your Dwarven Resilience trait. Instead, you have resistance to cold damage, and you ignore nonmagical difficult terrain caused by snow or ice.

Frost Breath. You can use your action to exhale a 15-foot cone of freezing air. Each creature in the area of exhalation must make a Constitution saving throw. The DC for this saving throw equals 8 + your Constitution modifier + your proficiency bonus. A creature takes 2d6 cold damage on a failed saving throw, and half as much damage on a successful one. The damage increases to 3d6 at 6th level, 4d6 at 11th level, and 5d6 at 16th level.

After you use your breath weapon, you can't use it again until you complete a short or long rest.

Eel, Gulper

This strange being of the depths appears to be little more than a large mouth, flaccid body and dangling tail which glows with an unnatural red light.

This larger version of its more common cousin makes its home in deep tropical and temperate waters well below 3,000 feet in depth. The gulper eel spends its life eating giant shrimp, and any other creatures which happen to arouse its senses.

Gulper eels spend most of their lives in the deepest and darkest parts of the oceans, rarely if ever venturing near the surface waters. Solitary creatures by nature, during mating season (colder months of the year), it is common to find a pair of these creatures dwelling together. During mating season, the female deposits her eggs (2–8) in the dirt and mass of plants on the ocean floor. Within two months the eggs hatch and the young swim free. Young are independent within 2 weeks after birth and venture out on their own shortly thereafter.

A gulper eel averages 10 feet in length but can grow to reach 30 feet or more. Its body is long, sleek, and black in color and its tail ends in a luminous organ. Its eyes are small for its body and close to its snout. It massive mouth is lined with rows of sharpened teeth.

Gulper eels attempt to bite their prey, holding it before swallowing it whole. Because a gulper eel can unhinge its jaw and stretch its stomach, it can swallow opponents larger than itself.

Eel, Gulper

Large beast, unaligned
Armor Class 14 (natural armor)
Hit Points 112 (15d10 + 30)
Speed swim 50 ft.

STR	DEX	CON	INT	WIS	CHA
17 (+3)	15 (+2)	14 (+2)	2 (–4)	12 (+1)	2 (–4)

Skills Perception +3, Stealth +4
Senses blindsight 60 ft., passive Perception 13
Languages —
Challenge 3 (700 XP)

Keen Smell. The eel has advantage on Wisdom (Perception) checks that rely on smell.

Water Breathing. The eel can only breathe underwater.

Actions

Bite. *Melee Weapon Attack:* +5 to hit, reach 5 ft., one target. *Hit:* 20 (5d6 + 3) piercing damage, and the target is grappled (escape DC 13). Until this grapple ends, the eel can bite only the grappled creature and has advantage on attack rolls to do so.

Swallow. The eel makes one bite attack against a Medium or smaller target it is grappling. If the attack hits, the target is swallowed, and the grapple ends. The swallowed target is blinded and restrained, it has total cover against attacks and other effects outside the eel, and it takes 10 (3d6) acid damage at the start of each of the eel's turns. The eel can have only one target swallowed at a time.

If the eel takes 25 damage or more on a single turn from the creature inside of it, the eel must succeed on a DC 12 Constitution saving throw at the end of that turn or regurgitate the swallowed creature, which falls prone in a space within 10 feet of the eel. If the eel dies, a swallowed creature is no longer restrained by it and can escape from the corpse using 15 feet of movement, exiting prone.

Elementals

Elemental, Acid

Acid Elemental

What was once a still puddle of green liquid rises up like a wave, lashing out with acid-dripping tendrils. In the midst of the pool, one can barely make out regions of darker green that form a vaguely human face.

Nestled among the various elemental there lies a plane composed entirely of acid. It is a place of noxious fumes and roiling, bubbling, pools. Plane jumpers do well to avoid this place as it is considered by many to be one of the deadliest, if not the deadliest, of the elemental-based planes.

Acid elementals rarely journey from their native plane, except when summoned. They do not like the Material Plane and when called to the place, are usually angered and always a bit uncomfortable. They have no trouble moving on land but prefer the sanctity of their native plane to all others. At rest, an acid elemental is a clear puddle of liquid with a slightly green hue. It can rise up like a wave in a manner similar to a water elemental, or ooze along solid surfaces by sending out tendrils and pulling itself along. Wherever it travels, it leaves behind a shallow trough that emits wisps of smoke.

Acid elementals are almost always encountered in large pools of acid when on the Material Plane and rarely leave these pools when combating foes. A favored tactic is to grab a foe and pull it into the elemental's acid pool, subjecting it to massive amounts of acid damage

Medium Acid Elemental

Medium elemental, neutral
Armor Class 13
Hit Points 68 (8d8 + 32)
Speed 20 ft., swim 80 ft.

STR	DEX	CON	INT	WIS	CHA
21 (+5)	16 (+3)	19 (+4)	6 (−2)	11 (+0)	11 (+0)

Skills Stealth +6
Damage Resistances bludgeoning, piercing, and slashing from nonmagical weapons
Damage Immunities acid, poison
Condition Immunities exhaustion, grappled, paralyzed, petrified, poisoned, prone, restrained, unconscious
Senses darkvision 60 ft., passive Perception 10
Languages —
Challenge 5 (1,800 XP)

Acid. A creature that touches the acid elemental or hits it with a melee attack while within 5 feet of it takes 5 (2d4) acid damage. Any nonmagical weapon made of metal or wood that hits the acid elemental corrodes. After dealing damage, the weapon takes a permanent and cumulative −1 penalty to damage rolls. If its penalty drops to −5, the weapon is destroyed. Nonmagical ammunition made of metal or wood that hits the acid elemental is destroyed after dealing damage. The acid elemental can eat through 2-inch-thick, nonmagical wood or metal in 1 round.

Fumes. Creatures who begin their turn within 5 feet of the acid elemental must succeed on a DC 15 Constitution saving throw or be poisoned until the start of their next turn. On a successful saving throw, the creature is immune to the elemental's fumes for 24 hours.

Vulnerability to Water. For every 5 feet that the elemental moves in water, or for every gallon of water splashed on it, it takes 1 fire damage.

Actions

Slam. Melee Weapon Attack: +8 to hit, reach 5 ft., one target. *Hit:* 9 (1d8 + 5) bludgeoning damage plus 14 (4d6) acid damage. In addition, nonmagical armor worn by the target is partly dissolved and takes a permanent and cumulative −1 penalty to the AC it offers. The armor is destroyed if the penalty reduces its AC to 10.

Elemental Sizes

Acid elementals of a similar size have identical statistics, but both larger and smaller elementals are sometimes summoned if a conjurer's magic is puissant enough to bring them from their home plane. The following is used to modify the statistics of the average acid elemental presented above to create a new creature.

Small Acid Elemental

The small acid elemental has the following changes:
• Its Challenge Rating is 3 (700 XP) and its size is Small.

- Its Armor Class is 12, a Strength score of 15 (+2), and it has 60 (8d6 + 32) hit points.

- The DC for its acidic Fumes is 15.

- The Slam attack has a +4 to hit, and deals 6 (1d8 + 2) bludgeoning damage plus 7 (2d6) acid damage.

Large Acid Elemental

The large acid elemental has the following changes:

- Its Challenge Rating is 7 (2,900 XP) and its size is Large.

- Its Armor Class is 15, its Strength score is 22 (+6), its Constitution score is 20 (+5), and it has 94 (9d10 + 45) hit points.

- The DC for its acidic Fumes is 16.

- The Slam attack has a +9 to hit, and deals 19 (3d8 + 6) bludgeoning damage plus 21 (6d6) acid damage.

Huge Acid Elemental

The huge acid elemental has the following changes:

- Its Challenge Rating is 9 (5,000 XP) and its size is Huge.

- Its Armor Class is 15, its Strength score is 22 (+6), its Constitution score is 20 (+5), and it has 103 (9d12 + 45) hit points.

- The DC for its acidic Fumes is 16.

- The Slam attack has a +10 to hit, and deals 19 (3d8 + 6) bludgeoning damage plus 28 (8d6) acid damage.

Greater Acid Elemental

The greater acid elemental has the following changes:

- Its Challenge Rating is 11 (7,200 XP) and its size is Huge.

- Its Armor Class is 16, its Strength and Constitution scores are 22 (+6), and it has 137 (11d12 + 66) hit points.

- The DC for its acidic Fumes is 18.

- The Slam attack has a +10 to hit, and deals 24 (4d8 + 6) bludgeoning damage plus 35 (10d6) acid damage.

Elder Acid Elemental

The elder acid elemental has the following changes:

- Its Challenge Rating is 13 (10,000 XP) and its size is Huge.

- Its Armor Class is 17, its Strength and Constitution scores are 22 (+6), and it has 162 (13d12 + 78) hit points.

- The DC for its acidic Fumes is 18.

- The Slam attack has a +11 to hit, and deals 24 (4d8 + 6) bludgeoning damage plus 49 (14d6) acid damage.

Elemental, Gravity

Gravity Elemental

This creature resembles a miniature black hole hovering several feet off the ground. It is a circular region of absolute blackness, with a bizarre distortion around its edges as it warps light waves. Four spiraling, rotating arms of debris and light surround the circular region of darkness. Its facial features are small points of light, almost like stars.

A gravity elemental embodies the very force that controls and holds together the fabric of the universe. The actual elemental is a tiny, superdense ball of matter deep within a zone of darkness and spiraling arms of debris that comprise the body of the elemental. A gravity elemental has mass and size, but no effective weight.

Gravity elementals originate on a weird, recently discovered plane that scholars affectionately call the Plane of Gravity. The elemental's home plane is a flat, rocky place with little life, no known water sources, and no plant life or foliage. The plane is always shrouded in darkness. Dense pockets of intense gravity and areas of little or no gravity dot the barren landscape. Gravity elementals seem to be able to converse with others of their kind by manipulating gravity itself.

Gravity elementals attack primarily by flailing at their opponents with multiple arms, each one a mixture of fluctuating fields of micro-gravity and debris that has been sucked into its gravity well. These creatures can also attack by adjusting the local gravity fields around themselves.

Medium Gravity Elemental

Medium elemental, neutral
Armor Class 13
Hit Points 75 (10d8 + 30)
Speed 0 ft., fly 40 ft.

STR	DEX	CON	INT	WIS	CHA
10 (+0)	10 (+0)	17 (+3)	4 (–3)	11 (+0)	11 (+0)

Skills Perception +3, Stealth +6
Damage Resistances bludgeoning, piercing, and slashing from nonmagical weapons
Damage Immunities poison
Condition Immunities exhaustion, grappled, paralyzed, petrified, poisoned, prone, restrained, unconscious
Senses darkvision 60 ft., passive Perception 13
Languages —
Challenge 5 (1,800 XP)

Distortion. The gravity elemental's Armor Class includes its Constitution modifier. In addition, the gravity elemental can hide when only lightly obscured by bending light around it.

Singularity. The gravity elemental is immune to spells and effects that would push, pull, or move it.

Actions

Gravity Field. The gravity elemental manipulates the very forces of nature and chooses one of the effects below.

Lift. The gravity elemental uses an action to manipulate the surrounding gravity to lift up to two objects weighing no more than 100 pounds that are within 20 feet of it. It can then use a bonus action to hurl both objects at a creature it can detect within 20 feet. The targets must make a DC 14 Dexterity saving throw, taking 12 (2d8 + 3) bludgeoning damage on a failed saving throw, or half as much damage on a success. A gravity elemental can drop an object it is lifting without taking an action.

Hold. The gravity elemental increases local gravity. Creatures within 20 feet of the elemental must succeed on a DC 14 Strength saving throw or be restrained until the beginning of the elemental's next turn.

Crush (2/day). The gravity elemental greatly increases local gravity within a 20-foot radius of itself. All creatures, other than the elemental, within that area make a DC 14 Constitution saving throw, taking 30 (5d10 + 3) force damage on a failed saving throw, or half as much damage on a success.

Engulf. The gravity elemental attempts to engulf one target it can see within 5 feet of it that is at least one size smaller than it. That target makes a DC 14 Dexterity saving throw. On a successful saving throw, the target is pushed 5 feet in a random direction. On a failed save, the gravity elemental enters that target's space, and the target is grappled and restrained. While restrained, a target has total cover from attacks coming from outside the elemental, and at the beginning of each of the elemental's turns, a target takes 19 (3d10 + 3) force damage. If this damage drops a target to 0 hit points, it is rendered down to its constituent atoms and cannot be brought back to life by any magic short of *true resurrection* or *wish*.

A grappled target can attempt to break free with a DC 14 Strength saving throw at the end of each of its turns, ending the effect on a success and moving 5 feet in a random direction.

Reactions

Deflection. The gravity elemental uses its reaction to deflect missile weapons that are at least one size smaller than it when it is hit with a ranged weapon attack. The damage the elemental takes from the attack is reduced by 9 (1d6 + 6). If the damage is reduced to 0, the gravity elemental can destroy the missile entirely, or cause the missile to orbit around it, and the elemental can make a ranged attack with the weapon or piece of ammunition it just caught, as part of the same reaction. The elemental has a +6 to hit with the attack, which has a normal range of 20 feet and a long range of 60 feet.

Elemental Sizes

The bizarre Plane of Gravity is host to multitudes of strange variations on the above elemental. The following variations vary in size and the strength of their manipulation of gravity.

Small Gravity Elemental

The small gravity elemental has the following changes:

- Its Challenge Rating is 3 (700 XP) and its size is Small.

- It has 52 (8d6 + 24) hit points, and a range of 15 feet for its Lift, Hold, and Crush abilities.

- The DC for all its abilities is 13.

- Its Lift ability can lift up to 50 pounds per object, and deals 7 (1d8 +3) bludgeoning damage for each of its two attacks.

- Its Crush ability can only be used once per long rest and deals 19 (3d10 + 3) force damage.

- Its Engulf ability deals 14 (2d10 + 3) force damage.

- The Deflection ability reduces damage by 8 (1d6 + 5) and has a +5 to hit when making the attack with the deflected ranged weapon.

Large Gravity Elemental

The large gravity elemental has the following changes:

- Its Challenge Rating is 7 (2,900 XP) and its size is Large.

- It has an Armor Class of 14, a Constitution score if 18 (+4), 95 (10d10 + 40) hit points, and a range of 30 feet for its Lift, Hold, and Crush abilities.

- The DC for all its abilities is 15.

- Its Lift ability can lift up to 150 pounds per object, and deals 17 (3d8 + 4) bludgeoning damage for each of its two attacks.

- Its Crush ability can be used once per short or long rest, and deals 48 (8d10 + 4) force damage.

- Its Engulf ability deals 26 (4d10 + 4) force damage.

- The Deflection ability reduces damage by 10 (1d6 + 7), and has a +7 to hit when making the attack with the deflected ranged weapon.

Huge Gravity Elemental

The huge gravity elemental has the following changes:

- Its Challenge Rating is 9 (5,000 XP) and its size is Huge.

- It has an Armor Class of 14, a Constitution score of 18 (+4), 126 (12d12 + 48) hit points, and a range of 40 feet for its Lift, Hold, and Crush abilities.

- The DC for all its abilities is 16.

- Its Lift ability can lift up to 200 pounds per object, and deals 22 (4d8 + 4) bludgeoning damage for each of its two attacks.

- Its Crush ability can be recharged on a 6, and deals 53 (9d10 + 4) force damage.

- Its Engulf ability deals 31 (5d10 + 4) force damage.

- The Deflection ability reduces damage by 11 (1d6 + 8), and has a +9 to hit when making the attack with the deflected ranged weapon.

Greater Gravity Elemental

The greater gravity elemental has the following changes:

- Its Challenge Rating is 11 (7,200 XP) and its size is Huge.

- It has an Armor Class of 15, a Constitution score of 20 (+5), 161 (14d12 + 70) hit points, and a range of 40 feet for its Lift, Hold, and Crush abilities.

- The DC for all its abilities is 17.

- Its Lift ability can lift up to 250 pounds per object, it can lift and throw up to 3 objects, and deals 23 (4d8 + 5) bludgeoning damage for each of its attacks.

- Its Crush ability can be recharged on a 5 or 6, and deals 83 (12d12 + 5) force damage.

- Its Engulf ability deals 38 (6d10 + 5) force damage.

- The Deflection ability reduces damage by 12 (1d6 + 9), and has a +9 to hit when making the attack with the deflected ranged weapon.

Elder Gravity Elemental

The elder gravity elemental has the following changes:

- Its Challenge Rating is 13 (10,000 XP) and its size is Huge.

- It has an Armor Class of 15, a Constitution score of 20 (+5), 172 (15d12 + 75) hit points, and a range of 40 feet for its Lift, Hold, and Crush abilities.

- The DC for all its abilities is 18.

- Its Lift ability can lift up to 300 pounds per object, it can lift and throw up to 3 objects, and deals 27 (5d8 + 5) bludgeoning damage for each of its attacks.

- Its Crush ability can be recharged on a 5 or 6, and deals 87 (15d10 + 5) force damage.

- Its Engulf ability deals 43 (7d10 + 5) force damage.

- The Deflection ability reduces damage by 13 (1d6 + 10), and has a +10 to hit when making the attack with the deflected ranged weapon.

Elemental, Lightning

Lightning Elemental

This creature appears as a bluish globe of electrical energy. Lightning plays off and around its body.

Lightning elementals are native to the Plane of Air, the Positive Energy Plane, and a rumored elemental plane situated in between (the Plane of Lightning). They are sometimes summoned to the Material Plane by wizards or clerics, but more often than not slip through a rift between the Material Plane and elemental plane during a lightning storm.

A lightning elemental can release small globes of electricity that hover around its body. An opponent that moves within 5 feet of a globe causes it to arc and discharge.

Medium Lightning Elemental

Medium elemental, neutral
Armor Class 15
Hit Points 67 (9d8 + 27)
Speed 0 ft., fly 50 ft.

STR	DEX	CON	INT	WIS	CHA
14 (+2)	20 (+5)	16 (+3)	4 (–3)	11 (+0)	11 (+0)

Damage Resistances acid, fire; bludgeoning, piercing, and slashing damage from nonmagical weapons
Damage Immunities lightning, poison
Condition Immunities exhaustion, grappled, paralyzed, petrified, poisoned, prone, restrained, unconscious
Senses darkvision 60 ft., passive Perception 10
Languages Auran
Challenge 6 (2,300 XP)

Lightning*.* A creature that touches the lightning elemental or hits it with a melee attack while within 5 feet of it takes 7 (2d6) lightning damage.

Water Susceptibility*.* For every 5 feet that the lightning elemental moves in water, or for every gallon of water splashed on it, it takes 1 cold damage.

Actions

Multiattack*.* The lightning elemental makes two slam attacks.

Slam*. Melee Weapon Attack:* +8 to hit, reach 5 ft., one target. *Hit:* 14 (2d8 + 5) lightning damage.

Lightning Bolt*. Ranged Spell Attack:* +8 to hit, range 20/60 ft., one target. *Hit:* 36 (7d8 + 5) lightning damage.

Globe Lightning (1/Short or Long Rest)*.* The lightning elemental discharges 3 globes of electricity that hover in its space for 1 minute. Whenever a creature enters or starts its turn within 5 feet of the elemental, one of the globes discharges. The target must make a DC 15 Dexterity saving throw, taking 9 (1d8 + 5) lightning damage on a failed saving throw, or half as much damage on a successful one. As each globe discharges, it disappears.

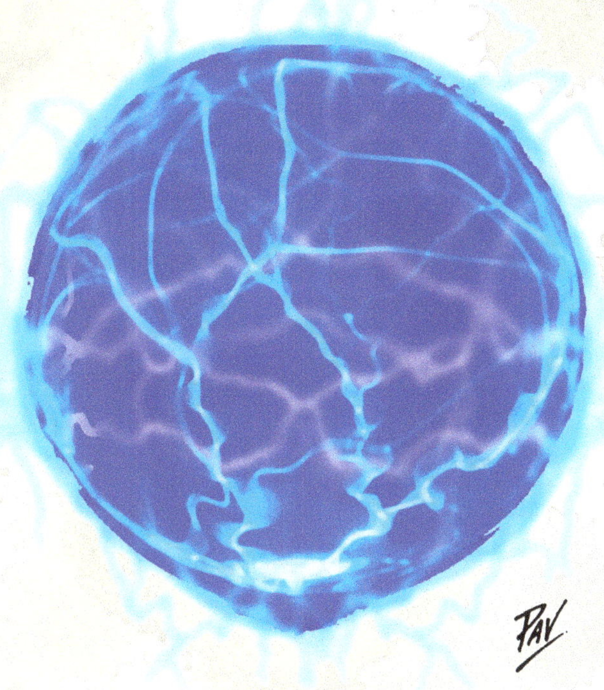

Elemental Sizes

No two lightning elementals are alike, but the different strengths of these elementals depend on their sizes. Use the following information to modify the above statistics to create lesser or greater lightning elementals.

Lesser Lightning Elemental

The lesser lightning elemental has the following changes:

- The lesser lightning elemental's Challenge Rating is 3 (700 XP), its Armor Class is 14, and it has 45 (6d8 + 18) hit points.

- Its Dexterity is 18 (+4)

- The DC for its abilities is 14.

- Its Slam has a +6 to hit, and deals 8 (1d8 + 4) lightning damage on a hit.

- Its Lightning Bolt has a +6 to hit, and deals 22 (4d8 + 4) lightning damage on a hit.

- The Globe Lighting ability can only be used once per long rest and deals 7 (1d6 + 4) lightning damage per discharge.

Greater Lightning Elemental

The greater lightning elemental has the following changes:

- The greater lightning elemental's Challenge Rating is 9 (5,000 XP), its Armor Class is 17, and it has 90 (12d8 + 36) hit points.

- Its Dexterity is 25 (+7)

- The DC for its abilities is 19.

- Its Slam has a +11 to hit, and deals 20 (3d8 + 7) lightning damage on a hit.

- Its Lightning Bolt has a +11 to hit, and deals 47 (9d8 + 7) lightning damage on a hit.

- The Globe Lightning ability recharges on a 5 or 6, and deals 16 (2d8 + 7) lightning damage per discharge.

Elemental, Obsidian

This creature is a powerfully built, roughly humanoid-shaped monolith of black stone. Its hands end in wicked, serrated and jagged claws. No facial features can be discerned.

In a realm where elemental water and elemental fire conjoin, there exists a pocket plane known as the Plane of Obsidian; a plane of barren wastes and blackened rock, of razor-sharp obelisks and fields of sharpened glass. Creatures native to this plane appear as blackened obsidian with jagged, serrated, or clear-cut angles and edges. Some have barbed spikes adorning their elemental forms.

Obsidian elementals are usually encountered on their home plane or on the Plane of Fire. Still, some can be found on the Obsidian Plain in the Plane of Molten Skies (see the *City of Brass* by **Necromancer Games**). Most, however, prefer the serenity that the Plane of Obsidian offers, and thus they rarely venture forth unless summoned.

Obsidian elementals are deadly combatants and strike with their sharpened claws, ripping and tearing at their opponents. They are relentless in their attacks and never give quarter.

Medium Obsidian Elemental

Medium elemental, neutral
Armor Class 15 (natural armor)
Hit Points 66 (7d8 + 35)
Speed 20 ft.

STR	DEX	CON	INT	WIS	CHA
18 (+4)	8 (−1)	20 (+5)	4 (−3)	11 (+0)	11 (+0)

Damage Resistances cold, fire; bludgeoning, piercing, and slashing damage from nonmagical weapons
Damage Immunities poison
Condition Immunities exhaustion, paralyzed, petrified, poisoned, unconscious
Senses darkvision 60 ft., passive Perception 10
Languages Terran
Challenge 5 (1,800 XP)

Brute. A melee weapon attack deals one extra die of its damage when the obsidian elemental hits with it (included in the attack).

Death Throes. When the obsidian elemental dies, it explodes, and each creature within 30 feet of it must make a DC 16 Dexterity saving throw, taking 17 (5d6) slashing damage and 17 (5d6) fire damage on a failed saving throw, or half as much damage on a successful one.

Molten Glass. A creature that hits the obsidian elemental with a melee attack while within 5 feet of it takes 7 (2d6) fire damage.

Actions

Multiattack. The obsidian elemental makes two claw attacks.

Claw. *Melee Weapon Attack:* +7 to hit, reach 5 ft., one target. *Hit:* 13 (2d8 + 4) slashing damage plus 4 (1d8) fire damage.

Elemental Sizes

The quasi-plane of obsidian is home to multitudes of obsidian elementals. Use the following to modify the above statistics to represent the varied power of the denizens of that plane.

Small Obsidian Elemental

The small obsidian elemental has the following changes:

• Its Challenge Rating is 2 (450 XP), its size is Small, and it has 45 (6d6 +

24) hit points.

• It has a Strength score of 16 (+3) and a Constitution score of 18 (+4).

• Its Armor Class is 14.

• Its Death Throes feature deals 10 (3d6) fire damage and 10 (3d6) slashing damage, and the DC for that ability is 14.

• Its Claw attack has a +5 to hit, and deals 10 (2d6 + 3) slashing damage plus 3 (1d6) fire damage.

Large Obsidian Elemental

The large obsidian elemental has the following changes:

• Its Challenge Rating is 8 (3,900 XP), its size is Large, and it has 94 (9d10 + 45) hit points.

• It has a Strength score of 20 (+5).

• Its Armor Class is 16.

• Its Death Throes feature deals 21 (6d6) fire damage and 21 (6d6) slashing damage, and the DC for that ability is 16.

• Its Claw attack has a +8 to hit, and deals 18 (3d8 + 5) slashing damage plus 9 (2d8) fire damage.

Huge Obsidian Elemental

The huge obsidian elemental has the following changes:

• Its Challenge Rating is 11 (7,200 XP), its size is Huge, and it has 137

(11d12 + 66) hit points.

- It has a Strength score of 20 (+5), and a Constitution score of 22 (+6).

- Its Armor Class is 17.

- Its Death Throes feature deals 31 (9d6) fire damage and 31 (9d6) slashing damage, and the DC for that ability is 18.

- Its Claw attack has a +9 to hit, and deals 23 (4d8 + 5) slashing damage plus 13 (3d8) fire damage.

Greater Obsidian Elemental

The greater obsidian elemental has the following changes:

- Its Challenge Rating is 14 (11,500 XP), its size is Huge, and it has 175 (14d12 + 84) hit points.

- It has a Strength score of 20 (+5), and a Constitution score of 22 (+6).

- Its Armor Class is 18.

- Its Death Throes feature deals 42 (12d6) fire damage and 42 (12d6) slashing damage, and the DC for that ability is 19.

- Its Claw attack has a +10 to hit, and deals 23 (4d8 + 5) slashing damage plus 13 (3d8) fire damage.

Elder Obsidian Elemental

The elder obsidian elemental has the following changes:

- Its Challenge Rating is 17 (18,000 XP), its size is Huge, and it has 225 (18d12 + 108) hit points.

- It has a Strength score of 23 (+6), and a Constitution score of 22 (+6).

- Its Armor Class is 19.

- Its Death Throes feature deals 52 (15d6) fire damage and 52 (15d6) slashing damage, and the DC for that ability is 20.

- Its Claw attack has a +12 to hit, and deals 33 (6d8 + 6) slashing damage plus 22 (5d8) fire damage.

Elemental, Time

This creature appears as a formless cloud of yellowish-red vapor or dust about 5 feet in diameter.

Time elementals are creatures from a plane most sages are unaware even exists. A time elemental is a powerful creature formed of pure time and matter such as is unknown to even the most learned of sages. It is unknown how or why time elementals enter the Material Plane, as they cannot be summoned using the standard summoning spells.

Time elementals attack by forming misty or smoky arms from their forms and lashing at opponents or by spraying a fine mist onto their opponents so as to induce aging. Against particularly powerful opponents, a time elemental uses its alter age ability or (if of the royal sort) summons additional time elementals to its aid.

Common Time Elemental

Medium elemental, neutral
Armor Class 17 (natural armor)
Hit Points 97 (13d8 + 39)
Speed 50 ft., fly 50 ft. (hover)

STR	DEX	CON	INT	WIS	CHA
16 (+3)	20 (+5)	16 (+3)	14 (+2)	14 (+2)	11 (+0)

Damage Resistance bludgeoning, piercing, and slashing from nonmagical weapons

Damage Immunities poison, psychic
Condition Immunities exhaustion, grappled, paralyzed, petrified, poisoned, prone, restrained, unconscious
Senses darkvision 60 ft., passive Perception 12
Languages telepathy 120 ft.
Challenge 7 (2,900 XP)

Cell Death. Damage dealt by the elemental can only be healed magically. In addition, a creature that is slain by a time elemental can only be restored to life by a *true resurrection* or *wish* spell.

Foresight. A time elemental can see a few seconds into the future. This ability prevents it from being surprised.

Immunity to Temporal Magic. Time elementals are immune to all time-related spells and effects that are not cast by other time elementals.

Actions

Multiattack. The time elemental makes two slam attacks.

Slam. *Melee Weapon Attack:* +8 to hit, reach 5 ft., one target. *Hit:* 14 (2d8 + 5) bludgeoning damage.

Multi-Manifestation (Recharge 5–6). The time elemental summons 1d4 duplicate manifestations of itself from alternate dimensions. Each of these manifestations have the same statistics of the time elemental but can only use melee attacks. Each manifestation can move and attack immediately after it is summoned. Attacks that deal damage to one manifestation deal the same damage to the elemental and the other manifestations.

The elemental can have no more than four manifestations under its control at any time. The manifestations disappear at the start of the elemental's next turn.

Time Jaunt. A time elemental can slip through the time stream and appear anywhere on the same plane of existence as if by *teleport*. This

ability transports the time elemental and up to four other creatures of the elemental's choice that are within 30 feet of it. Unwilling creatures must succeed on a DC 15 Wisdom saving throw to avoid being carried away.

Noble Time Elemental

Large elemental, neutral
Armor Class 18 (natural armor)
Hit Points 123 (13d10 + 52)
Speed 50 ft., fly 50 ft. (hover)

STR	DEX	CON	INT	WIS	CHA
18 (+4)	20 (+5)	18 (+4)	18 (+4)	18 (+4)	15 (+2)

Saving Throws Con +9, Wis +9, Cha +7
Skills Insight +9, Perception +9, Stealth +10
Damage Resistance bludgeoning, piercing, and slashing from nonmagical weapons
Damage Immunities poison, psychic
Condition Immunities exhaustion, grappled, paralyzed, petrified, poisoned, prone, restrained, unconscious
Senses darkvision 60 ft., passive Perception 19
Languages telepathy 120 ft.
Challenge 13 (10,000 XP)

Cell Death. Damage dealt by the elemental can only be healed magically. In addition, a creature that is slain by a time elemental can only be restored to life by a *true resurrection* or *wish* spell.

Foresight. A time elemental can see a few seconds into the future. This ability prevents it from being surprised.

Immunity to Temporal Magic. Time elementals are immune to all time-related spells and effects that are not cast by other time elementals.

Actions

Multiattack. The time elemental makes two slam attacks.

Slam. Melee Weapon Attack: +10 to hit, reach 5 ft., one target. *Hit:* 18 (3d8 + 5) bludgeoning damage.

Alter Age (1/day). The elemental can attempt to age a target creature within 5 feet of it. The target must make a DC 17 Constitution saving throw or be aged 1d4 x 10 years. The aging effect can be reversed with a *greater restoration* spell, but only within 24 hours of it occurring.

Multi-Manifestation (Recharge 5–6). The time elemental summons 1d4 duplicate manifestations of itself from alternate dimensions. Each of these manifestations have the same statistics of the time elemental but can only use melee attacks. Each manifestation can move and attack immediately after it is summoned. Attacks that deal damage to one manifestation deal the same damage to the elemental and the other manifestations.

The elemental can have no more than four manifestations under its control at any time. The manifestations disappear at the start of the elemental's next turn.

Temporal Displacement (1/day). The time elemental can remove a target creature from the current timeline. The target must succeed on a DC 18 Constitution saving throw, or disappear in a flash of white energy. For a number of minutes equal to the time elemental's Wisdom modifier, it is as if the displaced creature never existed. The creature is completely undetectable while in this state.

A displaced creature can use its action to attempt to end the displacement. When it does so, it makes a DC 18 Intelligence check. If it succeeds, it escapes, and the effect ends.

When the effect ends, the creature reappears in the same space it was in before being displaced. If the space is occupied when the creature returns, it appears in the nearest open space and takes no damage.

Time Jaunt. A time elemental can slip through the time stream and appear anywhere on the same plane of existence as if by *teleport*. This ability transports the time elemental and up to four other creatures of the elemental's choice that are within 30 feet of it. Unwilling creatures must succeed on a DC 15 Wisdom saving throw to avoid being carried away.

Royal Time Elemental

Large elemental, neutral
Armor Class 20 (natural armor)
Hit Points 380 (40d10 + 160)
Speed 50 ft., fly 50 ft. (hover)

STR	DEX	CON	INT	WIS	CHA
18 (+4)	20 (+5)	18 (+4)	21 (+5)	21 (+5)	20 (+5)

Saving Throws Con +10, Wis +11, Cha +11
Skills Insight +11, Perception +11, Stealth +11
Damage Resistance bludgeoning, piercing, and slashing from nonmagical weapons
Damage Immunities poison, psychic
Condition Immunities exhaustion, grappled, paralyzed, petrified, poisoned, prone, restrained, unconscious
Senses darkvision 60 ft., passive Perception 21
Languages telepathy 120 ft.
Challenge 17 (18,000 XP)

Cell Death. Damage dealt by the elemental can only be healed magically. In addition, a creature that is slain by a time elemental can only be restored to life by a *true resurrection* or *wish* spell.

Foresight. A time elemental can see a few seconds into the future. This ability prevents it from being surprised.

Immunity to Temporal Magic. Time elementals are immune to all time-related spells and effects that are not cast by other time elementals.

Actions

Multiattack. The time elemental makes two slam attacks.

Slam. Melee Weapon Attack: +11 to hit, reach 5 ft., one target. *Hit:* 23 (4d8 + 5) bludgeoning damage.

Alter Age (1/day). The elemental can attempt to age a target creature within 5 feet of it. The target must make a DC 17 Constitution saving throw or be aged 1d4 x 10 years. The aging effect can be reversed with a *greater restoration* spell, but only within 24 hours of it occurring.

Multi-Manifestation (Recharge 5–6). The time elemental summons 1d4 duplicate manifestations of itself from alternate dimensions. Each of these manifestations have the same statistics of the time elemental but can only use melee attacks. Each manifestation can move and attack immediately after it is summoned. Attacks that deal damage to one manifestation deal the same damage to the elemental and the other manifestations.

The elemental can have no more than four manifestations under its control at any time. The manifestations disappear at the start of the elemental's next turn.

Temporal Displacement (1/day). The time elemental can remove a target creature from the current timeline. The target must succeed on a DC 18 Constitution saving throw, or disappear in a flash of white energy. For a number of minutes equal to the time elemental's Wisdom modifier, it is as if the displaced creature never existed. The creature is completely undetectable while in this state.

A displaced creature can use its action to attempt to end the displacement. When it does so, it makes a DC 18 Intelligence check. If it succeeds, it escapes, and the effect ends.

When the effect ends, the creature reappears in the same space it was in before being displaced. If the space is occupied when the creature returns, it appears in the nearest open space and takes no damage.

Time Jaunt. A time elemental can slip through the time stream and appear anywhere on the same plane of existence as if by *teleport*. This ability transports the time elemental and up to four other creatures of the elemental's choice that are within 30 feet of it. Unwilling creatures must succeed on a DC 15 Wisdom saving throw to avoid being carried away.

Elemental Dragons

Elemental Air Dragon

This massive creature resembles a huge dragon composed of air and vapor. Its great wings are translucent and look like wisps of smoke. Its eyes are hollow sockets of mist though a glint of bright sunlight can occasionally be seen dancing across their surfaces. Its great tail appears as wisps of smoke or vapor and seems to trail off into nothingness.

The Plane of Air is home to many creatures. Yet none are as feared as the elemental air dragons. Their great form and majestic aura strike fear into the bravest of souls. Elemental air dragons are as evil as their brethren (the other elemental dragons) and take joy and pride in swooping over a settlement or village and destroying it with their great wing buffet. Watching the frightened creatures flee in terror provokes some sort of perverse excitement in these dragons. Luckily, elemental air dragons rarely enter the Material Plane. Elemental air dragons dislike cloud dragons and mist dragons and seek to slay them whenever encountered. The average air elemental dragon is 30 feet long.

Elemental air dragons attack by swooping on their prey, unleashing a blast of superheated air, and then flying away. An elemental air dragon rarely, if ever, touches the ground. It often employs its cyclone buffet to knock more powerful creatures prone, then swoops in to blast them with its breath weapon or rend them with its claws and bite.

Elemental Air Dragon

Huge elemental, neutral evil
Armor Class 15
Hit Points 312 (25d12 + 150)
Speed 40 ft., fly 80 ft.

STR	DEX	CON	INT	WIS	CHA
27 (+8)	20 (+5)	23 (+6)	16 (+3)	15 (+2)	19 (+4)

Saving Throws Dex +11, Con +12, Wis +8, Cha +10
Skills Arcana +9, Nature +9, Perception +14, Stealth +11
Damage Resistances lightning, thunder; bludgeoning, piercing, and slashing from nonmagical weapons
Damage Immunities poison
Condition Immunities exhaustion, grappled, paralyzed, petrified, poisoned, prone, restrained, unconscious
Senses blindsight 60 ft., darkvision 120 ft., passive Perception 24
Languages Auran, Common
Challenge 17 (18,000 XP)

Innate Spellcasting. The elemental dragon's innate spellcasting is Charisma (spell save DC 18, +10 to hit with spell attacks). It can cast the following spell requiring no material components.

At will: *gust of wind*
3/day each: *call lightning, wind wall*
1/day each: *control weather, plane shift*

Legendary Resistance (3/day). If the dragon fails a saving throw, it can choose to succeed instead.

Actions

Multiattack. The dragon makes three attacks: one with its bite and two with its claws.

Bite. *Melee Weapon Attack:* +14 to hit, reach 10 ft., one target. *Hit:* 19 (2d10 + 8) piercing damage plus 10 (3d6) fire damage.

Claw. *Melee Weapon Attack:* +14 to hit, reach 5 ft., one target. *Hit:* 15 (2d6 + 8) slashing damage.

Tail. *Melee Weapon Attack:* +14 to hit, reach 15 ft., one target. *Hit:* 17 (2d8 + 8) bludgeoning damage.

Scalding Breath (Recharge 5–6). The dragon releases a 60-foot cone of superheated air that wraps around corners. Creatures within the area must make a DC 21 Constitution saving throw, taking 63 (18d6) fire damage on a failed saving throw, or half as much damage on a successful one.

Whirlwind (Recharge 5–6). The dragon creates a cyclone in a 30-foot radius centered on itself. Creatures, other than the dragon, within the area can only move half their normal movement, nonmagical ranged attacks automatically fail, and all nonmagical unprotected flames are automatically extinguished. Large or smaller creatures within the area must also succeed on a DC 21 Strength saving throw. On a failed saving throw, the creature takes 20 (3d8 + 7) bludgeoning damage and is knocked prone and pushed 30 in a random direction. On a successful saving throw, the creature takes half damage and is not otherwise affected.

The dragon can take 3 legendary actions, choosing from the options below. Only one legendary action option can be used at a time and only at the end of another creature's turn. The dragon regains spent legendary actions at the start of its turn.

Detect. The dragon makes a Wisdom (Perception) check.

Tail Attack. The dragon makes a tail attack.

Wing Attack (Costs 2 Actions). The dragon beats its wings. Each creature within 15 feet of the dragon must succeed on a DC 21 Dexterity saving throw or take 15 (2d6 + 8) bludgeoning damage and be knocked prone. The dragon can then fly up to half its flying speed.

Elemental Earth Dragon

This creature resembles a 30-foot-long dragon composed of stone and earth. Its great wings glisten like polished stone. Its eyes are deep gray and its roar seems to shake the very earth itself.

Elemental earth dragons are the strongest of the elemental dragons. Using their great stone tail or earthen claws, they can destroy almost anything in short order. The majority of their time is spent burrowing through the Plane of Earth devouring gems, minerals, and silicate life forms. On occasion, they are summoned to the Material Plane by evil (and foolish) spellcasters who usually live just long enough to regret their mistake. Elemental earth dragons are evil (perhaps the evilest of the elemental dragons in addition to being the strongest) and despise most other forms of life. They rarely associate with other creatures, though a few have been known to have dealings with the occasional earth elemental. Elemental earth dragons cannot enter water; they must burrow under it or walk around it. The average elemental earth dragon is 30 feet long. Its roar can be heard up to 5 miles away.

Elemental earth dragons prefer to attack from ambush and secret rather than using a direct frontal assault. An elemental earth dragon lies in wait using its freeze ability or meld into stone ability and springs to attack when its prey comes into range. They are also fond of burrowing

into the ground and surfacing under their prey, thereby gaining total surprise. Slain opponents are processed and absorbed into the body of the elemental earth dragon.

Elemental Earth Dragon

Huge elemental, neutral evil
Armor Class 20 (natural armor)
Hit Points 362 (25d12 + 200)
Speed 40 ft., burrow 40 ft., fly 80 ft.

STR	DEX	CON	INT	WIS	CHA
28 (+9)	10 (+0)	26 (+8)	14 (+2)	16 (+3)	19 (+4)

Saving Throws Dex +6, Con +14, Wis +9, Cha +10
Skills Arcana +8, Nature +8, Perception +15, Stealth +6
Damage Vulnerabilities thunder
Damage Resistances bludgeoning, piercing, and slashing from nonmagical weapons
Damage Immunities acid, poison
Condition Immunities exhaustion, paralyzed, petrified, poisoned, unconscious
Senses tremorsense 60 ft., blindsight 60 ft., darkvision 120 ft., passive Perception 25
Languages Common, Terran
Challenge 19 (22,000 XP)

Earth Glide. The dragon can burrow through nonmagical, unworked earth and stone. While doing so, the elemental doesn't disturb the material it moves through.

False Appearance. While the dragon remains motionless, it is indistinguishable from a normal statue of a dragon.

Innate Spellcasting. The dragon's innate spellcasting ability is Charisma (spell save DC 18, +10 to hit with spell attacks). It can cast the following spells, requiring no material components.

At will: *meld into stone, stone shape*

3/day: *wall of stone*

1/day: *plane shift*

Legendary Resistance (3/day). If the dragon fails a saving throw, it can choose to succeed instead.

Siege Monster. The dragon deals double damage to objects and structures.

Actions

Multiattack. The dragon can make three attacks: one with its bite and two with its claws.

Bite. *Melee Weapon Attack:* +15 to hit, reach 10 ft., one target. *Hit:* 20 (2d10 + 9) piercing damage plus 10 (3d6) fire damage.

Claw. *Melee Weapon Attack:* +15 to hit, reach 5 ft., one target. *Hit:* 16 (2d6 + 9) slashing damage.

Tail. *Melee Weapon Attack:* +15 to hit, reach 15 ft., one target. *Hit:* 18 (2d8 + 9) bludgeoning damage.

Shale and Stone Breath (Recharge 5–6). The dragon releases a 60-foot cone of sand and gravel. Creatures within the area must make a DC 22 Constitution saving throw, taking 35 (10d6) fire damage plus 35 (10d6) bludgeoning damage on a failed saving throw, or half as much damage on a successful one. A creature slain by this damage has its body pulverized; it can only be restored to life by *true resurrection* or *wish*.

The dragon can take 3 legendary actions, choosing from the options below. Only one legendary action option can be used at a time and only at the end of another creature's turn. The dragon regains spent legendary actions at the start of its turn.

Detect. The dragon makes a Wisdom (Perception) check.

Tail Attack. The dragon makes a tail attack.

Wing Attack (Costs 2 Actions). The dragon beats its wings. Each creature within 15 feet of the dragon must succeed on a DC 23 Dexterity saving throw or take 16 (2d6 + 9) bludgeoning damage and be knocked prone. The dragon can then fly up to half its flying speed.

Elemental Fire Dragon

This creature appears as a 30-foot-long dragon composed of fire. Its eyes burn with a white-hot flame and flames lick the dragon's great mouth as it roars. As it flies overhead, its wings send sheets of flame roaring into the sky and crashing into the ground.

One of the most feared creatures from the Plane of Fire is the dreaded elemental fire dragon. They make their homes in the heart of the many volcanoes that dot the elemental landscape. Composed entirely of flames, these magnificent creatures fear little and are respected and feared by those that have encountered them. Elemental fire dragons are malign, vicious, and thoroughly evil. They delight in killing and torturing others, especially magmin (whom they relish as a delicacy). They often employ salamanders to aid them in their adventures, but once they have accomplished their goals, any surviving salamanders are usually devoured. Elemental fire dragons cannot enter water or any other nonflammable liquid, but they can fly or step over it. The typical elemental fire dragon is at least 30 feet long.

Elemental fire dragons are ruthless adversaries. They care nothing for treasure or anything of value. An elemental fire dragon attempts to annihilate its opponents using any means possible.

Elemental Fire Dragon

Huge elemental, neutral evil
Armor Class 15
Hit Points 445 (33d12 + 231)
Speed 40 ft., fly 80 ft.

STR	DEX	CON	INT	WIS	CHA
27 (+8)	20 (+5)	25 (+7)	16 (+3)	13 (+1)	21 (+5)

Saving Throws Dex +12, Con +14, Wis +8, Cha +12
Skills Arcana +10, Nature +10, Perception +15, Stealth +12
Damage Vulnerabilities cold
Damage Resistances bludgeoning, piercing, and slashing from nonmagical weapons
Damage Immunities fire, poison
Condition Immunities exhaustion, grappled, paralyzed, petrified, poisoned, prone, restrained, unconscious
Senses blindsight 60 ft., darkvision 120 ft., passive Perception 25
Languages Common, Ignan
Challenge 21 (33,000 XP)

Fiery Aura. At the start of each of the dragon's turns, each creature within 15 feet of it takes 14 (4d6) fire damage, and flammable objects in the aura that aren't being worn or carried ignite. A creature that touches the dragon or hits it with a melee attack while within 5 feet of it takes 14 (4d6) fire damage.

Illumination. The dragon sheds bright light in a 30-foot radius and dim light in an additional 30 feet.

Innate Spellcasting. The dragon's innate spellcasting ability is Charisma (spell save DC 20, +12 to hit withy spell attacks). It can cast the following spells, requiring no material components:

At will: *fireball, heat metal*

3/day each: *fire storm*

1/day each: *incendiary cloud, plane shift*

Legendary Resistance (3/day). If the dragon fails a saving throw, it can choose to succeed instead.

Water Susceptibility. For every 5 feet that the dragon moves in water, or for every gallon of water splashed on it, it takes 1 cold damage.

Actions

Multiattack. The dragon can make three attacks: one with its bite and two with its claws.

Bite. *Melee Weapon Attack:* +15 to hit, reach 10 ft., one target. *Hit:* 19 (2d10 + 8) piercing damage plus 14 (4d6) fire damage.

Claw. *Melee Weapon Attack:* +15 to hit, reach 5 ft., one target. *Hit:* 15 (2d6 + 8) slashing damage.

Tail. *Melee Weapon Attack:* +15 to hit, reach 15 ft., one target. *Hit:* 17 (2d8 + 8) bludgeoning damage.

Elemental Fire Breath (Recharge 5–6). The dragon breathes a 60-foot cone of elemental fire. Creatures in the area must make a DC 22 Dexterity saving throw, taking 77 (22d6) fire damage on a failed saving throw, or half as much damage on a successful one.

Legendary Actions

The dragon can take 3 legendary actions, choosing from the options below. Only one legendary action option can be used at a time and only at the end of another creature's turn. The dragon regains spent legendary actions at the start of its turn.

Detect. The dragon makes a Wisdom (Perception) check.

Tail Attack. The dragon makes a tail attack.

Wing Attack (Costs 2 Actions). The dragon beats its wings. Each creature within 15 feet of the dragon must succeed on a DC 23 Dexterity saving throw or take 15 (2d6 + 8) bludgeoning damage and be knocked prone. The dragon can then fly up to half its flying speed.

Rain of Fire (Costs 3 Actions). The elemental fire dragon beats its wings, casting fire out in a 100-foot sphere around itself. All creatures within the area must make a DC 22 Dexterity saving throw, taking 14 (4d6) fire damage on a failed saving throw, or half as much damage on a successful one. Objects not held or worn are set alight and continue burning until extinguished.

Elemental Water Dragon

This creature resembles a massive dragon composed entirely of water. Its wings slosh and drip water as it moves them. Its great mouth opens into a maw of inky darkness. Water drips from its fangs.

From the Plane of Water comes the elemental water dragon (also called water wyrm by some sages). They make their homes in the deep oceans of the Material Plane and are rarely found far away from large expanses of water. An elemental water dragon is composed entirely of water and commands respect from the more intelligent sea creatures as well as those humanoids that ply their trade upon the waters. Elemental water dragons are evil and take great pleasure in demanding sacrifice from those that dare enter their realm. If the sacrifice placates the dragon, it lets the creature pass unabated; otherwise, it attacks with all of its might and most often destroys those that offend it or fail to appease its desires. Water dragons take great pleasure in capsizing and sinking ships. Particularly evil water dragons may accept a sacrifice and then sink the ship of those that crossed its path anyway. On occasion, a group of skum or other evil aquatic creatures can be found allied with an elemental water dragon, but this alliance is usually short-lived and often shaky. It generally ends with the elemental water dragon feeding on its former allies.

Elemental water dragons prefer to fight in or near water where they can use their transparency and water mastery abilities to full advantage. They prefer to attack from ambush, often lying in wait for their opponents and then springing from the waves to assault their foes.

Elemental Water Dragon

Huge elemental, neutral evil
Armor Class 17
Hit Points 310 (27d12 + 135)
Speed 40 ft., fly 60 ft., swim 80 ft.

STR	DEX	CON	INT	WIS	CHA
25 (+7)	24 (+7)	21 (+5)	16 (+3)	14 (+2)	19 (+4)

Saving Throws Dex +13, Con +11, Wis +8, Cha +10
Skills Arcana +9, Nature +9, Perception +14, Stealth +13
Damage Resistances acid; bludgeoning, piercing, and slashing from nonmagical weapons
Damage Immunities poison
Condition Immunities exhaustion, grappled, paralyzed, petrified, poisoned, prone, restrained, unconscious
Senses blindsight 60 ft., darkvision 120 ft., passive Perception 24
Languages Aquan, Common
Challenge 17 (18,000 XP)

Freeze. If the elemental water dragon takes cold damage, it partially freezes; its speed is reduced by 20 feet until the end of its next turn.

Innate Spellcasting. The dragon's innate spellcasting ability is Charisma (spell save DC 18, +10 to hit with spell attacks). It can cast the following spells, requiring no material components:

At will: *create or destroy water*
3/day: *control water*
1/day each: *control weather, plane shift*

Legendary Resistance (3/day). If the dragon fails a saving throw, it can choose to succeed instead.

Siege Monster. The dragon deals double damage to objects and structures.

Actions

Multiattack. The dragon can make three attacks: one with its bite and two with its claws.

Bite. *Melee Weapon Attack:* +13 to hit, reach 10 ft., one target. *Hit:* 18 (2d10 + 7) piercing damage.

Claw. *Melee Weapon Attack:* +13 to hit, reach 5 ft., one target. *Hit:* 14 (2d6 + 7) slashing damage.

Tail. *Melee Weapon Attack:* +13 to hit, reach 15 ft., one target. *Hit:* 16 (2d8 + 7) bludgeoning damage.

Steam Breath (Recharge 5–6). The dragon exhales a 60-foot cone of superheated steam that spreads around corners. Creatures within the area must make DC 19 Dexterity saving throws, taking 63 (18d6) fire damage on a failed saving throw, or half as much on a successful one. Being underwater does not provide resistance to this effect.

Bonus Actions

Drench. The elemental water dragon can extinguish any one nonmagical flame or one magical flame created by a 5th level or lower spell it can see within 15 feet of it.

Legendary Actions

The dragon can take 3 legendary actions, choosing from the options below. Only one legendary action option can be used at a time and only at the end of another creature's turn. The dragon regains spent legendary actions at the start of its turn.

Detect. The dragon makes a Wisdom (Perception) check.

Tail Attack. The dragon makes a tail attack.

Wing Attack (Costs 2 Actions). The dragon beats its wings. Each creature within 15 feet of the dragon must succeed on a DC 19 Dexterity saving throw or take 14 (2d6 + 7) bludgeoning damage and be knocked prone. The dragon can then fly up to half its flying speed.

Elusa Hound

This powerful wolf-like dog has coarse white fur and pale white skin, and a short, bushy tail. Its eyes are a sickly yellow in color and its teeth are bone white.

Elusa hounds are used by different creatures for different reasons; though ultimately there have but one purpose: tracking (and often killing) magic-wielders. These creatures can detect the emanations given off by arcane and divine spellcasters and use this scent to track them. The origins of the elusa hounds have mystified even the most learned of sages, for though they seem to be born of magic, no spellcaster in his or her right mind would ever create such a beast.

Renegade bands enthralled with the idea of ridding the world of spellcasters sometimes employ them. Civilized towns and cities likewise use them in places where magic is forbidden or policed by the local government. In other instances, they are used by spellcasters to ferret out rivals.

When given instructions to track and kill their target, a pack of elusa hounds uses tactics similar to other canine animals: circle the prey and attack simultaneously from the front, rear, and flanks. These beasts can easily be trained to pin or hold a foe rather than kill it. This tactic is often employed by military or government units when they wish to capture and interrogate a renegade spellcaster. When using these tactics, the elusa hound attempts to trip its foe and then pins it with a bite. Elusa hounds radiate a moderate aura of divination magic if examined with detect magic or the like.

Elusa Hound

Medium monstrosity, unaligned

Armor Class 12
Hit Points 26 (4d8 + 8)
Speed 50 ft.

STR	DEX	CON	INT	WIS	CHA
15 (+2)	15 (+2)	15 (+2)	6 (–2)	12 (+1)	8 (–1)

Skills Athletics +4, Perception +3, Survival +3
Senses darkvision 60 ft., passive Perception 13
Languages understands Common but can't speak
Challenge 1 (200 XP)

Arcane Sight. Elusa hounds can perceive magical auras from active spells, magical effects, and magic items within a radius of 120 feet. Once an elusa hound has seen one of the above, it has advantage on Wisdom (Survival) checks to track the origin of the effect for 24 hours.

Keen Hearing and Smell. The elusa hound has advantage on Wisdom (Perception) checks that rely on hearing or smell.

Actions

Bite. *Melee Weapon Attack:* +4 to hit, reach 5 ft., one target. *Hit:* 5 (1d6 + 2) piercing damage. If the target is a creature, it must succeed on a DC 11 Strength saving throw or be knocked prone and grappled. The elusa hound can only grapple one creature at a time.

Encephalon Gorger

This creature is a sleek, pale-skinned humanoid with leathery white, semi-translucent flesh. It is a bit taller than an average human. Its features are delicate and precise. The creature's arms and legs are spindly, and each ends in four digits. This creature is completely hairless and its eyes are small, with nictitating membranes.

Encephalon gorgers (sometimes known as cranial vampires) are malevolent creatures from another dimension or plane of existence. They are greatly feared by intelligent creatures, for they use such beings (their brain fluid to be exact) to power their great cities. Many of these creatures have constructed strongholds or outposts on the Material Plane, though it is unknown when they first appeared.

Encephalon gorgers dislike direct sunlight, though they are not harmed by it. When traveling aboveground during daylight hours, they usually cloak themselves in robes of gray or black. The gorger's leathery, whitish flesh is nearly translucent, and in older encephalon gorgers, one can faintly see veins and other organs pushing grayish-brown blood through its body. Its mouth is lined with short, needlelike teeth, with the canines being most pronounced (perhaps the reason these monsters are sometimes called cranial vampires).

Encephalon gorgers enter battle using their claws to slash and grapple their foes, going first for targets with the most delicious, intelligent brains. Once it grabs its prey, it sinks its teeth into the foe's head, draining it of cerebral fluid. However, an encephalon gorger will not put itself in danger by ignoring other threats around it, so generally, it only drinks when all of its other foes are either dead or engaged with others of its kind. Encephalon gorgers often make use of slave creatures and dumb beasts to engage an enemy's warriors while it sidles behind its chosen victim. Often times, an encephalon gorger attempts to capture rather than kill its prey, especially in the case of intelligent humanoids. Captured prey are taken to one of their alien cities, where they are handed over to the Breeders who tend the slave pits. Encephalon gorgers advance by character level; many have levels in wizard or psionic-oriented classes. At least one such gorger capable of interplanar travel is always present in any Prime Material Plane outpost.

Encephalon Gorger Society

Encephalon gorgers refer to themselves as Silians, and they make their homes deep beneath the surface world or hidden far away from prying eyes (cloaked by natural occurrences such as fog or mist or hidden by magic). Underground lairs resemble great domed cities, while those on the surface resemble iron fortresses of exquisite craftsmanship. Each lair, regardless of its location, has dozens of slave pits and breeding pens filled with captured, intelligent humanoids (or other creatures). The slaves are maintained by a specialized group of Silians called the Breeders. It is their job to tend to the food supply of the city at all times and to gauge the relative worth of each and every humanoid used by the gorgers for feeding.

Encephalon gorgers sometimes trade with other races, usually trading for slaves, who are taken to the Breeders. Other slaves are kept by particular encephalon gorgers and assigned menial tasks. Once such a slave has exhausted its usefulness, it is "recycled" in the food pens so long as it isn't dead. Dead slaves are discarded, then ground up into a bland paste that is fed to the other slaves.

Little is known of particulars regarding the gorger's society such as reproduction, lifespan, aging patterns, and so on. A few things that are known come from a group of adventurers that saw one of the iron fortresses and lived to tell about it. They spoke of large vats filled with cranial fluid maintained by the Breeders and of young Silian being grown in these vats. They also spoke of the horrid squalor of the breeding pits and the slaves kept in them.

Encephalon Gorger

Medium aberration, chaotic evil
Armor Class 16 (natural armor)
Hit Points 71 (11d8 + 22)
Speed 30 ft.

STR	DEX	CON	INT	WIS	CHA
12 (+1)	16 (+3)	14 (+2)	20 (+5)	15 (+2)	15 (+2)

Skills Perception +5, Stealth +6
Senses darkvision 60 ft., passive Perception 15
Languages Common, Deep Speech, telepathy 120 ft.
Challenge 7 (2,900 XP)

Alien Mind. Encephalon gorgers can maintain concentration on 3 simultaneous spell effects.

Mindsense. The encephalon gorger is aware of the presence of creatures within 300 feet of it that have an Intelligence of 3 or higher. It knows the relative distance and direction of each creature, as well as the creature's approximate Intelligence score (within 3 points). Creatures under the effects of magic that protects the mind cannot be detected by the encephalon gorger.

Mind Screen. The mind of an encephalon gorger is an alien and dangerous place. Should a creature attempt to scan the mind or read the thoughts of an encephalon gorger (with *detect thoughts*, telepathy, or the like), it must succeed on a DC 15 Intelligence saving throw or be driven insane, gaining a flaw from the Indefinite Madness table (see the SRD). On a successful save, the creature is confused for 1 minute (as the *confusion* spell).

Actions

Multiattack. The encephalon gorger makes two attacks with its claws and uses Mindfeed if it has a creature grappled.

Claws. *Melee Weapon Attack:* +6 to hit, reach 5 ft., one target. *Hit:* 10 (2d6 + 3) slashing damage If the target is Medium or smaller, it is grappled (escape DC 16). Until this grapple ends, the target is restrained, and the encephalon gorger can only use its Mindfeed on the grappled creature and has advantage on attack rolls to do so.

Mindfeed. *Melee Weapon Attack:* +6 to hit, reach 5 ft., one creature that is grappled by the encephalon gorger. *Hit:* 7 (1d8 + 3) piercing damage, and the target must succeed on a DC 15 Intelligence saving throw, or take 33 (6d10), and the target's Intelligence score is reduced by 1d4. The target dies if this reduces its Intelligence to 0. Otherwise, the reduction lasts until the target finishes a long rest.

Adrenal Surge (2/day). The encephalon gorger surges with adrenaline until the end of its turn. While under this effect, it gains a +2 bonus to its AC, it has advantage on Dexterity saving throw, and it gains an additional action on its turn (as the *haste* spell).

Eye Killer

This human-sized creature looks like a cross between a bat and a snake. Its upper torso resembles that of a large black bat while its lower torso appears to be that of a green and yellow scaled snake. Dark green fur covers its upper body. Its eyes are large, lidless white circles and are without pupils.

Eye killers are subterranean dwellers that hate daylight. They dwell underground in dark places, where very little light can touch their sensitive eyes. They are evil, malicious creatures that delight in killing others, particularly those that wander to close to their lair. Eye killers seem to communicate with each other through a series of low rumbles and growls. They do not speak any known language.

Eye killers are limbless spherical things at birth, but take form as they develop, reaching maturity within a year. The average adult eye killer reaches a length of 7 feet. Its bat-like wings are useless, as the eye killer cannot fly.

The eye killer is very territorial and attacks any living creature that enters an area currently under its watchful eye. If the intruders a wield light source (magical flame, a lantern, or the like), the eye killer attacks using its eye ray ability by absorbing the light (from the source) into its eyes and releasing it in a bright flash of yellow light at its chosen target; otherwise, it dispatches the trespassers by grappling with its tail and squeezing. Eye killers flee if confronted with bright light, but otherwise are relentless in combat and always fight to the death.

Eye Killer

Medium monstrosity, chaotic evil
Armor Class 13
Hit Points 65 (10d8 + 20)
Speed 30 ft.

STR	DEX	CON	INT	WIS	CHA
17 (+3)	16 (+3)	14 (+2)	2 (−4)	13 (+1)	12 (+1)

Skills Perception +5, Stealth +5
Senses darkvision 120 ft., passive Perception 15
Languages —
Challenge 2 (450 XP)

Sunlight Vulnerability. If a source of sunlight is brought within 5 feet of the eye killer, the eye killer becomes frightened for 1 minute. While frightened, the eye killer must end any grapple it is maintaining and use its action to Dash away from the source of sunlight.

Actions

Tail Slap. *Melee Weapon Attack:* +5 to hit, reach 5 ft., one target. *Hit:* 14 (2d10 + 3) bludgeoning damage and the target is grappled (escape DC 13). At the beginning of each of the eye killer's turns, a grappled creature takes 14 (2d10 + 3) bludgeoning damage.

Death Ray (1/day). If the eye killer begins its turn within an area of bright light or dim light, it can immediately douse that source of light if it is created by a spell of 3rd level or lower. When it does so, it absorbs and redirects the light in a 60-foot line that is 5 feet across. Creatures in the area must make a DC 13 Dexterity saving throw. On a failed saving throw, the target drops to 0 hit points and begins dying. On a successful saving throw, the target takes 10 (3d6) radiant damage.

Umbral Eye Killer

The umbral eye killer uses the above statistics, with the following changes:

- Its Challenge Rating is 5 (1,800 XP).

- Its Perception and Stealth skills are +6, its passive Perception is 16, and its Weapon Attack is at +6 to hit.

- It has the following additional abilities.

Innate Spellcasting. The umbral eye killer's innate spellcasting ability is Charisma (spell save DC 12, +4 to hit with spell attacks). It can cast *darkness* 3/day without material components.

See in Darkness. The umbral eye killer can see in magical and nonmagical darkness.

Eye of the Deep

This creature is a 5-foot wide orb dominated by a central eye and large serrated mouth. Hundreds of small seaweed-like bristles hang from the bottom of its body. Two large crab-like pincers protrude from its body, and two long, thin eyestalks sprout from the top of its orb.

Eyes of the deep are found only in the deepest parts of the ocean, though on occasion one moves too close to the shoreline and ends up beached on the sands. An eye of the deep stranded in this manner dies in 2d4 minutes unless placed back into the water.

An eye of the deep floats slowly through the oceans searching for its prey. It attacks using its eye rays; then it grasps an opponent with its pincers and subjects the victim to its bite attack. An eye of the deep's pincers are considered to be primary attacks.

Eye of the Deep

Medium aberration, lawful evil
Armor Class 14 (natural armor)
Hit Points 117 (18d8 + 36)
Speed 5 ft., swim 20 ft.

STR	DEX	CON	INT	WIS	CHA
14 (+2)	10 (+0)	14 (+2)	12 (+1)	13 (+1)	13 (+1)

Skills Perception +4
Senses darkvision 60 ft., passive Perception 14
Languages Aquan, Common, Deep Speech
Challenge 5 (1,800 XP)

Amphibious. The eye of the deep can breathe in both air and water.

Flyby. The eye of the deep doesn't provoke an opportunity attack when it flies out of an enemy's reach.

Hyper-Awareness. An eye of the deep's eye stalks allow it to see in all directions at once. It cannot be surprised.

Stun Cone. An eye of the deep's central eye produces a cone extending straight ahead from its front to a range of 30 feet. At the start of each of its turns, the eye of the deep decides which way the cone faces and whether the cone is active. All creatures in this area must succeed on a DC 15 Constitution saving throw or be stunned for 1 minute. A creature can repeat the saving throw at the end of each of its turns, ending the effect on itself on a success.

Actions

Multiattack. The eye of the deep makes three attacks: one with its bite and two with its pincers.

Bite. *Melee Weapon Attack:* +5 to hit, reach 5 ft., one target. *Hit:* 12 (3d6 + 2) piercing damage.

Pincers. *Melee Weapon Attack:* +5 to hit, reach 5 ft., one target. *Hit:* 15 (3d8 + 2) bludgeoning damage. The target is grappled (escape DC 12) if the eye of the deep isn't already grappling a creature, and the target is restrained until the grapple ends.

Eye Rays. Each of the creature's eyes stalks can produce a magical ray once per round. The creature can aim both of its eye rays in any direction and they have a range of 150 feet.

Paralytic Ray. Using its left eye, the eye of the deep unleashes a powerful paralytic beam. The target must make a DC 15 Wisdom saving throw or be paralyzed for 1 minute. A creature can repeat the saving throw at the end of each of its turns, ending the effect on itself on a success.

Enfeeblement Ray. Using its right eye, the eye of the deep unleashes a powerful ray of enfeeblement. The target must make a DC 15 Wisdom saving throw or deal half damage with all attacks that use Strength for 1 minute. A creature can repeat the saving throw at the end of each of its turns, ending the effect on itself on a success.

Major Image. The eye of the deep concentrates its eye rays together to project a *major image* illusion. The illusion is generated at any point within range and in the eye of the deep's line of sight. Seeing through the illusion requires a successful DC 15 Intelligence (Investigation) check.

Ferrous Worm

These semi-intelligent subterranean creatures are found almost exclusively in treasure hoards where masses of metallic coins are present. Originally from the Quasi-Elemental Plane of Minerals, ferrous worms require close contact with metallic objects in order to maintain their bodily functions, much like fish require water. In their homeworld, such contact is omnipresent, but when brought to the Prime Material Plane to serve their summoner's needs, ferrous worms depend on alternate sources of metal for survival. They burrow deeply into large accumulations of treasure, attacking anyone who disturbs their surrogate home.

Ferrous worms use the element of surprise to their tactical advantage, often clamping their metal teeth on several victims before their unsuspecting targets can react. Not only is the creature's bite quite destructive as its metal teeth are ground to fine points, but any humanoid bitten by a ferrous worm must make a saving throw or contract a blood disease. This disease is the result of a sudden injection of heavy minerals into the system, including lead, mercury, beryllium, and lithium. Over the next 1d4 days, victims experience abdominal pains, headaches, and short-term memory problems. After another 1d4 days, their condition worsens, resulting in seizures and a loss of 3d6 hit points per day until death. Though the hit point loss may be abated with curative magic, only a successful *cure disease* restores the victim to full health.

Ferrous worms are solitary creatures except during the brief mating season when they burrow long distances through mineral-rich earth to locate a mate. The mating ritual requires several days to compete; if encountered at this time, ferrous worms are non-hostile unless openly attacked.

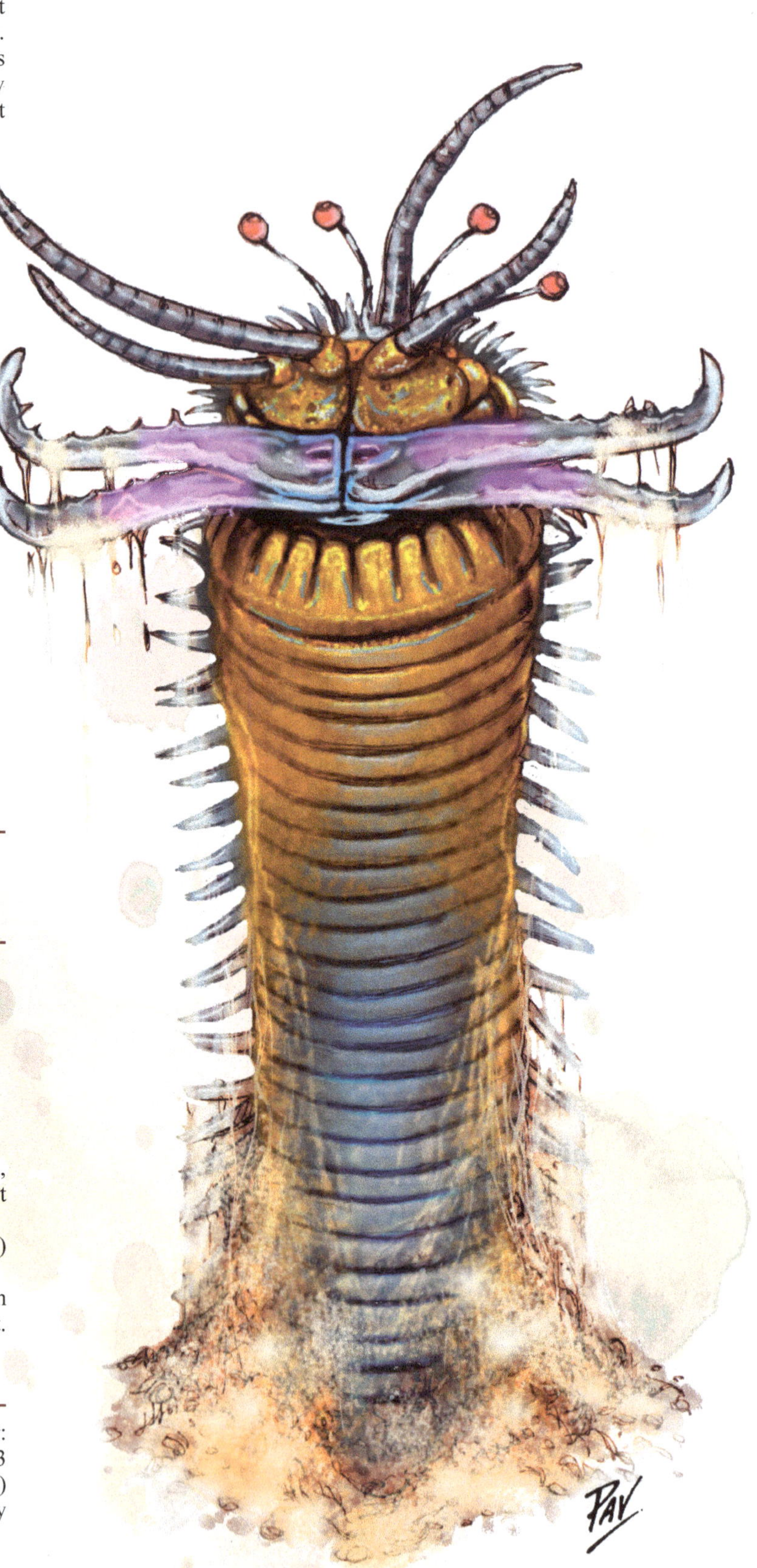

Ferrous Worm

Medium monstrosity, unaligned
Armor Class 16 (natural armor)
Hit Points 27 (5d8 + 2)
Speed 30 ft., burrow 30 ft.

STR	DEX	CON	INT	WIS	CHA
13 (+1)	17 (+3)	12 (+1)	12 (+1)	13 (+1)	5 (–3)

Saving Throws Con +3
Skills Perception +3, Stealth +7
Condition Immunities prone
Senses darkvision 60 ft., tremorsense 60 ft., passive Perception 14
Languages —
Challenge 3 (700 XP)

Earth Glide. The ferrous worm can burrow through nonmagical, unworked earth and stone. While doing so, the ferrous worm doesn't disturb the material it moves through.

Camouflage. The ferrous worm has advantage on Dexterity (Stealth) checks made to hide in rocky terrain and treasure piles.

Treasure Sense. The ferrous worm can pinpoint, by scent, the location of precious metals and stones, such as coins and gems, within 60 feet of it.

Actions

Bite. *Melee Weapon Attack:* +5 to hit, reach 5 ft., one creature. *Hit:* 10 (2d6 + 3) piercing damage, and the target must succeed on a DC 13 Constitution saving throw or be poisoned and take an additional 10 (3d6) poison damage each day until cured. The poison can only be cured by casting *lesser restoration*.

Fire Crab

*Fire crabs are invertebrates found roaming the fiery shores of the Elemental Plane of Fire and the Plane of Molten Skies (see **Rappan Athuk** by **Frog God Games**).*

Fire crabs can be found crawling the shores or swimming in pools and lakes of liquid flame. They are generally nonaggressive creatures and spend their time eating the heated rocks and plants found in the abovementioned planes. Food not eaten is carried and stored in their lair, which takes the form of a large burrow under the fiery waters or on the shores near their "water source." Such burrows are sometimes very large and can contain up to 20 of these creatures. On the Material Plane, fire crabs lair in volcanoes and near hot springs.

Fire crabs have large claws and in males, one claw is always larger (at least three times larger) than the other. Fire crabs have six segmented and spindly legs, blackish-red in color.

Fire crabs are highly territorial and defend their lair with great ferocity. Normally nonaggressive creatures, if their lair is threatened, they fight to the death. Against weaker prey, fire crabs usually just slash with their claws. Stronger foes are grabbed and squeezed by the fire crab. Once they grab an opponent, they hold on, allowing their fires to engulf the foe.

Diminutive Fire Crab

A dog-sized crab with a square-shaped reddish-brown carapace covered with dark-red and yellow markings scuttles forth, pincers raised. Tiny flames lick its body, erupting at irregular intervals from its underbelly. Its eyes are perched on the end of two large eyestalks that protrude from the center of the carapace.

Diminutive Fire Crab

Small elemental, unaligned
Armor Class 13 (natural armor)
Hit Points 22 (4d6 + 8)
Speed 20 ft., swim 20 ft.

STR	DEX	CON	INT	WIS	CHA
14 (+2)	14 (+2)	14 (+2)	2 (–4)	10 (+0)	2 (–4)

Damage Vulnerabilities cold
Damage Immunities fire
Condition Immunities charmed
Senses darkvision 60 ft., tremorsense 60 ft., passive Perception 10
Languages understand Ignan but can't speak
Challenge 2 (450 XP)

Heated Body. A creature that touches the fire crab or hits it with a melee attack while within 5 feet of it takes 3 (1d6) fire damage.

Actions

Multiattack. The diminutive fire crab makes two claw attacks.
Claws. *Melee Weapon Attack:* +4 to hit, reach 5 ft., one target. *Hit:* 4 (1d4 + 2) bludgeoning damage plus 3 (1d6) fire damage.

Medium Fire Crab

This crab is the size of a riding horse, with a square-shaped reddish-brown carapace covered with dark-red and yellow markings. Flames lick its body, erupting at irregular intervals from its underbelly. Its eyes are perched on the end of two large eyestalks that protrude from the center of the carapace.

Fire Crab

Medium elemental, unaligned
Armor Class 15 (natural armor)
Hit Points 75 (10d8 + 30)
Speed 30 ft., swim 30 ft.

STR	DEX	CON	INT	WIS	CHA
18 (+4)	10 (+0)	16 (+3)	2 (–4)	14 (+2)	2 (–4)

Skills Athletics +7
Damage Vulnerabilities cold
Damage Immunities fire
Condition Immunities charmed
Senses darkvision 60 ft., tremorsense 60 ft., passive Perception 12

Languages understand Ignan but can't speak
Challenge 5 (1,800 XP)

Heated Body. A creature that touches the medium fire crab or hits it with a melee attack while within 5 feet of it takes 7 (2d6) fire damage.

Actions

Multiattack. The medium fire crab makes two claw attacks

Claws. *Melee Weapon Attack:* +7 to hit, reach 5 ft., one target. *Hit:* 8 (1d8 + 4) bludgeoning damage plus 7 (2d6) fire damage. If both claw attacks hit in the same turn and the target is Large size or smaller, the target is grappled (escape DC 15). While grappled, the target is restrained and takes 7 (2d6) fire damage at the start of its turn. The fire crab can only grapple one target at a time and cannot perform a claw attack while grappling a target.

Constrict. If a target is grappled, the medium fire crab squeezes it and the target takes 8 (1d8 + 4) bludgeoning damage and 7 (2d6) fire damage.

Greater Fire Crab

A massive crab with a square-shaped reddish-brown carapace covered with dark-red and yellow markings scuttles forth, pincers raised. Tiny flames lick its body, erupting at irregular intervals from its underbelly. Its eyes are perched on the end of two large eyestalks that protrude from the center of the carapace.

Greater Fire Crab

Huge elemental, unaligned
Armor Class 17 (natural armor)
Hit Points 173 (15d12 + 75)
Speed 40 ft., swim 40 ft.

STR	DEX	CON	INT	WIS	CHA
22 (+6)	10 (+0)	20 (+5)	2 (−4)	16 (+3)	2 (−4)

Skills Athletics +10
Damage Vulnerabilities cold
Damage Immunities fire
Condition Immunities charmed
Senses darkvision 60 ft., tremorsense 60 ft., passive Perception 13
Languages understands Ignan but can't speak
Challenge 10 (5,900 XP)

Heated Body. A creature that touches the greater fire crab or hits it with a melee attack while within 5 feet of it takes 14 (4d6) fire damage.

Actions

Multiattack. The greater fire crab makes two claw attacks

Claws. *Melee Weapon Attack:* +10 to hit, reach 5 ft., one target. *Hit:* 12 (1d12 + 6) bludgeoning damage plus 14 (4d6) fire damage. If both claw attacks hit in the same turn and the target is Huge sized or smaller, target is grappled (escape DC 16). While grappled, a target takes 14 (4d6) fire damage at the start of its turn. The fire crab can only grapple one target at a time and cannot perform a claw attack while grappling a target.

Constrict. If a target is grappled, the greater fire crab squeezes it and the target takes 12 (1d12 + 6) bludgeoning damage and 14 (4d6) fire damage.

Fire Nymph

This creature appears as a beautiful female with long, flowing fiery-red hair. Her eyes are pale blue and her skin is lightly colored with a cinnamon hint to it.

A fire nymph is a beautiful creature that dwells on the Plane of Fire. It is akin to the nymph and dryad, though its origins obviously lie elsewhere. Fire nymphs rarely visit the Material Plane, though mages are known to request their company on occasion. A fire nymph usually wears translucent robes of white or ash.

Fire nymphs avoid combat if at all possible, but if pressed into action they rely on their innate spellcasting abilities and seek escape as soon as possible.

Fire Nymph

Medium elemental, chaotic neutral
Armor Class 13 (natural armor)
Hit Points 16 (3d8 + 3)
Speed 30 ft.

STR	DEX	CON	INT	WIS	CHA
10 (+0)	13 (+1)	12 (+1)	16 (+3)	17 (+3)	19 (+4)

Damage Immunities fire
Senses darkvision 60 ft., passive Perception 13
Languages Common, Ignan
Challenge 3 (700 XP)

Burn. Any creature that touches the nymph or hits it with a melee attack while within 5 feet of it takes 10 (3d6) fire damage.

Innate Spellcasting. The fire nymph's spellcasting ability is Charisma (spell save DC 14, +6 to hit with spell attacks). The fire nymph can innately cast each of the following spells, requiring no material components:

At will: *burning hands, flame blade, flaming sphere, produce flame*
1/day: *fire shield*

Magic Resistance. The fire nymph has advantage on saving throws against spells and other magical effects.

Actions

Multiattack. The fire nymph makes two attacks: one with its dagger and one with its fist.

Dagger. *Melee or Ranged Weapon Attack:* +3 to hit, reach 5 ft. or range 20/60 ft., one target. *Hit:* 3 (1d4 + 1) piercing damage plus 10 (3d6) fire damage.

Fist. Melee *Weapon Attack:* +3 to hit, reach 5 ft., one target. *Hit:* 3 (1d4 + 1) bludgeoning damage plus 10 (3d6) fire damage.

Fire Phantom

This humanoid has raging fire for hair and flame-encased fists. Elemental fire plays across its body exposing patches of charred flesh. Its eyes and tongue look like tiny balls of molten fire. Blackened teeth fill its mouth and flames dance in the back of its throat.

When a creature dies on the Elemental Plane of Fire, its soul often melds with part of the fiery plane and reforms as a fire phantom; a humanoid creature composed of rotted and burned flesh and elemental fire. Fire phantoms desire nothing more than to return to the Material Plane and destroy as many living creatures as possible by consuming them in the same flames that now house their spirit.

Fire phantoms are encountered in areas where fires are already burning (campfires, pyres, vigils, etc.). They step through a portal from the Plane of Fire into a fire on the Material Plane. This fire must be at least Small or larger; else any attempt by the fire phantom to enter the Material Plane through that fire automatically fails. Once it enters the plane, it often lies in wait in the fire for potential victims to come near it. A fire phantom hiding inside a fire is difficult to see requiring DC 18 Perception check.

A fire phantom waits inside its fire until it spots a living creature. It then rushes out, shrieking and hurling globes of fire. If faced with overwhelming odds or facing certain destruction, the fire phantom either moves as close as possible to as many foes as possible or attempts to draw in as many of its opponents as possible and uses it immolation ability. In normal melee, the fire phantom alternates between hurling globes of fire and pummeling a foe with its burning fists. When a fire phantom is wounded, flames dance and play around the wound. Fire phantoms fight until destroyed or all opponents are dead or flee.

Fire Phantom

Medium undead, chaotic neutral
Armor Class 14 (natural armor)
Hit Points 49 (9d8 + 9)
Speed 30 ft.

STR	DEX	CON	INT	WIS	CHA
19 (+4)	14 (+2)	13 (+1)	5 (–3)	12 (+1)	14 (+2)

Damage Vulnerabilities cold
Damage Immunities fire
Condition Immunities charmed, frightened, paralyzed, poisoned, unconscious
Senses darkvision 60 ft., passive Perception 11
Languages Ignan
Challenge 6 (2,300 XP)

Brutal Critical. The fire phantom can roll one additional weapon damage when determining the extra damage for a critical hit with a melee attack.

Death Throes. When the fire phantom dies, it explodes, and each creature within 30 feet of it must make a DC 14 Dexterity saving throw, taking 28 (8d6) fire damage on a failed save, or half as much damage on a successful one. The explosion ignites flammable objects in that area that aren't being worn or carried.

Fire Form. A creature that touches the fire phantom or hits it with a melee attack while within 5 feet of it takes 7 (2d6) fire damage.

Reckless. At the start of its turn, the fire phantom can gain advantage on all melee weapon attack rolls that turn but attack rolls against it have advantage until the start of its next turn.

Actions

Multiattack. The fire phantom makes two fist of fire attacks.

Fist of Fire. *Melee Weapon Attack:* +7 to hit, reach 5 ft., one target. *Hit:* 11 (2d6 + 4) bludgeoning damage plus 7 (2d6) fire damage.

Fire Blast. *Ranged Weapon Attack:* +7 to hit, range 60 ft., one target. *Hit:* 10 (3d6) fire damage.

Fire Whale
(Burning Leviathan)

Surfacing from the sea of flames rises, a titanic crimson whale mottled with a pattern of yellow and orange spots running down its dorsal fins. Its huge, angular mouth hangs open, exposing its hideous gaping gullet.

All manner of fiery aquatic life swims the Sea of Fire, including the majestic fire whales. These 30-foot-long mammals are relatively peaceful creatures, though if provoked they quickly become deadly adversaries.

Fire whales generally spend their time feeding on elemental invertebrates that move along the bottom of the Sea of Fire. When feeding, the fire whale dives to the bottom, flips on its side, and swims along, running its head through the fiery and oily sea floor scooping food into its mouth. Fire whales generally take in enough food to sustain themselves for 4 months (during breeding season).

Late in the year (by Material Plane standards) fire whales gather for their mating ritual. During this time as many as 7 fire whales can be encountered together. Sages are unsure as to the purpose of the "extra" fire whales, but each spends its share rolling and milling with the others during this ritual. Gestation for fire whales is generally 11 months after which time the mother gives birth to 1d2 calves. While the calves are growing, both they and the mother spend most of their time in the shallower ends of the Sea of Fire. After nearly 7 months, they migrate to deeper waters and most calves swim away and become independent. Young reach maturity around 6 years of age.

Fire whales are hunted by various races for their meat, blubber, and oil. Of the races that hunt them the most are the salamanders, volcano giants (see their entry in this book), and the efreet of the City of Brass.

Fire whales are generally peaceful creatures and rarely attack unless threatened. If forced into combat, a fire whale attacks with its bite and tail slap. Surface creatures that threaten a fire whale are subjected to its scalding blast attack.

Fire Whale

Huge elemental, unaligned
Armor Class 14 (natural armor)
Hit Points 175 (14d12 + 84)
Speed swim 40 ft.

STR	DEX	CON	INT	WIS	CHA
30 (+10)	13 (+1)	22 (+6)	2 (−4)	12 (+1)	6 (−2)

Skills Perception +5
Damage Immunities fire
Senses blindsight 120 ft., passive Perception 15
Languages —
Challenge 11 (7,200 XP)

Echolocation The whale can't use its blindsight while deafened.
Hold Breath. The whale can hold its breath for 30 minutes.
Keen Hearing. The whale has advantage on Wisdom (Perception) checks that rely on hearing.

Actions

Multiattack. The fire whale makes two attacks: one with its bite and one with its tail slap.

Bite. Melee *Weapon Attack:* +14 to hit, reach 5 ft., one target. *Hit:* 34 (7d6 + 10) piercing damage.

Tail Slap. Melee *Weapon Attack:* +14 to hit, reach 15 ft., one target. *Hit:* 23 (2d12 + 10) bludgeoning damage.

Scalding Blast (Recharge 5–6). A fire whale can release a blast of superheated air in a 60-foot cone from its blowhole that scalds or burns those contacting it. Each creature in that area must make a DC 16 Dexterity saving throw, taking 49 (14d6) fire damage on a failed save, or half as much on a successful one.

Fly, Giant

Bristling with coarse hairs, this enormous fly's legs twitch just before it launches into the air on buzzing wings. This human-sized insect has large, red, globular eyes, a body covered in hairy bristles, and two rapidly vibrating translucent wings.

Giant flies are larger relatives of normal flies. Like their lesser cousins, they are most often found in areas of garbage, litter, and refuse. A giant fly resembles a normal fly and can grow to a length of 12 feet, though most average about 6 feet long.

Giant flies attack by biting their opponents.

Giant Fly

Medium beast, unaligned
Armor Class 13
Hit Points 22 (3d8 + 9)
Speed 30 ft., fly 60 ft.

STR	DEX	CON	INT	WIS	CHA
12 (+1)	17 (+3)	16 (+3)	2 (–4)	7 (–2)	2 (–4)

Skills Perception +2
Senses darkvision 60 ft., passive Perception 12
Languages —
Challenge ½ (100 XP)

Keen Smell. The giant fly has advantage on Wisdom (Perception) checks that rely on smell.

Actions

Bite. *Melee Weapon Attack:* +5 to hit, reach 10 ft., one target. *Hit:* 10 (2d6 + 3) piercing damage. If the target is a creature it must succeed on a DC 13 Constitution saving throw or be diseased until the condition is cured. While the creature is diseased it is poisoned.. Every 24 hours that elapse, the target must repeat the saving throw, reducing its hit point maximum by 5 (1d10) on a failure. The disease is cured on a success. The target dies if the disease reduces its hit point maximum to 0. This reduction to the target's hit point maximum lasts until the disease is cured.

Fogwarden

This creature resembles a humanoid formed of fog and mist. The only discernible facial feature is its icy blue eyes.

The fogwarden is sometimes called the ice apparition, for much like the standard apparition, the fogwarden feeds on the fear of its victims. The fogwarden, however, is not undead. A fogwarden is usually found inhabiting the coldest and most desolate areas of the world. The fog surrounding it flashes with its life force. These flashes are often mistaken for the will-o'-wisp.

Fogwardens favor instilling fear and panic in their opponents to actual combat. In melee, the fogwarden attacks by launching a bolt of lightning at its foes. When a fogwarden is destroyed, it evaporates completely, leaving no trace of its existence.

Fogwarden

Medium aberration, neutral evil
Armor Class 14 (natural armor)
Hit Points 27 (5d8 + 5)
Speed fly 40 ft.

STR	DEX	CON	INT	WIS	CHA
11 (+0)	16 (+3)	12 (+1)	12 (+1)	11 (+0)	14 (+2)

Skills Perception +4
Damage Vulnerabilities radiant
Damage Immunities cold, lightning, poison
Condition Immunities poisoned
Senses darkvision 60 ft., passive Perception 14
Languages Auran, Common
Challenge 4 (1,100 XP)

Animate Dead. The electrical aura of the fogwarden can animate up to four dead creatures within 20 feet. The animated creatures resemble zombies and are under the control of the fogwarden. If the fogwarden is slain or moves more than 20 feet from a zombie, the animated creature collapses and cannot be animated again. The animated creatures use zombie statistics.

Electricity Discharge. A creature that touches the fogwarden or hits it with a melee attack while within 5 feet of it takes 14 (4d6) lightning damage. If the creature is wielding a metal weapon or wearing metal armor, it must succeed on a DC 14 Constitution saving throw or be stunned until the end of the fogwarden's next turn.

Gaseous Form. While in this form, the fogwarden's only method of movement is a flying speed of 10 feet. The Fogwarden can enter and occupy the space of another creature. The Fogwarden has resistance to nonmagical damage, is still hypersensitive to sunlight, and it has advantage on Strength, Dexterity, and Constitution saving throws. The Fogwarden can pass through small holes, narrow openings, and even mere cracks, though it treats liquids as though they were solid. The Fogwarden can't fall and remains hovering in the air even when stunned or otherwise incapacitated.

Innate Spellcasting. The fogwarden's spellcasting ability is Charisma (spell save DC 12, +4 to hit with spell attacks). The fogwarden can innately cast *animate dead* at will requiring no material components.

Sunlight Hypersensitivity. The fogwarden takes 20 radiant damage when it starts its turn in sunlight. While in sunlight, it has disadvantage on attack rolls and ability checks.

Actions

Shock. *Melee Spell Attack:* +4 to hit, reach 5 ft., one creature. *Hit:* 9 (2d8) lightning damage.

This tiny humanoid resembles a grey-skinned cross between a pixie and a goblin, with red and brown butterfly wings, like fresh blood splattered over older, dried blood.

Once upon a time, a well-meaning lawful good deity, whose name is lost to history, happened upon the abandoned servant-army of a chaotic evil deity and decided to devote spare time, over the course of several centuries, to the reformation of this evil servant species. The results were all but catastrophic, though not in the ways the deity might have expected. As it turned out, the corrupted fey were convinced to adopt the values of a lawful good life path such as justice, respect, honesty, valor, and generosity (and many others). Unfortunately, the god who had corrupted them had made them so intrinsically, innately chaotic evil, that even after they decided to be good, they were so bad at it that everything they did, nevertheless, still turned out to be evil. This earned them the name "the folly" because all the time spent teaching them goodness had turned out to be folly.

More often than fighting fair, the folly will murder or torment those weaker than them in the name of some dreadful misunderstanding of compassion. If faced with an actual challenge, they are likely to attempt to make friends. What the folly desire most is to become good enough to please the near-forgotten deity who tried to teach them. To this end, they seek noble and virtuous leaders to guide them, but woe betide the virtuous party who attempts to help them, and indeed, woe betide also the evil party who gets caught tricking them. The first will see horror and suffering everywhere in their wake, while the second are likely to be poisoned in their sleep in the name of "justice".

The folly wear little suits of gleaming armor and are always terribly honest and courteous in the horrible things they say. "Why did you burn that house down?" "You asked us to clean it! It's very clean now! Why, you almost can't tell there was ever a house there!"

The Folly

Tiny fey, chaotic evil
Armor Class 16 (natural armor)
Hit Points 71 (13d4 + 39)
Speed 15 ft., fly 30 ft.

STR	DEX	CON	INT	WIS	CHA
15 (+2)	14 (+2)	17 (+3)	12 (+1)	7 (–2)	19 (+4)

Saving Throws Dex +5, Con +6
Skills Arcana +4, Athletics +5, Perception +1, Persuasion +7
Senses darkvision 120 ft., passive Perception 11
Languages Common, Draconic, Sylvan
Challenge 5 (1,800 XP)

Innate Spellcasting. The folly's spellcasting ability is Charisma (spell save DC 15, +7 to hit with spell attacks). It can innately cast the following spells, requiring no material components:

At will: *acid splash, chill touch, eldritch blast, mage hand, minor illusion, poison spray, prestidigitation, shocking grasp, vicious mockery*

3/day each: *disguise self, flaming sphere, hideous laughter, invisibility, phantasmal killer, silent image, sleep, suggestion*

1/day: *dispel magic, fear, fireball, hypnotic pattern*

1/week each: *animate objects, arcane gate, polymorph* (10x normal casting time and requires at least 3 follies participating in the ritual)

1/month each: *earthquake, gate, reverse gravity* (100x normal casting time and requires at least 10 follies participating in the ritual)

Quick Breeding. The follies both breed and mature very quickly, but they also don't much care about self-preservation. Therefore, even though they often do things that get themselves killed, their population never seems to drop.

Wild Misperception. The follies misunderstand almost anything said to them in the most horrible possible way. For example, if asked, "Please make those children new shoes," they will happily slay the children and use their skins to make new shoes. They don't do this on purpose. They just get absolutely everything horribly, horribly wrong whenever it is at all possible to do so. Even when they do properly understand a request, they will find a horrible way to execute it. For example, if asked, "Please bring me a glass of water," they might steal a poor family's only nice glass or open a gateway to the elemental plane of water, flooding the town, just to fill the glass. Everything they can do wrong, they will.

Actions

+1 Tiny Longsword. *Melee Weapon Attack:* +6 to hit, reach 5 ft., one target. *Hit:* 4 (1d2 + 3) slashing damage.

+1 Tiny Shortbow. *Ranged Weapon Attack:* +6 to hit, range 40/160 ft., one target. *Hit:* 4 (1d2 + 3) piercing damage.

Forgotten One

This is a one-foot-tall creature with pointed ears, slanted eyes, and long lithe limbs. Its hair is brightly colored and decorated with leaves and twigs and it is dressed in greenish-brown clothes. It carries a tiny spear in its hands.

Forgotten ones are a sprite race related to pixies. These wee folk are natural spies and trackers and are routinely employed by powerful forest-guarding fey creatures such as unicorns, dryads, and nymphs. It is not uncommon for travelers in a fey forest to be followed by scores of forgotten ones, all moving unnoticed through the treetops as quickly and quietly as squirrels. While some forgotten ones keep track of the interlopers, others send messages back and forth to alert more powerful fey guardians to the presence of outsiders.

A forgotten one is about a foot tall with pointed ears, slanted eyes, and long, nimble limbs. Most forgotten ones weave twigs and leaves into their hair for decoration and to help conceal themselves in the treetops. Rangers are druids are especially fond of the forgotten ones, and often use them as intermediaries between themselves and the greater fey guardians of the forest.

Forgotten ones try to avoid combat with anything larger than themselves — they are well aware of their own limitations. If hard pressed or ordered into combat by a greater fey creature to defend their forest, forgotten ones will fight with courage not often attributed to creatures of such small size.

Forgotten One

Tiny fey, neutral
Armor Class 16 (natural armor)
Hit Points 7 (3d4)
Speed 20 ft.

STR	DEX	CON	INT	WIS	CHA
3 (–4)	19 (+4)	11 (+0)	14 (+2)	17 (+3)	20 (+5)

Damage Immunities poison
Condition Immunities poison
Senses darkvision 60 ft., tremorsense 90 ft., passive Perception 13
Languages Common, Elven, Sylvan
Challenge 1 (200 XP)

Innate Spellcasting. The forgotten one's spellcasting ability is Charisma (spell save DC 15, +7 to hit with spell attacks). The forgotten one can innately cast *blur* at will requiring no material components.

Environmental Awareness. The very earth speaks to a forgotten one. It cannot be surprised.

Poison Use. Forgotten Ones are skilled in the use of poison.

Actions

Spear. *Melee or Ranged Weapon Attack:* +6 to hit, reach 5 ft. or range 20/60 ft., one target. *Hit:* 7 (1d6 + 4) piercing damage plus 7 (2d6) poison damage.

Frogs

Frog, Giant Dire Abyssal

This frog appears to be about 12 feet long. Its skin is blackish-green and constantly oozes a milky slime from its body.

Giant Dire Abyssal Frogs come from the Plane of Slime and are wholly evil. They have a demonic aspect to them, with a spiny and usually poisonous hide. Their red eyes flicker with demonic intelligence.

Giant Dire Abyssal Frog
Large elemental, chaotic evil
Armor Class 16 (natural armor)
Hit Points 105 (10d10 + 50)
Speed 30 ft., swim 30 ft.

STR	DEX	CON	INT	WIS	CHA
20 (+5)	18 (+4)	20 (+5)	5 (–3)	10 (+0)	10 (+0)

Saving Throws Dex +7, Con +8
Skills Stealth +7, Perception +6
Damage Resistances acid, cold; bludgeoning, piercing and slashing from nonmagical weapons
Damage Immunities poison
Condition Immunities exhaustion, grappled, paralyzed, petrified, poisoned, prone, restrained, unconscious
Senses darkvision 60 ft., passive Perception 16
Languages —
Challenge 6 (2,300 XP)

Amphibious. The frog can breathe air and water.

Keen Smell. The frog has advantage on Wisdom (Perception) checks that rely on smell.

Poison Hide. A creature that touches the giant dire Abyssal frog or hits it with an unarmed or natural weapon attack takes 10 (3d6) poison damage from the milky, poisonous slime that oozes from its hide.

Standing Leap. The frog's long jump is up to 30 feet and its high jump is up to 20 feet, with or without a running start.

Actions

Multiattack. The giant dire Abyssal frog makes three attacks: one with its bite, one with its claws, and one with its tongue.

Bite. *Melee Weapon Attack:* +8 to hit, reach 5 ft., one target. *Hit:* 14 (2d8 + 5) piercing damage, and the target is grappled (escape DC 16). Until this grapple ends, the target is restrained and the frog can't bite another target.

Claws. *Melee Weapon Attack:* +8 to hit, reach 5 ft., one target. *Hit:* 15 (3d6 + 5) slashing damage.

Tongue. *Melee Weapon Attack:* +8 to hit, reach 15 ft., one target. *Hit:* 18 (2d12 + 5) slashing damage, and the target must succeed on a DC 16 Strength saving throw or be pulled up to 10 feet toward the giant dire Abyssal frog.

Swallow. The giant dire Abyssal frog makes one bite attack against a Large or smaller target it is grappling. If the attack hits, the target is swallowed, and the grapple ends. The swallowed target is blinded and restrained, it has total cover against attacks and other effects outside the giant dire Abyssal frog, and it takes 14 (4d6) acid damage at the start of each of the giant dire Abyssal frog's turns. The giant dire Abyssal frog can only swallow one target at a time.

If the giant dire Abyssal frog dies, a swallowed creature is no longer restrained by it and can escape from the corpse using 5 feet of movement, exiting prone.

Frog, Killer

This frog stands partially erect and has dark-green skin fading to light on its underbelly. A trio of defensive horn-like protuberances jut upward, one from its nose and each brow, and its smiling countenance reveals sharp fangs lining its entire gum line.

The killer frogs live, hunt, and mate near swampy lands, usually, but variants can be found in any moist or freshwater environment. Rabidly aggressive, their tiny minds view almost everything as food. They hunt smaller mammals, reptiles, other amphibians, or giant-sized insects and are rarely satiated. They typically avoid civilization, but it is not uncommon for villagers in the more remote areas to encounter one or more of the killer frogs, who are often responsible for missing dogs, livestock, or young children. Halflings have a love-hate relationship with the amphibian; they consider frog legs to be a delicacy, while the frogs share an equal taste for halfling legs.

Killer Frog

Small beast, unaligned
Armor Class 12 (natural armor)
Hit Points 11 (2d6 + 4)
Speed 30 ft., swim 30 ft.

STR	DEX	CON	INT	WIS	CHA
12 (+1)	13 (+1)	14 (+2)	2 (−4)	9 (−1)	6 (−2)

Skills Perception +3
Senses passive Perception 13
Languages —
Challenge ¼ (50 XP)

Amphibious. The frog can breathe air and water.

Keen Smell. The killer frog has advantage on Wisdom (Perception) checks that rely on smell.

Standing Leap. The frog's long jump is up to 15 feet and its high jump is up to 10 feet, with or without a running start.

Actions

Multiattack. The killer frog makes two attacks: one with its bite and one with its claws.

Bite. *Melee Weapon Attack:* +3 to hit, reach 5 ft., one target. *Hit:* 3 (1d4 + 1) piercing damage.

Claws. *Melee Weapon Attack:* +3 to hit, reach 5 ft., one target. *Hit:* 3 (1d4 + 1) slashing damage.

Frost Man

This creature appears to be a human dressed in loosely fitted animal skins and furs. It wears a patch over one eye, and its hair is long and unkempt. A short, rough beard of dark hair covers its jaw.

Frost men are hunters that make their home in the cold regions of the world. Each carries his personal belongings in small sacks and takes them wherever he goes. A frost man's body radiates cold out to 30 feet, though not enough to deal damage.

There is much speculation on the society of frost men. Other beings only encounter them as lone males. Speculation suggests that there must be villages somewhere with women and children, perhaps buried deep in cold mountain caves. Tribes that are aware of frost men fear them greatly for their deadly talent and refer to them as "ice demons."

Frost men appear in the outside world occasionally and wish only to go about their unknown business undisturbed. Anyone bothering them can expect to be attacked. A frost man usually opens combat with its ice blast before moving in to kill off anything not subsequently frozen to death.

Frost Man

Medium elemental, lawful evil
Armor Class 13 (studded leather)
Hit Points 27 (5d8 + 5)
Speed 30 ft.

STR	DEX	CON	INT	WIS	CHA
10 (+0)	12 (+1)	12 (+1)	10 (+0)	11 (+0)	11 (+0)

Skills Survival +2
Damage Vulnerabilities fire
Damage Immunities cold
Senses darkvision 60 ft., passive Perception 10
Languages Common, Nørsk
Challenge 1/2 (100 XP)

Actions

Morningstar. *Melee Weapon Attack:* +2 to hit, reach 5 ft., one target. *Hit:* 4 (1d8) piercing damage.

Longbow. *Ranged Weapon Attack:* +3 to hit, range 150/600 ft., one target. *Hit:* 5 (1d8 + 1) piercing damage.

Ice Blast (3/day). As a bonus action, the frost man can use its action to remove his eye patch, blasting everything in a 30-foot cone with a freezing mist. All creatures in the area of the cone must make a DC 13 Dexterity saving throw, taking 14 (4d6) cold damage on a failed save, or half as much on a successful save.

Frost Man Characters

Your skin is as cold as your icy home.

Ability Score Increase. Your Strength score increases by 2, and your Constitution score increases by 1.

Age. A frost man ages in a similar fashion to humans, but lives a few years longer.

Alignment. Frost men tend to remain neutral, but almost always lawful.

Size. You are similar to humans in size. Your size is Medium.

Speed. Your base walking speed is 30.

Darkvision. Your race is accustomed to frozen, long-lasting nights. You can see in dim light within 60 feet of you as if it were bright light, and in darkness as if it were dim light. You can't discern color in darkness, only shades of gray.

Icy Heart. You know the *ray of frost* cantrip. Constitution is your spellcasting ability for this spell. In addition, you can use an action to instantly freeze a melee weapon or 5 pieces of ammunition for 1 minute. When you hit with the melee weapon or the ammunition, you deal additional damage equal to your Constitution modifier and it counts as magical. Once the ammunition has been used, it ceases to be enchanted by your icy heart. Once you have used this ability, you can't do so again until you take a long rest.

Survivor. You have cold resistance and suffer no ill effects from temperatures as cold as –20 degrees Fahrenheit, and you have proficiency in the Survival skill.

Languages. You can speak, read, and write Common and one other language of your choice.

Fungal Folk Alchemist

A stout fungal being with malevolent red eyes glares at you. It holds a large puffball mushroom in its hand, and you notice many more hang at the ready on its volva.

These communal myconids make their homes in dense wet forests, feeding upon the decay of fallen trees and occasionally fallen creatures. They never stop growing throughout their lifespan but do reach a maximum size before growing beyond their ability to support their own weight, at which point their cap splits open, spilling spores into the soil to begin the cycle of life anew.

Fiercely protective of their food source, the fungal folk alchemists will attack any creature that wanders anywhere near its feeding ground, fearing competition for their decomposing trove. The fungal folk alchemists are so called because of their ability to harvest their own neurotoxic spores that grow within their very fibers. They collect the spores, grind them into a powder upon rocky surfaces, and finally coat them with the feathery gills from beneath their caps. An adhesive spittle is used to encapsulate the powder within the gills and also to adhere the completed puffballs to their volva for later use. As the fungal folk alchemist grows throughout its life, so too does the toxic properties of its spores, causing a surprising array of effects upon its hapless victims. The average fungal folk alchemist carries 1d6 neurotoxic puffballs attached to its body. Any creatures killed will be partially buried in the ground and left to decompose until considered ripe enough to feed upon.

Fungal Folk Alchemist I

Medium monstrosity, neutral evil
Armor Class 14 (natural armor)
Hit Points 6 (1d8+2)
Speed 30 ft.

STR	DEX	CON	INT	WIS	CHA
12 (+1)	16 (+3)	14 (+2)	12 (+1)	10 (0)	8 (−2)

Condition Immunities charmed, frightened, paralyzed, petrified, poisoned
Skills Stealth +5
Senses passive Perception 12
Languages Undercommon
Challenge 1 (200 XP)

Stalk-still. A fungal folk that remains perfectly still has advantage on Dexterity (Stealth) checks made to hide.

Actions

Stone Knuckles. *Melee weapon attack:* +5 to hit. *Hit:* 6 (1d6+3) slashing damage.

Spore Bomb. *Ranged weapon attack:* +3 to hit, range 30/60 ft. *Hit:* 2 (1d4) poison damage and the target must succeed on a DC 12 Constitution saving throw or see 4 versions of the fungal folk for 1 minute. An affected creature making an attack against one of the visions has a 25% chance to hit the real fungal folk. The affected creature can attempt the saving throw at the end of each of its turns, ending the effect on a success.

Fungal Folk Alchemist II

Medium monstrosity, neutral evil
Armor Class 14 (natural armor)
Hit Points 13 (2d8+4)
Speed 30 ft.

STR	DEX	CON	INT	WIS	CHA
12 (+1)	16 (+3)	14 (+2)	12 (+1)	10 (0)	8 (−2)

Condition Immunities charmed, frightened, paralyzed, petrified, poisoned

Skills Stealth +5
Senses passive Perception 12
Languages Undercommon
Challenge 3 (700 XP)

Stalk-still. A fungal folk that remains perfectly still has advantage on Dexterity (Stealth) checks made to hide.

Actions

Stone Knuckles. Melee weapon attack: +5 to hit. *Hit:* 6 (1d6+3) slashing damage.

Spore Bomb. Ranged weapon attack: +3 to hit, range 30/60 ft. *Hit:* 5 (2d4) poison damage and the target must succeed on a DC 12 Constitution saving throw or be paralyzed for 1 minute. The affected creature can attempt the saving throw at the end of each of its turns, ending the effect on a success.

Fungal Folk Alchemist III

Medium monstrosity, neutral evil
Armor Class 16 (natural armor)
Hit Points 39 (6d8+12)
Speed 30 ft.

STR	DEX	CON	INT	WIS	CHA
12 (+1)	16 (+3)	14 (+2)	12 (+1)	10 (0)	8 (−2)

Condition Immunities charmed, frightened, paralyzed, petrified, poisoned
Skills Stealth +6
Senses passive Perception 13
Languages Undercommon
Challenge 5 (1800 XP)

Stalk-still. A fungal folk that remains perfectly still has advantage on Dexterity (Stealth) checks made to hide.

Actions

Stone Knuckles. Melee weapon attack: +6 to hit. *Hit:* 6 (1d6+3) slashing damage.

Spore Bomb. Ranged weapon attack: +4 to hit, range 30/60 ft. *Hit:* 10 (4d4) poison damage and the target must succeed on a DC 14 Constitution saving throw or fall asleep for 1 minute. A sleeping creature is awakened if it takes damage or if another creature uses an action to awaken it.

Fungal Folk Alchemist IV

Medium monstrosity, neutral evil
Armor Class 16 (natural armor)
Hit Points 65 (10d8+20)
Speed 30 ft.

STR	DEX	CON	INT	WIS	CHA
12 (+1)	16 (+3)	14 (+2)	12 (+1)	10 (0)	8 (−2)

Condition Immunities charmed, frightened, paralyzed, petrified, poisoned
Skills Stealth +6
Senses 13
Languages Undercommon
Challenge 7 (2900 XP)

Stalk-still. A fungal folk that remains perfectly still has advantage on Dexterity (Stealth) checks made to hide.

Actions

Stone Knuckles. Melee weapon attack: +6 to hit. *Hit:* 10 (2d6+3) slashing damage.

Spore Bomb. Ranged weapon Attack: +4 to hit, range 30/60 ft. *Hit:* 15 (6d4) poison damage and the target must succeed on a DC 15 Constitution saving throw or be dominated for 1 minute. A dominated creature obeys all commands telepathically delivered by the fungal folk's spores. Each time the target takes damage it is allowed another saving throw.

Fungal Folk Alchemist V

Medium monstrosity, neutral evil
Armor Class 17 (natural armor)
Hit Points 104 (16d8+32)
Speed 30 ft.

STR	DEX	CON	INT	WIS	CHA
12 (+1)	16 (+3)	14 (+2)	12 (+1)	10 (0)	8 (−2)

Condition Immunities charmed, frightened, paralyzed, petrified, poisoned
Skills Stealth +7
Senses passive Perception 14
Languages Undercommon
Challenge 10 (5900 XP)

Stalk-still. A fungal folk that remains perfectly still has advantage on Dexterity (Stealth) checks made to hide.

Actions

Stone Knuckles. Melee Weapon Attack: +7 to hit. *Hit:* 10 (2d6+3) slashing damage.

Spore Bomb (Challenge 10): Ranged Weapon Attack: +8 to hit, range 30/60 ft. *Hit:* 15 (6d4) poison damage and the target must succeed on a DC 15 Constitution saving throw or drop to 0 hit points.

Gallows Tree

This creature appears as a massive, tall tree with thick branches from which hang several humanoid corpses tightly secured by their necks with greenish-brod bushy, and its trunk is mottled brown.

Gallows trees are sentient plants that sustain themselves on the internal organs and body fluids of living creatures. They use deception to lure potential prey into range at which time they unleash the gallows tree zombies attached to their branches to kill or capture the prey.

While mobile, a gallows tree prefers to remain in one spot for an extended length of time (usually until its food supply in the area runs out). From this location, it simply waits for prey and then attacks when such beings come into view. Gallows trees do not collect treasure but occasionally such items (the remnants of devoured prey) are found near a gallows tree.

A gallows tree normally stands idle, lowering its zombies to the ground when living prey come within 100 feet of the tree. If a foe comes within 15 feet of the tree itself, it lashes out with its sharpened branches and pummels the creature or attempts to wrap a branch around the foe. A grabbed foe is subjected to additional damage as the gallows tree pummels it with its other branches. Occasionally the tree works in concert with its zombies, grabbing a foe and holding it while its zombies pound it into goop. Slain creatures are dragged close to the tree, sliced open, and their innards devoured by the tree's roots.

Gallows Tree

Huge plant, unaligned
Armor Class 16 (natural armor)
Hit Points 287 (23d12 + 138)
Speed 30 ft.

STR	DEX	CON	INT	WIS	CHA
25 (+7)	10 (+0)	22 (+6)	10 (+0)	14 (+2)	6 (−2)

Saving Throws Con +11
Skills Perception +7, Stealth +5
Damage Resistance fire
Condition Immunities frightened, prone, stunned, unconscious
Senses tremorsense 60 ft., passive Perception 17
Languages Common, but cannot speak, telepathy 100 ft. with gallows tree zombies
Challenge 14 (11,500 XP)

Create Gallows Tree Zombie. When a creature dies within 15 feet of a gallows tree, The Gallow's Tree uses a sharpened tendril to slice open the creature's abdomen, thereby spilling the corpse's innards on the ground. The organs and fluids are then absorbed by the tree's roots. Corpses of a size other than Medium or Large are simply left to rot. Medium or Large corpses are filled with a greenish pollen fired from one of the tree's branches. The abdominal wound heals over the next 1d4 days, at which time the slain creature rises as a gallows tree zombie connected by a tether-vine to the gallows tree that created it. Gallows tree zombies possess none of their former abilities.

Gallows Tree Zombies. Each gallows tree has several gallows tree zombies connected to it. A Huge gallows tree may have no more than seven gallows tree zombies connected to it at one time. See the gallows tree zombie entry for details on that monster.

Actions

Multiattack. The gallows tree makes three slam attacks.

Slam. *Melee Weapon Attack:* +12 to hit, reach 15 ft., one target. *Hit:* 28 (6d6 + 7) bludgeoning damage and the target is grappled (escape DC 22) and restrained.

Gallows Tree Zombie

This creature is a humanoid with deathly gray-green skin dressed in tattered and torn clothes. Small plants, weeds, and fungi grow on the creature's body. A long, sinewy, greenish-brown noose connects the creature to the massive tree behind it.

Gallows tree zombies were once living humanoids slain and devoured by a gallows tree and reborn from the seedlings as a minion of said creature. They serve no purpose in life now other than killing or capturing living prey for the gallows tree that created them. These monsters retain small memories of their former lives and these scenes sometimes manifest in the zombie's mind, causing it great anger which it vents on the nearest living creature. Gallows tree zombies appear as humanoid creatures with deathly gray-green skin that feels coarse and rough to the touch. A long, sinewy cord of greenish-brown wraps around the zombie's throat and connects it to the gallows tree. Gallows tree zombies show no spark of life in their eyes but are not completely mindless. They are not undead even though their name suggests otherwise; therefore, they cannot be turned or rebuked.

Gallows tree zombies hang motionless from the tree that created them, being lowered to the ground only when a living creature comes within 100 feet of the gallows tree they are connected to. They are formidable opponents and relentlessly pound their foes with their club-like fists while breathing a cloud of choking spores. The zombies prefer uneven odds that favor them, so ganging up on an individual is the norm in battle. Slain foes are dragged back to the gallows tree, devoured by the tree, and eventually transformed into a gallows tree zombie to replace any that fell in battle.

Gallows Tree Zombie

Medium plant, unaligned
Armor Class 11 (natural armor)
Hit Points 52 (7d8 + 21)
Speed 20 ft.

STR	DEX	CON	INT	WIS	CHA
19 (+4)	10 (+0)	16 (+3)	4 (–3)	10 (+0)	1 (–5)

Damage Resistance fire
Damage Immunities poison
Condition Immunities poisoned; frightened, prone, stunned, unconscious
Senses darkvision 60 ft., passive Perception 10
Languages Common, but cannot speak, telepathy 100 ft. with gallows tree
Challenge 3 (700 XP)

Regeneration. The gallows tree zombie regenerates 5 hit points at the start of its turn if it has at least 1 hit point.

Tether-Vine. A gallows tree zombie is connected to the gallows tree that created it by a long, sinewy vine. This vine can be lengthened to allow the zombie to move up to 100 feet away from the tree. The vine is AC 12 and has 10 hit points. Harming the vine deals no damage to the gallows tree zombie or the gallows tree, but if severed, does prevent the zombie from regenerating any health at the start of its turn.

Actions

Multiattack. The gallows tree zombie makes two slam attacks.

Slam. *Melee Weapon Attack:* +6 to hit, reach 5 ft., one target. *Hit:* 11 (2d6 + 4) bludgeoning damage.

Spore Cloud (Recharge 6). A gallows tree zombie can breathe a cloud of poisonous, greenish spores at the space directly in front of it in a 5-foot cube. A creature caught in the cloud must succeed on a DC 13 Constitution saving throw or be poisoned for 1 minute. Until this poison ends, the target is slowed (as the *slow* spell). The target can repeat the saving throw at the end of each of its turns, ending the effect on itself on a success.

Gargoyles

Gargoyle, Four-Armed

A powerful gargoyle similar to its kin, but having four arms rather than two.

Four-armed gargoyles, like their brethren, often stand perched indefinitely without moving in an attempt to surprise their opponents. They have a great fondness for inflicting pain on their foes. When a four-armed gargoyle has the upper hand in battle, it often draws out the conflict as long as it can in order to deal as much pain and suffering as it can on its foes.

Four-Armed Gargoyle

Medium monstrosity, chaotic evil
Armor Class 15 (natural armor)
Hit Points 55 (10d8 + 10)
Speed 30 ft., fly 60 ft.

STR	DEX	CON	INT	WIS	CHA
15 (+2)	14 (+2)	12 (+1)	6 (–2)	11 (+0)	7 (–2)

Damage Resistances bludgeoning, piercing, and slashing from nonmagical weapons not made of adamantine
Damage Immunities poison
Condition Immunities exhaustion, petrified, poisoned
Senses darkvision 60 ft., passive Perception 10
Languages Terran
Challenge 4 (1,100 XP)

False Appearance. While the gargoyle remains motionless, it is indistinguishable from an inanimate statue.

Actions

Multiattack. The gargoyle makes four attacks: one with its bite, two with its claws, and one gore.

Bite. *Melee Weapon Attack:* +4 to hit, reach 5 ft., one target. *Hit:* 6 (1d8 + 2) piercing damage.

Claws. *Melee Weapon Attack:* +4 to hit, reach 5 ft., one target. *Hit:* 9 (2d6 + 2) slashing damage.

Gore. *Melee Weapon Attack:* +4 to hit, reach 5 ft., one target. *Hit:* 6 (1d8 + 2) piercing damage.

Gargoyle, Fungus

This creature looks like a winged statue, humanoid in shape, carved from molds, funguses, and mushrooms. Its arms and legs end in clawed hands and feet, and its mouth is lined with fangs carved from the same substances its body is.

Fungus gargoyles are thought to be gargoyles that have been transformed into their current state by an evil cult that pays reverence to various demons of slime, ooze, and fungus. These creatures are often found acting as guardians in temples dedicated to such demons.

Unlike normal plants, fungus gargoyles do not require food or air (they still require water, however), but sometimes eat their fallen enemies simply for the sheer pleasure of doing so (usually only evil-aligned fungus gargoyles do this). A typical fungus gargoyle stands about 5 or 6 feet tall and weighs up to 200 pounds. Though its shape can vary, most resemble ugly winged humanoids.

Fungus gargoyles typically ambush their prey, standing motionless until their opponent moves close. The fungus gargoyles then leap to the attack, slashing with their claws. Most fungus gargoyles try to stay airborne during combat rather than fight on the ground.

Fungus Gargoyle

Medium plant, neutral evil
Armor Class 14 (natural armor)
Hit Points 67 (9d8 + 27)
Speed 30 ft., fly 60 ft.

STR	DEX	CON	INT	WIS	CHA
18 (+4)	14 (+2)	17 (+3)	6 (–2)	11 (+0)	7 (–2)

Skills Perception +6, Stealth +5
Damage Resistances fire; bludgeoning, piercing, and slashing from nonmagical weapons that aren't adamantine

Damage Immunities poison
Condition Immunities exhaustion, petrified, poisoned
Senses passive Perception 16
Languages —
Challenge 5 (1,800 XP)

False Appearance. While the gargoyle remains motionless, it is indistinguishable from a weathered, inanimate statue that is covered in fungus, lichen, and moss.

Stench. Any creature that starts its turn within 10 feet of the gargoyle must succeed on a DC 13 Constitution saving throw or be poisoned until the start of its next turn. On a successful saving throw, the creature is immune to the gargoyle's stench for 24 hours.

Actions

Multiattack. The gargoyle makes three attacks: one with its bite and two with its claws.

Bite. *Melee Weapon Attack:* +7 to hit, reach 5 ft., one target. *Hit:* 13 (2d8 + 4) piercing damage.

Claws. *Melee Weapon Attack:* +7 to hit, reach 5 ft., one target. *Hit:* 11 (2d6 + 4) slashing damage.

Deadly Spores (Recharge 5–6). The fungus gargoyle exhales deadly spores in a 15-foot cone. Each creature in the area must make a DC 15 Constitution saving throw, taking 18 (4d8) poison damage on a failed save, or half as much damage on a successful one.

Gargoyle, Green Guardian

This winged humanoid creature is carved of a strange green stone with eyes rich black in color.

They prefer to remain still and then suddenly attack or dive into their prey. Green guardians attempt to hold their victims and then fly off with them.

Gargoyle, Green Guardian

Medium elemental, chaotic evil
Armor Class 15 (natural armor)
Hit Points 85 (10d8 + 40)
Speed 40 ft., fly 60 ft.

STR	DEX	CON	INT	WIS	CHA
15 (+2)	14 (+2)	18 (+4)	6 (–2)	11 (+0)	7 (–2)

Skills Perception +6
Damage Resistance bludgeoning, piercing, and slashing from nonmagical weapons that aren't adamantine
Damage Immunities poison
Condition Immunities exhaustion, petrified, poisoned
Senses darkvision 60 ft., passive Perception 16
Languages Common, Terran
Challenge 6 (2,300 XP)

False Appearance. While the gargoyle remains motionless, it is indistinguishable from an inanimate statue.

Magic Weapons. The gargoyle's attacks are magical.

Reanimation. The eyes of a green guardian gargoyle are made of two pieces of jet (500 gp each) that detect as both magic (faint conjuration) and evil. After being destroyed, a green guardian automatically reanimates

in 1d8+2 days unless the eye gems are crushed and disenchanted with both *dispel magic* and *remove curse*.

Swoop. If the green guardian flies at least 20 feet straight towards a target and then hits it with its gore attack on the same turn, the target takes an additional 9 (2d8) piercing damage. If the target is a creature, it must make a DC 13 Strength saving throw or be knocked prone.

Actions

Multiattack. The green guardian makes four attacks: one with its bite, two with its claws, and one with its gore.

Bite. *Melee Weapon Attack:* +5 to hit, reach 5 ft., one target. *Hit:* 11 (2d8 + 2) piercing damage.

Claws. *Melee Weapon Attack:* +45 to hit, reach 5 ft., one target. *Hit:* 9 (2d6 + 2) slashing damage. If both claws attacks hit the same target, then it is grappled (escape DC 12) and restrained. At the start of the gargoyle's next turn, it will attempt to fly off with the target.

Gore. *Melee Weapon Attack:* +5 to hit, reach 5 ft., one target. *Hit:* 13 (2d10 + 2) piercing damage.

Gargoyle, Margoyle

This creature looks like a hideously ugly humanoid chiseled from brown stone. Two large horns protrude from its head, just above its eyes. Four large, stony spikes jut from its shoulder blades. Its hands and feet end in sharpened claws.

A margoyle is a slightly larger version of the standard gargoyle. It is meaner, eviler, and deadlier than the normal gargoyle. Margoyles are most often encountered in subterranean regions and often have a pack of gargoyles with them. In such cases, the margoyle is looked upon as the master or leader of the group.

Gargoyle, Margoyle

Medium monstrosity, chaotic evil
Armor Class 15 (natural armor)
Hit Points 68 (8d8 + 32)
Speed 30 ft., fly 60 ft.

STR	DEX	CON	INT	WIS	CHA
17 (+3)	15 (+2)	19 (+4)	6 (−1)	10 (+0)	7 (−2)

Skills Stealth +4
Damage Resistances bludgeoning, piercing, and slashing damage from nonmagical weapons that aren't adamantine
Damage Immunities poison
Condition Immunities exhausted, petrified, poisoned
Senses darkvision 60 ft., passive Perception 10
Languages Terran
Challenge 4 (1,800 XP)

False Appearance. While a margoyle sits motionless, it is indistinguishable from natural stone and can't be detected as alive by any means.

Actions

Multiattack. The margoyle makes three attacks: one with its bite and two with its claws; it can gore once with its horns instead of using its bite.

Bite. *Melee Weapon Attack:* +5 to hit, reach 5 ft.; one target. *Hit:* 7 (1d8 + 3) piercing damage.

Claw. *Melee Weapon Attack:* +5 to hit, reach 5 ft., one target. *Hit:* 10 (2d6 + 3) slashing damage.

Gore. *Melee Weapon Attack:* +5 to hit, reach 5 ft., one target. *Hit:* 7 (1d8 + 3) piercing damage.

Gem Dog

This creature looks like a canine, but its fur gleams and shimmers in a brilliant hue as if the creature is made out of gems.

A gem dog is a canine-ish pack hunter that appears from a distance to be made out of gems. Long ago, a pack of wild dogs came to live in a region blasted by a battle between two powerful wizards. Like many of the wildlife in the region, the dogs were forever altered by their sojourn into so chaotically magical a land, though unlike most of the others, the gem dogs came out both uncorrupted by the less savory lingering enchantments and able to survive as a viable magical species all their own. Since then, they have spread throughout the land though they have never grown numerous.

Gem dogs remain carnivores as the wild dogs from which they mutated, but in addition to ordinary prey, gem dogs must also consume quality minerals to survive. They have no interest in diamonds but can smell jade, sapphires, rubies, emeralds, and alexandrite, among others, for miles. While they can gain sustenance from many silicates and other mineral sources (even sand), they far prefer the purest, clearest gem crystals when they can get them. Gem dogs will rarely threaten humanoids for any reason, but they will happily steal bags or stashes of gems whenever they can get to them. Starving gem dogs in a large pack might attack a party of travelers.

Gem dog jaws are freakishly strong for their size in order to crunch up delicious gemstones. Their teeth and claws are similarly freakishly hard. A gem dog can do a lot more harm than it looks like it should be able to, and combined with their skillful use of their blindingly glittering coats, gem dog packs take down surprisingly large prey from time to time. Gem dogs have crystalline spines along their backs that can be violently ejected at foes. The loss of the spines causes minor pain; therefore, they only shoot the projectiles if truly afraid.

Gem dogs can come in the colors of nearly any gemstone (even white, despite their disdain for diamonds), but usually, only 2–3 colors are represented in a single pack. The "gems" in gem dogs' fur and spines are worthless, crumbling within hours of being removed from a living gem dog (and even faster if the gem dog is slain). Gem dogs' hard, glittering outercoat is prickly and cold, but beneath that, gem dogs are soft and warm like regular dogs, especially on their bellies. If raised from puppyhood, it is said that gem dogs can be domesticated and trained, but between their high intelligence and sheer destructive power, few would be able to control one — especially when a friend's jewelry looks tasty.

Innate Spellcasting. The gem dog's spellcasting ability is Wisdom (spell save DC 16, +8 to hit with spell attacks). The gem dog can innately cast the following spells, requiring no material, verbal, or somatic components:

At will: *color spray, dancing lights, faerie fire*

3/day each: *blur, heat metal, hypnotic pattern, mirror image, misty step, moonbeam*

1/day: *hallucinatory terrain*

Magic Resistance. The gem dog has advantage on saving throws against spells and other magical effects.

Gem Dog

Small monstrosity, unaligned

Armor Class 16 (natural armor)
Hit Points 112 (15d6 + 60)
Speed 50 ft.

STR	DEX	CON	INT	WIS	CHA
22 (+6)	16 (+3)	18 (+4)	12 (+1)	18 (+4)	13 (+1)

Skills Perception +8, Stealth +7
Damage Resistances bludgeoning, piercing, and slashing damage from nonmagical weapons that aren't adamantine
Damage Immunities poison
Condition Immunities poisoned
Senses darkvision 60 ft., passive Perception 18
Languages —
Challenge 9 (5,000 XP)

Actions

Multiattack. The gem dog attacks once with its bite and twice with its claws, or it can make two Gem Spine Spray attacks.

Bite. *Melee Weapon Attack:* +10 to hit, reach 5 ft., one target. *Hit:* 28 (4d10 + 6) piercing damage.

Claw. *Melee Weapon Attack:* +10 to hit, reach 5 ft., one target. *Hit:* 15 (2d8 + 6) slashing damage.

Gem Spine Spray. *Ranged Weapon Attack:* +7 to hit, range 20/60 ft., one target. *Hit:* 30 (5d10 + 3) piercing.

Blinding Gleam. If the gem dog is in bright light, it can force one creature that it can see within 60 feet of it to make a DC 16 Dexterity saving throw if the gem dog isn't incapacitated. On a failed save, the creature is blinded for 1 minute as the gem dog reflects light into its eyes.

A creature that isn't surprised can avert its eyes to avoid the saving throw at the start of its turn. If it does so, it can't see the gem dog until the start of its next turn, when it can avert its eyes again. If it looks at the gem dog in the meantime, it must immediately make the save.

Genies

Genie, Abasheen

This being stands 8 feet tall in flowing robes of purple and gold. Its hair is black and tied back in a ponytail with a ribbon of gold.

Abasheen are genies from the Plane of Air and serve the nobles of that plane as diplomats, couriers, and emissaries. Some of the less scrupulous serve as spies and insurgents. They are extremely clever and often let their arrogance interfere with their assignments. Abasheen look down on all creatures from the Material Plane.

Abasheen and common djinn tolerate each other, but that is as far as it goes. They rarely work together and when they do, such pairings often degenerate into quarrels. The societal structure of the abasheen is unknown but it is believed to be vastly different than that of the other genies. No abasheen nobles are known to exist and the entire race seems to be servitor to the race of djinn.

An abasheen stands about 8 feet tall and is always dressed in flowing robes colored to denote their current station. Their skin is dark and their build powerful. All have dark hair, either black or brown, and most wear their hair braided or pulled into a ponytail, tied with ribbons of gold or silver.

Abasheen rely on their physical attack and spell-like abilities in combat. When combat starts, an abasheen commands one of its opponents (usually the one closest to it) to drop or flee (see the *command* spell). On its next action, it either bashes an opponent with its fists (if one is close enough) or attempts to charm an enemy spellcaster. During combat, an abasheen rarely touches the ground, preferring to remain airborne and above its opponents. They rarely fight to the death. Should combat turn against an abasheen it always attempts to escape, usually by plane shifting away.

Abasheen

Large elemental, neutral
Armor Class 16 (natural armor)
Hit Points 102 (12d10 + 36)
Speed 20 ft., fly 50 ft.

STR	DEX	CON	INT	WIS	CHA
16 (+3)	14 (+2)	16 (+3)	20 (+5)	18 (+4)	17 (+3)

Saving Throws Dex +5, Wis +7, Cha +6
Skills Perception +10
Damage Immunities lightning, thunder
Senses darkvision 60 ft., passive Perception 20
Languages Auran, Common, Infernal
Challenge 6 (2,300 XP)

Air Mastery. Airborne creatures attack at disadvantage against abasheen.

Elemental Demise. If the abasheen dies, its body disintegrates into a warm breeze, leaving behind only the equipment the abasheen was wearing or carrying.

Grant Wish. The genie can grant one creature's wish that is within 60 feet of it.

Innate Spellcasting. The abasheen's innate spellcasting ability is Intelligence (spell save DC 15, +7 to hit with spell attacks). It can innately cast the following spells, requiring no material components:

At will: *command, charm person, plane shift* (willing targets to elemental planes, Astral Plane, or Material Plane only)
1/day: *geas*

Actions

Multiattack. The abasheen makes two attacks with its falchion.

Falchion. *Melee Weapon Attack:* +6 to hit, reach 10 ft., one target. *Hit:* 12 (2d8 + 3) slashing damage.

Thunderclap (Recharge 5–6). The abasheen claps its hands together loudly, and a wave of thundering force emanates out from it in a 30-foot radius. Each creature in this area must make a DC 15 Constitution saving throw or be pushed back 10 feet and take 18 (4d8) thunder damage on a failed save, or half as much damage with no pushback on a successful one.

Genie, Seraph

This creature resembles a ten-foot-tall human with brick-red skin and coal-black hair, long and braided.

The seraphs are genies from the Plane of Fire, and the sworn enemies of the efreet. A violent war between the two genie races has spanned centuries and spilled into an uncountable number of planes. Any encounter between a seraph and an efreeti sparks a battle that only ends when one or the other is killed. Those that aid the efreeti are treated by seraphs as if they were efreeti themselves; no mercy is shown in battle to an ally of the hated fire genies. The seraphs often align themselves with djinn as they both share the efreeti as a common enemy.

A seraph prefers to use its spell-like abilities over melee weapons in combat, often allowing its opponents to move in close so the seraph can unleash its fire burst. A seraph facing overwhelming odds in battle attempts to flee; covering its escape by turning invisible or erecting a wall of fire between itself and its enemies.

A typical seraph stands 10 feet tall and weighs about 1,500 pounds.

Seraph Genie

Large elemental, neutral good
Armor Class 15 (natural armor)
Hit Points 119 (14d10 + 42)
Speed 40 ft., fly 30 ft.

STR	DEX	CON	INT	WIS	CHA
19 (+4)	16 (+3)	17 (+3)	15 (+2)	15 (+2)	19 (+4)

Saving Throws Int +5, Wis +5
Skills Arcana +5, Deception +7, Insight +5, Perception +5
Damage Vulnerabilities cold
Damage Immunities fire
Senses darkvision 60 ft., passive Perception 15
Languages Celestial, Common, Ignan; telepathy 100 ft.
Challenge 8 (3,900 XP)

Heat. A seraph's body generates heat. Creatures who touch the genie take 7 (2d6) fire damage. If the seraph genie uses a metal weapon adds this additional damage to the weapon's attacks. A seraph genie can suppress this effect for 1 hour as a bonus action.

Innate Spellcasting. A seraph genie's innate spellcasting ability is charisma (spell save DC 15, +7 to hit with spell attacks). It can cast the following spells without requiring material components.

At will: *detect evil and good, detect magic, flame blade, plane shift (self only), produce flame*

3/day each: *fireball, flame strike, invisibility, see invisibility, wall of fire*

1/day each: *fire storm, greater invisibility*

Actions

Multiattack. A seraph genie makes three scimitar attacks.

Scimitar. *Melee Weapon Attack:* +7 to hit, reach 5 ft., one target. *Hit:* 7 (1d6 + 4) slashing damage plus 7 (2d6) fire damage.

Fire Burst (Recharge 5–6). The seraph genie emits a blast of elemental fire in a 30-foot radius. All creatures in the area must make a DC 15 Dexterity saving throw, taking 28 (8d6) fire damage on a failed saving throw, or half as much on a successful one.

Ghoul, Cinder

This creature is a swirling humanoid cloud of burning ash and charred body parts. A red glow of burning embers can be glimpsed floating within the mass. This creature reeks of smoke and burnt flesh.

A creature that is burned to death by magical fire may rise again as a fiery undead being called a cinder ghoul. The lairs of old red dragons may be haunted by many of these pathetic, angry spirits, and many a wizard that has dispatched a foe with a well-placed fireball has been found mysteriously charred to death many months after the deed.

Cinder ghouls are barely intelligent, but they do have a very vivid recollection of the pain they endured in the moments before their death. Filled with anger as fiery as the flames that took their life, cinder ghouls harbor a strong hatred of fire and any living creature that has control over it.

Although it cannot speak, the sound of wailing and screaming and the rushing of fire-stoked wind constantly accompany a cinder ghoul.

In melee a cinder ghoul slams with the charred remains of its fists. If a cinder ghoul encounters an opponent that demonstrates any form of control over fire — either through casting a fire spell or using a magic item that produces fire — it attacks that opponent to the exclusion of all others.

Cinder Ghoul

Large undead, chaotic evil
Armor Class 18 (natural armor)
Hit Points 90 (12d10 + 24)
Speed fly 40 ft. (hover)

STR	DEX	CON	INT	WIS	CHA
16 (+3)	20 (+5)	15 (+2)	4 (–3)	12 (+1)	19 (+4)

Damage Resistances cold; bludgeoning, piercing, and slashing from nonmagical weapons
Damage Immunities fire
Condition Immunities charmed, exhaustion, paralyzed, poisoned, unconscious
Senses darkvision 60 ft., passive Perception 11
Languages —
Challenge 5 (1,800 XP)

Gaseous Form. While in this form, the cinder ghoul can't take any actions, speak, or manipulate objects. It is weightless, has a flying speed of 40 feet, can hover, and can enter a hostile creature's space and stop there. In addition, if air can pass through a space, the mist can do so without squeezing. It cannot pass through water. It has advantage on Strength, Dexterity, and Constitution saving throws, and it is immune to all nonmagical damage.

Magic Resistance. The cinder ghoul has advantage on saving throws against spells and other magical effects.

Actions

Slam. *Melee Weapon Attack:* +8 to hit, reach 5 ft., one target. *Hit:* 14 (2d8 + 5) bludgeoning damage plus 7 (2d6) fire damage.

Smoke Inhalation. One creature that isn't a construct or undead and is in the cinder ghoul's space must make a DC 15 Constitution saving throw. On a failed save, the target takes 10 (3d6) fire damage and its hit point maximum is reduced by an amount equal to the fire damage taken. The target dies if this reduces its hit point maximum to 0. This reduction of the target's hit point maximum lasts until the target finishes a long rest.

Ghoul, Dust

This monster appears as a dust-covered creature with decaying flesh pulled tight over its humanoid frame. Its teeth are pointed fangs and its hands end in wicked, dirt-covered and blood-soaked claws.

When a humanoid creature dies on the Parched Expanse on the Plane of Molten Skies, there is a good chance it returns from the afterlife as a dust ghoul — an undead flesh-eating creature composed of dust and earth.

Dust ghouls haunt the Parched Expanse, preying on unwary travelers who linger too long in their hunting grounds. These creatures savor the taste of human flesh and devour such a kill with great ferocity.

Dust ghouls predicate their arrival by animating dust into ghostly humanoids that immediately move to grapple potential prey. Dust ghouls then move in (often swooping in from above) and attempt to paralyze their foes with their shriek. Prey is then torn to pieces by the dust ghouls using its claws and fangs. If a dust ghoul is slain, it crumbles into a pile of dust.

Dust Ghoul

Medium undead, chaotic evil
Armor Class 16 (natural armor)
Hit Points 104 (16d8 + 32)
Speed 40 ft., fly 40 ft., burrow 20 ft.

STR	DEX	CON	INT	WIS	CHA
21 (+5)	16 (+3)	15 (+2)	14 (+2)	14 (+2)	16 (+3)

Damage Immunities poison
Condition Immunities charmed, exhaustion, frightened, paralyzed, poisoned
Senses darkvision 60 ft., passive Perception 18
Languages Common
Challenge 7 (2,900 XP)

Improved Critical. The ghoul's attacks score a critical hit on a roll of 19 or 20.

Actions

Multiattack. The dust ghoul makes three attacks: one with its bite and two with its claws.

Bite. Melee Weapon Attack: +8 to hit, reach 5 ft., one target. *Hit:* 14 (2d8 + 5) piercing damage.

Claws. Melee Weapon Attack: +8 to hit, reach 5 ft., one target. *Hit:* 15 (3d6 + 5) slashing damage.

Blinding Dust (1/day). Blinding dust and sand swirls magically around the ghoul. Each creature within 5 feet of the ghoul must succeed on a DC 15 Constitution saving throw or be blinded until the end of the creature's next turn.

Paralyzing Shriek (Recharge 5–6). The dust ghoul unleashes a hellish shriek. Each creature that is within 60 feet of the ghoul and can hear it must succeed on a DC 13 Constitution saving throw or be paralyzed for 1 minute. The target can repeat the saving throw at the end of each of its turns, ending the effect on itself on a success.

Giants

Giant, Cave

This massive giant has hideously primitive features and gray blotchy flesh. Unkempt, it wears nothing but filthy rags and carries a tremendous greatclub, and its eyes glare maliciously. Most disturbing, its protruding tusk-like teeth hang over its swollen lips, causing a steady stream of drool.

Dumber, stronger cousins of hill giants, cave giants live in small communal bands of no more than twelve individuals, with a single male leader that is usually stronger and certainly meaner than all others. They often take up residence in large hill or mountain caves, foraging for food such as mountain goats, bears, and wayward explorers. Extremely primitive and simple-minded, cave giants have no real concept of fire or creature comforts, so they eat their food raw.

Giant, Cave

Huge giant, chaotic evil
Armor Class 14 (natural armor)
Hit Points 137 (11d12 + 66)
Speed 40 ft.

STR	DEX	CON	INT	WIS	CHA
23 (+6)	10 (+0)	22 (+6)	6 (−2)	10 (+0)	7 (−2)

Skills Perception +3
Senses darkvision 120 ft., passive Perception 13
Languages Giant
Challenge 6 (2,300 XP)

Camouflage. The giant has advantage on Dexterity (Stealth) checks to hide in cavernous and rocky underground terrain.

Actions

Multiattack. The cave giant makes two greataxe attacks.
Greataxe. *Melee Weapon Attack:* +9 to hit, reach 10 ft., one target. *Hit:* 19 (2d12 + 6) slashing damage.
Rock. *Ranged Weapon Attack:* +9 to hit, range 60/240 ft., one target. *Hit:* 28 (4d10 + 6) bludgeoning damage. If the target is a creature, it must succeed on a DC 16 Strength saving throw or be knocked prone.

Reactions

Rock Catching. If a rock or similar object is hurled at the giant, the giant can, with a successful DC 10 Dexterity saving throw, catch the missile and take no bludgeoning damage from it.

Giant, Jack-in-Irons

Brutish, warty, hairy, and stinking of oil and iron, this creature has a jutting lower jaws and tusk-like teeth, not unlike an orc or hobgoblin of huge size wrapped in chains of iron. It wears belts of skulls and rotting heads about its throat and waist.

The jacks-in irons enjoy fastening gate chains and portcullis chains around their wrists, forearms and shins and tie chains about their throats, shoulders, and waists which hang with the heads of their many victims. Jacks-in-irons frequently operate as highwaymen, making their dwellings in ruined towers along abandoned roads. From this base, they roam out along old country trails ambushing unwary travelers, trade caravans and the knights assigned to protect them. They are known to take prisoners and hold them for high ransom.

Orcs and goblins often follow a jack-in-irons as their king or leader due to its massive size, brute strength, and penchant for wickedness — all of which are things that such evil creatures admire.

A jack-in-irons stands 20 to 25 feet tall and weighs 13,000 to 15,000 pounds. It prefers to dress in dark colors such as black or brown and always wears a multitude of chains about its body (as bracelets, necklaces, or slung about its shoulders). Its hair is dark and matted and many male jack-in-irons sport thick, bushy beards. Its eyes are purplish-black with light green irises.

Jack-in-irons speak Giant.

Bash, bash, bash, rinse and repeat if necessary until they are out of a DC 18 Dexterity saving throw or be grappled and restrained (escape DC 18) and the jack-in-irons giant cannot grapple another target. At the beginning of the giant's turn, it can smash a grappled target into the ground or another solid object within 15 feet of the giant, dealing 11 (1d8 + 7) bludgeoning damage.

Fist. *Melee Weapon Attack:* +10 to hit, reach 5 ft., one target. *Hit:* 14 (2d6 + 7) bludgeoning damage and the target must succeed on a DC 18 Strength saving throw or be knocked prone.

Rock. *Ranged Weapon Attack:* +10 to hit, range 60/240 ft., one target. *Hit:* 23 (3d10 + 7) bludgeoning damage.

Shake the Earth. Creatures within 10 feet of the jack-in-irons giant must succeed on a DC 18 Dexterity saving throw or fall prone.

Giant, Sand

This giant looks like a savage humanoid with dark tan skin, dark hair, and green eyes.

Sand giants are brutal, somewhat barbaric giants that prey on those weaker than themselves. They have dark tan skin, brown hair, and dark-brown or dark-green eyes. An adult male stands approximately 20 feet tall. Males tend to wear their hair and beards braided. Sand giants wear light clothes and light armor (if any). In times of battle or war, males may don chainmail. A typical sand giant's bag contains food, 3d4 mundane items, and a modest amount of cash (no more than 12d10 coins). Sand giants can live to be 500 years old.

attacks or out of enemies. Jacks-in-irons think of themselves as invincible and fight to the death.

Jack-in-Irons Giant

Huge giant, chaotic evil
Armor Class 15 (chain scraps)
Hit Points 138 (12d12 + 60)
Speed 40 ft.

STR	DEX	CON	INT	WIS	CHA
24 (+7)	12 (+1)	20 (+5)	9 (−1)	12 (+1)	8 (−1)

Senses darkvision 60 ft., passive Perception 11
Languages Giant
Challenge 7 (2,900 XP)

Actions

Multiattack. The jack-in-irons giant uses its shake the earth ability, and then makes two club attacks and either a chain or fist attack.

Club. *Melee Weapon Attack:* +10 to hit, reach 10 ft., one target. *Hit:* 16 (2d8 + 7) bludgeoning damage.

Chain. *Melee Weapon Attack:* +10 to hit, reach 15 ft., one target. *Hit:* 14 (2d6 + 7) bludgeoning damage and the target must succeed on

Sand giants make their homes in warm desert lands away from civilization. They live in organized tribes consisting of 8–9 families of 2–4 members each. On occasion, a tribe forms a raiding party that sets off to the nearest civilized place, returning at a later time with food, coins, and captives. For each adult in a sand giant's lair, there is a 40% chance that the lair has 1d3 captives of any humanoid race.

Sand giants favor their greatswords in combat. They usually begin combat by shaping a fist from the surrounding terrain and attacking with their greatswords in concert with the earthen fist. Sand giants do not throw rocks like many other giants do, but they can catch rocks or similar projectiles as other giants.

Sand Giant

Huge giant, neutral evil
Armor Class 16 (natural armor)
Hit Points 262 (21d12 + 126)
Speed 40 ft.

STR	DEX	CON	INT	WIS	CHA
28 (+9)	13 (+1)	22 (+6)	12 (+1)	12 (+1)	14 (+2)

Saving Throws Con +10, Wis +5
Skills Perception +5
Senses passive Perception 15
Languages Giant
Challenge 9 (5,000 XP)

Innate Spellcasting. The giant's innate spellcasting ability is Charisma (spell save DC 14, +6 to hit with spell attacks). It can innately cast the following spells, requiring no material components:
2/day: *move earth*
1/day: *earthquake*

Actions

Multiattack. The sand giant makes two attacks with its greatsword.
Greataxe. *Melee Weapon Attack*: +13 to hit, reach 15 ft., one target. Hit: 26 (5d6 + 9) slashing damage.
Fist of Sand (1/day). The giant slams its fist violently into the ground. All creatures within 10 feet of the giant must make a DC 16 Dexterity saving throw or be knocked prone and take 14 (4d6) bludgeoning damage on a failure, or half as much damage without being knocked prone on a success.

Giant, Sea

This huge being has bluish green skin and eyes that reflect light like two silvery moons. Rippling with muscle, this creature rises from the depths with a crash of waves on rocks.

Sea giants are the reclusive cousins of storm giants. They are most often found in the deepest depths of the seas where they make their dwelling in the cones of long-dead undersea volcanoes.

Sea giants have a druid-like power over the forces of the seas and are a living embodiment of its bounty and destructive wrath.

Sea giants seldom come into contact with surface-dwellers but have been known on rare occasions to exact bounties from coastal cities to ensure the safety of their navies and merchant vessels. Sea giants are most commonly encountered within a few hundred miles of their lair, tending to their domain and battling off incursions of sahuagin, aboleth, krakens and other such destructive forces of the undersea.

An adult male sea giant stands 10 feet tall and weighs about 6,000 pounds. Females are slightly shorter and lighter. Both have sea-green skin, dark-green or black hair, and silver eyes. Sea giants adorn themselves in loose flowing robes of white, blue, or green. Many wear wreaths of coral in their hair.

When battling at the surface of the seas, sea giants hurl rocks at great length against opposing ranged attackers, usually including crews of siege engines. When battling against surface ships their tactic is to disguise themselves by creating rough waters with their *control water* ability. They then hammer the hull with their mighty fists until it is holed, without ever revealing themselves to the crew. Once holed, they tear the hull apart and drown the crew.

When fighting beneath the waves they use their crushing pressure special ability to increase the water pressure around themselves in an effort to destroy interlopers and trespassers.

Sea Giant

Large giant, chaotic neutral
Armor Class 17 (natural armor)
Hit Points 178 (17d10 + 85)
Speed 40 ft., swim 30 ft.

STR	DEX	CON	INT	WIS	CHA
29 (+9)	14 (+2)	20 (+5)	17 (+3)	18 (+4)	19 (+4)

Saving Throws Con +9
Skills Acrobatics +6, Athletics +13, Intimidation +8, Perception +8, Stealth +6
Senses darkvision 120 ft., passive Perception 18
Languages Aquan, Common, Giant
Challenge 9 (5,000 XP)

Amphibious. The sea giant can breathe air and water.
Innate Spellcasting. The giant's innate spellcasting ability is Charisma (spell save DC 16, +8 to hit with spell attacks). It can innately cast the following spells, requiring no material components:

At will: *create or destroy water, detect magic*
5/day: *control water*
3/day: *control weather*

Actions

Multiattack. The sea giant makes two slam attacks.
Slam. *Melee Weapon Attack:* +13 to hit, reach 10 ft., one target. *Hit:* 18 (2d8 + 9) bludgeoning damage.
Rock. *Ranged Weapon Attack:* +13 to hit, range 60/240 ft., one target. *Hit:* 27 (4d8 + 9) bludgeoning damage.
Crushing Pressure (Recharge 5–6). The sea giant chooses an area of water no larger than a 50-foot cube with 30 ft. of it. The water pressure within the space magically increases, and creatures within the area treat it as difficult terrain. In addition, any creature who enters or begins its turn within the area must make a DC 18 Constitution saving throw, taking 18 (4d8) bludgeoning damage on a failed saving throw, or half as much damage on a successful one. The area remains affected by this magic for 1 minute, until the sea giant dismisses it as an action, or the sea giant dies.

Giant, Volcano

This 18-foot-tall, barrel-chested giant has leathery, reddish-brown skin and haunting amber eyes. The creature is tough and wiry, with the strength and texture of copper.

Volcano giants make their homes in the many twisting caves and subterranean rooms of volcanic cones, enlarging and reinforcing them for comfort and convenience.

Clothing for a volcano giant usually consists of little more than a simple wrap of fire lizard skin. Volcano giants wears ornaments made of bone, shell, and obsidian, and their general culture and society is similar to that of humanoid civilizations on tropical islands. Such island societies often get along well with local tribes of volcano giants, engaging in trade and peacefully coexisting. Should a tribe of volcano giants form an allegiance with a human tribe, the giants warn the humans of possible eruptions of their volcano to allow them time to escape the destruction.

Although volcano giants can be described as good-natured and peaceful people, their demeanor can change quickly. At a real or imagined affront, a volcano giant can erupt with a passion that is rivaled only by the fire and fury of the volcano in which it lives.

Volcano giants feel that their shadow is actually their soul, and do not tolerate any creature that dares to trod upon it. Volcano giants usually use gargantuan longspears in combat. They are fierce and brave warriors, not

backing down from any adversary. Many choose to open combat with their breath weapon so as to soften up their foes before attacking.

Volcano Giant

Huge giant, chaotic neutral
Armor Class 19 (natural armor)
Hit Points 187 (15d12 + 90)
Speed 40 ft.

STR	DEX	CON	INT	WIS	CHA
29 (+9)	15 (+2)	22 (+6)	16 (+3)	18 (+4)	18 (+4)

Saving Throws Con +11
Skills Acrobatics +7, Intimidation +9, Nature +8, Perception +9
Damage Vulnerabilities cold
Damage Immunities fire
Senses passive Perception 19

Languages Giant, Ignan
Challenge 13 (10,000 XP)

Heated Body. The volcano giant's attacks deal an additional 7 (2d6) fire damage (included in the attacks below).

Actions

Multiattack. The volcano giant makes one one-handed spear attack and one slam attack, or two slam attacks.

Spear. *Melee or Ranged Weapon Attack:* +14 to hit, reach 10 ft. or range 40/120 ft., one target. *Hit:* 23 (4d6 + 9) piercing damage plus 7 (2d6) fire damage, or 27 (4d8 + 9) piercing damage plus 7 (2d6) fire damage if used with two hands to make a melee attack.

Slam. *Melee Weapon Attack:* +14 to hit, reach 15 ft., one target. *Hit:* 19 (3d6 + 9) bludgeoning damage plus 7 (2d6) fire damage.

Rock. *Ranged Weapon Attack:* +14 to hit, range 60/240 ft., one target. *Hit:* 27 (4d8 + 9) bludgeoning damage plus 7 (2d6) fire damage.

Sulfuric Breath (Recharge 5–6). A volcano giant can exhale a cloud of warm and sulfuric gas in a 30-foot cone. All creatures in the area must succeed on a DC 19 Constitution saving throw or take 35 (10d6) acid damage and be poisoned for 1 minute.

Giant, Wood

This giant resembles a wood elf of about 10 feet tall. It has brownish-green skin, a bald head, and bright green eyes.

Wood giants are peaceful, good-natured giants found in the forested areas of the world. The average wood giant stands 9 feet tall, weighs 900 pounds, and resembles a large wood elf. Wood giants have large heads and prominent jaws; their elf-like ears sit high on their long, oval heads. Most wood giants (particularly males) are bald. Their skin is usually brownish-green. Wood giants dress in greens or browns and prefer neutral colors to the bright or dull colors of other races. Wood giants can live to be 400 years old.

Wood giants are on friendly terms with most benign creatures of the forest, particularly wood elves. Though contact outside their immediate clan is rare, they do occasionally have dealings with nearby tribes of wood elves. Wood giant villages are large and open expanses of land with few if any buildings or shelters. Wood giants prefer to spend their time under the warmth of the day and the serenity of the night. They do not associate with — and usually attack on sight — evil forest creatures.

Wood giants usually attack from ambush, hiding in dense undergrowth and firing at their prey with their bows before closing to melee with their greatswords.

Wood Giant

Large giant, chaotic good
Armor Class 16 (natural armor)
Hit Points 76 (9d10 + 27)
Speed 40 ft.

STR	DEX	CON	INT	WIS	CHA
20 (+5)	16 (+3)	17 (+3)	14 (+2)	14 (+2)	16 (+3)

Skills Acrobatics +5, Athletics +7, Perception +4, Stealth +5
Senses darkvision 60 ft., passive Perception 14
Languages Common, Giant, Sylvan
Challenge 4 (1,100 XP)

Innate Spellcasting. The giant's innate spellcasting ability is Charisma (spell save DC 13, +5 to hit with spell attacks). It can innately cast *alter self* at will, requiring no material components.

Actions

Multiattack. The wood giant makes two greatsword or two longbow attacks.

Greatsword. *Melee Weapon Attack:* +7 to hit, reach 10 ft., one target. *Hit:* 12 (2d6 + 5) slashing damage.

Longbow. *Ranged Weapon Attack:* +5 to hit, range 150/600 ft., one target. *Hit:* 12 (2d8 + 3) piercing damage.

Gibbering Abomination

This massive fleshy conglomeration is covered with madly staring eyes, gaping mouths in screaming faces, and pulsing orifices exuding foul-smelling substances.

A horrifying expanse of fused faces and parts of faces, the gibbering abomination is the result of foul arcane experiments studying the creation of chimerical creatures. It bears a close superficial resemblance to a gibbering mouther or lesser gibbering orb, and may be mistaken for one of those, but they are no true relation. Instead, the gibbering abomination has been cobbled together from the faces and organs of dozens of humanoid creatures; its innards are a bizarre tangle of brains, hearts, and other organs. The gibbering abomination is in constant pain as a result of the process that created it, haunted by half-remembered memories from the creatures it was composed from.

Gibbering abominations have clear memories of the experiments and procedures they suffered in their formation and value nothing more than their own personal freedom. Beyond that, their constant anguish has given them a hateful attitude toward other creatures.

Gibbering Abomination

Large aberration, chaotic evil
Armor Class 17 (natural armor)
Hit Points 200 (16d10 + 112)
Speed 10 ft., climb 10 ft.

STR	DEX	CON	INT	WIS	CHA
18 (+4)	16 (+3)	24 (+7)	10 (+0)	6 (−2)	19 (+4)

Saving Throws Con +12, Cha +9
Skills Perception +8, Stealth +8
Damage Resistance lightning, thunder; bludgeoning, piercing, and slashing from nonmagical weapons
Condition Immunities prone
Senses darkvision 60 ft., passive Perception 18
Languages Deep Speech
Challenge 16 (15,000 XP)

Innate Spellcasting. The gibbering abomination's spellcasting ability is Charisma (spell save DC 17, +9 to hit with spell attacks). It can cast the following spells at will, requiring no material components: *blur, color spray, confusion, dispel magic, fear, ray of frost, ray of enfeeblement, telekinesis.*

Amorphous. The gibbering abomination can move through a space as narrow as 1 inch wide without squeezing.

Arcane Frenzy. The gibbering abomination can use its innate spellcasting more frequently than other creatures. During a single turn, the gibbering abomination can use its action and bonus action to innately cast a spell. The gibbering abomination cannot cast the same spell twice during its turn.

Deathless. Unless the gibbering abomination is slain by a *disintegrate* spell or its remains are completely incinerated, the abomination returns to life with 1 hit point in 1 hour.

Hyper-Awareness. The gibbering abomination can't be surprised.

Pain Immunity. The gibbering abomination is immune to any effect or condition caused as a result of extreme pain or agony. This ability does not protect it against damage the abomination would suffer.

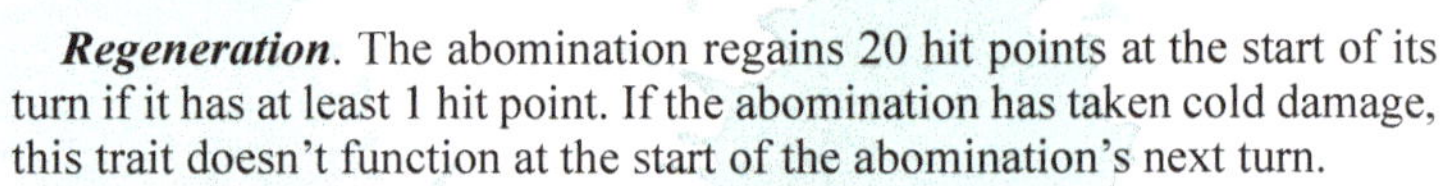

Regeneration. The abomination regains 20 hit points at the start of its turn if it has at least 1 hit point. If the abomination has taken cold damage, this trait doesn't function at the start of the abomination's next turn.

Actions

Multiattack. The gibbering abomination makes up to three bite attacks and uses Blood Drain on grappled creatures.

Bite. *Melee Weapon Attack:* +8 to hit, reach 5 ft., one target. *Hit:* 22 (4d8 + 4) piercing damage, and the target is grappled (escape DC 14), and it is restrained until this grapple ends. While grappling the target, the abomination has advantage on attack rolls against it and can't use this attack against other targets. The abomination can grapple up to three creatures.

Blood Drain. Each creature that is not a construct or undead, and that is grappled by the abomination must make a DC 18 Constitution saving throw. On a failed save, the target takes 10 (3d6) necrotic damage, its hit point maximum is reduced by an amount equal to the necrotic damage taken, and the abomination regains hit points equal to that amount. It dies if this effect reduces its hit point maximum to 0. This reduction to the target's hit point maximum lasts until the target finishes a long rest.

Disruptive Cacophony (Recharge 5–6). The abomination emits a horrible quasi-arcane chanting that can disrupt spellcasters within 90 feet of it. Any creature attempting to cast a spell that can hear the abomination's Disruptive Cacophony must succeed on a DC 18 Constitution saving throw or the spell fails. The disruption lasts until the start of the abomination's next turn.

Gibbering Orbs

Gibbering Orb, Lesser

These hideous masses of floating flesh appear to be covered with staring eyes and hungry mouths. The lesser gibbering orb is a pulsing mass of sickly greyish-green flesh, roughly 8 feet in diameter. The orb seems to fly in starts and fits, but this is a ruse, for the creature is nimble for its bulk. It may be a distant cousin to the eye of the deep or similarly orbed entities.

The lesser gibbering orb is either a smaller or younger version of the gibbering orb, or so similar it makes no difference for naming purposes. These odd beasts are not quite the force of nature their larger brethren are, but they are every bit as chaotic and hungry as the larger version. These creatures are very distinct, and no two lesser gibbering orbs encountered are the same, if the encounter is survived at all!

The gibbering orb has the ability to bite its foes by extending a pseudopod with one of its mouths protruding from the end. The orb can extend two of these at any one foe, or a total of six in any given round. At the same time, the legions of eyes have the ability to cast a host of spells at a rapid rate.

Like their larger kin, lesser gibbering orbs speak any language, and constantly babble and gurgle unintelligible gibberish to confuse and disorient their foes.

Lesser Gibbering Orb

Large aberration, chaotic evil
Armor Class 16 (natural armor)
Hit Points 136 (16d10 + 48)
Speed 5 ft., fly 30 ft.

STR	DEX	CON	INT	WIS	CHA
16 (+3)	17 (+3)	17 (+3)	20 (+5)	14 (+2)	21 (+5)

Skills Perception +12
Condition Immunities prone
Senses darkvision 60 ft., passive Perception 12
Languages all
Challenge 14 (11,500 XP)

Hyper-Awareness. A lesser gibbering orb can see in all directions at once and cannot be surprised.

Flyby. The lesser gibbering orb doesn't provoke an opportunity attack when it flies out of an enemy's reach.

Gibbering. The gibbering orb babbles incoherently while it can see any creature and isn't incapacitated. Each creature that starts its turn within 20 feet of the orb that can hear the gibbering must succeed on a DC 16 Wisdom saving throw. On a failure, the creature can't take reactions until the start of its next turn and rolls a d8 to determine what it does during its turn. On a 1 to 4, the creature does nothing. On a 5 or 6, the creature takes no action or bonus action and uses all its movement to move in a randomly determined direction. On a 7 or 8, the creature makes a melee attack against a randomly determined creature within its reach or does nothing if it can't make such an attack.

Esoteric Theft. When a creature dies by being swallowed whole (or when a creature killed by the lesser gibbering orb in some other fashion is eaten by it), the lesser gibbering orb absorbs the creature's known spells, prepared spells, and innate magic abilities. The orb can use one of the absorbed abilities per turn as a bonus action. Each originates from an eye that is not producing an eye ray that round. Stolen spells and innate magic abilities are lost after 24 hours.

Actions

Multiattack. The lesser gibbering orb makes three bite attacks.

Bite. *Melee Weapon Attack:* +8 to hit, reach 5 ft., one target. *Hit:* 21 (4d8 + 3) piercing damage. The target is grappled (escape DC 13) if the lesser gibbering orb isn't already grappling a creature, and the target is restrained until the grapple ends.

Swallow. The lesser gibbering orb makes one bite attack against a Medium or smaller target it is grappling. If the attack hits, the target is swallowed, and the grapple ends. The swallowed target is blinded and restrained, it has total cover against attacks and other effects outside the gibbering orb, and it takes 10 (3d6) acid damage at the start of each of the lesser gibbering orb's turns. The gibbering orb can have only one target swallowed at a time.

If the gibbering orb takes 30 damage or more on a single turn from the swallowed creature, the gibbering orb must succeed on a DC 13 Constitution saving throw at the end of that turn or regurgitate the creature, which falls prone in a space within 10 feet of the orb. If the lesser gibbering orb dies, a swallowed creature is no longer restrained by it and can escape from the corpse using 5 feet of movement, exiting prone.

Eye Rays. The orb casts three of the following spells as eye rays at random (reroll duplicates), choosing one to three targets it can see within 150 ft. of it. The spells have a save DC of 18 and a +10 to hit.

d20	Eye Ray
1	acid arrow
2	blindness/deafness
3	chill touch
4	color spray
5	enthrall
6	dispel magic
7	flaming sphere
8	grease
9	hypnotic pattern
10	inflict wounds
11	bestow curse
12	magic missile
13	ray of enfeeblement
14	ray of frost
15	shatter
16	sleep
17	slow
18	scorching ray
19	lightning bolt
20	hideous laughter

Gibbering Orb

These great masses of floating amorphous flesh appear to be covered in bloodshot, weeping eyes and disgustingly vile mouths. The gibbering orb is a pulsing mass of sickly greyish-green flesh, roughly 20 ft. in diameter. The orb distends and undulates as it flies, seeming to spasm through the air rather than fly. The creature does not seem to have a top or bottom, nor does it have any form of appendages for handling objects.

These great harbingers of insanity and chaos are fortunately very rare indeed. Locked away by whatever powers preserve order and sanity, the gibbering orbs occasionally make their way to the civilized world to satiate its ravenous hunger for sentient beings. While the gibbering orb looks like a mass of chaotic, insanely impossible flesh, it is a clever and very intelligent adversary. If any being is so foolish as to attack a gibbering orb, it hurls itself at its foes with complete abandon, somehow making tactical decisions despite its completely random approach to destruction.

Gibbering orbs speak all languages and frequently speak in several tongues at once to disorient their opponents. Gibbering orbs are incapable of speaking in a non-dominant role, their egos are too vast.

Gibbering orbs are 20 feet or more in diameter, weighing at least 8,000 pounds. Their coloration varies from a sickly, mottled gray to luminescent green or deep magenta at random intervals. The orbs flesh spasms and twitches constantly, and the entire surface is covered with eyes, mouths, and other incomprehensible appendages. The orb has no obvious top or bottom; as it hovers, the entire mass continuously rotates so no one side is ever in direct contact with opponents for longer than a few seconds.

Gibbering orbs are planar travelers; fortunately, they grow bored of one place quickly. The only time gibbering orbs maintain a residence for long in any one place is if they are guarding some location for their own amusement, or if they are stranded or bound to a location. Woe to those who stumble upon an orb that cannot leave of its own free will!

Gibbering orbs in combat are forces of nature. They attack with seeming abandon. Although they are incredibly intelligent, their ego does not allow them to comprehend the concept that other beings are as powerful as they are. Gibbering orbs consume their foes fully, drawing them into their various mouths; thus, any treasure found with a gibbering orb is on the inside of the creature.

Gibbering orbs are never found together. It is unknown how they reproduce, and such an event would most likely take place in a very secluded lair.

Gibbering Orb

Huge aberration, chaotic evil
Armor Class 26 (natural armor)
Hit Points 420 (29d12 + 232)
Speed 5 ft., fly 20 ft.

STR	DEX	CON	INT	WIS	CHA
30 (+10)	30 (+10)	26 (+8)	30 (+10)	23 (+6)	21 (+5)

Saving Throws Int +19, Wis +15, Cha +14
Skills Arcana +19, Perception +15
Damage Resistance cold, fire, force, lightning, necrotic, poison, psychic, radiant, thunder; bludgeoning, piercing, and slashing from nonmagical weapons
Condition Immunities charmed, exhaustion, frightened, paralyzed, petrified, poisoned, prone
Senses darkvision 60 ft., passive Perception 30
Languages all
Challenge 30 (155,000 XP)

Hyper-Awareness. A gibbering orb can see in all directions at once and cannot be surprised.

Flyby. The gibbering orb doesn't provoke an opportunity attack when it flies out of an enemy's reach.

Gibbering. The gibbering orb babbles incoherently while it can see any creature and isn't incapacitated. Each creature that starts its turn within 20 feet of the orb and can hear the gibbering must succeed on a DC 16 Wisdom saving throw. On a failure, the creature can't take reactions until the start of its next turn and rolls a d8 to determine what it does during its turn. On a 1 to 4, the creature does nothing. On a 5 or 6, the creature takes no action or bonus action and uses all its movement to move in a randomly determined direction. On a 7 or 8, the creature makes a melee attack against a randomly determined creature within its reach or does nothing if it can't make such an attack.

Magic Resistance. The gibbering orb has advantage on saving throws against spells and other magical effects.

Esoteric Theft. When a creature dies by being swallowed whole (or when a creature killed by the gibbering orb in some other fashion is eaten by it), the gibbering orb absorbs the creature's known spells, prepared spells, and innate magic abilities. The orb can use one of the absorbed abilities per turn as a bonus action. Each originates from an eye that is not producing an eye ray that round. Stolen spells and innate magic abilities are lost after 24 hours.

Actions

Multiattack. The gibbering orb makes six bite attacks.

Bites. *Melee Weapon Attack:* +19 to hit, reach 10 ft., one target. *Hit:* 37 (6d8 + 10) piercing damage. The target is grappled (escape DC 25) if the gibbering orb isn't already grappling a creature, and the target is restrained until the grapple ends.

Swallow. The gibbering orb makes one bite attack against a Large or smaller target it is grappling. If the attack hits, the target is swallowed, and the grapple ends. The swallowed target is blinded and restrained, it has total cover against attacks and other effects outside the gibbering orb, and it takes 21 (6d6) acid damage at the start of each of the gibbering orb's turns. The gibbering orb can have only one target swallowed at a time.

If the gibbering orb dies, a swallowed creature is no longer restrained by it and can escape from the corpse using 5 feet of movement, exiting prone.

Eye Rays. The orb casts three of the following spells as eye rays at random (reroll duplicates), choosing one to three targets it can see within 150 ft. of it. The spells have a save DC 22 and +14 to hit.

d20	Eye Ray
1	acid arrow
2	blindness/deafness
3	chill touch
4	prismatic spray
5	forcecage
6	dispel magic
7	irresistible dance
8	feeblemind
9	hypnotic pattern
10	inflict wounds
11	bestow curse
12	magic missile
13	ray of enfeeblement
14	ray of frost
15	finger of death
16	disintegrate
17	slow
18	scorching ray
19	lightning bolt
20	power word stun

Glass Wyrm

This creature appears to be formed of crystal or glass. Its scales are semi-transparent and appear razor-sharp. Its head is angular with two blade-like horns swept back across its crown. A glass fin-like crest starts near the base of its skull, runs down the center of its back and tapers off as it reaches the monster's tail. Its large wings are translucent and the sound of grating glass can be heard as the beast moves.

Glass wyrms are relatives of other dragons and are believed to have their origin on another plane of existence. They make their home beneath the surface world and enjoy the relative solitude of the underground world. Their lairs normally consist of a maze of twisting and winding corridors meant to confuse and befuddle trespassers. Their lairs are littered with scores and scores of gemstones and broken glass (thought to come from the glass wyrm's scales).

Glass wyrms sustain themselves on a diet of gemstones and natural minerals, and rarely eat meat (though their draconic heritage does occasionally rise to the surface thereby instilling the taste for such things in them).

In battle a glass wyrm relies on their breath weapon and natural attacks, switching between them as the battle warrants. Powerful foes are always targeted first and subjected to the monster's breath weapon. Some glass wyrms keep torches or other light sources scattered about their labyrinthine lairs so they can use their reflective hide to blind trespassers and enter combat quickly before their opponents can react.

Glass Wyrm

Large dragon, neutral

Armor Class 17 (natural armor)
Hit Points 105 (10d10 + 50)
Speed 30 ft., fly 60 ft.

STR	DEX	CON	INT	WIS	CHA
23 (+6)	10 (+0)	21 (+5)	14 (+2)	11 (+0)	19 (+4)

Saving Throws Dex +4, Con +9, Wis +4, Cha +8
Skills Arcana +6, Insight +4, Perception +8, Persuasion +8, Stealth +4
Damage Vulnerabilities thunder
Damage Resistances bludgeoning, piercing, and slashing from nonmagical weapons
Damage Immunities poison
Condition Immunities paralyzed, poisoned, unconscious
Senses darkvision 60 ft., passive Perception 18
Languages Draconic, Undercommon
Challenge 11 (7,200 XP)

Legendary Resistance (3/day). If the dragon fails a saving throw, it can choose to succeed instead.

Spell Reflection. Any time the glass wyrm is targeted by a *magic missile* spell, a line spell, or a spell that requires a ranged attack roll, roll a d6. On a 1 to 5, the dragon is unaffected. On a 6, the dragon is unaffected, and the effect is reflected back at the caster as though it originated from the dragon, turning the caster into the target.

Actions

Multiattack. The glass wyrm uses its blinding reflection ability, and makes one bite attack and two claw attacks.

Bite. *Melee Weapon Attack:* +10 to hit, reach 5 ft., one target. *Hit:* 15 (2d8 + 6) piercing damage.

Claw. *Melee Weapon Attack:* +10 to hit, reach 5 ft., one target. *Hit:* 17 (2d10 + 6) slashing damage.

Blinding Reflection. The glass wyrm reflects available light in a burst of radiance out to a 30-foot radius. Creatures that can see the glass wyrm in the area must succeed on a DC 17 Dexterity saving throw or be blinded for 1 minute. A blinded creature can attempt a DC 17 Constitution saving throw at the end of each of its turns, ending the blinded condition on a success.

The glass wyrm can't use this ability if it does not begin its turn within the dim light or bright light radius of a light source.

Glass Shards (Recharge 5–6). The glass wyrm breaths a 40-foot cone of glass razor-like glass shards. Creatures in the area must succeed on a DC 17 Dexterity saving throw, taking 54 (12d8) piercing damage on a failed saving throw, or half as much damage on a successful one.

Gloom Crawler

This giant, squid-like beast has thirty to forty tentacles, each about 30 feet long. At the end of each tentacle stares a small, round, lidless eye with a stark blue pupil. The creature's glossy flesh is inky-black with a slightly paler underside centered upon a vicious looking, monstrously-sized, hooked beak.

The gloom crawler is a solitary creature resembling a giant squid with blackened skin and a large mass of writhing squid-like tentacles. It makes its lair in underground caves, dungeons, and other such subterranean complexes far away from the daylight of the surface world and spends most of its time dormant, waking every so often to eat.

The gloom crawler moves along its underground world using the suction cups on its tentacles to pull itself along. The average gloom crawler has anywhere from thirty to forty tentacles, each averaging 15 to 30 feet long. In addition, each tentacle has a small eye near the tip that allows it to see in any direction at any time if it wishes. When prey is encountered the gloom crawler brings as many tentacles to bear on a foe as it can, using its smaller tentacles to move around during combat.

Gloom crawlers are omnivorous creatures sustaining themselves on a diet of subterranean plants, mosses, rodents, and other subterranean fauna. They do not, however, turn down the chance for a larger meal, such as that offered by a foolhardy adventurer that stumbles into a gloom crawler lair.

When an opponent first approaches a gloom crawler, it lashes out with its tentacles attempting to grab a foe. If successful, it hangs on and constricts that opponent while fighting off other foes with its other tentacles. A held foe is also pulled in close so the gloom crawler can bite with its beak. A gloom crawler can bring up to five tentacles to bear on a single 5-foot space.

Gloom Crawler

Huge monstrosity, neutral
Armor Class 17
Hit Points 136 (13d12 + 52)
Speed 20 ft., climb 20 ft.

STR	DEX	CON	INT	WIS	CHA
20 (+5)	24 (+7)	18 (+4)	4 (−3)	12 (+1)	2 (−4)

Skills Perception +9, Stealth +11
Senses darkvision 60 ft., passive Perception 19
Languages —
Challenge 10 (5,900 XP)

Hyper-Awareness. The gloom crawler has advantage on Wisdom (Perception) checks and on saving throws against being blinded.

Actions

Multiattack. The gloom crawler makes three tentacles attacks and one bite attack.

Bite. *Melee Weapon Attack:* +11 to hit, reach 5 ft., one target. *Hit:* 16 (2d8 + 7) piercing damage.

Tentacles. *Melee Weapon Attack:* +11 to hit, reach 15 ft., one target. *Hit:* 23 (3d10 + 7) bludgeoning damage, and the target is grappled (escape DC 19). At the beginning of the gloom crawler's turns, it can choose to pull a grappled creature 15 feet to its mouth or constrict its tentacles to deal 10 (1d10 + 5) bludgeoning damage to the grappled target. The gloom crawler can grapple up to three different targets.

Goblins, Elemental

Elemental goblins are a group of small humanoid creatures with a common origin and wildly divergent abilities. Long ago, in either a now-extinct species or a species very different from the elemental goblins' current forms (almost certainly not actual goblins), there lived 5 large family clans who came into dispute with one another. As the dispute grew violent, the 5 different clans each appealed to the gods for aid. For each clan, a different deity responded, each with different solutions. However, the members of all 5 clans were irrevocably altered into 5 new species.

Goblin, Fire

This halfling-sized humanoid has deep red skin and bright blue eyes, with orange and yellow hair that seems to waft naturally upward like a candle flame.

When the 5 clans quarreled so long ago, the fire goblins were at the heart of the quarrel. They wished to conquer and rule over the other tribes. Their prayers were answered by an evil god who twisted their hearts toward his own viewpoint even as he answered their pleas for increased prowess in battle. To this day, they seek to conquer all territories they encounter if tactically feasible, especially those of stone goblins. The fire goblins call their patron deity the Soul of Flame. It is unknown whether he is known by other names or guises in other lands.

Fire goblins are exceedingly militant in outlook and fair tacticians though they are less disciplined than some armies. In combat, they are clever and courageous, but their reason is sometimes marred by hot rage. They also enjoy their enemies' cries of suffering a bit more than is always useful. Watching them, it is obvious that their culture's universal and strict military training is always at war with their fierce inner passions.

Fire goblins are about the size of halflings, with deep red skin, bright blue eyes, and orange and yellow hair that tends to stay fairly short without being cut and grows almost straight up like a candle flame.

Fire Goblin

Small humanoid, neutral evil
Armor Class 15 (natural armor)
Hit Points 45 (10d6 + 10)
Speed 20 ft.

STR	DEX	CON	INT	WIS	CHA
14 (+2)	18 (+4)	13 (+1)	16 (+3)	10 (+0)	12 (+1)

Saving Throws Dex +7, Con +4
Skills Deception +4, Perception +3, Stealth +7
Damage Vulnerabilities cold
Damage Resistances lightning; bludgeoning, piercing, and slashing from nonmagical weapons
Damage Immunities fire
Senses darkvision 120 ft., passive Perception 13
Languages Common, Goblin, Sylvan
Challenge 7 (2,900 XP)

Flaming Arrows. Fire goblins are adept at manufacturing flaming arrows, and coupled with their produce flame cantrip, a fire goblin with prepared arrows (wrapped and treated to be easily flammable) may set up to 2 arrows on fire as a seamless part of each turn's attack, without requiring a separate action. Preparing an arrow for such a use still takes the normal amount of time but can be done in advance and saved for a later battle.

Innate Spellcasting. The fire goblin's spellcasting ability is Intelligence (spell save DC 14, +6 to hit with spell attacks). The fire goblin can innately cast the following spells, requiring no material components:

At will: *fire bolt, produce flame*
3/day each: *burning hands, flame blade, flaming sphere, heat metal*
1/day: *fireball, wall of fire*

Actions

Multiattack. The fire goblin can make two attacks with its flaming arrows using its shortbow.

Battleaxe. *Melee Weapon Attack:* +5 to hit, reach 5 ft., one target. *Hit:* 6 (1d8 + 2) slashing damage, or 7 (1d10 + 2) slashing damage if used with two hands.

Shortbow. *Ranged Weapon Attack:* +7 to hit, range 80/320 ft., one target. *Hit:* 7 (1d6 + 4) piercing damage plus 7 (2d6) fire damage.

Fire Breath (Recharge 5–6). The goblin exhales fire in a 20-foot cone. Each creature in that area must make a DC 15 Dexterity saving throw, taking 45 (10d8) fire damage on a failed save, or half as much damage on a successful one.

Goblin, Stone

This near-hairless humanoid is just smaller than a dwarf and has grey skin and eyes.

Of all the five clans, it was the stone goblins who chose most staunchly to stand their ground and face down the fire goblin threat. Their prayers for strength to resist were answered by a lawful god, who granted them unshakable discipline and many defensive abilities. In their worship of the elsewhere, seemingly unknown deity they call the Stone Heart, the stone goblins have grown fiercely traditional and closed-minded.

Stone goblins are serious, dour, uninspired, and intolerant of outsiders. In combat they are staunch but predictable, trusting in age-old, near-ritual tactical models. Their greatest strengths are a highly organized and smoothly functional command structure, as well as logistical preparations that are always flawless and extensive.

Stone goblins are the largest of the elemental goblins, nearly as tall and broad as dwarves. Their skin and eyes are always grey, with little variation even in shade. They grow no head or facial hair (other than eyebrows) and little body hair.

Stone Goblin

Medium humanoid, lawful neutral

Armor Class 14 (natural armor)
Hit Points 42 (5d8 + 20)
Speed 20 ft.

STR	DEX	CON	INT	WIS	CHA
16 (+3)	10 (+0)	18 (+4)	13 (+1)	16 (+3)	12 (+1)

Saving Throws Str +5, Con +6
Skills Athletics +5, Perception +5
Damage Vulnerabilities poison
Damage Resistances fire damage; bludgeoning, piercing, and slashing from nonmagical weapons
Damage Immunities acid
Senses darkvision 120 ft., passive Perception 15
Languages Common, Sylvan
Challenge 3 (700 XP)

Innate Spellcasting. The stone goblin's spellcasting ability is Wisdom (spell save DC 13, +5 to hit with spell attacks). The stone goblin can innately cast the following spells, requiring no material components:

At will: *acid splash, mending, resistance, true strike*
3/day each: *bane, bless, command, heroism, sanctuary, shield*
1/day: *meld into stone*

Magic Resistance. The stone goblin has advantage on saving throws against spells and other magical effects.

Actions

Warhammer. *Melee Weapon Attack:* +5 to hit, reach 5 ft., one target. *Hit:* 7 (1d8 + 3) bludgeoning damage, or 8 (1d10 + 3) bludgeoning damage if used with two hands.

Light Crossbow. *Ranged Weapon Attack:* +2 to hit, range 80/320 ft., one target. *Hit:* 6 (1d8 + 2) piercing damage.

Goblin, Water

This deep-blue-skinned humanoid, just smaller than a halfling, has long, flowing blue-green hair in a thick braid, and its fingers are webbed for swimming.

In the disagreement of the five clans, the water goblins were one of two clans who chose simply to pack up and leave the region. As they wept and mourned for their lost homeland, their cries of grief were answered by a sea deity, who taught them a calm, philosophical outlook and granted them many artistic gifts, as well as the ability to thrive where most could not: at sea. They call their deity the Song of the Waves. As with the others, the Song of the Waves may and may not be known in other ways, by other names, in other lands.

Water goblins prefer to live as peaceful merchants, artists, and performers, but when attacked, they loyally defend one another. When direly pressed, they have also been known to turn to piracy. In battle, water goblins are graceful of movement and especially good at dodging. They are generally open to dialogue and new ideas and always love to hear new stories and songs.

Water goblins come in many shades of green and blue (of skin, hair, and eyes), usually in darker tones. They have long, flowing, silky hair, which their culture discourages cutting. They wear it in thick braids while sailing or fishing. Water goblins have webbed fingers and toes and are, on average, a few inches shorter and a few pounds lighter than halflings.

At will: *mending, minor illusion, prestidigitation, ray of frost*
3/day each: *create or destroy water, fog cloud, grease, mage armor, purify food and drink, water breathing*
1/day: *water walk*

Actions

Scimitar. *Melee Weapon Attack:* +4 to hit, reach 5 ft., one target. *Hit:* 5 (1d6 + 2) slashing damage.
Shortbow. *Ranged Weapon Attack:* +4 to hit, range 80/320 ft., one target. *Hit:* 5 (1d6 + 2) piercing damage.

Reactions

Uncanny Dodge. When an attacker the water goblin can see hits it with an attack, it can use its reaction to halve the attack's damage against it.

Goblin, Wind

This pale humanoid has wispy hair and pastel-colored batwings. Though as tall as a halfling, it is unnaturally slim by comparison.

The wind goblins were once the most scholarly of all the elemental goblin clans. When the conflict between the clans began, they were quickly defeated and held hostage in an attempt to force the other clans to surrender. Each of the other clans, in turn, appeared to abandon the imprisoned wind goblins to their fate, until finally their prayers for freedom were answered by a chaotic deity they came to call the Mind and Breath. She helped them to escape and granted them wings with which to fly to freedom. Under her influence, the wind goblins have all become a bit strange.

Wind goblins will do anything for what they call "science", an undisciplined and poorly controlled combination of mad engineering and innate magics not even close to the scientific method. Nevertheless, their gadgets work (for the makers, not for other people), and wind goblins are not afraid to endanger themselves or others to test them. They seem, however, to basically mean well, and they can even be generous when they look up from their tinkering long enough to notice that other people are real. Perhaps fortunately for everyone, they have become highly nomadic and never stay in one place for long.

Wind goblins are similar in height to fire goblins but are naturally so slender that they weigh the least of all the elemental goblins. They come in all manner of pale colors, and their hair is wispy and soft, often resembling tufts of downy feathers. They have six limbs, the extra pair being strong, bat-like wings, and their flight tends toward a bat-like, chaotic bobbing as well. When building gadgets, wind goblins can also use the finger-like ends of their wings as clumsier extra hands while they work.

Wind Goblin

Small humanoid, chaotic neutral
Armor Class 14
Hit Points 36 (8d6 + 8)
Speed 20 ft., fly 40 ft.

STR	DEX	CON	INT	WIS	CHA
13 (+1)	19 (+4)	13 (+1)	20 (+5)	13 (+1)	11 (+0)

Saving Throws Int +7, Wis +3
Skills Arcana +7, Investigation +7
Damage Vulnerabilities acid

Water Goblin

Small humanoid, neutral
Armor Class 13 (natural armor, 16 with *mage armor*)
Hit Points 13 (3d6 + 3)
Speed 20 ft. swim 20 ft.

STR	DEX	CON	INT	WIS	CHA
13 (+1)	14 (+2)	13 (+1)	10 (+0)	12 (+1)	16 (+3)

Saving Throws Dex +4, Cha +5
Skills Acrobatics +4, Athletics +3
Damage Vulnerabilities lightning
Damage Resistances acid; bludgeoning, piercing, and slashing from nonmagical weapons
Damage Immunities cold
Senses darkvision 120 ft., passive Perception 11
Languages Common, Sylvan
Challenge 1/2 (100 XP)

Amphibious. Water goblins can breathe air and water.
Innate Spellcasting. The water goblin's spellcasting ability is Charisma (spell save DC 13, +5 to hit with spell attacks). The water goblin can innately cast the following spells, requiring no material components:

Damage Resistances poison; bludgeoning, piercing, and slashing from nonmagical weapons
Damage Immunities lightning
Senses darkvision 120 ft., passive Perception 11
Languages Common, Sylvan
Challenge 4 (1,100 XP)

Innate Spellcasting. The wind goblin's spellcasting ability is Intelligence (spell save DC 15, +7 to hit with spell attacks). The wind goblin can innately cast the following spells, requiring no material components:

At will: *dancing lights, mage hand, prestidigitation, shocking grasp*
3/day each: *detect magic, eldritch blast, faerie fire, gust of wind, identify*
1/day: *wind wall, call lightning*

Scientific Spellcasting. Wind goblins have a strange relationship with science and are able to use what they sincerely believe is scientific invention to mimic the abilities of spellcasters. They also describe arcane concepts in science-like jargon.

The following is a typical allocation of "scientific", gadget-based spells that a wind goblin might be able to cast, but specific spells vary from goblin to goblin. Wind goblin "science" magic never requires a verbal or material component. Instead, all spells require a gadget focus and the somatic component of turning the cranks and working the levers (etc.) on said focus. The process is usually loud and often smelly or smoky, with superfluous electrical arcing.

The wind goblin is a 4th level spellcaster. Its spellcasting ability is Intelligence (spell save DC 15, +7 to hit with spell attacks). It can cast the following spells, requiring only somatic components:

Cantrips (at will): *fire bolt, light, mending, message, minor illusion*
1st level (4/day*): *expeditious retreat, fog cloud, thunderwave*
2nd level (3/day*): *hold person, knock*
*The uses per day represent fuel-related limitations.

Actions

Dagger. *Melee or Ranged Weapon Attack:* +6 to hit, reach 5 ft. or 20/60 ft., one target. *Hit:* 6 (1d4 + 4) piercing damage.

Hand Crossbow. *Ranged Weapon Attack:* +6 to hit, range 30/120 ft., one target. *Hit:* 7 (1d6 + 4) piercing damage.

Goblin, Wood

Colored in dark browns and greens, this little humanoid appears outfitted for wilderness survival.

Wood goblins are the most compassionate of the elemental goblins, but they too decided to stay and resist the fire goblins' designs of conquest. Instead of hunkering down in fortresses, as the stone goblins did, the wood goblins preferred to remain mobile and to resist the fire goblins' evil wherever they encountered it. When they prayed to this end, they were answered by a deity that the wood goblins call Freedom's Will. Freedom's Will granted them abilities to counter the fire goblins' injustice through stealth, subtlety, and even kindness.

Wood goblins will only attack those they believe to be truly evil. Otherwise, they will always attempt a diplomatic solution before fighting. When they do decide to mete out justice, they use guerrilla and skirmishing tactics, ambushing foes and then melting silently back into the wilds. They use nonlethal traps to defend their homes, and they treat prisoners well when they take them.

Wood goblins are nocturnal and come in dark, woody colors, usually browns and greens, to blend with the nighttime wilderness. They are the smallest of the elemental goblins, though a wiry strength means they weigh a bit more than the wind goblins. They keep their curly hair in tight braids.

Wood Goblin

Small humanoid, neutral good
Armor Class 13 (natural armor)
Hit Points 18 (4d6 + 4)
Speed 20 ft.

STR	DEX	CON	INT	WIS	CHA
13 (+1)	15 (+2)	13 (+1)	16 (+3)	16 (+3)	10 (+0)

Saving Throws Dex +4, Int +5
Skills Athletics +3, Acrobatics +4, Medicine +5, Perception +5, Sleight of Hand +4, Stealth +4, Survival +5
Damage Vulnerabilities fire
Damage Resistances cold; bludgeoning, piercing, and slashing from nonmagical weapons

Damage Immunities poison
Condition Immunities poisoned
Senses darkvision 120 ft., passive Perception 15
Languages Common, Sylvan
Challenge 1 (200 XP)

Innate Spellcasting. The wood goblin's spellcasting ability is Wisdom (spell save DC 13, +5 to hit with spell attacks). The goblin can innately cast the following spells, requiring no material components:

At will: *detect poison or disease, poison spray, shillelagh, spare the dying*

3/day each: *barkskin, cure wounds, entangle, lesser restoration, protection from poison*

1/day: *spider climb*

Herbal Medicine. Due to their innate and magical affinity for plants and herbs, a wood goblin always has advantage on Wisdom (Medicine) skill checks. In addition, the wood goblin's innate *cure wounds* spells can be imitated herbally without limitation as long as the wood goblin has access to wild plants. However, the herbal versions require 15 minutes to prepare and must be fresh, and thus are not usable in combat.

Sneak Attack (1/turn). The wood goblin deals an extra 7 (2d6) damage when it has advantage and hits a target with a weapon on the attack roll, or when the target is within 5 feet of an ally of the wood goblin that isn't incapacitated and the wood goblin doesn't have disadvantage on the attack roll.

Actions

Rapier. *Melee Weapon Attack:* +4 to hit, reach 5 ft., one target. *Hit:* 6 (1d8 + 2) piercing damage.

Shortbow. *Ranged Weapon Attack:* +4 to hit, range 80/320 ft., one target. *Hit:* 5 (1d6 + 2) piercing damage.

Poison Cloud (1/day). A 10-foot radius of thick venomous gas extends out from the wood goblin. The gas spreads around corners, and its area is lightly obscured. It lasts for 1 minute or until a strong wind disperses it. Any creature that starts its turn in that area must succeed on a DC 11 Constitution saving throw or be poisoned until the start of its next turn and it takes 7 (2d6) poison damage. While poisoned in this way, the target can take either an action or a bonus action on its turn, not both, and can't take reactions.

Golems

Golem, Blood

This creature looks like a hideous, bloated slug, blood red in color. Two long spindly arms protrude from its upper body. It has no other discernible features.

Blood golems, contrary to their name, are not constructs: they are slug-shaped clots of living blood, animated by some ancient ritual by a now unknown and unremembered spellcaster.

A typical blood golem is 10 feet long and weighs 700 pounds.

When living prey is detected, the blood golem rises up and appears as a slug-like headless humanoid. It attacks with its arms.

Blood Golem

Large aberration, neutral
Armor Class 17 (natural armor)
Hit Points 102 (12d10 + 36)
Speed 20 ft.

STR	DEX	CON	INT	WIS	CHA
14 (+2)	19 (+4)	16 (+3)	2 (−4)	14 (+2)	1 (−5)

Damage Immunities fire, poison, psychic; bludgeoning, piercing, and slashing from nonmagical weapons that aren't adamantine
Condition Immunities charmed, exhaustion, frightened, paralyzed, petrified, poisoned
Senses darkvision 60 ft., passive Perception 10
Languages understands the languages of its creator but can't speak
Challenge 8 (3,900 XP)

Amorphous. The blood golem can move through a space as narrow as 1 inch wide without squeezing.

Berserk. When the blood golem starts its turn with 40 hit points or fewer, roll a d6. On a 6, the golem goes berserk. On each of its turns while berserk, the golem attacks the nearest creature it can see. If no creature is near enough to move to and attack, the golem attacks an object, with preference for an object smaller than itself. Once the blood golem goes berserk, it continues to do so until it is destroyed or regains all its hit points.

The golem's creator, if within 60 feet of the berserk golem, can try to calm it by speaking firmly and persuasively. The golem must be able to hear its creator, who must take an action to make a DC 15 Charisma (Persuasion) check. If the check succeeds, the golem ceases being berserk. If it takes damage while still at 40 hit points or fewer, the golem might go berserk again.

Blood Ooze. The blood golem takes up its entire space. Other creatures can enter the space, but a creature that does so is subjected to the blood golem's Engulf and has disadvantage on the saving throw.

Creatures inside the blood golem can't be seen and have total cover.

A creature within 5 feet of the blood golem can take an action to pull a creature or object out of the cube. Doing so requires a successful DC 12 Strength check, and the creature making the attempt takes 10 (3d6) necrotic damage.

The blood golem can hold only one Large creature or up to four Medium or smaller creatures inside it at a time.

Blood Sense. The blood golem can magically sense the presence of blood in living creatures up to 1 mile away. It knows the general direction they're in but not their exact locations.

Blood Splatter. Any time the golem is hit in combat, a gout of blood erupts from its body. All creatures within 10 feet of the golem must succeed on a DC 15 Dexterity saving throw or be blinded until the end of the creature's next turn.

Immutable Form. The golem is immune to any spell or effect that would alter its form.

Magic Resistance. The golem has advantage on saving throws against spells and other magical effects.

Magic Weapons. The golem's weapon attacks are magical.

Split. When a blood golem reaches its maximum hit points for its Hit Dice, it splits into two identical golems. Each golem has hit points equal to half the maximum hit points of the original golem. New golems are one size smaller than the original golem.

Actions

Multiattack. The golem makes two slam attacks.

Slam. *Melee Weapon Attack:* +7 to hit, reach 10 ft., one target. *Hit:* 13 (2d8 + 4) bludgeoning damage, and the target must make a DC 15 Constitution saving throw. On a failed save, the target takes 22 (4d8 + 4) bludgeoning damage plus 14 (3d6 + 4) necrotic damage; its hit point maximum is reduced by the amount equal to the necrotic damage, and the blood golem regains hit points equal to that amount. The reduction in the target's hit point maximum lasts until the target finishes a long rest. The target dies if this reduces its hit point maximum to 0.

Engulf. The blood golem moves up to its speed. While doing so, it can enter Large or smaller creatures' spaces. Whenever the blood golem enters a creature's space, the creature must make a DC 12 Dexterity saving throw.

On a successful save, the creature can choose to be pushed 5 feet back or to the side of the blood golem. A creature that chooses not to be pushed suffers the consequences of a failed saving throw.

On a failed save, the blood golem enters the creature's space, and the creature takes 10 (3d6) necrotic damage and is engulfed. The engulfed creature can't breathe, is restrained, and takes 21 (6d6) necrotic damage at the start of each of the blood golem's turns. When the blood golem moves, the engulfed creature moves with it.

An engulfed creature can try to escape by taking an action to make a DC 12 Strength check. On a success, the creature escapes and enters a space of its choice within 5 feet of the blood golem.

Golem, Ice

This icy statue stands a head taller than a normal human. A rime of frost coats it, and razor-sharp shards of ice adorn its limbs.

The ice golem is a humanoid formed of roughly chiseled ice, standing 10 feet tall and weighing around 800 pounds. Ice golems at rest appear to be normal ice sculptures and are often mistaken as such, but a DC 15 Wisdom (Perception) check will notice that the creature is alive.

An ice golem usually opens combat with its breath weapon. An ice golem never uses weapons or wears armor, preferring to attack with its powerful fists. Fire is an effective means of combating these creatures.

Ice Golem

Medium construct, neutral
Armor Class 14 (natural armor)
Hit Points 71 (11d8 + 22)
Speed 30 ft.

STR	DEX	CON	INT	WIS	CHA
16 (+3)	12 (+1)	14 (+2)	2 (−4)	10 (+0)	1 (−5)

Damage Immunities cold, poison, psychic; bludgeoning, piercing, and slashing from nonmagical weapons that aren't adamantine
Condition Immunities charmed, exhaustion, frightened, paralyzed, petrified, poisoned
Senses darkvision 60 ft., passive Perception 10
Languages understands the languages of its creator but can't speak
Challenge 5 (1,800 XP)

Icy Destruction. When the golem dies, it shatters in an explosion of jagged ice shards, and each creature within 15 feet of it must make a DC 13 Dexterity saving throw, taking 10 (3d6) piercing damage and 7 (2d6) cold damage on a failed save, or half as much damage on a successful one.

Immutable Form. The golem is immune to any spell or effect that would alter its form.

Magic Resistance. The golem has advantage on saving throws against spells and other magical effects.

Magic Weapons. The golem's weapon attacks are magical.

Actions

Multiattack. The golem can make two slam attacks.

Slam. *Melee Weapon Attack:* +6 to hit, reach 10 ft., one target. *Hit:* 10 (2d6 + 3) bludgeoning damage plus 7 (2d6) cold damage.

Cold Breath (Recharge 5–6). The golem exhales a blast of freezing wind in a 15-foot cone. Each creature in that area must make a DC 13 Dexterity saving throw, taking 18 (4d8) cold damage on a failed save, or half as much damage on a successful one.

Golem, Magnesium

Silvery-white powder shakes loose from this construct as it stomps across the floor. Its face is a featureless plane except for two gouges where there should be eyes.

Magnesium golems are silvery-white humanoids created by arcane spellcasters. As with other golems, they are incapable of thinking on their own, and are thus under control of the one that created them. They are created as guardians and keepers and can be given specific orders to guard a specific locale, item, or object or to attack a specific creature or type of creature.

The magnesium golem is a silvery-white humanoid formed of magnesium. The average magnesium golem stands about 6–7 feet tall and weighs 600 pounds. The magnesium golem's features are smooth and perfect, though it has no discernable ears, nose, or mouth. Its eyes appear to be nothing more than indentations in its body. Magnesium golems wear no clothing and never carry weapons, and it cannot speak or make any vocal noise. Unlike many other golems, the magnesium golem can move at the same speed as a human of its size.

Immutable Form. The golem is immune to any spell or effect that would alter its form.

Magic Resistance. The golem has advantage on saving throws against spells and other magical effects.

Magic Weapon. The golem's weapon attacks are magical.

Actions

Multiattack. The golem makes two slam attacks.

Slam. *Melee Weapon Attack:* +7 to hit, reach 5 ft., one target. *Hit:* 13 (2d8 + 4) bludgeoning damage.

Golem, Ooze

The ten-foot-tall column slides towards you. Its body swirls with changing colors and two pseudopods wave menacingly in the air.

Believed to be the creation of Masters of the Ooze (high-ranking priests and followers of The Faceless Lord), ooze golems appear as swirling conglomerations of oozes of columnar or humanoid shape. Their bubbling, shifting form stinks of dead animal matter and sulfur.

Ooze golems are often employed or summoned by evil spellcasters and given the task of guarding or protecting an area of great importance. They are sometimes found in the company of normal oozes. These golems are quite prevalent in temples dedicated to The Faceless Lord.

Ooze golems are 10-foot-tall amorphous creatures of swirling colors: gray, black, dull red, pale green, and brown. They can alter their shape so as to appear roughly humanoid, but their natural form resembles a column or pillar. Two large pseudopods extend from the central trunk and function

Magnesium Golem

Medium construct, neutral
Armor Class 15 (natural armor)
Hit Points 68 (8d8 + 32)
Speed 30 ft.

STR	DEX	CON	INT	WIS	CHA
19 (+4)	9 (−1)	18 (+4)	6 (−2)	10 (+0)	5 (−3)

Damage Immunities fire, poison, psychic; bludgeoning, piercing, and slashing from nonmagical weapons that aren't adamantine
Condition Immunities charmed, exhaustion, frightened, paralyzed, petrified, poisoned
Senses darkvision 60 ft., passive Perception 10
Languages understands the languages of its creator but can't speak
Challenge 5 (1,800 XP)

Aura of Sickness. Creatures who begin their turn within 10 feet of the golem must make a DC 15 Constitution saving throw. On a failed saving throw, the creature is poisoned for 1 minute. If a creature ends its turn outside the 10-foot area, it can repeat the saving throw, ending the effect on a success. If the creature succeeds or if the effect ends for it, it is immune to the golem's aura of sickness for 24 hours.

Fire Absorption. Whenever the golem is subjected to fire damage, it takes no damage and instead regains a number of hit points equal to the fire damage dealt.

as arms. No facial features are discernable in either form. In humanoid form, an ooze golem's lower torso ends in two powerful legs and almost-human feet. This creature can flatten its body and squeeze through cracks and openings up to 2-inches in size.

An ooze golem attacks by pummeling its opponents with its fists. It employs rudimentary tactics in battle and always fights until destroyed. An ooze golem often grabs a foe and hangs on; dealing acid damage each round the hold is maintained.

Ooze Golem

Large construct, neutral
Armor Class 15 (natural armor)
Hit Points 94 (9d10 + 45)
Speed 20 ft., climb 20 ft.

STR	DEX	CON	INT	WIS	CHA
18 (+4)	5 (−3)	20 (+5)	6 (−2)	10 (+0)	5 (−3)

Damage Immunities acid, cold, poison, lightning, psychic; bludgeoning, piercing, and slashing from nonmagical weapons
Condition Immunities blinded, charmed, deafened, exhaustion, frightened, paralyzed, poisoned, prone
Senses blindsight 60 ft. (blind beyond this radius), passive Perception 10
Languages understands the languages of its creator but can't speak
Challenge 7 (2,900 XP)

Acid. A creature that touches the golem or hits it with a melee attack while within 5 feet of it takes 9 (2d8) acid damage.

Amorphous. The golem can move through a space as narrow as 1 inch wide without squeezing.

Death Throes. When the ooze golem drops to 0 hit points, its body explodes in a 10-foot sphere. Creatures in that area must make a DC 15 Dexterity saving throw, taking 10 (3d6) acid damage on a failed saving throw, or half as much damage on a successful saving throw. The area of the golem's death throes remains acidic for 1 minute after death, and any creature that begins its turn in the area or enters it is affected as well.

Immutable Form. The golem is immune to any spell or effect that would alter its form.

Magic Resistance. The golem has advantage on saving throws against spells and other magical effects.

Magic Weapon. The golem's weapon attacks are magical.

Regeneration. The ooze golem regains 10 hit points at the beginning of each of its turns as long as it has at least 1 hit point.

Spider Climb. The golem can climb difficult surfaces, including upside down on ceilings, without needing to make an ability check.

Actions

Multiattack. The ooze golem makes two slam attacks.

Slam. Melee Weapon Attack: +7 to hit, reach 5 ft., one target. *Hit:* 13 (2d8 + 4) bludgeoning damage plus 9 (2d8) acid damage.

Golem, Tallow

This human-sized automaton has been carved from wax. Its face bears no discernible features and appears as a completely smooth surface.

The tallow golem is a humanoid construct composed entirely of wax. It stands about 6 feet tall and usually bears no facial features unless the creator chooses to render a lifelike "wax dummy," in which case the golem can appear quite real indeed. Wizards who specialize in the creation

of tallow golems refer to themselves as "chandlers." Unlike other golem-sculptors, chandlers consider their work a form of art. The golem wears whatever clothing (if any) that its creator desires, usually rags or trousers. It has no possessions and no weapons. The golem cannot speak or utter any sound. It moves slowly, but relentlessly.

A tallow golem attacks by pounding its foes with its massive fists.

Tallow Golem

Medium construct, neutral
Armor Class 15 (natural armor)
Hit Points 76 (9d8 + 36)
Speed 20 ft.

STR	DEX	CON	INT	WIS	CHA
19 (+4)	9 (−1)	18 (+4)	5 (−3)	11 (+0)	4 (−3)

Damage Vulnerabilities fire
Damage Immunities cold, poison, psychic; bludgeoning, piercing, and slashing damage from nonmagical weapons

Condition Immunities charmed, exhaustion, frightened, paralyzed, petrified, poisoned
Senses darkvision 60 ft., passive Perception 10
Languages understands the languages of its creator but can't speak
Challenge 6 (2,300 XP)

Immutable Form. The golem is immune to any spell or effect that would alter its form.

Magic Resistance. The golem has advantage on saving throws against spells and other magical effects.

Magic Weapon. The golem's weapon attacks are magical.

Actions

Multiattack. The tallow golem makes two slam attacks.

Slam. *Melee Weapon Attack:* +7 to hit, reach 5 ft., one target. *Hit:* 13 (2d8 + 4) bludgeoning damage plus 7 (2d6) poison damage. If the tallow golem rolls a natural 20, the target also suffers from discolored skin across its body and has disadvantage on Charisma skill checks. This further effect can be restored with magic such as *lesser restoration*.

Golem, Witch-Doll

This bizarre construct appears to be crafted from stuffed human skin, with large button-like platters in place of eye holes and crude stitching forming a pinched mouth. Knots of humanoid hair top its head and it is dressed in a patchwork of ill-fitting clothes. Large needles and pins pierce the creature where a humanoid's vital organs would be.

The witch-doll golem is a horrific hunter/assassin crafted in the likeness of a spellcaster's chosen foe. Witch-doll golems are designed to enact some vengeance on behalf of its creator and are thus made from some of the foe's personal effects (hair, blood, a bit of skin, fingernail clippings, etc.). It may be re-programmed should the witch-doll golem's master find a new enemy. The master merely adds new personal effects to the golem and fills it with new commands. The witch-doll golem then follows these commands mindlessly until it or its target is destroyed. Note that the witch-doll golem can only have one programmed target at one time.

A witch-doll golem stands twice the height of a human and weighs about 1,000 pounds. A witch-doll golem cannot speak.

When facing its programmed target, the witch-doll immediately attempts to establish a witch-doll link by pummeling the target with its fists or stabbing it with one of the needles in its body. It relentlessly attacks its foe with a ferocity unseen in most mindless automatons. Against other foes, the golem employs its fists and needles while attempting to keep its programmed target within range.

Witch-Doll Golem

Large construct, neutral
Armor Class 17 (natural armor)
Hit Points 94 (9d10 + 45)
Speed 30 ft.

STR	DEX	CON	INT	WIS	CHA
19 (+4)	14 (+2)	21 (+5)	7 (−2)	15 (+2)	11 (+0)

Skills Investigation +2, Perception +10, Survival +10
Damage Immunities poison, psychic; bludgeoning, piercing, and slashing damage from nonmagical weapons
Condition Immunities charmed, exhaustion, frightened, paralyzed, petrified, poisoned
Senses darkvision 60 ft., passive Perception 20

Languages understands the languages of its creator but can't speak
Challenge 10 (5,900 XP)

Find Target. The witch-doll golem knows the location of a specific target creature, or one creature cursed by its witch-doll curse ability, as long as that creature is within 1,000 feet of it. If the creature is moving, it knows the direction of that creature's movement. If the creature is beyond this distance, the witch-doll golem knows the direction that creature is in.

Immutable Form. The golem is immune to any spell or effect that would alter its form.

Magic Resistance. The golem has advantage on saving throws against spells and other magical effects.

Magic Weapon. The golem's weapon attacks are magical.

Actions

Multiattack. The witch-doll golem makes up to two attacks with its slam or its needle attack.

Slam. *Melee Weapon Attack:* +8 to hit, reach 5 ft., one target. *Hit:* 20 (3d10 + 4) bludgeoning damage.

Needle. *Melee or Ranged Weapon Attack:* +8 to hit, reach 5 ft. or range 20/60 ft., one target. *Hit:* 14 (3d6 + 4) piercing damage.

Witch-Doll Curse. The witch-doll golem chooses one creature it can see within 60 feet of it. The target must make a DC 17 Wisdom saving throw or be cursed. While cursed, the witch-doll golem deals an additional 13 (3d8) necrotic damage to the target when it hits with a weapon attack, and any damage the witch-doll golem takes from targets other than the cursed target is halved, and the cursed target takes the other half. The witch-doll golem can only have one active curse at a time.

The target remains cursed until the golem is destroyed or the target dies; magic such as *remove curse* can end the curse early.

Golem, Wood

This automaton is human-sized and resembles an ornately carved wooden statue.

Arcane spellcasters used several ancient texts to arrive at a process to create inexpensive yet still quite powerful golems. They had master craftsmen create wood statues with articulating limbs and then performed the proper spells to animate and control them. The statues vary in shape and form and usually have weapons of some sort held in each hand. The wood golems were designed to act both as an alarm and a protection against intruders.

Wood golems are usually programmed to close doors and avoid ranged weapons and spells but do not break off melee combat to avoid missile fire from other sources. They attack with their fists.

Wood Golem

Medium construct, neutral
Armor Class 13 (natural armor)
Hit Points 45 (7d8 + 14)
Speed 30 ft.

STR	DEX	CON	INT	WIS	CHA
16 (+3)	10 (+0)	15 (+2)	7 (–2)	11 (+0)	(–3)

Damage Vulnerabilities fire
Damage Immunities cold, lightning, poison, psychic; bludgeoning, piercing, and slashing damage from nonmagical weapons
Condition Immunities charmed, exhaustion, frightened, paralyzed, petrified, poisoned
Senses darkvision 60 ft., passive Perception 10
Languages understands the languages of its creator but can't speak
Challenge 3 (700 XP)

Alarm. Whenever a creature other than its creator comes within 60 feet of the golem, it releases an audible alarm sound which can be heard out to a range of 300 feet.

Immutable Form. The golem is immune to any spell or effect that would alter its form.

Magic Resistance. The golem has advantage on saving throws against spells and other magical effects.

Magic Weapon. The golem's weapon attacks are magical.

Actions

Multiattack. The wood golem makes two slam attacks.

Slam. Melee Weapon Attack: +5 to hit, reach 5 ft., one target. *Hit:* 12 (2d8 + 3) bludgeoning damage.

Gorgimera

This hideous creature has leathery dragon wings and three heads; a lion, a dragon, and a gorgon. Its hindquarters are that of a gorgon and its forequarters are that of a great lion.

A gorgimera is a chimerical creature with the heads of a lion, dragon, and gorgon. It has the hindquarters of a gorgon and the forequarters of a lion. It is a highly territorial predator whose hunting range often covers several square miles around its lair. The creature makes its home inside caves high atop mountains or deep inside caverns. A typical lair contains a mated pair and one or two young. A gorgimera's dragon head can be that of any of the evil dragons (see below). The lion head has no mane, and the scaled gorgon head is a deep navy blue with glowing red eyes.

A gorgimera prefers to attack from ambush. It usually attacks by biting with its lion head and dragon head, butting with its gorgon head, and slashing with its front leonine paws. In lieu of biting, the dragon head and gorgon head can emit their respective breath weapons.

Gorgimera

Large monstrosity, neutral
Armor Class 14 (natural armor)
Hit Points 114 (12d10 + 48)
Speed 40 ft., fly 50 ft.

STR	DEX	CON	INT	WIS	CHA
19 (+4)	13 (+1)	19 (+4)	4 (–3)	13 (+1)	10 (+0)

Saving Throws Dex +6, Con +9
Skills Perception +11
Senses darkvision 60 ft., passive Perception 21
Languages Draconic
Challenge 13 (10,000 XP)

Roll a d10 and refer to the table below for the color of the gorgimera's dragon head.

d10	Head Color	Breath Weapon
1–2	Black	40-foot-long, 5-foot-wide line of acid
3–4	Blue	40-foot-long, 5-foot-wide line of lightning
5–6	Green	20-foot cone of poisonous gas
7–8	Red	20-foot cone of fire
9–10	White	20-foot cone of cold

Flyby. The gorgimera doesn't provoke an opportunity attack when it flies out of an enemy's reach.

Keen Smell. The gorgimera has advantage on Wisdom (Perception) checks that rely on smell.

Charge. If the gorgimera moves at least 20 feet straight towards a creature and then hits with a gore attack on the same turn, the target takes an extra 9 (2d8) piercing damage. If the target is a creature, it must succeed on a DC 14 Strength saving throw or be pushed up to 10 feet away and knocked prone.

Actions

Multiattack. The gorgimera makes five melee attacks: two with its claws, two bites, and one gore attack. Alternatively, it can use its two breath weapons in place of the bite attacks.

Bite. *Melee Weapon Attack:* +9 to hit, reach 5 ft., one target. *Hit:* 17 (3d8 + 4) piercing damage.

Claws. *Melee Weapon Attack:* +9 to hit, reach 5 ft., one target. *Hit:* 11 (2d6 + 4) slashing damage.

Gore. *Melee Weapon Attack:* +9 to hit, reach 5 ft., one target. *Hit:* 13 (2d8 + 4) piercing damage.

Dragon Breath (Recharge 5–6). The dragon head exhales its breath based on the results from the table above. Each creature in the area affected must make a DC 18 Dexterity saving throw, taking 31 (7d8) damage on a failed save, of half as much on a successful one. Damage type determined by the table above.

Gorgon Breath. (Recharge 5–6). The gorgon head exhales petrifying gas in a 30-foot cone. Each creature in that area must succeed on a DC 18 Constitution saving throw or begin to turn to stone and berestrained. The restrained target must repeat the saving throw at the end of its next turn. On a success, the effect ends on the target. On a failure, the target is petrified until freed by a *greater restoration* spell or other magic.

Gremlins

This creature resembles a goblin with long floppy ears, a pinched wrinkled face, nasty claws, a mouth full of sharp teeth and a wicked glint in its eyes.

Gremlins are wicked fey beings who revel in destruction and creating mayhem. They are known to wreck machinery and equipment, often laying nasty traps behind, ensuring that repair is next to impossible. Due to their phase door ability, they can get inside even the most complicated and tight areas without fear of detection and remain as long as they like. Here they reside undetected until towers begin collapsing, forges explode, gates jam, and catapults begin to misfire. Once a village, city, or castle finds itself the unhappy host of a gremlin, it is almost impossible to root the creature out and remove it once and for all.

Individual gremlins tend to scout out new areas in which to wreak havoc. Within weeks their numbers double, especially in high population areas where they may remain undetected for an extended period of time.

A gremlin stands 3½ feet tall and weighs about 40 pounds.

When pressed into combat, gremlins fight with bites, claws and their wicked blades which are frequently slick with nasty venoms. They prefer to hide in shadows and lash out with their sneak attack and use their phase door ability to beat a hasty retreat.

Gremlin

Small fey, chaotic evil
Armor Class 14 (leather)
Hit Points 10 (3d6)
Speed 20 ft., climb 20 ft.

STR	DEX	CON	INT	WIS	CHA
7 (−2)	16 (+3)	11 (+0)	14 (+2)	14 (+2)	15 (+2)

Skills Acrobatics +5, Arcana +4, Perception +4, Sleight of Hand +5, Stealth +5
Senses passive Perception 14
Languages Common, Goblin, Sylvan
Challenge ¼ (50 XP)

Innate Spellcasting. The gremlin's innate spellcasting ability is Charisma (spell save DC 12, +4 to hit with spell attacks). It can cast the following spells without requiring material components.

At will: *arcane lock, knock*
3/day: *find traps*
1/day: *passwall*

Knot Expert. The gremlin has advantage on any check or saving throw to break free of any effect grappling or restraining it when the effect is made of rope or rope-like objects.

Actions

Bite. *Melee Weapon Attack:* +5 to hit, reach 5 ft., one target. *Hit:* 5 (1d4 + 3) piercing damage.

Shortsword. *Melee Weapon Attack:* +5 to hit, reach 5 ft., one target. *Hit:* 6 (1d6 + 3) piercing damage.

Gremlin Filcher

Gremlin filchers are a force to be reckoned with (when it comes to securing your valuables or hiring one to secure someone else's valuables). Their small size and high Stealth bonus allow them to easily slip unnoticed into most places. Their knack with ropes not only aids them in climbing into hard to reach spaces (which could be several given their small size) but also allows them to bind any person(s) who would stop them from their task at hand.

Gremlin Filcher

Small fey, chaotic evil
Armor Class 15 (studded leather)
Hit Points 45 (10d6 + 10)
Speed 20 ft.

STR	DEX	CON	INT	WIS	CHA
7 (−2)	17 (+3)	13 (+1)	14 (+2)	14 (+2)	15 (+2)

Saving Throws Dex +6, Int +5

Skills Acrobatics +6, Arcana +5, Perception +5, Sleight of
Hand +9, Stealth +9
Senses passive Perception 15
Languages Common, Goblin, Sylvan
Challenge 5 (1,800 XP)

Evasion. If the gremlin filcher is subjected to an effect that allows it to make a Dexterity saving throw to take only half damage, the filcher instead takes no damage if it succeeds on the saving throw, and only half damage if it fails.

Innate Spellcasting. The gremlin's innate spellcasting ability is Charisma (spell save DC 13, +5 to hit with spell attacks). It can cast the following spells without requiring material components.

At will: *arcane lock, knock*
3/day: *find traps*
1/day: *passwall*

Knot Expert. The gremlin has advantage on any check or saving throw to break free of any effect grappling or restraining it when the effect is made of rope or rope-like objects.

Sneak Attack. Once per turn, the filcher deals an extra 14 (4d6) damage when it hits a target with a weapon attack and has advantage on the attack roll, or when the target is within 5 feet of an ally of the gremlin that isn't incapacitated and the gremlin doesn't have disadvantage on the attack roll.

Actions

Multiattack. The filcher makes two shortsword attacks and one bite attack.

Bite. *Melee Weapon Attack:* +6 to hit, reach 5 ft., one target. *Hit:* 5 (1d4 + 3) piercing damage.

Shortsword. *Melee Weapon Attack:* +6 to hit, reach 5 ft., one target. *Hit:* 6 (1d6 + 3) piercing damage.

Bonus Actions

Cunning Action. The gremlin filcher can take the Dash, Disengage, or Hide actions.

Fast Hands. The gremlin filcher can use a bonus action to use an object or to make a Dexterity (Sleight of Hand) check to pickpocket one object on a target's body which it is not holding. The target makes an opposed Dexterity (Acrobatics) check if it is aware of the gremlin's presence, avoiding the attempt if the target wins. If the target is unaware of the gremlin, the filcher's attempt to pickpocket the target succeeds.

Gremlin, Fuath

This small, aquatic, vaguely humanoid creature exhibits keen interest in boaters and beachgoers. Its green, scaly skin and webbed fingers and toes befit its environment, and a thick yellow mane along its spine continues on to its long tail. The playful creature teases and splashes onlookers, ushering them into the water.

This scanty scourge of the sea (and other bodies of water) delights in trickery and causing misery. The size of a newborn human, it is capable of wreaking havoc and even murder. A fuath gremlin will sabotage boats just to watch the fear and mayhem as the passengers cling desperately to life on the open sea. The evil creature will attempt to drown anyone it entices into the water and can hasten the process by expelling a viscous, suffocating watery liquid from its throat, foiling the efforts of even the best swimmers. It attacks with two claws if close up and dealing with a flailing swimmer or from a distance with darts it fashions from stout underwater reeds and sharpened seashells.

Fuath Gremlin

Small fey, chaotic evil
Armor Class 13 (natural armor)

Hit Points 22 (4d6 + 8)
Speed 20 ft., climb 10 ft., swim 30 ft.

STR	DEX	CON	INT	WIS	CHA
7 (−2)	13 (+1)	14 (+2)	10 (+0)	13 (+1)	8 (−1)

Damage Resistances cold
Senses darkvision 60 ft., passive Perception 11
Languages Aquan
Challenge ½ (100 XP)

Sunlight Sensitivity. While in sunlight, the gremlin has disadvantage on attack rolls, as well as on Wisdom (Perception) checks that rely on sight.

Water Breathing. The fuath gremlin can only breathe underwater.

Actions

Multiattack. The fuath gremlin makes two attacks with its claws.

Claws. *Melee Weapon Attack:* +3 to hit, reach 5 ft., one target. *Hit:* 3 (1d4 + 1) slashing damage.

Dart. *Ranged Weapon Attack:* +3 to hit, range 20/60 ft., one target. *Hit:* 3 (1d4 + 1) piercing damage.

Congeal Water (1/day). One creature of the fuath gremlin's choice within 30 feet of it must succeed on a DC 10 Dexterity saving throw or be coated with a thick, viscous coating of clinging watery fluid for 1 minute. While coated with this substance, the target is restrained and must hold its breath to keep from drowning (reference the SRD for Suffocating rules). The target can repeat the saving throw at the end of each of its turns, ending the effect on itself on a success.

Gribbon

This wicked little creature looks like an oversized monkey with leathery bat wings. It clutches a needlelike dagger in its claws.

Gribbons, at first glance, resemble large monkeys with bat wings. Closer examination, however, reveals facial features of a more human than simian nature. Their bodies are covered with a coarse, brown fur, and their hands end in powerful and sharp claws. These creatures are fiercely territorial and prefer to swoop down from the treetops and assault trespassers without warning. Though they greatly prefer forests, gribbons have been known to reside in caves and caverns, especially those higher up with outcroppings where they can perch and survey their territory.

Gribbons are equally as likely to attack their opponents with weapons (preferring daggers and darts, though sometimes employing shortswords) as they are with their claws. Their favorite tactic is to grab an opponent, fly above the ground and drop it.

Gribbon

Small monstrosity, neutral evil
Armor Class 12
Hit Points 13 (3d6 + 3)
Speed 30 ft., fly 30 ft.

STR	DEX	CON	INT	WIS	CHA
12 (+1)	15 (+2)	13 (+1)	10 (+0)	10 (+0)	11 (+0)

Skills Stealth +4
Senses darkvision 60 ft., passive Perception 10
Languages Common
Challenge ½ (100 XP)

Pack Tactics. The gribbon has advantage on an attack roll against a creature if at least one of the gribbon's allies is within 5 feet of the creature and the ally isn't incapacitated.

Actions

Claw. *Melee Weapon Attack:* +4 to hit, reach 5 ft., one target. *Hit:* 4 (1d4 + 2) slashing damage.

Dagger. *Melee or Ranged Weapon Attack:* +4 to hit, reach 5 ft. or range 20/60 ft., one target. *Hit:* 4 (1d4 + 2) piercing damage.

Dart. *Ranged Weapon Attack:* +4 to hit, range 26/60 ft., one target. *Hit:* 4 (1d4 + 2) piercing damage.

Hamster, Giant

A green aura surrounds this enormous creature, which resembles nothing other than a bloodthirsty hamster. Its eyes blaze with monstrous hunger.

None know the origin of this terrifying creature, save that its coming brings nothing but sickness and death. Creatures who encounter the giant hamster are chased until they collapse from exhaustion, after which they are devoured. Even if a creature decides to fight the hamster dead on, the hamster's very existence weakens the defenders.

No matter how many humanoids the giant hamster eats, its hunger is never sated. It seeks specifically bipedal prey, but will not turn away a free meal if it is a beast or even a fiend or undead. Towns and cities are not free of the giant hamster's predations. In fact, it often seeks out these conglomerations of morsels as easy targets. Eventually, it moves on after all the townsfolk have either been devoured or fled.

Giant Hamster

Huge monstrosity, chaotic evil
Armor Class 16 (natural armor)
Hit Points 189 (18d12 + 72)
Speed 40 ft., burrow 20 ft.

STR	DEX	CON	INT	WIS	CHA
22 (+6)	12 (+1)	19 (+4)	11 (+0)	14 (+2)	8 (−1)

Skills Survival +7
Damage Resistances bludgeoning, piercing, and slashing from nonmagical weapons
Damage Immunities poison
Condition Immunities charmed, exhaustion, frightened
Senses darkvision 60 ft., passive Perception 12
Languages —
Challenge 15 (13,000 XP)

Magic Resistance. The giant hamster has advantage on saving throws against spells and other magical effects.

Radioactive Aura. Creatures who enter or begin their turn within 10 feet of the giant hamster take 7 (2d6) necrotic damage and must make a successful DC 15 Constitution saving throw or be poisoned for 1 minute. A poisoned creature can repeat the saving throw at the end of each of its turns, ending the effect on a success. If the saving throw is successful, or the effect ends for it, the creature is immune to being poisoned by the giant hamster's aura for 24 hours, but not to further necrotic damage.

Siege Monster. The giant hamster deals double damage to objects and structures.

Actions

Multiattack. The giant hamster makes one bite attack and two claw attacks.

Bite. Melee Weapon Attack: +11 to hit, reach 5 ft., one target. *Hit:* 15 (2d8 + 6) piercing damage and the target is grappled (escape DC 17). Until this grapple ends, the target is restrained and the hamster can't bite another target.

Claw. Melee Weapon Attack: +11 to hit, reach 10 ft., one target. *Hit:* 16 (3d6 + 6) slashing damage.

Energy Ray (Recharge 5–6). The giant hamster fires a ray of energy from its eyes in a 60-foot line that is 5 feet wide. Creatures in the area must succeed on a DC 15 Constitution saving throw or take 54 (12d8) necrotic damage and be sickened for 1 minute. While sickened, a creature reduces its maximum hit points by 5 at the start of each of its turns. Magic such as *lesser restoration* can cure the sickened effect early.

Swallow. One grappled creature must make a DC 17 Strength saving throw or it is swallowed and the grapple ends. While swallowed, the creature is blinded and restrained, it has total cover against attacks and other effects outside the hamster, and it takes 14 (4d6) acid damage and 14 (4d6) necrotic damage at the start of each of the hamster's turns. If the hamster takes 25 damage or more on a single turn from a creature inside it, the hamster must succeed on a DC 25 Constitution saving throw at the end of that turn or regurgitate all swallowed creatures, which fall prone in a space within 10 feet of it. If the hamster dies, a swallowed creature is no longer restrained by it and can escape from the corpse using 15 feet of movement, exiting prone.

Hell Moth

This creature looks like a giant gray moth with spiraling bands of red and black on its body. It has large, thin, reddish-hued wings.

The hell moth is thought to have come from another plane, though sages are not quite sure of its exact origin. The hell moth attacks living creatures that wander too close to its lair. It otherwise resembles a large moth with an 8-foot wingspan.

Hell moths wait for their prey to pass nearby before attacking. If facing multiple opponents, they attempt to bite and usually do not employ their engulfing ability. Multiple hell moths work in concert with one another against opponents. When a hell moth has successfully engulfed a foe, it sets its own body on fire in a display of self-immolation that consumes both it and its engulfed opponent.

Hell Moth

Large aberration, neutral evil
Armor Class 15 (natural armor)
Hit Points 52 (7d10 + 14)
Speed 10 ft., fly 60 ft.

STR	DEX	CON	INT	WIS	CHA
18 (+4)	17 (+3)	15 (+2)	6 (–2)	12 (+1)	10 (+0)

Damage Resistances fire
Senses darkvision 60 ft., passive Perception 11
Languages —
Challenge 5 (1,800 XP)

Damage Transfer. While the hell moth is grappling a creature, the hell moth takes only half the damage dealt to it, and the creature grappled by the hell moth takes the other half.

Keen Scent. The hell moth has advantage on Wisdom (Perception) checks based on scent.

Actions

Bite. *Melee Weapon Attack:* +7 to hit, reach 5 ft., one target. *Hit:* 8 (1d8 + 4) piercing damage.

Engulf. *Melee Weapon Attack:* +7 to hit, reach 5 ft., one Medium or smaller creature. *Hit:* The creature is grappled (escape DC 15). Until this grapple ends, the target is restrained and blinded, and the hell moth can't engulf another target.

Immolation (Recharges on a Short or Long Rest). The hell moth detonates, dealing 33 (6d10) fire damage to itself and any grappled creature.

Hellbender

An extremely scarce planar creature that looks somewhat like a cross between a salamander and a toad, the hellbender rarely leaves its natural plane willingly. The fiery-clawed creatures are usually enslaved and transported to a location where their special talent can be exploited; their massive, intensely hot claws drip fire and are capable of melting rock and stone quickly. They are weak minded and will finish whatever tunneling task they begin without considering other options. Their steely chitin hide protects them from rock slides and tunnel collapses, and if they become trapped within tons of rubble, they use their fiery pulse to burn their way out.

If the malevolent hellbender becomes idle, it looks for something to eat or kill. Hellbenders will turn on each other or other nearby creatures if they're not digging or tunneling. Hellbender masters often think twice about enslaving hellbenders once their work is done.

Hellbender

Large aberration, chaotic evil
Armor Class 18 (natural armor)
Hit Points 76 (8d10 + 32)
Speed 20 ft.

STR	DEX	CON	INT	WIS	CHA
20 (+5)	12 (+1)	19 (+4)	5 (–3)	9 (–1)	5 (–3)

Damage Resistances acid, poison
Damage Immunities fire
Senses darkvision 60 ft., passive Perception 9
Languages Hellbender
Challenge 5 (1,800 XP)

Actions

Multiattack. The hellbender makes two attacks with its claws.

Claw. Melee Weapon Attack: +8 to hit, reach 10 ft., one target. *Hit:* 10 (1d10+5) slashing damage plus 4 (1d8) fire damage.

Fiery Pulse (Recharge 5–6). The hellbender sends a burst of fire from all small pores in its chitin-like hide. Any creature within 5 feet of the hellbender must make a DC 15 Dexterity saving throw, taking 24 (7d6) fire damage on a failed save, or half as much damage on a successful one.

Hellcat

This small feline is all black, save for a small white patch on its chest and its red, pulsing eyes. However, in the blackest moments of the inky night, its true form is revealed: a red and black furred feline aberration with a spine of spikes.

Various cultures share a legend around a mystical feline creature that steals souls from those who do not leave blessings for the myth. This creature, called variously the *cath sìth*, *palug*, or *chapalu* might have a place in these legends. The hellcat appears, at first glance, as a common housecat, but this is belied by the feline's evil red gaze. The hellcat feeds off souls, often hunting in the night for the weakest humanoids, those lost or nearest death. (The hellcat can smell those near death.) Once located, the hellcat uses its Death Gaze to steal the creature's soul just before death. It will then stealthily flee, if possible, and dislikes being confronted, running into the dark as quickly as it can after tasting of the dead.

The hellcat does not discriminate, searching both urban and wilderness for humanoids of any nature, apparently preferring humans, elves, and other similar goodly races. Very few records of a hellcat stalking through the so-called evil humanoid territories exist, but whether this is a true correlation between the preferred diet of the hellcat or a lack of recordkeeping is unknown. Very rarely, a hellcat will form an alliance with a coven of evil witches or hags but will just as quickly dissolve such a friendship if the hellcat's life is threatened.

Hellcat

Tiny aberration, neutral evil
Armor Class 13 (natural armor)
Hit Points 44 (8d4 + 24)
Speed 40 ft., climb 30 ft.

STR	DEX	CON	INT	WIS	CHA
3 (–4)	15 (+2)	16 (+3)	11 (+0)	15 (+2)	18 (+4)

Saving Throws Int +2, Wis +4
Skills Perception +4, Stealth +4
Senses darkvision 60 ft., passive Perception 14
Languages understands Common but can't speak; telepathy 60 ft.
Challenge 2 (450 XP)

Death Sense. The hellcat can sense the exact location of any humanoid within 120 feet with less than half its hit points.

False Appearance. Unless it is using its Death Gaze ability, the hellcat is indistinguishable from a normal housecat.

Magic Resistance. The hellcat has advantage on saving throws against spells and other magical effects.

Actions

Multiattack. The hellcat makes one bite attack and one claw attack.

Bite. *Melee Weapon Attack:* +4 to hit, reach 5 ft., one target. *Hit:* 4 (1d4 + 2) piercing damage.

Claws. *Melee Weapon Attack:* +4 to hit, reach 5 ft., one target. *Hit:* 9 (2d6 + 2) slashing damage.

Death Gaze (Recharge 5–6). One target within 30 feet of the hellcat that it can see must make a DC 14 Constitution saving throw. On a failed saving throw, the target takes 27 (6d8) necrotic damage. If the creature drops to 0 hit points from this damage, it dies, and can only be restored to life by means of a *true resurrection* or *wish* spell.

Herald of Tsathogga

This creature appears to be a gigantic pale yellow-green frog with oversized monstrous eyes. In place of its legs and forelimbs are many long, writhing tentacles it uses to pull itself along the ground.

The dark, dismal tropical swamps and fens of the world are home to a horrible creature known only as the herald of Tsathogga. A vaguely froglike thing almost 20 feet across, the herald of Tsathogga is a nightmare creature that is spoken of only in hushed whispers. The creature is believed to have been created by the Frog God as punishment against humanity for wrongdoings done to Tsathogga and his worshippers.

Its warty, putrid skin is a pale yellow-green, and two monstrous eyes that have seen unknown secrets gaze from its fleshy face. The body of the thing resembles that of a massive toad, but rather than legs, the herald of Tsathogga drags itself through the murky terrain on ten thick tentacles. These tentacles are covered in tiny lancets that inject paralytic venom. Some who have seen the herald of Tsathogga swear that it is capable of flight, but these reports are dismissed as a madman's fantasy.

Though only one herald is thought to exist, rumors as of late, speak of at least three of these creatures in existence.

The herald of Tsathogga attacks first with its tentacles, attempting to paralyze or otherwise incapacitate as many opponents as possible. Paralyzed opponents are pulled to the creature's maw and bitten. Its tentacles are not coordinated enough to grab moving targets, so it cannot pick up opponents that have not been paralyzed.

Herald of Tsathogga

Huge aberration, chaotic evil
Armor Class 19 (natural armor)
Hit Points 299 (26d12 + 130)
Speed 10 ft., fly 60 ft.

STR	DEX	CON	INT	WIS	CHA
23 (+6)	16 (+3)	20 (+5)	7 (−2)	16 (+3)	12 (+1)

Saving Throws Dex +9, Con +11, Wis +9, Cha +7
Skills Perception +9
Damage Resistances thunder; bludgeoning, piercing, and slashing from nonmagical weapons
Senses darkvision 60 ft., passive Perception 19
Languages —
Challenge 18 (20,000 XP)

Bloated. If the Herald of Tsathogga attacks with more than four tentacles during a single turn, its movement speed is reduced to 0 and it falls prone. The herald can use half its movement on its next turn to rise from the prone position.

Regeneration. The Herald of Tsathogga regains 20 hit points at the start of its turn. If the herald takes fire or lightning damage, this trait doesn't function at the start of the herald's next turn. The herald dies only if it starts its turn with 0 hit points and doesn't regenerate.

Actions

Multiattack. The Herald of Tsathogga makes up to twelve attacks: one with its bite or swallow, one with its tongue, and it can make one attack with each of its ten tentacles.

Bite. *Melee Weapon Attack:* +12 to hit, reach 5 ft., one target. *Hit:* 15 (2d8 + 6) piercing damage, and the target is grappled (escape DC 16).

Until this grapple ends, the target is restrained and the herald can't bite another target.

Tongue. *Melee Weapon Attack:* +12 to hit, reach 30 ft., one target. *Hit:* 12 (1d12 + 6) slashing damage plus 9 (2d8) acid damage, and the target must succeed on a DC 16 Strength saving throw or be pulled up to 25 feet toward the Herald.

Tentacle. *Melee Weapon Attack:* +12 to hit, reach 20 ft., one target. *Hit:* 10 (1d8 + 6) bludgeoning damage. If the target is a creature other than an undead, it must succeed on a DC 19 Constitution saving throw or be paralyzed for 1 minute. The target can repeat the saving throw at the end of each of its turns, ending the effect on itself on a success.

Swallow. The Herald of Tsathogga makes one bite attack against a Large or smaller target it is grappling. If the attack hits, the target is swallowed and the grapple ends. The swallowed target is blinded and restrained, has total cover against attacks and other effects outside of the herald, and it takes 21 (6d6) acid damage at the start of each of the herald's turns. The herald can have only one target swallowed at a time.

If the herald takes 50 damage or more on a single turn from the swallowed creature, the herald must succeed on a DC 15 Constitution saving throw at the end of that turn or forcefully disgorge the creature, which falls prone in a space within 20 feet of the herald. If the herald dies, a swallowed creature is no longer restrained by it and can escape from the corpse using 15 feet of movement, exiting prone.

Bellow (Recharge 5–6). The Herald of Tsathogga emits a deafening, trilling croak. All creatures within 30 feet of the herald that can hear it must make a DC 19 Constitution saving throw, taking 28 (8d6) thunder damage on a failure, or half as much damage on a successful save. On a failed save, the creature is also deafened for 1 minute. A deafened creature can repeat the saving throw at the end of each of its turns, ending the effect on itself on a success.

Horned Lord, The

An aura of terror radiates from the figure on the throne as it regards you with burning red eyes. It is a clean, fleshless skeleton seemingly crafted from pale stone, a pair of great antlers rising from its bare skull, and it is clad in rich purple robes. In one hand it clutches a tall, wickedly curved scythe that pulses with evil energies.

The foul being known as the Horned Lord has troubled civilization for millennia, returning time and again from apparent destruction to once more lead his hordes in a war of conquest. So many times has the Horned Lord returned that his origins are lost the depths of legend, to the point that no one living knows the truth.

The Horned Lord's rising recurs every few generations, usually just as the tales of his last rise are beginning to fade from memory. He returns through some unusual process, often foretold by prophecy — accidentally awakened by adventurers, summoned by cultists, returned when the stars are right, and so on — inevitably accompanied by his feared minions, the twelve shadow captains. Once he has proclaimed his return, the Horned Lord begins to assemble an army of orcs, gnolls, humans, or other evil beings, corrupt the surrounding kingdoms through the acts of cultists or secret followers, and sets out once more on the path of conquest.

Just as surely as the Horned Lord rises, so he falls, but only after untold destruction and bloodshed. The coming of the Horned Lord inevitably heralds an end to civilization and the beginning of a barbaric dark age. Only when civilization has returned to its original level does the Horned Lord return and the cycle repeats itself.

The Truth

No one truly knows where the Horned Lord came from, and in fact, he rises up again only when stories about him have begun to fade from memory. The truth can be found, but it would require travel into the distant past, research into incredibly ancient books, or communication with the gods themselves. Countless millennia ago a monarch sought to build the greatest empire that the world had ever known. In doing so he made deals with many gods and wielded vast magical power, and as his power grew, so did his arrogance. When at last he had achieved his goal — a vast and unconquerable empire with him at its head — he was blinded by his pride and declared himself greater than the gods and turned his back on them. The emperor was to be the realm's only god, and all the deities of the past were to be forgotten, their priests slaughtered and their temples overthrown. As one might guess, the gods were mightily displeased and struck down the emperor, cursing both him and his realm. Soon his proud empire had crumbled to dust and barbarism ruled the land.

But the gods had not finished with the emperor, so great was his transgression. He was transformed into an undead thing, doomed to be reborn again and again, consumed by the desire for conquest — a desire that can never be fulfilled. Always would the Horned Lord see his dreams crumble, and perish among the ruins of civilization. Always would he return with the same dreams of conquest, only to be crushed and forgotten.

Dealing with the Horned Lord can provide PCs with a number of challenges. At the very least, he is your garden variety Evil Dark Lord™ determined to spread his evil like a stain across the land. On the other hand, should the adventurers learn something about his history and the cyclical nature of his appearances, they may deduce that this one is subtly different. Further research may reveal a way of lifting the Horned Lord's curse and possibly freeing him — and the entire world — from his endless cycle of war and destruction. This would, of course, require a fairly involved series of high-level adventures, possibly including direct contact and appeal to the gods themselves.

The Horned Lord

Medium undead, lawful evil

Armor Class 23 (natural armor, *robe of the archmagi*, *Harrowblade*, *cloak of protection*)
Hit Points 285 (38d8 + 114)
Speed 30 ft.

STR	DEX	CON	INT	WIS	CHA
10 (+0)	14 (+2)	16 (+3)	20 (+5)	22 (+6)	20 (+5)

Saving Throws Dex +9, Int +12, Wis +13, Cha +12
Skills Arcana +12, Deception +12, History +12, Insight +13, Intimidation +12, Perception +13, Persuasion +12, Religion +12
Damage Resistances force; bludgeoning, piercing and slashing damage from nonmagical weapons
Damage Immunities cold, necrotic, poison, psychic
Condition Immunities charmed, deafened, exhaustion, frightened, paralyzed, poisoned, unconscious
Senses truesight 120 ft., passive Perception 23
Languages Common
Challenge 22 (41,000 XP)

Special Equipment. The Horned Lord wears a *cloak of protection, ring of spell turning,* and a black *robe of the archmagi*. He has +1 to all saving throws while wearing the cloak. He also wields the infamous *Harrowblade* (see sidebar for more details).

Spellcasting. The Horned Lord is an 18th level spellcaster. Its spellcasting ability is Intelligence (spell save DC 22, +14 to hit with spell attacks). The Horned Lord has the following wizard spells prepared:

Cantrips (at will): *acid splash, chill touch, ray of frost*
1st level (4 slots): *detect magic, magic missile, shield, thunderwave*
2nd level (3 slots): *acid arrow, blur, detect thoughts, levitate*
3rd level (3 slots): *animate dead, dispel magic, fireball, lightning bolt*
4th level (3 slots): *confusion, ice storm*
5th level (3 slots): *cloudkill, scrying*
6th level (1 slot): *disintegrate, wall of ice*
7th level (1 slot): *finger of death, teleport*
8th level (1 slot): *dominate monster, power word stun*
9th level (1 slot): *power word kill*

Turn Resistance. The Horned Lord has advantage on saving throws against any effect that turns undead.

Magic Resistance. The Horned Lord has advantage on saving throws against spells and other magical effects.

Regeneration. The Horned Lord regains 1d6 hit points at the beginning of his turn if he has at least 1 hit point.

Harrowblade

Weapon (scythe), artifact (requires attunement)

This perpetually bloody weapon is a crooked scythe, a farming implement. It appears truly ancient, the blade filthy with ichor and long rust-covered. It stands 7 feet tall and exudes menace; it awakens a primal fear within all living creatures, causing their bowels to loosen in terror.

Unholy Aura. Living creatures cannot take long rests within 300 feet of *Harrowblade*. In addition, within 10 feet of *Harrowblade*, all holy water is destroyed, and creatures of CR 0 and plants that are not creatures die.

Magic Weapon. *Harrowblade* is a heavy, two-handed weapon that deals 2d6 slashing damage plus 4d6 cold damage on a hit, and you have a +3 bonus to attack and damage rolls made with the weapon. You score a critical hit if you roll a natural 19 or 20 on the attack roll with the weapon, and any living creature struck by the critical hit must make a DC 20 Wisdom saving throw, taking an additional 4d6 psychic damage on a failed saving throw, or half as much damage on a successful saving throw. Finally, *Harrowblade* also functions as a *mace of terror*, save that it has 7 charges and regains them at midnight.

Blessings of the Dead. You have a +1 bonus to your Armor Class while you wield *Harrowblade*, and have resistance to radiant damage. In addition, at the beginning of each of your turns, you regain 1d6 hit points if you have at least 1 hit point remaining.

Sentience. *Harrowblade* is a lawful evil magic weapon. It has hearing and vision to a distance of 120 feet and understands all the languages you do. It can communicate with emotions alone. It has an Intelligence of 10, a Wisdom of 14, and a Charisma of 16. *Harrowblade's* purpose is to enslave all living creatures and enthrone its wielder atop the new empire of tyranny it has helped create. It will rebel against a wielder whom it believes is not strong enough to carry out such a task.

Destruction. *Harrowblade* can be destroyed by a group of 7 lawful good clerics immersing *Harrowblade* into a bath of holy water, then each casting *holy aura* on the weapon. The combined might of these blessings is enough to shatter the blade of the magic weapon into fragments, leaving it nascent...until the Horned Lord rises again.

Actions

Multiattack. The Horned Lord makes three attacks with *Harrowblade*.

Harrowblade. *Melee Weapon Attack:* +12 to hit, reach 5 ft., one target. *Hit:* 12 (2d6+5) slashing damage plus 14 (4d6) cold damage. On a natural 19 or 20 attack roll, living creatures must make a DC 20 Wisdom saving throw, taking 14 (4d6) psychic damage on a failed save, or half as much damage on a successful one.

Dominate (Recharge 5–6). The Horned Lord speaks in a commanding voice, calling on all to bow down to him. Each creature within 60 feet of the Horned Lord must succeed on a DC 20 Wisdom saving throw or be incapacitated for 1 minute. A creature can repeat the saving throw at the end of each of its turns, ending the effect on a success. If a creature's saving throw is successful or the effect ends for it, the creature is immune to the Horned Lord's Dominate for the next 24 hours.

Legendary Actions

The Horned Lord can take 3 legendary actions, choosing from the options below. Only one legendary action can be used at a time and only at the end of another creature's turn. The Horned Lord regains spent legendary actions at the start of his turn.

Cantrip. The Horned Lord casts a cantrip.

Spell (Costs 2 Actions). The Horned Lord casts a prepared spell.

Stunning Wave (Costs 2 Actions). The Horned Lord unleashes a pulse of overwhelming evil energy. Each living creature within 20 feet of the Horned Lord must make a DC 20 Constitution saving throw or be stunned until the end of the Horned Lord's next turn.

Death Gaze (Costs 3 Actions). The Horned Lord chooses one creature within 60 feet of it that it can see. The creature must make a DC 18 Constitution saving throw. On a failure, the creature drops to 0 hit points. On a success, a creature takes 21 (6d6) psychic damage.

The Horned Lord's Lair

The Horned Lord instinctively makes his lair in a dark fortress, located in the heart of a wasteland far from civilization, and here, he marshals his evil forces, summons nightmarish demons, and performs unspeakable sacrifices. Guarded by hordes of evil humanoids and fiends, the Horned Lord can also perform several unique acts to help defend himself against those who dare to challenge him in his lair.

Lair Actions

On Initiative 20 (losing initiative ties), the Horned Lord takes a lair action to cause one of the following effects. The Horned Lord can't use the same effect two rounds in a row.

Miasmal Cloud. A dark miasma permeates the area in a 90-foot radius from the Horned Lord. All living creatures in the area must make a DC 20 Constitution saving throw or be poisoned until the end of Horned Lord's next turn.

Shades. The Horned Lord summons memories and shades from one living creature's past. The creature must make a DC 18 Wisdom saving throw or take 36 (8d8) psychic damage and gain a level of exhaustion.

Wall of Arms. The Horned Lord can make the ghostly limbs of past victims manifest in the air around foes in a 60-foot radius centered on him. Each creature in this area must make a DC 20 Dexterity saving throw or be restrained until the end of the Horned Lord's next turn.

Regional Effects

The region around the Horned Lord's lair is warped by his magic, creating one or more of the following effects:

Hot Lava. Fissures and magma eruptions spread across the area, destroying structures and causing 11 (2d10) fire damage per turn to anyone who falls into one.

Dark and Stormy. The sky grows gloomy and clouded, causing dim light conditions and occasionally lightly obscured patches of smoke and dark fog.

Sulfurous Gas. Vents of sulfurous gas release poison into the atmosphere. Anyone encountering such a vent must make a DC 12 Constitution saving throw or take 13 (3d8) poison damage and be poisoned for 1d6 hours.

If the Horned Lord dies, conditions surrounding the lair return to normal over the course of 1d10 days.

Hsagrath

A floating chain moves silently across the room as if held by an invisible will. Methodically, it patrols each corner of the room as if searching for something. If approached, the chain handle lifts and the levitating chain snaps backward, then forward again with lightning speed, making a loud cracking sound echoing in the darkness.

Hsagrath is an animated, spiked chain whip that hovers in the dark places of the world in search of victims. Formerly the weapon of a torture-loving fiend, Hsagrath was separated from its master. The construct is now autonomous and filled with hate. The embodiment of sadistic purpose, it desires victims, not to kill but to inflict pain to the cusp of death and guard them as they recover. Once recovered sufficiently, Hsagrath begins the terrible process again.

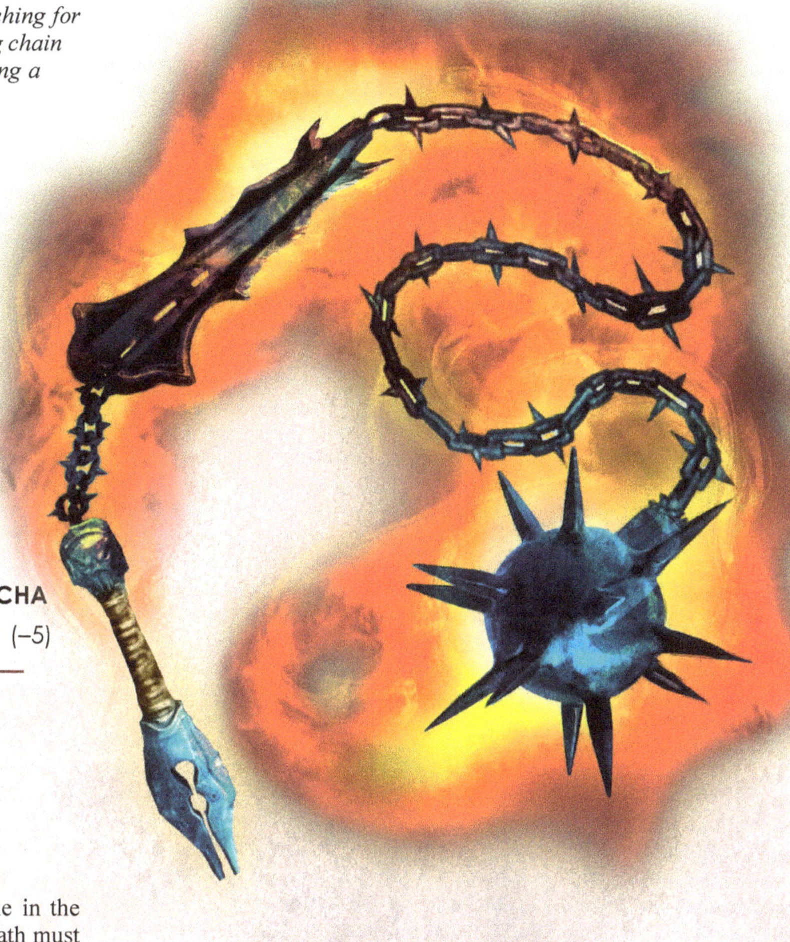

Hsagrath

Small construct, chaotic evil
Armor Class 17 (natural armor)
Hit Points 45 (10d8)
Speed 0 ft., Fly 50 ft. (hover)

STR	DEX	CON	INT	WIS	CHA
17 (+3)	12 (+1)	11 (+0)	9 (−1)	5 (−3)	1 (−5)

Saving Throw Dex +4
Damage Immunities: Poison, Psychic
Condition Immunities: Blinded, Charmed, Deafened, Frightened, Paralyzed, Poisoned
Senses: Blindsight 60 ft., Passive Perception 10
Languages —
Challenge 5 (1,800 XP)

Antimagic Susceptibility. The hsagrath is incapacitated while in the area of an antimagic field. If targeted by dispel magic, the hsagrath must succeed on a Constitution saving throw against the caster's spell save DC or fall unconscious for 1 minute.

False Appearance. While the hsagrath remains motionless and isn't flying, it is indistinguishable from a normal chain.

Fiendish Humor. When a target reaches 0 hit points, a hsagrath will release and seek a new target.

Actions

Whip. *Melee Weapon Attack:* +6 to hit, reach 30 ft., all targets within range. Hit: 7 (1d8+3) bludgeoning damage.

Nay Nay. *Melee Weapon Attack:* +6 to hit, reach 30 ft., one target. Hit: 12 (2d8+3) bludgeoning damage and the target is grappled (Escape DC 16). A grappled opponent takes 12 (2d8+3) bludgeoning damage at the beginning of its turn. The hsagrath can't make any other attacks while it has a creature grappled.

Huecuva

Rotting vestments hang across the withered flesh of this walking corpse, and its mouth hangs open in a silent scream.

Huecuva are the undead spirits of good clerics who were unfaithful to their god and turned to the path of evil before death. As punishment for their transgression, their god condemned them to roam the earth as the one creature all good-aligned clerics despise — undead. Huecuva resemble robed skeletons and are often mistaken for such creatures.

A huecuva attacks with its claws, raking and slashing at its opponents. It attacks relentlessly until either it or its opponent is dead. During combat, if a good-aligned cleric attempts to turn a huecuva and fails, the huecuva concentrates all attacks on that cleric, ignoring all other opponents until the cleric or the huecuva is dead.

A huecuva's natural weapons are treated as magic weapons for the purpose of overcoming damage reduction.

Huecuva

Medium undead, chaotic evil
Armor Class 14 (natural armor)
Hit Points 39 (6d8 + 12)
Speed 30 ft.

STR	DEX	CON	INT	WIS	CHA
13 (+1)	16 (+3)	14 (+2)	4 (−3)	12 (+1)	10 (+0)

Skills Perception +3, Stealth +5
Damage Resistances cold, necrotic; bludgeoning, piercing, and slashing from nonmagical weapons that aren't silvered
Damage Immunities poison
Condition Immunities exhaustion, frightened, poisoned
Senses darkvision 60 ft., passive Perception 13
Languages the languages it new in life
Challenge 2 (450 XP)

Shroud of Deception. During daylight hours only, a huecuva is transformed and looks, feels, and sounds like the living creature it once was. A creature that interacts with the huecuva must succeed on a DC 14 Intelligence (Investigation) check to realize the appearance of the huecuva is an illusion. Creatures with the Keen Smell trait automatically pass the check versus the illusion as the scent of the huecuva remains that of the grave.

Actions

Multiattack. The huecuva makes two attacks with its claws.

Claws. *Melee Weapon Attack:* +5 to hit, reach 5 ft., one target. *Hit:* 10 (2d6 + 3) slashing damage. If the target is a creature, it must succeed on a DC 12 Constitution saving throw against disease or become poisoned until the disease is cured. Every 24 hours that elapse, the poisoned target must repeat the saving throw, reducing its hit point maximum by 5 (1d10) on a failure. The disease is cured on a success. The target dies if the disease reduces its hit point maximum to 0. This reduction to the target's hit point maximum lasts until the disease is cured.

Iron Cobra

This creature resembles a small metallic cobra. Its body sheens with a silver hue and its eyes are small pinpoints of red light.

The iron cobra is a construct that resembles a small, 3-foot-long cobra. Its eyes give it an evil and determined — and almost intelligent — look. The iron cobra is most often used to guard a treasure or to act as a bodyguard to its creator, though on some occasions it can be ordered to track down and slay any creature who is within 1 mile and whose name is known by the creator.

The iron cobra attacks by biting its opponent.

Iron Cobra

Small construct, neutral
Armor Class 13 (natural armor)
Hit Points 27 (6d6 + 6)
Speed 40 ft.

STR	DEX	CON	INT	WIS	CHA
12 (+1)	15 (+2)	13 (+1)	5 (−3)	12 (+1)	1 (−5)

Skills Perception +3, Stealth +4
Damage Immunities poison, psychic; bludgeoning, piercing, and slashing from nonmagical weapons that aren't adamantine
Condition Immunities charmed, exhaustion, frightened, paralyzed, petrified, poisoned
Senses darkvision 60 ft., passive Perception 13
Languages understands the languages of its creator but can't speak
Challenge 1 (200 XP)

Find Target. The iron cobra knows the location of a specific target creature as long as that creature is within 1 mile of it. If the creature is moving, it knows the direction if that creature's movement. If the target is beyond this distance, the iron cobra can't locate the target creature.

Immutable Form. The iron cobra is immune to any spell or effect that would alter its form.

Magic Resistance. The iron cobra has advantage on saving throws against spells and other magical effects.

Magic Weapon. The iron cobra's weapon attacks are magical.

Poison. The iron cobra contains enough venom for three attacks. After that, it does not deal the poison damage listed in its bite attack.

Actions

Bite. *Melee Weapon Attack:* +4 to hit, reach 5 ft., one target. *Hit:* 7 (2d4 + 2) piercing damage, and the target must make a DC 11 Constitution saving throw, taking 10 (3d6) poison damage on a failed saving throw, or half as much damage on a successful one.

Jaguar, Saber-tooth

This hulking predator has two enlarged serrated canines jutting from its lower jaw, a thick neck, and robustly muscled forelimbs and shoulders. It has spotted fur that allows it to hide in tall grasses and ambush prey.

The sabertooth jaguar is a large predator, standing 4 feet at the shoulder, 7 feet long, and weighing over 400 pounds. It is different from other large felines in that its main upper canine teeth are large, curved, and serrated, which it uses in combination with its thickly muscled neck to deliver devastating slashing bites. Its forelimbs are also well-developed and longer than other feline creatures, with sharp claws.

The sabertooth jaguar's fur is covered in rosettes, small dark spots that function as camouflage in the dappled light of its forest habitat. The jaguar's existence in the forest means that it is an apex predator and is not preyed on in the wild. The feline is a strict carnivore, and often aims for the head of its prey, biting into the skull to deliver a fatal blow to the brain.

Saber-Tooth Jaguar

Large beast, unaligned
Armor Class 13
Hit Points 76 (9d10 + 27)
Speed 40 ft., climb 30 ft.

STR	DEX	CON	INT	WIS	CHA
20 (+5)	16 (+3)	16 (+3)	3 (−4)	12 (+1)	8 (−1)

Skills Perception +3, Stealth +7
Senses passive Perception 13
Languages —
Challenge 4 (1,100 XP)

Keen Smell. The jaguar has advantage on Wisdom (Perception) checks that rely on smell.

Pounce. If the jaguar moves at least 20 feet straight toward a creature and then hits it with a claw attack on the same turn, that target must succeed on a DC 15 Strength saving throw or be knocked prone. If the target is prone, the jaguar can make one bite attack against it as a bonus action.

Surprise Attack. If the sabertooth jaguar surprises a creature and hits it with an attack during the first round of combat, the target takes an extra 10 (3d6) damage from the attack.

Actions

Bite. *Melee Weapon Attack:* +7 to hit, reach 5 ft., one target. *Hit:* 27 (4d10 + 5) piercing damage.

Claw. *Melee Weapon Attack:* +7 to hit, reach 5 ft., one target. *Hit:* 12 (2d6 + 5) slashing damage.

Jynx

This creature resembles a 3-foot-tall elf with slightly longer ears and a pair of glittering insect-like wings. Its clothes are varying shades of green, and the creature carries a small shortsword.

Jynx are small whimsical, fun-loving forest fey thought to be an offshoot of the elven race. They live in small moss-covered caves within their forests, with such caves often being located near well-traveled roads and paths, but still well hidden from prying eyes. This location makes it much easier for the jynx to partake in one of their favorite pastimes — leading travelers astray. Jynx rarely try to harm the target of their pranks; they simply delight in sewing confusion and watching the target's reactions to such events. Those that despoil the forests, on the other hand, are led astray and often led into jynx-placed traps that seek to maim or even kill such creatures.

Jynx have good relations with other forest-dwelling humanoids and creatures (elves, sprites, pixies, etc.) and can often be found in their midst. They are on good terms with neutral and good-aligned druids and rangers as well.

A typical jynx stands around 3 feet tall and weighs about 40 pounds. Skin color is usually tan and hair color varies wildly from the deepest blacks to the brightest blondes. Eyes are most often deep blue or dark green. A jynx's lifespan is about 300 years.

Jynx tend to avoid melee combat, preferring to assault their enemies with their spell-like abilities and shortbows.

Jynx

Small fey, chaotic neutral
Armor Class 13
Hit Points 27 (6d6 + 6)
Speed 25 ft., fly 30 ft.

STR	DEX	CON	INT	WIS	CHA
7 (–2)	16 (+3)	13 (+1)	15 (+2)	14 (+2)	16 (+3)

Skills Acrobatics +5, Nature +4, Perception +4, Stealth +5
Senses darkvision 60 ft., passive Perception 14
Languages Common, Sylvan
Challenge 1 (200 XP)

Innate Spellcasting. The jynx's innate spellcasting ability is Charisma (spell save DC 13, +5 to hit with spell attacks). The jynx can cast the following spells without requiring material components:

At will: *detect evil and good, detect magic*
1/day each: *color spray, detect thoughts, dispel magic, entangle*

Actions

Shortbow. *Ranged Weapon Attack:* +5 to hit, range 80/320 ft., one target. *Hit:* 6 (1d6 + 3) piercing damage.

Shortsword. *Melee Weapon Attack:* +5 to hit, reach 5 ft., one target. *Hit:* 6 (1d6 + 3) piercing damage.

Jinx (1/Short or Long Rest). The jinx chooses one target that it can see within 60 feet of it to make a DC 13 Wisdom saving throw. On a failed saving throw, the creature is jinxed for 1 minute. While jinxed, the creature has disadvantage on all attack rolls, saving throws, and skill checks until the jinx ends. The jinx can be ended early with *remove curse*.

Kamasuhn

This regal creature resembles a muscular winged humanoid warrior with a proud eagle's head and four wing-like arms ending in delicately clawed hands. It bears a double-bladed polearm and is clad in elaborate armor, enameled in white and chased in gold.

The hawk-headed kamasuhn are celestial warriors, serving in the retinues of many different lawful good gods, and performing tasks for their patrons in the Material Plane. They are most often employed as guardians of dangerous or sacred places, or to retrieve lost treasures and artifacts. In this last capacity, kamasuhn have been known to assist adventuring parties in their various quests, so long as their new friends agree to aid the kamasuhn in retrieving the item in question and, if necessary, destroying it. If tasked to bring the item back to their patron, kamasuhn will reluctantly battle recalcitrant parties for the item's possession.

Though they are merciless in their persecution of evil creatures, neither asking nor giving quarter, kamasuhn are reluctant to take the lives of good creatures. If good creatures are threatened with death at a kamasuhn's hands, it will instead attempt to knock out the creature rather than kill it.

Kamasuhn

Large celestial, lawful good
Armor Class 17 (natural armor)
Hit Points 238 (28d10 + 84)
Speed 30 ft., fly 30 ft.

STR	DEX	CON	INT	WIS	CHA
15 (+2)	18 (+4)	16 (+3)	12 (+1)	14 (+2)	16 (+3)

Saving Throws Str +6, Wis +6
Skills Acrobatics +12, Insight +10, Intimidation +11, Perception +10, Persuasion +11, Religion +9
Damage Resistances necrotic; bludgeoning, piercing and slashing damage from nonmagical weapons
Condition Immunities charmed, exhaustion, frightened
Senses darkvision 60 ft., passive Perception 20
Languages Celestial, Common
Challenge 12 (8,400 XP)

Actions

Multiattack. The Kamasuhn makes two attacks with its glaive.

Glaive. Melee Weapon Attack: +6 to hit, reach 10 ft., one target. *Hit:* 13 (2d10 + 2) slashing damage.

Radiant Strike (Recharge 6). On a successful strike with its glaive, the kamasuhn unleashes a burst of radiant energy in a 60-foot radius. All creatures in this area must make a DC 13 Dexterity saving throw, taking 27 (6d8) radiant damage on a failed save, or half as much damage on a successful one.

Karina

Before your eyes, bathed in moonlight, the darkly beautiful elven woman transforms into a great snowy owl!

When the moon sheds its light on the land below, karina are able to transform to and from their owl shape. This isn't always as advantageous as it sounds, for a karina is unable to change during nights with a new moon and — more importantly — on foggy or cloudy nights when the moon is obscured. Accordingly, karina often make their lairs on mountain slopes high above the cloud line.

Karina act as raiders and kidnappers for evil fey, sneaking into settlements or isolated homesteads, stealing children and animals or simply terrorizing families. Karina are known to savor the flesh of mortals as well, stalking hunters and travelers through the forest for hours or days before finally swooping in to finish off their victims and feast on the remains. Though karina receive gold and magic in exchange for their captives, they appear to derive great perverse pleasure from the suffering they inflict.

While they are chaotic and thoroughly wicked, karina are not unwilling to deal with mortals. If a karina is unable or unwilling to come to an agreement with fellow fey in exchange for prisoners or plunder, she may turn to mortal clients, offering stolen lives and property in exchange for wealth or other services. Services may include acting on the karina's behalf in kidnappings, theft, burglary or even murder. Those who owe favors to a karina invariably regret their decision, for a karina's whims often end in disaster. Mortals who especially tickle a karina's fancy may find themselves as her lover, a position even more precarious than normal, but many greedy and lustful humans cannot resist a karina's otherworldly appeal.

Greatly feared by the folk of the northern forests, the karina is a fey shapeshifter, able to appear as either a beautiful elven woman with dark hair and pale skin or a giant snowy owl with fierce red eyes and deadly talons.

Karina

Medium fey, chaotic evil
Armor Class 17
Hit Points 88 (16d8 + 16)
Speed 30 ft., fly 60 ft. (owl form)

STR	DEX	CON	INT	WIS	CHA
10 (+0)	18 (+4)	13 (+1)	14 (+2)	20 (+5)	20 (+5)

Saving Throws Con +3, Wis +7
Skills Animal Handling +7, Insight +9, Perception +9, Persuasion +9, Stealth +8, Survival +9
Senses darkvision 60 ft., passive Perception 19
Languages Common, Elvish, Sylvan
Challenge 4 (1,100 XP)

Flyby. When in owl form, the karina does not provoke opportunity attacks when it flies out of an enemy's reach.

Innate Spellcasting. The karina's spellcasting ability is Wisdom (spell save DC 15, +7 to hit with spell attacks). The karina can innately cast the following spells, requiring no material components:

At will: *chill touch, dancing lights*
3/day each: *faerie fire, fog cloud*
1/day: *moonbeam*

Keen Hearing and Sight. Karina have advantage on Wisdom (Perception) checks based on sight or hearing.

Owl Form. As a bonus action when under moonlight, a Karina can transform either into or from owl form. In owl form, the karina gains fly 60 ft. and natural attacks (see below).

Actions

Multiattack. A karina makes two dagger attacks or one bite and one talon attack.

Bite (Owl Form Only). *Melee Weapon Attack:* +6 to hit, reach 5 ft., one target. *Hit:* 17 (3d8 + 4) piercing damage.

Dagger (Human Form Only). *Melee Weapon Attack:* +6 to hit, reach 5 ft., one target. *Hit:* 6 (1d4 + 4) piercing or slashing damage.

Talons (Owl Form Only). *Melee Weapon Attack*: +6 to hit, reach 5 ft., one target. *Hit:* 13 (2d8 + 4) slashing damage.

Kathlin

This creature resembles a blackish-brown warhorse that rears, exposing six muscular legs and terrible hooves.

Kathlins are powerful, six-legged horses that spend their time roaming the temperate plains they call home. They generally avoid contact with civilized races, preferring the seclusion of their homeland above all else.

Kathlin congregate in herds and two types of herds can be encountered; bachelor or mixed. A bachelor herd consists of all males. Each male in such a herd is young and hasn't reached full maturity yet. The second type of kathlin herd is a mixed herd that contains both females and males. In a mixed herd, there will always be at least one male for every three females (it's part of the harem-like structure of the kathlin society).

When a bachelor male reaches maturity, it leaves the bachelor herd and seeks out a mixed herd where it selects up to three females to mate with. Should the kathlin select a female that is mated with another male, a battle ensues. The male that wins this fight claims the female as its own.

Kathlins can be trained as mounts or beasts of burden. Young are usually easier to train than older kathlins, and males make better mounts than females. They can also be trained to serve as a mount in combat. They are fearless creatures and do quite well in such situations. Trained properly, a kathlin makes an excellent combat steed. When fighting, a kathlin rears back on its hind legs and slashes with its hooves or gnashes at a foe with its bite.

Non-domesticated or untrained kathlin back away from combat if overwhelmed. They do not do so out of fear but are intelligent enough to know when they are beaten.

Training a Kathlin

A kathlin requires training before it can bear a rider in combat. To be trained, a kathlin must have a friendly attitude toward the trainer. Training a friendly kathlin requires six weeks of work and a successful DC 15 Wisdom (Animal Handling) check.

Kathlin young are worth 5,000 gp on the open market. Professional trainers charge 1,000 gp to rear or train a kathlin.

Carrying Capacity: Carrying Capacity: A kathlin is unencumbered up to 300 pounds; lightly encumbered from 301 to 600 pounds; and encumbered from 601 to 900 pounds. It cannot carry more than 900 pounds, A kathlin can drag 4,500 pounds.

Kathlin

Large monstrosity, neutral good
Armor Class 12
Hit Points 34 (4d10 + 12)
Speed 60 ft.

STR	DEX	CON	INT	WIS	CHA
18 (+4)	15 (+2)	17 (+3)	5 (−3)	13 (+1)	8 (−1)

Senses darkvision 60 ft., passive Perception 11
Languages —
Challenge 2 (450 XP)

Brave. A kathlin has advantage on saving throws against being frightened.

Great Endurance. A kathlin can run at a gallop for up to 4 hours before succumbing to exhaustion.

Trampling Charge. If the kathlin moves at least 20 feet straight toward a creature and then hits it with a hooves attack on the same turn, that target must succeed on a DC 15 Strength saving throw or be knocked prone. If the target is prone, the kathlin can make another attack with its hooves against it as a bonus action.

Actions

Multiattack. The kathlin makes one hooves attack and one bite attack.

Bite. *Melee Weapon Attack:* +6 to hit, reach 5 ft., one target. *Hit:* 6 (1d4 + 4) piercing damage.

Hooves. *Melee Weapon Attack:* +6 to hit, reach 5 ft., one target. *Hit:* 13 (2d8 + 4) bludgeoning damage.

Kuah-Lij

This creature resembles a gnome that has been stretched vertically to a height of a human. Its features are knobby and elongated. Its hair is light and downy, more akin to a soft fur than anything else, and its skin is white with pale blue undertones.

The kuah-lij are a race of humanoids that inhabit a distant world orbiting a great red sun. They are lawful and organized, but a dying people due to a series of disasters on their homeworld, and now search for aid.

For several millennia, the kuah-lij lived in relative peace on an old world in an advanced civilization, though much of the technology was magic-based. This changed with a series of plagues that devastated the population, followed by a gradual, inexplicable advancement of the size of their oceans. Huge floods resulted. These cataclysms were followed by the invasion of a ferocious aquatic race resembling the aboleths. The aboleth-like creatures lurked in the deepest ocean trenches of the kuah-lij planet and attacked by coming up from the depths.

The kuah-lij, accomplished artisans, retaliated by building a series of magically enhanced sea craft to travel the deeps and attack these beings. Thus far they have arrived at a stalemate, and the kuah-lij now seek aid from other worlds and planes in their battle against their deepwater adversaries.

Individual kuah-lij commoners rely upon their military and combat specialists to protect them. With their focus on magical technology, they have easy access to a great many magical devices which they can use to defend themselves with as well.

The Kuah-lij were at one time a peaceful race of explorers, living in an organized society on a distant planet orbiting a great red sun. Though the course of their lives was regimented, their culture allowed them scope for individuality, and in fact, encouraged it. This, and the natural propensity of the kuah-lij for order, resulted in a society that had remained fresh and vigorous for over 10,000 years.

Kuah-lij young are placed into a public crèche to be raised within days of birth, to be raised by childcare specialists. As they grow and are educated, their affinities and talents are assessed, and at age 15 they are assigned a vocation, based on their talents, and an avocation, based on their preferences. They then study more intensely in these two areas, until they reach maturity at age 25. Kuah-lij youths have the option of changing vocation or avocation if they insist upon it, though this almost never occurs.

Upon reaching maturity, they fully enter society, where they spend 10 months of the year working at their vocation 10 hours per day, and the final two months on sabbatical, traveling, exploring, or doing whatever else strikes them as interesting. Their culture is based on a complex system of credit, with currency reserved only for dealing with non-kuahlij, and medicine, vacation time, and other services are all socialized, but due to their innately organized, cooperative mindset, there is remarkably little corruption within their culture.

Kuah-Lij

Medium humanoid (kuah-lij), lawful neutral
Armor Class 11
Hit Points 6 (1d8 +2)
Speed 30 ft.

STR	DEX	CON	INT	WIS	CHA
8 (−1)	13 (+1)	14 (+2)	16 (+3)	13 (+1)	8 (−1)

Skills Arcana +5

Senses passive Perception 11
Languages Aquan, Common, Elven, Gnome, Kuah-Lij
Challenge 1/8 (25 XP)

Gifted Craftsmen. A kuah-lij has proficiency in alchemist's supplies, jeweler's tools, and smith's tools.

Magical Sight. A kuah-lij can sense the presence of magic within 30 feet of it. It can use an action to see a faint aura around any visible creature or object in the area that bears magic, and it learns its school of magic, if any.

Actions

Dagger. *Melee or Ranged Weapon Attack:* +3 to hit, reach 5 ft. or range 20/60 ft., one target. *Hit:* 3 (1d4 + 1) piercing damage.

Light Crossbow. *Ranged Weapon Attack:* +3 to hit, range 80/320 ft., one target. *Hit:* 5 (1d8 + 1) piercing damage.

Lantern Goat

This creature resembles a goat with tangled and patchy gray-and-white hair, and horns and hooves that appear to be made of stone. Its eyes are stark white. Around its neck hangs a dented and ugly iron lantern, glowing with a foul amber light.

Lantern goats are undead wanderers thought to be the coalescence of souls of people who died while lost in the wilderness. Just as normal goats sometimes drift from the shepherd's care and fall prey to the dangers of the wild, so too do humans and demi-humans often meet with a dire end while trekking alone in the hills. Whether they die of exposure or become a predator's meal, these lost travelers usually journey in spirit form to the afterlife. Some, however, if they perish too close to a lantern goat, find their souls drawn into the fell receptacle the creature wears around its neck.

The scarred and battered lantern that hangs from the goat's neck serves to channel souls into the creature itself. As the goat moves through the hills, its lantern casts a sickening yellow glow that attracts the souls of the recently deceased. Lantern goats roam low mountains and foothills, damned to patrol the mortal realm in search of those who die alone.

How the lantern goat behaves in combat depends upon the number of adversaries it faces. Normally the goat preys on lone travelers, attacking them with its stony hooves and horns. If it encounters a group, the lantern goat emits a fear light from its lantern, intending to panic everyone in range and then pick them off individually.

Lantern Goat

Medium undead, chaotic evil
Armor Class 16 (natural armor)
Hit Points 93 (17d8 + 17)
Speed 40 ft., fly 60 ft.

STR	DEX	CON	INT	WIS	CHA
13 (+1)	18 (+4)	13 (+1)	6 (−2)	14 (+2)	17 (+3)

Skills Perception +8, Stealth +7
Damage Immunities poison
Condition Immunities exhaustion, poisoned
Senses darkvision 60 ft., passive Perception 18
Languages —
Challenge 6 (2,300 XP)

Charge. If the lantern goat moves at least 20 feet straight toward a target and then hits it with a head butt attack on the same turn, the target takes an extra 14 (4d6) bludgeoning damage. If the target is a creature, it must succeed on a DC 15 Strength saving throw or be knocked prone.

Fear Light. As a bonus action, the lantern goat can emit an ugly yellow light from the lantern around its neck. Any creature that can see the light within 30 feet of the lantern goat must make a DC 15 Wisdom saving throw, unless the lantern goat is incapacitated. On a failed save, the creature is frightened until the start of its next turn. If a creature's saving throw is successful, the creature is immune to the lantern goat's Fear Light for the next 24 hours.

Life Sense. The lantern goat can innately sense all living creatures within 60 feet of it.

Actions

Multiattack. The lantern goat makes three attacks: one with its head butt and two with its hooves.

Head Butt. *Melee Weapon Attack:* +7 to hit, reach 5 ft., one target. *Hit:* 11 (2d6 + 4) bludgeoning damage.

Hooves. *Melee Weapon Attack:* +7 to hit, reach 5 ft., one target. *Hit:* 9 (2d4 + 4) slashing damage

Reactions

Soul Capture. As a reaction, when a creature within 60 feet of the lantern goat that it can see dies, the lantern goat can draw the soul of that creature into the lantern around its neck unless the creature succeeds on a DC 15 Wisdom saving throw. On a failure, the creature's soul is drawn into the lantern, where it will be digested over the next 1 hour by the lantern goat. Once the hour has elapsed, the creature dies and can only be returned to life by a *resurrection*, *true resurrection*, or *wish* spell. The lantern can only be removed from the lantern goat or be destroyed — thus releasing the trapped soul — if the lantern goat is slain.

Lava Child

This creature is a stocky humanoid standing about 5 or 6 feet tall with sooty-black hair and green eyes. It wears crudely constructed hides of fur and leather. Its face has a curious, almost child-like appearance and seems to be imprinted with a permanent, non-changing smile. Its skin is pinkish-white.

Lava children make their lairs deep underground and usually in warmer climates. Some lava children build their communities in dying or burned out volcanoes as well. Their society as a whole is reclusive and rarely do lava children have dealings with outside races (magmin and fire elementals being the exception).

Lava children attack with their clawed hands and vicious bite. They direct their attacks against the most heavily armored foe (as their attacks can pass through armor) in an attempt to weaken their opponent's strongest (and probably front line) combatants.

Lava Child

Medium humanoid (elemental), neutral
Armor Class 13 (natural armor)
Hit Points 27 (5d8 + 5)
Speed 30 ft.

STR	DEX	CON	INT	WIS	CHA
13 (+1)	11 (+0)	13 (+1)	10 (+0)	11 (+0)	11 (+0)

Skills Perception +4
Damage Vulnerability cold
Damage Resistances force
Damage Immunities fire; bludgeoning, piercing, and slashing from metal weapons
Senses darkvision 60 ft., passive Perception 14
Languages Ignan, Lava Child
Challenge 2 (450 XP)

Heated Body. A creature that touches the lava child or hits it with a melee attack while within 5 ft. of it takes 7 (2d6) fire damage.

Metal Immunity. Lava children are unaffected by metal. They can walk through solid metal doors as if the door wasn't there. Metal weapons, even magical, have no effect on lava children. Lava children make all attacks with advantage against foes wearing metal armor.

Water Vulnerability. For every 1 gallon of water splashed on the lava child, it takes 3 cold damage.

Actions

Multiattack. The lava child makes one bite attack and one attack with its claws.

Bite. *Melee Weapon Attack:* +3 to hit, reach 5 ft., one target. *Hit:* 4 (1d6 + 1) piercing damage.

Claws. *Melee Weapon Attack:* +3 to hit, reach 5 ft., one target. *Hit:* 5 (1d8 + 1) slashing damage.

Leech, Cave

This large, bloated creature has a flattened, semi-translucent body of sickly yellow. Eight whip-like tentacles protrude from the monster's front, near its head. Hundreds of smaller tentacles line its body and seem to aid in locomotion. Its mouth is rounded and ringed with dozens of needlelike teeth.

Though not aquatic creatures, cave leeches are often found lairing near underground rivers, lakes, and streams. They are aggressive creatures whose sole purpose seems to be to kill and devour any living creature that stumbles into their territory.

Cave leeches often lair with others of their kind. Food is not shared among them, so each leech is effectively on its own when hunting prey. Quarrels over prey sometimes erupt between cave leeches lairing together; these disputes end when one of the leeches backs down or is driven away.

An adult cave leech measures about 8 feet long and its whip-like tentacles are each about 6 feet long. Cave leeches are often mistaken for ordinary giant leeches, especially when at rest because the creature folds its tentacles back against its body. They also do this when waiting to strike.

When a meal comes within range, the cave leech fires a tentacle out and attempts to grab its target. Grabbed prey is pulled in to the cave leech's mouth and bitten by its horrible teeth. Living creatures trapped by its tentacles are held and bitten, the leech draining blood with its bite. A victim that is completely drained of blood becomes a dried, rotting husk and its body is cast aside. Foes killed by its bite attack are often dragged to the cave leech's lair and fed to the young or drained of blood over several days. A cave leech sometimes uses the rotting husks of its victims to line its lair.

Cave Leech

Medium monstrosity, neutral
Armor Class 15 (natural armor)
Hit Points 112 (15d8 + 45)
Speed 30 ft., swim 30 ft.

STR	DEX	CON	INT	WIS	CHA
15 (+2)	11 (+0)	17 (+3)	3 (−4)	12 (+1)	6 (−2)

Skills Perception +4, Stealth +3
Senses darkvision 60 ft., tremorsense 60 ft. passive Perception 14
Languages —
Challenge 8 (3,900 XP)

Actions

Multiattack. The leech makes up to four tentacle attacks and can use blood drain on a grappled creature.

Tentacles. *Melee Weapon Attack:* +5 to hit, reach 5 ft., one target. *Hit:* 11 (2d8 + 2) bludgeoning damage. The target is grappled (escape DC 12) if the leech isn't already grappling a creature, and the target is restrained until the grapple ends. While grappling a creature, the leech can't use that tentacle. The leech has four tentacles

Blood Drain. *Melee Weapon Attack:* +5 to hit, reach 5 ft. one creature. Hit: 9 (2d6+2) piercing damage, and the leech attaches to the target. While attached, the leech doesn't attack. Instead, at the start of the leech's turns, the target loses 9 (2d6 + 2) hit points due to blood loss.

The leech can detach itself by spending 5 feet of its movement. It does so after it drains 25 hit points of blood from the target or the target dies. A creature, including the target, can use its action to make a DC 12 Strength check to rip the leech off and make it detach.

Leech, Giant

A large, bloated leech floats in the muck and slime.

These invertebrate parasitic relatives of the worm lurk in stagnant or slow-moving water, waiting for a suitable host. Giant leeches appear as larger versions of the common leech.

A giant leech attacks any living creature that comes within 30 feet of it. There is a 50% chance that any leech encountered carries filth fever.

Giant Leech

Medium beast (aquatic), unaligned
Armor Class 11
Hit Points 26 (4d8 + 8)
Speed 5 ft., swim 20 ft.

STR	DEX	CON	INT	WIS	CHA
11 (+0)	12 (+1)	14 (+2)	2 (–4)	10 (+0)	1 (–5)

Senses blindsight 30 ft., passive Perception 10
Languages —
Challenge 1 (200 XP)

Vulnerability to Salt. A handful of salt burns a giant leech as if it were a flask of acid, causing 1d6 acid damage per use.

Actions

Blood Drain. *Melee Weapon Attack:* +3 to hit, reach 5 ft. one creature. *Hit:* 4 (1d6 + 1) piercing damage, and the leech attaches to the target. While attached, the leech doesn't attack. Instead, at the start of the leech's turns, the target loses 5 (1d8 + 1) hit points due to blood loss.

The leech can detach itself by spending 5 feet of its movement. It does so after it drains 25 hit points of blood from the target or the target dies. A creature, including the target, can use its action to make a DC 10 Strength check to rip the leech off and make it detach.

Leprechaun

This creature resembles a tiny elf with long pointed ears and a pointed nose. It is dressed in brightly colored clothes of red and green and wears a wide-brimmed hat.

Leprechauns are short fey creatures, about 2 feet tall. They favor brightly colored clothes, particularly greens and reds. Leprechauns are a jovial people, enjoying fine food and drink; some leprechauns also enjoy a good smoke from a long-stemmed pipe. They are a tricky folk and enjoy jokes and pranks, although they usually do not appreciate being the victims of such acts. Most leprechauns are skilled pickpockets, and it is a favored prank of these wee folk to filch items from unsuspecting travelers in their domain and then taunt the intruders into pursuit. The leprechaun so involved in the prank often alternates between being visible and invisible as he teases and pesters his pursuers in a merry chase. Leprechauns tire of pranks quickly, however, and will give up the stolen item and sneak away. Some say leprechauns are descendants of halflings and pixies. Leprechauns summarily dismiss this rumor, however, scoffing at those who repeat it.

Leprechauns are fun-loving creatures and prefer to avoid combat. When facing opponents, a leprechaun usually turns invisible and flees. If forced into melee, a leprechaun uses its abilities to their fullest extent, seeking to drive an opponent off rather than kill it.

Leprechaun

Small fey, neutral
Armor Class 13
Hit Points 14 (4d6)
Speed 40 ft.

STR	DEX	CON	INT	WIS	CHA
7 (−2)	16 (+3)	11 (+0)	16 (+3)	15 (+2)	16 (+3)

Skills Deception +5, Perception +6, Persuasion +5, Sleight of Hand +5, Stealth +7
Damage Resistances bludgeoning, piercing, and slashing from nonmagical weapons
Condition Immunities charmed
Senses passive Perception 16
Languages Common, Sylvan
Challenge 2 (450 XP)

Innate Spellcasting. The leprechaun's innate spellcasting ability is Intelligence (spell save DC 13, +5 to hit with spell attacks). It can innately cast the following spells, requiring no material components:

At will: *dancing lights, hideous laughter, invisibility* (self only)*, mage hand, magic mouth, major image, minor illusion*

1/day each: *hypnotic pattern, major image*

Sneak Attack (1/turn). The leprechaun deals an extra 3 (1d6) damage when it hits a target with a weapon attack and has advantage on the attack roll, or when the target is within 5 feet of an ally of the leprechaun that isn't incapacitated and the leprechaun doesn't have disadvantage on the attack roll.

Actions

Dagger. *Melee or Ranged Weapon Attack:* +5 to hit, reach 5 ft. or range 20/60 ft., one target. *Hit:* 5 (1d4 + 3) piercing damage.

Leprechaun Traits

Leprechauns have a penchant for green, browns, grins, pranks, pots of gold, and lucky charms.

Ability Score Increase. Your Charisma score increases by 2, and your Dexterity score increases by 1.

Age. Leprechauns remain children for around the same amount of time as humans, but live as long as elves, if not longer.

Alignment. Leprechauns dislike rules, as a rule, and are almost never lawful. They are almost always, as a rule, neutral or chaotic, but don't usually hew towards good or evil to any real extent.

Size. You are average for fey but smaller than most other races. Your size is Small.

Speed. Your base walking speed is 30 feet.

Faeriefolk. You cannot be put to sleep or aged by magic.

Polymorph Object. You can touch as an action one nonmagical inanimate object not being held or worn by another creature and magically transform it into another nonmagical inanimate object of the same size. The object remains changed for 1 minute, or until you use an action to change it back to its true form. A transformed object functions normally for the duration.

Trickster Magic. You can cast the *dancing lights* cantrip. When you reach 3rd level, you can cast the *silent image* spell once per day. When you reach 5th level, you can cast *invisibility* spell once per day. Charisma is your spellcasting ability for these spells.

Languages. You can speak, read, and write Common and Sylvan.

Lich Shade

This creature appears as a rotting and skeletal humanoid dressed in tattered and worn robes with ancient runes etched on their surface. Its eyes blaze with a crimson fire.

The road a spellcaster travels in his or her quest for lichdom is not without danger. During the dark rituals invoked to achieve lichdom, the caster sometimes errs in his or her calculations or unleashes mystic forces best left untapped. When such an event occurs, the spellcaster is usually destroyed outright. Other times, something is born as a result of this failed ritual — a lich shade.

Lich shades are evil creatures who attempted to achieve lichdom but failed for whatever reason. The creature is not destroyed, nor does it become a lich, it becomes something in between — something in between mortal life and eternal unlife.

Lich shades retain portions of their life's memories and always retain full memory of the dark ritual they attempted while trying to become a lich. For this reason alone, they have grown to hate the living and particularly living spellcasters whom they blame (in some warp twisted way) for their current condition. A lich shade always attacks any opponents who have a spellcaster in their midst, often targeting that individual directly above all others.

A lich shade stands about 6 to 6½ feet tall and weighs about 160 pounds.

A lich shade attacks with its powerful claws, rending and tearing at its foes. If facing a spellcaster and it leeches one of its spells, it usually releases the first spell leeched as an eldritch bolt against its closest foe. Further leeched spells are used to heal the lich shade or cast back against its foes. If faced with certain defeat, a lich shade wills its own destruction, invoking its death throes ability, hoping to take several of its opponents with it.

A lich shade's natural weapons are treated as magic weapons for the purpose of overcoming damage reduction.

Lich Shade

Medium undead, neutral evil
Armor Class 16 (natural armor)
Hit Points 85 (9d8 + 45)
Speed 30 ft.

STR	DEX	CON	INT	WIS	CHA
11 (+0)	16 (+3)	20 (+5)	18 (+4)	16 (+3)	13 (+1)

Skills Arcana +7, History +7, Insight +6, Perception +6
Damage Resistances cold, lightning, poison; bludgeoning, piercing, and slashing damage from nonmagical weapons
Damage Immunities necrotic
Condition Immunities charmed, exhaustion, frightened, paralyzed, poisoned
Senses darkvision 60 ft., passive Perception 16
Languages Common, Infernal, plus up to four other languages
Challenge 8 (3,900 XP)

Death Throes. When the lich shade drops to 0 hit points, it explodes in a cloud of dust in a 10-foot radius. Creatures within this area must make a DC 16 Constitution saving throw. On a failed saving throw, the creature takes 22 (4d10) necrotic damage, and the creature's maximum hit points are reduced by the same amount. If a creature's maximum hit points are reduced to 0, it dies. Magic such as *greater restoration* is necessary to cure this effect. On a successful saving throw, the creature takes half damage and is poisoned for 1 minute, but its maximum hit points are unaffected.

Magic Resistance. The lich shade has advantage on saving throws against spells and other magical effects.

Magic Weapon. The lich shade's weapon attacks are magical.

Actions

Multiattack. The lich shade makes two claw attacks.

Claw. *Melee Weapon Attack:* +6 to hit, reach 5 ft., one target. *Hit:* 12 (2d8 + 3) slashing damage plus 11 (2d10) cold damage.

Reactions

Spell Leech. When a creature the lich shade can see within 30 feet of it casts a spell of 1st level or higher, the lich shade can counter the spell, as if the lich shade had cast *counterspell*. If the lich shade attempts to leech a spell of 4th level or higher, it must make an Intelligence ability check. The DC for this check is 10 + the spell's level.

If the spell leech is successful, the lich shade absorbs the magical energy and can use it only on its next turn in one of the following ways:

Cast. The lich shade can cast the spell as an action on its turn, using the original caster's spell save DC and spell attack modifier.

Eldritch Bolt. The lich shade chooses one creature it can see within 60 feet of it as an action. That creature must make a DC 16 Dexterity saving throw, taking 22 (4d10) force damage on a failed saving throw, or half as much damage on a successful one.

Heal. The lich shade uses an action to regain 22 (4d10) hit points, up to its maximum hit points.

If the lich shade does not use the absorbed magic, it fades at the end of its next turn.

Lizards

Lizard, Cavern

A 10-foot-long gray lizard with large wide feet and sapphire-gold bulging eyes stares. Balanced upon thick and muscled, its feet cling to surfaces upon small suction cup-like pads. Its head is angular and somewhat flat and its mouth sports a row of long, serrated teeth.

These large magical lizards, readily identified by large bulging sapphire-colored eyes, are found only in the darkest underground places and never venture to the surface world.

A cavern lizard is typically very aggressive and often travels far away from its lair in order to hunt. While not territorial, a cavern lizard is rarely encountered with others of its kind. Each cavern lizard often has a hunting ground covering up to 2 miles in the Under Realms.

A cavern lizard's lair is a large expanse of interconnected caves littered with the bones and scattered remains of its victims (including treasure). Hunting cavern lizards usually drag their kill back to their lair before devouring it. If young are present in the lair, the kill is divided between them. Young cavern lizards resemble their adult counterparts in all respects, save their eyes are a dull blue. During mating season (late summer, early fall) 1d6 eggs may be found in the lair. Eggs are round in shape, leathery to the touch, and gray in color.

Cavern lizards are aggressive ambush hunters. They prefer to scale the walls and wait for prey to pass underneath them where they drop down on their unsuspecting meal. In most battles, once a cavern lizard bites, it hangs on until its opponent is dead. If facing more than one foe, it won't employ this tactic so as not to leave itself defenseless against other aggressors. If cornered or extremely hungry, a cavern lizard fights to the death; otherwise, it retreats if facing a particularly powerful opponent.

Cavern Lizard

Large monstrosity, neutral
Armor Class 13 (natural armor)
Hit Points 93 (11d10 + 33)
Speed 30 ft., climb 20 ft.

STR	DEX	CON	INT	WIS	CHA
16 (+3)	14 (+2)	17 (+3)	3 (−4)	12 (+1)	2 (−4)

Skills Athletics +5, Stealth +4 (+6 in areas of natural stone or rock)
Senses darkvision 60 ft., passive Perception 11
Languages —
Challenge 3 (700 XP)

Surprise Attack. If the cavern lizard surprises a creature and hits it with an attack during the first round of combat, the target takes an extra 14 (4d6) damage from the attack.

Actions

Bite. *Melee Weapon Attack:* +5 to hit, reach 5 ft., one target. *Hit:* 14 (2d10 + 3) piercing damage plus the target is grappled (escape DC 13), and the cavern lizard can't grapple another target.

Lizard, Fire

This creature resembles a wingless red dragon. Its scales are gray and dappled in red and brown along its back. Its underbelly is bright red and its eyes are black with yellow pupils.

Fire lizards are often called "false dragons." Despite their general resemblance to dragons, sages have as yet found no evidence of these creatures being in any way related to them. Fire lizards do not associate with or keep company with dragons. A fire lizard averages 30 feet long but can grow to almost twice that size.

Fire lizards prefer to attack opponents with their claws and bite, though if outnumbered they resort to using their breath weapon.

Fire Lizard

Huge monstrosity, neutral
Armor Class 13 (natural armor)
Hit Points 138 (12d12 + 60)
Speed 30 ft.

STR	DEX	CON	INT	WIS	CHA
25 (+7)	10 (+0)	20 (+5)	2 (−4)	11 (+0)	10 (+0)

Damage Vulnerabilities cold
Damage Immunities fire
Senses darkvision 60 ft., passive Perception 10
Languages —
Challenge 12 (8,400 XP)

Rampage. When the fire lizard reduces a creature to 0 hit points with a melee attack on its turn, the fire lizard can take a bonus action to move up to half its speed and make a bite attack.

Actions

Multiattack. The fire lizard makes three attacks: one with its bite and two with its claws.

Bite. *Melee Weapon Attack:* +11 to hit, reach 5 ft., one target. *Hit:* 16 (2d8 + 7) piercing damage.

Claws. *Melee Weapon Attack*: +11 to hit, reach 10 ft., one target. *Hit:* 21 (4d6 +7) slashing damage.

Fire Breath (Recharge 5–6). The fire lizard exhales a blast of fire in a 20-foot cone. Each creature in that area must make a DC 16 Dexterity savings throw, taking 28 (8d6) fire damage on a failed save, or half as much on a successful one.

Lizard, Gnasher

This 10-foot-long stone-colored lizard has a large, wide gaping maw filled with double rows of dagger-like teeth. Its head is large and flat and sports a ridge of hardened bone that runs the length of its head before tapering off near the middle of its back. Its four legs end in large, flat clawed feet.

The gnasher is a deadly predator that often roams up to 3 miles from its lair in search of prey. Though its appearance lends to the façade of being a slow-moving lizard, it is in fact, rather graceful and quick. Those that make the mistake of assuming the gnasher is slow-moving rarely live to tell others of their mistake.

Gnasher lizards make their lairs in stony areas, typically forest clearings or mountain terrain, usually near (within several hundred feet if possible) a water source. They are carnivorous creatures and highly territorial, even attacking their own kind if one gnasher lizard intrudes upon the territory of another. Gnashers are solitary creatures and only come together to mate (during the spring or early summer months). Mating season is the only time more than one of these creatures is encountered together, and once the mating ritual is ended, each goes its own way. The female lays a clutch of 1d4+2 eggs which hatch within 3 months. Young reach maturity within 8 months and are left to their own devices.

A gnasher lizard is typically 10 feet long but can grow to a length of 20 feet or more. A typical gnasher weighs about 1,000 pounds. Though most are stone gray, some variants encountered have been colored greenish-brown or black. Its long fang-like teeth are razor-sharp and it uses these to tear its prey into pieces.

Gnasher lizards typically attack from ambush, using their surroundings to conceal themselves and springing out at the last second to catch their opponents by surprise. Gnashers attack any creature that wanders into their territory, including those larger than themselves, relying on their vorpal bite to quickly dispatch such creatures.

When it swallows a foe, a gnasher lizard typically holds it in its stomach for several rounds before regurgitating it into its mouth, snapping down on it with its razor-sharp teeth and then swallowing it again.

Gnasher Lizard

Large monstrosity, neutral
Armor Class 16 (natural armor)
Hit Points 152 (16d10 + 64)
Speed 30 ft.

STR	DEX	CON	INT	WIS	CHA
22 (+6)	14 (+2)	18 (+4)	2 (–4)	12 (+1)	10 (+0)

Skills Perception +4, Stealth +5
Senses darkvision 60 ft., passive Perception 14
Languages —
Challenge 7 (2,900 XP)

Surprise Attack. If the cavern lizard surprises a creature and hits it with an attack during the first round of combat, the target takes an extra 14 (4d6) damage from the attack.

Actions

Bite. *Melee Weapon Attack:* +9 to hit, reach 5 ft., one target. *Hit:* 22 (3d10 + 6) piercing damage and the target is grappled (escape DC 16), and the gnasher lizard can only grapple one creature at a time.

Thrash. The gnasher lizard rapidly shakes its head, and any grappled target takes 39 (6d10 + 6) slashing damage. If this damage is enough to drop the target to 0 hit points, the target is dismembered and portions of it are swallowed. A creature who suffers this cannot be brought back to life with anything less than *true resurrection*.

Lost Limb

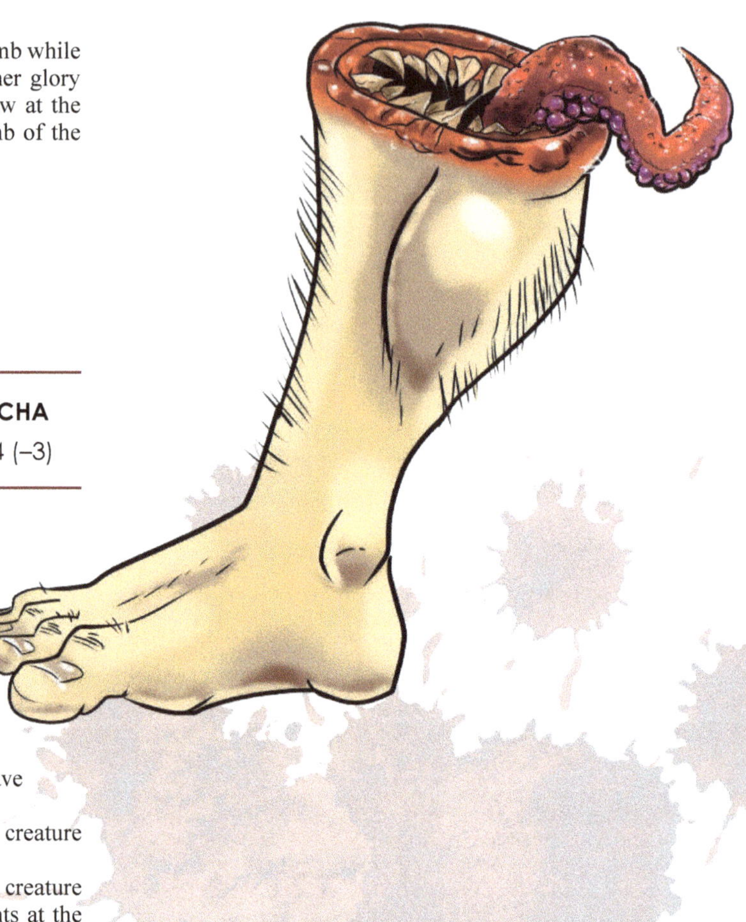

This limb is well muscled and vibrant with life. Its goal is to find a host 'partner'. The connecting end, the stump, is a toothy maw that will eat the limb it is replacing and fuse itself to the host.

The lost limb is said to be the remnant of humans who lose a limb while fighting in glorious and victorious battles. The limb seeks further glory and a host suitable to meet those requirements. The toothy maw at the end of the limb's stump is a toothy maw that consumes the limb of the new host.

Lost Limb

Small monstrosity, neutral
Armor Class 14 (natural armor)
Hit Points 16 (3d6 + 6)
Speed 30 ft., climb 30 ft.

STR	DEX	CON	INT	WIS	CHA
16 (+3)	16 (+3)	14 (+2)	4 (−3)	4 (−3)	4 (−3)

Skills Perception +1
Damage Immunities poison
Condition Immunities charmed, exhaustion, frightened, paralyzed, petrified, poisoned
Senses blindsight 60 ft., passive Perception 11
Languages —
Challenge 2 (450XP)

Adhesive. The lost limb adheres to the limb of its victim. A Huge or smaller creature adhered to the limb is also grappled (escape DC 13). Ability checks made to escape the grapple have disadvantage.

Compact. The lost limb may stay in the same space as another creature or character.

Fuse. Once the limb has consumed the limb it is replacing, the creature that it is attached to slowly begins to heal, regaining 5 hit points at the start of each of its turns. After 1 minute, the creature finally can control the limb and gains a +2 bonus to Strength as the limb becomes a permanent part of its body.

Grappler. The lost limb has advantage on attack rolls against any creature grappled by it.

Actions

Slam. *Melee Weapon Attack:* +5 to hit, reach 5 ft., one target. *Hit:* 5 (1d8 +1) bludgeoning damage and the target is grappled (escape DC 13) and restrained.

Consume. A creature grappled by the lost limb must make a DC 15 Constitution saving throw. On a failed save, the target takes 10 (2d6 + 3) necrotic damage as the lost limb starts to consume the limb of the target. The target takes an additional 10 (2d6) + 3 necrotic damage at the start of each of its turns but can repeat the saving throw at the end of each of its turns, ending the effect on a success. If the limb consumes more than one-quarter of the target's hit points, the target's limb is permanently replaced by the lost limb as it attaches to the joint (shoulder or hip) of the target.

Lurker Above

A black manta ray-like creature three times the size of a normal human flies toward you. Its body is black changing to gray on its inside or underbelly.

The lurker above is a subterranean carnivore that preys on any living creatures that enter its territory. These creatures are extremely territorial and are never encountered with others of their kind. Mating habits among lurkers are unknown to sages as no two of these creatures have ever been encountered together. A typical lurker above has a hunting territory of several square miles.

A lurker above waits for its prey, clinging to the ceiling, roof, or other such overhangs. When prey passes beneath it, the lurker above drops from its hiding place and wraps itself around its prey.

Lurker Below

The lurker below is an aquatic variety of lurker above that makes its lair in any body of water and in any climate (though it rarely lairs in extremely cold climates). Lurkers below are pale blue or black in color and are often mistaken for giant manta rays. Lurkers below cannot fly but have a swim speed of 40 feet. They are otherwise identical to their land-based counterparts detailed above.

Lurker Above

Huge aberration, neutral
Armor Class 13
Hit Points 68 (8d12 + 16)
Speed 10 ft., climb 5 ft., fly 40 ft.

STR	DEX	CON	INT	WIS	CHA
18 (+4)	16 (+3)	15 (+2)	2 (–4)	15 (+2)	9 (–1)

Skills Athletics +7, Stealth +6
Damage Resistances cold, fire; bludgeoning, piercing, and slashing from nonmagical weapons
Senses darkvision 60 ft., passive Perception 12
Languages —
Challenge 7 (2,900 XP)

Damage Transfer. While it is grappling a creature, the lurker above takes only half the damage dealt to it, and the creature grappled by the lurker above takes the other half.

Keen Scent. The lurker above has advantage on Wisdom (Perception) checks based on scent.

Sunlight Sensitivity. While in sunlight, the lurker above has disadvantage on attack rolls, as well as on Wisdom (Perception) checks that rely on sight.

Actions

Slam. *Melee Weapon Attack:* +7 to hit, reach 5 ft., one target. *Hit:* 17 (3d8 + 4) bludgeoning damage and the target is grappled (escape DC 15) and the lurker above cannot grapple or use its Slam attack on another target.

Smother. The lurker above wraps itself around one grappled creature of Large size or smaller, completely enclosing it. The grappled target is restrained, blinded, no longer able to speak or use spells with verbal components, and at risk of suffocating. At the start of each of the target's turns, the target takes 17 (3d8 + 4) bludgeoning damage.

Lynx, Giant

This big cat has thick back and forelegs, each with enormous, clawed, paws. Its tail is short and tufted. Its eyes glisten with divine power, and it wears a scarab beetle amulet around its thick neck.

While it appears as simply a very large feline creature, the giant lynx is, in fact, a celestial being — a servant of the Goddess of Beauty and Cats, Bast. Each is a dedicated creature, created by the Goddess to act as her emissaries on the Material Plane. The highest clerics of Bast can, if they are pious enough, gain the attention of one of these servants. These creatures are often the creature Bast sends to consecrate those deemed worthy enough to receive the blessing of lycanthropy, one of the greatest gifts that Bast can grant.

All rats and creatures who serve S'Surimiss, the Rat Queen, Goddess of Rats, treat giant lynxes as one of their greatest foes. Long are the tales of giant lynx hunting the children of the Rat Queen, and very few of those stories end well for those who worship S'Surimiss. A wererat servant of S'Surimiss who slays a giant lynx will find the blessings of the Rat Queen heavy upon their shoulders, making a cloak of the giant lynxes' pelt which S'Surimiss will transform into a potent magic item.

Giant Lynx

Large celestial, chaotic good
Armor Class 17 (natural armor)
Hit Points 123 (13d10 + 52)
Speed 40 ft., climb 30 ft.

STR	DEX	CON	INT	WIS	CHA
16 (+3)	22 (+6)	19 (+4)	17 (+3)	20 (+5)	20 (+5)

Saving Throws Wis +9, Cha +9
Skills Animal Handling +9, Insight +9, Perception +9, Stealth +10
Damage Resistances bludgeoning, piercing, and slashing from nonmagical weapons
Condition Immunities charmed, exhaustion, frightened
Senses darkvision 120 ft., passive Perception 19
Languages all, telepathy 120 ft.
Challenge 9 (5,000 XP)

Magic Resistance. The giant lynx has advantage on saving throws against spells and other magical effects.

Magic Weapons. The giant lynx's attacks are considered magical.

Spellcasting. The giant lynx is a 12th level spellcaster. The giant lynx's spellcasting ability is Wisdom (spell save DC 17, +9 to hit with spell attacks). It can cast the following cleric spells.

Cantrips (at will): *guidance, light, mending, resistance, sacred flame, thaumaturgy*

1st level (4 slots): *bless, cure wounds, detect evil and good, protection from evil and good*

2nd level (3 slots): *aid, hold person, lesser restoration, spiritual weapon*

3rd level (3 slots): *beacon of hope, dispel magic, revivify*

4th level (3 slots): *banishment, death ward, locate creature*

5th level (2 slots): *dispel evil and good, raise dead*

6th level (1 slot): *heal*

Actions

Multiattack. The giant lynx makes one bite attack and two claw attacks.

Bite. Melee Weapon Attack: +10 to hit, reach 5 ft., one target. *Hit:* 13 (2d6 + 6) piercing damage.

Claw. Melee Weapon Attack: +10 to hit, reach 10 ft., one target. *Hit:* 15 (2d8 + 6) slashing damage.

Change Shape. The giant lynx magically polymorphs into a humanoid or beast that has a challenge rating equal to or less than its own, or back into its true form. It reverts to its true form if it dies. Any equipment it is wearing or carrying is absorbed or borne by the new form (the giant lynx's choice). In a new form, the giant lynx retains its game statistics and ability to speak, but its AC, movement modes, Strength, Dexterity, and special senses are replaced by those of the new form, and it gains any statistics or capabilities (except class features, legendary actions, and lair actions) that the new form has but that it lacks.

Lythic

This creature appears to be a Medium sized humanoid composed of smoothly formed rock. Its features are human-like though emotionless.

Lythics are creatures from the Elemental Plane of Earth. There, they spend their time in huge underground caverns with others of their race or in the company of earth elementals. Some lythics serve the elder elemental lords as spies, using their skills of going unnoticed to sneak into the palaces of arch-rivals.

Lythics occasionally punch through a vortex or portal and wind up on the Material Plane. Other outer planes (save some of the more desolate Abyssal planes) hold no interest for the lythic. On the Material Plane, they spend their time underground or gliding through mountains, devouring minerals as they move along. Occasionally, a lythic's elemental master sends it on a mission into the Material Plane.

Lythics are not particularly fond of pechs and generally avoid them or attack on sight. They rarely associate with other elemental creatures.

Lythics are not particularly hostile unless threatened. When a party of would-be delvers enters its domain, the lythic often trails them by blending with surrounding stone. If detected, a lythic usually flees unless attacked. Once in combat, however, a lythic rarely backs down and often fights until it is killed or its opponents are dead or fleeing.

Lythic

Medium elemental, neutral
Armor Class 17 (natural armor)
Hit Points 45 (7d8 + 14)
Speed 30 ft., burrow 30 ft.

STR	DEX	CON	INT	WIS	CHA
17 (+3)	12 (+1)	15 (+2)	10 (+0)	11 (+0)	10 (+0)

Skills Perception +2, Stealth +3
Damage Vulnerabilities thunder
Damage Resistances bludgeoning, piercing, and slashing from nonmagical weapons
Damage Immunities poison
Condition Immunities exhaustion, paralyzed, petrified, poisoned, unconscious
Senses darkvision 60 ft., tremorsense 60 ft., passive Perception 12
Languages Terran
Challenge 3 (700 XP)

Blend With Stone. The lythic has advantage on Dexterity (Stealth) checks in rocky terrain, and can take the Hide action whenever it is within 10 feet of some sort of stone, and remains hidden unless it moves or attacks.

Earth Glide. The elemental can burrow through nonmagical, unworked earth and stone. While doing so, the elemental doesn't disturb the material it moves through.

Fury of the Earth. Whenever the lythic starts its turn with half its hit points or fewer, it flies into a berserker-like rage. On each of its turns while berserk, the lythic deals an additional 7 (2d6) damage with its slam attack.

Actions

Multiattack. The lythic makes two slam attacks.

Slam. *Melee Weapon Attack:* +5 to hit, reach 5 ft., one target. *Hit:* 12 (2d8 + 3) bludgeoning damage.

Magmoid

This elemental appears to be a massive of spherical ball entirely comprised of swirling liquid fire and rock.

Magmoids are giant balls of elemental magma that destroy or burn anything and everything they come in contact with. Though they are typically only found on the Planes of Earth or Fire or the Plane of Molten Skies (see the City of Brass by Necromancer Games for details on this demi-plane), occasionally one slips through a portal or nexus into the Material Plane (usually in the heart of a volcano) where it wreaks havoc upon all things that cross its path; be it creatures, structures, or anything else not immune to fire. Attempts by arcane spellcasters (foolish arcane spellcasters some would say) to control or harness the power of a magmoid, thus far have failed.

Magmoids seem to serve no purpose in the ecology of their native plane and are thought to be a living extension of the plane itself. Small bubbling pockets on the magmoid's form serve as sensory organs. A giant magmoid, measuring 30 feet across is thought to exist near the Sea of Fire, though none have ever seen it.

A magmoid attacks by spraying a blast of superheated magma at opponents or by slamming into and rolling over them. It often targets weapon-wielding creatures first and moves close enough where they can hit with their weapons. The magmoid knows that more than likely should a weapon hit its fiery form, it will be turned into a pile of slag in short order.

Magmoid

Large elemental, neutral
Armor Class 14 (natural armor)
Hit Points 120 (16d10 + 32)
Speed 40 ft.

STR	DEX	CON	INT	WIS	CHA
14 (+2)	17 (+3)	15 (+2)	4 (−3)	10 (+0)	5 (−3)

Damage Vulnerabilities cold
Damage Resistances bludgeoning, piercing, and slashing from nonmagical weapons
Damage Immunities fire, lightning, poison
Condition Immunities exhaustion, paralyzed, petrified, poisoned, prone, restrained, unconscious
Senses blindsight 60 ft., passive Perception 10
Languages Ignan, Terran
Challenge 8 (3,900 XP)

Illumination. The elemental sheds bright light in a 30-foot radius and dim light in an additional 30 feet.

Magma Form. The magmoid can move through a space as narrow as 1 inch wide without squeezing. A creature that touches the magmoid or hits it with a melee attack while within 5 feet of it takes 9 (2d8) fire damage. In addition, the magmoid can flow into a hostile creature's space and stop there. The first time it enters a hostile creature's space on a turn, that creature takes 9 (2d8) fire damage and catches fire; until someone takes an action to douse the flames, the creature takes 4 (1d8) fire damage at the start of each of its turns.

Melt Weapons. Any nonmagical weapon made of metal that hits the magmoid melts. After dealing damage, the weapon takes a permanent and cumulative −1 penalty to damage rolls. If its penalty drops to −5, the weapon is destroyed. Nonmagical ammunition made of metal or other flammable material is melted or burned and is destroyed after dealing damage.

Siege Monster. The magmoid deals double damage to objects and structures.

Actions

Multiattack. The magmoid makes two slam attacks.

Slam. *Melee Weapon Attack:* +6 to hit, reach 5 ft., one target. *Hit:* 10 (2d6 + 3) bludgeoning damage and 9 (2d8) fire damage. If the target is a creature or a flammable object, it ignites. Until a creature takes an action to douse the fire, the target takes 4 (1d8) fire damage at the start of each of its turns.

Magma Blast (Recharge 6). The magmoid hurls a blast of magma in a 60-foot line that is 5-foot-wide. Each creature in the line must make a DC 15 Dexterity saving throw, taking 18 (4d8) fire damage on a failure and half as much damage on a success. In addition, any creature or a flammable object in the line ignites. Until a creature takes an action to douse the fire, the target takes 4 (1d8) fire damage at the start of each of its turns.

Malignant Mouth

This long-forgotten magic mouth has been driven insane and twisted by its exposure to dark magic and the intense loneliness it has experienced.

Magic mouth spells are used to transmit welcomes, warnings, and messages to visitors. As these magical manifestations exist until they are dispelled, some are very ancient and forgotten. On rare occasions, long after the original spellcaster has died, the mouth gains sentience, becoming self-aware. Aware of its predicament and angry over being forgotten, it becomes vicious and utterly demented—a malignant mouth is born. Malignant mouths are usually found in ancient subterranean vaults, forgotten towers, and abandoned scriptoria (places of loneliness surrounded by ages of dark influences).

A malignant mouth remains partially bound by the spell which created it; thus, a malignant mouth will still be triggered to perform its intended duty. It will appear on a wall, object, or statue and delivers the message as intended, except the message is spoken in a twisted, tortured drawl or frenetic shriek. This disquieting noise will be punctuated by insane and painfully loud laughter.

Malignant Mouth

Medium monstrosity, chaotic neutral
Armor Class 16 (natural armor)
Hit Points 20 (4d8+2)
Speed 0 ft.

STR	DEX	CON	INT	WIS	CHA
12 (0)	6 (-2)	9 (0)	16 (–1)	14 (–1)	14 (+2)

Damage Resistances necrotic, poison
Condition Immunities charmed, frightened
Skills Performance +8
Senses tremorsense 120 ft., passive Perception 12
Languages all
Challenge 3 (700 XP)

Magic Resistance. The malignant mouth has advantage on saving throws against spells and other magical effects.

Actions

Bite. *Melee weapon attack:* +3 to hit, range 5 ft., one target. *Hit:* 9 (2d8) slashing damage.

Focused Shout. *Ranged weapon attack:* +6 to hit, range 60/120 ft., one target. *Hit:* 7 (2d6) force damage.

Cackle (Recharge 5–6). All creatures within a 30 ft. radius from mouth have one of the following effects. Roll 1d6 separately for each target.

d6	Effect
1	Confusion. Target must succeed on a DC 14 Wisdom saving throw or move in a random direction each turn, making a melee attack against the first target it encounters for 1d6 rounds.
2	Fear. Target must succeed on a DC 14 Wisdom saving throw or drop what it is holding and use its action and move to dash away from the mouth. The target can attempt a new saving throw at the end of each of its turns, ending the effect on a success.
3	Sleep. If the target has less than 5d8 hit points, it falls asleep as per the *sleep* spell.
4	Cure Wounds. The target is healed for 1d8+2 hit points.
5	Vomit. The target must succeed on a DC 14 Dexterity saving throw or be immobilized for 2d4 rounds. On a successful saving throw, the target moves at half speed for 1d4 rounds.
6	Tongue Lash. *Ranged Weapon Attack:* +8 to hit, range 10/20 ft., one creature. *Hit:* the target is pulled next to the malignant mouth, which can then make a bite attack against it with advantage.

Mammoth, Woolly

This massive elephant-like creature is covered in long, coarse hair, and its tusks sweep upward in great curves of yellowed ivory.

The woolly mammoth is a relative of both the common elephant and the mastodon. Like the mastodon, it is an herbivore and spends its days eating nuts, fruits, berries, and grasses. The typical mammoth consumes nearly 450 pounds of food and 50 gallons of water in a given day.

Mammoths travel in herds with the young moving in the center, protected and surrounded by the adults. If danger is present or a threat is imminent, the males move to face the danger, while the females encircle the young.

The woolly mammoth generally reproduces in the spring months with young being born about 22 months later. A young woolly mammoth resembles a miniature version of an adult, complete with fur, and underfur. It does not yet have the mighty tusks of the mammoth, though the tusks grow in quickly as the young mammoth reaches maturity (around age 12).

The mammoth has the same predators as the mastodon; the dire wolf, the smilodon, and man. Man hunts these creatures for the same reason they hunt the mastodon: meat, fur, ivory, or to capture young mammoths to be trained as mounts and beasts of burden.

The mammoth is a relative of the elephant and the mastodon though its head is slightly taller than an elephant's and slightly wider than a mastodon's. Its upward curving tusks are longer than those of the mastodon, and its trunk ends in two, small finger-like projections used for grasping branches, fruits, and other such small items. The mammoth stands about 22 feet tall and is covered in a thick coat of gray, brown, reddish-brown, yellowish-brown, or black fur with a coarse "under-fur" beneath it to protect it in harsh climates.

Mammoths generally avoid combat unless provoked or the herd is threatened. They have no natural fear of any creature, so do not flee. If the herd is threatened, mammoths fight by goring with their tusks or trampling. Mammoths fight to the death to protect their young.

Woolly Mammoth

Huge beast, unaligned
Armor Class 13 (natural armor)
Hit Points 73 (7d12 + 28)
Speed 40 ft.

STR	DEX	CON	INT	WIS	CHA
22 (+6)	9 (−1)	18 (+4)	3 (−4)	13 (+1)	6 (−2)

Damage Resistances cold
Senses passive Perception 11
Languages —
Challenge 5 (1,800 XP)

Keen Smell. The mammoth has advantage on Wisdom (Perception) checks that rely on smell.

Charge. If the mammoth moves at least 20 feet straight toward a creature and then hits it with a gore attack on the same turn, that target must succeed on a DC 17 Strength saving throw or be knocked prone. If the target is prone, the mammoth can make one stomp attack against it as a bonus action.

Actions

Multiattack. The mammoth makes two attacks: one with its gore and one with its slam.

Gore. *Melee Weapon Attack:* +9 to hit, reach 10 ft., one target. *Hit:* 16 (3d6 + 6) piercing damage.

Slam. *Melee Weapon Attack:* +9 to hit, reach 10 ft., one target. *Hit:* 15 (2d8 + 6) bludgeoning damage.

Stomp. *Melee Weapon Attack:* +9 to hit, reach 10 ft., one target. *Hit:* 16 (3d6 + 6) bludgeoning damage.

Mantidrake

This creature resembles a large, powerfully built lion with a dragon's head where its head would normally be, a pair of large scaly draconic wings, and a long serpentine tail that ends in a volley of sharpened spikes.

Mantidrakes were born from fell experiments and dark rituals that crossed evil dragons with manticores. The result: a creature that combines the best and worst traits of both of its parents. From a distance, a mantidrake is often mistaken for a normal manticore. Only when opponents close against it do they see that the creature is something different.

Mantidrakes, like dragons, are territorial predators and often claim a wide expanse of land as their hunting ground. Creatures that wander into a mantidrake's territory rarely go unnoticed, especially during the daylight hours when the mantidrake spends most of its time hunting. Slain prey is either devoured on the spot (if the mantidrake is hungry) or carried back to its lair and stored for later (or fed to the young if such creatures are present). Mantidrakes are generally solitary creatures though sometimes a pair may be encountered. Such an encounter is with a mated pair.

Female mantidrakes are just as common (or rare depending on how you classify this creature) as males and are just as likely to be encountered as both sexes are skilled hunters. When gestating, a female curtails the time she spends hunting to spend it in the lair preparing both herself and the lair for her young. Young are born live and by 2 years of age, they are independent enough to go out hunting on their own.

A typical mantidrake is about 10 to 12 feet long and weighs about 1,100 to 1,300 pounds. Its draconic head is scaled and is the same color as its dragon parent. The color slowly fades and meshes with the mantidrake's leonine body which is covered in dull tan fur, except for its underbelly which is scaled like a true dragon's. Its wings are of the same color as its dragon parent, dark, almost black (and in the case of a black dragon parent, the wings are actually black in color).

A mantidrake's environment varies based on its dragon heritage: black mantidrakes can be found in warm marshes, deserts, or underground; blue mantidrakes favor warm hills and mountains, rarely being found underground; green mantidrake s favor temperate or warm forests and underground settings; red mantidrakes favor warm mountains and underground settings; and white mantidrakes favor cold mountains, cold deserts, and underground environments.

Mantidrakes are aggressive combatants and begin most attacks with a blast from their deadly breath weapon. This is followed next by a volley of spikes or a claw/claw/bite routine against the closest opponent. Mantidrakes prefer to use their powerful wings to stay aloft and fight from the air where it can rain a combination of its breath weapon and deadly spikes down on its opponents.

Mantidrake

Large monstrosity, lawful evil
Armor Class 15 (natural armor)
Hit Points 147 (14d10 + 70)
Speed 30 ft., fly 50 ft.

STR	DEX	CON	INT	WIS	CHA
23 (+6)	15 (+2)	20 (+5)	9 (−1)	14 (+2)	13 (+1)

Saving Throws Dex +6, Con +9, Wis +6, Cha +5
Skills Perception +6
Damage Immunities see table below
Senses darkvision 60 ft., passive Perception 16

Languages Common, Draconic
Challenge 11 (7,200 XP)

Flyby. The mantidrake doesn't provoke an opportunity attack when it flies out of an enemy's reach.

Keen Smell. The mantidrake has advantage on Wisdom (Perception) checks that rely on smell.

Roll a d10 and refer to the table below to determine a mantidrake's draconic parent and breath weapon.

d10	Head Color	Breath Weapon	Immunity Type
1–2	Black	60-foot-long, 5-foot-wide line of acid	acid
3–4	Blue	60-foot-long, 5-foot-wide line of lightning	lightning
5–6	Green	30-foot cone of poisonous gas	poison
7–8	Red	30-foot cone of fire	fire
9–10	White	30-foot cone of cold	cold

Actions

Multiattack. The mantidrake makes three attacks: one with its bite and two with its claws.

Bite. *Melee Weapon Attack*: +10 to hit, reach 5 ft., one target. *Hit*: 15 (2d8 + 6) piercing damage.

Claws. *Melee Weapon Attack*: +10 to hit, reach 5 ft., one target. *Hit*: 15 (2d8 + 6) slashing damage.

Spikes. *Ranged Weapon Attack*: +6 to hit, range 5 ft., one target. *Hit:* 16 (4d6 + 2) piercing damage.

Dragon Breath (Recharge 5–6). The mantidrake exhales its breath based on the results from the table above. Each creature in the area affected must make a DC 18 Dexterity saving throw, taking 36 (8d8) damage on a failed save, of half as much on a successful one. Damage type determined by the table above.

Mastodon

This elephantine beast has a coat of thick fur and stands longer and lower to the ground than a typical pachyderm. Its tusks are long and curved, providing it with formidable natural weapons.

The great mastodon is a distant relative of the common elephant and is linked to that creature through the woolly mammoth. It is an herbivore and is found primarily in forested areas. Its teeth are rounded and pointed and make excellent "tools" for clipping leaves, branches, and twigs though its diet also includes things such as grasses, fruits, berries, and nuts. A typical mastodon consumes 400 pounds of food and 50 gallons of water each day. Mastodons generally deplete an area of its food supply before moving on, traveling in large herds with the young in the center, surrounded by the adults of the herd.

The mastodon does not have any particular season for reproducing, though most births seem to occur in the winter. Young are born with short, thick fur and weigh around 240 pounds. A young mastodon reaches maturity at about age ten.

The mastodon has three naturally occurring predators: the dire wolf, the smilodon, and man. The latter often hunts the great mastodon for its meat, fur, and the ivory of its tusks. Young mastodons are often captured alive and taken into captivity to be trained as mounts or beasts of burden.

The mastodon is a distant relative to the elephant though it is slightly longer and lower to the ground, with shorter and thicker legs than the common elephant. Its head is slightly longer and taller than an elephant's and the mastodon's entire body is covered in thick fur of brown, gray, reddish-brown, yellowish-brown, or black. Its long, upward curving tusks are formed of ivory and are white or yellowish-white in color. Its eyes range from gray to brown to green. An average mastodon stands 20 feet tall.

Mastodons are generally peaceful creatures and avoid combat. They have no natural fear of any creature, so they do not flee. If threatened or if their young are threatened, mastodons fight by goring with their tusks or trampling foes. Mastodons fight to the death to protect their young.

Training a Mastodon

A mastodon must be trained before it can bear a rider in combat. To be trained, a mastodon must have a friendly attitude toward the trainer. (This can be achieved through a successful Animal Handling check.) Training a friendly mastodon requires six weeks of work and another successful Animal Handling check (DC 20). Failure means that the beast is not fully trained and another 2 weeks of effort will be required to try the check again. Riding a mastodon requires an exotic saddle. A mastodon can fight while carrying a rider, but the rider cannot also attack unless he or she makes a successful Strength (Athletics) check. Mastodon young are worth 16,000 gp each on the open market. Professional trainers charge up to 2,500 gp to rear or train a mastodon.

Carrying Capacity. A mastadon is unencumbered up to 5,592 pounds; a lightly encumbered from 5,593 to 11,184 pounds; and encumbered from 11,185 to 16,800 pounds. A mastadon can drag 84,000 pounds.

Mastodon

Huge beast, unaligned

Armor Class 15 (natural armor)
Hit Points 270 (20d12 + 140)
Speed 40 ft.

STR	DEX	CON	INT	WIS	CHA
28 (+9)	10 (+0)	24 (+7)	2 (–4)	13 (+1)	6 (–2)

Senses passive Perception 11
Languages —
Challenge 9 (5,000 XP)

Keen Smell. The mastodon has advantage on Wisdom (Perception) checks that rely on smell.

Trampling Charge. If the mastodon moves at least 20 feet straight towards a creature and then hits with a gore attack on the same turn, that creature must succeed on a DC 19 Strength check or be knocked prone. If the target is prone, the mastodon can make one stomp attack against it as a bonus action.

Actions

Gore. *Melee Weapon Attack:* +13 to hit, reach 10 ft., one target. *Hit:* 27 (4d8 + 9) piercing damage.

Stomp. *Melee Weapon Attack:* +13 to hit, reach 10 ft., one target. *Hit:* 48 (6d12 + 9) bludgeoning damage and the target must succeed on a DC 17 Constitution saving throw or be stunned until the end of the mammoth's next turn.

Mephit, Lightning

This small creature appears to be a humanoid-shaped being composed of electricity. Bluish-white lighting arcs in small bursts from its body.

Lightning mephits come from the Elemental Plane of Air and Elemental Plane of Lighting. Rarely are they encountered elsewhere unless summoned or called by a spellcaster. If encountered on the Material Plane it is usually in the employ of some spellcaster who has called it to do his or her bidding. Occasionally, however, a lightning mephit stumbles into the Material Plane by way of a lightning storm (when said storm reaches into the Plane of Air and opens a temporary portal). Lightning mephits found anywhere except their home plane will be encountered in areas where lightning and storms are most prevalent. A lightning mephit is about 4 feet tall and weighs about 1 pound.

A lightning mephit begins combat with a lightning bolt attack, targeting the opponent closest to it. On the following round it breathes a cone of lightning on its foes if most are within range; otherwise, it moves to melee combat. Once in melee, a lightning mephit uses its natural attacks and shocking grasp, as well as its breath weapon (if it can catch most of its opponents in the cone).

A lightning mephit's natural weapons are treated as magic weapons for the purpose of overcoming damage reduction.

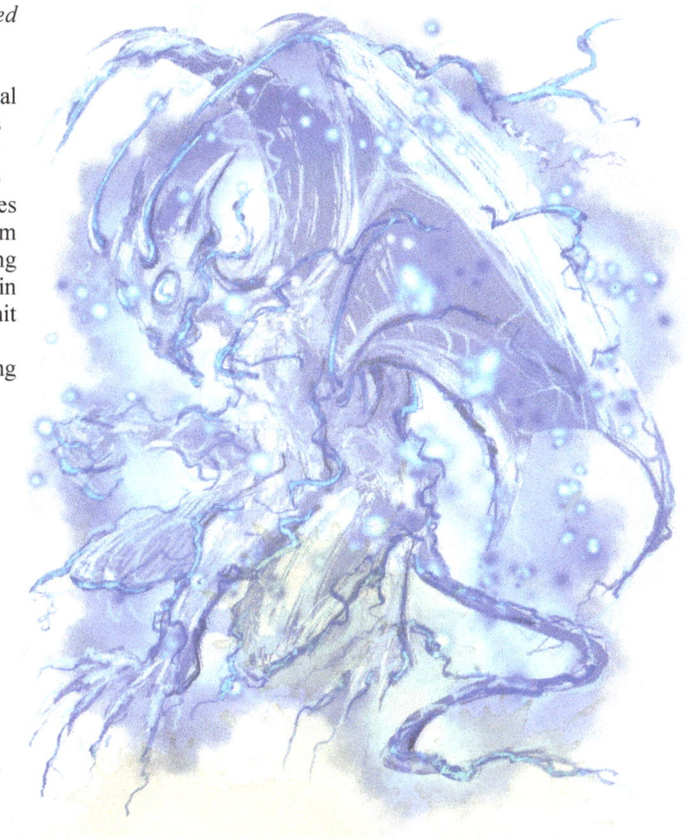

Lightning Mephit

Small elemental, neutral evil
Armor Class 13
Hit Points 21 (6d6)
Speed 30 ft., fly 30 ft.

STR	DEX	CON	INT	WIS	CHA
10 (+0)	17 (+3)	10 (+0)	6 (−2)	11 (+0)	15 (+2)

Skills Perception +4, Stealth +5
Damage Immunities lightning, poison
Condition Immunities poisoned
Senses darkvision 60 ft., passive Perception 14
Languages Auran
Challenge 1 (200 XP)

Death Burst. When the mephit dies, it explodes in a flare of lightning in a 15-foot radius. Creatures in the area must make a DC 12 Dexterity saving throw, taking 9 (2d8) lightning damage on a successful saving throw, or half as much damage on a failed one.

Innate Spellcasting. The mephit's spellcasting ability is Charisma (spell save DC 12, +4 to hit with spell attacks). It can innately cast *shocking grasp* at will requiring no material components.

Actions

Claws. *Melee Weapon Attack:* +5 to hit, reach 5 ft., one target. *Hit:* 5 (1d4 + 3) piercing damage plus 2 (1d4) lightning damage.

Lightning Breath (Recharge 6). The mephit exhales lightning in a 15-foot line that is 1-foot wide. All creatures within that area must make a DC 12 Dexterity saving throw, taking 9 (2d8) lightning damage on a failed save, or half as much damage on a successful one.

Mephit, Smoke

This small winged humanoid has soot-colored skin, crimson eyes, and dark wings. Small trails of smoke stream from its body as it flies along.

Smoke mephits are generally only encountered on the Plane of Molten Skies, though it is believed they originate from a plane or para-plane comprised entirely of smoke. They are generally lazy, but quick to anger. When encountered on the Material Plane it is usually because they have been summoned or called by a spellcaster to perform some task or chore. On such planes, smoke mephits generally prefer warmer climates and are never found in cold areas (unless specifically called by a spellcaster).

Smoke mephits enjoy combat and rush headlong into it, slashing with their claws. If a smoke mephit can draw its opponents to within 20 feet of its position, it uses its spell-like abilities to create an ember storm.

A smoke mephit stands about 4 feet tall and weighs about 2 pounds.

Smoke Mephit

Small elemental, neutral evil
Armor Class 12
Hit Points 21 (6d6)
Speed 30 ft., fly 30 ft.

STR	DEX	CON	INT	WIS	CHA
10 (+0)	14 (+2)	10 (+0)	6 (–2)	11 (+0)	15 (+2)

Skills Perception +4, Stealth +4
Damage Vulnerabilities cold
Damage Immunities fire, poison
Condition Immunities poisoned
Senses darkvision 60 ft., passive Perception 14
Languages Ignan
Challenge 1/2 (100 XP)

Death Burst. When the mephit dies, it explodes in a cloud of smoke. Each creature within 5 feet of the mephit must make a successful DC 10 Constitution saving throw or take 1d4 fire damage and be poisoned for 1 minute. A poisoned creature can repeat the saving throw at the end of each of its turns, ending the effect on a success.

Innate Spellcasting. The mephit can innately cast *blur* 1/day, requiring no material components. Its innate spellcasting ability is Charisma (spell save DC 12, +4 to hit with spell attacks).

Actions

Claw. *Melee Weapon Attack:* +4 to hit, reach 5 ft., one target. *Hit:* 4 (1d4 + 2) slashing damage plus 2 (1d4) fire damage.

Sooty Breath (Recharge 5–6). The mephit exhales black soot in a 15-foot cone. All creatures within that area must make a DC 12 Dexterity saving throw, taking 9 (2d8) fire damage on a failed save, or half as much damage on a successful one.

Ember Storm (1/day). A smoke mephit can create a downpour of white-hot embers that affects a 20-foot radius sphere centered on itself. All creatures caught in the storm must make a DC 12 Dexterity saving throw, taking 10 (3d6) fire damage on a failed save, or half as much damage on a successful one.

Mimi

This tiny fey resembles a one-foot-tall elf with small bee-like wings, silver hair, milk-white skin, and icy blue eyes. It is dressed in colorful garments of blue, silver, or green and carries a tiny shortsword in a scabbard slung across its backs, resting between its wings.

Mimis are one-foot-tall mischievous creatures that inhabit cold forests and fields and derive pleasure from playing tricks on creatures that wander into their icy realm. Mimi tricks are always harmless and include such things as throwing snowballs at a creature, creating a patch of ice on the ground and watching a creature slip and fall, or turning invisible and sneaking into a sleeping creature's camp wherein they put snow or ice in the creature's boots, clothes, or backpack.

While frolicsome, mimis are generally good-natured and friendly towards those they encounter. They often lend aid to creatures in need, especially those that have helped a mimi in the past. Mimis will not lend aid or assistance to creatures of a malign nature and tend to avoid such creatures if possible. They are on good terms with most other fey creatures, though they find brownies to be a little too "stiff" for their liking and buckawns to be a bit too gruff.

Druids and rangers can detect the presence of a mimi or group of mimis with a successful DC Survival check.

Mimis are nonaggressive creatures and rarely attack unless potential adversaries are inherently evil. They prefer to avoid combat if at all possible but if drawn in, they open using their frost fingers. Against more powerful opponents, mimis begin combat by blasting their foes with a cone of cold.

A persistent foe that wishes to continue the battle against a mimi (after being hit with its frost fingers or cone of cold) is subjected to a rapid decrease in the surrounding temperature. A mimi lowers the temperature just enough to possibly damage an adversary and maybe force it away; its goal is not to kill it.

Mimis usually turn invisible and flee if they cannot drive their opponents away.

Mimi

Tiny fey, neutral good
Armor Class 14
Hit Points 9 (2d4 + 4)
Speed 10 ft., fly 50 ft.

STR	DEX	CON	INT	WIS	CHA
4 (−3)	19 (+4)	14 (+2)	15 (+2)	13 (+1)	14 (+2)

Skills Perception +3, Stealth +6 (+8 in snowy terrain)
Damage Immunities cold
Senses darkvision 60 ft., passive Perception 11
Languages Common, Sylvan
Challenge 2 (450 XP)

Group Casting (1/day). A group of three or more mimis together can use *freezing sphere*.

Magic Resistance. The mimi has advantage on saving throws against spells and other magic effects.

Innate Spellcasting. The mimi's spellcasting ability is Charisma (spell save DC 12, +4 to hit with spell attacks). It can innately cast the following spells, requiring no material components:

At will: *invisibility, ray of frost*
2/day: *frost fingers* (as *burning hands*, but cold damage)
1/day: *cone of cold*

Actions

Shortsword. *Melee Weapon Attack:* +6 to hit, reach 5 ft., one target. *Hit:* 7 (1d6 + 4) piercing damage.

Lower Temperature. The mimi lowers the temperature in an area within 30 feet of it that is no larger than a 15-foot cube. Creatures who enter or begin their turn within the area must succeed on a DC 12 Constitution saving throw or take 11 (2d8 + 2) cold damage. If a creature takes cold damage, it has disadvantage on all attack rolls and ability checks for 1 minute.

Minotaur, Bleeding Horror

This creature appears as a hulking bull-headed humanoid whose body constantly drips and oozes thick blood. Its eyes are small pinpoints of red light and shine with evil. It wields a massive axe in its clawed hands.

A bleeding horror minotaur stands more than 7 feet tall and weighs about 700 pounds. Bleeding horror minotaurs prefer melee combat where their great strength serves them well.

Bleeding Horror Minotaur

Large undead, chaotic evil
Armor Class 14 (natural armor)
Hit Points 75 (10d10 + 20)
Speed 30 ft.

STR	DEX	CON	INT	WIS	CHA
19 (+4)	10 (+0)	15 (+2)	7 (−2)	10 (+0)	16 (+3)

Saving Throws Dex +3, Con +5, Wis +3
Skills Perception +6, Survival +6
Damage Resistances bludgeoning, piercing, and slashing from nonmagical weapons
Damage Immunities poison
Condition Immunities exhaustion, poisoned
Senses darkvision 60 ft., passive Perception 16
Languages Giant
Challenge 6 (2,300 XP)

Charge. If the minotaur moves at least 10 feet straight toward a target and then hits it with a gore attack on the same turn, the target takes an extra 9 (2d8) piercing damage. If the target is a creature, it must succeed on a DC 15 Strength saving throw or be pushed up to 10 feet away and knocked prone.

Horrific Appearance. All creatures who directly look at the minotaur must make a DC 14 Wisdom saving throw or be frightened for 1 minute. A creature can repeat the saving throw at the end of each of its turns, ending the effect on itself on a success. If a creature's saving throw is successful or the effect ends for it, the creature is immune to the minotaur's horrific appearance for the next 24 hours.

Magic Resistance. The minotaur has advantage on saving throws against spells and other magic effects.

Magic Weapons. The minotaur's attacks are magical.

Actions

Multiattack. The bleeding horror minotaur uses its gore attack, and makes one attack with its claw and one with its greataxe, or two with its claws.

Gore. *Melee Weapon Attack:* +7 to hit, reach 10 ft., one target. *Hit:* 13 (2d8 + 4) piercing damage.

Greataxe. *Melee Weapon Attack:* +7 to hit, reach 10 ft., one target. *Hit:* 11 (2d6 + 4) slashing damage.

Claws. *Melee Weapon Attack:* +7 to hit, reach 10 ft., one target. *Hit:* 13 (2d8 + 4) slashing damage.

Minotaur, Bronze

This massive bronze figure is shaped as a common minotaur although its sheer bulk and slow movements bely it is an automaton of some kind.

Tall, dark, and powerfully built, the bronze minotaur is an intimidating sight. Standing over 8 feet tall and weighing nearly 4,000 pounds, it is a massive, impressive guardian. Bronze minotaurs can understand simple commands from their creators. They follow these orders unswervingly.

Bronze Minotaur

Large construct, neutral

Armor Class 17 (natural armor)
Hit Points 110 (13d10 + 39)
Speed 20 ft.

STR	DEX	CON	INT	WIS	CHA
18 (+4)	10 (+0)	16 (+3)	3 (−4)	11 (+0)	1 (−5)

Damage Resistances bludgeoning, piercing, and slashing damage from nonmagical weapons that aren't adamantine
Damage Immunities fire, poison, psychic
Condition Immunities charmed, exhaustion, frightened, paralyzed, petrified, poisoned
Senses darkvision 60 ft., passive Perception 10
Languages understands the languages of its creator but can't speak
Challenge 10 (5,900 XP)

Fire Absorption. Whenever the bronze minotaur is subjected to fire damage, it takes no damage and instead regains a number of hit points equal to the fire damage dealt.

Immutable Form. The bronze minotaur is immune to any spell or effect that would alter its form.

Magic Resistance. The bronze minotaur has advantage on saving throws against spells and other magical effects.

Magic Weapon. The bronze minotaur's weapon attacks are magical.

Actions

Multiattack. The bronze minotaur makes two greataxe attacks.

Greataxe. *Melee Weapon Attack:* +8 to hit, reach 5 ft., one target. *Hit:* 23 (3d12 + 4) slashing damage.

Breathe Fire (Recharge 5–6). The bronze minotaur releases a 30-foot cone of flame. Creatures in the area must make a DC 16 Dexterity saving throw, taking 52 (15d6) fire damage on a failed saving throw, or half as much damage on a successful one.

Minotaur, Obsidian

This creature appears as a powerfully constructed minotaur, twice the size of a normal human and carved of obsidian. Its hands end in slightly oversized claws, and its feet are splayed hooves. Small pinpoints of bluish light can be seen in its eyes.

The obsidian minotaur is often employed by spellcasters as a guardian or killer and can be found performing such tasks. When employed as an assassin, the obsidian minotaur is quite effective, first striking fear into the heart of its opponent and then slaying it with no thought or consequence.

An obsidian minotaur stands 12 feet tall and weighs roughly 2,000 pounds.

As a guardian, the obsidian minotaur activates when trespassers enter an area it is programmed to protect. As an assassin, it actively hunts down the targeted victim. The creature attacks with its powerful claws, slashing and ripping its opponent's flesh. Against powerful foes, it employs its breath weapon.

Obsidian Minotaur

Large construct, neutral
Armor Class 16 (natural armor)
Hit Points 76 (8d10 + 32)
Speed 30 ft.

STR	DEX	CON	INT	WIS	CHA
21 (+5)	10 (+0)	18 (+4)	3 (−4)	11 (+0)	1 (−5)

Damage Immunities acid, fire, poison, psychic; bludgeoning, piercing, and slashing from nonmagical weapons that aren't adamantine
Condition Immunities charmed, exhaustion, frightened, paralyzed, petrified, poisoned
Senses darkvision 60 ft., passive Perception 10
Languages understands the languages of its creator but can't speak
Challenge 8 (3,900 XP)

Charge. If the obsidian minotaur moves at least 10 feet straight toward a target and then hits it with a gore attack on the same turn, the target takes an extra 9 (2d8) piercing damage. If the target is a creature, it must succeed on a DC 16 Strength saving throw or be pushed up to 10 feet away and knocked prone.

Immutable Form. The minotaur is immune to any spell or effect that would alter its form.

Magic Resistance. The minotaur has advantage on saving throws against spells and other magic effects.

Magic Weapons. The minotaur's weapon attacks are magical.

Actions

Multiattack. The obsidian minotaur makes one gore attack and two claw attacks.

Gore. Melee Weapon Attack: +8 to hit, reach 5 ft., one target. *Hit:* 14 (2d8 + 5) piercing damage plus 7 (2d6) fire damage.

Claw. Melee Weapon Attack: +8 to hit, reach 10 ft., one target. *Hit:* 12 (2d6 + 5) slashing damage plus 7 (2d6) fire damage.

Burning Breath (Recharge 5–6). An obsidian minotaur expels a cloud of superheated gas that fills a 10-foot cube adjacent to it.. The gas fades after the end of the minotaur's next turn. Creatures who enter the area or start their turn there must make a DC 16 Constitution saving throw. On a failed saving throw, the target takes 31 (9d6) fire damage and it is poisoned for 1 minute. On a successful saving throw, the target takes half the damage and is not poisoned.

Mohrg

Mohrgs are the animated corpses of mass murderers or similar villains who died without atoning for their crimes. They resemble zombies, but are far more dangerous, being somewhat more intelligent, much faster, and much stronger a zombie.

Mohrg

Medium undead, chaotic evil
Armor Class 12
Hit Points 112 (15d8 + 45)
Speed 30 ft.

STR	DEX	CON	INT	WIS	CHA
18 (+4)	14 (+2)	17 (+3)	11 (+0)	10 (+0)	8 (−1)

Damage Immunities poison
Condition Immunities charmed, exhaustion, frightened, paralyzed, petrified, poisoned, stunned
Senses darkvision 60ft., passive Perception 10
Languages —
Challenge 8 (3,900 XP)

Create Spawn. Any humanoid creature slain by the mohrg rises as a zombie at the beginning of the mohrg's next turn. If this occurs, the mohrg regains 10 hit points, and the morhg can immediately make one slam attack as a reaction.

Actions

Multiattack. The mohrg makes two slam attacks and one attack with its tongue.

Slam. Melee Weapon Attack: +7 to hit, reach 5 ft., one target. *Hit:* 13 (2d8 + 4) bludgeoning damage, and the target is grappled and restrained (escape DC15), and the morhg can't grapple another creature or use its slam attack.

Tongue. Melee Weapon Attack: +7 to hit, reach 5 ft., one target. *Hit:* The target must make a DC 16 Constitution saving throw. On a failed save, the target takes 21 (6d6) necrotic damage and is paralyzed for 1 minute. The creature can repeat the saving throw at the end of each of its turns, ending the effect on a success.

Mold, Brown

Found in dark caverns and remote subterranean passages, the brown mold waits patiently for victims to pass by. Less than an inch thick but spreading over a five foot patch of stone or wood, the tan to dark-brown mold seeks warmth to help it grow. Small bumps along its surface store thousands of spores waiting to be released into the air.

Any living creature that passes within 5 feet of the mold will be attacked by a burst cloud of millions of spores. Any caught within the 15-foot cloud may be overcome by the spores, dying within moments. The spores grow within their new host and crawl back to the main body of the mold, reattaching and adding needed nutrients. Each new victim adds another five feet to the mold's size.

The brown mold craves warmth and heat; attacking it with fire heals damage and doubles its size. Cold spells will kill the brown mold for good.

Brown Mold

Small mold, unaligned
Armor Class 5
Hit Points 5 (1d6 + 2)
Speed 0 ft.

STR	DEX	CON	INT	WIS	CHA
1 (−5)	1 (−5)	15 (+2)	1 (−5)	10 (+0)	1 (−5)

Damage Vulnerabilities cold, bludgeoning
Damage Immunities fire, poison; piercing from nonmagical weapons
Condition Immunities charmed, frightened, poisoned, stunned
Senses passive Perception 10
Challenge 2 (450 XP)

Fire Friend. A brown mold does not take damage from fire. Instead, it heals that amount. If the available healing is greater than the brown mold's maximum number of hit points, its maximum hit points increases by that amount.

Cold Sensitive. Magical cold damage instantly and automatically kills a brown mold.

Actions

Spore Burst. The brown mold releases spores that burst out in a cloud that fills a 15-foot cube centered on it, and the cloud lingers for 1 minute. Any creature that ends its turn in the cloud must make a DC 13 Constitution saving throw, taking 36 (8d8) necrotic damage on a failed save, or half as much damage on a successful one. Additionally, the target's hit point maximum is reduced by an amount equal to the damage taken. This reduction lasts until the target finishes a long rest. The target dies if this effect reduces its hit point maximum to 0.

Moose, Two-Toed Horned

The two-toed horned moose stands almost 7 feet at the shoulder, with majestic antlers towering over its already enormous form. A single protruding horn juts from above its steaming nostrils.

The two-toed horned moose is a solitary creature, who inhabits forested woodlands and plains. They are strict herbivores, eating both grasses and shoots of new growth trees, but also aquatic plants. The moose only gather in numbers during mating season, where bull moose fight for mating privileges. In contrast, female moose often keep their calves nearby until at least their first year, and sometimes longer.

Although the two-toed horned moose is an herbivore, its massive size combined with its horn and antlers mean that, when angered, it makes for a terrifying experience. When roused, the two-toed horned moose will lower its head and charge, crashing and piercing with its antlers and bludgeoning with its spade-like horn. The moose is not usually aggressive, save when confronted by intrusive humanoids or canine creatures. At these times, the moose will more often than not charge, as canine creatures are one of the moose's natural predators.

Two-Toed Horned Moose

Large beast, unaligned

Armor Class 12
Hit Points 68 (8d10 + 24)
Speed 60 ft.

STR	DEX	CON	INT	WIS	CHA
20 (+5)	16 (+3)	17 (+3)	7 (−2)	14 (+2)	11 (+0)

Skills Perception +4
Senses passive Perception 14
Languages —
Challenge 3 (700 XP)

Charge. If the moose moves at least 20 feet straight toward a target and then hits it with a ram attack on the same turn, the target takes an extra 7 (2d6) damage. If the target is a creature, it must succeed on a DC 15 Strength saving throw or be knocked prone. If the target is prone, the moose can make one attack with its hooves as a bonus action.

Actions

Ram. *Melee Weapon Attack:* +7 to hit, reach 5 ft., one target. *Hit:* 12 (2d6 + 5) bludgeoning damage.

Hooves. *Melee Weapon Attack:* +7 to hit, reach 5 ft., one target. *Hit:* 23 (4d8 + 5) bludgeoning damage.

Reactions

Kick. *Melee Weapon Attack:* +7 to hit, reach 5 ft., one target who moves within 5 ft. *Hit:* 14 (2d8 + 5) bludgeoning damage.

Mordnaissant

Floating before you is a horrid, shriveled human fetus nested within a translucent sphere of dark energy. Its jet-black eyes glitter with intensity as it twitches and spasms slightly, as if in great pain.

Occasionally when a woman with child dies violently in a place infused with unholy or negative energies, the unborn child within her does not perish, but instead continues to grow, vitalized by dark power, until it is capable of clawing its way free from its dead mother. This horrible creature, known as a mordnaissant, lives an existence of eternal pain, loneliness, and suffering and is relieved only by its ability to inflict harm on those around it. Mordnaissants avoid bright light if they can, though they suffer no ill effects from it.

Mordnaissant

Tiny undead, neutral evil
Armor Class 15
Hit Points 67 (15d4 + 30)
Speed 5 ft., fly 50 ft.

STR	DEX	CON	INT	WIS	CHA
3 (−4)	14 (+2)	15 (+2)	7 (−2)	14 (+2)	16 (+3)

Skills Perception +5
Damage Resistances bludgeoning, piercing, and slashing from nonmagical weapons
Damage Immunities poison
Condition Immunities charmed, exhaustion, frightened, paralyzed, poisoned, unconscious
Senses blindsight 60 ft., darkvision 60 ft., passive Perception 15
Languages —
Challenge 6 (2,300 XP)

Death Curse. If a mordnaissant dies, it releases a death curse on all creatures within 30 feet of it. Those creatures must make a DC 15 Wisdom saving throw. On a failed saving throw, the creature cannot regain hit points from spending hit dice and it has disadvantage on all saving throws for 24 hours. A *remove curse* or greater magic is necessary to end this curse early.

Shield of Agony. The mordnaissant's Armor Class includes its Charisma modifier.

Actions

Lash of Fury. *Ranged Spell Attack:* +5 to hit, range 30 ft., one target. *Hit:* 24 (5d8 + 2) necrotic damage and the target must make a DC 14 Constitution saving throw or lose 1d4 points of Intelligence. The target becomes incapacitated if this reduces its Intelligence to 0. Otherwise, the reduction lasts until the target finishes a long rest.

Pain Wail. The mordnaissant releases a wail. Creatures within 20 feet that can hear the mordnaissant must make a DC 14 Wisdom saving throw. On a failed saving throw, the target is stunned until the end of its next turn.

Moss

Memory Moss (Hazard)

Memory moss appears as a 5-foot square patch of black moss. It grows in temperate or warm climates and is sometimes encountered in subterranean realms. Memory moss cannot abide the cold or the arid clime of the desert and is never encountered in such environments.

When a living creature moves within 60 feet of a patch of memory moss, the moss attacks by attempting to steal that creature's memories. It can target a single creature each round. A targeted creature must succeed on a DC 14 Wisdom saving throw or lose all memories from the last 24 hours. This is particularly nasty to spellcasters, who lose all spells prepared within the last 24 hours. (Only those spells actually prepared in the last 24 hours are lost; spells prepared longer than 24 hours ago are not lost.)

Once a memory moss steals a creature's memories, it sinks back down and does not attack again for one day. If a creature loses its memories to the memory moss, it acts as if affected by a *confusion* spell for the next 1d4 hours. Lost memories can be regained by eating the memory moss that absorbed them. Doing so requires a DC 11 Constitution saving throw, with failure resulting in the creature being nauseated for 1d6 minutes and poisoned until it takes a long or short rest.

A creature that eats the memory moss temporarily gains the memories currently stored therein (even if they are not the creature's own memories). Such creatures can even cast spells if the memory moss has stolen these from a spellcasting creature. Any non-spellcaster that attempts to cast a spell gained in this way must succeed on an Intelligence check (DC 10 + spell level) or the spell fizzles away. After 24 hours, the memories fade (including any spells not yet cast). Creatures eating the memory moss to regain their own lost memories do not lose them after 24 hours. Cold or fire damage kills a patch of memory moss.

When first encountered there is a 25% chance that the memory moss has eaten within the last day and does not attack by stealing memories. In such a case, the moss contains 2d4 spells determined randomly from any spell caster's list with no spell over 4th level. When a living creature moves within 60 feet of a sated memory moss, it assumes a vaguely humanoid form and casts the stolen spells at its targets. The moss casts these spells as a sorcerer of the minimum level necessary to cast the stolen spell (save DC 10 + spell level, + spell level +2 to hit with spell attack).

Purple Moss (Hazard)

This plant is a distant cousin of yellow mold. It feeds on moisture, so any area in which it grows is always extremely dry. Purple moss emits a sweet smell to a range of 10 feet. Creatures with fewer than 22 hit points that enter that range must succeed on a DC 13 Constitution saving throw or fall asleep like that caused by the sleep spell. Victims that fall asleep are quickly covered by the moss. It takes 1 full round to cover a creature of Tiny size and one additional round for each size larger than Tiny. A creature covered by purple moss begins to suffocate and this does not cause them to wake up from the sleep effect. Slain victims are digested in 1d2 hours by acidic secretions from the moss. Purple moss can be destroyed by fire.

Mummy of the Deep

This rotting, bandaged humanoid slides with a slight gait as it moves. Its body is covered in tattered and torn bandages. Seaweed hangs from its unloving form and water drips in a constant state from its desiccated form.

A mummy of the deep is an undead creature that lairs in the depths of the sea. It is the result of an evil creature that was buried at sea for its sins in life. The wickedness permeating the former life has managed to cling even to unlife and revive the soul as a mummy of the deep.

Mummy of the Deep

Medium undead (aquatic), neutral evil
Armor Class 14 (natural armor)
Hit Points 52 (8d8 + 16)
Speed 20 ft., swim 20 ft.

STR	DEX	CON	INT	WIS	CHA
17 (+3)	10 (+0)	14 (+2)	6 (−2)	14 (+2)	15 (+2)

Saving Throws Con +5, Wis +5
Skills Athletics +6, Perception +5, Stealth +3
Damage Resistances fire; bludgeoning, piercing, and slashing from nonmagical weapons
Damage Immunities necrotic, poison
Condition Immunities charmed, exhaustion, frightened, paralyzed, poisoned
Senses darkvision 60 ft., passive Perception 15
Languages the languages it knew in life
Challenge 5 (1,800 XP)

Amphibious. Mummies of the deep can breathe air and water.

Innate Spellcasting (1/day). The mummy can innately cast *control water*, requiring no material components. Its innate spellcasting ability is Wisdom

Actions

Multiattack. The mummy can use its Dreadful Glare and makes one attack with its necrotizing strike.

Necrotizing Strike. *Melee Weapon Attack:* +6 to hit, reach 5ft., one target. *Hit:* 10 (2d6 + 3) bludgeoning damage plus 10 (3d6) necrotic damage. If the target is a creature, it must succeed on a DC 12 Constitution saving throw or be cursed with necrotic fever. The cursed target can't regain hit points, and its hit point maximum decreases by 10 (3d6) for every 24 hours that elapse. If the curse reduces the target's hit point maximum to 0, the target dies, and its body turns to pluff mud. The curse lasts until removed by the *remove curse* spell or other magic.

Dreadful Glare. The mummy targets one creature it can see within 60 feet of it. If the target can see the mummy, it must succeed on a DC 12 Wisdom saving throw against this magic or become frightened until the end of the mummy's next turn. If the target fails the saving throw by 5 or more, it is also paralyzed for the same duration. A target that succeeds on the saving throw is immune to the Dreadful Glare for all mummies (but no mummy lords) for the next 24 hours.

Drowning Breath. *Melee Weapon Attack:* +6 to hit, reach 5 ft., one target. *Hit:* The creature is grappled (escape DC 13). If the creature has not broken the mummy's grapple by the start of the mummy's next turn, the mummy uses its next action to press its lips against the creature's and regurgitates seawater into the creature's lungs. The creature immediately begins suffocating (see the fifth edition SRD for more information on suffocation). While suffocating, the creature can only use its actions to try and cough the seawater up, requiring a successful DC 12 Constitution saving throw to do so.

Netherspark

This creature looks like a 6-foot-tall humanoid whose form is composed of dark matter. Its head is featureless and sports no eyes, ears, nose, or mouth. It wears no clothes and bands of silver and white crackle and dance in its form.

Nethersparks are natives of the negative energy plane that sometimes find themselves lost in the Material Plane where they seek to transform positive energy into a negative charge. On their home plane, they are attracted to living organisms and seek to transform them into nothingness where both they and their home plane absorb the creature's positive essence. On the Material Planes, these creatures are often found haunting graveyards or in the employ of a powerful necromancer. Undead creatures are attracted to and can detect the presence of a netherspark within 60 feet.

A netherspark stands about 6 feet tall and weighs about 180 pounds. Its body is entirely composed of negative energy and dark matter. No facial features are discernable on its head, though the creature can see, hear, and speak.

A netherspark begins combat using its negative energy ray before closing into melee range. In close combat, the creature rains blow after blow down on its adversaries with its powerful fists. The creature continually moves around during combat attempting to expose as many targets as possible to its negative energy aura. A netherspark's natural weapons are treated as magic weapons for the purpose of overcoming damage reduction.

A netherspark's natural weapons, as well as any weapon it wields, are treated as evil-aligned for the purpose of overcoming damage reduction.

Netherspark

Medium elemental, neutral evil
Armor Class 15 (natural armor)
Hit Points 90 (12d8 + 36)
Speed 30 ft.

STR	DEX	CON	INT	WIS	CHA
19 (+4)	16 (+3)	16 (+3)	14 (+2)	16 (+3)	14 (+2)

Damage Resistances radiant
Damage Immunities necrotic
Condition Immunities charmed, exhaustion, frightened
Senses darkvision 60 ft., passive Perception 13
Languages Celestial, Common, Draconic, Infernal
Challenge 6 (2,300 XP)

Magic Resistance. The netherspark has advantage on saving throws against spells and other magic effects.

Necrotic Aura. Being composed of necrotic energy, a netherspark radiates an aura of such energy in a 10-foot radius. Any creature that's not an undead that enters or starts its turn within this area takes 7 (2d6) necrotic damage. Undead in the area instead regain 7 (2d6) hit points, up to their maximum hit points at the beginning of each of their turns.

Actions

Multiattack. The netherspark makes three slam attacks.

Slam. *Melee Weapon Attack:* +7 to hit, reach 5 ft., one target. *Hit:* 11 (2d6 + 4) necrotic damage.

Necrotic Ray. *Ranged Weapon Attack:* +6 to hit, range 40 ft., one target. *Hit:* 12 (2d8+3) necrotic damage. Undead take no damage but heal a number of hit points equal to what the ray would otherwise deal.

Necrotic Burst (Recharge 5–6). A netherspark can release a burst of necrotic energy in a 20-foot radius around it. Creatures in the area must make a DC 13 Constitution saving throw, taking 12 (2d8+3) necrotic damage on a failed save, or half as much damage on a successful one. Undead take no damage but heal a number of hit points equal to what the burst would otherwise deal.

Noble Streynor

The noble streynor is an evolved and magically active descendent of the prehistoric and extinct "brown streynor" first mentioned in the Emperor's Song Cycle by the poet and naturalist Nevigistro. Like their ancestors, noble streynors are herd animals most often found in their choice habitats where scrub plains give way to desert sands.

In that arid region, noble streynors graze on short, tough grasses, but they prefer to eat flowering cactus plants. The flesh inside their mouths is especially tough, enabling them safely to consume errant cactus needles. Noble streynors roam in herds of up to three dozen, placidly moving from one food source to the next. Though able to survive in diverse environments, noble streynors prefer areas less prone to precipitation, as their immune systems are weakened if their permeable hides spend too much time in the rain.

Noble streynors are hunted by the usual prey animals but do not often fall victim to them due to their magical ability to sense danger. At some point in its evolutionary past, the streynor was the subject of an alchemical experiment, and since then, every streynor is born with the inherent ability to detect potential predators within a 300-yard radius. Though not a particularly swift runner, a noble streynor can move quickly enough to avoid all but the fastest pursuer, given this advance warning. Despite its natural ability to avoid most threats, the noble streynor is still sought out by hunters who can sell the creature's frontal lobe for a high price to black-market magic users. Portions of a noble streynor's brain can be used to concoct various alchemical products and divination-based magic items, so they command high prices if the proper buyers can be found.

Noble Streynor

Large beast, unaligned
Armor Class 14
Hit Points 19 (3d10 + 3)
Speed 50 ft.

STR	DEX	CON	INT	WIS	CHA
18 (+4)	14 (+2)	13 (+1)	2 (–4)	17 (+3)	7 (–2)

Skills Perception +7
Senses darkvision 60 ft., passive Perception 17
Languages —
Challenge 3 (700 XP)

Keen Hearing and Smell. The noble streynor has advantage on Wisdom (Perception) checks that rely on hearing or smell up to 300 yards away.

Actions

Bite. *Melee Weapon Attack* +6 to hit, reach 5 ft., one target. *Hit*: 11 (3d4 + 4) piercing damage.

Nucklavee

A large skinless warhorse ridden by a similarly skinless rider approaches. As it nears, one can clearly see the rider growing straight out of the creature's back. The monster's internal organs, veins that carry its blackened blood, and corded muscles are all easily seen by one viewing the creature. A thin layer of reddish mucus covering its body gives off a putrid odor. Its eyes are stark white, while those of the rider are a hellish red. Its body is hairless save for its bushy, matted, and bloodstained horse-like tail.

An evil woodland creature that hates most other life is a good description of the nuckalavee. An evil woodland creature that kills all that cross its path, eats their flesh, and drinks their liquefied organs is an even better description of the nuckalavee. Nuckalavee are fearsome, aggressive combatants that relish the savagery and butchery of melee combat.

The true origin of the nuckalavee is shrouded in mystery and has been lost over time. Some believe it to be the offspring of a demon or devil and a female centaur. Others say the nuckalavee is the result of a curse placed upon a tribe of centaurs centuries ago by a mad and evil sorcerer. Whatever their origin, the nuckalavee is a deadly opponent, capable of felling even the mightiest of warriors.

Nuckalavee sustain themselves on a diet of flesh, blood, and liquefied organs. They digest no other foods or liquids (at least from what is known about these creatures). Prey is often captured or killed and dragged back to its lair where it is devoured. The typical nuckalavee lair is a crude structure formed of dirt, mud, and foliage. Contents range from bones, to rotting organs and flesh, to the treasure of those it has dragged back to its lair to feed upon. Often a lair contains a female and 1d2 young. Young nuckalavee resemble adults in all aspects, save they are smaller in size.

Nuckalavee relish the adrenaline of combat. They love the taste, sight, and smell of blood and seek to bleed their opponents as often and as much as they can. The "rider" always employs a bladed weapon (most often a longsword or greataxe) to deal damage, while the equine part of the nuckalavee slashes with its sharpened hoofs and bites with its razor-sharp teeth.

The nuckalavee opens combat with its poisonous breath, seeking to liquefy the organs of its foes before it moves to strike with hooves, bite, and weapon. They rarely attack from ambush, relishing in the fear their appearance strikes in the heart of opponents.

Nuckalavee

Large aberration, chaotic evil
Armor Class 17 (natural armor)
Hit Points 84 (8d10 + 40)
Speed 50 ft.

STR	DEX	CON	INT	WIS	CHA
20 (+5)	15 (+2)	20 (+5)	8 (−1)	15 (+2)	14 (+2)

Skills Perception +5, Stealth +5, Survival +5
Damage Resistances bludgeoning, piercing, and slashing from nonmagical weapons
Senses darkvision 60 ft., passive Perception 15
Languages Common, Sylvan
Challenge 8 (3,900 XP)

Charge. If the nuckalavee moves at least 20 feet straight toward a creature and then hits it with a greataxe attack, that target must succeed on a DC 16 Strength saving throw or be knocked prone. If the target is prone, the nuckalavee can make one attack with its hooves against it as a bonus action.

Horrific Appearance. Any creature that starts its turn within 20 feet of the nuckalavee must make a DC 13 Wisdom saving throw. On a failed save, the creature is frightened until the start of its next turn. If a creature's saving throw is successful, the creature is immune to the nuckalavee's horrific appearance for the next 24 hours.

Magic Resistance. The nuckalavee has advantage on saving throws against spells and other magic effects.

Actions

Multiattack. The nuckalavee makes four attacks: two with its greataxe, one bite attack, and one attack with its hooves.

Greataxe. *Melee Weapon Attack:* +8 to hit, reach 5 ft., one target. *Hit:* 12 (2d6 + 5) slashing damage.

Hooves. *Melee Weapon Attack:* +8 to hit, reach 5 ft., one target. *Hit:* 14 (2d8 + 5) slashing damage.

Bite. *Melee Weapon Attack:* +8 to hit, reach 5 ft., one target. *Hit:* 10 (2d4 + 5) piercing damage.

Poisonous Breath (Recharge 5–6). The nuckalavee exhales a cloud of caustic gas in a 20-foot cone. Creatures in this area must make a DC 15 Dexterity saving throw, taking 21 (6d6) acid damage on a failed save, or half as much damage on a successful one.

Oakman

This squat fey creature's brownish-green skin is as tough as tree bark. He has unkempt green hair, pale green eyes, and bulbous nose.

Oakmen are small fey that are said to be the spirits of oak trees. An oakman is a foul-tempered curmudgeon, gruff, and cantankerous. These grouchy creatures are usually seen sitting upon a thick branch in an oak tree, calling down insults and crude comments to those who pass by. Some say that the grumpy old oakmen are the male versions of the beautiful dryads. This may or may not be true, but it would certainly explain why dryads would rather take human mates.

Oakmen are generally content to sit in their trees and watch the world go by, venturing out only if their forest is threatened. They also enjoy creeping out of the forest to trick some fool human into eating magical cakes made from moss and mushrooms just to see what will happen to him.

Oakmen are scrappy and prone to combat despite their small size. They will fight if they must, but like most fey, prefer to use magic rather than melee.

Oakman

Small fey, chaotic neutral
Armor Class 12 (16 with *barkskin*)
Hit Points 33 (6d6 + 12)
Speed 20 ft., climb 30 ft.

STR	DEX	CON	INT	WIS	CHA
12 (+1)	14 (+2)	14 (+2)	11 (+0)	15 (+2)	14 (+2)

Skills Perception +4, Stealth +4
Senses darkvision 60 ft., passive Perception 14
Languages Common, Sylvan
Challenge 1 (200 XP)

Innate Spellcasting. The oakman's spellcasting ability is Charisma (spell save DC 12, +4 to hit with spell attacks). He can innately cast the following spells, requiring no material components:

At will: *druidcraft, shillelagh*
3/day each: *entangle, goodberry*
1/day each: *barkskin, pass without trace*

Magic Resistance. The oakman has advantage on saving throws against spells and other magical effects.

Moss. Using his unique knowledge of plants and herbal mixtures, an oakman can concoct unusual cakes from tree moss. A typical oakman has 3 (1d6) moss cakes of random type on his person. These moss cakes have a variety of effects and must be eaten by the target creature to take effect.

d6	Result
1	**Coloration.** This moss cake is quite harmless when eaten and does nothing more than cause the target's skin to become spotted. The spots can be of just about any color, though most tend to be brown, red, or blue. The spots last for 1 hour before fading.
2	**Healing.** This moss cake heals the target of 22 (5d8) damage.
3	**Lethargy.** The target falls into a state of apathy and becomes sluggish if it fails a DC 12 Constitution saving throw. On a failed save, the target suffers from three levels of exhaustion, which can be removed normally.
4	**Pain.** Eating this moss cake wracks the target with pain for 1 hour if it fails a DC 12 Constitution saving throw. During this time, the target moves at half speed, and has disadvantage on all attack rolls, ability checks, and saving throws for 1 hour.
5	**Poison.** Eating this moss cake poisons the target. The target must make a DC 12 Constitution saving throw. On a failed saving throw, the target takes 7 (2d6) poison damage and is poisoned for 1 hour. While poisoned, the target must repeat the saving throw at the beginning of each of its turns. On a failed saving throw, the target spends its action retching and vomiting.
6	**Sleep.** This moss cake puts the target to sleep for 1 hour if it fails a DC 12 Constitution saving throw.

Tree Stride. Once on his turn, the oakman can use 10 feet of his movement to step magically into one living tree within his reach and emerge from a second living tree within 60 feet of the first tree, appearing in an unoccupied space within 5 feet of the second tree. Both trees must be Large or bigger.

Actions

Club. *Melee Weapon Attack:* +3 to hit (+4 with *shillelagh*), reach 5 ft., one target. *Hit:* 3 (1d4 + 1) bludgeoning damage, or 6 (1d8 + 2) bludgeoning damage.

Oozes

Ooze, Amber

This creature resembles a small pool of liquid the color and consistency of mead.

Amber oozes were created by an evil wizard as a means of gaining control over the elders of a powerful city. He bred many of the creatures in secret and sealed them into kegs of ale, then hired merchants to distribute this ale throughout the city. The wizard was ultimately slain and the city saved by a band of heroic adventurers.

Unknown to the adventurers, the merchants had wanted to line their own pockets without the knowledge of their employer. Unaware of the plot they sold some of the kegs of ale in illegal markets. Now, many of the kegs containing amber oozes have been shipped to other cities and the creatures are spreading. When an amber ooze divides, one of the new creatures seeps out of the keg to find its own lair. Stacked in rows with other kegs of uncontaminated ale, amber oozes can quickly take over a storeroom or pantry.

An amber ooze is approximately 1 foot in diameter and is a dark amber color. The designs of the mad mage even provided the amber ooze with the scent of mead or heady ale. Amber oozes can lay in a state of hibernation for years, coming out of it only to replicate — a process they undergo once every few months — or when they are alerted by movement of the keg.

When a keg containing an amber ooze is tapped, the creature makes its way to the opening. Within the drawing of a few drinks, the amber ooze squeezes out of the tap and into the mug. As soon as the victim drinks, the ooze forces itself down the victim's throat and into its belly.

Amber Ooze

Tiny ooze, unaligned
Armor Class 8
Hit Points 13 (3d4 + 6)
Speed 10ft., climb 10 ft.

STR	DEX	CON	INT	WIS	CHA
12 (+1)	8 (−2)	14 (+2)	1 (−5)	1 (−5)	1 (−5)

Damage Immunities acid
Condition Immunities blinded, charmed, deafened, exhaustion, frightened, prone
Senses blindsight 60 ft. (blind beyond this radius), passive Perception 5
Languages —
Challenge 1/2 (100 XP)

False Appearance. The amber ooze is indistinguishable from a pint of ale or mead as long as it does not move.

Infuse. A victim that has ingested an amber ooze must make a DC 12 Constitution saving throw. On a successful saving throw, the amber ooze is expelled from the host's body into an unoccupied space within 5 feet of the host. On a failed saving throw, the amber ooze infuses itself into the host's body. The amber ooze has total cover from effects outside the host's body, and is blind and deafened.

While the amber ooze is infused, the host creature must succeed on a DC 12 Constitution saving throw at the beginning of each of its turns. On a failed saving throw, the host takes 7 (2d6) acid damage, or half as much damage on a successful saving throw. If this damage drops to host to 0 hit points, its insides are liquefied and another amber ooze is created.

An amber ooze can be forcibly removed with magic such as *lesser restoration*.

Actions

Attach. *Melee Weapon Attack:* +3 to hit, reach 5 ft., one creature. *Hit:* The amber ooze attaches to the target. While attached, the amber ooze makes its way up the body using its movement and attempts to infuse itself into a new host. A creature can use its action to attempt a DC 11 Strength (Athletics) check to pull the ooze from the creature it is attached to.

Ooze, Livestone

A large slab of moss-covered rock seems to ooze and move before you.

Livestone is a strange species of ooze that can solidify itself into a consistency that very closely resembles that of stone. In its solidified form, a livestone is indistinguishable from a normal boulder or slab of rock. No one is quite sure from where livestones originated, but ancient legends say that the dwarves accidentally unleashed these horrors on the surface world by digging into their subterranean lairs. Eventually, some livestones found their way to the surface. Livestones are incredibly long lived, solidifying and entering a form of hibernation and remaining that way indefinitely until a food source wanders too near. Livestones have a simple chameleon-like ability to mimic local stone by ingesting a small sample and adjusting its own color and texture to match. A hibernating livestone can become covered in moss and lichens to further the deception.

Livestones generally attack from ambush, waiting for a potential meal to pass before flowing into their ooze form and rushing up to engulf the prey. If the surprise attack fails, a livestone resorts to hammering with a hard-as-rock pseudopod.

Livestone

Large ooze (fungus), unaligned
Armor Class 10
Hit Points 168 (16d10 + 80)
Speed 20 ft.

STR	DEX	CON	INT	WIS	CHA
20 (+5)	10 (+0)	20 (+5)	2 (–4)	1 (–5)	1 (–5)

Damage Immunities acid, cold, fire, poison
Condition Immunities blinded, charmed, deafened, exhaustion, frightened, poisoned, prone
Senses blindsight 60 ft. (blind beyond this radius), passive Perception 5
Languages —
Challenge 5 (1,800 XP)

False Appearance. While the livestone is solidified and remains motionless, it is indistinguishable from a typical stone.

Stone Camouflage. The livestone has advantage on Dexterity (Stealth) checks made to hide in rocky terrain.

Actions

Multiattack. The livestone makes two attacks with its pseudopod.

Pseudopod. *Melee Weapon Attack:* +8 to hit, reach 5 ft., one target. *Hit:* 14 (2d8 + 5) bludgeoning damage. If the target is Medium or smaller, it is grappled (escape DC 15) and restrained until the grapple ends. The livestone can grapple two targets.

Engulf. The livestone engulfs a Medium or smaller creature grappled by it. The engulfed target is blinded, restrained, and unable to breathe, and it must succeed on a DC 15 Constitution saving throw at the start of each of the livestone's turns or take 14 (2d8 + 5) bludgeoning damage. If the livestone moves, the engulfed target moves with it. The livestone can have only one creature engulfed at a time.

Reactions

Solidify. As a reaction, the livestone can solidify all or part of itself into material with the same consistency of solid rock. The livestone adds 4 to its AC against one melee attack that would hit it. The livestone does not have to see the attack to use this ability. A livestone cannot take attack or move actions if its entire form is solidified. A livestone must use an action to desolidify itself.

Ooze, Magma

This creature appears to be a pool of bubbling and churning molten rock.

A magma ooze is encountered primarily on the Material Plane but is thought to have its origins on the Plane of Fire. They are almost always found in or near volcanoes and other warm or hot places. Magma oozes do not approach water and are never found near such sources. Magma oozes can grow to a length of 10 feet, with a thickness of about 6 inches.

Magma Ooze

Large ooze, unaligned
Armor Class 7
Hit Points 85 (9d10 + 36)
Speed 20 ft., climb 20 ft.

STR	DEX	CON	INT	WIS	CHA
16 (+3)	4 (–3)	18 (+4)	1 (–5)	6 (–2)	1 (–5)

Damage Immunities acid, cold, fire, lightning, poison, psychic, slashing
Condition Immunities blinded, charmed, deafened, exhaustion, frightened, prone
Senses blindsight 60 ft. (blind beyond this radius), passive Perception 8
Languages —
Challenge 6 (2,300 XP)

Amorphous. The magma ooze can move through a space as narrow as 1 inch wide without squeezing.

Superheated. Creatures that touch the magma ooze take 7 (2d6) fire damage. Any nonmagical weapon used to attack the magma ooze melts and warps. After dealing damage, the weapon takes a permanent and cumulative –1 penalty to damage rolls. If its penalty drops to –5, the weapon is destroyed. Nonmagical ammunition that hits the ooze is destroyed after dealing damage.

The ooze can melt through 2-inch-thick, nonmagical wood or metal in 1 round.

Spider Climb. The magma ooze can climb difficult surfaces, including upside down on ceilings, without needing to make an ability check.

Actions

Pseudopod. *Melee Weapon Attack:* +6 to hit, reach 5 ft., one target. *Hit:* 13 (3d6 + 3) bludgeoning damage plus 28 (8d6) fire damage. In addition, any nonmagical armor worn by the target is partially burned and melted and takes a permanent and cumulative –1 penalty to the AC it offers. The armor is destroyed if the penalty reduces its AC to 10.

Split. When a magma ooze that is Medium or larger is subjected to slashing damage, it splits into two new magma oozes if it has at least 10 hit points. Each new magma ooze has hit points equal to half the original ooze's, rounded down. New oozes are one size smaller than the original magma ooze.

Ooze, Metallic

A large pile of seemingly unguarded coins lies before you.

A metallic ooze appears as a 9-foot blob of protoplasm of varying hue and color, and come in a variety of sizes and colors: gold, silver, platinum, copper, brass, or bronze. Regardless of the color or size, metallic oozes resemble large piles of coins. The oozes use their appearance to lure would-be treasure hunters to their doom. Because of this, they are sometimes referred to as hoard oozes. Its form is coarse and rough giving it the appearance of piles of coins. A metallic ooze can flatten its body in order to squeeze through spaces and cracks where it normally could not go.

A metallic ooze can be found virtually anywhere, though it tends to inhabit dungeons, ruined temples, castles, and other buildings where treasure seekers seem to enjoy perfecting their craft. From a distance of 30 feet or more, a metallic ooze resembles a pile of loose coins (of whatever type its coloration most closely resembles). A creature can attempt a DC 20 Perception check to notice the ooze for what it is. This monster does not collect treasure, but the remnants of living creatures that meet their demise at the hands of this creature are often found scattered about its lair.

A metallic ooze lies still until it detects a potential meal within range. It then forms a pseudopod and pummels the opponent. Creatures killed by a metallic ooze are devoured. While a metallic ooze can cling to walls and ceilings (and often does drop on unsuspecting prey), it prefers to wander dungeon corridors and such on the ground, often waiting in one spot until living prey wanders too close.

Metallic Ooze

Large ooze, unaligned
Armor Class 9 (natural armor)
Hit Points 95 (10d10 + 40)
Speed 20 ft., climb 10 ft.

STR	DEX	CON	INT	WIS	CHA
17 (+3)	5 (−3)	19 (+4)	2 (−4)	6 (−2)	1 (−5)

Skills Stealth +3
Damage Immunities acid
Condition Immunities blinded, charmed, deafened, exhaustion, frightened, prone
Senses blindsight 60 ft. (blind beyond this radius), passive Perception 8
Languages —
Challenge 5 (1,800 XP)

False Appearance. The metallic ooze is indistinguishable from a pile of coins as long as it remains motionless.

Irritating Fumes. If a metallic ooze takes fire damage, it emanates a cloud of semi-transparent vapor that irritates the eyes and respiratory system of living creatures within 10 feet of it. All creatures other than undead or constructs within the area must succeed on a DC 15 Constitution saving throw or take 10 (3d6) acid damage and be poisoned for 1 minute. A poisoned creature can repeat the saving throw at the end of each of its turns, ending the effect on a success. The cloud disperses in 1 minute, or can be dispersed by a moderate or greater wind.

Spider Climb. The metallic ooze can climb difficult surfaces, including upside down on ceilings, without needing to make an ability check.

Actions

Slam. Melee Weapon Attack: +6 to hit, reach 5 ft., one target. *Hit:* 12 (2d8 + 3) bludgeoning damage plus 18 (4d8) acid damage, and the target must succeed on a DC 15 Constitution saving throw or be poisoned for 1 hour.

Ooze, Mudbog

What you originally thought was a patch of muddy water reveals itself to be a protoplasmic life-form resembling a giant brownish-black amoeba.

Mudbogs are strange, slow-moving, pudding-like creatures that dwell in swamps, fens, and wetlands. Situated comfortably in its hole along well-traveled paths, a mudbog is likely to be mistaken for a patch of muddy water or a wet spot in the road. Creatures attempting to simply walk over or through the "mud puddle" find themselves stuck fast and, worse yet, being consumed by the hungry ooze.

A mudbog doesn't really attack its opponents; its method of getting a meal is strictly passive. However, once a meal stumbles into its protoplasmic body, the mudbog is determined not to let it escape. They are brownish in color, resembling nothing more than brackish mud. These monsters use their coloration to their best advantage and use their acidic bodies to dig a hole, usually several feet deep, in which to lie in wait for a meal. The average mudbog is roughly 10 feet across and 3 feet deep.

A mudbog lacks the intelligence to collect treasure. However, the possessions of its victims can always be found in a heap at the bottom of the hole it has chosen as its home. Actually getting to the treasure involves somehow removing the mudbog from its hole.

Mudbog

Large ooze, unaligned
Armor Class 9
Hit Points 51 (6d10 + 18)
Speed 10 ft., swim 10 ft.

STR	DEX	CON	INT	WIS	CHA
20 (+5)	8 (–1)	17 (+3)	1 (–5)	10 (+0)	3 (–4)

<RULE.

Skills Stealth +1
Senses blindsight 60 ft. (blind beyond this radius), passive
  Perception 10
Damage Resistances fire
Damage Immunities acid, psychic
Condition Immunities blinded, charmed, deafened,
  exhaustion, frightened, prone
Languages —
Challenge 2 (450 XP)

Acid. A mudbog secretes a digestive acid that quickly dissolves organic material, but not metal or stone. A creature that attacks the mudbog takes 3 (1d6) acid damage. Any wood or other organic material that touches the mudbog is pitted. Wooden weapons suffer a cumulative –1 penalty to damage rolls made with it unless it is magical. When this penalty reaches –5, the weapon is destroyed.

Amorphous. The ooze can move through a space as narrow as 1 inch wide without squeezing.

False Appearance. The mudbog, while not moving, is indistinguishable from a muddy puddle.

Actions

Engulf. The mudbog moves up to its speed. While doing so, it can enter Medium or smaller creatures' spaces. Whenever the mudbog enters a creature's space, the creature must make a DC13 Dexterity saving throw.

On a successful save, the creature can choose to be pushed 5 feet back or to the side of the mudbog. A creature that chooses not to be pushed suffers the consequences of a failed saving throw. On a failed save, the creature is engulfed and the mudbog enters the creature's space. The creature takes 10 (3d6) acid damage. The engulfed creature can't breathe, is restrained, and takes 21 (6d6) acid damage at the start of each of the ooze's turns. When the mudbog moves, the engulfed creature moves with it.

An engulfed creature can try to escape by taking an action to make a DC13 Strength check. On a success, the creature escapes and enters a space of its choice within 5 feet of the ooze.

Ooze, Undead

This creature appears as a large, undulating mass of black goo from which rotted and broken bones protrude.

When an ooze moves across the grave of a restless and evil soul, a transformation takes place. The malevolent spirit, still tied to the rotting flesh consumed by the ooze, melds with the ooze. The result is a creature filled with hatred of the living and an intelligence and cunningness not normally known among its kind.

The undead ooze has an advantage over any other ooze: intelligence. It uses this new gift to its fullest in combat by attacking from surprise or by stalking its prey and attacking when the opportunity presents itself. The undead ooze attacks by slamming its body into its prey. It usually engulfs its foes or expels its skeleton allies to contend with its enemies.

Ooze, Undead

Huge undead, neutral evil
Armor Class 5
Hit Points 67 (9d12 + 9)
Speed 10 ft., fly 50 ft.

STR	DEX	CON	INT	WIS	CHA
12 (+1)	1 (–5)	13 (+1)	2 (–4)	12 (+1)	10 (+0)

Damage Immunities cold, necrotic, poison
Condition Immunities blinded, charmed, deafened,
  exhaustion, frightened, poisoned, prone
Senses blindsight 60 ft., passive Perception 11
Languages —
Challenge 5 (1,800 XP)

Amorphous. The ooze can move through a space as narrow as one inch without squeezing.

Ooze Mass. The ooze takes up most of its space. Other creatures can enter the space, but a creature that does so is subjected to the ooze's engulf and has disadvantage on the saving throw.

Creatures inside the ooze can be seen but have total cover.

A creature within 5 feet of the ooze can take an action to pull a creature or object out of the ooze. Doing so requires a successful DC 15 Strength check, and the creature making the attempt takes 9 (2d8) necrotic damage. If a skeleton is pulled out, it animates as if the skeletons ability was used.

Undeath. An undead ooze doesn't need air, food, drink, or sleep.

Actions

Pseudopod. Melee Weapon Attack: +4 to hit, reach 10 ft., one target. *Hit:* 14 (3d8 + 1) bludgeoning damage and 9 (2d8) necrotic damage.

Engulf. The ooze moves up to its speed. While doing so, it can enter Large or smaller creatures' spaces. Whenever the ooze enters a creature's space, the creature must make a DC 15 Dexterity saving throw.

On a successful save, the creature can choose to be pushed 5 feet back or to the side of the ooze. A creature that chooses not to be pushed suffers

Jelly, Mustard

This creature appears to be a yellowish-brown amoeba.

Mustard jelly appears to be a yellowish-brown form of the ochre jelly and is thought to be a distant relative of said creature. However, the mustard jelly is far more dangerous than its supposed relative because it is intelligent.

The mustard jelly gives off a faint odor of mustard plants to a range of 20 feet. Though it possesses intelligence, a mustard jelly cannot speak. A mustard jelly attacks by forming a pseudopod from its body and either slashing or enveloping its foes. Mustard jellies prefer to attack from ambush or where they have the upper hand on an opponent. If combat goes against a mustard jelly, it does not hesitate to flee, though often it uses this tactic to lure unsuspecting foes in closer.

A mustard jelly's natural weapons are treated as magic weapons for the purpose of overcoming damage reduction.

Mustard Jelly

Large ooze, unaligned

Armor Class 14 (natural armor)
Hit Points 136 (13d10 + 65)
Speed 30 ft.

STR	DEX	CON	INT	WIS	CHA
15 (+2)	10 (+0)	21 (+5)	10 (+0)	10 (+0)	10 (+0)

Skills Perception +6, Stealth +6
Damage Resistance cold
Damage Immunities force, lightning, poison
Condition Immunities blinded, charmed, deafened, exhaustion, frightened, poisoned
Senses blindsight 60 ft. (blind beyond this radius), passive Perception 16
Languages —
Challenge 6 (2,300 XP)

Amorphous. The jelly can move through a space as narrow as 1 inch wide without squeezing.

Energy Absorption. A mustard jelly is immune to force and lightning damage. If the jelly would have taken force or lightning damage, it is instead healed for the same amount it would have taken in damage.

Magic Weapons. The jelly's attacks are magical.

Spider Climb. The jelly can climb difficult surfaces, including upside down on ceilings, without needing to make an ability check.

Poison Aura. At the start of each of the jelly's turns, each creature within 10 feet of it takes 10 (3d6) poison damage. A creature that touches the jelly or hits it with a melee attack while within 5 feet of it takes 10 (3d6) poison damage.

Actions

Pseudopod. *Melee Weapon Attack:* +5 to hit, reach 5 ft., one target. *Hit:* 12 (3d6 + 2) bludgeoning damage and 10 (3d6) acid damage.

---

the consequences of a failed saving throw.

On a failed save, the ooze enters the creature's space, and the creature takes 18 (4d8) necrotic damage and is engulfed. The engulfed creature can't breathe, is restrained, and takes 27 (6d8) necrotic damage at the start of each of the ooze's turns. When the ooze moves, the engulfed creature moves with it.

An engulfed creature can try to escape by taking an action to make a DC 15 Strength check. On a success, the creature escapes and enters a space of its choice within 5 feet of the ooze.

Skeletons. An undead ooze can expel 1d6 skeletons from its mass, each appearing within 5 feet of the ooze. Skeletons can act in the round they are expelled. Slain skeletons are engulfed by the undead ooze and can be reanimated and expelled again in 1d2 hours. An undead ooze's form holds up to 10 skeletons of Medium size. These skeletons are included in the determination of the undead ooze's CR and experience points. They remain active even if the ooze is killed. Some undead oozes have unusual or larger skeletons inside of them.

Ophidian

This strange 6-foot-tall humanoid is covered with blue-green scales and its head is almost snake-like in appearance. It has no hair on its head or body. Where its hands should be are instead the snapping the heads of a cruel fanged vipers.

Common ophidians make up the bulk of the population in ophidian communities. They serve as the laborers, craftsmen, workers, citizens, guards, and militia. They initiate combat using their blinding spray to gain the advantage. Afterward, the creatures move in and attack with their snake-hands or weapons (if they happen to be wielding any).

Ophidian

Medium monstrosity, neutral evil
Armor Class 15 (natural armor)
Hit Points 32 (5d8 + 10)
Speed 30 ft.

STR	DEX	CON	INT	WIS	CHA
14 (+2)	17 (+3)	15 (+2)	12 (+1)	13 (+1)	12 (+1)

Skills Perception +3, Stealth +5
Damage Immunities poison
Senses darkvision 60 ft., passive Perception 13
Languages Common, Ophidian
Challenge 3 (700 XP)

Keen Smell. The ophidian has advantage on Wisdom (Perception) checks that rely on smell.

Actions

Snake Hands. *Melee Weapon Attack:* +5 to hit, reach 5 ft., one target. *Hit:* 7 (1d8 + 3) piercing damage, and the target must succeed on a DC 12 Constitution saving throw or be poisoned for 1 hour.

Blinding Spray. *(Recharge 5–6)*. The ophidian spews forth a 20-foot cone of viscous liquid. All creatures in this area must succeed on a DC 12 Dexterity saving or be blinded for 1 minute. The blinded target can repeat the saving throw at the end of each of its turns, ending the effect on itself on a success.

Orcs

Orc tribes are feared and reviled throughout the planes for their depravities and their penchant for destruction and mindless violence. The vast majority of orcs are easy enough to identify by their jutting jaw, yellowed tusks, squinting eyes and hairy, brutally muscular frames. Their skin color tends to run the gamut from blue-black to grey, with putrid slime-green being the most common. Many tribes of orcs, however, have adopted traits unique to their own species through interbreeding with other races, adaptation to climate and terrain, and the intervention of evil magicians or other-planar powers.

Orc, Black

This creature resembles a 7-foot-tall orc with bluish-black skin and red eyes.

Fully a head taller than an ordinary orc these foul brutes have been known to make other orcs cringe in fear. Unlike normal orcs, black orcs move in daylight as well as they do the darkness of their subterranean lairs (they do not have the light sensitivity penalty that normal orcs have).

Black orcs were taken in early ages by Orcus the Demon Lord of Undead and bred with demonic blood in a matter that would accommodate his diabolical needs. Black orcs refer to their dark master as "Old Man Death". These orcs fairly worship death and display the death's head prominently upon their standards and devices. They are often found in the service of necromancers and move easily in mixed groups of zombies, skeletons, and even ghouls.

Larger and more intelligent than their lesser kin, black orcs look down on other orc races as inferior to themselves. When forced to cooperate with other orc tribes in large forces black orcs consistently plot to overthrow the other tribe's chieftain and take command. This treachery is likely the reason there are so few bands of the black orc nation known to exist, as the infighting tends to keep their numbers down.

Black orcs stand 7 feet tall and weigh 200 to 280 pounds. Females tend to be about the same height, but are a bit lighter. Both males and females have blue-black skin with red eyes and more pronounced tusks than their smaller cousins.

Black orcs have a decent understanding of tactics. They are adept in the use of reach weapons such as longspears and glaives. Many of their number are proficient in the use of light crossbows. In melee, they prefer to gang up on powerful opponents and dispatch them quickly before moving on to lesser foes whenever possible. As they are often led by clerics and necromancers in the service of Orcus, they are likely to take prisoners if possible with the intent of sacrificing them to the Demon Lord of Undead at some future time.

Black Orc

Medium humanoid (black orc), chaotic evil
Armor Class 15 (scale mail)
Hit Points 16 (3d8 + 3)
Speed 30 ft.

STR	DEX	CON	INT	WIS	CHA
14 (+2)	12 (+1)	12 (+1)	9 (−1)	10 (+0)	9 (−1)

Skills Intimidation +3
Senses darkvision 60 ft., passive Perception 10
Languages Common, Orc
Challenge 1 (200 XP)

Blessing of Orcus. Black orcs have advantage on saving throws against the spells and effects of undead creatures.

Actions

Spear. *Melee or Ranged Weapon Attack:* +4 to hit, reach 5 ft. or range 20/60 ft., one target. *Hit:* 5 (1d6 + 2) piercing damage, or 6 (1d8 + 2) piercing damage when used with two hands to make a melee attack.

Light Crossbow. *Ranged Weapon Attack:* +3 to hit, range 80/320 ft., one target. *Hit:* 5 (1d8 + 1) piercing damage.

Black Orc Champion

Medium humanoid (black orc), chaotic evil
Armor Class 18 (plate)
Hit Points 97 (15d8 + 30)
Speed 30 ft.

STR	DEX	CON	INT	WIS	CHA
20 (+5)	14 (+2)	14 (+2)	9 (−1)	12 (+1)	18 (+4)

Saving Throws Wis +4, Cha +7

Skills Intimidation +7, Perception +4, Religion +2
Senses darkvision 60 ft., passive Perception 14
Languages Abyssal, Common, Orc
Challenge 7 (2,900 XP)

Blessing of Orcus. Black orcs have advantage on saving throws against the spells and effects of undead creatures.

Spellcasting. The black orc champion is a 7th level spellcaster. Its spellcasting ability is Charisma (spell save DC 15, +7 to hit with spell attacks). It has the following paladin spells prepared:

1st level (4 slots): *command, detect evil and good, false life, protection from evil and good, shield of faith*

2nd level (3 slots): *magic weapon, silence, protection from poison*

Unholy Strike. Once on each of the black orc champion's turns when it hits a creature with a weapon attack, the champion can cause the attack to deal an extra 13 (3d8) necrotic damage to the target.

Actions

Multiattack. The black orc champion makes two melee attacks.

Greatsword. *Melee Weapon Attack:* +8 to hit, reach 5 ft., one target. *Hit:* 12 (2d6 + 5) slashing damage.

Light Crossbow. *Ranged Weapon Attack:* +5 to hit, range 80/320 ft., one target. *Hit:* 6 (1d8 + 2) piercing damage.

Dreadful Glare (Recharges on a Short or Long Rest). Each enemy within 30 feet of the champion must succeed on a DC 15 Wisdom saving throw or drop whatever it is holding and become frightened for 1 minute. A frightened creature can repeat the saving throw on the end of each of its turns, ending the effect on a success.

Reactions

Parry. The black orc champion adds 3 to its AC against one melee attack that would hit it. To do so, the champion must see the attacker and be wielding a melee weapon.

Black Orc High Priest of Orcus

Medium humanoid (black orc), chaotic evil
Armor Class 16 (scale mail)
Hit Points 127 (15d8 + 60)
Speed 30 ft.

STR	DEX	CON	INT	WIS	CHA
16 (+3)	14 (+2)	18 (+4)	12 (+1)	20 (+5)	14 (+2)

Saving Throws Wis +9, Cha +6
Skills Arcana +5, Deception +6, Insight +9, Intimidation +6, Perception +9
Senses truesight 120 ft., passive Perception 19
Languages Abyssal, Common, Orc
Challenge 9 (5,000 XP)

Abyssal Blessing. The priest of Orcus gains 10 temporary hit points when it reduces a hostile creature that is not an undead to 0 hit points.

Blessing of Orcus. Black orcs have advantage on saving throws against the spells and effects of undead creatures.

Deadsight. The high priest of Orcus has truesight out to a range of 120 feet.

Spellcasting. The high priest of Orcus is a 10 level spellcaster. Its spellcasting ability is Wisdom (spell save DC 17, +9 to hit with spell attacks). It has the following cleric spells prepared:

Cantrips (at will): *chill touch, guidance, mending, resistance*

1st level (4 slots): *bane, cure wounds, false life, inflict wounds*

2nd level (3 slots): *aid, blindness/deafness, hold person, silence*

3rd level (3 slots): *animate dead, bestow curse, dispel magic, spirit guardians*

4th level (3 slots): *banishment, death ward, guardian of faith*

5th level (2 slots): *dispel evil and good, insect plague*

Unholy Strike. Once on each of the high priest's turns when it hits a creature with a weapon attack, the high priest can cause the attack to deal an extra 18 (4d8) necrotic damage to the target.

Actions

Multiattack. The high priest makes two melee attacks.

Mace. *Melee Weapon Attack:* +7 to hit, reach 5 ft., one target. *Hit:* 12 (2d8 + 3) bludgeoning damage.

Caress of Orcus (Recharge 5–6). *Melee Weapon Attack:* +7 to hit, reach 5 ft., one target. *Hit:* 12 (2d8 + 3) necrotic damage, and the target's Strength score is reduced by 1d4. The target dies if this reduces its Strength to 0. Otherwise, the reduction lasts until the target finishes a short or long rest.

If a non-evil humanoid dies from this attack, a shadow rises from the corpse in 24 hours under the priest's control, unless the humanoid is restored to life or its body is destroyed. The priest can have no more than three shadows under its control at one time.

Orc, Blood

This massive creature resembles a powerful orc with bestial jaws and oversized tusks. It wears black armor and carries a wicked greataxe caked in blood. Its armor and hair, like its weapon, is caked with dried blood.

Blood orcs are considered vicious killers even amongst other breeds of orcs. Distrusted in times of peace, their savage warriors are sought out in times of war for their brutality and ferocity. Blood orc bands decorate their standards and shields with the scalps and severed heads of opponents and are known to drink flagons of putrid blood before entering battle. Blood orcs always fight to the death, take few prisoners, and offer no quarter to their foes. Blood orcs have a special hatred for black orcs whom they see as traitors to the orcish god Grotaag.

A typical male blood orc stands over 6 feet tall and weighs around 200 pounds or more. Females tend to be slightly lighter and smaller. Blood orcs skin is dark reddish-black and their hair is black, dark brown, or crimson (rare, but it does occur). Eye color is always black. Blood orcs favor armor and clothes of black or dark red.

Skilled in combat, blood orcs are ruthless opponents, attacking with weapons and savage bite. They swarm foes and are known for assaulting the center of enemy forces, overbearing defenders with their brutal attacks. Their most common tactic is to form a shield wall with heavy wooden shields. The front rows of attackers break enemy lines with battleaxes while the rear ranks attack with longspears and glaives. Once melee is mixed and blood is in the air, the blood orcs drop both in favor of greataxes. When faced with magic-using opponents they spread themselves out to avoid being consumed by area of effect spells.

Blood Orc Society

Blood orcs are a primitive (even for orcs), barbaric race of people. Hunters and nomads by nature, they rarely settle in one place for long being always on the move following any source of food. Blood orc tribes and villages tend to congregate near one another for protection, food, and various other needs. Most tribes or villages also situate themselves near an abundant source of water. Other orc tribes avoid the blood orc nations, seeing them as savages and primitives. Trade between the blood orcs and other races is rare though blood orcs do tend to favor the company of gnolls, flinds, and hobgoblins (why, no one knows).

Each tribe or village is let by an elder warrior, a barbarian of great strength and power. Each tribe also includes at least a single shaman or witch doctor who tends to the wounded, predicts the future, and so on.

Blood Orc Elder Warrior

Medium humanoid (blood orc), chaotic evil
Armor Class 14 (chain shirt)
Hit Points 75 (10d8 + 30)
Speed 40 ft.

STR	DEX	CON	INT	WIS	CHA
21 (+5)	13 (+1)	16 (+3)	8 (−1)	6 (−2)	6 (−2)

Saving Throws Str +8, Con +6
Skills Intimidation +1, Perception +1, Survival +1
Senses darkvision 60 ft., passive Perception 11
Languages Common, Orc
Challenge 6 (2,300 XP)

Bloodfrenzy. When the blood orc begins its turn with half or fewer of its hit points, it can make a bite attack as a bonus action when it takes the attack action, it has advantage on Intelligence, Wisdom, and Charisma saving throws against spells and other effects, and the elder warrior has resistance to bludgeoning, piercing, and slashing damage.

Brute. A melee weapon deals one extra die of its damage when the elder warrior hits with it (included in the attack).

Actions

Multiattack. The elder warrior makes two melee attacks.

Bite. *Melee Weapon Attack:* +8 to hit, reach 5 ft., one target. *Hit:* 10 (2d4 + 5) piercing damage.

Greataxe. *Melee Weapon Attack:* +8 to hit, reach 5 ft., one target. *Hit:* 18 (2d12 + 5) slashing damage.

Terrorize (1/day). The elder warrior roars and displays its trophies, which are visible to all creatures within 30 feet that can see it. Creatures of the elder warrior's choice within that area must make a DC 16 Wisdom saving throw or be frightened of the warrior for 1 minute. While frightened, they are paralyzed. A frightened creature can repeat the saving throw at the end of each of its turns, ending the effect on a success.

Orc, Ghost-Faced

This creature looks like an orc whose face and head are painted in a grotesque skull-like pattern.

When they may be seen at all, ghost-faced orcs appear as normal orcs who paint their faces in grotesque skull like patterns. Invisible in shadow and darkness to all but one another due to unholy pacts with their dark god, their face paint gives them the impression of floating disembodied skulls.

Ghost-faced orcs are similar in every way to their common cousins — filthy, smelly, aggressive, and thoroughly cruel. Their hair ranges from black to slate grey to shock white. Their equipment is ill-kempt and crudely made, leaving most to forage for better gear amongst their victims. Ghost-face orcs are seldom seen above ground except on moonless nights.

Most are warriors, fighters or barbarians and favor greataxes and longspears to any other weapon. They on occasion carry shortbows for hunting or ambushes.

Ghost-Faced Orc Society

Ghost-faced orcs differ little from their kin with the exception that a larger portion of their population are clerics in service of Grotaag. As such these battle priests hold a revered place in society. The priesthood is referred to as the Ghost Face Cabal which is made up of the highest level clerics amongst the tribe. The cabals outfit themselves and their most powerful slayers with enchanted weapons, armor and potions.

Blood Orc

Medium humanoid (blood orc), chaotic evil
Armor Class 14 (chain shirt)
Hit Points 13 (2d8 + 4)
Speed 30 ft.

STR	DEX	CON	INT	WIS	CHA
15 (+2)	13 (+1)	14 (+2)	8 (−1)	6 (−2)	6 (−2)

Skills Intimidation +0
Senses darkvision 60 ft., passive Perception 8
Languages Common, Orc
Challenge ¼ (50 XP)

Bloodfrenzy. When the blood orc begins its turn with half or fewer of its hit points, it can make a bite attack as a bonus action when it takes the Attack action, and it has advantage on Intelligence, Wisdom, and Charisma saving throws against spells and other effects.

Actions

Bite. *Melee Weapon Attack:* +4 to hit, reach 5 ft., one target. *Hit:* 4 (1d4 + 2) piercing damage.

Greataxe. *Melee Weapon Attack:* +4 to hit, reach 5 ft., one target. *Hit:* 8 (1d12 + 2) slashing damage.

Ghost-Faced Orc

Medium humanoid (ghost-faced orc), chaotic evil
Armor Class 12 (leather)
Hit Points 9 (2d8)
Speed 30 ft.

STR	DEX	CON	INT	WIS	CHA
15 (+2)	12 (+1)	10 (+0)	7 (–2)	10 (+0)	6 (–2)

Skills Intimidation +0, Perception +2, Stealth +3 (+5 in dim light or darkness)
Senses darkvision 120 ft., passive Perception 12
Languages Common, Orc
Challenge ¼ (50 XP)

Shadow Stealth. When in dim light or darkness, the ghost-faced orc can Hide as a bonus action.

Actions

Greataxe. *Melee Weapon Attack:* +4 to hit, reach 5 ft., one target. *Hit:* 8 (1d12 + 2) slashing damage.

Shortbow. *Ranged Weapon Attack:* +3 to hit, range 80/320 ft., one target. *Hit:* 4 (1d6 + 1) piercing damage.

Ghost-Faced Battle Priest

Medium humanoid (ghost-faced orc), chaotic evil
Armor Class 15 (studded leather)
Hit Points 88 (16d8 + 16)
Speed 30 ft.

STR	DEX	CON	INT	WIS	CHA
17 (+3)	16 (+3)	12 (+1)	8 (–1)	20 (+5)	8 (–1)

Saving Throws Wis +8, Cha +2
Skills Intimidation +2, Perception +8, Religion +2, Stealth +6 (+9 in dim light or darkness)
Senses darkvision 120 ft., passive Perception 18
Languages Common, Orc
Challenge 8 (3,900 XP)

Shadow Stealth. When in dim light or darkness, the ghost-faced orc can Hide as a bonus action.

Spellcasting. The battle priest is a 9th level spellcaster. Its spellcasting ability is Wisdom (spell save DC 16, +8 to hit with spell attacks). It has the following cleric spells prepared:

Cantrips (at will): *chill touch, guidance, mending, resistance, thaumaturgy*

1st level (4 slots): *bane, command, cure wounds, inflict wounds, protection from evil and good*

2nd level (3 slots): *blindness/deafness, enhance ability, hold person, silence, spiritual weapon*

3rd level (3 slots): *bestow curse, dispel magic, protection from energy, spirit guardians*

4th level (3 slots): *banishment, death ward*

5th level (1 slot): *insect plague*

Actions

Multiattack. The battle priest makes two melee attacks.

Mace. *Melee Weapon Attack:* +6 to hit, reach 5 ft., one target. *Hit:* 12 (2d8 + 3) bludgeoning damage.

Reactions

Summon Demon (1/day). When the battle priest drops a hostile target to 0 hit points, the battle priest can attempt to summon a chaaor demon. It has a 45% chance of succeeding on this attempt. The summoned demon appears in an unoccupied space within 60 feet of the battle priest and can't summon other demons. It remains for 1 minute, until it or the battle priest is slain, or until the battle priest takes an action to dismiss it.

Orc, Greenskin

This creature looks like an ugly orc with green slime colored skin, small tusks, and canine-like eyes.

Wiry and quick, these slime-green orcs have long ears, smallish tusks, and coyote-like eyes. They shoot first and eat later.

Greenskins are a wicked orcish species of arboreal hunters. More stealthy and agile than their common cousins they are slighter of build but suffer no penalties from daylight or bright light. They are generally open and friendly to other evil humanoid races and often set up trade routes with said creatures. They make their homes among the dense foliage of the forest building their wooden huts from the trees and branches. Some tribes even build their entire village among the treetops (as a defense measure against land-based adversaries). Greenskin orcs stand about 6 feet tall. Females are slightly smaller. Hair color is always black or greenish-black.

Eye color varies but is usually dark brown, dark green, or occasionally deep, rich blue.

Greenskins are highly proficient in the use stealth and surprise, attacking with their ranged weapons when an enemy is sighted. They seek to disable and weaken foes with arrows before closing to finish the job with their wicked longswords.

Greenskin Orc Society

Greenskins tend to get along well with most other species of orcs being smart enough to take orders and wise enough to keep their mouths shut. They often serve roles in mixed tribes as scouts and skirmishers. Greenskins are mortal enemies of elves and the bane of fey and enchanted woodland creatures. They torture such beings mercilessly should they manage to take one alive. Despite their skill with the longbow, greenskin warriors are equally proficient with the longsword and hunting knife.

Greenskins tend to hunt in packs, using their scent ability to track their quarry. Their hunting packs are competitive with one another, each member seeking to be the one to make the kill. Greenskins are likely to have 1d2 trained worgs among them. Greenskin lairs often have as many as two dozen of these foul creatures living and sleeping amongst their masters filthy sleeping rags.

Greenskin tribes are known to hire themselves out to civilized masters as scouts and even irregular and regular missile units. They are also likely to serve evil druids and despotic ranger lords.

Greenskin Orc

Medium humanoid (greenskin orc), chaotic evil
Armor Class 13 (leather)
Hit Points 11 (2d8 + 2)
Speed 35 ft.

STR	DEX	CON	INT	WIS	CHA
15 (+2)	15 (+2)	12 (+1)	7 (−2)	10 (+0)	6 (−2)

Skills Intimidation +0, Perception +2, Stealth +4 (+6 in forests), Survival +2
Senses darkvision 60 ft., passive Perception 12
Languages Common, Orc
Challenge ¼ (50 XP)

Arboreal Hunter. The greenskin orc has advantage on Dexterity (Stealth) checks when in temperate or warm forests.

Actions

Longsword. *Melee Weapon Attack:* +4 to hit, reach 5 ft., one target. *Hit:* 6 (1d8 + 2) slashing damage or 7 (1d10 + 2) slashing damage when used with two hands.

Longbow. *Ranged Weapon Attack:* +4 to hit, range 150/600 ft., one target. *Hit:* 6 (1d8 + 2) piercing damage.

Greenskin Orc Elfhunter

Medium humanoid (greenskin orc), chaotic evil
Armor Class 17 (studded leather)
Hit Points 105 (14d8 + 42)
Speed 35 ft.

STR	DEX	CON	INT	WIS	CHA
17 (+3)	20 (+5)	15 (+2)	9 (−1)	14 (+2)	8 (−1)

Saving Throws Str +6, Dex +8
Skills Acrobatics +8, Intimidation +2, Nature +2, Perception +5, Stealth +8 (+11 in forests), Survival +5
Senses darkvision 60 ft., passive Perception 15
Languages Common, Elvish, Orc, Sylvan
Challenge 5 (1,800 XP)

Arboreal Hunter. The greenskin orc has advantage on Dexterity (Stealth) checks when in temperate or warm forests.

Favored Enemy. The elfhunter has advantage on Wisdom (Perception) and Wisdom (Survival) checks to track or notice any variety of elf or fey creature.

Forest Hunter. When the elfhunter hits a creature with a weapon attack, the creature takes an extra 3 (1d6) damage.

Land Stride. The elfhunter can move through nonmagical difficult terrain without using extra movement and can pass through nonmagical plants without being slowed by them and without taking damage from them even if they have thorns, spines, or a similar hazard.

Spellcasting. The elfhunter is an 8th level spellcaster. Its spellcasting ability is Wisdom (spell save DC 13, +5 to hit with spell attacks). It has the following ranger spells prepared:

1st level (4 slots): *cure wounds, detect magic, jump, longstrider*
2nd level (3 slots): *find traps, pass without trace, silence*

Actions

Multiattack. The green orc elfhunter makes two attacks with its longsword or two with its longbow.

Longsword. *Melee Weapon Attack:* +6 to hit, reach 5 ft., one target. *Hit:* 7 (1d8 + 3) slashing damage or 8 (1d10 + 3) slashing damage when used with two hands.

Longbow. *Ranged Weapon Attack:* +8 to hit, range 150/600 ft., one target. *Hit:* 9 (1d8 + 5) piercing damage.

Phasma

A floating semi-transparent humanoid dressed in grayish robes slowly moves toward you. Its face is either nonexistent or concealed behind a translucent gray mask. A faint pulsating white light surrounds its form.

A phasma is an undead creature spawned when a humanoid or monstrous humanoid fails its Fortitude saving throw against a phantasmal killer spell and dies as a result. Phasmas are extremely evil and highly aggressive with a hatred for living creatures (especially arcane spellcasters) that knows no bounds. A phasma is usually found haunting an area within 500 feet of where it was slain when it was alive. It is not bound to this area and may travel or move wherever it pleases, though for some reason, a phasma rarely leaves the area where it died.

A phasma feeds on the mental strength of living creatures. By sapping a foe's mental strength it weakens its mind, thereby opening it up to the true power of the phasma, the ability to kill an opponent the same way it died — by a phantasmal killer effect. Creatures slain are left where they fall: the phasma has no use for the opponent anymore.

A phasma appears as a 6-foot-tall incorporeal humanoid dressed in gray robes. A translucent and pale white light surrounds its entire body. A phasma speaks the same languages it did in life and Common (though it rarely engages in communication with living creatures, other than perhaps to hurl insults and curses at its opponents).

A phasma engages any living foe it encounters. It begins melee using its incorporeal touch in order to feed on an opponent's mental strength, often focusing its incorporeal touch on a different opponent each round. Once it feels it has weakened the will of its foes enough, it uses its phantasmagoria ability to try and kill its foes immediately.

Phasma

Medium undead, chaotic evil
Armor Class 15
Hit Points 117 (18d8 + 36)
Speed 0 ft., fly 40 ft. (hover)

STR	DEX	CON	INT	WIS	CHA
6 (−2)	20 (+5)	15 (+2)	15 (+2)	17 (+3)	20 (+5)

Damage Resistance acid, cold, fire, lightning, thunder; bludgeoning, piercing and slashing from nonmagical weapons that aren't silvered
Damage Immunities necrotic, poison
Condition Immunities charmed, exhaustion, frightened, grappled, paralyzed, petrified, poisoned, prone, restrained
Senses darkvision 60 ft., passive Perception 13
Languages the languages it knew in life
Challenge 15 (13,000 XP)

Innate Spellcasting. The phasma's spellcasting ability is Charisma (spell save DC 18, +10 to hit with spell attacks). It can innately cast the following spells, requiring no material components:

At will: *detect evil and good*
3/day each: *dispel magic, protection from evil and good*
1/day each: *banishment, (un)holy aura*

Flyby. The phasma doesn't provoke opportunity attacks when it flies out of an enemy's reach.

Incorporeal Movement. The phasma can move through other creatures and objects as if they were difficult terrain. It takes 5 (1d10) force damage if it ends its turn inside an object.

Sunlight Sensitivity. While in sunlight, the phasma has disadvantage on attack rolls, as well as on Wisdom (Perception) checks that rely on sight.

Actions

Multiattack. The phasma makes two phantom touch attacks.

Phantom Touch. *Melee Weapon Attack:* +10 to hit, reach 5 ft., one target. *Hit:* 41 (8d8 + 5) necrotic damage, and the target's Wisdom score is lowered by 1d6 and the phasma gains 5 temporary hit points. The target dies if this reduces its Wisdom to 0. Otherwise, the reduction lasts until the target finishes a long rest. In addition, the target must make a DC 18 Wisdom saving throw. On a failure, the target can't take reactions and must roll a d10 at the start of each of its turns to determine its behavior for that turn.

d10	Behavior
1	The creature uses all its movement to move in a random direction. To determine the direction, roll a d8 and assign a direction to each die face. The creature doesn't take an action this turn.
2–6	The creature doesn't move or take actions this turn.
7–8	The creature uses its action to make a melee attack against a randomly determined creature within its reach. If there is no creature within its reach, the creature does nothing this turn.
9–10	The creature can act and move normally.

At the end of each of its turns, the creature can repeat the saving throw, ending the effect on itself on a success.

Phantasmagoria (Recharge 6). The phasma taps into the nightmares of each creature it can see that is within 30 feet of it, creating an illusory manifestation of each target's deepest fears, visible only to that creature. Each creature must make a DC 18 Wisdom saving throw, taking 33 (6d10) psychic damage on a failed save, or half as much damage on a successful one. A creature that succeeds on the saving throw is immune to the phasma's Phantasmagoria for the next 24 hours.

Phlogiston Bush

This creature resembles a bush with silvery-green leaves and dark, twisted branches. The sweet smell of cinnamon lingers in the air around it. Four tendrils writhe and slash from its central form.

The phlogiston bush (known as a fire shrub by some sages) is an immobile plant found only in temperate regions. Phlogiston bushes gain nourishment from the body fluids and organs of living creatures, particularly the bones and muscle tissue of such creatures. Being plants, they do gain sustenance from sunlight and the soil, so they can go long periods of time (reportedly up to two weeks or so) without eating, but given the chance, a phlogiston bush catches and kills any living creature that wanders too close to it. These plants generate a pleasing odor noticeable to a range of about 30 feet. It uses this odor to lure semi-intelligent creatures (such as ordinary animals) into range where it can use its tendrils and fire bolt attack.

These plants rely on living creatures to spread, so on occasion, when not looking for a meal, a phlogiston bush releases a small blast of seedlings in a 5-foot cone directly in front of it. A creature in the area that fails a DC 15 Wisdom (Perception) check fails to observe that tiny seeds of silvery-green hue are clinging to its body. After 1d4 hours, the seedlings drop off and take root in the immediate area, blooming into a new phlogiston bush in just under 2 months.

A phlogiston bush lies dormant until unsuspecting prey comes within range. It then slashes with its tendrils or releases a single fire bolt at its opponent. In combat, the phlogiston bush attempts to grab its prey with a tendril. Grabbed prey is held until it escapes, dies, or the plant is killed. Creatures slain by a phlogiston bush are entwined in its tendrils and slowly digested over the next 6 to 8 hours until there is nothing left. (Digestive acids secreted from the plant break down the bones of the victim.) Being mindless, a phlogiston bush fights until either it or its prey is slain.

Phlogiston Bush

Medium plant, unaligned
Armor Class 13 (natural armor)
Hit Points 32 (5d8 + 10)
Speed 0 ft.

STR	DEX	CON	INT	WIS	CHA
17 (+3)	13 (+1)	14 (+2)	2 (–4)	12 (+1)	2 (–4)

Damage Resistances fire
Condition Immunities blinded, deafened
Senses blindsight 60 ft., passive Perception 11
Languages —
Challenge 2 (450 XP)

Death Throes. If a phlogiston bush is reduced to 0 or fewer hit points, it explodes in a concussive blast of fire in a 10-foot radius. All creatures within the area must make a DC 13 Dexterity saving throw, taking 17 (5d6) fire damage on a failed save, or half as much damage on a successful one.

Actions

Multiattack. The phlogiston bush makes two attacks with its tendrils.
Tendrils. *Melee Weapon Attack:* +5 to hit, reach 5 ft., one target. *Hit:* 17 (4d6 + 3) slashing damage.
Fire Bolt. *Ranged Weapon Attack:* +5 to hit, range 40 ft., one target. *Hit:* 10 (3d6) fire damage.

Phooka

These small hairy creatures resemble a cross between a goblin and a child's fuzzy play bear. They have wide-set glowing golden eyes and long pointed ears like those of a donkey. They have a mouth to match their ears, complete with buck teeth.

Phookas are tricksters and jokesters. They revel in playing tricks on unwary travelers, leading them on merry chases or getting them lost deep in the forest. They are not necessarily malicious though some phooka do lean towards evil and murder.

A phooka's trickery may include turning itself into an enchanted pony and offer a stranger a ride, only to lead it through brambles and thorns at top speed, or to lead travelers to enchanted springs that cause them to fall into a deep slumber and strip them of all their belongings and clothes, then leave behind clues as to where their possessions are hidden.

Phooka are deeply attuned to nature and animals and have a bond with their natural surroundings. If slain, all plant matter within one square mile of the phooka withers and dies.

A phooka stands about 3 feet.

Phooka

Small fey, chaotic neutral
Armor Class 14 (natural armor)
Hit Points 27 (6d6 + 6)
Speed 30 ft.

STR	DEX	CON	INT	WIS	CHA
10 (+0)	17 (+3)	12 (+1)	13 (+1)	15 (+2)	18 (+4)

Skills Perception +6, Stealth +5
Senses passive Perception 16
Languages Common, Sylvan
Challenge 2 (450 XP)

One with Nature. When a phooka is slain through violence, all plants within a 100-foot radius of where it fell die and no new ones grow naturally in that area for 1 year.

Tree Stride. Once on its turn, the phooka can use 10 feet of its movement to step magically into one living tree within its reach and emerge from a second living tree within 60 feet of the first tree, appearing in an unoccupied space within 5 feet of the second tree. Both trees must be Large or bigger.

Actions

Dagger. *Melee or Ranged Weapon Attack*: +5 to hit, reach 5 ft. or range 20/60 ft., one target. *Hit:* 5 (1d4 + 3) piercing damage.

Phycomid

A small blob of decomposing matter covers the ground. Several small mushrooms sprout from the patch.

A patch of phycomids is often found growing in garbage heaps, refuse, and other such places. A typical patch of phycomids covers an area of 2 feet. The actual number of mushroom-growths varies with the actual size of the patch. The mushroom caps are usually white, red, purple, or yellow in color, and the phycomid's body is milky white.

The phycomid attacks by extruding a small tube from its body and firing a glob of acid at a foe. The phycomid has a range increment of 5 feet and can fire a globule to a maximum range of 20 feet.

Phycomid

Small plant (fungus), unaligned
Armor Class 12 (natural armor)
Hit Points 27 (6d6 + 6)
Speed 10 ft.

STR	DEX	CON	INT	WIS	CHA
8 (−1)	10 (+0)	13 (+1)	2 (−4)	11 (+0)	1 (−5)

Skills Stealth +4
Damage Immunities fire, psychic
Condition Immunities frightened, prone, stunned, unconscious
Senses tremorsense 30 ft., passive Perception 10
Languages —
Challenge ½ (100 XP)

Actions

Fluid Globule. *Ranged Weapon Attack:* +2 to hit, range 20 ft., one target. *Hit:* 7 (2d6) acid damage.

Debilitating Spores (3/day). The phycomid ejects spores in a 10-foot radius. All creatures within this area must succeed a DC 13 Constitution saving throw, or take 10 (3d6) necrotic damage and have its hit point maximum reduced by an amount equal to the damage taken. The reduction lasts until the target finishes a long rest.

Quantum

This creature seems to have no true shape as its outline flickers and changes seemingly at random. At first, it appears to have four tentacles, then in a flicker, eight more appear and waver menacingly before shimmering once more out of existence. Its general shape is serpentine, with an uncertain number of tentacles dangling beneath it. The only constants are its six glowing eyes, three on each side of what must be its head.

The quantums hail from beyond and between all planes. The first quantum is said to have followed a lost band of adventurers back after they became lost on a planar journey.

A quantum exists simultaneously in many dimensions at once, which gives it a flickering, seemingly insubstantial shape as if some mad god is continually creating and re-creating it on a whim. If its form could somehow be stabilized into only three dimensions, a quantum would resemble a flattened jellyfish with a knob at the top containing six unblinking eyes. It has an oblong body with many tentacles radiating out from beneath its body. The exact number of tentacles cannot be known, however, since stabilizing a quantum's shape is a task yet to be undertaken and may not even be possible.

Quantums move by avoiding space entirely. A quantum hovers like some eerie jellyfish but doesn't fly by conventional means. Instead, a quantum actually teleports short distances faster than the eye can detect, and in this manner, it appears to be hovering. A quantum can also teleport across greater distances. At one moment a quantum can be in one space and then in an instant it is somewhere else, having never been at any point between. The flickering form of a quantum allows it to attack with one tentacle, two, six, or as many as it needs. Attack-capable limbs seem to manifest themselves as they are needed, then vanish again as if they had never existed.

A quantum lashes out at its foes with its tentacles. Against a particularly powerful opponent, it uses its disintegration attack. When facing multiple foes, a quantum uses its quantum form to better its odds or make its escape.

Quantum

Huge aberration, neutral
Armor Class 20 (natural armor)
Hit Points 448 (39d12 + 195)
Speed fly 40 ft.

STR	DEX	CON	INT	WIS	CHA
30 (+10)	18 (+4)	20 (+5)	11 (+0)	14 (+2)	17 (+3)

Saving Throws Wis +8, Cha +9
Skills Acrobatics +16, Insight +14, Perception +14, Religion +12
Damage Immunities bludgeoning, piercing, and slashing from nonmagical weapons
Senses darkvision 60 ft., passive Perception 24
Languages Common, Quantum
Challenge 20 (25,000 XP)

Displacement. The quantum projects a magical illusion that makes it appear to be standing near its actual location, causing attack rolls against it to have disadvantage. If it is hit by an attack, this trait is disrupted until the end of its next turn. This trait is also disrupted while the quantum is incapacitated or has a speed of 0.

Innate Spellcasting. The quantum's spellcasting ability is Charisma (spell save DC 17, +9 to hit with spell attacks). It can innately cast *dimension door* 1/day, requiring no material components.

Quantum Form (3/day). A quantum can move in such a way as to appear in two places at once, at a distance no greater than 30 feet. This is a bonus action that provokes an attack of opportunity and lasts only one round. While occupying two spaces simultaneously, each representation of the quantum can perform one action normally. Using this ability, the same quantum could attack two different opponents, or attack one opponent while opening a door to escape, and so on. At the end of the round, both instances of the quantum return to the space it originally occupied before activating this ability.

Actions

Multiattack. The quantum makes two attacks with its tentacles.

Tentacles. *Melee Weapon Attack:* +16 to hit, reach 15 ft., one target. *Hit:* 31 (6d6 + 10) bludgeoning damage.

Disintegration (3/day). *Melee Weapon Attack:* +16 to hit, reach 15 ft., one target. *Hit:* the target must make a DC 18 Constitution saving throw, taking 140 (40d6) force damage on a failed save, or 42 (12d6) force damage on a successful one. If the damage reduces the target to 0 hit points, it is disintegrated.

Raggoth

A sleek black-furred creature leaps from the underbrush, its gaping mouth showing a full allotment of sharpened fangs. It has a lupine head and six muscular legs. Its body is long and ends in a thick-furred tail.

Raggoths are aggressive predators with voracious appetites and a killing instinct that makes them quite deadly in battle. Though its hunting area typically covers only about a mile around its lair, raggoths are known to track their prey up to 10 or more miles. Whether this only occurs when food is scarce or if the raggoth simply hunts and tracks its prey for the sheer thrill of the hunt is unknown.

Raggoths, by their very nature, are solitary though sometimes they will work together to track down an elusive target or work together to bring down a particularly powerful opponent. Typically, two raggoths working in concert are a mated pair.

Raggoths dwell in thick forests and make their home amidst the foliage or in shallow caves and caverns. If a mated pair is encountered, there is a chance (40%) that 1d4 young are present. Young are born live and are fully dependent on their mother for the first year of their life. Around 12 to 18 months, they begin to gain their independence but do not fully leave the lair until they are around 2 years of age. A young raggoth reaches maturity around 4 years of age.

A raggoth is about 8 feet long and weighs about 450 pounds. Its fur is jet black, its nails and teeth are dull white, and its eyes are dull yellow.

Raggoths are ambush hunters and always use stealth tactics when hunting and tracking their prey. When spotted, a raggoth moves slowly toward its target and then quickly bursts from its hiding spot at its opponent. If the raggoth doesn't fell its opponent in the first round, it lets loose its tormenting howl to weaken its prey before attempting to finish it off with its terrible claws and bite. A raggoth fights to the death only if cornered or defending its lair.

Raggoth

Large monstrosity, neutral evil
Armor Class 17 (natural armor)
Hit Points 136 (13d10 + 65)
Speed 40 ft.

STR	DEX	CON	INT	WIS	CHA
22 (+6)	16 (+3)	20 (+5)	6 (–2)	12 (+1)	14 (+2)

Saving Throws Dex +6, Con +8
Skills Perception +4, Stealth +6
Damage Resistances bludgeoning, piercing, and slashing from nonmagical weapons
Senses darkvision 60 ft., passive Perception 14
Languages —
Challenge 8 (3,900 XP)
Keen Smell. The raggoth has advantage on Wisdom (Perception) checks that rely on smell.

Actions

Multiattack. The raggoth makes three attacks: one with its bite and two with its claws.

Bite. *Melee Weapon Attack:* +9 to hit, reach 5 ft., one target. *Hit:* 15 (2d8 + 6) piercing damage.

Claws. *Melee Weapon Attack:* +9 to hit, reach 5 ft., one target. *Hit:* 20 (4d6 + 6) slashing damage, and the target is grappled (escape DC 17) and restrained.

Tormenting Howl (Recharge 5–6). The raggoth unleashes a piercing howl. All creatures within 60 feet of the raggoth that can hear it must succeed on a DC 15 Wisdom saving throw or be frightened for 1 minute. A creature can repeat the saving throw at the end of each of its turns, ending the effect on itself on a success. If a creature's saving throw is successful or the effect ends for it, the creature is immune to the raggoth's Tormenting Howl for 24 hours.

Rakklethorn Toad

A cat-sized toad, about three feet long with dozens of small needlelike thorns protruding from its back, hops forth. Its mottled brown and green skin glistens with a dull sheen, while its gray eyes study knowingly.

Relatives of poisonous toads, rakklethorns live in small squiggles in murky swamps. Rakklethorn toad squiggles are fiercely territorial, and battles between them are frequent. Occasionally, however, the rakklethorn toads enter a mating frenzy. Several packs merge and form a great swarm of noisy frogs that sweeps through the marshes like a wave. After a mating frenzy, females release hundreds of jelly-like eggs into the waters. Of all those eggs, only a very small fraction live long enough to hatch into tadpoles.

A rakklethorn toad attacks by arching its back and firing a volley of thorns at an opponent. It rarely ever closes to melee, preferring to attack at range. If confronted in close quarters, a rakklethorn toad usually flees or if cornered, attacks with its bite.

Rakklethorn Toad

Small monstrosity, neutral

Armor Class 13 (natural armor)
Hit Points 13 (3d6 + 3)
Speed 20 ft.

STR	DEX	CON	INT	WIS	CHA
10 (+0)	15 (+2)	12 (+1)	2 (–4)	10 (+0)	6 (–2)

Damage Immunities poison
Condition Immunities poisoned
Senses darkvision 60 ft., passive Perception 10
Languages —
Challenge 1/2 (100 XP)

Keen Smell. The rakklethorn toad has advantage on Wisdom (Perception) checks that rely on smell.

Actions

Bite. *Melee Weapon Attack:* +4 to hit, reach 5 ft., one target. *Hit:* 4 (1d4 + 2) piercing damage.

Thorn Volley. *Ranged Weapon Attack:* +4 to hit, range 50 ft., one target. *Hit:* 5 (1d6 + 2) slashing damage, and the target must succeed on a DC 11 Constitution saving throw or become poisoned for 1 hour.

The Ravager

The Ravager was created eons ago by a primeval race of beings who believed in the unity of three forces: body, mind, and spirit. In their ongoing war with another race of savages, they created several weapons of terrible power. The greatest of these is the living beast known only as the Ravager.

This beast was given incredible vitality, and the power to manipulate its own body to assume a form most advantageous to it: a crawling weasel-like form that can burrow, a hulking apelike humanoid form with greater reach and strength, and a winged form to allow it greater mobility and agility.

After being used once or twice on the battlefield, those who created it realized its awesome danger and contained it in the strongest prison they could devise, suspended in time until it would once again be needed.

However, due to the subsequent influence of Orcus near the vault where the Ravager was contained, the wards were damaged, and a taint of evil infected its quarantine. This has resulted in it reproducing asexually and has granted the Ravager an astonishing capacity for growth. For every week that it lives, it permanently gains 1 hit die. There is no known limit to how far this advancement can go before it either devastates the planet it lives on or collapses under its own weight.

The Ravager (Crawler Form)

This enormous creature stands 18 feet high at the shoulders and has a body 30 feet long. Its body is long and narrow, with eight stubby legs ending in ebon claws the size of large falchions. Its mouth is filled with sharp black teeth, and its eyes are jet-black orbs the size of dinner platters, set above a delicate muzzle like that of a bulldog. The body is hairless, covered with a thick, leathery crimson hide.

The Ravager (Crawler Form)

Gargantuan monstrosity, neutral
Armor Class 27 (natural armor)
Hit Points 984 (48d20 + 480)
Speed 50 ft., burrow 20 ft.

STR	DEX	CON	INT	WIS	CHA
30 (+10)	23 (+6)	30 (+10)	6 (−2)	24 (+7)	23 (+6)

Saving Throws Dex +15, Con +19
Skills Perception +16
Damage Resistance acid, cold, fire, lightning, thunder; bludgeoning, piercing, and slashing from nonmagical weapons
Condition Immunities charmed, frightened, paralyzed, petrified, poisoned
Senses darkvision 120 ft., tremorsense 60 ft., passive Perception 26
Languages —
Challenge 30 (155,000 XP)

Charge. If the Ravager moves at least 20 feet straight toward a creature and then hits it with a claw attack on the same turn, the target must succeed on a DC 25 Strength saving throw or be knocked prone. If the target is prone, the Ravager can make one claw attack against it as a bonus action.

Form-Shifting. The Ravager can physically alter its physiology to take on one of the three listed forms: the crawler, the brawler, or the flier. Doing so takes one minute, and during this period it cannot take any other actions, though it is not considered incapacitated.

Improved Critical. The Ravager's bite and claws score a critical hit on a roll of 19 or 20.

Legendary Resistance (3/day). If the Ravager fails a saving throw, it can choose to succeed instead.

Magic Disruption. Every time the Ravager comes into contact with magical effects, there is a chance that it disrupts it. This effect functions as per the dispel magic spell cast using a 7th level spell slot with a +7 spell casting ability modifier.

Magic Weapons. The Ravager's melee attacks are magical.

Rampage. When the Ravager reduces a creature to 0 hit points with a melee attack on its turn, the Ravager can take a bonus action to move up to half its speed and make a bite attack.

Regeneration. The Ravager regains 15 hit points at the start of its turn. If the Ravager takes damage from an artifact or from a legendary action, this trait doesn't function at the start of the Ravager's next turn. The Ravager only dies if it starts its turn at 0 hit points and doesn't regenerate.

Tunneler. The Ravager can burrow through solid rock at half of its burrowing speed, leaving a 10 foot-wide, 16-foot-high tunnel in its wake.

Vampiric Healing. Whenever the Ravager hits with a melee attack, it regains hit points equal to half the damage it inflicts on its opponent, up to its hit point maximum.

Actions

Multiattack. The Ravager makes one bite and four claw attacks.

Bite. *Melee Weapon Attack:* +19 to hit, reach 10 ft., one target. *Hit:* 34 (7d6 + 10) piercing damage.

Claws. *Melee Weapon Attack:* +19 to hit, reach 15 ft., one target. *Hit:* 45 (10d6 + 10) slashing damage.

Legendary Actions

The Ravager can take 3 legendary actions, choosing from the options below. Only one legendary action option can be used at a time and only at the end of another creature's turn. The Ravager regains spent legendary actions at the start of its turn.

Attack. The Ravager makes one claw or bite attack.

Move. The Ravager moves up to half of its speed.

Charge. The Ravager charges at a target of its choice.

The Ravager (Brawler Form)

Towering 35 feet high is a massive, apelike creature, resting on two sets of powerfully muscled legs. A third set of arms, thick and corded with muscle, bulges out from its massive shoulders, ending with massive black claws. The mouth is filled with jagged black teeth, and glistening black eyes are set over a wide muzzle. Its skin is deep red, somewhat lighter on the underbelly.

The Ravager (Brawler Form)

Gargantuan monstrosity, neutral

Armor Class 27 (natural armor)
Hit Points 738 (36d20 + 360)
Speed 70 ft.

STR	DEX	CON	INT	WIS	CHA
30 (+10)	23 (+6)	30 (+10)	6 (–2)	24 (+7)	23 (+6)

Saving Throws Dex +15, Con +19
Skills Perception +16
Damage Resistance acid, cold, fire, lightning, thunder; bludgeoning, piercing, and slashing from nonmagical weapons
Condition Immunities charmed, frightened, paralyzed, petrified, poisoned
Senses darkvision 120 ft., tremorsense 60 ft., passive Perception 26
Languages —
Challenge 30 (155,000 XP)

Charge. If the Ravager moves at least 20 feet straight toward a creature and then hits it with a claw attack on the same turn, the target must succeed on a DC 25 Strength saving throw or be knocked prone. If the target is prone, the Ravager can make one claw attack against it as a bonus action.

Form-Shifting. The Ravager can physically alter its physiology to take on one of the three listed forms: the crawler, the brawler, or the flier. Doing so takes one minute, and during this period it cannot take any other actions, though it is not considered incapacitated.

Improved Critical. The Ravager's bite and claws score a critical hit on a roll of 19 or 20.

Legendary Resistance (3/day). If the Ravager fails a saving throw, it can choose to succeed instead.

Magic Disruption. Every time the Ravager comes into contact with magical effects, there is a chance that it disrupts it. This effect functions as per the dispel magic spell cast using a 7th level spell slot with a +7 spellcasting ability modifier.

Magic Weapons. The Ravager's melee attacks are magical.

Rampage. When the Ravager reduces a creature to 0 hit points with a melee attack on its turn, the Ravager can take a bonus action to move up to half its speed and make a bite attack.

Regeneration. The Ravager regains 15 hit points at the start of its turn. If the Ravager takes damage from an artifact or from a legendary action, this trait doesn't function at the start of the Ravager's next turn. The Ravager only dies if it starts its turn at 0 hit points and doesn't regenerate.

Tunneler. The Ravager can burrow through solid rock at half of its burrowing speed, leaving a 10 foot-wide, 16-foot-high tunnel in its wake.

Vampiric Healing. Whenever the Ravager hits with a melee attack, it regains hit points equal to half the damage it inflicts on its opponent, up to its hit point maximum.

Actions

Multiattack. The Ravager makes one bite and four claw attacks. It can also make a smash attack if it is grappling a creature.

Bite. *Melee Weapon Attack:* +19 to hit, reach 15 ft., one target. *Hit:* 34 (7d6 + 10) piercing damage.

Claws. *Melee Weapon Attack:* +19 to hit, reach 15 ft.,

one target. *Hit:* 45 (10d6 + 10) slashing damage and the target is grappled (Escape DC 23). Until this grapple ends, the creature is restrained.

Smash. If a target is grappled at the beginning of its turn, the Ravager may smash it into the ground for 37 (6d8 + 10) bludgeoning damage.

Legendary Actions

The Ravager can take 3 legendary actions, choosing from the options below. Only one legendary action option can be used at a time and only at the end of another creature's turn. The Ravager regains spent legendary actions at the start of its turn.

Attack. The Ravager makes one claw or bite attack.
Move. The Ravager moves up to half of its speed.
Charge. The Ravager charges at a target of its choice.

The Ravager (Flier Form)

With a crack and boom, this creature spreads a pair of great leathery wings over 50 feet in span. Its body is lean and covered with rippling muscle beneath a thick, leathery crimson hide. Its claws and teeth are black, as are its eyes.

The Ravager (Flier Form)

Gargantuan monstrosity, neutral
Armor Class 27 (natural armor)
Hit Points 738 (36d20 + 360)
Speed 20 ft., fly 140 ft.

STR	DEX	CON	INT	WIS	CHA
30 (+10)	30 (+10)	30 (+10)	6 (−2)	24 (+7)	23 (+6)

Saving Throws Dex +19, Con +19
Skills Perception +16
Damage Resistance acid, cold, fire, lightning, thunder; bludgeoning, piercing, and slashing from nonmagical weapons
Condition Immunities charmed, frightened, paralyzed, petrified, poisoned
Senses darkvision 120 ft., tremorsense 60 ft., passive Perception 26
Languages —
Challenge 30 (155,000 XP)

Charge. If the Ravager moves at least 20 feet straight toward a creature and then hits it with a claw attack on the same turn, the target must succeed on a DC 25 Strength saving throw or be knocked prone. If the target is prone, the Ravager can make one claw attack against it as a bonus action.

Flyby. The Ravager doesn't provoke an opportunity attack when it flies out of an enemy's reach.

Form-Shifting. The Ravager can physically alter its physiology to take on one of the three listed forms: the crawler, the brawler, or the flier. Doing so takes one minute, and during this period it cannot take any other actions, though it is not considered incapacitated.

Improved Critical. The Ravager's bite and claws score a critical hit on a roll of 19 or 20.

Legendary Resistance (3/day). If the Ravager fails a saving throw, it can choose to succeed instead.

Magic Disruption. Every time the Ravager comes into contact with magical effects, there is a chance that it disrupts it. This effect functions as per the dispel magic spell cast using a 7th level spell slot with a +7 spellcasting ability modifier.

Magic Weapons. The Ravager's melee attacks are magical.

Rampage. When the Ravager reduces a creature to 0 hit points with a melee attack on its turn, the Ravager can take a bonus action to move up to half its speed and make a bite attack.

Regeneration. The Ravager regains 15 hit points at the start of its turn. If the Ravager takes damage from an artifact or from a legendary action, this trait doesn't function at the start of the Ravager's next turn. The Ravager only dies if it starts its turn at 0 hit points and doesn't regenerate.

Tunneler. The Ravager can burrow through solid rock at half of its burrowing speed, leaving a 10 foot-wide, 16-foot-high tunnel in its wake.

Vampiric Healing. Whenever the Ravager hits with a melee attack, it regains hit points equal to half the damage it inflicts on its opponent, up to its hit point maximum.

Actions

Multiattack. The Ravager makes one bite and four claw attacks.
Bite. *Melee Weapon Attack:* +19 to hit, reach 15 ft., one target. *Hit:* 34 (7d6 + 10) piercing damage.
Claws. *Melee Weapon Attack:* +19 to hit, reach 15 ft., one target. *Hit:* 45 (10d6 + 10) slashing damage.

Legendary Actions

The Ravager can take 3 legendary actions, choosing from the options below. Only one legendary action option can be used at a time and only at the end of another creature's turn. The Ravager regains spent legendary actions at the start of its turn.

Attack. The Ravager makes one claw or bite attack.
Move. The Ravager moves up to half of its speed.
Charge. The Ravager charges at a target of its choice.

Ravager Spawn (Crawler Form)

Ravager Spawn (Crawler Form)

Huge monstrosity, neutral
Armor Class 25 (natural armor)
Hit Points 558 (36d12 + 324)
Speed 40 ft., burrow 10 ft.

STR	DEX	CON	INT	WIS	CHA
27 (+8)	20 (+5)	29 (+9)	5 (−3)	24 (+7)	18 (+4)

Saving Throws Dex +12, Con +16
Skills Perception +14
Damage Resistance acid, cold, fire, lightning, thunder; bludgeoning, piercing, and slashing from nonmagical weapons
Condition Immunities charmed, frightened, paralyzed, petrified, poisoned
Senses darkvision 120 ft., tremorsense 60 ft., passive Perception 24
Languages —
Challenge 23 (50,000 XP)

Charge. If the Ravager moves at least 20 feet straight toward a creature and then hits it with a claw attack on the same turn, the target must succeed on a DC 25 Strength saving throw or be knocked prone. If the target is prone, the Ravager can make one claw attack against it as a bonus action.

Form-Shifting. The Ravager can physically alter its physiology to take on one of the three listed forms: the crawler, the brawler, or the flier. Doing so takes one minute, and during this period it cannot take any other actions, though it is not considered incapacitated.

Improved Critical. The Ravager's bite and claws score a critical hit on a roll of 19 or 20.

Legendary Resistance (3/day). If the Ravager fails a saving throw, it can choose to succeed instead.

Magic Disruption. Every time the Ravager comes into contact with magical effects, there is a chance that it disrupts it. This effect functions as per the dispel magic spell cast using a 5th level spell slot with a +5 spellcasting ability modifier.

Magic Weapons. The Ravager's melee attacks are magical.

Rampage. When the Ravager reduces a creature to 0 hit points with a melee attack on its turn, the Ravager can take a bonus action to move up to half its speed and make a bite attack.

Regeneration. The Ravager regains 10 hit points at the start of its turn. If the Ravager takes damage from an artifact or from a legendary action, this trait doesn't function at the start of the Ravager's next turn. The Ravager only dies if it starts its turn at 0 hit points and doesn't regenerate.

Tunneler. The Ravager can burrow through solid rock at half of its burrowing speed leaving a 10 foot-wide, 16-foot-high tunnel in its wake.

Vampiric Healing. Whenever the Ravager hits with a melee attack, it regains hit points equal to half the damage it inflicts on its opponent, up to its hit point maximum.

Actions

Multiattack. The Ravager makes one bite and four claw attacks.

Bite. *Melee Weapon Attack:* +15 to hit, reach 15 ft., one target. *Hit:* 29 (6d6 + 8) piercing damage.

Claws. *Melee Weapon Attack:* +15 to hit, reach 15 ft., one target. *Hit:* 36 (8d6 + 8) slashing damage.

Ravager Spawn (Brawler Form)

This represents the Ravager soon after it is generated and before it has grown to its much more powerful form.

Ravager Spawn (Brawler Form)

Huge monstrosity, neutral
Armor Class 24 (natural armor)
Hit Points 450 (36d12 + 216)
Speed 50 ft.

STR	DEX	CON	INT	WIS	CHA
30 (+10)	20 (+5)	23 (+6)	5 (−3)	24 (+7)	18 (+4)

Saving Throws Dex +12, Con +13
Skills Perception +14
Damage Resistance acid, cold, fire, lightning, thunder; bludgeoning, piercing, and slashing from nonmagical weapons
Condition Immunities charmed, frightened, paralyzed, petrified, poisoned
Senses darkvision 120 ft., tremorsense 60 ft., passive Perception 24
Languages —
Challenge 23 (50,000 XP)

Charge. If the Ravager moves at least 20 feet straight toward a creature and then hits it with a claw attack on the same turn, the target must succeed on a DC 25 Strength saving throw or be knocked prone. If the target is prone, the Ravager can make one claw attack against it as a bonus action.

Form-Shifting. The Ravager can physically alter its physiology to take on one of the three listed forms: the crawler, the brawler, or the flier. Doing so takes one minute, and during this period it cannot take any other actions, though it is not considered incapacitated.

Improved Critical. The Ravager's bite and claws score a critical hit on a roll of 19 or 20.

Legendary Resistance (3/day). If the Ravager fails a saving throw, it can choose to succeed instead.

Magic Disruption. Every time the Ravager comes into contact with magical effects, there is a chance that it disrupts it. This effect functions as per the dispel magic spell cast using a 5th level spell slot with a +5 spellcasting ability modifier.

Magic Weapons. The Ravager's melee attacks are magical.

Rampage. When the Ravager reduces a creature to 0 hit points with a melee attack on its turn, the Ravager can take a bonus action to move up to half its speed and make a bite attack.

Regeneration. The Ravager regains 10 hit points at the start of its turn. If the Ravager takes damage from an artifact or from a legendary action, this trait doesn't function at the start of the Ravager's next turn. The Ravager only dies if it starts its turn at 0 hit points and doesn't regenerate.

Tunneler. The Ravager can burrow through solid rock at half of its burrowing speed leaving 10 foot-wide, 16-foot-high tunnel in its wake.

Vampiric Healing. Whenever the Ravager hits with a melee attack, it regains hit points equal to half the damage it inflicts on its opponent, up to its hit point maximum.

Actions

Multiattack. The Ravager makes one bite and four claw attacks. It can also make a smash attack if it is grappling a creature.

Bite. *Melee Weapon Attack:* +17 to hit, reach 10 ft., one target. *Hit:* 31 (6d6 + 10) piercing damage.

Claws. *Melee Weapon Attack:* +17 to hit, reach 15 ft., one target. *Hit:* 38 (8d6 + 10) slashing damage and the target is grappled (Escape DC 21).

Smash. If a target is grappled at the beginning of its turn, the Ravager may smash it into the ground, doing 31 (6d6 + 10) bludgeoning damage.

Ravager Spawn (Flier Form)

This represents the Ravager soon after it is generated and before it has grown to its much more powerful form.

Ravager Spawn (Flier Form)

Huge monstrosity, neutral
Armor Class 26 (natural armor)
Hit Points 450 (36d12 + 216)
Speed 20 ft., fly 100 ft.

STR	DEX	CON	INT	WIS	CHA
27 (+8)	25 (+7)	23 (+6)	5 (−3)	24 (+7)	18 (+4)

Saving Throws Dex +14, Con +13
Skills Perception +14
Damage Resistance acid, cold, fire, lightning, thunder; bludgeoning, piercing, and slashing from nonmagical weapons
Condition Immunities charmed, frightened, paralyzed, petrified, poisoned
Senses darkvision 120 ft., tremorsense 60 ft., passive Perception 24
Languages —
Challenge 22 (41,000 XP)

Charge. If the Ravager moves at least 20 feet straight toward a creature and then hits it with a claw attack on the same turn, the target must succeed on a DC 25 Strength saving throw or be knocked prone. If the target is prone, the Ravager can make one claw attack against it as a bonus action.

Flyby. The Ravager doesn't provoke an opportunity attack when it flies out of an enemy's reach.

Form-Shifting. The Ravager can physically alter its physiology to take on one of the three listed forms: the crawler, the brawler, or the flier. Doing so takes one minute, and during this period it cannot take any other actions, though it is not considered incapacitated.

Improved Critical. The Ravager's bite and claws score a critical hit on a roll of 19 or 20.

Legendary Resistance (3/day). If the Ravager fails a saving throw, it can choose to succeed instead.

Magic Disruption. Every time the Ravager comes into contact with magical effects, there is a chance that it disrupts it. This effect functions as per the dispel magic spell cast using a 5th level spell slot with a +5 spellcasting ability modifier.

Magic Weapons. The Ravager's melee attacks are magical.

Rampage. When the Ravager reduces a creature to 0 hit points with a melee attack on its turn, the Ravager can take a bonus action to move up to half its speed and make a bite attack.

Regeneration. The Ravager regains 10 hit points at the start of its turn. If the Ravager takes damage from an artifact or from a legendary action, this trait doesn't function at the start of the Ravager's next turn. The Ravager only dies if it starts its turn at 0 hit points and doesn't regenerate.

Tunneler. The Ravager can burrow through solid rock at half of its burrowing speed leaving a 10 foot-wide, 16-foot-high tunnel in its wake.

Vampiric Healing. Whenever the Ravager hits with a melee attack, it regains hit points equal to half the damage it inflicts on its opponent, up to its hit point maximum.

Actions

Multiattack. The Ravager makes one bite and four claw attacks.

Bite. *Melee Weapon Attack:* +15 to hit, reach 15 ft., one target. *Hit:* 29 (6d6 + 8) piercing damage.

Claws. *Melee Weapon Attack:* +15 to hit, reach 15 ft., one target. *Hit:* 36 (8d6 + 8) slashing damage.

Reigon

This powerful creature resembles a gorilla with thick, brownish-black fur. Its face is white and its eyes are brown. Its mouth is lined with rows of sharp teeth with the canines being slightly longer than the rest. Its hands end in wickedly sharp black nails.

A reigon is an aggressive predatory biped that dwells in dark forests away from general civilization, but not so far away that a small band of these creatures can't go out hunting in the night hours. A reigon's diet consists of berries, plants, forest game (both large and small), and sometimes humanoids (particularly if a supply, such as a small town or village, is readily available).

Reigons are tribal, territorial, and never associate with creatures outside their own tribe or family (including other reigons). If two reigon tribes move into the same area, a small war usually ensues with the victor claiming rights to the area and any survivors of the defeated side moving on to greener pastures. If a common threat presents itself, however, reigon tribes will band together in order to remove said threat before each tribe goes its own way.

A reigon tribe makes its home in thickly wooded areas usually well-hidden and out of the way, but fairly close to a natural source of water. Once seated, a tribe rarely moves, unless a new tribe moves into the area and forces them to flee or food and water become extremely scarce. Reigon lairs are simple wooden structures covered with bark, cloth, leaves, and vines.

A reigon stands about 8 feet tall and weighs around 600 pounds. Its entire body, save for its face and palms are covered in thick fur. A reigon generally lives for about 40 years, with young reaching maturity around 4 to 6 years of age.

Reigons speak their own guttural language consisting of grunts, growls, and howls.

Reigons attack from ambush, using their chameleon psi-like ability to hide and wait for their targets to wander close by. Once in range, a reigon leaps to the attack, slashing and biting with its claws (though occasionally, a reigon employs a club). If an opponent isn't killed immediately it is assaulted in the following rounds by a barrage of psi-like abilities, most notably a reigon's mind thrust or concussion blast.

Slain prey is dragged or carried back to the reigon's lair and either stored for later consumption or distributed among the other reigon's in the lair.

Reigon

Large monstrosity (psionic), chaotic evil
Armor Class 14 (natural armor)
Hit Points 59 (7d10 + 21)
Speed 30 ft., climb 30 ft.

STR	DEX	CON	INT	WIS	CHA
19 (+4)	15 (+2)	16 (+3)	17 (+3)	12 (+1)	10 (+0)

Skills Perception +3, Stealth +4
Senses darkvision 120 ft., passive Perception 13
Languages Reigon
Challenge 3 (700 XP)

Chameleon. Whenever the reigon takes the hide action, it has advantage on Dexterity (Stealth) checks as it uses psionic illusions to assist its attempt. Creatures with truesight automatically notice the reigon while it attempts to hide.

Keen Smell. The reigon has advantage on Wisdom (Perception) checks that rely on smell.

Actions

Multiattack. The reigon makes one bite attack, and two greatclub attacks or two claw attacks.

Bite. *Melee Weapon Attack:* +6 to hit, reach 10 ft., one target. *Hit:* 13 (2d8 + 4) piercing damage.

Claws. *Melee Weapon Attack:* +6 to hit, reach 10 ft., one target. *Hit:* 11 (2d6 + 4) slashing damage.

Greatclub. *Melee Weapon Attack:* +6 to hit, reach 10 ft., one target. *Hit:* 13 (2d8 + 4) bludgeoning damage.

Mindthrust (1/day). One creature the reigon can see within 60 feet of it must make a DC 13 Intelligence saving throw. On a failed saving throw, the target takes 25 (4d10 + 3) psychic damage, or half as much damage on a successful saving throw.

Concussion Blast (1/day). The reigon releases a blast of psionic force in a 15-foot cone. Creatures in the area must make a DC 13 Constitution saving throw. On a failed saving throw, the target takes 21 (4d8 + 3) force damage and is stunned until the end of their next turn. On a successful saving throw, the target takes half damage and is not stunned.

Reliquary Guardian

A 12-foot-tall statue of exquisite craftsmanship, a pair of finely carved wings folded over its back, holds a large greatsword over an altar to ancient gods before it.

Reliquary guardians are constructs found guarding the bones of saints or protecting religious icons and relics against would-be thieves or plunderers. They stand unmoving unless activated by intrusion into their protected sanctuary by unbelievers. At this time they activate and reap great ruin upon foes with divine magic and deadly blows from their weapon or fists.

Reliquary guardians are aligned with the faith of their creator. All weapons and spells used are thus aligned accordingly whether on the law-chaos axis, the good-evil axis, or both. There are no true neutral aligned reliquary guardians known to exist.

Imbued with a spark of intellect by the deity involved in their creation, reliquary guardians may travel great distances and even seek to cross into other planes of existence in order to retrieve the icons placed in their protection. They may possibly enlist the aid of heroes in their quest to return certain relics to their rightful sanctuary.

A reliquary guardian stands 12 feet tall and weighs 5,000 pounds. It speaks Common, and at least one other language (Abyssal or Infernal if evil-aligned or Celestial if good-aligned).

A reliquary guardian begins combat by making a pronouncement against its foes. Those that survive or manage to escape it relatively unharmed are assaulted by a barrage of spell-like abilities and repeated blows by the reliquary guardian's mighty greatsword.

Reliquary Guardian

Large construct, lawful evil

Armor Class 19 (natural armor)
Hit Points 170 (20d10 + 60)
Speed 30 ft., fly 60 ft.

STR	DEX	CON	INT	WIS	CHA
19 (+4)	12 (+1)	17 (+3)	10 (+0)	17 (+3)	21 (+5)

Skills Perception +7
Damage Immunities bludgeoning, piercing, and slashing from nonmagical weapons that aren't adamantine
Condition Immunities charmed, exhaustion, frightened, paralyzed, petrified, poisoned
Senses darkvision 60 ft., passive Perception 17
Languages speaks and understands the languages of its creator
Challenge 12 (8,400 XP)

Divine Blessing. The reliquary guardian deals an additional 14 (4d6) damage with its weapon attacks, included below. This damage is either radiant, if lawfully aligned, or necrotic, if chaotically aligned.

Immutable Form. The reliquary guardian is immune to any spell or effect that would alter its form.

Innate Spellcasting. The reliquary guardian's innate spellcasting ability is Charisma (spell save DC 17, +9 to hit with spell attacks). It can innately cast the following spells, requiring no material components:

At will: *chill touch* (17th level, if chaotically aligned), *protection from evil and good, sacred flame* (17th level, if lawfully aligned)

3/day each: *lightning bolt, flame strike* (deals necrotic instead of radiant if chaotically aligned), *spirit guardians, spiritual weapon*

1/day each: *commune, dispel evil and good, dispel magic*

Magic Resistance. The reliquary guardian has advantage on saving throws against spells and other magical effects.

Magic Weapons. The reliquary guardian's weapon attacks are magical.

Actions

Multiattack. The reliquary guardian makes two attacks with either its greatsword or its slam attack.

Greatsword. *Melee Weapon Attack:* +8 to hit, reach 10 ft., one target. *Hit:* 18 (4d6 + 4) slashing damage and 14 (4d6) necrotic or radiant damage.

Slam. *Melee Weapon Attack:* +8 to hit, reach 10 ft., one target. *Hit:* 22 (4d8 + 4) bludgeoning damage and 14 (4d6) necrotic or radiant damage.

Pronouncement (1/day). All creatures within 120 feet of the reliquary guardian that can hear it must succeed on a DC 17 Wisdom saving throw. On a failed saving throw, the target takes 66 (12d10) thunder damage and is stunned for 1 minute. On a successful saving throw, the target takes half damage and is not stunned. A stunned creature can repeat the saving throw at the end of each of its turns, ending the effect on a success.

Retch Hound

This large, muscular dog has sickly brownish-yellow fur, matted or torn in places. Small sores cover its body, each oozing a thick, yellowish-green liquid. Its mouth is filled with long, pointed yellow teeth, some broken off on the ends. Most disturbingly, it has four large yellow eyes evenly aligned across its canine head.

Retch hounds are large, yellowish, sickly looking hounds, about the size of war dogs. They are highly aggressive and powerfully built carnivores that love the taste of human flesh and bones. Their appearance lends to the façade of a sickly dog, which sometimes works to the retch hound's advantage when hunting its prey.

Retch hounds are often found in the service of powerful fighters and warriors, who use the dogs to guard prisoners, lead hunting expeditions, and perform other such services. A retch hound is only as loyal to its master as it has to be to ensure its own survival. While the dog won't necessarily seek escape at the earliest possible time, it often turns on its master at some point. Retch hounds raised in captivity are often more loyal to their masters than those captured in the wild. A typical retch hound stands 4 to 4½ feet tall at the shoulder and weighs about 150 pounds.

Retch hounds hunt their prey in packs. Using an eerie howl, they seem to coordinate and communicate with one another during these hunts. A favored tactic of a retch hound pack is to encircle a foe and then hit it from all sides at once. Usually, the largest hound in the pack is the leader. When slain, a retch hound melts into a pile of stinking and bubbling slime.

Retch Hound

Medium monstrosity, neutral evil
Armor Class 15 (natural armor)
Hit Points 45 (7d8 + 14)
Speed 40 ft.

STR	DEX	CON	INT	WIS	CHA
14 (+2)	15 (+2)	15 (+2)	5 (–3)	12 (+1)	4 (–3)

Skills Perception +5
Damage Immunities acid, poison
Condition Immunities poisoned
Senses darkvision 60 ft., passive Perception 15
Languages —
Challenge 3 (700 XP)

Keen Senses. The retch hound has advantage on Wisdom (Perception) checks that rely on hearing, sight, or smell.

Pack Tactics. Retch hounds have advantage on an attack roll against a creature if at least one of the hound's allies is within 5 feet of the creature and the ally isn't incapacitated.

Actions

Bite. *Melee Weapon Attack:* +4 to hit, reach 5 ft., one target. *Hit:* 9 (2d6 + 2) piercing damage plus 7 (2d6) acid damage.

Retch (Recharge 5–6). The retch hound exhales acidic bile in a 15-foot cone. Each creature in that area must make a DC 12 Dexterity saving throw, taking 21 (6d6) acid damage on a failed save, or half as much on a successful one.

Revenant, Hybrid

The thing stirs, revealing itself to be a rotting, skeletal humanoid but with several obviously animal bones in place of its normal skeleton, including the frightening visage of a great wolf's skull.

When a humanoid soul dies in especial rage, torment, and injustice, it is known that such spirits sometimes return to seek vengeance. Such vengeance can take many forms, but one of the most wretched of these is the hybrid revenant. It is believed that hybrid revenants occur when two or more creatures, at least one of them humanoid, die on the same spot, in similar throes of torment, at any time within a decade or so of one another. While the first soul's will to rise was not enough on its own, the addition of a second or third like-minded victim is enough in aggregate for a single, hybrid, undead body to rise.

However, such an unnatural merging, born always of mind-shattering torment, sears the mind of the newly risen undead, and it no longer remembers clearly what happened to it or how to achieve the justice it craves. In unending, hellish agony, the hybrid revenant wanders the land, howling out the horror of its unnatural existence and tainting all it passes with the corruption of its despair. A hybrid revenant attacks only in self defense, but it howls whenever it witnesses the meaningless suffering it has unwittingly caused, and it has no control over its explosive despair. If the humanoid portion of the entity is helped to find clarity and peace, the animal portion will naturally pass on as well.

A hybrid revenant usually resembles a semi-skeletal large humanoid, with some of its humanoid parts replaced by animal bones. For example, one revenant might be entirely humanoid save for a wolf skull in place of a human head, while another might be humanoid on top and elk on the bottom, like a hideous, skeletal centaur. Some may be clothed in rags, while others might be bare bones or still hung with strips of rotting flesh. The revenant's large size usually stems from the combination of two or more corpses, but the unnatural forces holding the hybrid revenant together can sometimes resize and reshape various parts for a whole that appears strangely complete as if it might have been a hybrid being in life though it was not.

Hybrid Revenant

Large undead, neutral evil
Armor Class 18 (natural armor)
Hit Points 209 (22d10 + 88)
Speed 40 ft.

STR	DEX	CON	INT	WIS	CHA
21 (+5)	10 (+0)	19 (+4)	10 (+0)	3 (−4)	9 (−1)

Saving Throws Con +8, Int +4
Damage Immunities necrotic, poison
Condition Immunities exhaustion, fright, poison, unconsciousness Resistances
Senses darkvision 120 ft., passive Perception 6
Languages understands Common, but cannot speak
Challenge 12 (8,400 XP)

Explosive Despair. The suffering of the hybrid revenant is so great that it explodes outward around itself from time to time, at random, as a palpable and deadly force. At the beginning of the hybrid revenant's initiative, roll 1d6. On a one, the hybrid revenant doubles over in apparent pain, incapacitated for this round. At the same time, necrotic withering hurtles outward from the revenant in a 30-foot radius. Each creature in this area must make a DC 17 Constitution saving throw, taking 71 (13d10) damage on a failed save, or half as much damage on a successful one.

Taint on the Land. If the hybrid revenant is merely slain, the restless spirits that formed it will not be satisfied. Deprived of a body, they will remain in waiting for another like-minded soul to join them, and the process will begin again (and in the meantime, the location of its corpse will attract other undead to the area). The hybrid revenant may be forcibly laid to rest after its body is slain by casting hallow on any physical remains. However, a hybrid revenant may also be laid to rest through roleplay, for a party and GM so inclined, by learning the revenant's tale and providing some form of solace, justice, epiphany, or catharsis.

Actions

Multiattack. The hybrid revenant attacks once with its bite and twice with its claws.

Bite. *Melee Weapon Attack:* +9 to hit, reach 5 ft., one target. *Hit:* 18 (2d12 + 5) piercing damage.

Claws. *Melee Weapon Attack:* +9 to hit, reach 5 ft., one target. *Hit:* 14 (2d8 + 5) slashing damage.

Wail of the Yawning Void (Recharge 4–6). When a hybrid revenant howls, those who hear its cry are consumed by the nameless, gaping loss within the revenant's soul. All creatures within 60 feet of the revenant that can hear it must succeed on a DC 17 Wisdom saving throw or be stunned for 1 minute. A creature can repeat the saving throw at the end of each of its turns, ending the effect on a success. If the saving throw is successful, or the effect ends on it, the creature is immune to the revenant's Wail of the Yawning Void for 24 hours.

Rhinoceros

Rhinoceros, Prehistoric (Elasmotherium)

This creature has massive legs and a stout body with a thick coat of brown fur. Two curving horns rise from the tip of its elongated nose.

A giant beast grazes peacefully with its herd. But be careful, for these creatures are highly territorial, and will attack if you enter their domain. If something threatens the herd, the females will circle the young, while the males will seek out the intruders. They have been known to sweep riders from their horses with their horn and toss them into the air repeatedly until the rider is killed.

Ancient tales describe the Elasmotherium as an intelligent beast, able to distinguish right from wrong, and representations of it were placed in courtrooms and on the caps of judges. In northern lands, a white Elasmotherium was considered to be an omen of a harsh winter.

Distinguished by a massive horn on its head, the Elasmotherium is the size of a mammoth and covered in a grey-brown fur. Long legs allow Elasmotherium to gallop like a horse, charging full-speed at its enemies in order to gore them with its horn. The horn is used for defense of its territory and mates, and for driving away competitors in their grazing grounds.

The Elasmotherium stands 7-feet tall at the shoulder and reaches lengths of up to 16-feet long. At a weight of 10,000 pounds, this massive beast packs a powerful punch when it charges. The horn can reach lengths of 5 feet and is made of hardened keratin, rather than bone. The tip of the horn forms a sharp point, easily penetrating the defenses of unwary enemies.

Prehistoric Rhinoceros (Elasmotherium)

Large beast, unaligned
Armor Class 15 (natural armor)
Hit Points 237 (19d10 + 133)
Speed 50 ft.

STR	DEX	CON	INT	WIS	CHA
27 (+8)	10 (+0)	25 (+7)	2 (−4)	13 (+1)	2 (−4)

Skills Perception +9
Senses passive Perception 19
Languages —
Challenge 12 (8,400 XP)

Keen Smell. The Elasmotherium has advantage on Wisdom (Perception) checks that rely on smell.

Siege Monster. The Elasmotherium deals double damage to objects and structures.

Trample. If the Elasmotherium moves at least 20 feet straight toward a creature and then hits it with a gore attack on the same turn, that target must succeed on a DC 18 Strength saving throw or be knocked prone. If the target is prone, the Elasmotherium can make stomp on the target as a bonus action.

Actions

Gore. *Melee Weapon Attack:* +12 to hit, reach 5 ft., one target. *Hit:* 43 (10d6 + 8) piercing damage.

Stomp. *Melee Weapon Attack:* +12 to hit, reach 5 ft., one target. *Hit:* 34 (4d12 + 8) bludgeoning damage and the target must succeed on a DC 17 Constitution saving throw or be stunned for 1 minute. The stunned creature can repeat the saving throw on each of its turns, ending the effect on a success.

Rhinoceros, Prehistoric (Embolotherium)

This enormous, heavily armored creature stands well over 8 feet tall and has a large blunt horn protruding from its snout, arcing almost straight up from the nose.

This creature sports an enormous bony protuberance, over 2 feet in length. The blunt horn coupled with the embolotherium's extreme height and immense weight makes for an excellent siege weapon. Many a town's wooden walls have become so many matchsticks when faced with a herd of charging embolotherium.

The embolotherium's horn, along with functioning as a bludgeoning weapon, also functions as a resonating chamber, allowing the creature's voice to be heard over very long distances. The herds of embolotherium often communicate in this fashion and have a deep, complicated social component to their herds, often with observed hierarchies. Most scholars believe they lack the intelligence to take advantage of this ability, and observations have supported that to date.

Prehistoric Rhinoceros (Embolotherium)

Large beast, unaligned
Armor Class 13 (natural armor)
Hit Points 76 (9d10 + 27)
Speed 40 ft.

STR	DEX	CON	INT	WIS	CHA
22 (+6)	8 (−1)	16 (+3)	2 (−4)	11 (+0)	6 (−2)

Senses passive Perception 10
Languages —
Challenge 3 (700 XP)

Charge. If the embolotherium moves at least 20 feet straight toward a target and then hits it with a gore attack on the same turn, the target takes an extra 11 (2d10) bludgeoning damage. If the target is a creature, it must succeed on a DC 16 Strength saving throw or be knocked prone.

Siege Monster. The embolotherium deals double damage to objects and structures.

Actions

Gore. *Melee Weapon Attack:* +8 to hit, reach 5 ft., one target. *Hit:* 28 (4d10 + 6) bludgeoning damage.

Rhinoceros, Woolly

This creature has massive legs and a stout body with a thick coat of brown fur. From the tip of its elongated nose rise two curving horns.

The woolly rhino is an herbivore of the Pleistocene Epoch, feeding mainly on various plants, nuts, berries, and bark, as well as large quantities of water. Thus, it is usually found in areas plentiful with water, such as riverbanks, lakes, and even marshes and swamps. The woolly rhino usually forages in the morning, so encounters are more common at this time. It is mostly a solitary creature, though chance encounters at a common foraging area may lead to encounters with more than one creature. Herds tend to gather near watering grounds, with the females surrounding the young.

Woolly rhinos mate during the late summer or early fall. Gestation lasts about 450 days after which time the female gives birth to a single calf. Calves are dependent on their mother for about the first two years of their life. Around three years of age, the calf becomes completely independent and reaches maturity by age five.

The woolly rhino averages about 11 feet long and has two ivory horns, the longest averaging about three feet in length. Its body is covered with a thick layer of black, brown, ruddy, or yellowish-brown fur that enable it to withstand its harsh climate. The creature has poor eyesight and relies on its senses of hearing and smell to locate sources of food and warn of impending danger.

The woolly rhino is generally passive but reacts violently if it or its herd is threatened. It attacks by goring and trampling its foes, often opening combat with a charge.

Woolly Rhinoceros

Large beast, unaligned
Armor Class 14 (natural armor)
Hit Points 172 (15d10 + 90)
Speed 30 ft.

STR	DEX	CON	INT	WIS	CHA
21 (+5)	10 (+0)	22 (+6)	3 (−4)	13 (+1)	2 (−4)

Skills Perception +7
Senses passive Perception 17
Languages —
Challenge 6 (2,300 XP)

Improved Critical. Gore attacks score a critical hit on a roll of 19 or 20.

Keen Smell. The woolly rhinoceros has advantage on Wisdom (Perception) checks that rely on smell.

Charge. If the woolly rhinoceros moves at least 20 feet straight toward a creature and then hits it with a gore attack on the same turn, the target takes an extra 9 (2d8) piercing damage. If the target is a creature, it must succeed on a DC 15 Strength saving throw or be knocked prone. If the target is prone, the woolly rhinoceros can make one stomp attack against it as a bonus action.

Actions

Gore. *Melee Weapon Attack:* +8 to hit, reach 5 ft., one target. *Hit:* 14 (2d8 + 5) piercing damage.

Stomp. *Melee Weapon Attack:* +8 to hit, reach 5 ft., one target. *Hit:* 18 (2d12 + 5) piercing damage.

Riptide Horror

This vile, grayish-tan tubeworm is longer than a man. It has six eyeless heads, and each mouth is lined with inward-curving, serrated teeth. Six long grayish-tan tentacles protrude from the middle of its body.

The terrifying riptide horror is a giant, sightless tubeworm found in sea caves or deep within desolate marshes. They are carnivorous creatures and have a voracious appetite that is only sated with meat, preferably that of warm-blooded humanoids or reptiles.

Opportunistic ambush hunters, riptide horrors wait for prey to come to them. They can go several weeks without eating, and sometimes do, but if a meal is readily available, the horror does not hesitate to kill and devour it. Such a meal is placed in a "reserve" stomach-like sac. When the food supply is low, the riptide horror delves into its reserve and draws sustenance from the stored food.

Riptide horrors mate once a year, usually in flooded sea caves. The female crawls into the male's lair and deposits a sticky, greenish-tan mass of eggs on the wall of the cave. The male fertilizes the eggs, and in 4 months, the eggs begin to hatch. Juveniles are excellent swimmers and leave the cave as soon as they hatch. As a riptide horror ages, its body secretes a substance that forms a shell-like carapace on its dorsal side.

Riptide horrors prefer to attack from ambush; sitting unmoving until potential prey moves within range. Often, they use their Spider Climb ability to cling to sea cave walls where their unsuspecting prey walks underneath them. Once prey wanders too close, the riptide horror lashes out with its tentacles and attempts to grab its meal. Grabbed foes are subjected to its paralytic poison and are bitten by its razor-sharp teeth.

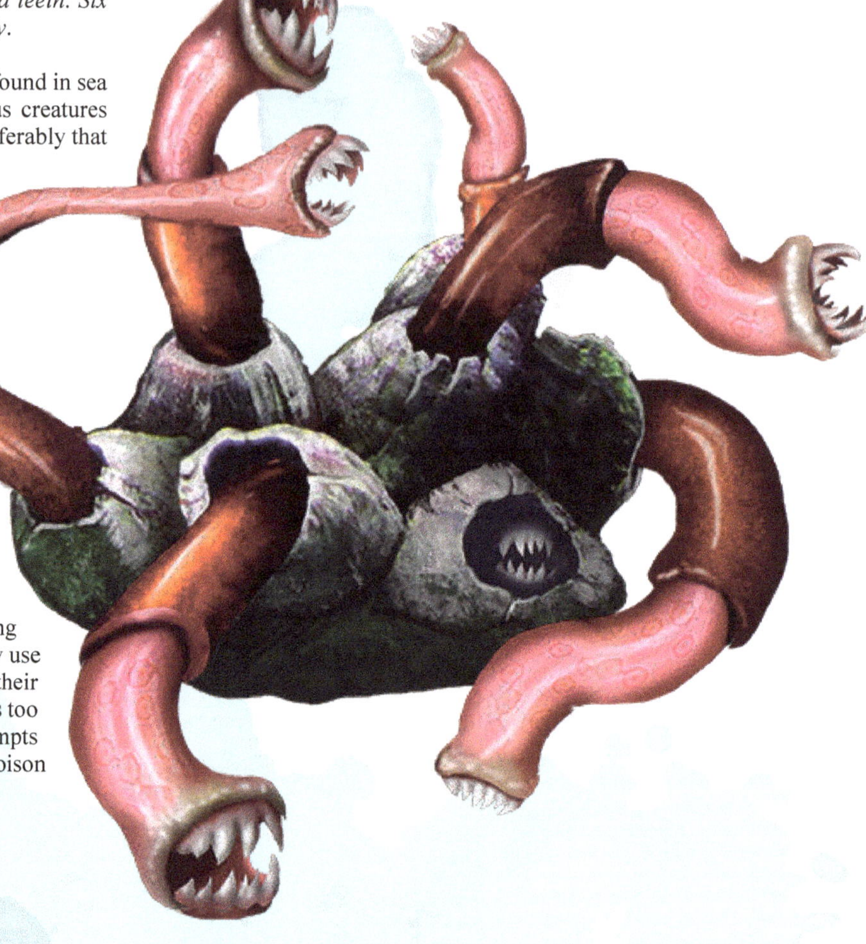

Riptide Horror

Medium monstrosity, lawful evil
Armor Class 15 (natural armor)
Hit Points 95 (10d8 + 50)
Speed 20 ft., swim 40 ft.

STR	DEX	CON	INT	WIS	CHA
17 (+3)	15 (+2)	20 (+5)	8 (−1)	9 (−1)	8 (−1)

Skills Perception +2, Stealth +5
Damage Vulnerabilities lightning
Damage Resistances bludgeoning, piercing, and slashing from nonmagical weapons
Condition Immunities blinded
Senses blindsight 60 ft. (blind beyond this radius), passive Perception 12
Languages —
Challenge 7 (2,900 XP)

Amphibious. The riptide horror can breathe air and water.

Spider Climb. The riptide horror can climb difficult surfaces, including upside down on ceilings, without needing to make an ability check.

Actions

Multiattack. The riptide horror makes six attacks: three with its tentacles plus three bites.

Tentacles. *Melee Weapon Attack:* +6 to hit, reach 10 ft., one target. *Hit:* 7 (1d8 + 3) bludgeoning damage and the target is grappled (escape DC 14). Until the grapple ends, the target is restrained, and the target must succeed on a DC 16 Constitution saving throw or become poisoned for 1 hour. While the target is poisoned, it is paralyzed. The riptide horror can have up to 6 creatures grappled with its six tentacles.

Bite. *Melee Weapon Attack:* +6 to hit, reach 5 ft., one target. *Hit:* 10 (2d6 + 3) piercing damage.

Sabrewing

A 6-foot-tall muscular humanoid with black, rubbery flesh stretches two large, leathery wings in place of its arms. Rigid plates of razor-sharp bone jut from the wing's outer edge. It perches on long, muscular legs that end in three-toed clawed feet. Peers menacingly through golden pupil slits, its wide, snarling grimace exposes rows of sharp teeth.

Sabrewings are winged humanoids from an unknown outer plane believed to be formed of rock and lined with razor-sharp blades of all shapes and sizes. These creatures delight in killing those weaker than themselves and often travel the outer planes preying on such creatures when they encounter them. Evil spellcasters and powerful outsiders (demon lords, arch-devils, lesser dukes, and so on) sometimes employ these creatures as assassins because of the sabrewing's skill at killing and the creature's desire to do nothing else. They are not averse to venturing to the Material Plane to answer an evil summons, and often do so, usually with the intent of fulfilling the bargain and then killing the summoner (if possible). If called by a powerful outsider, a sabrewing will not attempt to kill its summoner, as it's smart enough to know when it's outmatched. In such cases, they simply do their job and then return to their native plane.

Little is known of their native plane, but one adventurer that has supposedly seen this place speaks of huge citadels and fortresses constructed of iron and earth surrounded by "forests of steel blades." This information has never been substantiated and plane jumpers have been unable to locate such a plane. (Perhaps the sabrewings do not actually have their own native plane but implanted such false information to detour those that would seek them out.)

Sabrewings prefer to attack from the air, using speed to their advantage while also staying out of the reach of their opponents. Before combat, sabrewings usually cast magic weapon or greater magic weapon on their wings before engaging in combat so they can use their wings to the utmost advantage Multiple sabrewings work in concert with one another to bring down foes; one draws an opponent's attention while another swoops in from behind and slashes with its deadly wings.

Sabrewing

Medium fiend, neutral evil
Armor Class 15 (natural armor)
Hit Points 66 (7d8 + 35)
Speed 30 ft., fly 60 ft.

STR	DEX	CON	INT	WIS	CHA
20 (+5)	15 (+2)	20 (+5)	12 (+1)	14 (+2)	15 (+2)

Skills Perception +5, Survival +4
Damage Resistances cold, fire, lighting; bludgeoning, piercing, and slashing from nonmagical weapons
Senses darkvision 120 ft., passive Perception 15
Languages Common, Sabrewing
Challenge 5 (1,800 XP)

Flyby. The sabrewing doesn't provoke an opportunity attack when it flies out of an enemy's reach.

Magic Weapons. The sabrewing's weapon attacks are magical.

Actions

Multiattack. The sabrewing makes two attacks with its wings.

Wings. *Melee Weapon Attack:* +8 to hit, reach 5 ft., one target. *Hit:* 14 (2d8 + 5) slashing damage, and the target begins bleeding out. While the target is bleeding out, it must succeed on a DC 15 Constitution saving throw at the beginning of its turns, or its maximum hit points are reduced by 7 (2d6). Bleeding out continues until the target or another creature uses an action to make a successful DC 15 Wisdom (Medicine) check, or if the target receives magical healing.

Sand Kraken

A huge, bloated, eyeless, and formless octopus rises from the sand. From its pale-yellow, shapeless body sprout ten long tentacles tipped with cruel barbed pads.

Sand krakens are dangerous creatures encountered only in remote wastelands. A sand kraken keeps its body well concealed, buried deep in sand or loose rock, and inaccessible to most attacks. The creature never moves from the place where it digs its first burrow, and once it settles in, it will never again see the light of day. The only parts of a sand kraken that are usually seen are its tentacles, and by then it is often too late.

Sand krakens are omnivores but prefer meat to any other food. Once it captures and kills its prey, it pulls the carcass down into its sandy lair and devours it with its great central maw. For this reason, a number of scholars speculate a biological relationship between sand krakens and dustdiggers.

For most of its life, a sand kraken remains dormant and silent, buried several feet below the surface of the ground. When it senses prey, its tentacles swiftly rise to the surface. A sand kraken uses its initial attacks to immobilize its prey by constriction. Each tentacle has its own secondary brain and can attack independently. While tentacles can be harmed and severed, the only true way to kill a sand kraken is to dig it up and destroy its body.

Sand Kraken

Large aberration, neutral
Armor Class 13 (natural armor)
Hit Points 85 (9d10 + 36)
Speed 20 ft., burrow 30 ft.

STR	DEX	CON	INT	WIS	CHA
18 (+4)	10 (+0)	18 (+4)	5 (–3)	13 (+1)	6 (–2)

Skills Perception +4, Stealth +6
Senses darkvision 60 ft., tremorsense 120 ft., passive Perception 14
Languages —
Challenge 7 (2,900 XP)

Buried Camouflage. A sand kraken has advantage on Dexterity (Stealth) checks and it has total cover from attacks as long as it remains buried.

Keen Smell. The sand kraken has advantage on Wisdom (Perception) checks that rely on smell.

Tentacles. A sand kraken has 10 tentacles, each of which can grapple one creature. Each tentacle has an AC of 20, 15 hit points, and immunity to poison and psychic damage. Severing or destroying a tentacle deals no damage to the sand kraken, and severed tentacles regrow at a rate of 1 per day.

Actions

Multiattack. The sand kraken makes three tentacle attacks.

Bite. *Melee Weapon Attack:* +7 to hit, reach 5 ft., one target. *Hit:* 30 (4d12 + 4) piercing damage. If the target is a creature, it must succeed on a DC 15 Constitution saving throw against disease or become poisoned until the disease is cured. Every 24 hours that elapse, the target must repeat the saving throw, reducing its hit point maximum by 5 (1d10) on a failure. The disease is cured on a success. The target dies if the disease reduces its hit point maximum to 0. This reduction to the target's hit point maximum lasts until the disease is cured.

Tentacles. *Melee Weapon Attack:* +7 to hit, reach 30 ft., one target. *Hit:* 13 (2d8 + 4) bludgeoning damage. The target is grappled (escape DC 15) and restrained. Until the grapple ends, a grappled target takes 13 (2d8 + 4) bludgeoning damage at the beginning of each of the sand kraken's turns.

Scylla

This massive sea monster is about 20 feet long with a rounded lower body, four large fins, a short tail, and six heads, each perched on top of a long snake-like neck.

Scyllas are thought to be related to hydras, though no proof exists connecting the two. They are found in climates from temperate to warm (they don't like the cold) and prefer to lair in natural underwater caves and caverns, only emerging when hungry. A scylla is a predatory creature, existing on a diet of large fish such as shark, octopus or squid, or unlikely swimmers and sailors. Prey is usually devoured in the same spot it is killed; rarely does a scylla return to its lair with prey except when nursing its young.

Scyllas are solitary creatures, and even during mating season, it is rare to actually encounter more than one of these creatures. The mating ritual lasts but a short time with the male swimming away afterward, never to return to the lair. Young are born about 6 months later and reach maturity in just under a year. Young scyllas are noncombatants and do not possess the heat ability of adult scyllas.

A scylla is gray-blue to dark gray in color with a lighter shaded underbelly. Its fins are gray-blue to dark gray. Its eyes are golden or gray and each mouth is lined with triple rows of whitish-gray teeth. Scyllas can grow to a length of 50 feet.

Scyllas attack their foes with vicious bites from their multiple heads. When facing more than one opponent, a scylla uses its heat ability to boil the water surrounding it and burn its foes. Scyllas prefer to attack when it is most advantageous, such as surfacing under a foe. If combat goes against a scylla it dives beneath the waves and swims away. A cornered or hungry scylla, or one defending its lair, always fights to the death.

Scylla

Huge monstrosity, neutral

Armor Class 16 (natural armor)
Hit Points 94 (9d12 + 36)
Speed 10 ft., swim 50 ft.

STR	DEX	CON	INT	WIS	CHA
20 (+5)	14 (+2)	19 (+4)	10 (+0)	14 (+2)	10 (+0)

Skills Perception +10, Stealth +6, Survival +6
Damage Immunities fire
Senses darkvision 60 ft., passive Perception 20
Languages Aquan, Common
Challenge 9 (5,000 XP)

Heat. A creature who touches a scylla takes 7 (2d6) fire damage.
Multiple Heads. The scylla has six heads. It has advantage on saving throws against being blinded, charmed, deafened, frightened, stunned, or knocked unconscious.
Water Breathing. The scylla can only breathe underwater.
Water Dependency. A scylla can survive on land for 6 hours before suffocating.

Actions

Multiattack. The scylla makes three bite attacks.
Bites. *Melee Weapon Attack:* +9 to hit, reach 10 ft., one target. *Hit:* 23 (4d8 + 5) piercing damage.
Superheat Water (Recharge 5–6). The scylla uses one of the following options.
Scalding Blast. The scylla releases a line of scalding water that is 60 feet long and 5 feet wide. Creatures in the area must make a DC 16 Dexterity saving throw, taking 35 (10d6) fire damage on a failed saving throw, or half as much damage on a successful saving throw.
Boil Water. The water surrounding a scylla in a radius of 10 feet rises to a boil. All creatures within the area must make a DC 16 Constitution saving throw, taking 24 (7d6) fire damage on a failed saving throw, or half as much damage on a successful one. The area remains at a boil for 1 minute, even if the scylla moves to another space.

Sea Serpents

Nearly as old as the dragons that roam the sky, sea serpents are great snakelike creatures that have roamed the oceans for ages. Unlike the classical dragon, these great, scaly, serpentine beasts are generally agreed to be a product of evolution though many suspect magical influence, either deliberate or natural, somewhere in their evolution.

Whatever their origins, sea serpents are a highly-varied species, with great variation in size, coloration, intellect, and temperament. However, all sea serpents bear certain similarities. They are long, sinuous, warm-blooded creatures that closely resemble snakes in appearance, though they all have two sets of flippers, which may be large or so small and atrophied as to be nearly unnoticeable. Sea serpents are aquatic creatures, though some can make their way about on land. All sea serpents can breathe both water and air with equal efficiency, another fact that distinguishes them from marine mammals and reptiles. Further, all sea serpents are sentient, with an intellect ranging from little greater than moronic to supragenius level.

One trait that sea serpents share in common with their draconic brethren is a sense of innate superiority, a feeling that they are masters of the sea, at least in whatever manner they choose to pursue their expertise.

Unlike dragons, however, sea serpents are not distinguished by color or age category. And while some species are as acquisitive as dragons, others have no interest in hoarding wealth and live lives little better than beasts.

All sea serpents can speak and understand Aquatic, and many know Draconic as well. The more intelligent species may also learn the languages of marine civilizations or the languages of sea-traveling surface-dwellers.

Due to their physical similarities, sea serpents use fairly consistent tactics in combat situations. All sea serpents have venomous bites, and they use this to their advantage to slow or immobilize multiple attackers so they can concentrate on one foe. In addition to their lethal bite, all sea serpents have the ability to ensnare prey in their coils as a giant constrictor does and crush the life out of them. The larger sea serpents may even use this constriction attack against sea vessels, and mariners in their smoky dens delight in recounting tales of horror and woe of great serpents that splinter hulls and then devour the helpless sailors in the water.

Because they are sentient beings, sea serpents can often be reasoned with even if the reasoning is no more complex than simple intimidation. They are adaptable to circumstances, and none throw themselves into battle rashly.

Sea Serpent, Brine

This serpentine creature is about 20 feet long, nose to tail, with two sets of large flippers and a wide body. A finned crest runs the length of its back, head to tail. The body is dark blue with a lighter underbelly, often tinged with rust or green highlights.

The brine sea serpent is a relatively stupid and aggressive predator of the deeps and is the only sea serpent with a breath weapon.

The brine sea serpent lives in caves in the ocean floor, where it maintains a hoard much like a dragon. It often lives in seas known for their stormy conditions, since it enjoys feeding on humans capsized from boats. Sometimes it even attacks ships directly if it is hungry. It also searches sunken ships for objects of interest to add to its hoard. The eyes of a brine serpent are small, but it possesses large ears and has exceptional hearing.

Against lone prey, the brine sea serpent likely closes and attack with its bite.

When confronting larger groups, it uses its breath weapon first — the brine sea serpent has a special organ that harvests sodium from seawater and stores it in concentrated form in a gland in its cheek. It generally avoids constricting attacks unless attacking large opponents that do not die from its poisonous bite. The brine sea serpent may also use the constriction attack against small sea vessels if it is very hungry.

Brine Sea Serpent

Huge dragon, chaotic evil
Armor Class 18 (natural armor)
Hit Points 195 (17d12 + 85)
Speed 0 ft., swim 60 ft.

STR	DEX	CON	INT	WIS	CHA
21 (+5)	15 (+2)	20 (+10)	7 (−2)	13 (+1)	14 (+2)

Saving Throws Str +10, Dex +7, Con +9
Skills Athletics +10, Perception +6
Damage Immunities acid
Condition Immunities prone
Senses darkvision 60 ft., passive Perception 16
Languages Aquan, Draconic
Challenge 13 (10,000 XP)

Amphibious. The brine sea serpent can breathe air and water.

Actions

Multiattack. A brine sea serpent attacks once with its bite and once with its tail.

Bite. *Melee Weapon Attack:* +10 to hit, reach 5 ft., one target. *Hit:* 21 (3d10 + 5) piercing damage plus 10 (3d6) acid damage, and the target is grappled (escape DC 18). If the brine sea serpent already has a creature grappled with its bite, it can only bite that creature, and it has advantage on that attack.

Tail Slap. *Melee Weapon Attack:* +10 to hit, reach 15 ft., one target. *Hit:* 18 (3d8 + 5) bludgeoning damage and the target must succeed at a DC 18 Strength saving throw or be pushed 10 feet away and knocked prone.

Brine Blast (Recharge 6). The brine serpent releases a 50-foot cone of briny acid. Creatures in the area must make a DC 18 Dexterity saving throw. On a failed saving throw, the target takes 72 (16d8) acid damage.

Legendary Actions

The brine sea serpent can take up to 3 legendary actions, choosing from the options below. Only one legendary action option can be used at a time and only at the end of another creature's turn. The serpent regains spent legendary actions at the start of its turn.

Tail Attack. The brine serpent uses its tail attack.

Coiling Maneuver (Costs 2 Actions). The brine sea serpent attempts to grapple a Large or smaller target. The target must make a DC 18 Strength saving throw or be grappled and restrained. The sea serpent can't use its other legendary actions or its Tail Slap if it's grappling a target. At the beginning of each of the brine serpent's turns, the grappled target takes 18 (3d8 + 5) bludgeoning damage.

Sea Serpent, Deep Hunter

This serpent is about 60 feet long and 10 feet thick. Its body scales are smooth, each about the size of a large shield, and the entire serpent is deep green to jet black in color, with eyes a solid, nearly black red color.

The immense deep hunter serpent lives in deep oceans and delights in hunting down and killing the most fearsome creatures of the sea. The deep hunter lives on the ocean floor, usually near thermal vents and volcanic areas where it is relatively warm. However, when hunting it may be encountered just about anywhere at sea; its preferred prey are krakens and the largest whales, though it may attack any other fearsome sea predator — the more dangerous, the better.

The deep hunter sea serpent is seldom seen near the surface, as its prey tends to stick to deep waters. It does not initiate combat against creatures it sees as its inferiors, but if it does regard a creature as a threat, it uses stealth to surprise its prey when possible and launches into a full-scale assault using all of its physical attacks to the best of its ability.

Deep Hunter Sea Serpent

Gargantuan dragon, lawful neutral
Armor Class 19 (natural armor)
Hit Points 385 (22d20 + 154)
Speed 0 ft., swim 80 ft.

STR	DEX	CON	INT	WIS	CHA
26 (+8)	14 (+2)	25 (+7)	7 (–2)	13 (+1)	14 (+2)

Saving Throws Str +15, Dex +10, Con +14
Skills Athletics +15, Perception +8
Damage Immunities poison
Condition Immunities poisoned, prone
Senses darkvision 60 ft., passive Perception 18
Languages Aquan, Draconic
Challenge 21 (33,000 XP)

Amphibious. The deep hunter serpent can breathe air and water.

Siege Monster. The deep hunter serpent deals double damage to objects and structures.

Actions

Multiattack. A deep hunter serpent attacks once with its tail and either bites or uses its swallow attack.

Bite. *Melee Weapon Attack:* +15 to hit, reach 10 ft., one target. *Hit:* 34 (4d12 + 8) piercing damage plus 22 (4d10) poison damage, and the target is grappled (escape DC 23) and restrained. The deep sea hunter can't make a bit attack while it has a creature grappled with its bite.

Tail Slap. *Melee Weapon Attack:* +15 to hit, reach 20 ft., one target. *Hit:* 30 (4d10 + 8) bludgeoning damage and the target is pushed 15 feet away and knocked prone.

Swallow. A Large or smaller target grappled by the serpent's bite attack is swallowed and the grapple ends. While swallowed, the creature is blinded and restrained, it has total cover against attacks and other effects outside the deep hunter serpent, and it takes 42 (12d6) acid damage at the start of each of the deep hunter serpent's turns. If the deep hunter takes 30 damage or more on a single turn from a creature inside it, the serpent must succeed on a DC 25 Constitution saving throw at the end of that turn or regurgitate all swallowed creatures, which fall prone in a space within 10 feet of the serpent. If the serpent dies, a swallowed creature is no longer restrained by it and can escape from the corpse using 15 feet of movement, exiting prone.

Legendary Actions

The deep hunter sea serpent can take up to 3 legendary actions, choosing from the options below. Only one legendary action option can be used at

a time and only at the end of another creature's turn. The serpent regains spent legendary actions at the start of its turn.

Tail Attack. The deep hunter serpent uses its Tail Slap.

Coiling Maneuver (Costs 2 Actions). The deep hunter sea serpent attempts to grapple a Huge or smaller target. The target must make a DC 23 Strength saving throw or be grappled and restrained. The sea serpent can't use its other legendary actions or its Tail Slap if it's grappling a target. At the beginning of each of the brine serpent's turns, the grappled target takes 30 (4d10 + 8) bludgeoning damage.

Unhinge Jaw (Costs 3 Actions). The deep hunter uses its bite attack on all creatures of Large size or smaller in a 10-foot cube within 15 feet of the deep hunter. If the attack hits on any of the creatures, it can use its swallow ability.

Sea Serpent, Fanged

This serpent is 12 to 15 feet long and 5 feet thick. Its body scales are thickened and hardened, which slows it somewhat in water but provides good protection. The serpent's most outstanding features, however, are the rows of long, sharp teeth that fill its mouth. It has large, lidless red eyes with white pupils.

The fanged sea serpent is a vicious predator of the seas feared for its tendency to travel in packs and swarm over creatures much larger than itself. Fanged sea serpents are nomadic, traveling with ocean currents. They prefer to hunt in groups, which they can surround and attack from all sides. Fanged sea serpents have been known to attack their own kind, but only when starving.

Fanged sea serpents on their own usually live on large fish and avoid confronting intelligent opposition unless they believe their victims to be helpless. However, when they are in groups, they become much more aggressive, and attack creatures much larger than themselves. They prefer to use swarm tactics, surrounding their target and attacking simultaneously from all directions; in the water, where they can also

Fanged Sea Serpent

Large dragon, neutral evil
Armor Class 15 (natural armor)
Hit Points 93 (11d10 + 33)
Speed 0 ft., swim 40 ft.

STR	DEX	CON	INT	WIS	CHA
18 (+4)	13 (+1)	16 (+3)	5 (−3)	11 (+0)	6 (−2)

Skills Athletics +7, Perception +3
Damage Immunities poison
Condition Immunities poisoned, prone
Senses darkvision 60 ft., passive Perception 13
Languages Aquan, Draconic
Challenge 5 (1,800 XP)

Amphibious. The fanged serpent can breathe air and water.

Actions

Bite. *Melee Weapon Attack:* +7 to hit, reach 5 ft., one target. *Hit:* 10 (1d12 + 4) piercing damage plus 7 (2d6) poison damage, and the target is grappled (escape DC 15). Until this grapple ends, the target is restrained and the sea serpent cannot grapple another target. While the fanged serpent has a creature grappled in its bite, it cannot bite a different creature, and has advantage on bite attacks against the grappled creature.

Roll. One target that the fanged serpent has grappled takes 21 (6d6) slashing damage as the fanged serpent rolls quickly. After this damage is dealt, the target is no longer grappled.

Sea Serpent, Gilded

This serpent is about 8 feet long and 2 feet thick. Its body scales are small and smooth, with the brilliant luster of gold. It has a long, narrow crocodilian snout and a cluster of antenna-like whiskers sweeping back from just above its jaws.

One of the rarest of sea serpents, the gilded serpent is known for its glittering golden hide and is often hunted for this skin and for the powerful narcotic that can be made from its venom. In the wild, gilded sea serpents live on the most secluded islands and hidden lagoons, where they nest in sandy lairs and shallow, sun-warmed waters. Wealthy coastal lords have been known to acquire gilded sea serpent eggs or infants and raised them captivity. These serpents are usually revered as holy or prized as status symbols; captive gilded serpents that are mistreated quickly lose the will to live and die.

The golden hide of a gilded serpent can be harvested and made into a single set of scale mail that fits a Medium or smaller creature. This armor is considered masterwork and has the same properties as mithril scale armor.

Golden Bliss

Golden Bliss (Inhaled). A creature subjected to this poison must succeed on a DC 13 Constitution saving throw or be poisoned for 1 minute. While poisoned, the target is stunned and has advantage on Intelligence, Wisdom, and Charisma saving throws against spells and magical effects. The poisoned target can repeat the saving throw at the end of each of its turns, ending the effect on a success.

The poison of the gilded serpent can be milked or harvested as well, then made into a powerful narcotic drug called golden bliss.

Gilded sea serpents flee danger when they can, using their ability to swim swiftly to evade danger as quickly as possible. If cornered or surprised, however, they lash out with their bite and use their constriction attack if their prey is small enough. The venom of a gilded sea serpent numbs the flesh to pain and induces a state of catatonic stupor.

Gilded Sea Serpent

Medium dragon, neutral
Armor Class 14 (natural armor)
Hit Points 52 (8d8 + 16)
Speed 0 ft., swim 30 ft.

STR	DEX	CON	INT	WIS	CHA
16 (+3)	12 (+1)	14 (+2)	5 (−3)	11 (+0)	7 (−2)

Skills Athletics +5, Perception +2
Damage Immunities poison
Condition Immunities poisoned, prone
Senses darkvision 60 ft., passive Perception 12
Languages Draconic
Challenge 4 (1,100 XP)

Amphibious. The gilded serpent can breathe air and water.

Actions

Bite. Melee Weapon Attack: +5 to hit, reach 5 ft., one target. *Hit:* 14 (2d10 + 3) piercing damage and if the target is a creature, it must succeed at a DC 14 Constitution saving throw. On a failed saving throw, the target is poisoned for 1 minute. While poisoned, the target is also stunned. A poisoned creature can repeat the saving throw at the end of each of its turns, ending the effect on a success.

Constrict. Melee Weapon Attack: +5 to hit, reach 5 ft., one creature. *Hit:* 12 (2d8 + 3) bludgeoning damage and the target is grappled if it is Medium-sized or smaller (escape DC 13). At the beginning of each of the serpent's turn, the grappled creature takes 12 (2d8 + 3) bludgeoning damage.

Sea Serpent, Shipbreaker

This devastating serpent is over 120 feet long and 15 feet thick. Its body scales are dark gray-brown, festooned with barnacles, seaweed, and other sea life. Its maw is the size of a large wagon, with teeth the size of greatswords.

The legendary shipbreaker is thought to be the largest of the sea serpents, a true behemoth that rules the seas. It is a fearless hunter that enjoys attacking the largest seagoing vessels and crushing them in its mighty coils. It is believed by many sailors and seafarers that the shipbreaker is a unique creature (i.e., that only one of these mighty beasts exists), and apparently (and thankfully) it seems to spend most of its time hibernating.

A shipbreaker attacks ships and huge-sized creatures as its primary prey. It ignores smaller creatures except as snacks, or if directly threatened by one. Its favorite tactic is to ambush a ship or approach it at speed, then wrap it in its coils and crush it. It then feasts on the sailors in the water at its leisure. The shipbreaker is most often sighted deep at sea, usually just before it approaches and breaks up a naval vessel into kindling.

It is unknown what language the shipbreaker speaks or understands, if any, since none have ever reported successfully speaking with it. A shipbreaker's broad flat flippers allow it to slowly propel itself onto and across dry land.

Shipbreaker Sea Serpent

Gargantuan dragon, chaotic neutral
Armor Class 19 (natural armor)
Hit Points 663 (34d20 + 306)
Speed 20 ft., swim 60 ft.

STR	DEX	CON	INT	WIS	CHA
30 (+10)	10 (+0)	29 (+9)	11 (+0)	17 (+3)	11 (+0)

Saving Throws Str +19 Dex +9, Con +18, Wis +12
Damage Immunities cold, poison; bludgeoning, piercing, and slashing from nonmagical weapons.
Condition Immunities frightened, paralyzed, poisoned, restrained
Skills Perception +22, Stealth +18
Senses blindsight 120 ft., darkvision 120 ft., passive Perception 22
Languages Deep Speech, Draconic
Challenge 30 (155,000 XP)

Amphibious. The sea serpent can breathe air and water.

Keen Scent. This sea serpent can notice creatures by scent in a 180-foot radius underwater and can detect blood in the water at a range of up to a mile.

Legendary Resistance (3/day). If the sea serpent fails a saving throw, it can choose to succeed instead.

Siege Monster. The sea serpent deals double damage to objects and structures.

Actions

Multiattack. The sea serpent can use its frightful presence and make two attacks: one with its bite and one with its tail.

Size	Outcome
Medium	The craft must make a generic DC 20 saving throw to avoid being destroyed. If the craft fails the save by 5 or more, it capsizes and all on board must make a DC 18 Dexterity saving throw to avoid being pulled under with the ship. If the save is successful, the ship takes 120 (20d10 + 10) damage and those on board must make a successful DC 17 Dexterity saving throw. On a failed save, the passenger takes 48 (7d10 + 10) bludgeoning damage and is knocked prone (or overboard if they are near the ship's edge), or half as much without being knocked prone on a success.
Large	The craft must make a generic DC 18 saving throw to avoid being capsized. If it fails the save by 5 or more, the ship capsizes and all on board must make a DC 16 Dexterity saving throw to avoid being pulled under with the ship. If the save is successful, the ship takes 103 (17d10 + 10) damage and those on board must make a DC 14 Dexterity saving throw. On a failed save, the passenger takes 37 (5d10 + 10) bludgeoning damage and is knocked prone (or overboard if they are near the ship's edge), or half as much without being knocked prone on a success.
Huge	The craft must make a generic DC 16 saving throw to avoid being capsized. If it fails the save by 5 or more, the ship capsizes and all on board must make a DC 15 Dexterity saving throw to avoid being pulled under with the ship. If the save is successful, the ship takes 81 (13d10 + 10) damage and those on board must make a DC 12 Dexterity saving throw. On a failed save, the passenger takes 26 (3d10 + 10) bludgeoning damage and is knocked prone (or overboard if they are near the ship's edge), or half as much without being knocked prone on a success.
Gargantuan	The craft must make a generic DC 14 saving throw to avoid being capsized. If it fails the save by 5 or more, the ship capsizes and all on board must make a DC 13 Dexterity saving throw to avoid being pulled under with the ship. If the save is successful, the ship takes 65 (10d10 + 10) damage and those on board must make a DC 10 Dexterity saving throw. On a failed save, the passenger takes 15 (1d10 + 10) bludgeoning damage and is knocked prone (or overboard if they are near the ship's edge), or half as much without being knocked prone on a success.

Bite. *Melee Weapon Attack:* +19 to hit, reach 20 ft., one target. *Hit:* 45 (10d6 + 10) piercing damage and 28 (8d6) poison damage.

Ram. *Melee Weapon Attack:* +19 to hit, reach 10 ft., one target. *Hit:* 65 (10d10 + 10) bludgeoning damage.

Tail. *Melee Weapon Attack:* +19 to hit, reach 30 ft., one target. *Hit:* 37 (6d8 + 10) bludgeoning damage.

Frightful Presence. Each creature of the sea serpent's choice that is within 120 feet of the sea serpent and aware of it must succeed on a DC 23 Wisdom saving throw or become frightened for 1 minute. A creature can repeat the saving throw at the end of each of its turns, ending the effect on itself on a success. If a creature's saving throw is successful or the effect ends for it, the creature is immune to the sea serpent's Frightful Presence for the next 24 hours.

Capsize. If the sea serpent moves at least 30 feet straight toward a watercraft (boat, ship, ferry, etc.) and then hits it with a ram attack on the same turn, there is a chance that it will capsize. All occupants of the watercraft must make Dexterity saving throw when the craft is rammed (see below). To determine if the watercraft capsizes, consult the following table:

Size	Outcome
Small	The craft is destroyed, all on board must make a successful DC 23 Dexterity saving throw to avoid being stunned. On a failed save, passengers each take 65 (10d10 + 10) bludgeoning damage, are trapped in the wreckage, and are stunned for 1 minute, or half as much on a successful save and are thrown clear of the wreckage.

Legendary Actions

The sea serpent can take 3 legendary actions, choosing from the options below. Only one legendary action can be used at a time and only at the end of another creature's turn. The sea serpent regains spent legendary actions at the start of its turn.

Detect. The sea serpent makes a Wisdom (Perception) check.

Tail Attack. The sea serpent makes a tail attack.

Breach (Costs 3 Actions). The sea serpent dives deep below the surface of the water then swims rapidly upward, propelling itself out of the water, often clearing the surface, before violently slamming into the surface with great force. Each creature within 60 feet of the sea serpent must succeed on a DC 23 Dexterity saving or take 27 (5d10) bludgeoning damage and be knocked prone.

Sea Serpent, Spitting

The body length of these serpents is roughly 15 to 18 feet, with a girth of up to 3 feet. They are covered with rough-edged scales of brown, green, or blue coloration, giving their hides a mottled appearance. Their heads are short, with thick, muscular necks concealed beneath a webbed fringe.

Spitting sea serpents are a fiercely territorial, if not terribly intelligent, species that can be a great hazard on unfamiliar coasts. They are renowned for their great ability to spit globs of acidic spittle onto creatures that threaten them. The spitting sea serpent always tries to use its spitting attack against any that anger it, using its bite and constriction attacks against food or as a last resort.

A spitting sea serpent prefers to dwell in shallow coastal waters and coastlines, and avoids deep water where they are ill-equipped to handle encounters with large marine predators, against which their ability to spit is ineffective. They prefer to live in wild, uncivilized lands, and fiercely protect their hunting grounds from intrusion by any other predators.

Spitting Sea Serpent
Large dragon, chaotic evil
Armor Class 16 (natural armor)
Hit Points 97 (13d10 + 26)
Speed 10 ft., swim 40 ft.

STR	DEX	CON	INT	WIS	CHA
20 (+5)	13 (+1)	14 (+2)	8 (−1)	13 (+1)	6 (−2)

Skills Athletics +8, Perception +4
Damage Immunities acid, poison
Condition Immunities poisoned, prone
Senses darkvision 60 ft., passive Perception 14
Languages understands Aquan but seldom speaks
Challenge 8 (3,900 XP)

Amphibious. The spitting sea serpent can breathe air and water.

Actions

Multiattack. A spitting sea serpent spits once and bits once, or it can make a constrict attack.

Bite. *Melee Weapon Attack:* +8 to hit, reach 5 ft., one creature. *Hit:* 14 (2d8 + 5) piercing damage plus 10 (3d6) poison damage.

Constrict. *Melee Weapon Attack:* +8 to hit, reach 5 ft., one creature. *Hit:* 23 (4d8 + 5) bludgeoning damage and the target is grappled if it is Medium-sized or smaller (escape DC 16). At the beginning of each of the serpent's turn, the grappled creature takes 23 (4d8 + 5) bludgeoning damage.

Spit. *Ranged Weapon Attack:* +8 to hit, range 60 ft., one target. *Hit:* 15 (3d6 + 5) acid damage. This attack can be used underwater.

Seahorse, Giant

This aquatic creature resembles an ordinary seahorse with a vaguely equine-shaped head, fins emerging from the base of its head and a curling tail but it extends to a length of 8 feet or more.

Giant seahorses are larger versions of the common seahorse that spend their days swimming slowly along feeding on crustaceans and other such aquatic life. The average giant seahorse is about eight feet long and weighs 300 pounds.

Giant seahorses eat a variety of aquatic life, including plants, shrimp, and other small aquatic life. They are slow swimmers and never pursue their prey.

Giant seahorses reproduce through internal fertilization and do so four times each year (once per season). During reproduction, the female giant seahorse lays between 300 and 700 eggs in the male's incubation pouch (which resembles the pouch of a kangaroo). After 20 days, the eggs hatch, and the young remain in the pouch until they are capable of swimming on their own (about ten days). Newborn giant seahorses are about one foot long and reach maturity in eight months. About 30% of all young seahorses die before birth (either the eggs don't hatch or the young die before emerging from the pouch). Giant seahorses are monogamous and mate for life.

A giant seahorse is about 8 feet long from the top of its head to the tip of its tail. Its body is covered with fine scales and its head is horse-like with a long snout. Its back is lined with small dorsal fins. (These aid it in swimming.) Near the base of its head are pectoral fins that help the giant seahorse turn while swimming. A giant seahorse ranges in color from yellow to dull green or brown. Its eyes are almost always brown with the occasional giant seahorse having blue eyes.

Giant seahorses are not aggressive creatures and only attack if cornered or if a member of the herd is threatened. In combat, a giant seahorse butts an opponent with its bony head. Most, however, simply flee when confronted.

Training a Giant Seahorse

A giant seahorse requires training before it can bear a rider in combat. To be trained, a giant seahorse must have a friendly attitude toward the trainer. Training a seahorse as an aquatic mount requires six weeks of work and a successful DC 15 Wisdom (Animal Handling) check. Riding a seahorse requires an exotic saddle. A seahorse can fight while carrying a rider. Seahorse eggs are worth 2,000 gp apiece on the open market, while young are worth 4,000 gp each. Professional trainers charge 1,000 gp to rear or train a giant seahorse.

Carrying Capacity. A giant seahorse is unencumbered up to 300 pounds, lightly encumbered from 301–600 pounds, and encumbered from 601–900 pounds. A giant seahorse can drag 4,500 pounds.

Giant Seahorse

Large beast, unaligned
Armor Class 12
Hit Points 26 (4d10 + 4)
Speed 0 ft., swim 30 ft.

STR	DEX	CON	INT	WIS	CHA
16 (+3)	15 (+2)	13 (+1)	2 (–4)	13 (+1)	10 (+0)

Senses darkvision 60 ft., passive Perception 11
Languages —

Challenge ½ (100 XP)

Water Breathing. The giant seahorse can only breathe underwater.

Actions

Tail Slap. *Melee Weapon Attack:* +5 to hit, reach 5 ft., one target. *Hit:* 7 (1d8 + 3) bludgeoning damage.

Head Butt. *Melee Weapon Attack:* +5 to hit, reach 5 ft., one target. *Hit:* 7 (1d8 + 3) bludgeoning damage.

Shadelock

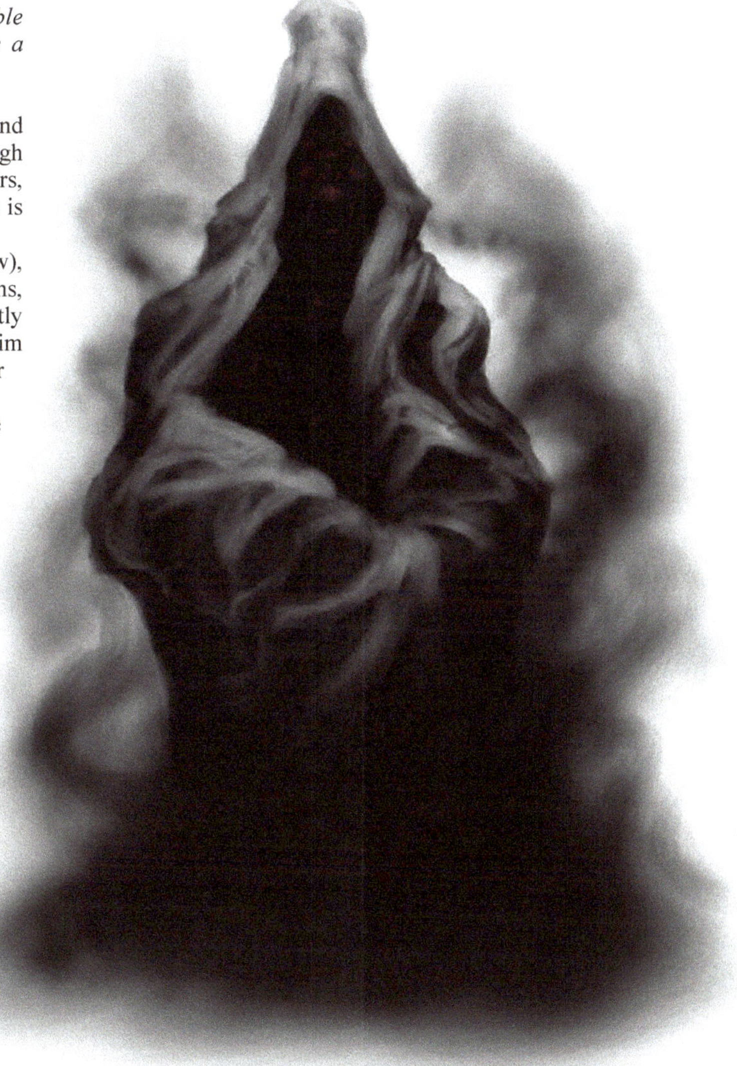

A gaunt, robed figure stands before you, its features almost invisible in a deep hood. The essence of pure shadow swirls around it like a great cloak.

Shadelockes are mysterious creatures that dwell in gloomy places and possess a natural ability to harness the shadows to their own ends. Though they are usually solitary, shadelockes are sometimes encountered in pairs, working together to confuse and mislead their foes into thinking there is only one, then attacking when the opportunity presents itself.

While they may not belong in the material world (see below), shadelockes seem quite at home living in forsaken forests, bleak dungeons, or ruins — hiding among the shadows — occasionally emerging to quietly observe nearby mortals or to stalk and terrify. Some fear-filled tales claim that the shadelockes also kidnap their victims, spiriting them off to their own nightmarish dimension.

Scholars are uncertain about the shadelockes' origins and true nature, for they utterly refuse to communicate with those not of their species. Attempts to magically compel them to talk result in an incomprehensible flood of verbal and mental gibberish. If discovered in their silent observations — lurking in the gloom, silently following their victims along streets or lonely roads, staring intently through windows in the dark of night — they will invariably attack, trying to slay anyone who has seen them. If outnumbered or badly wounded, a shadelocke will flee, and under no circumstances will it surrender or parley. In very rare circumstances, shadelockes have been captured, but these individuals never communicate and invariably die in short order.

Investigators have had to turn to folklore to learn more of the shadelockes, but even here legends are contradictory. The most common tale is that shadelockes are servitors of a mysterious Shadow King who dwells in a dark realm of shadow adjacent to but separate from the known planes. The shadelockes are tasked with gathering information on dwellers in the Material Plane, spreading fear and dread to keep the Shadow King's realm safe from intrusion and occasionally kidnapping mortals into the shadow realms for experimentation and amusement. Some stories postulate that the Shadow King has other, even more terrifying, minions that no one has ever lived to describe.

Shadelocke

Medium aberration, chaotic neutral

Armor Class 16 (natural armor)
Hit Points 108 (24d8)
Speed 30 ft., fly 30 ft. (hover)

STR	DEX	CON	INT	WIS	CHA
8 (−1)	18 (+4)	10 (+0)	12 (+1)	16 (+3)	18 (+4)

Saving Throws Dex +7, Cha +7
Skills Arcana +7, Insight +9, Perception +9, Stealth +10
Damage Vulnerabilities radiant
Damage Resistances cold, necrotic
Damage Immunities psychic; bludgeoning, piercing and slashing damage from nonmagical weapons
Senses darkvision 60 ft., passive Perception 19
Languages Common
Challenge 8 (3,900 XP)

Aura of Gloom. When not subjected to full daylight or its magical equivalent, shadelockes have advantage on all Dexterity (Stealth) checks.

Innate Spellcasting. The shadelocke's spellcasting ability is Charisma (spell save DC 15, +7 to hit with spell attacks). The shadelocke can innately cast the following spells, requiring no material components:

At will: *chill touch, detect thoughts, mage hand, minor illusion*
3/day each: *blink, darkness, major image*
1/day each: *dominate person, fly, true seeing*

Actions

Multiattack. The shadelocke makes two shadow touch attacks.

Shadow Touch. *Melee Weapon Attack:* +7 to hit, reach 5 ft., one creature. *Hit:* 22 (4d8+4) cold damage.

Shadow Captain

The black-armored figure has no face save a pair of burning points of light. Its breastplate is emblazoned with the sigil of a skull that sprouts massive stag's horns.

When the eternally cursed undead creature known as the Horned Lord (p. 200) rises, he is inevitably accompanied by his 12 minions, the deadly shadow captains. These creatures may be the undead remains of the Horned Lord's old followers, but some have suggested that they are equally wicked individuals from other lands and eras, cursed to serve him for all eternity. A few have even gone so far as to speculate that the shadow captains are actually undead entities sent by the gods to further the Horned Lord's torment, acting ostensibly as his minions, but also adding to his misery and the realization of his unending doom.

Regardless of their origin, the shadow captains carry out the Horned Lord's will — leading his armies, exterminating enemies, engaging in acts of corruption and espionage using their *alter self* ability. Many tales have been told about rulers, advisors, valued counselors, lovers and other intimate associates who were, in the end, revealed to be shadow captains, following the Horned Lord's dread commands.

Shadow Captain

Medium undead, lawful evil
Armor Class 19 (half plate, shield)
Hit Points 156 (24d8 + 48)
Speed 30 ft.

STR	DEX	CON	INT	WIS	CHA
18 (+4)	14 (+2)	14 (+2)	10 (+0)	16 (+3)	10 (+0)

Saving Throws Str +8, Wis +7
Skills Perception +11, Stealth +10
Damage Resistances lightning; bludgeoning, piercing, and slashing from nonmagical weapons
Damage Immunities cold, necrotic, poison
Condition Immunities charmed, exhaustion, frightened, paralyzed, poisoned, unconscious
Senses darkvision 60 ft. passive Perception 21
Languages Common
Challenge 12 (8,400 XP)

Alter Self. The shadow captain can assume a different form at will. The magic that provides the shadow captain with this ability is so powerful that only a *true seeing* spell can discern what lies under the illusion.

Innate Spellcasting. The shadow captain's spellcasting ability is Wisdom (spell save DC 15, +7 to hit with spell attacks). The shadow captain can innately cast the following spells, requiring no material components:
At will: *alter self, resistance, sacred flame*
3/day each: *bane, inflict wounds, shield of faith*
1/day each: *animate dead, contagion*

Regeneration. The shadow captain regains 10 hit points at the start of its turn. If the shadow captain takes acid or fire damage, this trait doesn't function at the start of its next turn. The shadow captain dies only if it starts its turn with 0 hit points and doesn't regenerate.

Actions

Multiattack. The shadow captain makes two longsword attacks.
Longsword. *Melee Weapon Attack:* +8 to hit, reach 5 ft., one target. *Hit:* 15 (2d10 + 4) slashing damage plus 22 (4d10) cold damage.
Draining Touch. *Melee Weapon Attack:* +6 to hit, reach 5 ft., one target. *Hit:* 15 (3d8 + 2) cold damage. The target must succeed on a DC 14 Constitution saving throw or its hit point maximum is reduced by an amount equal to the damage taken. This reduction lasts until the target finishes a long rest. The target dies if this effect reduces its hit point maximum to 0.

Shadow Hunter

The shadow hunter is a great, dark serpent that hunts in deep caverns beneath the earth. An adult specimen is over 40 feet long and nearly 5 feet thick in its midsection. In bright light, it can be seen to be covered with nonreflective black scales, and its underbelly is the dark red of clotted blood. Shadow hunters have the supernatural ability to blend in with shadows, both to protect themselves and to stalk and ambush prey. Unlike normal snakes, shadow hunters often work in groups of two or three to corner prey in passages.

Shadow hunters generally prefer to hunt in networks of twisting passages that allow them to move around their intended prey, or even approach it from multiple directions. They are particularly fond of elf flesh but eats any Small to Large creature as long as it is living, organic, and animal-based (i.e., not a plant or fungus). When they attack, they prefer to strike and envenom their prey, holding on and chewing the poison into their opponent until it stops struggling. If there is more than one foe present, they do not try to grab their prey, preferring to strike at those that threaten it, retreating if need be to return later to consume their hopefully dead prey.

Shadow Hunter

Huge monstrosity, neutral
Armor Class 14 (natural armor)
Hit Points 105 (10d12 + 40)
Speed 30 ft., climb 50 ft., swim 30 ft.

STR	DEX	CON	INT	WIS	CHA
23 (+6)	15 (+2)	19 (+4)	5 (–3)	14 (+2)	3 (–4)

Skills Perception +6, Stealth +6
Condition Immunities prone
Senses darkvision 60 ft., tremorsense 60 ft., passive Perception 16
Languages —
Challenge 9 (5,000 XP)

Keen Smell. The shadow hunter has advantage on Wisdom (Perception) checks that rely on smell.

Shadow Stealth. While in dim light or darkness, the shadow can take the Hide action as a bonus action.

Actions

Bite. *Melee Weapon Attack:* +10 to hit, reach 10 ft., one target. *Hit:* 15 (2d8 + 6) piercing damage and 27 (6d8) poison damage. The target must succeed on a DC 15 Constitution saving throw or be poisoned for 1 hour.

Constrict. *Melee Weapon Attack:* +10 to hit, reach 5 ft., one target. *Hit:* 17 (2d10 + 6) bludgeoning damage and the target is grappled (escape DC 16). Until this grapple ends, the creature is restrained, and the shadow hunter can't constrict another target.

Shadow Hunter Hatchling

Medium monstrosity, neutral
Armor Class 13 (natural armor)
Hit Points 55 (10d8 + 10)
Speed 30 ft., climb 40 ft., swim 20 ft.

STR	DEX	CON	INT	WIS	CHA
16 (+3)	13 (+1)	12 (+1)	5 (–3)	10 (+0)	3 (–4)

Skills Perception +4, Stealth +3
Condition Immunities prone
Senses darkvision 60 ft., tremorsense 60 ft., passive Perception 14
Languages —
Challenge 2 (450 XP)

Keen Smell. The shadow hunter has advantage on Wisdom (Perception) checks that rely on smell.

Shadow Stealth. While in dim light or darkness, the shadow can take the Hide action as a bonus action.

Actions

Bite. *Melee Weapon Attack:* +5 to hit, reach 5 ft., one target. *Hit:* 6 (1d6 + 3) piercing damage and 10 (3d6) poison damage. The target must succeed on a DC 13 Constitution saving throw or be poisoned for 1 hour.

Shark, Oil

An immense, eyeless shark over 20 feet long feet darts through the flames, its blackish-blue, metallic scales gleam with blackish oil.

The Sea of Fire located on the Plane of Molten Skies and the Plane of Fire is home to strange aquatic life (if they can be called that), but perhaps none is stranger than the mighty oil shark. These creatures spend their days swimming beneath the burning surface of the Sea of Fire, searching for prey. Their diet consists of other aquatic creatures found in the Sea of Fire such as fire crabs, oil worms, and the great fire whales. The latter is a particular favorite of the oil shark, and while the typical great fire whale outweighs (and is generally larger) than the typical oil shark, an oil shark pack has been known to attack and kill a lone fire whale with ease. Oil sharks have never been encountered outside the Plane of Molten Skies or Plane of Fire though sages believe the oil shark can exist in normal water.

Oil sharks are completely blind and rely completely upon their "sonar" to hunt their prey. Oil sharks generally behave as other sharks; circling their prey before striking with their powerful jaws. Non-aquatic prey (i.e., creatures that breathe air) are often grasped in its jaws and dragged below the surface of the burning sea where it drowns in the oily waters. Their oily hides allow them to glide smoothly and quickly through normal water.

Oil sharks are a delicacy of volcano giants and are often hunted by such creatures. The thick, metallic hide of an oil shark is prized by salamanders and they often hunt these creatures, kill them, and sculpt armor from the hide. Oil shark armor is detailed in the sidebar.

Oil Shark

Huge monstrosity, neutral

Armor Class 15 (natural armor)
Hit Points 114 (12d12 + 36)
Speed swim 60 ft.

STR	DEX	CON	INT	WIS	CHA
22 (+6)	15 (+2)	17 (+3)	1 (−5)	12 (+1)	2 (−4)

Skills Perception +4
Damage Vulnerabilities cold
Damage Immunities fire
Senses blindsight 60 ft., passive Perception 14
Languages —
Challenge 6 (2,300 XP)

Blood Frenzy. The shark has advantage on melee attack rolls against any creature that doesn't have all its hit points.

Keen Smell. The oil shark has advantage on Wisdom (Perception) checks that rely on smell.

Liquid Fire. The oil shark is only known to inhabit the Sea of Fire in the Plane of Molten Skies and the Plane of Fire, and therefore can breathe in liquid fire and underwater.

Actions

Bite. *Melee Weapon Attack:* +9 to hit, reach 5 ft., one target. *Hit*: 28 (4d10 + 6) piercing damage plus 14 (4d6) fire damage.

Silid

A small goblin-like humanoid emerges from the shadows. It is dressed in drab garments that match its pale gray, leathery skin. An unkempt shock of short black hair frames its bat-like face. It has slightly pointed ears and bulbous red pupils, and its long and slender arms end in four-fingered hands.

These small subterranean dwellers enjoy ambushing and waylaying their opponents. They slay their victims, steal their possessions, and leave their bodies to whatever happens to wander along looking for a meal. Cruel, mean-spirited creatures, silids care nothing for themselves or anything else. They seem to take great pleasure in bringing misery to others, particularly adventurers. Silids rarely interact with other races. They are an untrustworthy lot, and most other races avoid contact with them.

Silids live in groups (called stripes) of up to 40 individuals. Each stripe is a loose organization of silids, with a single leader that controls and governs the remainder of the stripe. The leader is almost always the meanest, cruelest, and sneakiest silid of the bunch. Under his command, the silids conduct raids and hunt their subterranean realm for surface-dwellers that have wandered into their territory. When hunting or harassing travelers, silids often don armor (either leather or padded) and carry weapons.

Silids skulk about their underground world in search of surface-dwellers. Surface-dwellers seem to love exploring the Underdark, so there rarely is a shortage of opponents for the mean-spirited silid. Often, a band of silids trails an adventuring party before attacking; waiting until the terrain is just right (silids prefer small, cramped areas because they gain the advantage on larger opponents). When the attack commences, a silid blurs itself and usually employs one of the following tactics.

The silids attack from ambush, attempting to maim or kill as many of their opponents as they can. Or, the silids rush from all angles and swarm their opponents. The latter tactic is usually only used when a large group of silids is present (such as when a party of adventurers stumbles into a silid lair).

Silid

Small humanoid, chaotic evil
Armor Class 13 (leather armor)
Hit Points 16 (3d6 + 6)
Speed 30 ft.

STR	DEX	CON	INT	WIS	CHA
13 (+1)	15 (+2)	14 (+2)	10 (+0)	9 (−1)	9 (−1)

Skills Stealth +4
Senses darkvision 60 ft., passive Perception 9
Languages Goblin, Undercommon
Challenge 1 (200 XP)

Innate Spellcasting. The silid's innate spellcasting ability is Charisma (spell save DC 9, +1 to hit with spell attacks). It can innately cast *blur* 1/day, requiring no material components.

Surprise Attack. If the silid surprises a creature and hits it with an attack during the first round of combat, the target takes an extra 10 (3d6) damage from the attack.

Actions

Shortsword. *Melee Weapon Attack:* +4 to hit, reach 5 ft., one target. *Hit:* 5 (1d6 + 2) piercing damage.

Spear. *Melee or Ranged Weapon Attack:* +3 to hit, reach 5 ft. or range 20/60 ft., one target. *Hit:* 4 (1d6 + 1) piercing damage.

Skeleton Knight

Once bound to their master as a personal guard, a skeletal knight returns when called to defend its lord once again. Only the master knows the command word that will cause the skeletal knight to reassemble to its humanoid form from the pile of bones, armor scraps, and rusted weapons that is its dormant state. When the master calls, one to four skeletal knights will rise and fight with whatever weapon is grasped during reanimation. When encountered, a skeletal knight is often found with either a greatsword, longsword, or a battle axe and wears bits of scale mail, chainmail, or plate armor.

A skeletal knight cannot speak, but it understands the language of its master. Once created, it will defend its lord as it did in life, unceasingly and without fail. If a skeletal knight is inactive for 24 hours, it will collapse into a giant pile once again to await the master's next call.

Skeletal Knight

Medium undead, lawful evil
Armor Class 15 (armor scraps)
Hit Points 37 (5d8 + 15)
Speed 30 ft.

STR	DEX	CON	INT	WIS	CHA
13 (+1)	15 (+2)	17 (+3)	7 (−2)	8 (−1)	6 (−2)

Damage Vulnerabilities bludgeoning
Damage Immunities poison
Condition Immunities: exhaustion, poisoned
Senses darkvision 60 ft., passive Perception 9
Languages understand its master's language in life but cannot speak
Challenge 2 (450 XP)

Actions

Melee Weapon. *Melee Weapon Attack:* +3 to hit, reach 5 ft., one target. *Hit:* varies, damage is determined by weapon. *Battleaxe or longsword:* 5 (1d8 + 1) slashing damage, or 6 (1d10 + 1) slashing damage if used with two hands. *Greatsword:* 9 (2d6 + 1) slashing damage.

Skeletons

Skeleton, Black

This creature looks like a skeleton with glistening black bones, seemingly constructed of blackened steel. Small red pinpoints of light burn in its hollowed eye sockets.

Black skeletons were first encountered in Rappan Athuk (see the adventure, Rappan Athuk V from Necromancer Games). Much more powerful than standard skeletons, these minions of evil are often employed as guardians or protectors to keep sealed some ancient knowledge best left undiscovered. They are intelligent monsters and are not subject to the mindless commands that can be given to such undead as skeletons or zombies. They have a clear mind and sometimes go against the commands and wishes of those they serve, if it benefits the black skeleton in question.

Black skeletons are the remnants of living creatures slain in an area where the ground is soaked through with evil. The bodies of fallen heroes are contaminated and polluted by such evil and within days after their death, the slain creatures rise as black skeletons, leaving their former lives and bodies behind. Black skeletons are intelligent and do maintain some memories of their former lives.

Black skeletons wear any clothes or armor they had in life, and some still carry their gear or weapons (most discard their weapons in favor of two shortswords as soon as they can).

Black skeletons attack with two shortswords in battle with little more than the intention of cutting their foes to pieces. They are intelligent opponents and will use tactics during battle, often sending several of their number against a foe's front, while the others move into position to flank their adversaries. Black skeletons are smart enough to know when the battle is lost and withdraw from combat, though rarely. Most simply fight to the death, driven by some unseen hatred for the living.

Black Skeleton

Medium undead, chaotic evil
Armor Class 17 (chain shirt)
Hit Points 71 (13d8 + 13)
Speed 40 ft.

STR	DEX	CON	INT	WIS	CHA
11 (+0)	19 (+4)	13 (+1)	13 (+1)	10 (+0)	14 (+2)

Skills Perception +4, Stealth +6
Damage Vulnerabilities bludgeoning, radiant
Damage Resistances cold
Damage Immunities necrotic, poison
Condition Immunities exhaustion, poisoned
Senses darkvision 60 ft., passive Perception 14
Languages the languages it knew in life but can't speak
Challenge 4 (1,100 XP)

Shortsword Masters. Black skeletons gain defensive bonuses (+2 to AC) and bonuses to attack (+2 to hit) when wielding two shortswords (included in the statistics).

Actions

Multiattack. The black skeleton makes two claw attacks or two shortsword attacks.

Claw. *Melee Weapon Attack:* +6 to hit, reach 5 ft., one target. *Hit:* 8 (1d8 + 4) slashing damage, and the target's Strength score is reduced by 1d4. The target dies if this reduces its strength to 0. Otherwise, the reduction lasts until the target finishes a short or long rest.

Shortsword. *Melee Weapon Attack:* +8 to hit, reach 5 ft., one target. *Hit:* 11 (2d6 + 4) piercing damage, and the target's Strength score is reduced by 1d4. The target dies if this reduces its strength to 0. Otherwise, the reduction lasts until the target finishes a short or long rest

Skeleton, Lead

This creature appears to be an animated skeleton whose bones have been coated with metal.

Lead skeletons appear simply to be skeletons coated with metal. Despite their outward appearance, they are actually golem-like constructs and not undead. Therefore, they cannot be turned.

Lead skeletons appear as 6-foot-tall skeletons constructed of metal. Some have gemstones encrusted in the body and eye sockets. A lead skeleton is expensive to create. Those who choose to create such creatures prefer the added fear and awe the skeletons tend to receive, and have a great deal of additional wealth and time.

Lead skeletons can be programmed to attack only certain creatures or be programmed to accept certain passwords or types of clothing. More complex programming tends to fail. While lead skeletons might not have the same abilities as other golems, their immunities and speed make them extraordinarily dangerous. They use their fists to inflict large amounts of damage and attack a single target until it is dead.

Lead Skeleton

Medium undead, neutral
Armor Class 18 (natural armor)
Hit Points 66 (12d8 + 12)
Speed 30 ft.

STR	DEX	CON	INT	WIS	CHA
21 (+5)	18 (+4)	13 (+1)	2 (−4)	10 (+0)	1 (−5)

Damage Immunities acid, cold, fire, lightning, poison; bludgeoning, piercing, and slashing from nonmagical weapons that aren't adamantine
Condition Immunities charmed, exhaustion, frightened, paralyzed, petrified, poisoned
Senses darkvision 60 ft., passive Perception 10
Languages understands the languages it knew in life but can't speak
Challenge 6 (2,300 XP)

Immutable Form. The skeleton is immune to any spell or effect that would alter its form.

Magic Resistance. The skeleton has advantage on saving throws against spells and other magical effects.

Magic Weapons. The skeleton's weapon attacks are magical.

Actions

Multiattack. The lead skeleton makes two slam attacks.

Slams. Melee Weapon Attack: +8 to hit, reach 5 ft., one target. *Hit:* 14 (2d8 + 5) bludgeoning damage.

Skulleton

This being looks like a humanoid skull with several small gems inset in its eye sockets and mouth.

Skulletons are undead creatures believed to have been created by a lich or demi-lich, for the creature greatly resembles the latter in that it is nothing more than a pile of dust, a skull, and a collection of bones. The gemstones inset in its eye sockets and in place of its teeth are not gemstones at all, but are painted glass (worthless). The skulleton is thought to have been created to frighten off would-be tomb plunderers or convince them they have defeated the skulleton's creator rather than a minor servitor and tomb guardian.

A skulleton lies in wait for its prey. When a living creature touches a skulleton, it uses its dust attack to incapacitate and confuse the intruders. If the intruders have not fled, it moves in to bite with its gem-encrusted teeth.

Skulleton

Tiny undead, neutral evil
Armor Class 12 (natural armor)
Hit Points 21 (6d4 + 6)
Speed fly 10 ft.

STR	DEX	CON	INT	WIS	CHA
6 (–2)	10 (+0)	13 (+1)	10 (+0)	12 (+1)	14 (+2)

Skills Perception +5
Damage Immunities poison
Condition Immunities exhaustion, poisoned
Senses darkvision 60 ft., passive Perception 15
Languages understands the languages of its creator but can't speak
Challenge ¼ (50 XP)

Actions

Bite. *Melee Weapon Attack:* +2 to hit, reach 0 ft., one target. *Hit:* 3 (1d6) piercing damage. If the target is a creature, it must succeed on a DC 11 Constitution saving throw against disease or be poisoned until the disease is cured. For every 24 hours that elapse, the target must repeat the saving throw, reducing its hit point maximum by 5 (1d10) on a failure. The disease is cured on a success. The target dies if the disease reduces its hit point maximum to 0. This reduction to the target's hit point maximum lasts until the disease is cured.

Dust (2/day). The skulleton can use its crumbled remains to attack any creature that comes within 10 feet of it. The skulleton billows forth a cloud of dust that surrounds it in a 10-foot radius. All creatures in this area must succeed on a DC 12 Constitution saving throw or be poisoned for 1 minute. The target can repeat the saving throw at the end of each of its turns, ending the effect on itself on a success.

Sloth Viper

This large emerald snake has bands of gold and black ringing its body and a black-tipped tail.

The sloth viper is a lightning-quick predator most often found in dense, thick jungles or overgrown swamplands. The typical sloth viper is 9–10 feet long, though they can grow to a length of 20 or more feet. They subsist on a diet of small animals, preferring birds, lizards, and small mammals to others. They are fearless, however, and do not hesitate to attack much larger prey such as cheetahs, leopards, and even lions. Once the sloth viper has fed, it often recoils high above the ground, under the thicket and blanket of leaves, branches, and limbs where it sleeps for the next 1d6 days.

The sloth viper is a solitary predator; rarely is more than one encountered. If such an encounter takes place, they are often a mated pair, with a nest of eggs nearby. A sloth viper's lair is a dense thicket of natural underbrush and trees. A typical nest contains 1d4 emerald colored eggs.

Sloth vipers are hunted by some humanoids for their scales and poison (which is rumored to be valued by spellcasters for its properties).

Sloth vipers are ambush hunters and wait patiently among the limbs and branches of trees for potential prey to pass underneath it. When unsuspecting prey is in range, the viper either drops on it from above or snaps down quickly with its vicious bite, recoiling back into the trees afterward.

Sloth Viper

Large monstrosity, neutral

Armor Class 16 (natural armor)
Hit Points 38 (7d10)
Speed 30 ft., climb 30 ft., swim 30 ft.

STR	DEX	CON	INT	WIS	CHA
13 (+1)	16 (+3)	11 (+0)	2 (–4)	12 (+1)	2 (–4)

Skills Perception +3, Stealth +5
Senses darkvision 60 ft., passive Perception 13
Languages —
Challenge 2 (450 XP)

Actions

Bite. *Melee Weapon Attack:* +5 to hit, reach 5 ft., one target. *Hit:* 7 (1d8 + 3) piercing damage, and the target must succeed on a DC 13 Constitution saving throw. On a failed saving throw, the target takes 14 (4d6) poison damage and the target is poisoned for 1 minute. On a successful saving throw, the target takes half damage and isn't poisoned.

While the target is poisoned, its speed is halved, it can't use reactions, and it can take only one action or one bonus action on each of its turns, and regardless of abilities or magic items, it can't make more than one melee or ranged attack during its turn. If the creature attempts to cast a spell with a casting time of 1 action, roll a d20. On an 11 or higher, the spell doesn't take effect until the creature's next turn, and the creature must use its action on that turn to complete the spell. If it can't, the spell is wasted.

Sloth, Giant

This massive sloth is brownish-black, and its fur has a greenish tint to it. Its eyes are white.

Giant sloths grow up to be 10 feet long and weigh up to 450 pounds. The fur of a giant sloth is stained green by algae.

A giant sloth attacks by biting and rending its opponent with its claws.

Giant Sloth

Huge beast, neutral
Armor Class 15 (natural armor)
Hit Points 76 (8d12 + 24)
Speed 15 ft., climb 30 ft.

STR	DEX	CON	INT	WIS	CHA
22 (+6)	10 (+0)	17 (+3)	2 (–4)	12 (+1)	5 (–3)

Skills Athletics +9
Senses passive Perception 11
Languages —
Challenge 5 (1,800 XP)

Keen Scent. The giant sloth has advantage on Wisdom (Perception) checks based on scent.

Actions

Multiattack. The giant sloth makes one bite attack and two claw attacks.

Bite. *Melee Weapon Attack:* +9 to hit, reach 5 ft., one target. *Hit:* 15 (2d8 + 6) piercing damage.

Claw. *Melee Weapon Attack:* +9 to hit, reach 10 ft., one target. *Hit:* 17 (2d10 + 6) slashing damage, and the target must make a DC 17 Strength saving throw or be knocked prone.

Winglessly flying forth, a monstrously-sized anaconda-like serpent descends from the sky. Its 30-foot body is nearly two-feet thick and covered in muddy brown scales with strange patterns and symbols on its dorsal side. Large glowing yellow orbs set in its wide, triangular head emit a haunting glare and arching its tail aggressively, it exposes a vicious-looking barbed stinger.

Wizards and other sages well-versed in arcane lore agree that the sepia snake was the inspiration for the spell sepia snake sigil. The similarities between the creature and the spell are simply too great to be coincidental. Though a sepia snake can be found just about anywhere, it usually makes its lair deep underground in abandoned mines, dungeons, or subterranean caverns. It has been said that to look into the eyes of the sepia snake is to look into one's own doom.

A sepia snake begins combat by using its gaze on what it believes to be its most dangerous opponents so it can safely deal with them later. In melee, a sepia snake tries to avoid direct combat and will rely on its Flyby Attack feat to keep it out of danger. A sepia snake can emit a brown, web-like substance from its throat that immobilizes its opponent. Held, cocooned, or otherwise incapacitated foes are poisoned to soften them up for consumption.

Sepia Snake

Huge monstrosity, neutral
Armor Class 16 (natural armor)
Hit Points 147 (14d12 + 56)
Speed 40 ft., fly 50 ft.

STR	DEX	CON	INT	WIS	CHA
23 (+6)	16 (+3)	19 (+4)	4 (–3)	13 (+1)	19 (+4)

Saving Throws Dex +7, Con +8
Skills Perception +9, Stealth +7
Damage Resistance bludgeoning, piercing, and slashing from nonmagical weapons
Damage Immunities poison
Condition Immunities poisoned, prone
Senses darkvision 120 ft., passive Perception 19
Languages —
Challenge 9 (5,000 XP)

Flyby. The sepia snake doesn't provoke an opportunity attack when it flies out of an enemy's reach.

Gaze. When a creature that can see the sepia snake's eyes starts its turn within 30 feet of the sepia snake, the snake can force it to make a DC 16 Constitution saving throw if the sepia snake isn't incapacitated and can see the creature. On failure, the creature is frightened for 1 minute.

Unless surprised, a creature can avert its eyes to avoid the saving throw at the start of its turn. If the creature does so, it can't see the sepia snake until the start of its next turn, when it can avert its eyes again. If the creature looks at the sepia snake in the meantime, it must immediately attempt the save. While averting its eyes, any attacks on the sepia snake are done at disadvantage.

Actions

Multiattack. The sepia snake makes two melee attacks: one with its bite and one with its tail sting.

Bite. *Melee Weapon Attack:* +10 to hit, reach 10 ft., one target. *Hit:* 15 (2d8 + 6) piercing damage. The target is grappled (escape DC 16) if the sepia snake isn't already grappling a creature, and the target is restrained until the grapple ends. While the snake has a creature grappled with its bite, it can't bite a different creature.

Tail Sting. *Melee Weapon Attack:* +10 to hit, reach 10 ft., one target. *Hit:* 19 (2d12 + 6) piercing damage and 27 (6d8) poison damage, and the target must make a successful DC 16 Constitution saving throw or is paralyzed for 1 minute. The creature can repeat the saving throw at the end of each of its turns, ending the effect on itself with a success.

Cocoon (Recharge 5–6). A sepia snake can fire a line of webbing to a range of 20 feet. Creatures in this area must make a DC 16 Dexterity saving throw. On a failure, the creature is restrained by webbing. If a creature is completely covered in webbing, it must make a successful DC 16 Constitution saving throw or be placed in a state of magical suspended animation for 1d4 + 12 days. During this time, the creature does not need food or water.

In one round, the sepia snake can spit enough webbing to cover one Medium or smaller creature. For each size category larger than Medium, the snake must fire another line of webbing to completely encase an opponent.

As an action, creatures hit by the webbing but not completely covered can make a DC 16 Strength check, bursting the webbing on a success. A creature that is completely wrapped in the webbing cannot break free and must rely on others to remove the webs. The webbing can be attacked and destroyed (AC 10; hp 10; vulnerability to fire damage; immunity to bludgeoning, poison, and psychic damage).

Spell Parrot

The bird appears to be an entirely ordinary parrot. When it speaks, however, it utters the words of a magical spell, and arcane energy begins to swirl around it.

Spell parrots are an exceedingly rare and unexplained phenomenon. They look, think, and act primarily like parrots, despite high intelligence for an animal. No one knows why they are able to do what they do though it is clear that the ability they possess is as likely to be a burden as a boon to them. When spell parrots first hear and mimic a spellcaster, they rarely seem to understand or expect the results of their mimicry. Older wild spell parrots have usually learned how to utilize their strange and unpredictable powers but rarely will do so unless threatened.

Spell parrots can be tamed as pets, but since they occur spontaneously (within any of the larger parrot species), it is difficult to discover one young enough to socialize it properly. Careful training by someone with exceptional animal handling skills can result in a spell parrot that only mimics spells at a signal from its humanoid handler. However, they can be cantankerous creatures, and moody, with questionable senses of humor, and even the best-trained spell parrot may choose to disobey its handler.

Like mundane parrots, spell parrots often live a little longer than humans, and while they cannot become fluent in humanoid languages, they can memorize small vocabularies and engage in rudimentary verbal communication. Talking to a well-trained spell parrot is similar in clarity, depth, grammar, and logic to communication with a small toddler.

Spell Parrot

Tiny monstrosity, unaligned
Armor Class 12
Hit Points 3 (2d4 − 2)
Speed 10 ft., fly 50 ft.

STR	DEX	CON	INT	WIS	CHA
2 (−4)	14 (+2)	8 (−1)	2 (−4)	12 (+1)	6 (−2)

Skills Perception +3
Senses passive Perception 13
Languages —
Challenge 3 (700 XP)

Spell Mimicry. Whenever the spell parrot hears a cantrip or a 1st through 5th level spell that has a verbal component being cast, it can attempt to mimic the casting of that spell on its next turn. The spell parrot ignores any somatic or material component that the spell requires.

When the spell parrot attempts to mimic the spell, roll a d6. If the spell is a cantrip or 1st level spell, the casting succeeds if the result is a 3–6. If the spell is 2nd level or higher, the casting succeeds on the result of a 5 or 6. Once the spell parrot mimics a spell, it forgets the spell. The spell parrot uses the original caster's spell save DC and spell attack bonus, and the spell must have a valid target for the spell parrot to use as the target of the mimicked spell.

Actions

Bite. *Melee Weapon Attack:* +4 to hit, reach 5 ft., one target. *Hit:* 1 piercing damage.

Elder Spell Parrot

An elder spell parrot is capable of attempting to mimic even higher level spells. It has the following changes:

- Its Challenge Rating is 6 (2,300 XP).

- It has 7 (5d4 − 5) hit points.

- Its Spell Mimicry feature is as follows:

Spell Mimicry. Whenever the spell parrot hears a cantrip or a 1st through 8th level spell that has a verbal component being cast, it can attempt to mimic the casting of that spell on its next turn. The spell parrot ignores any somatic or material component that the spell requires.

When the spell parrot attempts to mimic the spell, roll a d6. If the spell is a cantrip or a 1st through 3rd level spell, the casting succeeds if the result is a 3–6. If the spell is 4th through 6th level, the casting succeeds on the result of a 5 or 6. If the spell is 7th or 8th level, the casting succeeds only on a 6. Once the spell parrot mimics a spell, it forgets it. The spell parrot uses the original caster's spell save DC and spell attack bonus, and the spell must have a valid target for the spell parrot to use as the target of the mimicked spell.

Spiders

Spider Climb. The spider can climb difficult surfaces, including upside down on ceilings, without needing to make an ability check.

Web Sense. While in contact with a web, the spider knows the exact location of any other creature in contact with the same web.

Web Walker. The spider ignores movement restrictions caused by webbing.

Actions

Bite. *Melee Weapon Attack:* +4 to hit, reach 5 ft., one target. *Hit:* 3 (1d3 + 2) piercing damage, and the target must attempt a DC 13 Constitution saving throw taking 1 (1d3) poison damage on a failure. If the target misses its saving throw by 5 or more, it is poisoned for 1 hour.

Spider, Demon

Created in the bowels of the underworld, the extremely rare demon spider is one of the largest varieties of its kind. Although not actually a demon, the creature has been given its name by survivors because of its appearance and especially malevolent attitude; it not only kills to feed itself, it enjoys the hunt and subsequent torture of its victim.

Demon Spider

Large monstrosity, chaotic evil
Armor Class 16 (natural armor)
Hit Points 102 (12d10 + 36)
Speed 30 ft., climb 30 ft.

STR	DEX	CON	INT	WIS	CHA
10 (+0)	17 (+3)	16 (+3)	5 (−3)	12 (+1)	3 (−4)

Spider, Albino Cave

This tiny hunting spider is about the size of a man's fist. It is pallid white, often with irregular light brown blotches on its abdomen, which helps it blend in with the toadstools and fungus which is its home. The albino cave spider normally feeds on normal and dire rats, but it attacks anything that comes within range.

Albino cave spiders hunt rats in caves or in deep underground regions where the sun never reaches. These tiny killers are extremely sensitive to movement, and despite their unique coloring, are highly adept at hiding and stealthy stalking.

The albino cave spider is mildly toxic, as some of the other Under Realm predators have discovered. They use their poisonous bite to sicken prey and follow until they can feast on the remains.

Male and female cave spiders are roughly the same size, with females being slightly larger. The females are the predominant hunters, with the males tending to the web-nest when an egg sac is present. Both sexes are extremely protective of the egg sac and attack larger foes when it is threatened.

Spider, Albino Cave

Tiny beast, unaligned
Armor Class 15 (natural armor)
Hit Points 2 (1d4)
Speed 20 ft., climb 10 ft.

STR	DEX	CON	INT	WIS	CHA
4 (−3)	14 (+2)	10 (+0)	2 (−4)	10 (+0)	3 (−4)

Skills Stealth +6
Damage Vulnerabilities fire
Damage Resistances cold, lightning
Damage Immunities poison
Condition Immunities poisoned
Senses darkvision 120 ft., passive Perception 11
Challenge 8 (3,900 XP)

Magic Resistance. The spider has advantage on saving throws against spells and other magical effects.

Magic Weapons. The spider's weapon attacks are magical.

Spider Climb. The spider can climb difficult surfaces, including upside down on ceilings, without needing to make an ability check.

Web Sense. While in contact with a web, the spider knows the exact location of any other creature in contact with the same web.

Web Walker. The spider ignores movement restrictions caused by webbing.

Actions

Multiattack. The spider can make one bite attacks and two puncture attacks with its legs.

Bite. *Melee Weapon Attack:* +6 to hit, reach 5 ft., one target. *Hit:* 8 (1d10 + 3) piercing damage, and the target must make a DC 12 Constitution saving throw, taking 18 (4d8) poison damage on a failed save, or half as much damage on a success. If the poison damage reduces the target to 0 hit points, the target is stable but poisoned for 1 hour, even after regaining hit points, and is paralyzed while poisoned in this way.

Puncture. *Melee Weapon Attack:* +6 to hit, reach 10 ft., one target. *Hit:* 14 (2d10 + 3) piercing damage.

Spider, Prism

Alarmed and posturing aggressively, the great spider changes from a mottled brown to a shifting array of colorful patterns pulsing across its surface as it attacks.

Prism spiders are exceedingly rare giant spiders of mysterious origin. Like most spiders, they are predatory, and though most are reclusive hunters of wild game, some have learned to see humanoids as a food source. When this happens, it is often sadly the case that these beautiful animals must be put down. Sadder still, despite their rarity, prism spiders are sometimes poached for their carapaces. In death, a prism spider's carapace retains the color and immunity it had in the moment it died, and the carapace of a prism spider who died fighting may be crafted into a set of full plate, offering the wearer resistance to whatever immunity the carapace holds. Carapaces sell for 1,000 gp, and finished prism spider armor for twice as much. (It is otherwise identical to regular

full plate, but able to be additionally enchanted at regular price, if desired.)

A prism spider is hardly helpless prey for the harvesting. With its bite and spined legs alone, prism spiders are formidable foes. Add to that their prismatic powers and few would-be poachers escape with their lives. Failed poaching, however, can be what leads a prism spider to see humanoids as food, and thus need to be dealt with for the safety of surrounding communities.

When calm, a prism spider is a mottled black and brown in color and looks like an ordinary giant spider. Once the spider is alarmed or aggressive, however, it begins to change colors in brilliant and beautiful patterns, some speckled, striped, diamond-patterned, or even swirled. No one knows if the prism spider changes color deliberately, due to some incomprehensible spider logic, or whether the changes are merely random.

Prism Spider

Small monstrosity, unaligned
Armor Class 14 (natural armor)
Hit Points 71 (11d6 + 33)
Speed 30 ft., climb 30 ft.

STR	DEX	CON	INT	WIS	CHA
19 (+4)	16 (+3)	16 (+3)	2 (−4)	13 (+1)	6 (−2)

Skills Perception +9, Stealth +11, Survival +9
Damage Immunities varies
Condition Immunities varies
Senses blindsight 10 ft., darkvision 60 ft., passive Perception 19
Challenge 9 (5,000 XP)

Shifting Power. As the prism spider shifts color, its immunities and attacks change. Roll a d6 at the start of the spider's turn and consult the table below. Use the result in place of one of the spider's attacks.

1d6	Color/ Immunity	Other
1	Green/ Acid	***Spit Acid.*** The spider spits a 30-foot line of acid that is 5 feet wide. Each creature in the line must make a DC 16 Dexterity saving throw, taking 31 (9d6) acid damage on a failed save, or half as much damage on a successful one.
2	Orange/ Fire	***Inferno Shield.*** The spider is wreathed in intense, thick flames, shedding bright light in a 20-foot radius and dim light for an additional 20 feet. Whenever a creature within 5 feet of the spider hits it with a melee attack before the end of the prism spider's next turn, the shield erupts, dealing 27 (6d8) fire damage to the creature.
3	Grey/ Disease	***Fetid Bite.*** When the prism spider makes a bite attack, the target must succeed on a DC 17 Constitution saving throw against disease or become poisoned until the disease is cured. Every 24 hours that elapse, the target must repeat the saving throw, reducing its hit point maximum by 16 (3d10) on a failure. The disease is cured on a success. The target dies if the disease reduces its hit point maximum to 0. This reduction to the target's hit point maximum lasts until the disease is cured

1d6	Color/Immunity	Other
4	Blue/Lightning	**Shocking Aura.** Until the end of the spider's next turn, creatures who enter or begin their turns within 15 feet of the prism spider must make a DC 16 Dexterity saving throw, taking 27 (6d8) lightning damage on a failed saving throw, or half as much damage on a successful one. Creatures wearing metal armor have disadvantage on this saving throw.
5	White/Cold	**Hoarfrost.** Until the beginning of the spider's next turn, creatures who enter or begin their turns within 15 feet of the prism spider must make a DC 16 Constitution saving throw. On a failed saving throw, the target takes 28 (8d6) cold damage. A creature who takes cold damage from this effect has their movement speed halved, cannot take reactions, and can only take one action or one bonus action on their turn. They can only make one melee or ranged attack on their turn, regardless of other class features or magic items.
6	Purple/ —	**Heal.** The spider magically heals itself for 36 (8d8) damage, and it has advantage on saving throws against spells and other magical effects until the end of its next turn.

Spider Climb. The prism spider can climb difficult surfaces, including upside down on ceilings, without needing to make an ability check.

Web Sense. While in contact with a web, the spider knows the exact location of any other creature in contact with the same web.

Web Walker. The spider ignores movement restrictions caused by webbing.

Actions

Multiattack. The spider uses one of its shifting power abilities and makes a bite attack.

Bite. Melee Weapon Attack: +8 to hit, reach 5 ft., one creature. *Hit:* 13 (2d8 + 4) piercing damage.

Web (Recharge 5–6). Ranged Weapon Attack: +7 to hit, range 30/60 ft., one creature. *Hit:* The target is restrained by webbing. As an action, the restrained target can make a DC 14 Strength check, bursting the webbing on a success. The webbing can also be attacked and destroyed (AC 10; hp 10; the same resistances that the prism spider is benefiting from at that time; immunity to bludgeoning, poison, and psychic damage).

Spider, Skull

This tiny creature appears to be a humanoid skull with eight spidery legs.

Skull spiders are tarantula-like creatures that reside in the skulls of their victims. The two front legs of a skull spider contain poisoned barbs that they use to sting their victims. The weak and fleshy body of a skull spider is about the size of a grapefruit and is easily damaged. Its eyes grow on the end of long, slender stalks. Skull spiders take up residence within skulls as a means of protecting themselves in a manner similar to hermit crabs.

Their eyestalks protrude through the empty eye sockets of their skull, and their legs have a backwards curve in the first joint that enables them to extend out of the bottom of the skull to allow rapid locomotion. Skull spiders can also fold their legs under their skull so they cannot be seen. Many an adventurer has been unnerved by the sight of dozens of skulls seemingly sprouting long, spidery legs and skittering toward them.

A colony of skull spiders is led by a king and queen, which are the only two members of the colony that are capable of reproducing. After a victim is subdued, the queen deposits an egg in the skull. Queen skull spiders are always 3 HD. The larva hatches, consumes the brain over a period of weeks, and then enters a pupae stage. After several months, when the corpse is sufficiently deteriorated, the new skull spider hatches, uses its strong legs to detach the skull, and goes to join its colony.

Skull spiders always attack en masse, swarming over their victims in great numbers and stinging them repeatedly.

Skull Spider

Tiny beast, unaligned
Armor Class 17 (natural armor)
Hit Points 2 (1d4)
Speed 20 ft., climb 10 ft.

STR	DEX	CON	INT	WIS	CHA
6 (−2)	20 (+5)	10 (+0)	2 (−4)	10 (+0)	2 (−4)

Skills Perception +4, Stealth +7
Senses darkvision 60 ft., passive Perception 14
Languages —
Challenge ½ (100 XP)

Pack Tactics. The spider has advantage on an attack roll against a creature if at least one of the spider's allies is within 5 feet of the creature and the ally isn't incapacitated.

Actions

Sting. Melee Weapon Attack: +7 to hit, reach 5 ft., one target. *Hit:* 7 (1d4 + 5) piercing damage, and the target must succeed on a DC 10 Constitution saving throw or become poisoned for 1 hour.

Spökvatten

The misty form of the stag suddenly transforms into that of a tall, graceful elven woman, rising from the cold waters of the lake.

The wicked fey known as the spökvatten lives in lonely ponds, streams, and waterfalls, lying in wait for its prey. In its natural form, a spökvatten resembles a beautiful elven woman with pale skin, long black hair, and pupilless black eyes. When prey (animals or humanoids) approaches, the spökvatten can transform into a cold, clinging mist. When hunting animals, the creature can simply envelop its prey in a chill grasp, paralyzing and killing it. Intelligent prey requires more subtlety, and in such cases, the spökvatten can take on the shape of any animal or humanoid — impersonating an especially impressive target for hunters, a lost child, or an especially attractive individual to draw its quarry closer.

The spökvatten's victims are drawn close to the creature's lair, and if possible, into the icy water where they will be easier to subdue. Slain and frozen victims are consumed later at the spökvatten's leisure or stored under the cold water for future use.

Spökvatten

Medium fey, neutral evil
Armor Class 14
Hit Points 78 (12d8 + 24)
Speed 30 ft., swim 30 ft.

STR	DEX	CON	INT	WIS	CHA
9 (–1)	18 (+4)	14 (+2)	10 (+0)	16 (+3)	18 (+4)

Skills Deception +10, Insight +6, Nature +3, Perception +9, Persuasion +10, Stealth +10
Damage Immunities cold
Senses darkvision 60 ft. passive Perception 19
Languages Aquan, Sylvan
Challenge 5 (1,800 XP)

Shapechanger. The spökvatten can use its action to magically polymorph into a Large cloud of mist, into a beast or humanoid of challenge rating 2 or lower, or back into its true form (that of a Medium fey). Anything it is carrying or wearing transforms with it. It reverts to its true form if it dies.

While in beast or humanoid form, the fey retains its game statistics and ability to speak, but its AC, movement modes, Strength, Dexterity, and special senses are replaced by those of the new form, and it gains any statistics and capabilities (except class features, legendary actions, and lair actions) that the new form has but that it lacks.

In mist form, the spökvatten can only use its icy fog ability, and it is unable to speak or manipulate objects. It is weightless, has a flying speed of 20 feet, can hover, and can enter a hostile creature's space and stop there. In addition, if air can pass through a space, the mist can do so without squeezing, and it can't pass through water. It has advantage on Strength, Dexterity, and Constitution saving throws, and it is immune to all nonmagical damage.

Actions

Cold Touch. *Melee Spell Attack:* +7 to hit, reach 5 ft., one target. *Hit:* 26 (4d10 + 4) cold damage. The target must succeed on a DC 15 Constitution saving throw or be paralyzed for 1 minute. The target can repeat the saving throw at the end of each of its turns, ending the effect on itself on a success.

Icy Fog (Recharge 5–6). The spökvatten exhales a cloud of freezing mist in a 15-foot cone. Each creature in that area must make a DC 15 Dexterity saving throw, taking 36 (8d8) cold damage on a failed save, or half as much damage on a successful one.

Stone Delver

A grotesque horror that tunnels through the underground with its four powerful arms, the stone delver constantly searches for more prey to feed its insatiable hunger.

The creature stands on its short back legs when it tunnels, using its four arms and razor-sharp claws to dig through earth and stone. However, it can travel on all six limbs quickly, often rushing foes in a silent charge. The stone delver's carapace exterior is as hard as granite, shielding it from rock slides and tunnel collapses.

Although it primarily survives on flesh from plentiful subterranean races, it is always searching for gems to consume. The valuable crystals have a regenerative power, restoring lost hit points or healing damage within a few hours after consumption. The stone delver can be distracted by gems if thrown or displayed by characters. Deep within the ground, the stone delver's lair often has a hidden hoard of raw and uncut gems.

Six Limb Charge. If the stone delver moves at least 20 feet straight towards a target and then hits it with a claw attack on the same turn, the target takes an extra 10 (3d6) slashing damage. If the target is a creature, it must succeed on a DC 16 Strength saving throw or be knocked prone.

If the stone delver hit its initial target on the same turn and knocked it prone, it can use a bonus action to make up to four claw attacks against targets that are adjacent to the initial target.

Tunneler. The stone delver can burrow through solid stone at half its burrowing speed leaving a 5 foot wide, 10-foot-high tunnel in its wake.

Actions

Multiattack. The stone delver makes three claw attacks.

Claw. *Melee Weapon Attack:* +8 to hit, reach 10 ft., one target. *Hit:* 10 (1d10+5) slashing damage.

Stone Delver

Large monstrosity, chaotic evil
Armor Class 19 (natural armor)
Hit Points 114 (12d10 + 48)
Speed 30 ft., burrow 30 ft.

STR	DEX	CON	INT	WIS	CHA
21 (+5)	14 (+2)	18 (+4)	7 (–2)	10 (+0)	9 (–1)

Senses darkvision 120 ft., tremorsense 120 ft., passive Perception 10
Languages Stone Delver
Challenge 7 (2,900 XP)

Stormwarden

This humanoid has dark hair and eyes. Its skin is sapphire colored, and its hair is long. A long beard dominates its countenance. It is dressed in hide armor and furs.

Stormwardens dwell high in the mountains and hills away from civilization. They are hunters by nature and spend their time hunting and trapping game, though they never do so to an abundance, only enough to sustain themselves. They are isolationists and solitary, rarely found in groups of more than 6 individuals. Their hair color and eye color range across the spectrum just as a normal human, though most tend to have dark hair and eyes.

Stormwardens prefer to avoid combat, but if provoked, they open combat using their longswords, attempting to slay their opponents before escaping to their lair. If melee goes against a stormwarden, it alters the weather and attempts to escape.

Stormwarden

Medium humanoid, chaotic neutral
Armor Class 12 (hide armor)
Hit Points 45 (7d8 + 14)
Speed 30 ft.

STR	DEX	CON	INT	WIS	CHA
14 (+2)	10 (+0)	14 (+2)	16 (+3)	13 (+1)	10 (+0)

Skills Survival +3
Damage Resistances lightning, thunder
Senses darkvision 60 ft., passive Perception 11
Languages Common, Draconic, Giant
Challenge 1 (200 XP)

Innate Spellcasting. The stormwarden's spellcasting ability is Intelligence (spell save DC 13, + 5 to hit with spell attacks). The stormwarden can innately cast the following spells, requiring only verbal components:

At will: *thaumaturgy*
1/day: *fog cloud*

Actions

Longsword. *Melee Weapon Attack:* +4 to hit, reach 5 ft., one target. *Hit:* 6 (1d8 + 2) slashing damage, or 7 (1d10 + 2) slashing damage if used with two hands.

Longbow. *Ranged Weapon Attack:* +2 to hit, range 150/600 ft., one target. *Hit:* 4 (1d8) piercing damage.

Stormscream (1/day). The stormwarden unleashes a deafening scream filled with the fury of the storm in a 15-foot cone. Each creature in that area must make a DC 12 Constitution saving throw. On a failed save, a creature takes 9 (2d8) thunder damage and is pushed 10 feet away from the stormwarden. On a successful save, the creature takes half as much damage and isn't pushed.

Stormwarden Traits

Your stormwarden character has the following racial traits.

Ability Score Increase. Your Intelligence score increases by 2, and your Constitution score increases by 1.

Age. Stormwardens mature at the same rate as humans and reach the age of majority around the age of 20. They often live to be more than 150 years of age.

Alignment. Reclusive, passive, and attuned to nature, stormwardens tend to neutral alignment. It is not unusual to find a stormwarden that has been touched by the storm (or lightning), and is unpredictable and given to chaotic actions and choices.

Darkvision. You have acute vision that can pierce the darkest storm. You can see in dim light within 60 feet of you as if it were bright light, and in darkness as if it were dim light. You cannot discern color in darkness, only shades of gray.

Size. Stormwarden, much like humans, vary widely in height and build, from just over 5 feet to well over 6 feet tall. Your size is Medium.

Speed. Your base walking speed is 30 feet.

Blessing of the Storm. You know the *thaumaturgy* cantrip. When you reach 3rd level, you can cast *fog cloud* as a 2nd level spell once with this trait and regain the ability to do so when you finish a long rest. When you reach 5th level, you can cast *call lightning* as a 3rd level spell with this trait and regain the ability to do so when you finish a long rest. Intelligence is your spellcasting ability for these spells.

Discharge. You have advantage on saving throws made against effects that deal lightning damage.

Languages. You can speak, read, and write Common and your choice of either Draconic or Giant.

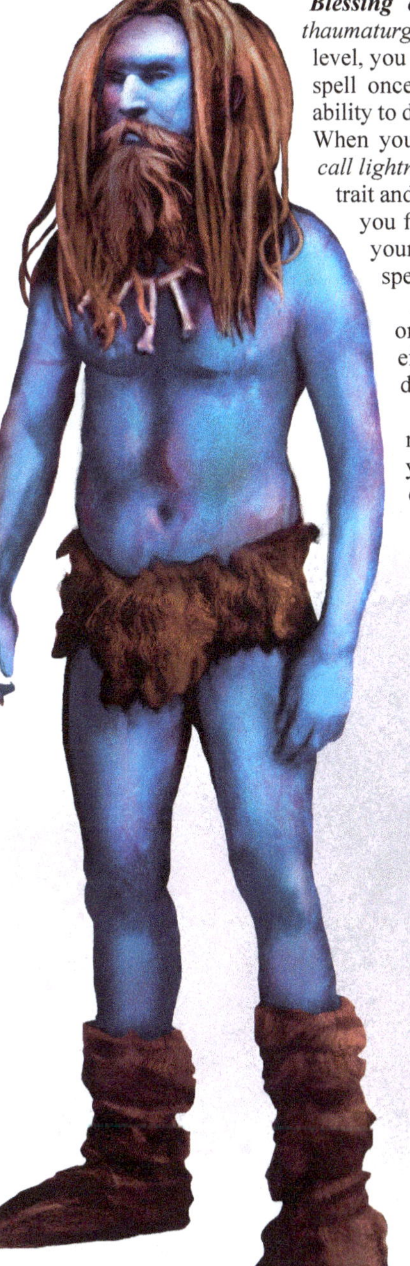

Swarm of Grigs

Winged man-shaped creatures with blue skin and cricket legs buzz about in a dense mass both hypnotic and frightening.

A grig swarm is a large mass of flying grigs. Normally grigs don't gather into groups larger than 80 or so creatures. But sometimes when several tribes come together, they join as a grig swarm.

The individual grigs that make up the swarm have light blue skin, forest-green hair, and brown hairy legs, and usually wear tunics or brightly colored vests with buttons made from tiny gems. A grig stands 1½ feet tall and weighs about 1 pound.

A grig swarm normally attacks by surrounding and enveloping its opponents. Before closing to melee range, a swarm uses its entangle ability to bind its foes. If facing destruction, a swarm often turns invisible and flees.

Swarm of Grigs

Medium swarm of Tiny fey, neutral good
Armor Class 14 (natural armor)
Hit Points 110 (20d8 + 20)
Speed 30 ft., fly 40 ft.

STR	DEX	CON	INT	WIS	CHA
5 (−3)	14 (+2)	12 (+1)	10 (+0)	13 (+1)	16 (+3)

Saving Throws Dex +5, Cha +6
Skills Acrobatics +5, Perception +4, Performance +6, Stealth +8
Senses passive Perception 14
Languages Common, Sylvan
Challenge 6 (2,300 XP)

Innate Spellcasting. The swarm of grig's innate spellcasting ability is Charisma (spell save DC14, +6 to hit with spell attacks). It can cast the following spells innately, without requiring material components.

At will: *druidcraft*
3/day each: *disguise self, entangle, invisibility*

Surprise Attack. If the swarm of grigs surprises a creature and hits it with an attack during the first round of combat, the target takes an extra 28 (8d6) damage from the attack.

Swarm. The swarm can occupy another creature's space and vice versa, and the swarm can move through any opening large enough for a grig. The swarm can't regain hit points or gain temporary hit points.

Actions

Shortsword. *Melee Weapon Attack:* +5 to hit, reach 5 ft., one target. *Hit:* 12 (3d6 + 2) piercing damage, or 5 (1d6 + 2) piercing damage if the swarm has half its points or fewer.

Fiddle (Recharge 5–6). The swarm of grigs begins playing a lively tune with its fiddles. Creatures within 30 feet that can hear the fiddle must make a DC 13 Wisdom saving throw or be charmed for 1 minute. While charmed by the swarm, the target uses its action to dance in place, capering comically. The creature can repeat the saving throw at the end of each of its turns, ending the effect on a success. If the saving throw is successful, or the effect ends for it, the creature is immune to that grig's Fiddle ability for 24 hours.

Swarm of Poisonous Frogs

Each frog in the hopping army bears black stripes on its hind legs and sickly, yellowish eyes.

Poisonous frog swarms are composed of small, fierce, poisonous frogs. The swarm moves collectively, hopping or jumping toward their prey.

Single poisonous frogs mate during the second half of the year. The male attracts a female through a series of unique mating calls consisting of strange guttural sounds. When a female answers the call, she lays a clutch of 1d6 eggs in a damp, dark area covered with leaves. The male fertilizes the eggs and protects them during their incubation period. Two weeks later the eggs hatch and the male carries the tadpoles to the water on its back. Tadpoles reach maturity in two to three months.

A single poisonous frog is a small dark-green frog with black bands or stripes on its hind legs. These stripes function as a warning to predators that the frog is poisonous. The skin of a poisonous frog is very smooth to the touch. The middle digit on each of its extremities is slightly shorter than the others.

Poisonous frog swarms attack by engulfing their prey and subjecting it to the frog's deadly poison. Creatures that begin their turn in a poisonous frog's space suffer swarm and poison damage.

Swarm of Poisonous Frogs

Medium swarm of Tiny beasts, unaligned
Armor Class 13
Hit Points 76 (17d8 – 8)
Speed 20 ft., swim 20 ft.

STR	DEX	CON	INT	WIS	CHA
1 (–5)	13 (+1)	8 (–1)	1 (–5)	8 (–1)	3 (–4)

Skills Perception +1, Stealth +3
Damage Immunities poison
Condition Immunities poisoned
Senses passive Perception 11
Languages —
Challenge 1 (200 XP)

Amphibious. The swarm can breathe air and water.

Keen Smell. The swarm has advantage on Wisdom (Perception) checks that rely on smell.

Standing Leap. The swarm's long jump is up to 10 feet and its high jump is up to 5 feet, with or without a running start.

Swarm. The swarm can occupy another creature's space and vice versa, and the swarm can move through any opening large enough for a poisonous frog. The swarm can't regain hit points or gain temporary hit points.

Actions

Bite. *Melee Weapon Attack:* +3 to hit, reach 0 ft., one target. *Hit:* 11 (3d6 + 1) piercing damage, and the target must succeed on a DC 12 Constitution saving throw or be poisoned for 1 hour.

Tainted Servant of Tsathogga

Tainted Servant of Tsathogga

Medium humanoid (corrupt), chaotic evil
Armor Class: 17 (natural armor)
Hit Points: 45 (10d10)
Speed: 30 ft., Swim 30 ft.t

STR	DEX	CON	INT	WIS	CHA
17 (+3)	12 (+1)	11 (+0)	9 (−1)	12 (+1)	8 (−2)

Damage Resistances: Bludgeoning, Cold
Damage Vulnerability: Radiant
Senses: Darkvision 30 ft., Passive Perception 14
Languages —
Challenge 5 (1,800 XP)

Amphibious: A tainted servant of Tsathogga can breathe air or water.

Slimy: Any attempt to grapple a tainted servant of Tsathogga is made with disadvantage. Any contested grapple checks made by a tainted servant of Tsathogga have advantage. All touch attack spells against a tainted servant of Tsathogga are made with disadvantage.

Actions

Frog's Claw. *Melee weapon attack:* +6 to hit, range 5 ft., one target. *Hit:* 7 (1d8+3) slashing damage.

Chaotic Croak (Recharge 5-6). A tainted servant of Tsathogga can croak, forcing all enemies within 50 ft. to attempt a DC 14 Wisdom saving throw. Any who fail use their action on their next turn to make an attack against the nearest creature if possible. A creature that fails its saving throw and cannot attack the nearest creature does not use its action on its turn.

Tsathogga's Spit (2/day). tainted servant of Tsathogga can spit a viscous glob at a target. On a successful hit, the target becomes restrained (Escape DC 14).

Tsathogga's Gift (1/day). A tainted servant of Tsathogga releases a 20 ft. sphere of poisonous gas through its skin. Any other creature that starts its turn within the range must make a successful DC 12 Constitution saving throw or take 7 (2d6) poison damage. This sphere follows the tainted servant and dissipates after 1 miunte.

Thaumaturmite

Created by accident in the laboratory of a magic-user renowned for his repertoire of *polymorph* spells, the magical insect known as the thaumaturmite is capable of dramatically altering its physical dimensions. The thaumaturmite may be encountered in either of its two forms, a 2-inch-long bug often mistaken for an exotic beetle, or a 6-feet-long menace weighing over 500 pounds. The creature can alter shape at will. No one knows which of these two shapes is the creature's true form, as it seems no more inclined to choose one shape or the other at any given time. Likewise, its choice of form often seems inappropriate or chaotic; a giant thaumaturmite has been encountered crammed into a small sewer pipe, while the tiny form sometimes foolishly attempts to attack human-sized targets.

Possessing an insect-level intelligence, the thaumaturmite seeks mainly to feed and to procreate. In its smaller form, it eats fabric and cloth, especially that worn by spellcasters. A single thaumaturmite typically chews 2d12 holes in a piece of fabric during a single feeding session. They are capable of damaging magic items such as an *elven cloak*, rendering the item non-magical if left to feed unnoticed. In its larger state, the thaumaturmite eats meat of all kinds, attacking any living creature when it needs to satisfy its hunger. It almost always favors spellcasters as food, using its special antenna to detect those of such vocations.

Thaumaturmite, lesser

Small monstrosity, unaligned
Armor Class 10
Hit Points 10 (3d6)
Speed 30 ft., climb 30 ft.

STR	DEX	CON	INT	WIS	CHA
10 (+0)	15 (+2)	10 (+0)	3 (−4)	5 (−3)	5 (−3)

Condition Immunities prone
Senses darkvision 30 ft., passive Perception 7
Languages —
Challenge 1 (200 XP)

Magic Scent. The thaumaturmite can pinpoint, by scent, the location of any magical cloth within 30 feet of it.

Consume magic. Any magical cloth that the thaumaturmite hits starts to corrode. Each time the thaumaturmite bites into a magical cloth which is worn or carried, the bearer of the item must make a successful DC 12 Dexterity saving throw or the item starts corroding. After two failed savings throws the item loses its magical qualities.

Spider Climb. The thaumaturmite can climb difficult surfaces, including upside down on ceilings, without needing to make an ability check.

Magic Resistance. The thaumaturmite has advantage on saving throws against spells and other magical effects.

Actions

Bite. *Melee weapon attack*: +4 to hit, reach 5 ft., one target. *Hit*: 9 (2d6 + 2) piercing damage.

Thaumaturmite, greater

Medium monstrosity, unaligned
Armor Class 15
Hit Points 27 (6d8)
Speed 30 ft., climb 30 ft.

STR	DEX	CON	INT	WIS	CHA
13 (+1)	17 (+3)	10 (+0)	3 (−4)	5 (−3)	5 (−3)

Condition Immunities prone
Senses darkvision 60 ft., passive Perception 7
Languages —
Challenge 5 (1,800 XP)

Magic Scent. The thaumaturmite can pinpoint, by scent, the location of any magical cloth within 30 feet of it.

Consume magic. Any magical cloth that the thaumaturmite hits starts to corrode. Each time the thaumaturmite bites into a magical cloth which is worn or carried, the bearer of the item must make a successful DC 12 Dexterity saving throw or the item starts corroding. After two failed savings throws the item loses its magical qualities.

Spider Climb. The thaumaturmite can climb difficult surfaces, including upside down on ceilings, without needing to make an ablity check.

Magic Resistance. The thaumaturmite has advantage on saving throws against spells and other magical effects.

Actions

Bite. *Melee weapon attack*: +6 to hit, reach 5 ft., one target. *Hit*: 25 (5d8+3) piercing damage.

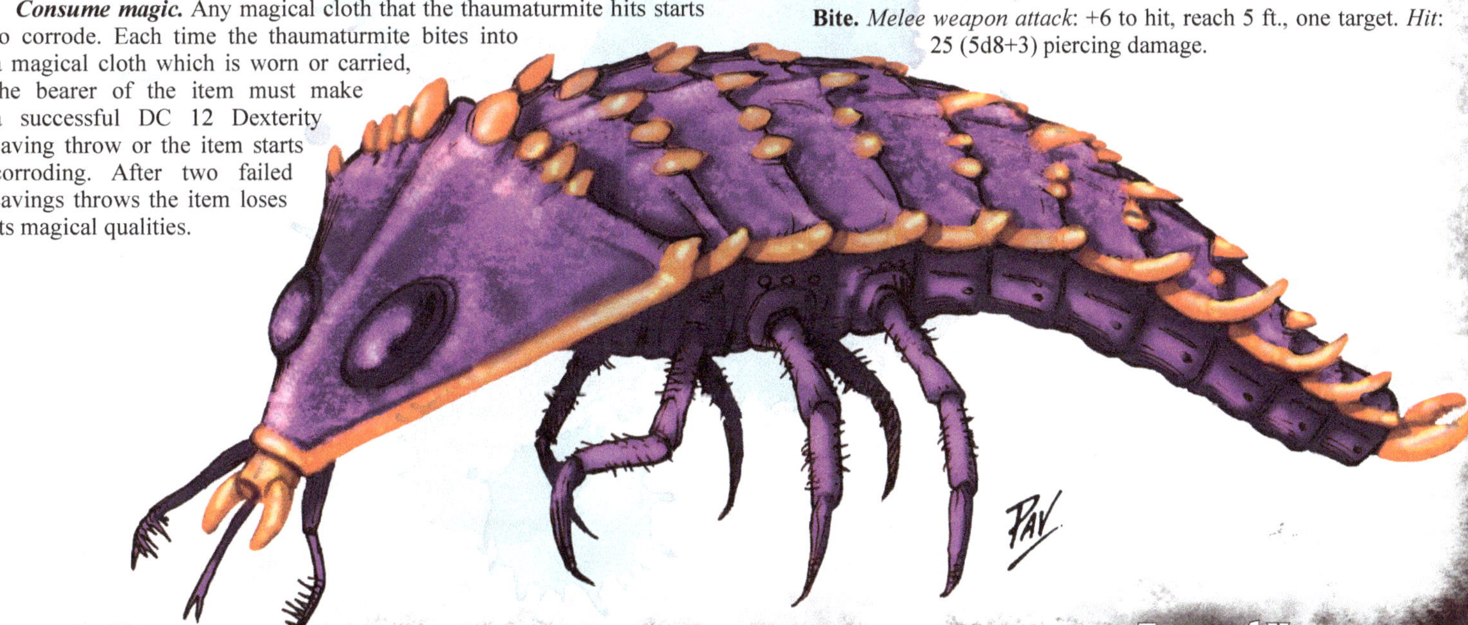

Tick, Giant

Giant ticks appear as 3-foot-long ticks. They are otherwise similar to normal ticks.

Giant ticks attack by dropping on their prey from above and stabbing with a hollow mouth tube. If subjected to fire or immersed in water, a giant tick detaches from its victim.

Giant Tick

Small beast, unaligned
Armor Class 13 (natural armor)
Hit Points 10 (3d6)
Speed 10 ft., climb 20 ft.

STR	DEX	CON	INT	WIS	CHA
11 (+0)	10 (+0)	11 (+0)	2 (−4)	10 (+0)	2 (−4)

Senses darkvision 60 ft., passive Perception 10
Challenge ¼ (50 XP)

Keen Smell. The tick has advantage on Wisdom (Perception) checks that rely on smell.

Red Ache. Creatures bitten by a giant tick must make a DC 15 Constitution saving throw or become infected with this disease. Within 4 hours of infection, the infected creature will develop red welts that are hot to the touch all over their skin. Their joints will swell and their bones will ache painfully. While infected, the creature has disadvantage on Strength checks, Strength saving throws, and attack rolls that use Strength. The saving throw can be repeated after every long rest and if successful in 2 consecutive tries (two long rests in a row), the creature is cured and the effects of the disease end. A *greater restoration* spell will also cure the disease.

Actions

Blood Drain. *Melee Weapon Attack:* +2 to hit, reach 5 ft., one target. *Hit*: 2 (1d4) piercing damage and the tick attaches to the target. While attached, the tick doesn't attack. Instead, at the start of each of the ticks's turns, the target loses 2 (1d4) hit points due to blood loss.

The tick can detach itself by spending 5 feet of its movement. It does so after it drains 10 hit points of blood from the target or the target dies. A creature, including the target, can use its action to detach the tick.

Transposer

This creature looks like a featureless humanoid whose arms end in large sucker-like membranes.

Transposers are thought to be of an alien culture; how they came to the Material Plane remains a mystery to sages. Most transposers avoid contact with sentient races, preferring to live in seclusion among their own kind. When it first encounters potential prey, a transposer uses its innate ability to cast *alter self* to lure its target into its trap.

Transposer

Medium aberration, neutral
Armor Class 12 (natural armor)
Hit Points 49 (9d8 + 9)
Speed 30 ft.

STR	DEX	CON	INT	WIS	CHA
15 (+2)	13 (+1)	12 (+1)	8 (–1)	12 (+1)	12 (+1)

Skills Deception +3, Perception +3
Senses darkvision 60 ft., passive Perception 13
Languages Common, Deep Speech
Challenge 3 (700 XP)

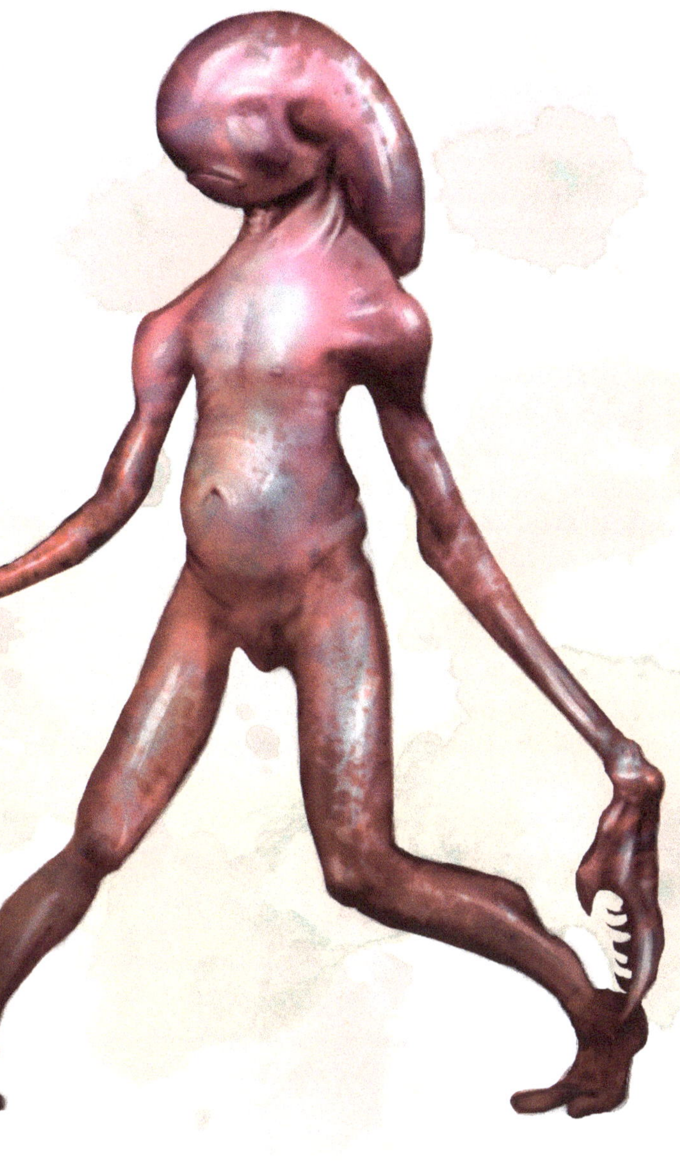

Innate Spellcasting. The transposer's innate spellcasting ability is Charisma (spell save DC 11, +3 to hit with spell attacks). It can innately cast *alter self* at will requiring no material components.

Transposition. An opponent hit by a transposer's slam attack must make a DC 13 Constitution saving throw or become linked to the transposer. A transposer can have no more than 4 linked creatures at a time. While linked, the transposer knows the exact location of the target as long as it is on the same plane of existence.

While the transposer remains linked to a target, any damage the transposer takes is halved, and each linked target takes an equal amount. If a transposer's linked target regain hit points, the amount received by the target is halved, and the transposer regains an equal amount of hit points.

A *remove curse* or *dispel magic* cast on the linked target can end the link. If *dispel magic* is cast on the transposer, one random link is severed. Otherwise the link lasts until the targert dies or the transposer chooses to end the link.

Actions

Multiattack. The transposer makes two attacks with its slam.
Slam. *Melee Weapon Attack:* +4 to hit, reach 5 ft., one target. *Hit:* 9 (2d6 + 2) bludgeoning damage.

Troblin

This hideous humanoid creature is a twisted amalgamation of extra limbs, thickened hide, and protruding growths.

A troblin is a twisted creature, born of the union of a troll and a goblin. Due to the horrid side effects of their diminished regenerative abilities, the overall appearance of a troblin is difficult to quantify. No two troblins look exactly alike. One troblin may be covered in tough scars that have thickened its skin, while another may have two forearms sprouting from the elbow of one arm. Other troblins may have two arms on one side, or two feet on one leg.

Troblin bands build their lairs in forested areas away from more civilized lands. They are hunter-gatherers and use the land as a means of survival, hunting deer, elk, moose, and other game animals.

In general, troblins stand 5 feet tall, with crooked noses, long arms and legs, and large flapping feet. A troblin shares in the characteristics of both its parents, resembling a very tall goblin with troll-like facial features. Its skin is blotched in shades of green, grey, and dull yellow. Its eyes range from pale red to an ochre color. Troblins dress in drab-colored clothing and furs made from the hides of animals.

Troblins are a disorganized lot and rarely engage in any sort of formal tactics or strategy. When a troblin war band encounters opponents, they simply attack with as much strength and ferocity as they can muster. Troblins are even more craven and cowardly than goblins, and a lone troblin usually runs from any combat in which it is outnumbered.

Troblin Mutations

Each troblin has 1d4 random mutations brought about by its bizarre regeneration (duplicate mutations stack, as detailed in the mutation). Increase the troblin's Challenge Rating to 2 (450 XP) unless otherwise noted, and roll on the table below for each mutation.

Should a troblin be slain but not prevented from regenerating back to life, it always gains 1 mutation, and has a 35% chance of gaining an additional 1d4 more mutations.

d20	Mutation
1–2	**Dual Forearm**. The troblin's claw attack deals 1d8 damage instead of 1d6. If the troblin already possesses this mutation, increase the damage die size an additional time. In addition, it can wield two-handed weapons with that arm alone.
3–4	**Oversized Jaw**. The troblin's bite attack deals 2d4 damage instead of 1d4. If the troblin already possesses this mutation, add an additional 1d4 to the damage for each stacking mutation.
5–6	**Massive Scarring**. Increase the troblin's Armor Class by 1. This mutation can stack.
7	**Increased Muscle Mass**. Each of the troblin's melee weapon attacks deals 1d4 additional damage of the same type. Each time this mutation is rolled, increase the bonus by one die step (1d4 to 1d6, 1d6 to 1d8, etc.).

d20	Mutation
8	**Redundant Vital Organs**. Once per short or long rest, if the troblin takes 14 damage or less that would reduce it to 0 hit points, it is reduced to 1 hit point instead. Each time this mutation is rolled, increase the number of times the troblin can use this ability by 1.
9	**Shortened Tendons**. The troblins has proficiency in the Acrobatics skill, and has advantage on checks and saving throws against being grappled.
10	**Extra Arm**. The troblin grows an additional arm. It can make one additional claw when it takes the attack action. Each time this mutation is rolled, the number of claw attacks increases.
11	**Hollow Bones**. The troblin has vulnerability to bludgeoning damage, but gains proficiency in the Stealth skill and has a movement speed of 35 feet. If this mutation is rolled a second time, the troblin doubles its proficiency bonus when rolling Dexterity (Stealth) checks. If this mutation is rolled a third time, reroll.
12	**Large Eyes**. The troblin doubles the range of its darkvision, to a maximum of 120 feet.
13	**Two Heads**. The troblin has proficiency in the Perception skill, and advantage on saving throws against being blinded. If the troblin already possesses this mutation, add a vestigial face to the troblin's body. This grants the troblin advantage on Wisdom (Perception) checks that rely on sight or smell, in addition to the other benefits. Reroll if this mutation is rolled a third time.
14–19	No Mutation.
20	**Greater Regeneration**. The troblin's regeneration trait regains 10 hit points instead of 5 hit points. For each 10 hit points above the original 5 this trait regains for the troblin, increase the troblin's Challenge Rating by 1.

Troblin

Medium giant, chaotic evil
Armor Class 13 (natural armor)
Hit Points 52 (8d8 + 16)
Speed 30 ft.

STR	DEX	CON	INT	WIS	CHA
15 (+2)	12 (+1)	15 (+2)	8 (−1)	9 (−1)	7 (−2)

Senses darkvision 60 ft., passive Perception 9
Languages Giant
Challenge 1 (200 XP)

Regeneration. The troblin regains 5 hit points at the start of its turn. If the troblin takes acid or fire damage, this trait doesn't function at the start of the troblin's next turn. The troblin dies only if it starts its turn with 0 hit points and doesn't regenerate.

Actions

Multiattack. The troblin makes one greatclub attack and one bite attack, or one claws attack and one bite attack.

Greatclub. *Melee Weapon Attack:* +4 to hit, reach 5 ft., one target. *Hit:* 6 (1d8 + 2) bludgeoning damage.

Bite. *Melee Weapon Attack:* +4 to hit, reach 5 ft., one target. *Hit:* 4 (1d4 + 2) piercing damage.

Claws. *Melee Weapon Attack:* +4 to hit, reach 5 ft., one target. *Hit:* 5 (1d6 + 2) slashing damage.

Trolls

Troll, Cave

This ugly humanoid appears to be about 6 feet tall. Its leathery skin is blackish-gray and its eyes are yellow. It has long, upright ears, almost elven in nature. Its arms and legs are spindly and end in wicked-looking claws.

Cave trolls are cousins of the typical troll and are found in all types of subterranean realms. Though smaller in stature, they are as deadly as their surface-dwelling brethren, possessing an accelerated metabolism and a consequently voracious appetite. They sustain themselves on whatever they can find in their underground realms. They rarely venture to the surface world, preferring the security and tranquility of the darkness they inhabit. If extremely hungry, or if food is scarce, a cave troll will venture to the surface and attack whatever it finds near its lair.

Cave trolls stand 6 feet tall and weigh 300 pounds. They do not walk with the same hunched gait of their larger relatives but stand upright and move with blinding speed.

Cave trolls often use deception when they first encounter prey, especially of the intelligent variety. Their troll heritage often leads to the misconception that they are slow in combat, which they gladly allow their opponents to believe — until the cave troll strikes or moves. Only then is the ruse negated and the true nature of the troll revealed.

Cave Troll

Medium giant, chaotic evil
Armor Class 15 (natural armor)
Hit Points 76 (9d8 + 36)
Speed 60 ft., climb 20 ft.

STR	DEX	CON	INT	WIS	CHA
14 (+2)	19 (+4)	18 (+4)	8 (−1)	9 (−1)	7 (−2)

Skills Perception +1
Senses darkvision 60 ft., passive Perception 11
Languages Giant
Challenge 4 (1,100 XP)

Haste. When in need, a cave troll is capable of startling bursts of speed. It has advantage on Dexterity saving throws and gains an additional action on each of its turns. That action can be used only to take the Attack (one claw), Dash, Disengage, Hide, or Use an Object action.

Regeneration. The cave troll regains 6 hit points at the start of its turn. If the cave troll takes acid or fire damage, this trait doesn't function at the start of the cave troll's next turn. The cave troll dies only if starts its turn with 0 hit points and doesn't regenerate.

Spider Climb. The cave troll can climb difficult surfaces, including upside down on ceilings, without needing to make an ability check.

Actions

Multiattack. The cave troll makes three attacks: one with its bite and two with its claws.

Bite. *Melee Weapon Attack:* +6 to hit, reach 5 ft., one target. *Hit:* 7 (1d6 +4) piercing damage.

Claw. *Melee Weapon Attack:* +6 to hit, reach 5 ft., one target. *Hit:* 9 (2d4+4) slashing damage.

Troll, Ice

This large, powerful creature has semitransparent flesh of light blue. Its body is completely hairless and its cold, piercing eyes are stark white.

Ice trolls are relatives of normal trolls but are decidedly more cunning, ruthless, evil, and despicable. They make their homes in very cold climates, always near a pool of water (either natural or troll-made). The strongest (and sometimes most intelligent) member of a band is usually the leader.

Unlike their trollish cousins, ice trolls do not rush headlong into battle. They prefer to attack the weakest opponents first if they can. If combat goes against an ice troll, it does not hesitate to flee.

Ice trolls savor the taste of human flesh and construct their lairs near civilized areas where humans are plentiful. Ice trolls often set traps for humans and either devour them immediately or capture them and carry them back to their lair. Captured humans are caged and fattened up before they are eaten.

An ice troll stands about 8 feet tall and weighs 450 pounds.

Troll, River

Similar in many respects to their swamp-loving kin, river trolls prefer a less slimy existence and choose to live in forested regions near rivers and streams, or under bridges.

River trolls patrol the banks of large rivers, looking to hunt the forest creatures that use the river for sustenance. Very rarely, the river trolls are indigent enough to use crude nets or spears to harvest fish and other aquatic foods from the river itself.

River trolls are more frequently found as a group, as they are somewhat smaller than a normal troll (though only other trolls really notice this). They will work together with those of their own kind, but not with other common trolls.

River trolls are adept swimmers and like to lurk underwater for prey near bridges, if possible.

River Troll

Large humanoid, chaotic evil
Armor Class 15 (natural armor)
Hit Points 57 (6d10 + 24)
Speed 30 ft., swim 40 ft.

STR	DEX	CON	INT	WIS	CHA
17 (+3)	14 (+2)	19 (+4)	6 (−2)	9 (−1)	7 (−2)

Ice Troll

Large giant, chaotic evil
Armor Class 12 (natural armor)
Hit Points 68 (8d10 + 24)
Speed 30 ft.

STR	DEX	CON	INT	WIS	CHA
19 (+4)	12 (+1)	16 (+3)	9 (−1)	10 (+0)	6 (−2)

Skills Perception +2
Damage Vulnerabilities fire, slashing
Damage Immunities cold
Senses darkvision 60 ft., passive Perception 12
Languages Giant
Challenge 4 (1,100 XP)

Slashing Susceptibility. If an attack made with a slashing weapon scores a critical hit on the ice troll, the troll must succeed on a DC 13 Constitution saving throw or lose a limb. Roll a d6. On a roll of 1–3, the troll loses an arm, and on a roll of 4–6 the troll loses a leg. It is GM's choice as to whether it was the right or left arm or leg.

Regeneration. The ice troll regains 10 hit points at the start of its turn. If the troll is not making physical contact with ice or near-freezing water, this trait doesn't function at the start of the troll's next turn. The cave dies only if starts its turn with 0 hit points and doesn't regenerate.

Actions

Multiattack. The cave troll makes three attacks: one with its bite and two with its claws.

Bite. *Melee Weapon Attack:* +6 to hit, reach 5 ft., one target. *Hit:* 7 (1d6 + 4) piercing damage plus 7 (2d6) cold damage.

Claw. *Melee Weapon Attack:* +6 to hit, reach 5 ft., one target. *Hit:* 8 (1d8 + 4) slashing damage.

Skills Athletics +5, Perception +3
Damage Immunities poison
Senses darkvision 60 ft., passive Perception 13
Languages Giant
Challenge 4 (1,100 XP)

Amphibious. The river troll can breathe both air and water.

Keen Smell. The river troll has advantage on Wisdom (Perception) checks that rely on smell.

Poison Skin. The river troll's skin contains a powerful poison. Any time the troll touches another creature, the creature takes 7 (2d6) poison damage (included in attacks).

Regeneration. The river troll regains 10 hit points at the start of its turn as long as it is at least partially submerged in water; strong rainfall also allows the troll's regeneration to function. If the troll takes acid or lightning damage, this trait doesn't function at the start of the troll's next turn. The troll only dies if it starts its turn with 0 hit points and doesn't regenerate.

Actions

Multiattack. The river troll makes three attacks: one with its bite and two with its claws.

Bite. *Melee Weapon Attack:* +5 to hit, reach 5 ft., one target. *Hit:* 6 (1d6 + 3) piercing damage plus 7 (2d6) poison damage.

Claw. *Melee Weapon Attack:* +5 to hit, reach 5 ft., one target. *Hit:* 10 (2d6 + 3) slashing damage plus 7 (2d6) poison damage.

Troll, Rock

This giant creature stands nearly twice as tall as a normal man. Its hide is earth-colored and its hair is dark. Its eyes are deep brown. The creature's arms and legs are long and thin and end in sharpened talons. Its feet end in three-toed feet.

Rock trolls are relatives of the normal troll and make their lairs deep within the subterranean realms of the earth. Most underground creatures avoid rock trolls, as they are completely malign and evil, attacking any living creature, especially when hungry. They are quite fond of human and halfling flesh. Unlike common trolls, rock trolls cannot regenerate lost limbs (though they do possess the ability to quickly heal damage).

Rock trolls are 10 feet tall and weigh about 600 pounds. They resemble their smaller relatives in most respects. The rock troll's hide is stone gray or brown, its hair is black or brown, and its eyes are dull brown.

Rock trolls attack any living thing that enters their territory, usually doing so for food. They have no strategy or organization in their attacks; a rock troll flails relentlessly at its foes with its powerful claws until either it or its opponent is dead.

Troll, Rock

Large giant, chaotic evil
Armor Class 15 (natural armor)
Hit Points 150 (12d10 + 84)
Speed 30 ft., burrow 20 ft.

STR	DEX	CON	INT	WIS	CHA
24 (+7)	10 (+0)	24 (+7)	6 (−2)	9 (−1)	6 (−2)

Skills Perception +3
Damage Resistances force, poison; bludgeoning, piercing, and slashing from nonmagical weapons
Senses darkvision 60 ft., passive Perception 13
Languages Giant
Challenge 11 (7,200 XP)

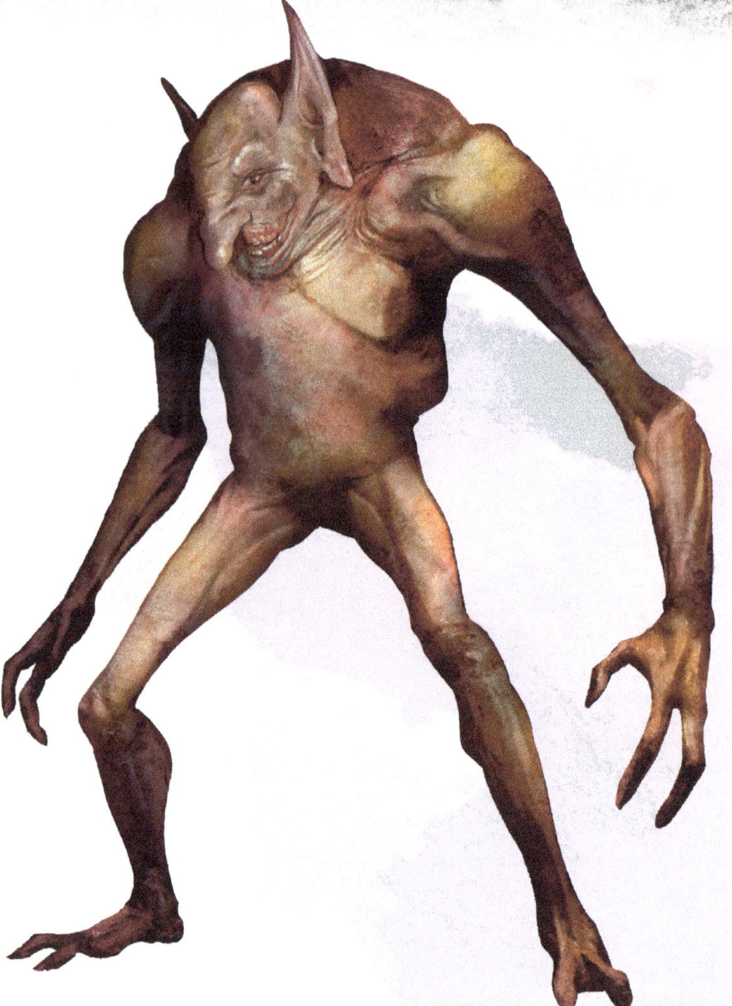

Keen Smell. The troll has advantage on Wisdom (Perception) checks that rely on smell.

Regeneration. The rock troll regains 10 hit points at the start of its turn if it has at least 1 hit point and is underground touching earth or rock. If the rock troll takes acid or fire damage, this trait doesn't function at the start of the troll's next turn.

Rend. If the troll hits the target with both claws on the same turn, the troll rends the target, dealing an additional 22 (4d10) slashing damage to the target.

Sunlight Vulnerability. The rock troll begins to turn to stone and its speed is halved when it starts its turn in true sunlight (magical light does not have the same effect). The rock troll must make a DC 17 Constitution saving throw at the end of its next turn. If it fails this saving throw, it completely turns to stone and is petrified. The troll must repeat the saving throw for each turn it remains in sunlight.

The petrified effect is permanent unless dispelled (but only if done out of direct sunlight).

Tough Hide. The rock troll has extremely thick, tough skin that protects it from nonmagical weapons.

Actions

Multiattack. The rock troll makes three melee attacks: one with bite and two claws. If both claw attacks hit the same target on the same turn, the troll rends the creature with its claws, inflicting additional slashing damage.

Bite. *Melee Weapon Attack:* +11 to hit, reach 5 ft., one target. Hit: 16 (2d8 + 7) piercing damage.

Claws. *Melee Weapon Attack:* +11 to hit, reach 5 ft., one target. *Hit:* 18 (2d10 + 7) slashing damage.

Troll, Swamp

This large hulking brute has long, thick arms and legs, both of which end in sharpened and filthy claws. Its body is covered with moss and fungus, and its hair is dark brownish-green. Large, upward-curving fangs jut from its lower jaw.

Swamp trolls are large, stocky, dark gray or brown hunched humanoids. Their flesh is slick and slimy like moss. Swamp trolls make their lairs deep in swampland and marshes away from more settled areas, but not far enough away where they cannot hunt humans if game and other food run scarce in the swamps.

Swamp trolls are 7-foot-tall hunched humanoids and weigh about 400 pounds.

Swamp trolls are aggressive predators that attack living creatures on sight (especially when a swamp troll is hungry). When hunting a swamp troll moves quietly along, easing closer to its prey and then finally striking with its claws and bite when within range. Swamp trolls rarely fight to the death unless threatened or hungry.

Swamp Troll

Large giant, chaotic evil
Armor Class 14 (natural armor)
Hit Points 63 (6d10 + 30)
Speed 30 ft., swim 30 ft.

STR	DEX	CON	INT	WIS	CHA
18 (+4)	14 (+2)	20 (+5)	6 (–2)	9 (–1)	4 (–3)

Skills Athletics +8, Perception +1, Stealth +4 (+6 in swampy terrain)
Senses darkvision 60 ft., passive Perception 11
Languages Giant
Challenge 2 (450 XP)

Keen Smell. The swamp troll has advantage on Wisdom (Perception) checks that rely on smell.

Regeneration. The troll regains 3 hit points at the start of its turn. If the troll takes acid or fire damage, this trait doesn't function at the start of the troll's next turn. The troll dies only if it starts its turn with 0 hit points and doesn't regenerate.

Slimy. The swamp troll is covered swampy muck. Creatures attempting to grapple a swamp troll have disadvantage.

Swamp Stride. The swamp troll ignores nonmagical difficult terrain caused by swamp water or vegetation.

Actions

Multiattack. The swamp troll makes one bite attack and two claw attacks.

Bite. *Melee Weapon Attack:* +6 to hit, reach 10 ft., one target. *Hit:* 14 (3d6 + 4) piercing damage.

Claws. *Melee Weapon Attack:* +6 to hit, reach 10 ft., one target. *Hit:* 11 (2d6 + 4) slashing damage.

Tsathar

This vile creature resembles an upright, humanoid frog with gray flesh and reddish-gold eyes. Its humanoid arms end in wicked claws.

Tsathar (pronounced "suh-Thar") are a race of froglike humanoids that dwell in fetid swamps and dark caverns deep beneath the earth. They worship a strange and terrifying demonic being known as Tsathogga, and often hunt down and capture individuals of other humanoid races to serve as sacrifices or victims in their foul breeding pits.

Tsathar prefer to use short, barbed spears and kukris in combat. They sometimes employ nets as well. They charge into combat with maniacal fury, and rarely use elaborate tactics unless a scourge or priest is present to control them. They favor leather armor crafted from hides of the frogs they breed. Priests favor the wicked kukri in battle.

A typical tsathar stands 6 feet tall and weighs about 300 pounds. A tsathar scourge is slightly bulkier, of equivalent height but weighing about 350 pounds.

Tsathar Society

Tsathar prefer to live in fetid lairs deep underground or in dark swamps. When they dwell above ground, they are nocturnal. Some few surface-dwelling tsathar have joined cults of assassins.

Tsathar communities are led by priests that lead the tsathar in their reverence of the demon-god Tsathogga, a foul toadlike demonic being.

Tsathar are sexless and reproduce by implanting an egg into a host, which can be any form of living creature. Normally, creatures are captured or bred to serve as hosts — dire rats and giant frogs being common hosts. It is said that priests must be born of an egg implanted into a humanoid or other creature of great intelligence.

Tsathar

Medium monstrosity (aquatic), chaotic evil
Armor Class 13 (leather armor)
Hit Points 16 (3d8 + 3)
Speed 30 ft., swim 30 ft.

STR	DEX	CON	INT	WIS	CHA
13 (+1)	14 (+2)	12 (+1)	12 (+1)	12 (+1)	10 (+0)

Skills Stealth +4
Senses darkvision 60 ft., passive Perception 11
Languages Abyssal, Tsathar
Challenge ½ (100 XP)

Amphibious. The tsathar can breathe air and water.

Keen Smell. The tsathar has advantage on Wisdom (Perception) checks that rely on smell.

Slimy. Tsathar continuously cover themselves with muck and slime. Creatures attempting to grapple a tsathar do so with disadvantage.

Standing Leap. The tsathar's long jump is up to 20 feet and its high jump is up to 10 feet, with or without a running start.

Actions

Multiattack. The tsathar makes two melee attacks: one with its bite and one with its claws, or one with its bite and one with its spear.

Bite. *Melee Weapon Attack:* +3 to hit, reach 5 ft., one target. *Hit:* 3 (1d4 + 1) piercing damage.

Claws. *Melee Weapon Attack:* +3 to hit, reach 5 ft., one target. *Hit:* 3 (1d4 + 1) slashing damage, and the target must succeed on a DC 13 Constitution saving throw or become the living host to a tsathar egg, which over the course of the egg maturing, migrates to the chest cavity of the host. The host creature must make another DC 13 Constitution saving throw after 24 hours of the egg having been implanted. A failed saving throw results in the host becoming violently ill, followed by a deep coma-like state that lasts 2d6 + 2 days. At the end of each day, the host can attempt another saving throw with a success indicating that its body has managed to destroy the egg through normal immune response. At the end of the incubation period, the host awakes to excruciating pain as the young tsathar, freed from its egg, tears its way out of the host, who is reduced to 0 hit points in the process.

A DC 16 Wisdom (Medicine) check can be attempted to surgically extract an egg from the host. A *lesser restoration* spell will also cure the condition and purge the host of the egg.

Spear. *Melee Weapon Attack:* +3 to hit, reach 5 ft. or 20/60 ft., one target. *Hit:* 4 (1d6 + 1) piercing damage, or 5 (1d8 +1) piercing damage if used with two hands to make the melee attack.

Tsathar Monk

Medium monstrosity (aquatic), chaotic evil
Armor Class 14
Hit Points 52 (8d8 + 16)
Speed 30 ft., swim 30 ft.

STR	DEX	CON	INT	WIS	CHA
15 (+2)	18 (+4)	14 (+2)	12 (+1)	16 (+3)	11 (+0)

Skills Nature +5, Perception +5, Religion +5
Senses darkvision 60 ft., passive Perception 15
Languages Abyssal, Tsathar
Challenge 2 (450 XP)

Amphibious. The tsathar can breathe air and water.

Keen Smell. The tsathar has advantage on Wisdom (Perception) checks that rely on smell.

Slimy. Tsathar continuously cover themselves with muck and slime. Creatures attempting to grapple a tsathar does so with disadvantage.

Standing Leap. The tsathar's long jump is up to 20 feet and its high jump is up to 10 feet, with or without a running start.

Actions

Multiattack. The tsathar can make three melee attacks: two with its claws and one bite. It can use its flurry of blows or stunning strike ability in place of one of the claw attacks.

Bite. *Melee Weapon Attack:* +6 to hit, reach 5 ft., one target. *Hit:* 7 (1d6 + 4) piercing damage.

Claws. *Melee Weapon Attack:* +6 to hit, reach 5 ft., one target. *Hit:* 8 (1d8 + 4) slashing damage, and the target must succeed on a DC 13 Constitution saving throw or become the living host to a tsathar egg, which over the course of the egg maturing, migrates to the chest cavity of the host. The host creature must make another DC 13 Constitution saving throw after 24 hours of the egg having been implanted. A failed saving throw results in the host becoming violently ill, followed by a deep coma-like state that lasts 2d6 + 2 days. At the end of each day, the host can attempt another saving throw with a success indicating that its body has managed to destroy the egg through normal immune response. At the end of the incubation period, the host awakes to excruciating pain as the young tsathar, freed from its egg, tears its way out of the host, who is reduced to 0 hit points in the process.

A DC 16 Wisdom (Medicine) check can be attempted to surgically extract an egg from the host. A *lesser restoration* spell will also cure the condition and purge the host of the egg.

Flurry of Blows (3/day)*. Melee Weapon Attack:* +6 to hit, reach 5 ft., one target. *Hit:* 14 (3d6 + 4) bludgeoning damage, and the target suffers one of the following effects of its choice:

Prone. The target must succeed on a Dexterity saving throw (DC 14) or be knocked prone.

Pushed. The target must make a Strength saving throw or be pushed up to 15 feet away from the tsathar.

Agog The target can't take reactions until the end of the tsathar's next turn.

Stunning Strike (3/day)*. Melee Weapon Attack:* +6 to hit, reach 5 ft., one target. *Hit:* 8 (1d8 + 4) bludgeoning damage, and the target must succeed on a DC 14 Constitution saving throw or be stunned until the end of the tsathar's next turn.

Reactions

Deflect Missiles. If the tsathar has one hand free, it can use its reaction in response to being hit with a ranged weapon attack. It reduces the damage by 14 (1d10 + 9). If it reduces the damage to 0, it can catch the missile if it is small enough for it to hold with one hand.

Tsathar Priest

Medium monstrosity (aquatic), chaotic evil
Armor Class 14 (frog hide)
Hit Points 52 (8d8 + 16)
Speed 30 ft., swim 30 ft.

STR	DEX	CON	INT	WIS	CHA
10 (+0)	14 (+2)	14 (+2)	12 (+1)	17 (+3)	11 (+0)

Skills Nature +5, Perception +5, Religion +5
Senses darkvision 60 ft., passive Perception 15
Languages Abyssal, Tsathar
Challenge 4 (1,100 XP)

Amphibious. The tsathar can breathe air and water.

Keen Smell. The tsathar has advantage on Wisdom (Perception) checks that rely on smell.

Slimy. Tsathar continuously cover themselves with muck and slime. Creatures attempting to grapple a tsathar does so with disadvantage.

Standing Leap. The tsathar's long jump is up to 20 feet and its high jump is up to 10 feet, with or without a running start.

Fetid Shroud of the Frog God. The priest of Tsathogga is surrounded by a fetid, swirling shroud of foul corruption. At the start of each of the priest's turns, each creature within 5 feet of it takes 7 (2d6) poison damage. A creature that touches the priest or hits it with a melee attack while within 5 feet of it takes 7 (2d6) poison damage.

Fetid Strike. Once on each of the priest's turns when it hits a creature with a weapon attack, it can cause the attack to deal an extra 9 (2d8) poison damage to the target.

Spellcasting. The tsathar priest is a 5th level spellcaster. Its spellcasting ability is Wisdom (spell save DC 13, +5 to hit with spell attacks). It has the following cleric spells prepared:

Cantrips (at will): *guidance, poison spray, resistance, thaumaturgy*
1st level (4 slots): *bane, bless, cure wounds, detect magic, inflict wounds*
2nd level (3 slots): *enhance ability, hold person, silence*
3rd level (3 slots): *bestow curse, dispel magic, stinking cloud*

Actions

Kukri*. Melee Weapon Attack:* +4 to hit, reach 5 ft., one target. *Hit:* 5 (1d6 + 2) slashing damage.

Bite. *Melee Weapon Attack:* +4 to hit, reach 5 ft., one target. *Hit:* 5 (1d6 + 2) piercing damage.

Claws. *Melee Weapon Attack:* +4 to hit, reach 5 ft., one target. *Hit:* 6 (1d8 + 2) slashing damage, and the target must succeed on a DC 13 Constitution saving throw or become the living host to a tsathar egg, which over the course of the egg maturing, migrates to the chest cavity of the host. The host creature must make another DC 13 Constitution saving throw after 24 hours of the egg having been implanted. A failed saving throw results in the host becoming violently ill, followed by a deep coma-like state that lasts 2d6 + 2 days. At the end of each day, the host can attempt another saving throw with a success indicating that its body has managed to destroy the egg through normal immune response. At the end of the incubation period, the host awakes to excruciating pain as the young tsathar, freed from its egg, tears its way out of the host, who is reduced to 0 hit points in the process.

A DC 16 Wisdom (Medicine) check can be attempted to surgically extract an egg from the host. A *lesser restoration* spell will also cure the condition and purge the host of the egg.

Tsathar Sorcerer

Medium monstrosity (aquatic), chaotic evil
Armor Class 14 (frog hide)
Hit Points 27 (5d8 + 5)
Speed 30 ft.

STR	DEX	CON	INT	WIS	CHA
10 (+0)	14 (+2)	13 (+1)	12 (+1)	11 (+0)	15 (+2)

Skills Nature +3, Perception +4, Survival +3
Senses darkvision 60 ft., passive Perception 14
Languages Abyssal, Tsathar
Challenge 2 (450 XP)

Spellcasting. The tsathar sorcerer is a 5th level spellcaster. Its spellcasting ability is Charisma (spell save DC 12, +4 to hit with spell attacks). It knows the following sorcerer spells:

Cantrips (at will): *dancing lights, light, prestidigitation, ray of frost, shocking grasp*

1st level (4 slots): *fog cloud, magic missile, shield*

2nd level (3 slots): *scorching ray, spider climb*

3rd level (2 slots): *lightning bolt*

Amphibious. The tsathar can breathe air and water.

Keen Smell. The tsathar has advantage on Wisdom (Perception) checks that rely on smell.

Slimy. Tsathar continuously cover themselves with muck and slime. Creatures attempting to grapple a tsathar do so with disadvantage.

Standing Leap. The tsathar's long jump is up to 20 feet and its high jump is up to 10 feet, with or without a running start.

Actions

Bite. *Melee Weapon Attack:* +2 to hit, reach 5 ft., one target. *Hit:* 2 (1d4) piercing damage.

Claws. *Melee Weapon Attack:* +2 to hit, reach 5 ft., one target. *Hit:* 2 (1d4) slashing damage, and the target must succeed on a DC 13 Constitution saving throw or become the living host to a tsathar egg, which over the course of the egg maturing, migrates to the chest cavity of the host. The host creature must make another DC 13 Constitution saving throw after 24 hours of the egg having been implanted. A failed saving throw results in the host becoming violently ill, followed by a deep coma-like state that lasts 2d6 + 2 days. At the end of each day, the host can attempt another saving throw with a success indicating that its body has managed to destroy the egg through normal immune response. At the end of the incubation period, the host awakes to excruciating pain as the young tsathar, freed from its egg, tears its way out of the host, who is reduced to 0 hit points in the process. A DC 16 Wisdom (Medicine) check can be attempted to surgically extract an egg from the host. A *lesser restoration* spell will also cure the condition and purge the host of the egg.

Spear. *Melee Weapon Attack:* +2 to hit, reach 5 ft. or 20/60 ft., one target. *Hit:* 3 (1d6) piercing damage, or 4 (1d8) piercing damage if used with two hands to make the melee attack.

T'Shann

The slug-like thing has a cylindrical body and a mass of dripping, writhing tentacles at its head. It is brownish gray, with patches of green and black blotches scattered unevenly over its body. Its underside is pasty off-white in color and ripples with the muscular contractions that move the creature along.

T'shanns are slug-like creatures that burrow through earth and stone to consume the minerals trapped in the rock. They range anywhere from 2 to 4 feet long. A t'shann burrows through stone by extruding powerful digestive enzymes through its mouth and skin, that let it dissolve the stone, and then slurping it up for consumption. It can use this ability to attack creatures that threaten it.

The most unusual aspect of a t'shann is its ability to cause confusion by its mere presence. The simple but alien brain of a t'shann emits waves in such a frequency that more advanced creatures suffer from severe disorientation if they come too close. T'shanns rarely attack. They are content to burrow through rock and dirt, blissfully unaware of the rest of the world. If attacked, however, a t'shann defends itself with all the natural weapons available to it.

T'shann

Small aberration, neutral
Armor Class 8 (natural armor)
Hit Points 32 (5d6 + 15)
Speed 10 ft., burrow 10 ft.

STR	DEX	CON	INT	WIS	CHA
10 (+0)	4 (–3)	16 (+3)	2 (–4)	10 (+0)	12 (+1)

Senses blindsight 60 ft. (blind beyond this radius), passive Perception 10
Languages —
Challenge 1 (200 XP)

Acidic Secretions. A creature who touches the t'shann takes 5 (2d4) acid damage. Any nonmagical weapon made of metal or wood that hits the t'shann corrodes. After dealing damage, the weapon takes a permanent and cumulative –1 penalty to damage rolls. If its penalty drops to –5, the weapon is destroyed. Nonmagical ammunition made of metal or wood that hits the t'shann is destroyed after dealing damage.

In addition, nonmagical armor worn by the target of any of the t'shann's attacks is partly dissolved and takes a permanent and cumulative –1 penalty to the AC it offers. The armor is destroyed if the penalty reduces its AC to 10.

Alien Thoughts. When a creature enters or starts its turn within 30 feet of the t'shann, the creature must make a DC 13 Wisdom saving throw, unless the t'shann is incapacitated. On a failed saving throw, the creature can't take reactions until the start of its next turn and rolls a d8 to determine what it does during that turn. On a 1–4, the creature does nothing. On a 5 or 6, the creature takes no action but uses all its movement to move in a random direction. On a 7 or 8, the creature makes one melee attack against a random creature, or it does nothing if no creature is within reach.

Actions

Slam. *Melee Weapon Attack:* +2 to hit, reach 5 ft., one target. *Hit:* 2 (1d4) bludgeoning damage plus 5 (2d4) acid damage.

Spew Acid. *Ranged Weapon Attack:* +2 to hit, range 10 ft., one target. *Hit:* 5 (2d4) acid damage.

Tunnel Worm

This massive creature appears to be a 30-foot-long sleek black centipede with a long segmented body and many slender legs. Its huge mandibles are serrated and razor-sharp, and its eyes are multifaceted. A ring of chitinous bone protects its oversized head.

The tunnel worm is a burrowing creature related to the monstrous centipede. It is a very aggressive predator and hunter, though it can sustain itself by scavenging. Its preferred food is fresh, raw meat. Tunnel worms are very aggressive and attack anything that enters their territory.

Tunnel worms live in mazelike complexes of burrows connected by passages they have chewed out over time; these burrows are often filled with the rotting remains of past prey, used by the worm to incubate its offspring. The favored tactic of the tunnel worm is to lurk beneath the surface of the ground or behind a wall until it senses a creature moving by, whereupon it burrows out to surprise and attack its prey (treat this attack as a charge attack). A tunnel worm that has taken more than half its hit points in damage retreats to its lair unless it is cornered, in which case it fights to the death.

A typical tunnel worm is 30 feet long but can grow to a length of 60 feet.

Tunnel Worm

Huge monstrosity, neutral
Armor Class 13 (natural armor)
Hit Points 149 (13d12 + 65)
Speed 20 ft., burrow 20 ft.

STR	DEX	CON	INT	WIS	CHA
21 (+5)	13 (+1)	21 (+5)	1 (−5)	10 (+0)	6 (−2)

Condition Immunities prone
Senses darkvision 60 ft., tremorsense 60 ft., passive Perception 10
Languages —
Challenge 5 (1,800 XP)

Rend Armor. When the tunnel worm hits a creature wearing nonmagical armor or carrying a shield with its bite attack, the armor or shield takes a permanent −1 penalty to the AC it offers. Armor reduced to an AC of 10 or a shield that drops to +0 bonus is destroyed.

Actions

Bite. Melee Weapon Attack: +8 to hit, reach 10 ft., one target. *Hit:* 26 (6d6 + 5) piercing damage, and the target is grappled (escape DC 16). Until this grapple ends, the target is restrained. The tunnel worm can bite only the grappled creature and has advantage on attack rolls to do so.

Undead Swordsman

This armored skeleton stands in a battle-ready pose, its weapon held high as cold blue light shines in its eye sockets.

Some skeletons retain their intelligence and cunning, making them formidable warriors. These undead are far more powerful than their mindless kin.

Undead Swordsman

Medium undead, neutral evil
Armor Class 16 (chainmail armor)
Hit Points 27 (5d8 + 5)
Speed 30 ft.

STR	DEX	CON	INT	WIS	CHA
17 (+3)	13 (+1)	13 (+1)	9 (−1)	10 (+0)	12 (+1)

Skills Perception +4
Damage Immunities cold, necrotic, poison
Condition Immunities exhaustion, paralysis, poison
Senses darkvision 60 ft., passive Perception 14
Languages understands the languages it knew in its life but can't speak
Challenge 2 (450 XP)

Actions

Greatsword. *Melee Weapon Attack:* +5 to hit, reach 5 ft., one target. *Hit:* 10 (2d6 + 3) slashing damage.

Weird, Lightning

The snakelike creature crackles and thrashes like a bolt of lightning. It flares with electrical brilliance as tiny arcs travel up and down its form.

The Plane of Lightning is not only home to the lightning elementals, but also home to the serpent-like lightning weirds. The plane itself is an inhospitable place to those without some protection against electricity. Lightning weirds spend their time riding electrical storms on their native plane.

Casters often summon lightning weirds to do their bidding; confining them into pools of lightning until their task is complete. These creatures sometimes find their way through a portal into the Material Plane and will be found in areas of concentrated lightning strikes.

Lightning weirds resemble 10-foot-long serpents composed of yellow or white crackling lightning. Their body is long and thin and is always in motion. Brilliant flares of electricity function as the creature's eyes, and small bolts of electricity constantly leap and dance from its form.

Lightning weirds lash out of their crackling pools as soon as an opponent moves too close. Foes are usually grabbed and pulled into the pool where the weird holds on and waits for the creature to die. The lightning weird always chooses a heavily armored or metal-armored foe over an opponent in light or no armor. These creatures hate lightning quasi-elementals and attack them on sight.

Lightning Weird

Large elemental, chaotic evil
Armor Class 18 (natural armor)
Hit Points 90 (12d10 + 24)
Speed 50 ft.

STR	DEX	CON	INT	WIS	CHA
17 (+3)	20 (+5)	15 (+2)	10 (+0)	12 (+1)	14 (+2)

Damage Resistances bludgeoning, piercing, and slashing from nonmagical weapons
Damage Immunities acid, lightning, poison, thunder
Condition Immunities exhaustion, grappled, paralyzed, petrified, poisoned, prone, restrained, unconscious
Senses blindsight 30 ft., passive Perception 11
Languages Auran, Common, Weirdling
Challenge 7 (2,900 XP)

Electricity. If a creature attacks the lighting weird with a melee weapon, that creature takes 9 (2d8) lightning damage.

Lightning Mote. A lightning weird's mote is a crackling, dancing, arcing, ball of electricity that occupies a 5-foot space. Creatures that start their turn within 5 feet of the lightning mote take 13 (3d8) lightning damage; creatures wearing metal armor must make a successful DC 15 Constitution saving throw if they take lightning damage from being near the mote. On a failed saving throw, the target is stunned until the end of its next turn. The lightning can move its mote up to 30 ft. as a bonus action. The mote must remain within 90 ft.

Reform. When reduced to 0 hit points, a lightning weird collapses back into its pool. Four rounds later, it reforms at full strength minus any damage taken from fire-based attacks and effects (including attacks by earth or fire elemental creatures).

Transparent. Even when the lightning weird is in plain sight, it takes a successful DC 15 Wisdom (Perception) check to spot a lightning weird that has neither moved nor attacked. A creature that tries to enter the lightning weird's space while unaware of the lightning weird is surprised by the lightning weird.

Actions

Bite. *Melee Weapon Attack:* +8 to hit, reach 5 ft., one target. *Hit:* 14 (2d8 + 5) piercing damage plus 9 (2d8) lightning damage.

Command Elemental. One air elemental that the lightning weird can see within 60 feet of it must make a DC 13 Wisdom saving throw. On a failed saving throw, the air elemental is charmed for 1 minute. While charmed, the air elemental follows the lightning weird's commands.

Wights

Wight, Barrow

This creature appears as a rotting humanoid with leathery, gray skin drawn tight over its frame. Its eyes glow crimson. The creature's clothes appear as rotting and tattered rags.

Barrow wights are undead creatures akin to normal wights, but they are always found in or near barrows, usually guarding the treasure contained therein. They hate living creatures and attempt to destroy anyone who invades their resting place.

A barrow wight is a twisted, insane creature standing about 6 feet tall.

A barrow wight attempts to use its gaze attack on the closest creature to it when it is first encountered. Creatures not affected by its gaze are pummeled with its fists.

Barrow Wight

Medium undead, chaotic evil
Armor Class 14 (studded leather)
Hit Points 45 (6d8 + 18)
Speed 30 ft.

STR	DEX	CON	INT	WIS	CHA
16 (+3)	14 (+2)	16 (+3)	10 (+0)	13 (+1)	15 (+2)

Skills Perception +3, Stealth +4
Damage resistances necrotic; bludgeoning, piercing and slashing from nonmagical weapons that are not silvered
Damage immunities poison
Condition immunities exhaustion, poisoned
Senses darkvision 60 ft., passive Perception 13
Languages the language it knew in life
Challenge 3 (700 XP)

Gaze of Insanity. If a creature starts its turn within 30 feet of the barrow wight and the two of them can see each other, the barrow wight can force the creature to make a DC 13 Wisdom saving throw if the barrow wight is not incapacitated. On a failed save, the creature is affected by a short-term madness effect for 1 minute. Determine the effect from the table below.

d100	Effect (lasts 1 minute)
01–20	The target retreats into its mind and becomes paralyzed. The effect ends if the creature takes any damage.
21–30	The creature is incapacitated, and can only scream, laugh, or weep hysterically.
31–40	The creature is frightened and must use its actions to flee from the source of the fear.
41–50	The creature babbles incoherently and cannot speak normally or cast spells.
51–60	The creature must use its action to attack the nearest creature.
61–70	The creature hallucinates vividly, incurring disadvantage on all ability checks.
71–75	The creature does whatever anyone tells it to do that isn't obviously self-destructive.
76–80	The creature experiences an overpowering urge to eat something strange, such as dirt, offal, or slime.
81–90	The creature is stunned.
91–00	The creature falls unconscious.

The target can repeat the saving throw at the end of each of its turns. A successful save ends the effect and renders the target immune to the same barrow wight's insanity gaze for 24 hours.

A creature that isn't surprised can avert its eyes to avoid the saving throw at the start of its turn. If the creature does so, it can't see the barrow wight until the start of its next turn, when it can avert its eyes again. If the creature looks at the barrow wight in the meantime, it must immediately make the save.

Sunlight Sensitivity. While in sunlight, the wight has disadvantage on attack rolls, as well as on Wisdom (Perception) checks that rely on sight.

Actions

Slam. *Melee weapon attack:* +5 to hit, reach 5 ft., one creature. *Hit:* 6 (1d6+3) bludgeoning damage plus 6 (1d6 + 3) necrotic damage. The target must succeed on a DC 13 Constitution saving throw or its hit point maximum is reduced by an amount equal to the necrotic damage taken.

This reduction lasts until the target takes a long rest. The target dies if this effect reduces their hit point maximum to zero.

A humanoid slain by this attack rises 1d4 rounds later as a barrow wight under the control of the wight that killed it unless the humanoid is restored to life or its body is destroyed. The wight can have no more than three barrow wights under its control at one time.

Wight, Blood

This creature looks like a tattered and desiccated humanoid about 8 feet covered in fresh blood which seems to ooze and weep from its body. Its clothes hang in rags and are soaked in blood as well. Its hands end in sharpened claws and its eyes display no signs of life.

When a living creature bleeds to death on unholy ground, its corpse sometimes returns to life as a blood wight. Evil priests of Orcus, Jubilex, Lucifer and various other demon princes and devil lords often hold dark rituals where they bleed a living creature to death in order to create a blood wight. Blood wights generally detest living creatures, but if created by a clerical or necromantic ritual, the created blood wight will not harm its creator (unless attacked first). Blood wights are solitary creatures though occasionally more than one of these creatures is encountered (particularly when they have been created by an evil cleric or necromancer).

A blood wight stands 8 to 10 feet tall and weighs 400 to 550 pounds. It appears much as it did in life but its body constantly weeps and oozes blood, even leaving footprints as it moves across the ground. Blood wights that could speak in life retain the knowledge of all languages they knew, but for the most part blood wights do not communicate either with others of their kind or with living creatures (including their creator).

A blood wight enters combat slashing with its claws. Given a chance, it grabs the closest opponent and engulfs it, holding it inside its body until it drowns. Drowned foes are ejected from the blood wight's body into a heap on the ground (the blood wight later devours any creature it kills).

Blood Wight

Large undead, neutral
Armor Class 16 (natural armor)
Hit Points 95 (10d10 + 40)
Speed 30 ft.

STR	DEX	CON	INT	WIS	CHA
20 (+5)	15 (+2)	18 (+4)	13 (+1)	13 (+1)	16 (+3)

Skills Perception +7, Stealth +5
Damage Resistances fire, necrotic; bludgeoning, piercing, and slashing from nonmagical weapons that aren't silvered
Damage Immunities poison
Condition Immunities exhaustion, poisoned
Senses darkvision 60 ft., passive Perception 17
Languages the languages it knew in life
Challenge 8 (3,900 XP)

Magic Weapons. The wight's weapon attacks are magical.
Sunlight Sensitivity. While in sunlight, the wight has disadvantage on attack rolls, as well as on Wisdom (Perception) checks that rely on sight.

Actions

Multiattack. The blood wight makes one claw attack and one life drain attack.

Claws. *Melee Weapon Attack:* +8 to hit, reach 10 ft., one target. *Hit:* 14 (2d8 + 5) slashing damage. If the target is a Medium or smaller creature, it is grappled (escape DC 15). The wight can grapple only one target.

Engulf. The wight engulfs one creature it has grappled, and the grapple ends. While engulfed, the creature is blinded and restrained, it has total cover against attacks and other effects outside the wight, and it takes 27 (6d8) necrotic damage at the start of each of the wight's turns. If the wight takes 30 damage or more on a single turn from a creature inside it, the wight must succeed on a DC 15 Constitution saving throw at the end of that turn or regurgitate all engulfed creatures, which fall prone in a space within 5 feet of the wight. If the wight dies, all engulfed creatures explode out from the corpse, falling prone 15 feet away.

Life Drain. *Melee Weapon Attack:* +8 to hit, reach 5 ft., one creature. *Hit:* 11 (2d6 + 4) necrotic damage. The target must succeed on a DC 15 Constitution saving throw or its hit point maximum is reduced by an amount equal to the damage taken. This reduction lasts until the target finishes a long rest. The target dies if this effect reduces its hit point maximum to 0. A humanoid slain by this attack rises 24 hours later as a zombie under the wight's control, unless the humanoid is restored to life or its body is destroyed. The wight can have no more than twelve zombies under its control at one time.

Wight, Sword

These wicked and depraved creatures lived and died by the sword, and now, their dark taint passes through their weapons to tear at your soul.

Much like the standard wight, these undead abominations are warped and twisted caricatures of their former selves. The sword wight bears a massive greatsword, and the cold touch of the grave courses through the creature, through the weapon, into the hapless target.

Sword Wight

Medium undead, lawful evil
Armor Class 16 (chainmail)
Hit Points 66 (12d8+12)
Speed 30 ft.

STR	DEX	CON	INT	WIS	CHA
12 (+1)	12 (+1)	13 (+1)	11 (+0)	13 (+1)	15 (+2)

Skills Perception +4, Stealth +4
Damage resistances necrotic; bludgeoning, piercing and slashing from nonmagical weapons that are not silvered
Damage immunities poison
Condition immunities exhaustion, poisoned
Senses darkvision 60 ft., passive Perception 14
Languages the languages it knew in life
Challenge 5 (1,800 XP)

Improved Critical. Greatsword attacks score a critical hit on a roll of 19 or 20.

Magical Weapons. Attacks by the sword wight using its weapons are considered to be magical.

Sunlight Sensitivity. While in sunlight, the sword wight has disadvantage on attack rolls, as well as on Wisdom (Perception) checks that rely on sight.

Weapon Master. When using its greatsword attack, a sword wight may reroll any 1 on damage dice, keeping the second result.

Actions

Multiattack. The sword wight makes two greatsword attacks or two longbow attacks. It can use its life drain in place of one greatsword attack.

Greatsword. Melee Weapon Attack: +4 to hit, reach 5 ft., one target. *Hit:* 8 (2d6 + 1) slashing.

Life Drain. Melee Weapon Attack: +4 to hit, reach 5 ft., one creature. *Hit:* 4 (1d6 + 1) necrotic damage. The target must succeed on a DC 15 Constitution saving throw or its hit point maximum is reduced by an amount equal to the damage taken. This reduction lasts until the target finishes a long rest. The target dies if this effect reduces its hit point maximum to 0.

A humanoid slain by this attack rises 24 hours later as a zombie under the wight's control, unless the humanoid is restored to life or its body is destroyed. The wight can have no more than twelve zombies under its control at one time.

Longbow. Ranged Weapon Attack: +4 to hit, range 150/600 ft., one target. *Hit:* 5 (1d8 + 1) piercing damage.

Reactions

Parry. The sword wight adds 2 to its AC against one melee attack that would hit it. To do so, the sword wight must see the attacker and be wielding a melee weapon.

Wizard's Shackle

This tiny creature appears to be a gray-green leech.

The wizard's shackle is a 6-inch long, leech-like creature. Though it is small in size, it is greatly feared by spellcasters, for its bite drains arcane magic from a caster's mind. In some rare instances, evil spellcasters have harvested these monsters and set them loose in an enemy spellcaster's tower or laboratory.

A wizard's shackle attacks from ambush. It favors hiding on ledges, bookshelves, doors, and other such places where it can drop on spellcasters that pass underneath it. A wizard's shackle injects an anesthetic when it bites, so it is possible that its bite goes unnoticed (DC 12 Perception check to notice).

Wizard's Shackle

Tiny monstrosity, neutral
Armor Class 11
Hit Points 16 (3d4 + 9)
Speed 5 ft.

STR	DEX	CON	INT	WIS	CHA
1 (−5)	12 (+1)	16 (+3)	1 (−5)	11 (+0)	2 (−4)

Senses blindsight 30 ft., passive Perception 10
Languages —
Challenge 1/2 (100 XP)

Arcane Sense. A wizard's shackle can automatically detect the location of any active spell or magical item within 30 feet not hidden behind 10 feet of dirt, 5 feet of stone, 1 foot of common metal, or 5 inches of lead.

Magic Resistance. The wizard's shackle has advantage on saving throws against spells and magical effects.

Actions

Bite. *Melee Weapon Attack:* +3 to hit, reach 5 ft., one creature. *Hit:* 3 (1d4 + 1) piercing damage and the wizard's shackle attaches to the target. While it is attached, any time the target attempts to cast a cantrip or spell, it takes 10 (3d6) psychic damage and must make a DC 10 Constitution saving throw. On a failed saving throw, the target fails to cast the spell and if a spell slot was used, it is wasted.

The wizard's shackle can be removed as an action by the target or another creature. If a creature or creature to which the wizard's shackle is attached attempts to remove the wizard's shackle, the attached target must succeed on a DC 13 Constitution saving throw. On a failed saving throw, the target is unconscious for 1 minute.

Wolf, Ghoul

This creature resembles a wolf with matted dark fur torn away in places. Its flesh is sickly gray where its fur is torn away. Its eyes are stark white.

Ghoul wolves are carnivorous undead wolves that delight in hunting living creatures, catching them, and tearing them to shreds. These creatures are most often found haunting desolate moors and marshes.

Ghoul wolves hunt in packs, surrounding their prey and circling as they move in for the kill.

Ghoul Wolf

Large undead, chaotic evil
Armor Class 13 (natural armor)
Hit Points 52 (8d8 + 8)
Speed 50 ft.

STR	DEX	CON	INT	WIS	CHA
16 (+3)	13 (+1)	13 (+1)	7 (−2)	11 (+0)	8 (−1)

Skills Perception +4
Damage Immunities poison
Condition Immunities charmed, exhaustion, poisoned
Senses passive Perception 14
Languages —
Challenge 2 (450 XP)

Keen Hearing and Smell. The ghoul wolf has advantage on Wisdom (Perception) checks that rely on hearing or smell.

Pack Tactics. The ghoul wolf has advantage on attack rolls against a creature if at least one of the ghoul wolf's allies is within 5 feet of the creature and the ally isn't incapacitated.

Actions

Multiattack. The ghoul wolf makes two attacks: one with its bite and one with its claws.

Bite. *Melee Weapon Attack:* +5 to hit, reach 5 ft., one creature. *Hit:* 10 (2d6 + 3) piercing damage.

Claws. *Melee Weapon Attack:* +5 to hit, reach 5 ft., one target. *Hit:* 8 (2d4 + 3) slashing damage. If the target is a creature other than an elf or undead, it must succeed on a DC 13 Constitution saving throw or be paralyzed for 1 minute. The target can repeat the saving throw at the end of each of its turns, ending the effect on itself on a success.

Zombie, Basilisk

In the distance you see a shape moving across a rugged, stony terrain. Its six sickly looking legs move in a deliberate manner dropping flakes of scaly skin and and chunks of rotted flesh. After a sudden stop you know it has detected your presence and turns toward you. Too late you realize that the creature is a basilisk and you are looking right at its dark eyes. Frozen, not petrified, but from fright, you wonder how you survived its lithic stare. When it attacks it you understand, it is no longer a. living monster but a shell brought back to life for nefarious purpose.

Basilisk Zombie

Medium undead, neutral evil
Armor Class 12 (natural armor)
Hit Points 52 (8d8 + 16)
Speed 20 ft.

STR	DEX	CON	INT	WIS	CHA
16 (+3)	8 (−1)	15 (+2)	2 (−4)	8 (−1)	7 (−2)

Damage Immunities poison
Condition Immunities poisoned
Senses darkvision 60 ft., passive Perception 9
Languages —
Challenge 3 (700 XP)

Undead Fortitude. If damage reduces the zombie to 0 hit points, it must make a Constitution saving throw with a DC of 5 + the damage taken, unless the damage is radiant or from a critical hit. On a success, the zombie drops to 1 hit point instead.

Actions

Bite. *Melee Weapon Attack:* +5 to hit, reach 5 ft., one target. *Hit:* 10 (2d6 + 3) piercing damage plus 7 (2d6) necrotic damage.

Zombie, Behir

The sleek body and its lightning fast limbs have decayed to bits of flesh clinging loosely to old bone. Fearsome and dangerous in life, it has become horrifying in its undead form. Glimpsed between ribs, freshly killed and swallowed-whole corpses dance their last dance as they are churned about within the great beast's belly.

Behir Zombie

Huge undead, neutral evil
Armor Class 17 (natural armor)
Hit Points 168 (16d12 + 64)
Speed 50 ft., climb 40 ft.

STR	DEX	CON	INT	WIS	CHA
23 (+6)	10 (+0)	18 (+4)	3 (−4)	7 (−2)	5 (−3)

Saving Throws Wis +2
Damage Immunities lightning, poison
Condition Immunities exhaustion, poisoned
Senses darkvision 90 ft., passive Perception 8
Languages —
Challenge 11 (7,200 XP)

Undead Fortitude. If damage reduces the zombie to 0 hit points, it must make a Constitution saving throw with a DC of 5 + the damage

taken, unless the damage is radiant or from a critical hit. On a success, the zombie drops to 1 hit point instead.

Actions

Multiattack. The zombie makes two attacks: one with its bite and one with its constrict.

Bite. *Melee Weapon Attack:* +10 to hit, reach 5 ft., one target. *Hit:* 17 (2d10 + 6) piercing damage.

Constrict. *Melee Weapon Attack:* +10 to hit, reach 5 ft., one Large or smaller creature. *Hit:* 17 (2d10 + 6) bludgeoning damage plus 17 (2d10 + 6) slashing damage. The target is grappled (escape DC 16) if the zombie isn't already constricting a creature, and the target is restrained until this grapple ends.

Swallow. The zombie makes one bite attack against a Medium or smaller target it is grappling. If the attack hits, the target is also swallowed, and the grapple ends. While swallowed, the target is blinded and restrained, it has total cover against attacks and other effects outside the zombie, and it takes 21 (6d6) necrotic damage at the start of each of the zombie's turns. A behir zombie can have only one creature swallowed at a time.

If the zombie dies, a swallowed creature is no longer restrained by it and can escape from the corpse by using 15 ft. of movement, exiting prone.

Zombie, Brine

This creature appears as a rotting humanoid dressed in tattered and ragged clothing. Its semi-bloated body glistens from the slimy mixture of water and seaweed that hangs from its form. The creature's rotting flesh is blue-green in color. No semblance of life burns in its eyes.

Brine zombies are the remnants of a ship's crew that has perished at sea. They are mindless creatures, not very pleasant to look at, and relentless in their attacks on the living. The spark of evil that brought them back from the ocean depths drives them to seek the living so they may join them in their watery graves. Brine zombies appear much as they did in life.

Brine zombies attack an opponent with their cutlasses or fists in melee. If a brine zombie successfully grabs an opponent, it dives overboard and attempts to drown the victim by pinning its adversary underwater.

Brine Zombie

Medium undead, neutral evil
Armor Class 11 (natural armor)
Hit Points 27 (5d8 + 5)
Speed 20 ft., swim 30 ft.

STR	DEX	CON	INT	WIS	CHA
14 (+2)	8 (–1)	13 (+1)	2 (–4)	10 (+0)	10 (+0)

Damage Resistances fire
Damage Immunities poison
Condition Immunities poisoned
Senses darkvision 60 ft., passive Perception 10
Challenge 1 (200 XP)

Undead Fortitude. If damage reduces the zombie to 0 hit points, it must make a Constitution saving throw with a DC of 5 + the damage taken, unless the damage is radiant or from a critical hit. On a success, the zombie drops to 1 hit point instead.

Actions

Scimitar. *Melee Weapon Attack:* +4 to hit, reach 5 ft., one target. *Hit:* 5 (1d6 + 2) slashing damage.

Slam. *Melee Weapon Attack:* +4 to hit, reach 5 ft. one target. *Hit:* 9 (2d6 + 2) bludgeoning damage.

Zombie, Plague

This creature looks like a desiccated humanoid with grayish, leathery flesh. It is naked except for thin strands of tattered cloth. These strips of linen are crusted in dried blood and pus that oozes from sickly boils and other plague-born afflictions of the zombie's skin.

Plague Zombie

Medium undead, neutral evil
Armor Class 8
Hit Points 22 (3d8 + 9)
Speed 20 ft.

STR	DEX	CON	INT	WIS	CHA
13 (+1)	6 (–2)	16 (+3)	3 (–4)	6 (–2)	5 (–3)

Saving Throws Wis +0
Damage Immunities poison
Condition Immunities poisoned
Senses darkvision 60 ft., passive Perception 8
Languages understands the languages it knew in life but can't speak
Challenge ½ (100 XP)

Death Burst. If the plague zombie is dropped to 0 hit points, it explodes in a burst of decaying flesh. Any creature within 15 feet of the plague zombie must make a saving throw against its Zombie Rot.

Zombie Rot. A creature who takes a bite or claw attack, or who is within 15 feet of the plague zombie when it drops to 0 hit points, must make a DC 13 Constitution saving throw. On a failed save, the creature contracts zombie rot.

Zombie, Purple Worm

This undead monster's long form is wrapped in a lattice of dry leathery hide. A loathsome smell and rotting bits of viscera seep out through gaping tears and holes upon its diseased and faded purple flesh.

Purple Worm Zombie

Gargantuan undead, neutral evil
Armor Class 18 (natural armor)
Hit Points 247 (15d20 + 90)
Speed 50 ft., burrow 30 ft.

STR	DEX	CON	INT	WIS	CHA
28 (+9)	7 (−2)	22 (+6)	1 (−5)	8 (−1)	4 (−3)

Saving Throws Wis +4
Damage Immunities poison
Condition Immunities poisoned
Senses blindsight 30 ft., tremorsense 60 ft., passive Perception 9
Languages —
Challenge 15 (13,000 XP)

Tunneler. The worm can burrow through solid rock as half its burrow speed leaving a 10-foot-diameter tunnel in its wake.

Undead Fortitude. If damage reduces the zombie purple worm to 0 hit points, it makes a Constitution saving throw with a DC of 5 + the damage taken, unless the damage is radiant or from a critical hit. On a success, the zombie drops to 1 hit point instead.

While it has zombie rot, the creature cannot regain hit points except via magical means, and it has vulnerability to slashing damage as its flesh rots. At the end of each long rest after being infected, the creature's maximum hit points are reduced by 3 (1d6) and it can repeat the saving throw, ending zombie rot on a success. Any reduction to the creature's hit point maximum is permanent until the zombie rot has been cured. The reduction ends after the creature's next long rest after being cured. If this reduction drops the creature to 0 hit points, the creature dies and rises as a plague zombie in 1d4 hours.

Actions

Multiattack. The plague zombie makes one bite attack and one slam attack.

Bite. *Melee Weapon Attack:* +3 to hit, reach 5 ft., one creature. *Hit:* 4 (1d6 + 1) piercing damage, and the creature must make a DC 13 Constitution saving throw or contract zombie rot.

Slam. *Melee Weapon Attack:* +3 to hit, reach 5 ft., one creature. *Hit:* 4 (1d6 + 1) bludgeoning damage, and the creature must make a DC 13 Constitution saving throw or contract zombie rot.

Actions

Multiattack. The worm makes two attacks: one with its bite and one with its stinger.

Bite. *Melee Weapon Attack*: +14 to hit, reach 10 ft., one target. *Hit*: 22 (3d8 + 9) piercing damage. If the target is a Large or smaller creature, it must succeed on a DC 19 Dexterity saving throw or be swallowed by the worm. A swallowed creature is blinded and restrained, it has total cover against attacks and other effects outside the worm, and it takes 21 (6d6) necrotic damage at the start of each of the worm's turns.

If the worm dies, a swallowed creature is no longer restrained by it and can escape from the corpse by using 20 feet of movement, exiting prone.

Tail Stinger. *Melee Weapon Attack*: +14 to hit, reach 10 ft., one creature. *Hit*: 19 (3d6 + 9) piercing damage, and the target must make a DC 19 Constitution saving throw, taking 42 (12d6) poison damage on a failed save, or half as much damage on a successful one.

Zombie, Pyre

A rotting corpse walks forward without the usual hesitation and stuttering steps. After a few steps, it bursts into flames that lick its entire body, although it does not seem harmed in the slightest bit.

Pyre zombies are the sad, tortured remains of those who were killed just before being burned alive. When the soul departed, their bodies were taken over by some malignant spirit. The spirit fortified the bodies from destruction by the fire, and the undead forms escaped the pyre to wreak vengeance on the living.

Pyre zombies are not harmed by fire, but neither do they seek it out.

Pyre Zombie

Medium undead, neutral evil
Armor Class 12 (natural armor)
Hit Points 19 (3d8 + 6)
Speed 30 ft.

STR	DEX	CON	INT	WIS	CHA
13 (+1)	6 (−2)	16 (+3)	3 (−4)	6 (−2)	5 (−3)

Damage Immunities fire, poison
Condition Immunities exhaustion, poisoned
Senses darkvision 60 ft., passive Perception 8
Languages understands the languages it knew in life but can't speak
Challenge 3 (700 XP)

Undead Fortitude. If damage reduces the zombie to 0 hit points, it makes a Constitution saving throw with a DC of 5+ the damage taken, unless the damage is radiant or from a critical hit. On a success, the zombie drops to 1 hit point instead.

Magic Resistance. The zombie has advantage on saving throws against spells and other magical effects.

Violent Combustion. Whenever the zombie is hit, it violently explodes. Every creature with a 5-foot radius must make a DC 13 Dexterity saving throw, taking 7 (2d6) fire damage on a failed save, or half as much on a successful one.

Actions

Slam. *Melee Weapon Attack:* +3 to hit, reach 5 ft., one target. *Hit:* 9 (2d6 + 1) bludgeoning damage plus 7 (2d6) fire damage.

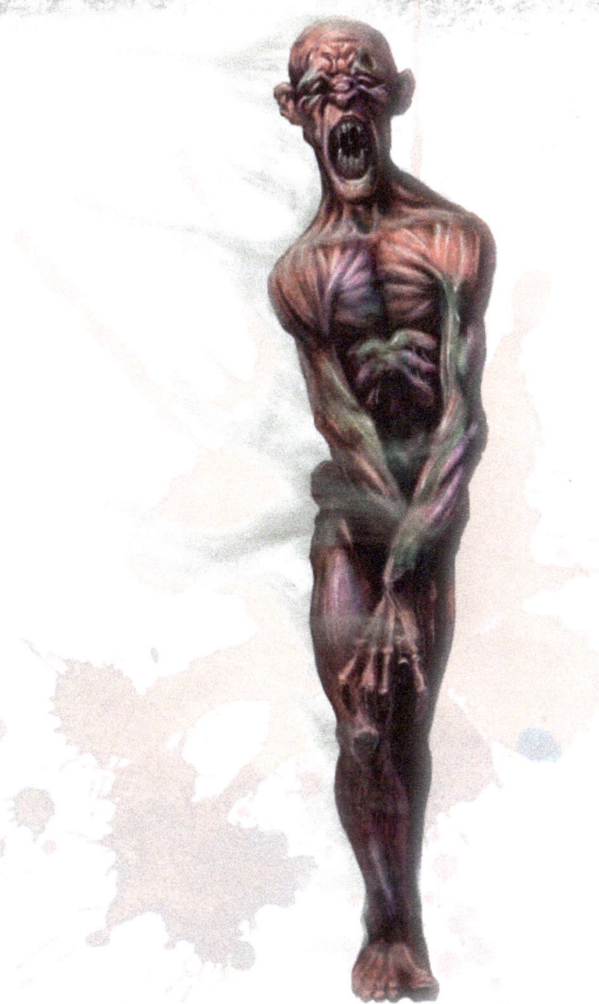

Zombie, Spellgorged

The shambling zombie shuffles forward, opens its mouth in a silent moan, and suddenly spits out a gout of searing fire.

It is the ultimate humiliation for a spellcaster to be reduced to a mindless, rotting husk used only to store the spells of a rival. Created with the use of a *create undead* spell, a spellgorged zombie is a programmed being, which appears much like a normal zombie. It must be made from a corpse that was in life an arcane or divine spellcaster. Spellgorged zombies may be used to store spells much like a *ring of spell storing* with the notable exception that they may be programmed to exhaust these spells by the spellcaster through a series of set commands.

Spellgorged Zombie

Medium undead, neutral evil
Armor Class 10
Hit Points 75 (10d8 + 30)
Speed 20 ft.

STR	DEX	CON	INT	WIS	CHA
13 (+1)	10 (+0)	16 (+3)	3 (−4)	6 (−2)	5 (−3)

Saving Throws Wis +0
Damage Immunities poison
Condition Immunities poisoned

Senses darkvision 60 ft., passive Perception 8
Languages understands the languages it knew in life but can't speak
Challenge 1 (200 XP)

Spell Storing. The zombie can store any spells cast into its mouth as if it were a *ring of spell storing*. The zombie can store up to 5 levels worth of spells at a time. The spells stored in the zombie uses the slot level, spell save DC, spell attack bonus, and the spellcasting ability of the original caster. Once the spell is released by the zombie it is no longer stored in it, freeing up space for additional spells.

Undead Fortitude. If damage reduces the zombie to 0 hit points, it must make a Constitution saving throw with a DC of 5 + the damage taken, unless the damage is radiant or from a critical hit. On a success, the zombie drops to 1 hit point instead.

Actions

Slam. *Melee Weapon Attack:* +3 to hit, reach 5 ft., one target. *Hit:* 4 (1d6 + 1) bludgeoning damage.

Zombie, Vrock

The body of a slain demon animated with unholy power. This creature has no further link to its Abyssal masters but is instead a servant of the dark force behind its animation. Decayed and diseased it remains a powerful enemy.

Vrock Zombie

Large fiend (undead), chaotic evil
Armor Class 15 (natural armor)
Hit Points 104 (11d10 + 44)

Speed 40 ft., fly 60 ft.

STR	DEX	CON	INT	WIS	CHA
17 (+3)	15 (+2)	18 (+4)	8 (−1)	13 (+1)	8 (−1)

Saving Throws Dex +5, Wis +4, Cha +2
Damage Resistances cold, fire, lightning; bludgeoning, piercing, and slashing from nonmagical weapons
Damage Immunities poison
Condition Immunities poisoned
Senses darkvision 120 ft., passive Perception 11
Languages understands Abyssal but can't speak
Challenge 6 (2,300 XP)

Magic Resistance. The vrock has advantage on saving throws against spells and other magical effects.

Undead Fortitude. If damage reduces the zombie vrock to 0 hit points, it must make a Constitution saving throw with a DC of 5 + the damage taken, unless the damage is radiant or from a critical hit. On a success, the zombie drops to 1 hit point instead.

Actions

Multiattack. The vrock makes two attacks: one with its beak and one with its talons.

Beak. *Melee Weapon Attack:* +6 to hit, reach 5 ft., one target. *Hit:* 10 (2d6 + 3) piercing damage.

Talons. *Melee Weapon Attack:* +6 to hit, reach 5 ft., one target. *Hit:* 14 (2d10 + 3) slashing damage.

Spores (Recharge 6). A 15-foot radius cloud of toxic spores extends out from the vrock. The spores spread around corners. Each creature in that area must succeed on a DC 14 Constitution saving throw or become poisoned. While poisoned in this way, a target takes 5 (1d10) poison damage at the start of each of its turns. A target can repeat the saving throw at the end of each of its turns, ending the effect on itself on a success. Emptying a vial of holy water on the target also ends the effect on it.

Stunning Screech (1/day). The vrock emits a horrific screech. Each creature within 20 feet of it that can hear it and that isn't a demon must succeed on a DC 14 Constitution saving throw or be stunned until the end of the vrock's next turn.

Monsters by Challenge Rating

CR 1/8

Conshee
Kuah-Lij

CR 1/4

Beetle, Stench
Frog, Killer
Gremlin
Orc, Blood
Orc, Ghost-Faced
Orc, Greenskin
Skulleton
Tick, Giant

CR 1/2

Abyssal Larva
Barbegazi (Ice Gnome)
Beetle, Gelid
Beetle, Saw-Toothed
Beetle, Water
Blindheim
Boarfolk
Dwarf, Frost
Fly, Giant
Frost Man
Goblin, Elemental Water
Gremlin, Fuath
Gribbon
Mephit, Smoke
Ooze, Amber
Phycomid
Rakklethorn Toad
Seahorse, Giant
Spider, Albino Cave
Spider, Skull
Tsathar
Wizard's Shackle
Zombie, Plague
Dragon, Vulgar Mouse

CR 1

Archer Bush
Bat, Mobat
Beaver, Armor Plated
Beetle, Blister
Beetle, Cave
Beetle, Ravager
Cadaver
Clubnek

Defender Globe
Demon, Barizou (Assassin Demon)
Dragon, Copper Mouse
Dragon, Smoke
Elusa Hound
Forgotten One
Fungus Man Alchemist I
Goblin, Elemental Wood
Iron Cobra
Jynx
Leech, Giant
Lynx, Giant
Mephit, Lightning
Oakman
Orc, Black (Black Orc of Orcus)
Silid
Stormwarden
Swarm, Poisonous Frog
Thaumaturmite, Lesser
Troblin
T'Shann
Zombie, Brine
Zombie, Spellgorged

CR 2

Allip
Asrai
Brownie
Cartyatid Column
Clamor
Crabman
Decapus
Demon, Geruzou (Slime Demon)
Dragon, Silver Mouse
Elemental, Obsidian (Small)
Eye Killer
Fire Crab (Diminutive)
Hellcat
Huecuva
Kathlin
Lava Child
Leprechaun
Lost Limb
Mimi
Mold, Brown
Ooze, Mudbog
Phlogiston Bush
Phooka
Shadow Hunter (Hatchling)
Skeletal Knight
Sloth Viper
Troll, Swamp
Tsathar Monk
Tsathar Sorceror

Undead Swordsman
Wolf, Ghoul

CR 3

Amphisbaena
Beaver, Prehistoric
Belabra
Blood Bush
Bog Beast
Burning Ghat
Cadejo, Dark
Cadejo, Light
Crystalline Horror
Demon, Azizou (Pain Demon)
Demon, Mehrim (Goat Demon)
Dragon, Wyrmling Cloud
Eel, Gulper
Elemental, Acid (small)
Elemental, Gravity (Small)
Elemental, Lightning (Lesser)
Eye Killer (Umbral)
Ferrous Worm
Fire Nymph
Fungus Man Alchemist II
Gallows Tree Zombie
Goblin, Elemental Stone
Golem, Wood
Lizard, Cavern
Lythic
Malignant Mouth
Moose, Two-Toed Horned
Ophidian
Reigon
Retch Hound
Rhinoceros, Prehistoric (Embolotherium)
Spell Parrot
Transposer
Troll, Cave
Wight, Barrow
Zombie, Basilisk
Zombie, Pyre

CR 4

Badger, Prehistoric Honey
Basilisk, Crimson
Bison, Bighorn
Cadaver Lord
Corpse Candle
Corpse Rook
Deer, Onyx
Demonic Mist
Dragon, Electrum Mouse

Dragon, Gold Mouse
Dragon, Wyrmling Dungeon
Dragon, Wyrmling Gray
Fogwarden
Gargoyle, Four-Armed
Gargoyle, Margoyle
Giant, Wood
Goblin, Elemental Wind
Jaguar, Saber-tooth
Karina
Noble Streynor
Sea Serpent, Gilded
Skeleton, Black
Troll, Ice
Troll, River
Tsathar Priest

CR 5

Ape, Woods
Beetle, Deathwatch
Beetlor
Blood Orchid
Carrion Moth
Death Cow
Devil Dog
Dragon, Platinum Mouse
Dragon, Wyrmling Mist
Elemental, Gravity (Medium)
Elemental, Obsidian (Medium)
Eye of the Deep
Fire Crab
Folly, The
Fungus Man Alchemist III
Gargoyle, Fungus
Ghoul, Cinder
Golem, Ice
Golem, Magnesium
Hell Moth
Hellbender
Hsagrath the chain whip
Mammoth, Woolly
Mummy of the Deep
Ooze, Livestone
Ooze, Metallic
Ooze, Undead
Orc, Greenskin (Elfhunter)
Sabrewing
Sea Serpent, Fanged
Sloth, Giant
Spökvatten
Stone Delver
Tainted Servant of Tsathogga
Thaumaturmite, Greater
Tunnel Worm
Wight, Sword

CR 6

Chaos Beast
Demonic Knight
Elemental, Acid (Medium)
Elemental, Lightning (Medium)
Fire Phantom
Frog, Giant Dire Abyssal
Gargoyle, Green Guardian
Genie, Abasheen
Giant, Cave
Golem, Tallow
Lantern Goat
Minotaur, Bleeding Horror
Mordnaissant
Netherspark
Ooze, Jelly, Mustard
Ooze, Magma
Orc, Blood (Elder Warrior)
Shark, Oil
Skeleton, Lead
Swarm, Grig
Zombie, Vrock Demon

CR 7

Beetle, Rhinocerous
Cateprism
Crypt Thing
Demon, Guardian (daemon)
Drake, Salt
Elemental, Acid (Large)
Elemental, Gravity (Large)
Elemental, Time (Common)
Encephalon Gorger
Fungus Man Alchemist IV
Ghoul, Dust
Giant, Jack-in-Irons
Goblin, Elemental Fire
Golem, Ooze
Lizard, Gnasher
Lurker Above
Orc, Black (Black Orc Champion)
Riptide Horror
Sand Kraken
Weird, Lightning

CR 8

Aerial Assault Gnome
Bedlam
Dragon, Young Cloud
Elemental, Obsidian (Large)
Genie, Seraph
Golem, Blood
Leech, Cave
Lich Shade

Magmoid
Minotaur, Obsidian
Mohrg
Nucklavee
Orc, Ghost-Faced (Battle Priest)
Raggoth
Sea Serpent, Spitting
Shadelock
Spider, Demon
Wight, Blood

CR 9

Blood Orchid Savant
Bog Creeper
Brass Man
Carrion Claw
Demon, Balban (Brute Demon)
Demon, Derghodemon (Cockroach Demon)
Dragon, Young Dungeon
Drake, Splinter
Elemental, Acid (Huge)
Elemental, Gravity (Huge)
Elemental, Lightning (Greater)
Gem Dog
Giant, Sand
Giant, Sea
Mastodon
Orc, Black (Black Orc Priest of Orcus)
Rhinoceros, Woolly
Scylla
Shadow Hunter
Snake, Sepia
Spider, Prism

CR 10

Cinder Knight
Demon, Aeshma (Rage Demon)
Demon, Chaaor (Beast Demon)
Devouring Mist
Dragon, Young Gray
Dragon, Young Mist
Fire Crab (Greater)
Fungus Man Alchemist V
Gloom Crawler
Golem, Witch-Doll
Minotaur, Bronze

CR 11

Demon, Greruor (Frog Demon)
Elemental, Acid (Greater)
Elemental, Gravity (Greater)
Elemental, Obsidian (Huge)
Fire Whale (Burning Leviathan)

Glass Wyrm
Mantidrake
Troll, Rock
Zombie, Behir

CR 12

Angel, Chalkydri
Angel, Empyreal (Fallen)
Bulette, Blue
Bulette, Red
Kamasuhn
Lizard, Fire
Reliquary Guardian
Rhinoceros, Prehistoric (Elasmotherium)
Shadow Captain

CR 13

Bone Crawler
Bulette, Black
Bulette, Green
Elemental, Acid (Elder)
Elemental, Gravity (Elder)
Elemental, Time (Noble)
Giant, Volcano
Gorgimera
Revenant, Hybrid
Sea Serpent, Brine

CR 14

Amalgamation
Biclops
Elemental, Obsidian (Greater)
Gallows Tree
Gibbering Orb, Lesser

CR 15

Beetle, Requiem
Bulette, Translucent
Dragon, Adult Cloud
Dragon, Adult Mist
Hamster, Giant
Phasma
Zombie, Purple Worm

CR 16

Demon, Gharros (Scorpion Demon)
Dragon Crab
Dragon, Adult Dungeon
Gibbering Abomination

CR 17

Bulette, Gold
Colussus, Jade
Demon, Choronzon (Chaos Demon)
Dragon, Adult Gray
Elemental Dragon, Air
Elemental Dragon, Water
Elemental, Obsidian (Elder)
Elemental, Time (Royal)

CR 18

Dragon, Fly
Herald of Tsathogga

CR 19

Dragon, Wrath
Elemental Dragon, Earth

CR 20

Abyssal Harvester
Demon Lord, Sonechard (General of Orcus)
Dragon, Ancient Mist
Quantum

CR 21

Devil, Gorson (The Blood Duke)
Dragon, Ancient Dungeon
Dragon, Ancient Gray
Elemental Dragon, Fire
Sea Serpent, Deep Hunter

CR 22

Demon Lord, Kostchtchie (Demon Prince of Wrath)
Dragon, Ancient Cloud
Horned Lord
Ravager Spawn (Flier Form)

CR 23

Ravager Spawn (Brawler Form)
Ravager Spawn (Crawler Form)

CR 24

Demilich, Advanced
Devil, Cerberus

CR 26

Demon Lord, Dagon
Demon Lord, Maphistal (Second of Orcus)

CR 27

Demon Lord, Pazuzu (Demon Prince of Air)

CR 30

Gibbering Orb
Ravager (Brawler Form)
Ravager (Crawler Form)
Ravager (Flier Form)
Sea Serpent, Shipbreaker

CR 35+

Demon Lord, Orcus
Demon Lord, Tsathogga (The Frog God)

Monsters by Type

Aberration

Abyssal Harvester
Bedlam
Belabra
Blindheim
Blood Orchid
Blood Orchid Savant
Bone Crawler
Carrion Moth
Chaos Beast
Clamor
Crystalline Horror
Decapus
Encephalon Gorger
Eye of the Deep
Fogwarden
Gibbering Abomination
Gibbering Orb
Gibbering Orb, Lesser
Hell Moth
Hellbender
Herald of Tsathogga
Nucklavee
Quantum
Sand Kraken
Shadelock
Transposer
T'Shann

Beast

Badger, Prehistoric Honey
Beaver, Armor Plated
Beaver, Prehistoric
Beetle, Blister
Beetle, Cave
Beetle, Deathwatch
Beetle, Ravager
Beetle, Requiem
Beetle, Rhinocerous
Beetle, Saw-Toothed
Beetle, Stench
Beetle, Water
Bison, Bighorn
Eel, Gulper
Fly, Giant
Frog, Killer
Gem Dog
Hamster, Giant

Jaguar, Saber-tooth
Leech, Cave
Leech, Giant
Lynx, Giant
Mammoth, Woolly
Mastodon
Moose, Two-Toed Horned
Noble Streynor
Rhinoceros, Prehistoric (Elasmotherium)
Rhinoceros, Prehistoric (Embolotherium)
Rhinoceros, Woolly
Seahorse, Giant
Sloth, Giant
Spell Parrot
Spider, Albino Cave
Spider, Skull
Swarm, Poisonous Frog
Tick, Giant

Celestial

Angel, Chalkydri
Angel, Empyreal (Fallen)
Kamasuhn
Construct
Amalgamation
Brass Man
Cartyatid Column
Colussus, Jade
Golem, Blood
Golem, Ice
Golem, Magnesium
Golem, Ooze
Golem, Tallow
Golem, Witch-Doll
Golem, Wood
Hsagrath the chain whip
Iron Cobra
Minotaur, Bronze
Minotaur, Obsidian
Reliquary Guardian
Dragon
Dragon, Adult Cloud
Dragon, Adult Dungeon
Dragon, Adult Gray
Dragon, Adult Mist
Dragon, Ancient Cloud
Dragon, Ancient Dungeon
Dragon, Ancient Gray
Dragon, Ancient Mist
Dragon, Cloud

Dragon, Copper Mouse
Dragon, Dungeon
Dragon, Electrum Mouse
Dragon, Fly
Dragon, Gold Mouse
Dragon, Gray
Dragon, Mist
Dragon, Mouse
Dragon, Platinum Mouse
Dragon, Silver Mouse
Dragon, Smoke
Dragon, Vulgar Mouse
Dragon, Wrath
Dragon, Wyrmling Cloud
Dragon, Wyrmling Dungeon
Dragon, Wyrmling Gray
Dragon, Wyrmling Mist
Dragon, Young Cloud
Dragon, Young Dungeon
Dragon, Young Gray
Dragon, Young Mist
Drake, Salt
Drake, Splinter
Glass Wyrm
Sea Serpent, Brine
Sea Serpent, Deep Hunter
Sea Serpent, Fanged
Sea Serpent, Gilded
Sea Serpent, Shipbreaker
Sea Serpent, Spitting

Elemental

Beetle, Gelid
Cateprism
Cinder Knight
Defender Globe
Elemental Dragon, Fire
Elemental Dragon, Air
Elemental Dragon, Earth
Elemental Dragon, Water
Elemental, Acid (Medium)
Elemental, Acid (Elder)
Elemental, Acid (Greater)
Elemental, Acid (Huge)
Elemental, Acid (Large)
Elemental, Acid (small)
Elemental, Gravity (Medium)
Elemental, Gravity (Elder)
Elemental, Gravity (Greater)
Elemental, Gravity (Huge)

Elemental, Gravity (Large)
Elemental, Gravity (Small)
Elemental, Lightning (Medium)
Elemental, Lightning (Greater)
Elemental, Lightning (Lesser)
Elemental, Obsidian (Medium)
Elemental, Obsidian (Elder)
Elemental, Obsidian (Greater)
Elemental, Obsidian (Huge)
Elemental, Obsidian (Large)
Elemental, Obsidian (Small)
Elemental, Time (Common)
Elemental, Time (Noble)
Elemental, Time (Royal)
Fire Crab
Fire Crab (Diminutive)
Fire Crab (Greater)
Fire Nymph
Fire Whale (Burning Leviathan)
Frost Man
Gargoyle, Four-Armed
Gargoyle, Green Guardian
Gargoyle, Margoyle
Genie, Abasheen
Genie, Seraph
Lava Child
Lizard, Fire
Lythic
Magmoid
Mephit, Lightning
Mephit, Smoke
Netherspark
Weird, Lightning

Fey

Asrai
Brownie
Cadejo, Dark
Cadejo, Light
Conshee
Folly, The
Forgotten One
Gremlin
Gremlin, Fuath
Jynx
Karina
Kuah-Lij
Leprechaun
Mimi
Oakman
Phooka
Spökvatten
Swarm, Grig

Fiend

Abyssal Larva
Demon Lord, Dagon
Demon Lord, Kostchtchie (Demon Prince
of Wrath)
Demon Lord, Maphistal (Second of Orcus)
Demon Lord, Orcus
Demon Lord, Pazuzu (Demon Prince of Air)
Demon Lord, Sonechard (General of Orcus)
Demon Lord, Tsathogga (The Frog God)
Demon, Aeshma (Rage Demon)
Demon, Azizou (Pain Demon)
Demon, Balban (Brute Demon)
Demon, Barizou (Assassin Demon)
Demon, Chaaor (Beast Demon)
Demon, Choronzon (Chaos Demon)
Demon, Derghodemon (Cockroach Demon)
Demon, Geruzou (Slime Demon)
Demon, Gharros (Scorpion Demon)
Demon, Greruor (Frog Demon)
Demon, Guardian (daemon)
Demon, Mehrim (Goat Demon)
Demonic Knight
Demonic Mist
Devil Dog
Devil, Cerberus
Devil, Gorson (The Blood Duke)
Frog, Giant Dire Abyssal
Hellcat
Sabrewing

Giant

Biclops
Giant, Cave
Giant, Jack-in-Irons
Giant, Sand
Giant, Sea
Giant, Volcano
Giant, Wood
Troblin
Troll, Cave
Troll, Ice
Troll, River
Troll, Rock
Troll, Swamp

Humanoid

Aerial Assault Gnome
Barbegazi (Ice Gnome)
Dwarf, Frost
Goblin, Elemental Fire
Goblin, Elemental Stone
Goblin, Elemental Water
Goblin, Elemental Wind
Goblin, Elemental Wood
Orc, Black (Black Orc Champion)
Orc, Black (Black Orc of Orcus)
Orc, Black (Black Orc Priest of Orcus)
Orc, Blood
Orc, Blood (Elder Warrior)
Orc, Ghost-Faced
Orc, Ghost-Faced (Battle Priest)
Orc, Greenskin
Orc, Greenskin (Elfhunter)
Silid
Stormwarden
Tainted Servant of Tsathogga

Mold

Mold, Brown

Monstrosity

Amphisbaena
Ape, Woods
Basilisk, Crimson
Bat, Mobat
Beetlor
Boarfolk
Bog Beast
Bulette, Black
Bulette, Blue
Bulette, Gold
Bulette, Green
Bulette, Red
Bulette, Translucent
Carrion Claw
Clubnek
Corpse Rook
Crabman
Death Cow
Deer, Onyx
Dragon Crab
Elusa Hound
Eye Killer
Eye Killer (Umbral)
Ferrous Worm
Fungus Man Alchemist
Fungus Man Alchemist I
Fungus Man Alchemist II
Fungus Man Alchemist III
Fungus Man Alchemist IV
Fungus Man Alchemist V
Gloom Crawler
Gorgimera
Gribbon
Kathlin
Lizard, Cavern
Lizard, Gnasher
Lurker Above
Malignant Mouth

Mantidrake
Ophidian
Raggoth
Rakklethorn Toad
Ravager
Ravager (Brawler Form)
Ravager (Crawler Form)
Ravager (Flier Form)
Ravager Spawn (Brawler Form)
Ravager Spawn (Crawler Form)
Ravager Spawn (Flier Form)
Reigon
Retch Hound
Riptide Horror
Scylla
Shadow Hunter
Shadow Hunter (Hatchling)
Shark, Oil
Sloth Viper
Snake, Sepia
Spider, Demon
Spider, Prism
Stone Delver
Thaumaturmite
Thaumaturmite, Greater
Thaumaturmite, Lesser
Tsathar
Tsathar Monk
Tsathar Priest
Tsathar Sorceror
Tunnel Worm
Wizard's Shackle

Ooze

Ooze, Amber
Ooze, Jelly, Mustard
Ooze, Livestone
Ooze, Magma
Ooze, Metallic
Ooze, Mudbog

Plant

Archer Bush
Blood Bush
Bog Creeper
Gallows Tree
Gallows Tree Zombie
Gargoyle, Fungus
Moss, Memory
Moss, Purple
Phlogiston Bush
Phycomid

Undead

Allip
Burning Ghat
Cadaver
Cadaver Lord
Corpse Candle
Crypt Thing
Demilich, Advanced
Devouring Mist

Fire Phantom
Ghoul, Cinder
Ghoul, Dust
Horned Lord
Huecuva
Lantern Goat
Lich Shade
Lost Limb
Minotaur, Bleeding Horror
Mohrg
Mordnaissant
Mummy of the Deep
Ooze, Undead
Phasma
Revenant, Hybrid
Shadow Captain
Skeletal Knight
Skeleton, Black
Skeleton, Lead
Skulleton
Undead Swordsman
Wight, Barrow
Wight, Blood
Wight, Sword
Wolf, Ghoul
Zombie, Basilisk
Zombie, Behir
Zombie, Brine
Zombie, Plague
Zombie, Purple Worm
Zombie, Pyre
Zombie, Spellgorged
Zombie, Vrock Demon